NO SAFE PLACE

THE DARK HEART OF YORKSHIRE

DI HASKELL & QUINN CRIME THRILLER SERIES
BOOK 8

BILINDA P. SHEEHAN

Copyright © 2025 by Bilinda P. Sheehan

All rights reserved.

No part of this book may be reproduced in any form or by any electronic or mechanical means, including information storage and retrieval systems, without written permission from the author, except for the use of brief quotations in a book review.

No part of this book can be used in the training of Generative AI LLMs without the express and written permission of the copyright holder.

The locations used in this book are real. Details may have been changed for story purposes.

This book was created entirely by human imagination and hard work.

ALSO BY BILINDA P. SHEEHAN

Watch out for the next book coming soon from Bilinda P. Sheehan by joining her mailing list.

A Wicked Mercy - DI Haskell & Quinn Crime Thriller

Death in Pieces - DI Haskell & Quinn Crime Thriller Book 2

Splinter the Bone - DI Haskell & Quinn Crime Thriller Book 3

Hunting the Silence - DI Haskell & Quinn Crime Thriller Book 4

Hidden in Blood - DI Haskell & Quinn Crime Thriller Book 5

Place of Temptation - DI Haskell & Quinn Crime Thriller Book 6

Lake of Tears - DI Haskell & Quinn Crime Thriller Book 7

No Safe Place - DI Haskell & Quinn Crime Thriller Book 8

Dark is the Mind - DI Haskell & Quinn Crime Thriller Book 9

All the Lost Girls - A Gripping Psychological Thriller

Wednesday's Child - A Gripping Psychological Thriller

NO SAFE PLACE

PART 1

1

PROLOGUE

THE IDEA of spending so much time in Scotland filled Willow with dread. Her parents had insisted she needed to go with them, even though she was more than capable of staying home and...

The screech of brakes pulled her from her thoughts. Getting up from the nest she'd created for herself on the bed, she peered out the window in time to see Terry Phillips heave himself out of his Land Rover. Even from a distance, it was easy to see he was pissed off about something. He paused, huffing a breath as he dragged a tissue from inside his jacket and dabbed at his mottled complexion. He used the time to peer up at the house, and as his eyes scanned over the upstairs windows, Willow ducked out of view.

Terry was a creep. There was always something going on behind those scrunched up piggy eyes.

Grabbing her headphones, Willow slid her

iPhone into the pocket of her green hoodie. If Terry was here, that meant he was back on the warpath. And Willow wasn't about to miss the fireworks that would inevitably erupt. With any luck, Andy would get caught up in the action. He might even get hurt. The thought of seeing her brother injured by Terry Phillips filled her with a twisted sense of satisfaction.

Willow descended halfway down the stairs before the hushed voices of her mother and brother drifted up to her.

Crouching on the steps, she peered through the stair rail into the kitchen. Mum stood with her body pressed against Andy's back. They were so close that not even a slip of paper could have fitted between them. *Gross.* Willow pulled a face as she watched her mother run her hands up his arms before beginning to massage his shoulders.

The way they behaved around each other was unnatural. It had taken Willow a long time to finally reach that conclusion. It wasn't as though she had anything to compare their relationship to. At least, not until she'd started spending time at her friends' houses. Other mothers were not so touchy-feely with their kids.

She'd mentioned it once to her mate Sandra, but the way Sandra had looked at Willow, like she'd completely lost her mind, had brought an end to the conversation. She'd mentally vowed never to mention it to anyone ever again.

She shrank back from view as her mother leaned

over to get a closer look at a catalogue on the table. Something Andy said made Mum laugh and the sound made Willow cringe. She never laughed like that when dad cracked a joke.

The door rattled in its frame making Willow jump. She'd almost forgotten why she'd abandoned her homework in the first place. Terry Phillips hammered on the door again. From the corner of her eye, she watched as Mum sprang away from Andy, a look passing between them that Willow knew only too well.

Leaning back against the steps, she feigned nonchalance as her mother left the kitchen. Their eyes locked for a split second when Mum reached the hall. Was that guilt? Whatever emotion Willow thought she saw, it was gone when Terry let his frustration pour forth in another volley of knocks that shook the house to its foundations.

Breaking eye contact, Willow stared down at her phone, pointedly ignoring her mother as she opened the front door.

"Where is he?" Terry's voice boomed through the hall. "You tell your rat bastard of a husband to get his arse out here now."

"Terry, stop! What do you think you're doing?"

"I haven't got time for your placating bullshit, Anna. I want to speak to him."

Willow watched through her curtain of dark hair as her mother tried to block Terry's path. Not that she could actually stop him. Terry pushed her aside as though she were nothing more than an irritating fly to be swatted away. He charged down the hall, poking his head into the living room before making a beeline for the kitchen.

Unease curdled the contents of Willow's stomach. Terry was the kind of mad that made people do stupid shit. Whatever thoughts she might have had earlier were gone. Terry was mad enough to do some real damage and whatever her feelings about her brother might be, she didn't want him to get killed. Gripping her phone, she contemplated calling the police. It wouldn't be the first time.

Andy appeared in the door just as Terry reached the end of the hall.

"Where's your father, Andy?" Terry's mouth was set in a grim line, his fists balled by his sides. Willow tried to imagine what she would do if Terry punched her brother.

"He's—" Before Andy could finish the sentence the sound of wheels crunching over the drive made Terry swing back to the door.

"I'm going to fucking kill him..." Terry raced for the driveway, his speed surprising considering his size. Then again, bulls were fast too, and they were huge muscle-bound monsters. When she was five, Andy had persuaded her that the bull in the back field was terribly lonely and painfully shy. Naively, Willow had believed him. She had gone to the field with her favourite tea set and a plan to pick daisies to make flower crowns for them both.

Unsurprisingly, the bull had not wanted a playmate. And when he'd seen her skipping around in her little red coat, he had given chase. Seeing Terry stalk through the hall to her father reminded her of the moment she'd spotted the bull charging towards her.

"Andrew!" Mum's voice rang out. The world slowed as Willow watched events unfold from her place on the stairs.

She heard her father's voice outside. "You've got some nerve coming here, Terry, after I told you to stay away. Did you think I was bluffing when I said I'd press charges?"

Willow crept down the stairs, following her family outside onto the drive. Her father held his shotgun in his hands and had squared off against Terry. In spite of Terry's promise to kill her father, he was the one nursing a bloody nose.

"You said you wouldn't interfere with the sale," Terry said, swiping at the blood dribbling down his lip with the back of his hand. "You swore you'd let it go through. Just because you want to throw your life away trying to run a money-pit like this place doesn't mean I want to do the same."

"You lied to them, Terry. Nobody made you. You did that all by yourself. I merely set them straight."

"You bastard!" Terry jerked forward.

It only took her father a moment to raise the shotgun to rest against his shoulder. He levelled the gun at his oldest friend's chest. The threat was enough to halt Terry in his tracks.

"Get the fuck off my property, Terry. I never want to see you darken my door again, you hear?"

Terry backed off, his hands held in the air. But it was the look on his face that frightened Willow. It was the look of someone who would have happily pulled the trigger had the tables been turned.

"I'll kill you for this, Andrew. I'll fucking kill you and I'll laugh while I'm doing it." Terry backed off to his car and climbed in behind the wheel. He gunned the engine, the sound echoing around the yard.

Her father kept the gun levelled at Terry as though he half expected him to act on his promise there and then. He didn't relax until Terry had reversed and swung the car violently back towards the road.

"What did you do this time, Andrew? You said you'd sorted it all out." There was a note of real fear in Mum's voice.

"I did. It's not my fault that things went to shit."

Willow tuned out as her parents started to bicker. From the corner of her eye, she caught her brother watching her, the way he tracked her movements making her uncomfortable. Rather than let him know he was getting under her skin, she slid her headphones on over her ears and slipped back into the house.

NO SAFE PLACE

SITTING on the bottom of the stairs, she slid her stockinged feet back and forth across the tile floor. Her mother and father were arguing in the kitchen. Turning up the volume on her iPhone, she let a Nine Inch Nails song wash over her. With the beat pounding in her ears, it was almost comical watching her parents wave their arms around, their faces contorted in rage.

They'd been at it since Terry had left. Willow had taken a walk across the field out back in the hopes it would have blown over by the time she returned. Instead, in her absence, her the argument had only gained steam.

Her father's face contorted as he turned away and stormed across the kitchen. His complexion was normally a bit ruddy, but today it practically glowed purple. It reminded Willow of the Ribena berries adverts she skipped on YouTube. If he kept looking like that, he was going to wind up having some kind of seizure. Marilyn had looked a little like that when she'd had her seizure in school. It had scared Willow shitless watching her friend flop around on the floor.

Something touched her shoulder, and she jerked forward. Andy lifted his hands, as if in surrender. His mouth moved but Willow couldn't hear anything he said. Grudgingly, she slipped her Skullcandy headphones off her ears and let them hang around her neck.

"Terry really knows how to kick the hornets' nest." He kept his voice deliberately low. Why he was bothering to keep quiet made no sense; it wasn't as though their parents would hear them. A brass band could march through the hall and they would still continue to psychologically score points against one another.

"Whatever." Willow rolled her eyes and got up from her place on the stairs. "I'm going to my room." Andy let her pass, but she could feel him following close behind her on the stairs.

She reached the landing and picked up her pace, her socked feet moving quickly over the carpeted floor. Turning into her bedroom she started to close the door, but Andy jammed his shoulder against the wood, halting her.

Raised voices drifted up the stairs as the fight downstairs continued.

"Get out!" She pressed herself against the door and used her weight to push it closed. For one perfect moment she thought she'd managed it, only for Andy to decide he was done screwing around.

Rather than leave, he thumped the door hard, sending her crashing back onto the floor.

"Asshole!" Pain speared up through her wrist and arm as she landed awkwardly. Their parents' fight continued but the sound became muted as Andy closed the door behind him, sealing them inside the room together. Willow waited for someone to come and check on her. The noise of her landing on the floor should have been enough to get their attention. Then again, they never heard her. Nobody did.

Grinning at her, Andy sauntered into the room as if he owned the place. Willow's blood began to boil. Andy was the golden child. In their parent's eyes he could do no wrong. When he'd announced that he was going to study some bullshit Agriculture course in Newcastle, they'd all but thrown a parade in his honour. But if they knew what their precious little angel child was really up to, they might not have been so thrilled.

He threw himself down on her bed and propped his arms behind his head, the picture of ease.

"Get out, Andy, or I swear—"

"Or what? The parentals are too busy ripping chunks out of each other to care about you. It's just you and me, Wills." His smile turned predatory. "Come and lie here with me." He patted the bedspread next to him. "Like we used to."

An icy finger of fear traced a pattern down Willow's spine. Scooting backwards on the floor, she shook her head. "No thanks. Don't you have to head back to Uni? Won't what's-her-name be eager to see you?"

"Her name is Cecelia. And she's always eager to see me." He sighed and turned his long-suffering expression upwards to the ceiling. "Cece is a nice girl, unlike you."

"Fuck you!" Willow spat the words out before she could stop herself.

Andy sat up and swung his legs onto the floor. "Come here."

"No. Get out, Andy. I mean it." Seeing the look that crossed his face, Willow quickly added, "I've got a load of homework to finish. Andy, please..."

"I said come here." The edge in his voice turned her stomach. "I want to play a game."

"This isn't right. Please, just leave me alone." Willow hated the way her voice shook.

"We can do it the nice way, or—"

"I'll tell them about you," Willow said, fear making her tongue loose.

Andy started to laugh, the sound causing the hairs to stand on the back of her neck. She knew what would come next if she didn't do something to stop him.

"They won't believe you. You're the problem child, remember? They'll think you're using again."

"No, I mean I'll tell them what you're really up to." Willow met his gaze head on. His smile slowly faded as her meaning sank in.

"You don't know shit."

"I know a lot more than you think. And I've got the proof, too. You really should pick a better password."

She expected him to swear at her. She expected violence and rage. Instead, she was greeted with silence. And Willow wasn't sure which was worse. At least anger was predictable. This, whatever it was, scared her.

Her heart climbed into her throat as he stared her down. And then, like somebody flipped a switch inside his brain, Andy's expression shifted, and he stood. "You're no fun, Wills. I preferred you when you were getting high." Pausing at the door, he stared down at her, his gaze unreadable. When his phone beeped, Willow jumped. "Later loser." He slammed the door behind him, leaving her alone.

She stayed frozen in place on the floor, not knowing if he was really gone or if he was just fucking with her. It wouldn't be the first time he'd tricked her. She closed her eyes in a pathetic attempt to stop the memory from replaying in her brain. But it replayed anyway, as it always did when she didn't want it to.

The only thing that had worked to quiet the memories was when she would get high. But she'd given that up.

As the minutes slowly ticked by, she grew braver. Getting slowly to her feet, she grabbed her chair and dragged it cautiously to the bedroom door. Her hands shook as she pushed the backrest beneath the doorknob, securing it.

Finally, she stepped back. Her heart continued to thump in her chest. Satisfied he was really gone, Willow felt tears well in her eyes. She would not cry. She'd done enough of that in the past.

But as she stood alone in the middle of her bedroom, the tears came anyway.

FOUR DAYS Later

WILLOW COULDN'T SLEEP. Wind howled around the house, rattling the windows in their frames. Through an open gap in the curtains, she could see the trees outside as they swayed and bent practically double. It didn't take long for the rain to come. It fell heavy and hard, hammering off the tiled roof over her head.

Squeezing her eyes shut, she tried to concentrate on her own breathing, but the noise of the storm was much too loud for that. Rolling onto her side, she snatched her headphones from the bedside table. A noise from downstairs caused her to still. She stayed propped on one elbow, straining to see in the darkness of her room as she waited for another noise.

It's just the storm. Stop being a baby.

Rolling her eyes at her own foolishness, she flopped onto her back and settled the headphones over her ears. Music would drown out the sounds of the storm and it would help her sleep. The light from the phone screen burned her eyes but it only took a second to find the album she needed. Sliding the phone under her pillow, she closed her eyes as the music swelled in her ears.

IT WAS STILL DARK when she woke again. Something had pulled her from sleep, but her brain felt like mush. The lingering cobwebs of her dreams clung to her mind, making it difficult to discern reality from fantasy. The music was muffled, the headphones having slid off one ear as she'd tossed and turned in the bed.

A dull thud pulled her consciousness to the surface. Glancing towards the door, she expected to see it closed. Instead, it sat ajar. For a moment, she could have sworn she saw a face peering through the gap. Then it was gone.

Fear spiked her adrenaline. Sitting bolt upright in the bed, she pulled the covers close to her body. Her movements knocked the headphones completely from her head and down onto the floor next to the bed.

It was a dream. It had to be a dream. But a dream didn't explain the door being partially open. She had definitely closed it; she was certain of it. It was part of her nightly ritual. She always closed the door and placed the chair beneath the doorknob and—

But Andy was back in Newcastle now. He'd gone back up there the day after Terry Phillips had called to the house. And with him no longer in the house, she had stopped ritually putting the chair behind the door.

The wind rattled the windows, making her jump, and the door drifted closed as though moved by an invisible hand.

The wind. The wind had blown the door open. Relief made her sag back against the pillows.

You are such an idiot. And she did feel like a fool. Imagine being such a drama queen that you conjured a face in the darkness. Pulling her phone from its place under the pillow, she contemplated sending a message to the group chat but quickly chickened out. She would never hear the end of it if she shared her silly scare.

Scooting up in bed, she reached for her cold cup. She'd wanted a Stanley Cup, but her parents had refused on the grounds that it was a ridiculous expense. She'd found a dupe online, and while it wasn't perfect, something was better than nothing. She sipped at the contents but was disappointed to discover the water was lukewarm. So much for being a cold cup.

Of course, if Andy had asked for one, Mum would have turned the world upside down to get it for him.

Swinging her legs out of the bed, she took the cup with her and made her way to the hall. The house was cloaked in darkness, and she felt along the wall to the top of the stairs. Something moved in the gloom at the bottom of the steps. Willow's heart leapt into her throat as she watched the shadows coalesce into a human shape. It moved steadily up the stairs towards her.

Dropping her cup, she fled.

"Mum! Dad!" She barely took a breath as she ran

for her parents' bedroom door. They would know what to do.

"Mum!"

Exploding through the bedroom door, she was surprised to find the lights on. She turned to the bed and faltered.

"Mummy..." Her voice broke off in a whimper as Willow took in the sight of her mother tied spreadeagled to the bed. Her face was bloodied, her blonde hair streaked with red. One of her eyes was swollen almost entirely shut. She turned her head in Willow's direction and opened her mouth, but only blood bubbled past her lips.

Willow took a step towards the bed, her hands reaching automatically for her mother.

She felt the air shift behind her. adrenaline tuning her nerves to every micro movement in the environment. She tried to turn, but he was on her before she could take a step. His weight and momentum took her down, and Willow hit the carpet, the air rushing from her lungs before she could think to scream.

Scrambling forwards, she clawed at the floor with such desperation that she didn't feel her nails break as they tore against the carpet fibres.

Fight.

She wanted to live. Her exams were coming up, and she had so many plans. So many things she wanted to do. So many places she wanted to visit.

Something struck the side of her head. Hard

enough to cause an explosion of white that obscured her vision.

No, not like this. She had so much left to do.

There was so much of her life left to live.

She'd never been in love.

Never even kissed a boy she liked.

"Mummy…"

The darkness closed around her, narrowing her vision to a pin prick of light.

She was afraid.

So utterly afraid.

And so completely alone.

He hit her again.

Willow knew she was going to die.

And she was terrified.

CHAPTER TWO

"JEZZA, pull that mask down over your mouth, man. What the heck do you think you're playing at? Do you want people to recognise you?"

Jeremy glared at Mark and quickly realised the combined darkness from the interior of the van and the balaclava covering most of his face prevented Mark from seeing his expression.

"I told you before, I'll pull it down when we get out." Jeremy huffed a breath. The mask was much too warm and made breathing virtually impossible in the stuffy van. "Why do I have to ride in the back anyway? It's like Satan's ball sack back here."

"Because I didn't fancy us all being crammed up here in the front like sardines in a can." Mark settled down into his seat. From Jeremy's position in the back, he could only see the top of his mate's head. "Plus, it's much better this way, you know, in case of dash cam footage," Mark said airily, as though that explained everything. As far as Jeremy was concerned it explained nothing.

"Simon, mate, turn up the radio. I fucking love this song," Mark barked the order at the tall, lanky bloke hunched over the steering wheel. Simon did as he was told without question.

It had been a long time since Jeremy had done anything like this. His misspent youth had been put behind him long ago.

The van rattled over a pothole, and Jeremy swore violently as he was tossed from his precarious position on top of Mark's toolbox. He hit the floor of the van with a dull thud, pain spreading quickly up through his arse and into his spine.

"Hold on back there," Mark called back. The two men upfront started to laugh.

Grumbling under his breath, Jeremy pulled himself back onto the toolbox. Grease smeared his hands, and he swore under his breath as he wiped it away on his black Nike jogging bottoms.

This was madness. He did not belong here, not anymore. Yet he'd agreed to this run. There had been a time when doing things like this had felt exciting. Now, the thrill was well and truly dead.

But what choice did he have? Kelly had just entered her second trimester. He still remembered the day she'd told him he was going to be a dad. Just thinking about it caused a swell of pride and joy to expand in his chest. He had responsibilities now. She was counting on him. But getting laid off from his IT job had not exactly done them any favours financially.

Sweat beaded beneath the balaclava. Without thinking, he jammed his fingers beneath the itchy wool fabric and scratched. The smell of grease invaded his nostrils, and he swore silently.

When Mark had approached him about the job, he'd thought somebody up there must be looking out for him. But now that he was here, in the back of the dark van, he was sure he'd made a huge mistake.

Was Mark taking advantage of his change in circumstances and just using him for his unique skillset? Definitely.

Whatever friendship had existed between them was long dead. Mark wasn't the forgiving type, and when Jeremy had snatched Kelly out from under his friend's nose, Mark had cut him off. Until now.

He was no fool. Mark would screw him over the first chance he got. There had been a time when they would have done anything for each other, but that time was gone.

The van's progress slowed to a crawl. When Simon killed the engine, the van continued to coast before coming to a rocking halt. Jeremy crouched next to the doors and waited for Mark to open them. The sound of another car engine falling silent told Jeremy that the rest of the crew had arrived.

Quiet laughter drifted through the heavy doors to where Jeremy sat. Anger spread in his chest as he listened to the others making plans. After what felt like an age, his anger finally got the better of him and he rapped on the doors.

The laughter and happy chatter ceased instantly. Boots on gravel told Jeremy that somebody was approaching. A moment later, the doors swung open to reveal Mark and a couple of the others gathered in the lane with their vans and trailers.

"What the fuck, Jezza? Have you lost your mind. Someone might hear."

"They'll hear you lot first," Jeremy said, his tone sour. "Have you all gone soft? Why are you out here laughing and joking like we're going to a football match and that we're not about to go and nick some stuff."

"We were being careful," Mark said. His glanced back at the others and they nodded. "You really have gone rusty, haven't you?"

"Fuck off," Jeremy said under his breath.

Mark's smile faded from his lips. In the darkness, his eyes were black and glittering. "Come again?"

"Give over, Mark. Stop trying to come on all tough just because—"

Mark grabbed him by the front of his black jacket and jerked him from the van. Jeremy hit the ground hard enough to feel gravel dig into his palms.

"What the fuck, Mark—" Jeremy didn't get the chance to finish speaking. Mark yanked him upright. He barely managed to keep his footing as his oldest friend slammed him against the door of the vehicle.

"You think this is an act?" Mark's smile had returned, but it lacked warmth.

Jeremy made to grab at his mate, but Mark slammed him against the door again, the metal groaning under the assault.

Gasping for air as Mark tightened the grip on his neck, Jeremy tried to shrug out of the other man's grip but found it impossible.

Mark was still as short as ever. He only came up to Jeremy's chin, and in the past, Jeremy had used his size to intimidate his vertically challenged friend. But now. the tables had turned, and Jeremy found himself at the mercy of the other man.

In his dark clothes, Mark appeared gaunt. Where he had once been slim, he was now wiry and strong.

When had Mark become so powerful? Jeremy thought. Come to think of it, when had Mark become so aggressive?

"Look, I was just saying—" Jeremy's voice was high-pitched and breathy.

"You just thought you could be the big man," Mark said. He leaned in, pressing up into Jeremy's face until his nose was inches away. The smell of sour cream and onion crisps wafted over Jeremy's face, and he struggled not to retch. "I brought you in as a favour. But I'm not seeing any gratitude, Jezza. Instead, all I'm hearing is bellyaching and a whole lot of bitching."

"I'm sorry," Jeremy said. He hated being forced to apologise to Mark. It felt wrong. He'd always been the stronger one, the tougher one, more outgoing one. As teenagers, Jeremy had taken Mark under his wing, helping him find his place in the gang. And when Mark had stepped out of line, Jeremy had been only too happy to correct him.

Now, everything was different.

Rather than wilt when Jeremy left the gang, Mark had grown. He was harder now, tougher, stronger. And, Jeremy realised as he glanced over Mark's shoulder to the others gathered nearby, well respected.

Mark shoved against him and Jeremy lost his footing so that he hung from Mark's grip. Belatedly, Jeremy realised he needed to get his old school friend back on side, and sharpish.

"What was that?" Mark asked, adding a little shake that caused Jeremy's teeth to rattle in his head. "I can't hear you."

"I'm sorry, mate," Jeremy managed to squeeze the words out.

Mark stared at him, his gaze flat and emotionless. He let go suddenly, and Jeremy slumped to the stony ground. The sharp gravel dug into his knees as he struggled to catch his breath.

"That's what I thought," Mark said. His mouth stretched into a wide cruel grin. Turning to the others, he started to hand out orders.

Readjusting his jacket, Jeremy slowly climbed to his feet. Mark elbowed him out of the way as though he were nothing more than excess baggage taking up precious space. Rubbing his throat, Jeremy watched as the necessary tools were distributed.

Mark handed out signal repeaters and consoles—necessary for hacking the central locking systems in the cars they'd planned to steal—and from the back of the van, he pulled out a couple of crowbars and other useful items.

"What do you need me to do?" Jeremy asked, as the others cleared off, their footsteps fading into the darkness.

"You can come with me," Mark said. "Unless you've got some other smart-arse response?"

Jeremy shook his head and gazed down at his shoes.

"Here then, take this." Mark thrust a baseball bat into his hands before reaching back into the van and pulling out a crowbar and a sawn-off shotgun.

"Shit, mate, what are you planning to do with that?" Jeremy stared at the shotgun as fear curled in the pit of his stomach.

"This?" Mark gazed down at the gun. "This is just in case."

"In case of what?"

"In case we run into trouble." Mark narrowed his eyes at him. "What's your problem? You used to be cool with this kind of thing."

"That was a long time ago," Jeremy said quietly. "But even then, you weren't carrying a gun, Mark."

Mark shrugged. "Times change. These farmers

are often armed. I'm just levelling the playing field is all."

Jeremy contemplated continuing the argument but the look on Mark's face suggested he should let it drop. Mark closed the van doors quietly and locked up. "You and me, we're going to have a look inside the house. I know a good way in."

"How could you know a way into the house?"

"A little birdy told me about it. I did my homework, checked some things out and I happen to know there's something better in the house. And that's why I need you." There was something in the sly way he spoke that made Jeremy uneasy.

"I thought this was all about stealing the Range Rover and quad bikes?"

"Mostly. But I happen to know this bloke has a safe in the bedroom."

"So that's why you asked me to come in." Jeremy felt his stomach fall as he followed Mark along the path.

"Now you're catching on." Mark punched him playfully on the arm. "I knew the old Jezza was in there somewhere."

"I don't do stuff like that anymore, Mark. I went legit."

"Well, tonight you do."

Jeremy bit his tongue and followed Mark. They left the lane and vaulted over a low wall that sat alongside a field. Jeremy followed his old friend as they kept low and ran across the open space that lay at the back of the house.

A few moments later, Jeremy hopped the fence that led into the garden that lay to the back of the property. "Looks like they're still up," he whispered. He stared up at the house. All but one of the windows were wreathed in darkness. "We can't go in if they're up."

"Ignore it," Mark said quietly. "They leave that light on all the time. It doesn't mean anything."

"Are you sure?" Jeremy asked as they crept closer to the house. He expected the rest of the house lights to come on at any moment, and the owner to appear at the window. He waited a few moments, but nothing happened. Slowly but surely, his heart rate slowed to a crawl. Maybe Mark was right and no one was home.

It made sense. Mark was a risk-taker, and always had been, but he wasn't stupid. He wouldn't want to get caught red handed.

"Of course I'm fucking sure," Mark whispered. "Now come on. We don't have all night."

Jeremy traced his friend's footsteps up to a small side door. "If we break that glass, they're going to hear us."

"We don't need to break anything." Mark grinned at him.

With a gloved hand, Mark reached out and pushed on the door, allowing it to swing inwards with an eerie creak.

"I've got a really bad feeling about this," Jeremy said. His heartbeat had started to pick up its pace as he stared into the impenetrable gloom beyond the doorway.

"You've got a bad feeling about everything," Mark said. He fished a flashlight out of his rucksack. "You need to lighten up." He flicked the flashlight on and aimed the beam directly in Jeremy's face. "Get it? Lighten up."

Jeremy wasn't having any of it. The situation was too serious. "Mark, think about it. Who leaves their door open?"

Chuckling, Mark glanced at him. "You'll see soon enough."

"We should leave. We'll take the Range Rovers and--"

"Jezza, you've heard it said that you shouldn't look a gift horse in the mouth. Well this, my friend, is the gift horse."

"This doesn't feel right," Jeremy said beneath his breath. If Mark heard him, he certainly gave no indication of it. Instead, the smaller man slipped inside and disappeared into the shadows. Seeing no other option, Jeremy followed.

The smell hit him as he moved into a large farm style kitchen. The putrid stench coated the inside of his mouth, invading his nose and clinging to his hair. Raising his arm, he buried his mouth and nose in the crook of his elbow to block the worst of it, but to no avail. It was everywhere, and no matter what Jeremy did, there was no escaping the putrid air.

He spotted Mark moving quickly and quietly ahead of him. The other man seemed utterly unconcerned by the smell that surrounded them.

Hurrying to catch up, Jeremy touched Mark's shoulder before he could slip out into the hall. "What the fuck is that smell?"

When Mark glanced back at him, Jeremy swore he spotted something akin to joy pass through his accomplice's eyes. It was gone in an instant and the callous expression returned, making Mark appear almost inhuman.

Jeremy took a step back as Mark shrugged away from him. "No clue. Maybe something died in the walls, or under the floorboards." There was something in the tone of his voice that made Jeremy's hair rise on the back of his neck.

If it were true, Jeremy thought, the dead something would have to be huge. And how could anyone live alongside a stench so foul? How could they sleep in a house with this foul odour invading every corner of it?

"Nah, this ain't right," Jeremy said. "There's something really off about all of this, Mark. I think we should cut our losses and go." He thought about Kelly at home. And, in that moment, he wished he'd never agreed to this stupid idea.

"If you fucking bail on me now, I'll put a tip into the police that this here was your doing," Mark said.

His voice was low and controlled and the flat, dead look was back in his eyes.

"You can't threaten me like that," Jeremy spluttered, indignation warming his cheeks beneath the balaclava.

"Yeah, I can. And you know I mean it." There was a coldness to Mark's voice that chilled Jeremy to the bone.

"You wouldn't." Jeremy tried to play down his concern.

"With you out of the picture, mate, Kelly is fair game." Mark leaned closer. "And with you inside and that little baby on the way, it wouldn't take much to have her begging on her knees. Desperate times and all that. She'd do whatever I wanted."

"You leave her out of this." Jeremy's voice was thick with emotion.

Mark's laughter washed over him like a bucket of ice water.

"Whatever." Jeremy pushed past Mark and made for the hall. As he shoved open the door and stepped out onto the flagstones, he was hit by the sour smell like a slap in the face. It was stronger here, the pungent scent making him think that somebody had allowed raw meat to rot in the space. He swept the beam from his flashlight along the hall floor, the light instantly picked out a wide rusty streak that ran the length of the corridor.

Jeremy stumbled, and it took all of his strength to

remain on his feet. He backed up into Mark who forced him forwards with a rough shove.

Mark followed him into the hall, the sweep of the flashlight picking out the dark brown streaks smeared across the floor. He moved his beam over the walls, showing the splatters that had spread across the beige paint. Amid the splatters, Jeremy could make out a handprint.

"Jesus Christ." Jeremy's eyes watered as he stared at the mess. "We need to leave, Mark."

"No, we need to finish. He's already dead."

Jeremy turned slowly and stared at the man opposite. He couldn't make out Mark's facial features beneath the balaclava, but he could see from the nonchalant shrug that Mark didn't care.

"You knew?"

"I told you I'd done my homework. Of course I knew."

"So, you've seen this before? You knew and you brought us back here?" Another thought struck him suddenly. "Did you do this?"

Mark shook his head. "Nah. Come on, we need to get a move on."

Mark took the stairs, moving up them quickly and confidently. His familiarity with the space made Jeremy doubt the veracity of his story. He contemplated moving down the hall, following the blood to its ultimate conclusion. But at the last moment he changed his mind. Whatever lay at the end of that rust-coloured path was not something he needed to see.

Jeremy turned away and followed Mark up the stairs. He reached the upper landing quickly and quietly. The smell was equally as terrible up here and Jeremy found his steps slowing as he approached the room Mark was moving around in.

Jeremy pushed open the bedroom door with his flashlight to reveal what had once been a pleasant, bright space. A large four-poster bed dominated the centre of the room.

Mark was working at the opposite side of the room. He'd already lifted a large canvas from the wall and was standing to one side, his gaze pinned on Jeremy as he crept into the space.

From the corner of his eye, Jeremy could see the mound on the bed. He kept his gaze trained on Mark, refusing to turn his head towards the scene spread out in the centre of the room.

"Poor bitch," Mark said nonchalantly. "Come on, I need you to open this for me." He gestured to a safe that was set into the wall.

"Mark, I don't think I can--"

"Jesus H Christ. Do I have to do everything myself?"

"This isn't right, we need to call someone." Jeremy accidentally glanced in the direction of the bed. His gorge rose in his throat as his brain quickly assimilated the image of the woman spread across the bed.

With eyes watering, Jeremy spun away and ran for the door. Mark beat him to it, catching him in the doorframe. He wrapped his arm around Jeremy's head and frog-marched him back into the middle of the room.

"You'll do this, Jezza, mate, or you'll wind up like that silly bitch on the bed." Mark tightened his grip on Jeremy's neck, forcing him to look towards the bed. Jeremy caught a glimpse of blonde hair tarnished with brown rust. Hands that were a purple-black colour splayed out on the bedspread.

"I'm going to be sick…"

"For fuck's sake." Mark pushed him in the direction of the en-suite. "When did you get so fucking soft?"

Stumbling and struggling to take shallow breaths, Jeremy thrust open the door. The sight that greeted him appeared as though it had bled straight from his nightmares and into reality.

The remains of a naked, kneeling body was draped over the edge of the bath tub. A dark film had formed over the surface of the bathwater, making it appear as though the body was slowly being sucked into the oily depths.

"Never seen human soup before?" Mark said from the bedroom.

Unable to keep it in any longer, Jeremy vomited.

"See, if we call someone now, they'll know you were here."

Gagging, Jeremy fought the acrid vomit that

burned in his nose and prickled in the back of his throat. Half moaning, half crying, he turned away. But when he closed his eyes, he could still see the body.

"Are you going to do as you're told?" Mark crouched in front of him.

Jeremy nodded, barely able to see through his blurred vision.

"Good lad." Mark patted him on the back as he shoved him in the direction of the safe.

Jeremy wiped his eyes with the back of his gloved hand. The smell in the room was stuck in the back of his throat, and every breath he took made the situation worse. It was the image of the small body on its knees, half in and half out of the bath, that had burned itself onto the inside of his eyelids.

"Did you do this?" Jeremy kept his gaze averted from the remains on the bed as he crossed to the safe. It had been years since he'd tried to crack one open. He wasn't even sure he could do it anymore. Some skills needed to be used frequently, or they were lost over time, and Jeremy was sure his expertise in safe cracking had all but disappeared by now.

If he couldn't crack it, then what? Would Mark be true to his word? Would he tell the police that everything here was his doing? Or would he do worse?

"Me? Nah, mate. Can't say that I'm too upset though. Whoever did these three in did us all a favour. This score will be the best we've ever had."

So, the question remained, did Jeremy believe what Mark was saying? He gagged again as he studied the safe. Combination lock. A digital lock, despite the obvious difficulties it would have posed, would have been easier. They usually came with a reset button, designed to assist forgetful owners in retrieving their precious items. That design fail-safe allowed him to change the code without too much difficulty.

But a combination lock, like the one facing him, required a special touch. There had been a time in his life when he had taken great pride in his ability to pop open a combination safe in a matter of minutes. But as rusty as he was now, he wasn't convinced he would manage to crack even one of the numbers, never mind all three.

If it hadn't been set securely into the wall, Jeremy would have suggested that they take it with them. At least then, he would have had time to work on the lock without the stress of being in a house with three decomposing bodies. But he had a feeling Mark would not be interested in trying to move the safe.

He glanced over his shoulder at Mark, who had dragged the vanity stool over to the side of the bed. Jeremy watched him, noting the way he rummaged through the deceased occupant's belongings without a care in the world.

Despite Mark's assertions that the murders were not his handiwork, Jeremy found his ease around the dead bodies suspicious. How could he be so cold and callous?

"I'm not going to get this open," Jeremy said finally.

Mark barely looked at him. "Yeah, you are."

"Mark, it's not like the movies. It's really fucking complicated."

"Why do you think I brought you in? Nobody else can break a safe like you, mate. So, hop to it."

Jeremy made to step away from the safe, but Mark levelled the sawn-off shotgun at his chest. "That wasn't a request, Jezza. Open the safe or you're going to become so much human soup, like the body in the bathroom."

Jeremy contemplated his options. "And if I really can't do it."

Mark shrugged. "I believe in you..."

Unable to see another option, Jeremy turned back to the safe. As impossible as it appeared, he had to do it.

Mark slid a bag across the floor to him. "These might help."

CHAPTER THREE

SHIVERING, Drew pulled his coat on and huddled down inside it. They'd promised to fix the heating in the office sooner rather than later and yet, more than a *week* later, they still showed no signs of reconnecting the system.

It was practically Baltic. Drew took a chance and shot a sneaky look in the direction of Gregson's office, but the blinds were shut, making it impossible to tell if the Monk was feeling the cold like the rest of them. Knowing the Monk, he'd have icicles hanging from his nose hairs before he'd admit that there was a problem.

Drew leaned back in his chair and surveyed the rest of the room. Most of the desks sat empty, the other officers suddenly occupied with work that took them outside the confines of the ice tundra the office had turned into.

Pinching the bridge of his nose, Drew returned

his attention to the report. Perhaps if he stared down at it for long enough, he could intimidate it into making sense. No such luck.

With a sigh, he stretched. Despite spending the better part of an hour on it, he wasn't making any headway.

"Guv, Jodie has an update on the CCTV from the local business in the area of the attack." Arya's voice cut through Drew's concentration.

"Great." He spun around on his chair and stood. Anything that would get him out of the Arctic Circle was good, as far as he was concerned.

"Jodie told me not to say anything but you're not going to like what she's got for you," Maz said.

"Sounds like another depressing dead end," Drew said under his breath. Rather than dwell on the depressing titbit of news Arya had shared with him, Drew decided to make his own fun.

"When did it stop being Ms Meakin and become Jodie?"

Rosy colour spread across Maz's face and disappeared into his hairline. "Most of us are on a first name basis, so..." He fumbled his way over the words. "Sorry, guv, won't happen again."

"I'm just having a laugh, Arya. No need to be so serious."

Maz nodded, but Drew could tell from the serious set of his colleague's mouth that he'd made a significant misstep. Just another perfect example of putting my foot in it, he thought. He followed close on Maz's heels as the DS made for Jodie's domain.

The moment they crossed the hall and stepped into the room, Drew felt the change in temperature instantly. While the rest of the office was forced to operate in near freezing temperatures, Jodie's office space was positively balmy. Not that the heating system was working on this side of the hall either. The warmth, Drew noted, had more to do with the sheer volume of computer equipment Ms Meakin was operating.

Several large server banks had been moved into the office. And Jodie's personal computer setup would have put any high budget sci-fi show to shame. Drew followed Maz to the desk. Just what did she need with so much computer gear? And how much of their operational budget was going to its upkeep?

Jodie never bothered to look up from her place at the computer. "Sit." The command pulled a small smile from Drew as he stood next to her desk.

"DS Arya says you've got something to show me." As Drew spoke, he watched in abject fascination as her fingers flew over the keyboard. Each keystroke added to the lines of characters crossing the screen at the kind of speed Drew couldn't hope to follow.

"Sit."

Drew glanced at Arya who rubbed his hand awkwardly across the back of his neck. "Jodie..."

She sighed and with a couple of extra flourishes on the keyboard the screen disappeared. "Do you realise what you've interrupted?" She barely glanced in Drew's direction and instead directed her ire in Maz's direction. "Do you know how hard it is to try and trace a signal that is being passed through several countries simultaneously?"

Maz shook his head.

"Well, I do," she said. "I'll have to start over."

"Do I want to know what you're trying to trace?" Drew eyed her computer screen with the kind of wariness he usually only reserved for poisonous snakes, or the tofu curries his sister tried to pass off as real chicken.

She spun around in her chair and faced him. "Probably best to just let me see what I can come up with. If it's useful, great. If not, then it won't matter."

He contemplated arguing with her and then changed his mind. She was a force of nature, which considering the work they did was not a bad thing. Drew shot a surreptitious look in Arya's direction, confirming his earlier suspicions. The man was clearly smitten. On the other hand, Drew couldn't tell if Jodie reciprocated Maz's feelings, or if she was trying to keep her distance by doing her best impression of a human porcupine.

"So, what bad news do you have for me re the CCTV footage?" Drew said.

She shot a sour look in Arya's direction, an expression that said, *I told you not to say anything*. From the corner of his eye, Drew caught Maz shrug at her. Watching them communicate silently between each other left Drew in the awkward position of having to either comment on it or pretend he didn't see it. He chose the latter.

"They knew what they were doing," Jodie said. "They picked this spot in particular because most of the businesses in the area don't have working CCTV."

"And how would they know that?" Drew folded his arms over his chest.

"They've probably got connections in the area," Maz said.

"Or they're the reason the CCTV doesn't work on that stretch of road."

"What kind of a radius are we talking here?" Drew leaned over her shoulder, his gaze darting over the aerial map of the area surrounding the attack on DI Appleton.

Despite Melissa telling him that it wasn't his fault, Drew still felt the weight of guilt resting on his shoulders. He could have done more. He should have done more.

"It's this whole block." Jodie indicated a section on the map.

"And what about the traffic cameras on both ends. There's a junction right there. Can we not pull some footage from the cameras there?"

Jodie shot him a withering look. "I thought of that already. But it seems the cameras were knocked out due to a collision at the junction."

"What kind of collision?"

"I had to request the footage from East Yorkshire Motor Service. I just got it this morning."

"And?" Drew tried to keep the impatience from his voice.

Jodie tapped through the footage quickly. "Looks like somebody decided to skip the traffic queue coming into the junction. They hop the kerb back here." Jodie spooled backwards on the CCTV from a bus before hitting play.

The angle was poor. Leaning closer, Drew squinted at the screen. A white Ford Transit van skipped the line of cars and careened into the lights. Despite doing damage, made obvious by the sudden shift in the pole, the van reversed and then accelerated into the pole a second time.

"They misjudged their escape here." From the bus camera, Drew spotted the Ford van as it attempted to reverse a third time. It clipped a car on the right, causing it to spin into oncoming traffic. Within seconds, the junction was in complete chaos.

Drew kept his attention fixed on the white Ford van as it ploughed through the commotion, leaving behind its front bumper. A moment later, the van disappeared from the bus camera's view.

"Can you track it?"

"No need," Jodie said. Her fingers moved seamlessly over the keyboard. "Somebody reported a van on fire in a field a few miles outside Scarborough."

"But the camera was probably still working,"

Drew said, nodding towards the still image of the mobile traffic camera. "I've seen worse."

"After they cleaned up the mess on the junction, they disabled the lights and the camera for repair." Jodie hit a key and a clear image of a photo ID showing a serious looking middle-aged man with a ginger beard appeared on the screen.

"Do we know who that is? Is he legit?"

Jodie nodded. "I did a cross-reference check. It all looks above board. The camera was due to be replaced, but due to budget constraints that hasn't yet happened."

"Shit," Drew said. "Have we got *anything*?"

Jodie looked sceptical. "Not really."

"What about putting out an appeal for people in the area who might have dash cam footage from the night?" Maz looked from Drew to Jodie.

"That could work," Jodie said. "As long as we can find someone with the right angles and the necessary footage."

"You two can arrange that," Drew said. "There's someone I need to have a chat with." He started for the door and then thought better of it. "And someone should bring in the bloke who disabled the camera on the lights."

"I've already looked into him, he's clean," Jodie said.

Drew smiled at her. "I'd still feel better if we brought him in for a friendly chat."

"But I—" Jodie's protest was cut off as Maz nudged her shoulder.

"Consider it done, guv," Arya said. "I'll have a uniform bring him in."

"Good." Some of the tension left Drew's shoulders.

"Do you need anything else?" Maz made a half-hearted attempt to stand.

"No. Stay here and assist Ms Meakin."

The relief on Maz's face was palpable as he sat back down. "We won't let you down, guv."

Shaking his head, Drew left the two of them to discuss their next move. Heading back to his desk, he grabbed his keys and signed out of his computer. Scrolling through his text messages with Harriet, he found the number she'd given him.

He didn't make the call until he'd left the office. Sliding in behind the steering wheel, he listened to the dial tone. It felt like a lifetime, but the phone finally clicked into voicemail.

"Dr Tony Sheridan. Please leave your name and number and I'll get back to you as soon as possible."

"Dr Sheridan, my name is DI Drew Haskell with North Yorkshire police. I was given your number by a colleague. Dr Harriet Quinn. She said if I had an issue I could contact you. I'd appreciate if you could give me a call back at your earliest convenience." He left his number and hung up.

Leaning back, he let his head loll back against the headrest. Was he doing the right thing? Harriet wasn't due back from Ireland for at least a few more days. And considering the complicated emotional maze she was navigating there, he did not want to heap more misery on her. But he needed some guidance.

He stared at the phone, willing it to ring. When it didn't, he sighed and started the engine. He'd gone this long; he could wait a little longer.

CHAPTER FOUR

HE WATCHED from the safety of the car as she got into her Kia and reversed from the driveway before leaving. Getting out, he scanned the residential street before strolling across the road.

It took him only a moment to duck down the alley at the side of the house. Two minutes later, he had let himself in through the back gate.

With the bitch at work, he would have the house to himself. He kept a close eye on the neighbours' windows. He didn't need some nosey curtain twitchers letting her know he'd been around. He shoved the key into the lock and let himself in through the back door.

It swung open to reveal a messy kitchen. The sink was piled high with dishes. She was a grubby bitch. And to think she had kicked him out of his own house. And for what?

It wasn't his fault things were rough on the work

front. Times were hard, and most people were struggling to keep their heads above water. Yet, she had blamed him, instead of putting the blame squarely where it belonged; the fucking government were the ones running the country into the ground.

The smell of her perfume still lingered in the kitchen. It tugged at his senses and when his body responded, it only served to make him angrier. Crossing to the fridge, he pulled the door open and scanned its contents.

Too lazy to do a proper shop, he noted. He grabbed two cans of Coke from the door and jammed them into the pockets of his hoodie. Reaching back in, he grabbed the last Dairylea Dunker and ripped off the lid. Licking the soft cheese from the top, he felt his rage deepen. For a moment, he contemplated leaving the discarded lid inside the fridge, a little inconvenience that would irritate her and make her question the kids.

In the end, he took the lid and dropped it into the bottom of the bin. Carrying the plastic container of cheese with him through the house, he moved to the living room. His gaze drifted over the space. She'd changed everything around since he'd last been here. Crossing to the couch, he slumped down between the cushions and flicked on the telly.

Spreading crumbs around, he surfed through the channels, allowing his greasy fingers to linger over the buttons.

Once he'd finished his snack and drunk the last

of his Coke, he stood, leaving the television switched on as he started up the stairs. His bladder was full, a side effect of the Coke.

When he reached the landing, he ignored the two bedrooms to the left and started for the bathroom, but then paused, his attention fixed on the master bedroom at the end of the hall.

Pushing the door open, he was unsurprised to find the smell of her perfume stronger in here. Stepping inside, he closed the door behind him and crossed to her side of the bed. Leaning down, he brought his face to her pillow, inhaling the scent of her shampoo and the faint tang of her skin. His dick twitched in response.

The sight of his side of the bed, void of any of his personal belongings, sent a spike of hatred through him. How could she destroy their family? How could she be so stupid, so selfish? Depriving their children of their father.

Gritting his teeth, he yanked back the covers. A pair of satin pyjamas were folded neatly beneath the top pillow. She'd never worn anything like this for him. When they'd been together, she had always favoured oversized shapeless t-shirts that emphasised her lumpy body. Scooping up the scanty scrap of silk fabric that turned out to be a camisole, he stared at it. In his mind he could picture her wearing it. Silly cow probably thought she looked good wearing it, too.

He contemplated jamming it down the toilet, clogging up the bowl. The look of shock on her face would be priceless. Chuckling to himself, he made it halfway across the floor before halting. If he did that, she would know he'd been here. It would do nothing but cause problems and hinder his ability to come and go from the house whenever she was out.

His bladder niggled.

No. He could do better.

Moving to the en-suite bathroom, he left the thin silk top hanging on the door handle. Pausing at the toilet, he unzipped his jeans and tugged out his semi-hard penis. There was something erotic about being here without her knowing it.

It took a moment for his body to respond and when it did, he let his head loll back as piss splashed against the side of the bowl. When he was finished, he didn't bother to shake himself off. Instead, he reached over to the silk pyjama top hanging on the door and wrapped the fabric around his sensitive glans as he shook out the final droplets. He then then proceeded to use the camisole to dry the remaining urine from the head of his penis.

Only when he was satisfied did he tuck himself away, but he didn't bother to zip up his jeans. Walking back into the bedroom, he discarded the camisole on the end of the bed and pulled open the top drawer in the dresser.

Bingo.

The inside of the drawer was filled with her knickers and bras. Taking out a small selection, he carried them back to the bed. Climbing on top of the sheets, he lay out on her side of the bed and shimmied his jeans down over his hips until his arse was pressed into the mattress. Grabbing the first lacy thong, he wrapped it around his length and began to masturbate.

He would make her pay. She would be sorry for the way she'd treated him. As he closed his eyes, the memory of what he'd done to the prostitute rose in his mind. It had been over much too quickly. He'd taken her so completely by surprise that she hadn't even attempted to fight back.

If he was honest, the experience had been a little disappointing. He'd expected more. If she had fought back... The idea sent a cold shiver through him. He wanted a fight. He wanted to feel them struggle beneath him. He wanted to watch the realisation that they were trapped filling their eyes. He wanted to feel the panic as it took hold, feel their strength slowly ebb away as they struggled to survive. And then, the moment when they finally surrendered, when they finally knew there would be no escape, he would lock eyes with them and watch as their hope was extinguished right before he took everything from them.

The bitch would fight back. That much he knew for certain. If it had been her in the bed... he would have taken his time. Drawing it out, making it last. And when the time came, she would have known that he held her life in his hands. She would be sorry then.

A combination of rage and imagining the things he would do to her if he had the chance meant he didn't last very long.

Using the underwear he'd taken from the drawer, he cleaned himself up, revelling in the sticky mess that soaked into her intimate garments. Satisfied, he settled down among the pillows and drifted off for a nap.

The incessant buzz of his phone pulled him from his sleep. Rolling over, he reached for the phone, but it wasn't in its usual spot. Unsettled, his eyes sprang open, and he stared at unfamiliar surroundings. It took him a moment to reorder his thoughts. His gaze landed on the soiled underwear, and he smiled.

The buzzing phone ceased, and he sat up. The light had dimmed outside and the drone from the television downstairs drifted up to him.

"Shit." His voice was harsh and guttural as he noted the time on the bedside table. He snatched up his phone, panic swelling in his chest as he noted the number of missed calls and texts from her.

The last text caused the blood in his veins to turn icy. She was on her way home.

"Fuck!" He sprang from the bed, the mattress springs protesting with a noise he recognised from when he'd still lived here.

Gathering up the underwear, he folded them haphazardly and stuffed them back into the dresser drawer. There was no time to relish the petty act. It wouldn't take her long to do the school pick-up and then return home.

He turned and stared at the bed. Stupid, stupid. Struggling to straighten the sheets, he replaced her pyjamas where he'd found them. The bed didn't look as pristine as it had when he'd arrived. The art of bed making had never been one of his strengths.

With one final look at the bedroom, he left and clattered down the stairs, grabbing the empty Coke cans from where he'd discarded them on the couch. He dumped his rubbish into the bin. Returning to the living room, he switched off the television and plumped up the cushions.

It wasn't perfect, but it would have to do. She wouldn't notice, anyway. Not right away, and that was what he wanted. He wanted her to discover the little changes throughout the evening.

He left the television remote in front of the television rather than replacing it where he'd found it in the little remote holder on the coffee table. From the moment she'd bought the holder, he had hated it. A pointless waste was what he'd thought when she'd returned home with it one evening. She'd seen it on some Yummy Mummy social media. He hadn't bothered to ask which one. As far as he could tell, one vapid internet slut was like every other.

Sidling back into the kitchen, he rummaged in the fridge a final time. A chilled pizza sat on the middle shelf, and he removed it. A kernel of guilt took root in his chest. This was probably intended as tea for the kids. Even for him, the idea of stealing food from his own children didn't sit well with him. For a moment, he contemplated replacing it and then changed his mind. Fuck her. If she was too lazy to go out and do a proper shop like a real mother would, that wasn't his fault.

Perhaps this would teach her a lesson. If she was going to keep custody of his children, she needed to take better care of them. And anyway, he glanced down at the pizza, his lip curling with contempt, this was cheap junk food. Growing children need better, healthier food.

Slamming the fridge closed, he made his way to the back door and let himself out into the rain-soaked garden. The leaden sky hung low overhead and heavy water droplets began to fall from the clouds. Tugging up his hood, he hurried around the side of the house just as a car pulled into the drive.

Swearing silently, he pressed his back against the red brick of the house and prayed she had remembered to bring her keys for the front door. If she hadn't, then it was game over.

Excited whoops met his ears, and he cringed back, wishing he could become invisible.

The clang of the front door made his heart sing. He waited a few minutes more, the rain soaking in through his clothes, before he darted out of his hiding place next to the house. The second he hit the street, he moved in the opposite direction of his car.

It had been stupid to leave it across the road.

Stupid and careless. He made his way up the street, allowing his heart rate to slow down before he crossed the road and sauntered back the way he'd come.

Anyone looking out their window would see a man hurrying along in the rain. Nothing suspicious about that. Upon reaching the car, he slid in behind the steering wheel and slumped down in the driver's seat, his gaze fastened to the house across the road. There was no sign of the bitch, or any of the kids for that matter.

Starting the engine, he deliberately kept his speed low as he pulled out into the street. Don't give it away now.

His breathing slowed into a more relaxed pace as he turned off the street and headed for home. He'd done it.

His mind was already coming up with plausible excuses for ignoring her calls and messages. It was simple really. He'd just tell her a job had come up. Two birds with one stone. If she suspected him of being in the house, the lie would put paid to those suspicions.

His phone rang again, and he glanced down at it on the passenger seat next to the pizza, a smile playing around his mouth. The bitch. He contemplated answering, then changed his mind. She could wait. He was going home to have his tea.

CHAPTER FIVE

MELISSA STRUGGLED with the sleeve on her freshly pressed, white shirt, her muscles crying out as she fought against the pain that lingered in her body.

Dorothy Appleton, or Dot as she preferred to be called, watched from the opposite side of the bed. "I really don't agree with all of this." She pursed her lips. "You're doing it all wrong. Here, let me help." Melissa's mother stood and moved quickly to her side.

Mum's steel grey hair was cut short and as per usual was styled immaculately. They shared the same blue eyes but that was where the similarities ended. Where her mother's features were small and delicate, Melissa's were pronounced.

"I don't know why you insist on wearing such drab colours," Mum said, tutting softly as she tried to assist Melissa.

"Mum, I'm fine." She gritted her teeth, forcing her arm to twist in the direction she wanted. Her mother sighed and jerked the shirt harshly. Pain rocketed up from Melissa's elbow, spearing through her bruised shoulder before it spread through her battered and cracked ribs. She felt as though someone had doused her in molten metal.

After the beating, Melissa had called her brother Roger. But as was typical of her brother, he was too busy with 'family commitments', mainly his wife and two kids and the woman he was seeing on the side, not to mention his own case load.

With no one else to turn to, Melissa had been forced to do the unthinkable. The call to her mother had been as uncomfortable as she'd expected. And even now, it left a bitter taste in her mouth.

Tears prickled at the back of her eyeballs, and she squeezed her eyes shut. She wouldn't cry. Not over something so stupid. She had nothing to complain about. What was a little pain, and discomfort when Chelsea was lying on a cold slab in the morgue?

"You don't have to be a hero." Mum's voice cut through the noise in Melissa's head, reminding her that she wasn't alone and therefore couldn't succumb to the vortex of emotions that raged inside her.

"Why couldn't you have taken the same path as Roger? At least then you wouldn't be stuck here, injured, and alone."

"I like it here," Melissa said. She swallowed her

discomfort and shrugged into her jacket. It cost her to keep her expression devoid of pain, but the less she let her mother see how badly she was hurt, the better.

"Well now that it's over between you and Drew, why don't you come home? I'm sure the DCI can spare you. And if you do come home, Daddy can put a word in for you with the Met. I'm sure they'd find something useful for you there."

Melissa's eyes snapped open, and she glared at her mother. "I've worked hard to get where I am. Going to the Met would be a step backwards."

"But that's because you wasted so much time moving all over the place." Mum wafted her hand airily. "Anyway, Daddy, would make sure it wasn't too much of a step down for you. He's very well respected, you know."

Melissa shook her head. "Mum, for the last time, no."

Her mother huffed a sigh. "Fine." She raised her hands in fake surrender. "My lips are sealed." Mutiny glittered in her blue eyes as she looked Melissa up and down.

The door to the hospital room swung open and a dark-haired nurse appeared. The smile on her face faded as soon as she saw Melissa up and dressed. "You're supposed to rest."

"I tried to tell her that, but will she listen?" Mum's expression switched instantly. Gone was the calculated expression from a moment ago, replaced instead with a broad smile.

Gripping the end of the bed, Melissa tried to keep the contents of her stomach where they belonged. She did not have the energy to keep fighting everyone but if she had to spend even one more minute in this hospital room, she was going to start screaming. And if she started, she was certain she would never stop.

"Ms Appleton, you need to get back into bed."

"It's DI Appleton," Melissa grumbled. "And I'm going home." She caught the glint in her mother's eye and shook her head. "My *own* home. My apartment. I'm not going home with you."

"But, Melissa—"

"End of discussion." She tried to put the same kind of force into her voice that she sometimes used at work, but where Maz or Olivia might have relented, her mother was made of sterner stuff and could not be dissuaded.

"I want it put on record that I'm completely against this madness. You need to be with people who care about you. People who can look after you."

The nurse joined in. "DI Appleton, you're in no fit state to be up on your feet. The injuries you sustained are serious."

"I know they're serious," Melissa said through her teeth. "I'm the one who sustained them." Tightening her grip on the end of the bed, she straightened her shoulders. "What I really need is for everyone to stop arguing with me so I can go home."

She pulled in a deep breath but the pain in her ribs flared into life, cutting the air off mid-way. Sweat beaded on her scalp before it slipped down her neck and along her spine.

"You've not been discharged. The doctor will have to see you and he's not going to like it." The nurse sounded huffy.

"I'm discharging myself," Melissa said, hating the breathy tone of her voice. It made her appear weak, incompetent, and she was neither of those things.

And then, as though she'd conjured him from the air itself, Drew appeared in the doorway. His dark gaze raked over the scene, shrewdly getting the lay of the land in an instant.

"Ey-up!" Drew grinned at her. "I thought I'd drop by and see how you're doing." His gaze bounced from Melissa to the mutinous nurse.

Mum, Melissa noted, had ducked behind the door out of sight.

"Are you going home?" Drew's eyebrows rose upwards.

Melissa nodded. The nurse shook her head.

"She needs time to heal," the nurse said. Turning to Melissa, she added, "You need to get back into bed."

"Maybe you should do as your told." There was an undertone of mirth in Drew's voice, and it cut Melissa to the quick. What did he have to be so upbeat about? It wasn't that long since she'd broken it off with him and here he was, bouncing in the door like a puppy, happy as could be.

Had he already started something with Harriet? The idea of it twisted like a knife in Melissa's guts. No. She would not go down that path. She had made a promise to herself; no more being the consolation prize. She was worth more than that.

She pulled herself up a little straighter, catching the way Drew's grin dimmed as he registered the awkward pause. Melissa sighed, gradually slowing her heart rate. "Not you too..."

"Perhaps she'll listen to you." Ever one for a dramatic entrance, Mum stepped out from her spot behind the door. "Good to see you again, Drew."

"Mrs Appleton, lovely to see you again, too." Drew shot a wary look in Melissa's direction, one that said, *'you should have warned me,'* and *'I'm out of my depth here'*. Not that she blamed him. The last time he'd met her mother, it had ended disastrously.

"Now what have I said about calling me Mrs Appleton? It's Dot and I won't hear anything else." She beamed at him and Melissa was impressed by how easily her mother switched on the charm. It was a talent that she herself had never managed to master.

She busied herself with the jacket on the bed. Putting it on would only result in more pain and there was no chance she was willing to appear that vulnerable in front of Drew, not after everything that had happened between them. Closing her eyes, she tried to block out the mindless chatter between her mother and her ex.

"We should get going," she said, abruptly interrupting their conversation. Melissa stared pointedly at her mother and prayed she would read the desperation in her voice.

"Don't be so rude, Melissa. Drew came to see you. The least you could do is spare the man five minutes of your time." Mum turned her hundred-watt smile on Drew. "I'll nip out for a coffee and give you two a chance to catch up." The possessive way she placed her hand on Drew's arm made Melissa's blood boil.

Stretching a thin smile over her lips, Melissa attempted to control her anger. "I'm sure DI Haskell here has better things to be doing with his time. Anyway, you said you'd give me a lift home."

"I said I could take you home," Mum said. "To your real home. Not that flea pit of a flat that you've been renting."

"She tried to persuade me to stay there while I've been up here caring for her." Dorothy returned her attention to Drew. "But I took one look at the place and called Alex and asked him to book me into a nearby hotel. You remember Alex, don't you, Drew? Melly's father. I can't say he was too thrilled when Melissa said you two were seeing each other. Anyway, that's all over with now and Melly can finally come home where she belongs."

"Mum, please." Melissa balled her fingers into a fist, digging her short nails into the flesh of her palm. Pain was an easy distraction, and it allowed her to control the tears that threatened to spill. She would not allow herself to cry in front of Drew. Not now, not ever.

"Melly." Mum placed a hand against her cheek. "Oh sweetheart, the doctor said you weren't ready to leave. Until they give you the all-clear, I'm not taking you anywhere."

Melissa caught the smug smile on the nurse's face.

"Then I'll find my own way home." Melissa pulled away from her mother and made to grab her bag from the bed. The simple act of stretching her arm out pulled a gasp from her. Pain, an icy dagger that speared through her ribcage and sealed the air in her lungs, caused her eyes to water. Gritting her teeth, she curled her fingers around the straps of the hold-all and slid the bag to the edge of the bed.

Before the weight of the bag could cause her anymore pain, Drew was there. His warm fingers closed over hers, halting her progress.

"Drew, please..." Rather than meet his gaze, Melissa closed her eyes.

"Melly, you're only going to hurt yourself. You can't leave. Tell her Drew, she might listen to you."

Melissa's resolve began to weaken. Calling her mum had been a mistake.

"Melissa is going to stay with me."

Melissa's eyes snapped open, and she stared at the man next to her. The warmth from his hand that still covered hers helped to push the pain to the back of her mind.

"What?" The word came out of Melissa as a squeak.

Drew smiled at her, the corners of his eyes crinkling. "It's for the best. She won't be alone; I'll be there to keep an eye on her. And if anything goes wrong, I'll bring her straight back here."

"But you're not even together," Mum interjected. "It makes more sense for Melly to come home. That way she can get a fresh start, and--"

"Is that what you want?" Drew asked Melissa.

"No," she said, ignoring the dagger-filled look mum threw in her direction. "I just want to get out of here. I can't rest in this place."

"I get it," Drew said. He blew out a breath and took the bag from her. "It's settled, then. We'll get you discharged, and you'll come home with me."

"That isn't a good idea," the nurse said.

"I promise to keep a close eye on the patient," Drew said. "Scout's honour."

His disarming grin seemed to have the desired effect on the nurse because she returned his smile. "All right, but only because you're the one saying it, DI Haskell. I'll see what I can do with the doctor."

"Thanks, Francesca, you're an angel."

She rolled her eyes at him, but judging by her body language, she was lapping up the attention.

It was unusual to see Drew like this. He was normally so serious. Reserved, even. This was an unfamiliar side of him.

As the nurse left, Mum turned to Drew. "Do you think you could give me a moment with my daughter?"

Melissa contemplated asking him to stay but then decided against it. If they did not have the conversation now, Mum would just find some other, inopportune time to spring it on her.

Drew glanced in her direction and Melissa nodded. "It's fine. I'll be done in a few."

"I'll chase up the discharge papers." He turned his smile on Mum. "Always a pleasure to see you, *Mrs Appleton*. I hope the next time we meet, it will be under better circumstances."

Mum's smile was withering but she held her hand out. "I don't foresee many opportunities for meeting in our future, DI Haskell. Have a good day."

Drew's smile remained in place. The old Drew would have soured, his expression reflecting his true emotions. Instead, he shrugged and went to the door. "If you need me, I'm just out here."

"Thanks," Melissa said. Mum's rage was barely contained, and as Drew closed the door behind him, Melissa felt it grow out of control, sucking up all the oxygen in the room so that it was difficult to take a satisfying breath.

"This is a mistake, Melissa." Mum's prim tone grated against the headache that had started in the back of Melissa's skull. "You should be coming home with me. Daddy and I will sort you out, don't you worry about that."

Melissa opened her mouth to argue but her mother decided to bulldoze straight over her. "Doing anything else would be a mistake. DI Haskell means well, but he's a bit useless really." Mum shook her head. "I don't know what you ever saw in him. He's not exactly the brightest bulb in the box, is he? And going home with him, well, it's just going to confuse things between you. He'll get the wrong end of the stick, and you'll have to pick up the pieces again--"

"Mum!" Melissa balled her hands into fists in a poor attempt at keeping her anger in check. Seeing the look of shock on her mother's face helped take the edge off, and Melissa let her voice drop. "Enough. Please." Closing her eyes, she sank onto the edge of the bed. "I know you mean well. And I know you want to help."

"You're my daughter. I hate seeing you make mistakes because you're too stubborn to do what's best."

"But that's the problem, Mum. You never listen to me. You don't have the first clue about what I actually want in my life."

"Of course I do. You're my daughter. I know you better than you know yourself."

Melissa shook her head and let her chin drop to her chest. "You haven't got a fucking clue." She lifted her gaze. "I love you and Dad, I really do. But I'm not Roger. I'll never do things the way you want me to."

"I know that." Mum rolled her eyes.

"I have to do what's right for me."

"And you think going home with DI Haskell is right for you?" Mum's arched eyebrow threatened to spike Melissa's blood pressure.

"I don't know. Maybe. Yeah. For now, at least. I belong here. There are things I need to do."

Mum sighed. "Fine. But I want you to know that I think you're making a mistake." She shook her head. "You're an adult now. I can't force you to change your mind, no matter how foolish I think you're being." She gathered up her coat and handbag. "When you come to your senses, your father and I will be waiting." She paused at the door. "But don't wait too long. We won't be around forever."

Before Melissa could respond, her mother disappeared out into the hall. The click-clack of her low heels receded down the hall. Blowing out her cheeks, Melissa leaned back against the pillows. If Drew hadn't turned up when he did, would her mother have worn her down, eventually?

The idea left her uncomfortable.

"You all right?" Drew poked his head around the door.

"I'll be better when I'm out of here."

"Then let me be the bearer of good news." He held up a set of forms. "Once you sign these, you're officially free."

Melissa reached for the papers and regretted the movement instantly. Wincing, she let her arm drop back to her side. She caught the wary look on Drew's face and shook her head. "I'll be fine, Drew, really. I just can't be here anymore. It's too painful." She let her gaze fall to her lap.

Without a word, he set the papers and pen in front of her.

CHAPTER SIX

DREW SET the bag down in the boot of the car and watched Melissa struggle to get into the front seat. His offer of a place to stay had been made impulsively, but now that he'd said it, he couldn't take it back. No matter that a part of him considered it a huge mistake. Then again, it wasn't exactly a normal scenario they found themselves in.

Sliding into the driver's seat, he studied her profile. She was chalk white, her lips compressed in a tight line that belied her earlier protestations that her pain was manageable.

"Are you sure this is a good idea?" He didn't want to keep questioning her, but she really did not look well at all.

"Drew, please..." She sighed and glanced at him. The dark blue smudges below her eyes emphasised the exhaustion that shadowed her gaze. "I don't want to be here anymore. I can't lie in that bed any longer knowing Chelsea's body is a few floors below in the morgue's cold storage."

Without needing to be told a second time, Drew started the engine and reversed out of the car space. Melissa continued to stare at him for a moment or two, before she finally settled back into the passenger seat.

He knew what it was like. When he'd woken up in the hospital after Freya had tried to kill them both, it had been nigh impossible to rest knowing she was so close but completely out of reach.

They left the city behind. Melissa's easy breathing made Drew think she'd drifted off to sleep. Mist spattered over the windscreen and Drew let his speed drop as they reached the A171, cutting through the countryside to Whitby. Turning on the car radio, he turned the volume down, so as not to wake Melissa. But between the hum of the road and the steady back and forth swish of the wipers he had to strain to hear the news report.

"I never asked why you decided to move all the way out here," Melissa said, her voice dropping into the void left when the news report ended.

"Sorry, did I wake you?"

Melissa shook her head. "I wasn't asleep." The silence stretched like an elastic, broken only when Melissa spoke again. "Why did you move out here? I never had you pegged for a fan of rural life."

"I'm not, really," he said. "I've just always liked the idea of living by the sea. And after everything that happened with Matthews, I realised life was too short not to take a chance."

From the corner of his eye, he watched as she bit her lip and stared down at her hands. "How do you do it?" she said.

"Do what?" He glanced at her in surprise.

"How do you just let it all go? The fear, the pain, the guilt." On the last word, her voice dropped until it was a whisper that trembled in the air.

Drew hesitated. How could he answer her. Everything seemed so utterly irrelevant. He'd asked himself the exact same question; first after Freya and then later when Matthews had tried to cut him into pieces on the plastic tarp in his living room.

"I don't know that you can," he said finally. It wasn't the answer Melissa wanted but at least it was honest.

"Do you still feel..." Melissa trailed off, uncertainty in the awkward shrug of her shoulders. But Drew knew what she was asking without her ever needing to say the words.

"I still carry that guilt over Freya. Nobody will ever convince me that I shouldn't, that I couldn't have seen it coming. I knew how sick she was. I knew how fragile her state of mind was, but I was just so glad to have her home." He kept his gaze trained on the road ahead.

"At least I can talk about her now without wanting to rip the world apart, without wanting to punish those around me for getting on with their lives." He shrugged and glanced quickly in Melissa's direction before returning his attention to the traffic. "And that's progress. At least that's what Harriet says."

Melissa's sigh was so quiet that he very nearly missed it. But it wasn't the typical exasperated sound he was used to hearing whenever Dr Quinn's name was mentioned. This one sounded, at least to him, like pure resignation.

"Why don't you like her?"

"I don't know her," Melissa said quickly. "Not like you do." The last was added as an afterthought but the implication was clear.

Drew laughed. "You never wanted to know her. Never gave yourself the chance."

Melissa shrugged and winced, regret etched into her screwed up features and the shallow way she took a breath. "It's not easy to come into a team that's already formed. You, Maz, and Olivia. Then there's Gregson, who clearly favours you. And the cherry on top was Dr Quinn. Someone who should have been an outsider, but you all behaved like she had always been there. Like she was just part of the gang. Like she was one of us."

"She is."

"No," Melissa said, straightening up in her seat. From the corner of his eye, Drew could see the beads of sweat that glistened on her forehead and the ashy colour that spread over her face. "No, she was never one of us. She's an outsider. A civilian. Always was, always will be."

"Harriet earned her place with us, fair and square."

The silence grew between them, uncomfortable and stifling in its stillness. Finally, unable to bear it anymore, Drew coughed.

"You weren't always so opposed to civilian help."

Melissa shrugged. "Things change."

"And Chelsea?" It was a low blow, and he knew it. But that didn't change the fact that he wanted to understand what had changed.

Melissa blew out a low, pained breath. When Drew looked at her, he could see tears glittering on her cheeks.

"Shit, I'm sorry."

"You don't have to be," she said. "It's not your fault." She glanced at him, a sideways look that in the past would have melted his heart. "It's not because Harriet is a civilian. It never was. Maybe in another life, in some other place she and I would be friends..." She shook her head. "But not here."

"Harriet is an asset to the team."

Melissa nodded. "I know. I can see that. She belongs here."

"Then if you know all of this, why are you so opposed to her assistance?"

"She makes me feel like an outsider." The words were whispered, and Drew took his eyes from the road to look over at her, uncertain if he'd heard her correctly.

"I don't understand."

"You wouldn't," she said wryly. "You've never had to feel that way. You've never been on the outside."

"That's not fair, Melissa."

She studied him for a moment. "You asked, Drew. I never promised the reason would be fair, or even rational." Her laughter was bitter and hurt his ears.

He parked outside the house and killed the engine before turning to face her.

"I think it was a mistake to come back here," she said finally.

"I don't think you should be alone," Drew said.

"I didn't mean a mistake to come here," she said laughing. "Although, that was also probably a mistake but for a completely different reason." She took a steadying breath.

"Then what?"

"I think it was a mistake to come back to North Yorkshire. Stupid, really. There was a part of me that genuinely believed we could pick right up where we left off. As though all that intervening time had never happened. As though you hadn't suffered a life altering loss."

She buried her face in her hands and began to cry. Drew felt like a pointless pillock, so he waited, unsure of his next move. The conversation was a necessary one, but that didn't make it any less painful.

He waited until Melissa's tears quietened before deciding to speak again. "You have as much right to be here as any of us."

Melissa ran the back of her hand over her eyes and laughed. "You almost sound believable."

"It's the truth."

She shook her head and stared out the passenger window at the house wreathed in darkness. "I was always an outsider, even in the beginning. I didn't fit in like you or the others. It's why I went in the first place." She looked over at him. "Do you think..." she trailed off and he could see how uncertain she had become.

"Go on."

"Do you think things would have been different if I'd stayed?"

It was Drew's turn to feel as though the earth had suddenly shifted beneath his feet, solid ground giving way to sinking sand. One wrong step and he would be lost. It would be easy to lie. A kindness, really.

But they were past that now, weren't they?

"No. Things would never have worked between us."

Melissa nodded, her face ashen. "I know. I think I knew even then." She touched her fingers to his arm. "Why did you go along with it this time?"

The question was a painful one and Drew wasn't sure if he was ready to admit the truth out loud. As though she could sense this, Melissa started to open her door.

"It's all right," she said softly. "I get it."

"What?"

When she smiled it was not an expression of joy, but instead one of pure sadness. "I made you a coward."

"You didn't make me do anything," he said quickly. "It was something I chose for myself."

"We both did, I suppose." She sighed. "Christ, what is it about feeling like shit that makes you want to put every aspect of your life under the microscope?"

"I was the same," Drew said, feeling like a prisoner on death row who had received a last-minute reprieve from the chair. "It screws with your head."

"It definitely does that," Melissa grumbled under her breath as she struggled against the breeze that threatened to pull the door from her hold.

Drew hurried around to her side of the car, offering her his hand as she climbed unsteadily to her feet. She glared at the proffered hand and pushed him aside.

"I'm no invalid, Drew." The words were spoken through gritted teeth.

Stepping back, he watched her struggle over to the door as he grabbed the bags from the boot. As soon as they were inside, Melissa dropped heavily into the second-hand armchair Drew had picked up when he'd first moved in. Her eyes fluttered shut and he could see a shadow of pain that crossed her features.

"Do you want me to get you something to eat? I mean there's not much, but I can rustle something up."

There was no answer. Her breathing had deepened, her visage relaxed as she lay with her head against the back of the chair. Grabbing a throw from the back of the sofa, Drew draped it gently over her body and crept from the room.

CHAPTER SEVEN

PC JAY VARMA pulled off the A169 into the wide yard in front of the farmhouse and parked the car. A Land Rover was parked haphazardly on the opposite side of the yard and as Jay killed the engine, he saw a man climb from the driver's side.

"Took you long enough!" Jay was greeted with the harsh words as soon as he opened his door.

"Excuse me?"

"I called it in over an hour ago. Do you lot think the rest of us have got nothing better to do with our time than wait around for you to get off your arse and respond?"

"I came as soon as I was free," Jay said, keeping his voice steady. It wasn't unusual for him to be met with hostility. "You were the one who made the call for a welfare check?"

The ruddy-faced man nodded. "Well, it wasn't the bloody tooth-fairy."

"What did you say your name was?" Jay glanced up at the two-storey farmhouse noting a faint glow in one of the upstairs windows.

"I gave all of this information to the operator. Terry Phillips. I live a few miles that way."

"And when was the last time you saw the occupants, Mr Phillips?" Jay let his gaze drift over their surroundings. He spotted a shed, the front door of which was partially ajar. He crossed the yard, taking note of the broken padlock on the ground which was half buried in the gravel. Without touching anything, he peered around the edge of the door. The shed was empty but a couple of oil stains on the concrete floor suggested that hadn't always been true.

"Four weeks ago," Terry said. "Shouldn't you be looking at the house?"

Ignoring the second question, Jay withdrew from the shed and ambled towards the house. "And that's unusual?"

"Andrew was supposed to come by my place a couple of days ago—"

"And Andrew is the owner of the property?" Jay interjected.

"Aye, Andrew Hadfield."

"Four weeks is a long time. You said on the phone that you and Andrew were close." Jay glanced back at the man shadowing his footsteps.

"We're good friends." Terry bristled. "Four weeks is highly unusual. I normally see Andrew every other day, out and about. But me and the missus were away on holiday. We've got an apartment in Spain. And Andrew was away in Scotland."

"Maybe they haven't returned yet." Jay circled back to the front door.

"Well, maybe…"

"And when did you return?"

"Two days ago. But Andrew and I had arranged to meet when I got back." Terry sighed and glanced up at the house. "I swung by here yesterday but there was no one around then, either. And I can't get Andrew on the phone. Even if he's away, he'd answer the phone."

"Who else lives in the property with Mr Hadfield?"

"His wife Anna and their two kids. Well, they're not really kids anymore. Willow is still in school. She's had a few issues. Fell in with a bad crowd." Terry sighed. "But she's doing better these days, got her head in the books studying for her GCSEs. And young Andy is doing his first year away in university. Got into Uni in Newcastle studying Agriculture with Farm Business Management. Andrew is so proud of him. In fact, he never stops banging on about it. Says Andy is going to take over the farm when he retires."

"And you can't reach any of the family?"

Terry shook his head. "No one."

Jay nodded. "Please wait here." He indicated a spot next to the Land Rover and walked away before Terry Phillips could argue further.

He made his way to the front door and rapped smartly on the heavy wood. When no answer came, he knocked a second time. He attempted to peer through the side window, but his view was obscured by a fancy voile, the type his own mother favoured.

Rounding the side of the house, Jay scanned the surroundings for anything that might be out of place. The flowerbeds beneath the windows on the ground floor seemed to be churned up but that wasn't what caught his attention as he made his way to the back of the house. The rubber surround on one of the double-glazed panes of glass had been carelessly replaced, leaving some of the rubber hanging out on the window ledge.

The window itself was too high to get a good view into the house, but Jay couldn't ignore the unease that settled over him as he studied the property. He continued his progress around the house and spotted a set of French doors. The blinds on the doors were shut, making it impossible to see into the house. He knocked, and the door moved beneath the weight of his fist. With his elbow, he pushed harder on the door and it swung inwards. He moved forward but spotted the dead flies littering the cream lounge carpet and halted.

His stomach knotted as he poked his head inside. A wave of fetid heat hit him like a slap to the face and he stumbled backwards. He'd attended the scene of a sudden death when he'd first started working for the police. An elderly gentleman had passed away while seated in his living room armchair. With no family to check on him, it had been sometime before the neighbour had noted his absence. When she'd gone round to check, the smell that poured out through the letterbox had given away the grim truth. She'd raised the alarm and Jay and a senior officer had responded to the call.

That smell had been the same as this. The same cloying, viscous rot that thickened the air, invading the nose and mouth, turning each breath to a sticky soup that caught in the back of the throat. It was impossible to avoid.

Reaching for his radio, Jay called it in.

CHAPTER EIGHT

MAZ SAT BACK against his seat and stared at the screen. The words had started to blur. Nothing made sense anymore. Stretching his arms back, he tried to sort the pieces together in his head so they could form something approaching a coherent theory. But nothing worked. There was clearly something he was missing.

He got up from his chair, his feet carrying him in the direction of Jodie's office. The low hum of her computers greeted him before he stepped into the warm space.

Jodie was nowhere to be found. Crossing to her workstation, Maz stared at the dark monitor, the lines of code moving of their own volition as various programs ran in the background.

"What are you doing?" There was a sharp edge to Jodie's voice as she entered the room.

Maz whirled to face her and smiled apologetically. "I was looking for you. I was going to ask if you wanted a coffee, but I see you're way ahead of me."

Jodie nodded stiffly and crossed to her desk. She set the steaming mug down on the desk and paused.

It dawned on Maz that he was blocking her path, and he hastily stepped aside. "Sorry."

Jodie hurried into her space, her fingers flying over the keyboard. The windows with the lines of code disappeared in an instant.

"Can I help you with something?" She glanced up at him. Maz realised with a start that her glasses were slightly askew. In his eyes, it only added to her charm.

"It's not making any sense," he said.

Jodie gestured to the seat next to her desk. "Sometimes, when things don't make sense to me, talking about the problem helps."

Maz dropped into the seat, allowing his momentum to swing the chair around before it came to a stop and he was once again facing Jodie. The ghost of a smile hovered on her lips and Maz's heart flipped in response.

"I don't imagine you run into many problems you can't solve," he said.

Jodie thought about it for a moment before shrugging. "You'd be surprised. Between us," she leaned conspiratorially towards him, "there are a lot of things I can't do. At least not if I want to keep my job." Her full smile, when it crept over her face, made Maz think of a sunrise he'd witnessed as a child when they'd visited relatives in India.

She straightened up. "Is it about the files you've been reviewing?"

Maz glanced up at her in surprise. "How did you know?"

Her smile turned sheepish. "I saw you struggling through it when I went to get coffee. I thought about asking you if you fancied a break, but you were so engrossed, I decided not to."

Maz found himself wishing she *had* asked him. "There are too many holes in the report."

"Which one?" Jodie asked, returning her attention to the computer.

"The official report on the system about the night DI Appleton was attacked. It's just not adding up for me."

Jodie nodded and let her fingers drift rapidly over the keys. The file appeared on the screen, and she took a moment to peruse the text. Her face was a mask of concentration. A cute little notch appeared between her brows as she stared at the screen.

Maz read the report over her shoulder, hoping to find something different this time.

"See?" He slumped back and pressed his hands to his face. "It doesn't make sense. There's clearly something missing."

"Who found DI Appleton?" she asked.

"I have no idea. Probably some good Samaritan who was passing by. There's nothing about it in the report, not that it matters. Someone will have followed up on it but there's never usually anything important."

Jodie's expression was grim as she returned her attention to the screen.

"I don't see any evidence of a statement." Her brow furrowed again as she continued to type.

"Like I said, that's not important." Maz swivelled around in the chair. "The forensic report was oddly sparse.

After more tapping on the keyboard, Jodie sat back triumphantly. "I've found the call."

"What call?"

She shot him an incredulous look and heat crawled into Maz's face. "You mean the list of call logs for that night?" He shook his head. "I looked that over. I couldn't find anything remotely matching the attack on DI Appleton."

Jodie's expression turned withering. "I don't give up as easily. The files for the call logs are there but someone erased a group of them from the list."

Maz straightened up. "Erased them? Who the heck would do that?"

Jodie shrugged. "I mean, I could try and find out if you think it would help?"

"It would definitely help."

"Don't get your hopes up but I might be able to track down a system ID." She returned to the screen.

Maz waited expectantly. "How long will it take?"

"How long is a piece of string?" She riveted her

attention to the screen and nodded absently at what she saw there.

"You've got something?"

Jodie grimaced and sat back. "Just the system ID."

"And what does that tell us?"

"Not much I'm afraid. I can't cross reference the numbers until whoever owns that particular ID logs in again."

"Great." Maz swore under his breath but the look on Jodie's face pulled him up short. "What is it?"

"Do you know how difficult it is to cover your tracks like that?"

He shrugged. "It's just a deleted call log."

Jodie chewed her lip and drummed her fingers against the desk's surface. "It's not that simple. I mean, it is, but the rest of it..."

"What are you trying to say?"

"I'm saying that whoever did this didn't want to be found."

"But you can figure it out, yeah? I mean, this is your whole thing."

"True." Jodie sounded sceptical. She got to her feet. "I need to speak with the DCI."

As she moved around Maz, he caught her hand. "Woah, wait. What aren't you telling me?"

Jodie's gaze met his before it dropped to the place where his hand was wrapped around hers. Sucking in a breath, she steadied herself. "Do you want to get a drink sometime?"

Her question knocked Maz off kilter. He swallowed hard. His brain refused to cooperate. He'd never been asked out by a woman before. He was the one who always did the asking.

"Sure." He squeezed the word out before the voice in the back of his head talked him out of it.

Jodie's face broke into a wide grin. "Great, we'll arrange it." And then she was gone. Maz stared at the place where his hand had touched hers. So engrossed was he in the question she'd asked him, he hadn't even noticed when she'd pulled free of his grip.

Getting to his feet, he tracked her progress. She disappeared into the Monk's office. It was weird. Her behaviour was strange. They'd found something together and yet she had rabbited off before they could examine it more thoroughly.

Maybe her invitation for a drink had been nothing more than an attempt to throw him off guard. That thought alone was enough to deflate him, and he sloped back to his desk. Slumping back into his seat, he stared down at the reports.

Well, if Jodie could find the information so easily, then so could he. His mother had always told him that he had a talent for computers. She'd been baffled when he'd decided to join the police force instead of going on to study computer science as they'd discussed.

Stretching his arms, he cracked his knuckles and set to work on the computer. How hard could it be?

Buoyed by a sense of purpose, he clicked through to the call logs and began to scroll.

BLEARY EYED, he glared at the screen. Two hours had already passed, and he was still no closer to figuring out who had taken the call the night of DI Appleton's attack. The idea of having to go and speak to each operator individually just to figure out which one had taken the call did not sit well with him. There had to be some other way to narrow it down.

Jodie had left the Monk's office forty minutes previously, her expression grim. He'd tried to catch her eye but if she'd seen him, she'd given no indication of it and had instead hurried back to her own office. He'd thought of following her but as he'd stood, he'd caught sight of her scurrying from her office with her bag and coat in hand.

And now, he was stuck here, no further along than he had been hours before.

With a sigh, he settled back in his chair and closed his eyes. A hand dropped onto his shoulder, and he yelped, the sudden jerky movement almost sent him sprawling to the floor. He managed to right himself before that happened.

Twisting in the chair, he glared up at Olivia.

"What's eating you?" She cocked her head to one side and glanced past him to the documents spread out on the desk. Her gaze tracked up to the computer screen and she raised a quizzical brow.

"Nothing," Maz said, moodily. It wasn't her fault that his mother had lied to him.

"Well, something's got your knickers in a twist, so come on, spit it out."

"Don't you have your own crap to get on with?" He crossed his arms over his chest and cocked an arrogant eyebrow at her. The collar on her shirt was mostly closed but he could just see the reddish pink edge of her scar as it peeked over the top.

She caught him staring and her hand rose to adjust the collar. Maz tore his eyes away and sheepishly stared down at his desk.

"You can be a complete arse sometimes, do you know that?"

He did, in fact, know this and he hated himself for it. It had been a defence mechanism he'd developed when he'd been a child. It wasn't exactly easy to be the youngest child of six siblings. Not to mention the age gap. Twelve years didn't seem like much now that he was older, but back then it had proven to be a veritable chasm. By the time he was old enough to walk and talk, the rest of his siblings were teenagers, and they had wanted nothing to do with their snot nosed younger brother.

"Sorry," he said reflexively.

Olivia had already turned to walk away and Maz called after her. "I'm working on the DI Appleton material." Olivia didn't stop. "I might have found something." That brought her up short and she turned to face him.

"What kind of thing?" Suspicion glinted in her eyes.

Maz beckoned her over and proceeded to fill her in on what little information he'd managed to glean. By the time he'd finished, he sat back and stared at her expectantly. She would dismiss it, he knew that. It was far too thin to be worth examining.

"We should go and speak with them," Olivia said.

"I told you already, it's just a wild goose chase. I'd wind up looking like a fool."

Olivia shook her head. "You're getting soft, Maz. Where's your sense of adventure? The thrill of the chase and all that? Come on, we can do this."

"You only want to go because you've been grounded on desk duty."

"Exactly," Olivia said. "And this is perfect. Not even the DCI can say no to something like this."

"Technically, he could," Maz said. "Anyway, it's tenuous at best. We can't just go questioning a bunch of our own on a hunch."

Olivia fell silent next to him.

"It's a dead end," he said.

"Not necessarily."

"Yeah, it is. I'll ask Jodie in the morning what she—"

"If questioning the operators is too much, couldn't we just request a list of who was on duty that night from Force Control?"

Heat crept up Maz's neck and into his face. Why hadn't he thought of that?

"Judging by the look on your face I'm going to assume my brilliance just blew your mind." Olivia grabbed her jacket and slid her arms into the sleeves.

"Where are you going?"

"I'm going to request a hard copy of that list. Are you coming or not?"

"The DCI won't be happy about this."

"Nope, but he'll only know if he catches us leaving." When she realised Maz wasn't moving, Olivia paused. "Come on, this is something we can do. This is real policing. We don't need everything to be spoon fed to us."

Sighing, Maz got to his feet. "Fine, but I do the talking. I'm the DS, remember?"

Olivia pulled a face, but Maz was surprised when she didn't argue with him.

Grabbing his keys, he gathered up his papers and handed them over to her. "You take these. And we can brainstorm what excuse we'll use to get the information."

"Why can't I drive?"

"Because you're supposed to be on desk duty," Maz reminded her. "And anyway, you seem to think the speed limit is only a suggestion and I happen to like my car as it is."

Maz started out of the office and Olivia trailed behind him. "We'd be quicker walking," she grumbled.

CHAPTER NINE

DAVID STOOD in the floodlit driveway and stared at his phone. Not that there was anything to see. Harriet's last text had said she was returning home. Guilt gnawed in his gut as he read back through her messages.

The tabloids had painted her in a less than flattering light. Not that he'd believed everything they'd printed, but the same couldn't be said for everyone. And he had to think of his own career. There was no denying that associating with her would pose a professional risk. He was still weighing up the pros and cons of pursuing a relationship with her.

DI Haskell's team had initially appeared to abandon her. But the arrest of Lila Uxley had changed things. The DI had always appeared protective of Dr Quinn. Possessive might be a better word. Yes, definitely possessive. When he'd shown up on her doorstep and just barged in... Even now, David could feel the anger coil in the pit of his stomach. The man had the cheek of the devil.

What had been worse was watching Harriet run out into the night after Drew. Perhaps distancing himself from her wasn't such a terrible thing.

"David!" Tasha's shout roused him from his contemplation. Lifting his gaze from the bright glare of his screen, he watched the CSI cross the grass. Her white, bulky Tyvek suit reflected the harsh lights set up in the front garden, giving her an unearthly glow. The sight of her reminded him of the scene from Ghost Busters when Gozer had taken on the form of the Stay-Puft Marshmallow man and ambled down the street, leaving destruction in its wake. Much like Tasha, he mused.

The stark white hood framed her heart-shaped face, making her skin look practically translucent. Her chestnut locks were safely tucked out of sight. She frowned at him, the furrow between her dark brows marring her pretty face. When she smiled, it was always slightly lopsided, made all the more pronounced by the fact that she had only one dimple. He missed her smile.

The fact hit him like an open palmed slap.

"We need to get a move on." She slid a pair of gloves on over her small, delicate hands. "The others have already gone in." There was barely a hint of her Eastern European accent. Had she deliberately worked to rid herself of her history? It wasn't exactly a question he could ask her.

"How are you?" David slid his phone into the pocket of his jeans and zipped up the front of his suit.

Tasha narrowed her eyes at him. She, more than anyone else he knew, had the uncanny ability to see straight through him. It had unnerved him in the beginning, but not anymore.

"Why are you asking?"

"Just trying to be a friend," he said. "There's not always an ulterior motive, Tash." He knew he'd made a mistake the moment he'd used the nickname. Stupid, stupid mistake.

"Oh, so it's, Tash, now, is it? You are so transparent, David. You say you want to be friends but what next, eh? More of your games? You need to make up your mind. In the meantime, we have a job to do." She huffed a breath before stomping away in the direction of the house.

Perhaps he didn't miss her smile as much as he'd thought.

DESPITE THE MASK HE WORE, the thick, foetid air inside the house threatened to overwhelm his senses. The team had already begun work on cataloguing and examining the scene downstairs.

Upstairs, however, was a little complicated. Pausing on the landing at the top of the stairs, David studied his surroundings, keeping a close watch on the other officers as they carefully photographed and took samples from the blood spatter on the walls.

"David, what are we going to do with the contents from the bath?" Even covered head to toe, with his voice muffled by the mask he wore, David would have known Gunther anywhere.

Crossing the plates that had been carefully laid over the carpeted floor, David paused in the bathroom doorway and took in the sight that awaited him. In all his years working as a crime scene technician, he'd only ever once seen something that had come close to the magnitude of this scene. A criminal gang had decided that instead of burying their enemies, they would dispose of the bodies in plastic barrels. Even now, David could remember the smell when the lids had been opened. The scene in this family home made him think of those bodies. But even the violence of that criminal scene could not compare to the cruelty that had befallen this unlucky trio.

"We'll have to empty it and bring it with us," he said. "Parts of the body have disintegrated into the water. They'll have to be separated out and tested—"

"David, there's a DS here who wants to speak with you," one of the SOCOs called up the stairs.

"Who is it?"

"DS Scofield."

With a sigh, David backtracked on the plates. "Fine." He turned his attention back to the scene. "You all right to start draining the bath once they've finished logging and photographing everything in here?"

Gunther grimaced. "Do we have something to put the liquid into?"

David gave him a curt nod. "I'll have something sent up."

"Boss, he insists he needs a word."

"Yeah. I'm on my way." With one more backwards glance at the scene, David escaped down the stairs.

FIVE MINUTES LATER, he was back outside in the fresh air. He bagged his gloves and suit before approaching the DS standing at the edge of the driveway.

"DS Scofield, is it?"

"I was told this was a break-in gone awry."

"Not from what I've seen," David said. "Then again, we're not done in there yet, so everything is subject to change."

"The attending officers said there were signs of a break in, and the neighbour confirmed all the machinery and cars were gone."

"I've got a team going through the sheds for evidence. But these people were butchered. You don't see that kind of violence at a typical burglary."

"Any identification on the bodies?"

David grimaced. "It's going to take time to be certain. All three bodies will need to be identified with dental records. But purely guessing, I'm going to say it's the three occupants of the property."

DS Scofield crossed his arms over his chest. "How sure are you this isn't like the other robberies in the area?"

David closed his eyes, a flash of the scene inside the bathroom blooming behind his eyelids. He mentally batted the image aside. Allowing emotions in would only inhibit his ability to work. And the people inside the house did not need his feelings muddying the crime scene.

"If this was done by the same group that was at all the other scenes, then this is a significant escalation, DS Scofield."

"I was worried you would say something like that," Scofield said. "All right, as soon as I can take a walk through the scene, I'd like to have a look. I'll get things rolling on my end."

David watched the large man stride away, the crunch of his boots on the gravel echoing in the still night air. This was the kind of case he would like to talk to Harriet about. Her insight would, no doubt, be transfixing. But texting her out of the blue now might be a little awkward.

"Boss, they need you back at the upstairs scene."

"Huh?" David paused and glanced at the Tyvek suit-wearing SOCO in the door of the house.

"You're needed upstairs."

"I'm on my way." He left the phone in his pocket and grabbed another white coverall. There would be plenty of time to think about Dr Quinn. Right now, he needed to focus on the scene that awaited him.

CHAPTER TEN

JEREMY STOOD beneath the spray of the shower head. Water hot enough to redden his skin pelted down over his hair and ran into his eyes, blurring his vision. Not that he minded. It was safer to not see anything. Not that physical blindness could hold at bay the visions that plagued his mind.

Every time he closed his eyes, every time he allowed his mind to wander, he saw those visions again. Kelly had served him up a Frey Bentos steak and kidney pie the night before and the layers of half-baked pastry floating in the greasy liquid below propelled him right back to that house. He'd barely made it to the bathroom before he'd puked his guts up.

When Kelly had asked him what was wrong, he couldn't very well tell her now, could he? He hated himself enough without her looking at him like he was a stranger, a criminal. Instead, he'd made up some barely coherent story about his sickness being connected to her pregnancy. Before the job, he'd skim-read something to that effect in a baby book. His life was separated into two distinct parts now; the time before the job, when life had been filled with promise and hope, and the time after, when it was filled with lies and horror.

Raising his hands, he scrubbed them over his face. Fuck. Why had he agreed to the job? Things had been bad. Money was tight and he did not want to see Kelly unduly worried about the predicament they found themselves in. But now, things were worse. Much worse. The house of horrors was forever seared into his brain. No amount of Call of Duty could wipe away those memories.

And there was the guilt to contend with. He'd wanted to call the police. As much as he didn't like the cops, the moment he'd been faced with the scene inside that house, the urge to dial 999 had swept over him like the childish urge to run into your mother's arms after a fall. But Mark's voice came back to him.

"Do you think they'll believe you? Believe that you had nothing to do with this? Are you soft in the head?" Mark had jabbed his index finger against Jeremy's temple. *"What'll Kelly do then, eh? When you're locked up? Good looking bird like Kelly, she won't hang around, mate. And that kid of yours will have some new bloke to call daddy."*

Jeremy thudded his forehead against the white

shower tiles. Move on. Just forget about it and move on. If only memories were so easily erased.

"Are you going to be much longer?" Kelly's voice cut through his thoughts. His hands shook as he twisted the knob and cut the flow of water. Without the heat from the spray, cold air closed in around him, cloaking his skin so that goosebumps rose over his arms and torso.

"Just a minute!" He grabbed the towel from the rack, the musty smell conjuring visions in the darkest recesses of his mind.

Opening the bathroom door, he met Kelly in the doorway. "I thought you were never coming out." She smiled at him, her deep brown eyes mischievous. She trailed a finger over the bare skin of his chest. Before the burglary he wouldn't have been able to resist her touch, but now it left him cold. "Are you sure you're all right?"

Swallowing around the lump in his throat, he nodded. "Yeah, of course. I'm fine. Just tired. Tough week."

She nodded sympathetically. "If you're not up to coming with me, you don't have to. It's only a check-up.

Jeremy shook his head. There was only one way through this, and it was with distraction. Sitting at home would only give his brain the opportunity to replay the scenes over and over in his mind. At least if they went out as planned, he would have other things to concentrate on.

"Nah, we've been looking forward to this for ages. And anyway, it'll be good for us."

"Good for you," she said with a smile. "You're not the one who has to get freezing jelly smeared all over them." She patted the small rounding on her belly. She hadn't yet popped, but the changes were there if you knew what to look for.

"True enough," he said, forcing himself to sound brighter than he felt. He covered her hand with his own and leaned down to place a gentle kiss against her soft lips. She sighed, pushing up on tiptoe to meet him. His hand slid down from her belly to her hips, holding her gently in place against the doorframe as she impatiently tried to close the distance between them. Jeremy loved how responsive she was.

Here with her, there was nothing else in his mind. All the darkness, the terrible thoughts, the memories of death that had consumed his every waking moment fled as he kissed her.

With his free hand, he cupped her cheek, sliding his fingers upwards to tangle in her hair. Jeremy tilted her head gently and ran his tongue lightly over her lips. She opened to him and their kiss deepened. Her arms curled around his neck, pulling him closer. He leaned into her, the towel slipping down his hips.

He loved her. God, how he loved her. Everything he'd been experiencing suddenly seemed foolish. He'd done it all for them, for the family they were creating. Clarity came as Kelly wriggled against him.

Mark was right. Nothing else mattered but the

woman in his arms and their child. Acknowledging it helped to chase away the remnants of the memories from his mind. He could do this because it wasn't about him.

Breathless, Kelly pulled away. "You need to get ready."

"We could be a little late." He pressed his lips to her ear and rolled his naked hips against her.

She gasped and arched her neck, giving him better access to the sensitive spot between her neck and shoulder. "Jeremy…"

Sighing, he buried his head against her neck and drank in her soft scent. "I'm sorry I've been such an arse." His voice was muffled but she heard him.

Placing her hands on his shoulders, she pushed him away until she could see his face. "You can tell me anything. You know that, right?" There was a furrow between her brows. It shamed Jeremy to see it. He was the cause of it. Reaching up, he smoothed the frown away.

"I know."

She waited but he said nothing else. She didn't need to know the truth of what he had done.

He said, "I'm fine. Really."

"You sure?"

Nodding, he pulled her closer. He would do better. Anything else would be too much like failure. His father had been a waste of space, and it had fucked Jeremy up for a long time. Kelly had saved him, and despite the issues they faced, he wouldn't let history repeat itself. He would be everything his own father had never been.

Dropping into a crouch, he pushed up Kelly's top and pressed his lips to her stomach. "Sorry, baby. I won't be a grumpy prick."

"Jeremy, language! The baby can hear you."

Tilting his head up, he grinned at her. "I don't think it's going to remember this."

"Well, you don't know."

Laughing, he tightened his grip on her hips and whispered against her tummy. "Don't be fooled by your mum. She's no angel. Got a mouth on her like a sailor when—"

"Jeremy!" Giggling, she half-heartedly pushed him away. "Go and get ready. We're already late."

He made it halfway down the hall before he stopped and turned back around. "I do love you."

Kelly paused her progress down the stairs. "And I love you." She narrowed her eyes, her gaze probing his. "Are you sure there's nothing you want to tell me?"

He shook his head. "Nah, I'm just being a soppy bastard."

She cocked her head to the side. "Promise?"

"I promise." He smiled at her and hoped it would be enough to reassure her.

She studied him for a moment, before finally returning his smile. "All right, then. How long do you think you'll be?"

"Not long. I've just got to get dressed."

Her phone buzzed in her hand, and she looked down at the screen. "That's Carrie. She wants to know if we're going to find out the sex of the baby." Kelly started off down the stairs, leaving Jeremy alone.

He could do this. He would do this. Their future depended on it.

CHAPTER ELEVEN

FLIPPING THROUGH THE REPORT, Martina shot a sideways glance at the burly figure of the DS next to her. "Sir, are you sure this is something we should be handling?"

Ambrose's eyebrows drew together over his deep-set eyes, his mouth fixing into a grim line. But he never lifted his gaze from the road ahead. "What kind of question is that?"

Martina bit her tongue and swallowed the question which hovered on the tip of her tongue. Questioning your superior was never a good idea, no matter how friendly they might be. Then again, it was Ambrose; he wasn't just any superior officer. What she didn't know about him could have fit on the back of a postage stamp. And in the past, he'd always welcomed her insight, no matter how contrary to his own.

"Well, it's just that it feels like something DI Haskell's team might handle."

"We've been working on these thefts for months now. Why would Haskell suddenly sweep in to take it out from under us?"

"Because this isn't like the others..." Martina pushed her hair back over her shoulder and decided to push on, consequences be damned. "Three dead bodies, sir. This is a serious escalation."

"People have been killed before during a burglary. Just last year an elderly farmer was tied to a kitchen chair and beaten because he wouldn't give the intruders his PIN number."

"That was different. He died of a stroke."

"But it still counts."

Martina shook her head. "Not like this." She swallowed past the lump in her throat and turned over the image of the young girl in the bath. Nobody deserved to die like that.

Ambrose sighed. "I see what you're saying, I really do. But I spoke to the boss man, and he says this is ours."

Martina twisted against the seatbelt and stared at the man next to her. "But Haskell's team has got the manpower, not to mention the budget for something like this. And we both know they wouldn't kick us off if they took over the main bulk of the case."

"Things are a little unsettled with the unit."

Martina opened her mouth to ask another question but before she could form the words, Ambrose cut her off.

"Don't quote me but I reckon it's got something to do with the fuss that kicked off over Dr Quinn. And some of the other smaller forces have been complaining about the resources diverted to the task force. Not everyone is supportive of the idea of one team getting all the glory while everyone else is left to pick over the scraps."

She couldn't argue with him there. She'd heard the whispers herself, the rumblings of disquiet that spread through the force. Heck, even she had initially thought they were getting far too much special treatment. But that had been before she'd had the time to work with them. Before she'd got the opportunity to see firsthand just why a team like this was needed.

"But they get results," she said, hating the whiny quality in her voice.

"No arguments here." Ambrose spun the wheel and eased the car into a tight parking space. "But you and I both know, results are not always enough. It's a political minefield and everyone is too busy trying to get one over on each other. Teams like the one Haskell is running might get the results in the end but the cost is often too high for the top brass to stomach." He sighed and killed the engine. "You ready for this?"

Martina's gaze flicked up to the block of apartments they had parked in front of. "Not especially, no." It was never easy breaking this kind of news to the next-of-kin. And this case would be a difficult one. How did you explain to a teenager that his entire family was gone? Everyone he had ever known and loved, wiped out. And for what?

Martina conjured an image of her own parents. Things were hard and she knew the inevitable outcome for her mum. When it happened, there would be the fallout to contend with from her dad. A future where they were no longer in her life wasn't one she wanted to imagine, no matter how inevitable it might be. No matter how difficult her present circumstances.

"How do you think he'll react?" She closed the file on her lap.

"How would you react?"

Martina grimaced. "I hate this bit."

"Aye, you and me both, lass. You and me both."

MARTINA STOOD to one side and allowed Ambrose to take the lead. She'd had her fair share of breaking bad news to loved ones and. knew this was going to be a difficult one.

Ambrose rapped on the heavy, white fire door a second time and shot a sideways look in Martina's direction. She shrugged in response, looking up and down the corridor. The fluorescent light cast harsh shadows in odd angles, and its almost imperceptible flicker strained her eyes.

Finally, the sound of a lock being pulled back reached them and a moment later the door swung inwards. A sleep-tousled young woman stood on the threshold. Bleary eyed, she scrubbed a hand over her eyes, causing the grey t-shirt she wore to ride up her tanned thighs.

For a moment, Martina wondered if the woman was even fully awake. Perhaps she was still half asleep and didn't realise she'd answered the door to two complete strangers with her lacy thong in full view.

The young woman yawned. "Yeah?"

"We were hoping to speak with Andy Hadfield." Ambrose took a small step back, giving her more space on the doorstep.

"Andy's asleep. Who are you?"

"My name is DS Ambrose Scofield, and this is my colleague DC Martina Nicoll."

The sleepy expression disappeared from her face, and she straightened up. "Police?" The word came out in a squeak, belying the remnants of sleep in her eyes.

"Perhaps we could come in and you could wake Andy up." Martina took a step forward, crowding the doorway, catching the woman off guard.

"Of course. I just…" She glanced down the hall in the direction of the rooms that lay inside.

"You go and get Andy and we'll—" Before Martina had finished speaking, the creak of a door opening and closing softly in the depths of the apartment seemed to be the wake-up call the woman in the door needed.

"You can wait in the living room," she said, taking a step back to clear the path for the detectives. "I'll be right back."

She directed Ambrose and Martina down the hall and closed the front door. The detectives entered an open plan living space. At one end of the room was a small sofa. It looked like something out of an Ikea catalogue, Martina thought as she swept her gaze over the space.

There were a couple of framed movie posters on the white walls. She recognised Alfred Hitchcock's *The Birds*, and *Vertigo*. There were a few others with writing in what looked to her like Italian, but she didn't know the movies they represented.

A thud from somewhere in the apartment had Martina throw a curious look at Ambrose. He shrugged and continued his perusal of the space.

A large flatscreen television dominated one wall, and beneath it, Martina spotted an X-box and a PlayStation. She didn't know much about gaming consoles, but she elbowed Ambrose and directed his attention to the set-up.

"They look new." She moved slowly towards the kitchen area and spotted an expensive looking barista style coffee machine sitting on the Formica counter top.

"They are," Ambrose said. "There's a new Nintendo here too."

"And that coffee maker wasn't cheap." Martina directed his attention to the machine in the kitchen.

"Julie would kill for one of those," Ambrose said.

"Maybe you should get her one."

Ambrose pulled a face. "If I bought her one of those, I'd have to remortgage the house." He sighed wistfully and stared at the machine.

Another thud came from deep in the apartment. The noise seemed familiar somehow, but Martina couldn't put her finger on why.

"Are you sure it's Julie who wants one?" she teased Ambrose.

"Well, I wouldn't say no either. But it's not going to happen. Julie wants to save up for a new kitchen. One of those women she follows on Instagram had a new one put in and now all she talks about are tiled backsplashes and something called an Aga."

"What do you think is taking so long?" Martina asked, pacing the floor.

Ambrose shrugged. "Maybe he's a heavy sleeper."

"I doubt it." She shook her head and paused to stare out at the city skyline. Dawn had arrived, and raked pink fingers of light through the heavy, pillowy clouds that sat low over the city. The view was arresting.

"Anything strike you as odd about the set-up?" Martina let her gaze slide over the room as she waited for Ambrose to reply.

"It's damn good for student accommodation,"

Ambrose said finally. "There was nothing like this when I went to college."

"Me either," Martina said. "I guess times really do change."

The door swung open, and a lanky young man strode into the room, his large hands fumbling with the buttons on his jeans. He wore a grey T-shirt, and to Martina's eyes it looked suspiciously like the same T-shirt the woman had been wearing when she'd answered the door to them.

"What's the meaning of this?" The irritation and aggression in his body language took Martina by surprise. She wasn't used to dealing with such open hostility, especially considering the situation. On the young man standing before them, the display of emotion felt inauthentic. Like a small boy playing dress up in his father's suits and ties.

"Andy Hadfield?" Ambrose kept his tone genial. "I'm DS Ambrose Scofield and this is—"

"I don't give a fuck who you are, what do you want?" Andy's gaze found Martina's and he gave up on trying to fasten his belt. Instead, he allowed it to hang open like some kind of challenge.

His rude response rendered Ambrose momentarily stunned into silence. Martina stepped forward and gestured to the couch. "Perhaps we should take a seat."

"I don't want to take a seat," Andy said, looking her up and down. He folded his arms over his slim torso and puffed out his chest, reminding Martina of a preening budgie.

She took a closer look at him as he stared at her. His grey eyes were bloodshot and, as she drew closer to him, she could smell alcohol rolling off his breath. That at least explained his behaviour. He wasn't entirely sober.

"I think it would be for the best, mate," Ambrose said, recovering himself. "We can all sit down together and—"

Andy levelled his attention on Ambrose. "I said, I don't want a seat and I'm not your fucking mate. Spit it out, whatever it is, and then fuck off out of my apartment so I can go back to bed with my girlfriend."

"We've got some bad news, Andy."

<<<<<<<<<<<<<<<<<<<<<<<<<<<<<<<

His demeanour shifted entirely. "What kind of bad news?"

"It's your parents." Martina took a deep breath. "I'm sorry to be the one to tell you this, but they were found dead."

He stared at her, his grey gaze glassy. "Is this some sort of joke?" The anger in his voice seemed at odds with his body language, but Martina couldn't pinpoint exactly what it was about the contradiction that made her uneasy. "I don't know who put you up to this but I'm not going to play along," he said.

"Mr Hadfield--" Martina started to speak but her cut her off with a shake of his head.

"Who put you up to this? I want to know. It's a sick joke."

"I can assure you this is no joke." Ambrose's tone was placating. "This is difficult news to take in, but I need you to hear me and understand what I'm telling you, Andy. Can you do that for me?"

Andy stared at him, his expression a confused mixture of disbelief and irritation. "I'll call them right now."

"Andy, I know this is hard, but you can't call them."

Martina admired Ambrose's calm, yet authoritative manner. It was something she hadn't quite mastered yet, herself.

Andy looked between them, a tremor starting in his hands before it spread through his body. "You're wrong. This is a joke. It has to be."

"When did you last have contact with your parents?" Ambrose took a step forward, herding Andy over to the couch.

"I can't be certain," Andy said, dropping down into the cushions. From where Martina stood, he looked like a deflated balloon, discarded after a birthday party. "You're sure this isn't some kind of mistake? Maybe I should call them to be sure."

Ambrose took up the seat next to Andy on the couch, his large frame somehow folding into the remaining space like a magic trick. "I know this is hard, but I need you to think back to when you last spoke to them."

Andy stared at his clasped hands and hung his head. "Yeah, sure, of course. It was a few weeks ago, I think."

Martina retreated to the kitchen to fetch some tissues as Andy squeezed his eyes shut and his shoulders began to shake. "This can't be real."

She returned with the tissues and handed them over without a word. Andy took them and pressed them to his eyes without meeting her gaze.

"What happened?" His voice was muffled through the tissue. "Was it a break in?"

Martina glanced at Ambrose, but his attention was firmly fixed on the man next to him.

"We're not sure yet," Ambrose said. "We're still gathering information."

"What do you mean you're not sure? You must know if it was a break in or something else." Andy looked from Ambrose's face and back to Martina.

"Can you think of any reason why someone would want to hurt your parents?"

Andy glanced down at the balled-up tissue in his hands and proceeded to pull the thin layers apart, allowing small flakes of it to drift towards the rug. "Not exactly."

"You don't sound certain," Martina probed.

Andy shrugged. "There was some interest from a private firm that wanted to buy up most of the farm, but Dad refused to sell." Andy kept his attention fixed on the tissue. "The neighbours weren't best pleased by it."

"Which neighbours?"

"The Phillips for starters," Andy said. "Terry turned up on Dad's doorstep several times. Mum had to call the police on one occasion because it got so heated."

"Did the Phillips disapprove of your father's intentions?"

"Terry tried to do a deal with the company, but Dad's farm was the only useable land. They said they would only take Terry's land if Dad would sell up as well." Andy's hands began to tremble. "You don't think Terry Phillips would have hurt them, do you?"

"At this point we're just gathering information," Ambrose said smoothly.

Andy shook his head. "I just can't believe it." He looked ashen as he scrubbed his hands over his face. "This doesn't feel real."

"And what about your sister?" Martina asked.

Andy stared blankly at her. "My sister? What about her?"

"Can you think of anyone who might want to hurt her?"

"Hurt Willow? No. Nobody. She mostly kept to herself. She didn't have any friends. Not really. A bit too introverted if you ask me." He sighed. "God, it must have been terrifying for her."

"Well, if you can think of anything at all that might help with the enquiry, we'd really appreciate if you'd get in contact with us," Ambrose said, climbing to his feet. "We'll be assigning you a FLO—" Seeing the blank look on Andy's face, Ambrose explained, "A FLO is a Family Liaison Officer. They'll keep you in the loop for any major developments. Anything you need to tell us, you can pass it along to the FLO and they'll make sure we're informed."

"I really don't think that's necessary," Andy said dismissively.

Martina found herself scrutinising his behaviour a little closer. He had spent a lot of time mopping his face and his eyes, but she couldn't see any evidence of tears. Dismissing the thought as nothing more than her being too hypervigilant, she decided his reaction was probably typical of someone who had just suffered a particularly gruesome shock.

Andy followed them to the front door.

"All the same," Ambrose said pausing in the hall, "we'll send the FLO over later today so you can become acquainted with them. Is there anything you'd like to ask?"

Andy started to shake his head and then changed his mind. "Do you need me to identify them or anything?"

Ambrose shook his head. "That won't be necessary."

Andy nodded thoughtfully. "Just one more question," he said.

Martina froze with her hand on the door.

"Did it hurt?"

Ambrose shot her a sideways look before he

returned his attention to Andy. "Excuse me? Did what hurt?"

"I know it's a weird question," Andy said, "But it's something that will play on my mind if I don't ask."

When neither officer replied, he looked from Ambrose's face to Martina's. "Did they suffer?"

"I'm not sure that's something you need to think about," Ambrose said.

Andy nodded. "No, I suppose not. It's just, you can't help the way your brain reacts to these things, can you?"

Ambrose patted him on the shoulder. "We'll be in touch, Mr Hadfield. And once again, I'd just like to say how sorry we are for your loss."

Andy's expression was impossible to read as he let them out into the hall. Mumbling her apologies, Martina followed Ambrose and waited until they were back out in the crisp early morning light.

"That didn't strike you as odd?" she asked, finally breaking the silence that had developed between them.

"Everyone deals with grief differently." His voice was gruff, and despite the dismissal, Martina could tell from the troubled expression on his face that he was as unsettled by the experience as she was.

CHAPTER TWELVE

MELISSA GROANED. Why was it taking so long for her body to recover? It felt like a lifetime had passed since she'd been in that alley. Of course, when nighttime fell, and she was alone, it was as if no time had passed at all. The slightest noise put her right back on that stinking, glass-covered ground. She battled against panic and fear every time she closed her eyes, but that only made it worse. She'd been forced to sleep with the lights on, just like she had when she'd been five years old and had believed a monster lived under her bed.

Propping her body up in the doorway of her apartment, she surveyed the carnage. Her mother had chosen not to stay, and had only dropped by long enough to pick up a few extra things when Melissa had been in hospital, but the flat still looked like it had been ransacked by a Roman legion.

"I can help you get things straightened up," Drew said behind her.

Shaking her head, Melissa crossed the threshold and hobbled to the nearest armchair. "No, this is my mess."

"That's not the point..."

"Drew, it's fine. I'm just glad to be home."

"Well, I still don't think you should stay here alone. You can barely make a cup of tea without almost passing out." His lips compressed into a thin line of disapproval. It was the kind of expression that made her think of her father. Not that Drew and her father had anything in common. They couldn't have been more opposite if they tried. It had been a point of pride for Melissa that Drew was so completely different, especially when she thought back over her past relationships.

"I don't need you smothering me any more with your mother hen routine." Her tone was far harsher than she'd intended, a product of her pain meds wearing off. "Sorry, I didn't mean it like that." She sighed and closed her eyes. The dark alley flashed on the inside of her eyelids, and she gasped, sitting bolt upright in the chair.

"What is it?"

"I just..." She shook her head. "It's nothing. I'm fine, Drew, honest. You should go. You need to go to the office and see if there's any progress."

"You keep seeing it don't you?"

"What?" The question took her by surprise. She'd been so careful to keep it hidden from him.

"That night. It keeps replaying in her head. You're probably seeing flashes of the attack, reliving it over and over."

Melissa stared at him like he'd grown a second head. She could rule out the possibility of him being a mind reader, and yet...

"It's the same thing that happened to me after the Star Killer tried to skin me like a rabbit. Every time I closed my eyes, there he was, slicing off another piece." Drew visibly shuddered.

"How did you stop it?"

"Time," he said. "Harriet helped." As soon as he said her name, he cringed. "Sorry—"

Melissa shook her head. "You don't have to apologise. You can say her name." She glanced down at her broken and bruised hand. "I'm glad you had her to help you through it. I don't think I'll be so lucky."

"Harriet would be happy to speak with you," Drew said, before he added, "but only if you'd like her to."

"Maybe..." Melissa grinned. "Probably not. You know me, I'm too stubborn for my own good."

"True."

Silence sat between them. Had it always been this awkward or was this something new? Melissa couldn't be entirely certain, but she was willing to bet it had always been this way. She'd just refused to acknowledge it.

"I know you gave a statement…" Drew stared down at the ground. "But I know you, Mel. There are things you're not sharing."

"I've told you everything I know."

"There's nothing you're holding back in the hopes of—"

"The hopes of what?" Her voice rose. "You really think I'm holding back information? For what reason? So I can come back to work and break the case all on my own? Chelsea is dead, Drew. That little girl is lying on a cold slab instead of being tucked up in her own bed. And all because I fucked up. She's dead because I didn't share what was going on. Maybe if I had—"

"She would still be dead, Mel. You and I both know it. They were going to kill her no matter what you did. She was talking to Angelica, sharing too much information. It's not your fault."

"Thanks, but I know the truth. She's dead because of me. If I could have stopped her that first day, if I'd just stopped her leaving, she would still be alive."

"And her mother and brother would probably be dead instead. They wanted to send a message. There was nothing you could have done to stop it."

"I could have caught them." Melissa's voice wavered. "If David Grantly had given me what I needed—"

"In a perfect world, none of this would happen. But that's not possible."

Melissa swallowed past the lump in the back of her throat. "You should go. If I can't work, then I need you out there hunting that bastard down."

"Mel, you really shouldn't be alone."

"I'm not going to do anything stupid, if that's what you're worried about. I need space, Drew. I know you mean well, but I need time and space."

Drew folded his arms over his broad chest. "I—"

"Drew, I say this with love, but please fuck off."

He chuckled and Melissa felt some of the tension leave her body. At least he still understood her sense of humour.

"Fine, I'll go. But only because you said, please. I'll drop by—"

Melissa held her hand up, halting him. "Only come if you have news. If I need you, I'll call."

Hurt flickered in his eyes but it was gone in an instant. "If you're sure."

"I'm positive. I need time to lick my wounds. But if there's a development, promise you'll bring me in."

"You know I can't do that."

"Drew."

"Gregson would have my hide."

"Please."

Blowing out a breath, he nodded. "Fine. If we learn something, I'll let you know."

"Promise?"

"Yeah."

"Good. Now go."

"I'm going, I'm going. Christ, don't be so obnoxious." Grinning at her, he crossed to the door. As he stepped out into the hall, Melissa's chest tightened. There was something so final about it. They would see each other again, she knew that, but it would be different.

"Drew..."

"Yeah?" He turned, his hand on the door.

"Thanks." She swallowed. "I wouldn't change a second of it."

His smile was tinged with sadness, as though he could feel it too. "Me neither."

And then he was gone, leaving Melissa with the horrors in her mind.

CHAPTER THIRTEEN

MAZ SQUEEZED his eyes shut and tilted his head back. For two days now, they had been going through the list of operators who had worked the night DI Appleton had been attacked, and it seemed that none of them had taken the call in question.

"This is ridiculous," Maz muttered beneath his breath. The scratch of Olivia's pen on paper could barely be heard above the general din of the canteen.

"I'm going to get a coffee and a sandwich. You want anything?" Maz pushed to his feet.

"We're missing a name," Olivia said finally. She glanced down at the paper and chewed thoughtfully on the top of her Bic biro.

"How can you be sure?" Maz asked. He leaned over her shoulder and scanned the spidery scratchings she'd littered over the page, but it looked about as readable as hieroglyphs.

"Because the numbers don't add up." Olivia nudged him in the thigh and Maz winced.

"What was that for?"

"We need to know who else was on that night. Maybe someone who wasn't supposed to be at work was pulling an extra shift."

"And who do you--" Maz cut off as Olivia waved someone over.

"Alex, how are things?"

Maz glanced up at the young man that crossed the room in their direction. His face was lit up with a bright smile.

"Livi, where the heck have you been? I haven't seen you in ages."

Olivia was on her feet and the two met in a warm embrace on the opposite side of the table.

Rolling his eyes, Maz made off in the direction of the sandwich counter as the two started to catch up.

As Maz paid for his tuna sandwich, the woman at the counter inclined her head in the direction of Olivia and Alex. "I think your mate is looking for you," she said as she took his money.

Maz glanced over his shoulder in the direction of Olivia, who was waving him over.

"I think you might be right." Grabbing his cup of coffee and the sandwich, Maz slowly made his way back to the table.

Alex was sitting on the opposite side, with Olivia perched next to him.

"Maz, you disappeared before I could introduce

you," Olivia said. There was an excited gleam in her eyes as she quickly made the intros.

"Nice to meet you, mate," Maz said, doing his best to channel DI Haskell. Clearly it wasn't working, because Olivia threw him a sideways look. Maz settled into his seat.

"So, Livi, tells me you two are trying to work out who was at Force Control the night DI Appleton was attacked."

"*Livi* shouldn't go around telling just anyone." Maz sighed. He was tired, irritable, and bloody hungry, and the last thing he wanted to do right now was waste more time talking to another person who would have no information for them. At this rate, they would probably be better off speaking with the canteen staff. They would know who was on that night, and...

Maz jerked his head up and glanced at Alex. "Sorry, could you repeat that?"

Olivia glared at Maz, but she didn't say anything. Not that she needed to; he could see the wrath in her eyes. No doubt he'd be in for an earful on the way back to the office.

"I said I was on that night, too. A few of us caught some extra shifts." Alex glanced back at Olivia. "I'm saving to go on holiday to Marbella. You should come."

Olivia pursed her lips. "The last time I agreed to go away with you and your mates, Alex, it took me a month to get over the hangover." She laughed and it struck Maz then that it had been a while since he'd really seen Olivia smile or even laugh. Since the incident, she had been more subdued. It didn't help that she was always on desk duty these days and he did not see as much of her as he once had. Not that it should have made a difference. They were friends. He should have made more of an effort.

Shame burned in his cheeks as he watched her giggle conspiratorially with Alex.

"You don't happen to remember who else was on that night, do you?" Olivia injected the question smoothly into the conversation.

Alex screwed up his face and listed off a few names, most of which were on the list they had collected. But one stuck out as unfamiliar.

"I don't suppose you took the call about DI Appleton?"

Alex shook his head. "No, but I remember how shocked everyone was when we heard about it. I mean, you hear about officers getting attacked quite regularly, but what happened to your DI..." Alex whistled low and shook his head. "It's just awful."

Olivia leaned in towards him and lowered her voice. "You don't happen to know who exactly took the call?"

Alex's cheeks flushed with colour and for a moment. Maz wondered if the heightened flush was caused by anger or something else. A moment later, it became plainly obvious what emotion Alex was struggling with.

"I know this is going to sound weird, but there were two calls." He ran his hand self-consciously up the back of his neck, a self-soothing gesture.

"Is it odd to receive two calls?" Maz couldn't keep the scepticism from his voice.

"No, it happens all the time. Usually for RTAs or house fires, we receive several calls. But the weird part about this was that somebody had already sent an ambulance and police cars by the time the official call came in from some passerby who happened upon DI Appleton and the scene. We spoke about it afterwards, but nobody admitted to taking the first call, which considering how serious it was, was weird." He shifted uncomfortably in his chair.

"Do you discuss all the calls that come in?" Maz asked.

Alex glanced over at him. "Not really. I mean, sure, sometimes we do. Especially when it's something like the attack. When one of us is hurt, we all feel it."

"But if anyone would know who took that call, it would be you, Alex." Olivia's voice was heavily laced with flattery. She touched his hand gently. "You've always been able to ferret out everybody's secrets."

Alex visibly relaxed, his smile smoothing out the furrow that had appeared between his brows. "Well, if I had to guess, I would suggest you have a chat with Celeste Jackson. She was on that night, and right around the time the first call would have come in, she disappeared for about fifteen minutes."

"What's so significant about that?" Maz asked.

"We're allowed to go on breaks, especially if we've had to deal with a particularly difficult call. You get to go out and take a breather. Most of us get a cup of tea and grab a smoke out back. I went on a break around then. I got a call from some girl..." He cut himself off and shook his head. "It doesn't matter. It was just a rough call. Anyway, I went out back for a sneaky ciggie and Celeste was outside arguing with someone on the phone."

"You didn't catch who she was talking to, did you?" Olivia shot Maz a meaningful look.

"I just assumed it was her boyfriend. They're always fighting." He glanced at Olivia. "The on-again-off-again type. It's ridiculous the number of times we've told her just to dump the loser, but she won't."

"So, if this was common, why was it different that night?" Maz asked.

"Because I heard her saying she wouldn't do 'it', but the moment she realised I was outside, she ended the call sharpish. I asked if she was ok, but she shrugged it off and suggested she'd had a tough call." Alex sighed. "We normally talk about it, but she wasn't interested in sharing and hurried back inside after that."

"And was there anything else she did that struck you as suspicious that night?"

Alex glared at him. "It sounds like you're fishing

for some kind of evidence that Celeste did something wrong."

"I'm not fishing for anything of the sort," Maz said indignantly.

Olivia placed her hand on Alex's arm. "Alex, chill. We're just looking for people who can help us. We have no interest in getting Celeste in trouble. It's not like that, so don't worry, ok?"

Alex shifted in his seat and shook his head. "This doesn't feel right, Livi. It kind of feels like you're looking for a way to scapegoat Celeste, and I'm not interested in helping you do that. She didn't hurt DI Appleton, that much is clear by the very fact that she was here at work the entire time."

"Nobody thinks she hurt, DI Appleton," Olivia said quickly. "Really, Alex, you're being a little bit ridiculous."

He glared at her and then got to his feet. "I'm being ridiculous? You're the ones in here questioning us when we're just trying to do our bloody jobs. I'd call *that* ridiculous."

"Alex--"

"No, I'm not interested, Olivia. This conversation is done. I wish you luck in finding the person responsible, but you're barking up the wrong tree here and you know it." Before she could say another word, he was gone, leaving Olivia and Maz alone.

"Well, that went disastrously," Olivia said. She sighed and sat back in her chair with a glum expression.

"Are you kidding me? That was the closest we've come to real information since we got here."

"But we don't actually have anything useful," Olivia said. "It's just hearsay."

"True," Maz said. "But if the DCI gives us the go ahead, we can use it to question Celeste."

Olivia nodded but the look on her face was still downcast.

"Come on, Livi, what can I do to cheer you up?" Maz asked, a broad grin stretching his mouth.

Olivia's chin jerked up. "For starters, you can never call me that again." She got to her feet and Maz followed suit. "And secondly, you can buy me a proper coffee, not the shit they serve here."

"That doesn't seem fair," Maz said, trailing her. "Why does he get to call you cutesy nicknames?"

"Because I've known Alex since I was five, when he would paddle around in my kiddie pool in the nip."

"Wait, what?" Maz hurried to catch up to her, but Olivia managed to stay ahead of him.

"WE NEED to take this to the boss," Maz said as he passed the paper cup full of coffee over to Olivia.

Pulling a face at him, she started towards the car. "I think that's a mistake." She sipped at the coffee gingerly, and despite her care still managed to burn the tip of her tongue. "Holy shit, it's like lava."

Maz grinned at her. "Well don't be so bloody impatient then." He paused at his side of the car and stared at her over the roof. "Why is it a mistake?"

"Because the moment we do that, we lose the element of surprise. And that's honestly all we have right now."

"DI Haskell would never compromise the integrity of the investigation."

"That's not what I mean, Maz, and you know that. Something like this needs to be treated with kid-gloves. The DI will insist we do things by the book."

Maz started to protest but Olivia cut him off with a shake of her head. "If you pull your head out of your arse for a minute, you'll realise I'm right."

"Look, you're not even supposed to be out here. If we go ahead and question Celeste without the guv's say so, things are going to get really messy."

Shame burned in Olivia's cheeks as she read between the lines of what he was saying.

"Shit, Maz, no need to be an asshole about it." She slipped in behind the steering wheel. "I already feel shit about everything that happened. I know I screwed up before, but you can't keep holding that over my head."

"That's not what this is about."

"Yeah, it is," she said. "I made a mistake and now you all think I'm reckless and—"

"Olivia, that's not what I mean." Maz ran his hand over his eyes, a gesture Olivia recognised as belonging to DI Haskell.

"If we're correct, it means one of our own helped to put DI Appleton in the hospital. Best case scenario, she wasn't directly involved, she was just the messenger. Worst case..."

He didn't have to finish his thought because Olivia knew exactly what the worst-case scenario meant for them. They had a leak. As much as she hated to admit it, Maz was right. They needed to speak to the guv. They were in over their heads. And Olivia needed to prove that she'd turned over a new leaf.

"You're right," she said.

"Excuse me?" Maz half turned in his seat to stare at her.

"You heard me, Arya."

"No, I don't think I did. For a minute there, I thought you said I was right. The Olivia Crandell I know would never admit that."

Rolling her eyes, Olivia started the car. "Yeah, yeah, you're right. Don't get too used to it."

Maz groaned. "I knew it was too good to be true. No chance you'd just let it go."

"This is huge, Maz. If we go in all guns blazing, we'll lose the only real lead we've had since all of this started." Gripping the steering wheel, Olivia stared at the half empty car park. "I'm not a huge fan of DI Appleton, but she's one of us. We should at least try and get a lay of the land before we take it to the boss. At least that way when we go to him, we'll have something concrete to tell him."

Maz sat with his arms folded over his chest, refusing to meet her gaze.

"Come on, Maz. You know I'm right about this. We don't have anything real. And with the mood DI Haskell has been in lately, he'll have our arse in a sling if we bring him a bunch of hearsay and speculation."

"Fine."

"Really?" Olivia couldn't keep the excitement from her voice.

"Yes, really." The frustration in Maz's voice was palpable, and a kernel of guilt sprouted in Olivia's gut.

She reversed out of the car space.

"Where do we start?" Maz asked.

"By trying to fill in some of the blanks."

CHAPTER FOURTEEN

DREW PICKED up his phone and quickly punched in Dr Sheridan's number. Harriet had said the man was reliable, but despite leaving a message, Drew had yet to hear from Dr Tony Sheridan.

The phone rang twice before being picked up. The sound of rustling paper and plastic travelled down the line and was followed by a slightly out of breath male voice.

"I forgot to ask for a portion of spring rolls."

"Sorry, what?" Drew glanced down at his screen, convinced he had somehow entered the incorrect number. "Dr Sheridan?"

"I know you've probably added them anyway. I don't know why I forgot. Recent events have me a little more harebrained than usual and my Mini is back in the garage."

He sighed, giving Drew the break in the conversation he needed to interject. "You are Dr Sheridan, correct?"

"Yes." Tony's quiet voice turned wary. "You're not Delun." There was a pause and the faint sound of traffic in the distance travelled down the line. "And you don't sound like anyone else who works in the Chinese Takeaway." There was an accusatory tone to his voice, as though Drew had deliberately tried to trick him into revealing more information than he had wanted to impart.

"My name is DI Drew Haskell. Dr Harriet Quinn gave me your number and said you might be willing to offer some assistance if I ran into trouble."

"Oh, Dr Quinn." The rustling of paper and plastic resumed in earnest. "How is Harriet? I haven't heard from her in..." The noise stopped and Drew could practically visualise the man on the other end of the line scratching his head while he tried to recall the necessary details. "Well, it's quite some time, anyway."

"She's taking some time off," Drew said. "She's in Ireland at the moment."

"Time off? That doesn't sound like the Harriet Quinn I know." Tony sounded marginally more jovial than he had previously.

"Well, after everything that happened at the university and with the press camped on her front doorstep, she needed some time to work things out in her head."

"What situation at the university?"

"You don't know?" Drew wondered if calling up Dr Sheridan was such a good idea. From what Drew had witnessed so far, the doctor was more a bumbling idiot than a sharp-witted profiler capable of going toe-to-toe with one of the worst serial killers in Canada's history.

"With things as they are here, I haven't had much time for reading the newspapers." Drew detected a level of strain in the other man's voice.

"Anything my team can help with?"

Silence followed Drew's offer, and he wondered if Dr Sheridan had hung up.

"No, this is something that only I can deal with." A pregnant pause followed. "Is Harriet all right?"

Drew wished he could be certain of the answer to that question, but the truth was, he didn't honestly know how Harriet was. He knew what she told him on the phone. However, her radio silence was disconcerting. He knew deep down that she needed time, and he was willing to give it to her. Whatever she needed, he would gladly let her have it, so long as it meant she would come back to the team... back to him.

"It's been difficult." He'd been aiming for neutrality but missed it by a mile. He roughly sketched out Harriet's situation without sharing too much information. If Dr Sheridan wanted to, he could always look it up for himself.

"I can imagine," Dr Sheridan said finally. "That's a nightmare scenario for anyone who values their privacy and Harriet does, perhaps more than most." He sighed. "It can't have been easy for any of you." There was a depth of empathy reflected in his voice that surprised Drew. For the first time since they'd started talking, he understood why Harriet had suggested he speak with Tony if he found himself in need.

"Well, DI Haskell, what can I help you with?"

Drew opened his mouth to reply and faltered. Now that he had the psychologist on the phone, he wasn't sure where to start. If it were Harriet on the other end of the line, knowing what to say would come easily. They would talk around the problem until finally his mind would put enough of the puzzle pieces together so that he could explain the issue.

With Dr Sheridan, Drew found himself at a loss.

"Just start at the beginning, DI Haskell. That might make things a little easier."

So, Drew did just that. He explained all he knew of the situation involving Melissa and the attack that had put her in the hospital fighting for her life. While he didn't have all the details, he had enough to sketch an image for Dr Sheridan.

When he finished, Drew waited, with nothing but the even breaths of the man on the other end of the line for company.

"And you said this is a county lines drugs operation?" Sheridan said finally.

"That's what DI Appleton thinks. She's been

pursuing this group for some time now. It became a professional obsession."

"She sounds very driven."

"She's one of the most dedicated officers I know."

"And you're sure this is county lines?"

Drew detected an edge of incredulity in Dr Sheridan's voice. "What are you getting at, Dr Sheridan?"

"Please, call me, Tony. Everyone else does. And I'm not doubting the veracity of your DI Appleton. Nor am I questioning your interpretation of the facts, DI Haskell."

"What then?"

"Well, it's all a bit personal, isn't it?"

"I'm not sure I follow."

"I could be wrong, I very frequently am," Tony laughed. "And I suppose without seeing the crime scene reports and photographs, I'm fishing in the dark."

"I can send them over if you'd be willing to take a look," Drew said.

"That would be very helpful. Just going on what you've told me, the attack on DI Appleton sounds like it's personal."

"Are you suggesting DI Appleton has some kind of personal connection to the gang?"

"God, no!" Tony sounded genuinely shocked. "But the murder of the young girl..."

Drew swallowed around the lump in his throat. He'd attended the postmortem personally and even now, when he closed his eyes, he could see the disfigured face of the child staring, unseeing, at the clinically white ceiling.

"She was an asset."

Drew snapped back to the present and realised belatedly that Tony had continued to speak whilst he was lost in his own morbid thoughts.

"People like that don't value the kids who work for them," Tony was saying. "As far as they're concerned, for every one they lose, there are ten more to take their place."

Drew ran his hand down his face. "It's my understanding that they go through a kind of wooing period. Wouldn't that suggest the kids have an inherent value?"

Tony's voice became muffled before growing clear again. "True, but it rarely lasts very long."

"What does that have to do with the attack on DI Appleton and her informant?" Drew asked.

"They could have killed the informant at any time. And they could have killed DI Appleton."

"I don't think I emphasised the level of injuries DI Appleton sustained," Drew said. "She very nearly didn't make it."

"But if they'd wanted her dead, DI Haskell, she would be dead. No ifs, buts, or maybes about it. DI Appleton survived because the head of the gang wanted her to. And the young girl feels like a message. A warning."

"You think it's a threat?"

"Maybe. I'm not sure," Tony said, sounding a little flustered. "I don't do my best work on an empty stomach." He let out a long breath. "I need some more time to think about it and look at the files." His voice faded on the line as though he'd set the handset down and wandered away. His voice was muffled and distorted and Drew could barely hear him. "Where did I put it…"

"Dr Sheridan? Tony."

"Leave it with me, DI Haskell." Tony's voice boomed back on the line, an excited hitch to his breath as he spoke rapidly. "As soon as I have something more concrete for you, I'll get back in touch." The line went dead abruptly, leaving Drew to stare at the phone in his hand in bewilderment. Sheridan might be good at his job but how anyone got along with him, Drew couldn't fathom.

But Harriet had recommended him and Drew trusted her implicitly. If Dr Tony Sheridan was worthy of her praise, then he would just have to believe it.

CHAPTER FIFTEEN

OLIVIA LEANED over the bathroom sink and splashed cold water onto her face. It had been a long few days. She'd spent so long going through the records and combing through each one of Celeste Jackson's calls, she was surprised she could see at all.

Pulling the eyedrops from her back pocket, she tipped her head back as the bathroom door swung open behind her. The cold drops stung as she let them hit her eyeball before her automatic urge to blink kicked in.

Holding open her other eye she quickly repeated the process.

A throat clearing behind her made Olivia flinch. With her vision blurred, she tried to make out the vaguely human shaped figure reflected in the mirror.

"Why are you talking to everyone in the Force Control room about me?" The woman's voice, despite the directness of the question, was timid.

Olivia swore under her breath as she tried to swipe at her streaming eyes with the back of her hand.

"Sorry, I'm a little—"

"Oh, did I catch you at a bad time?" There was no mistaking the sarcasm in the voice at her back.

As her vision started to return, Olivia realised with a sinking feeling in her gut that the woman behind her was Celeste Jackson. She'd promised Maz to stay away from her. Not an easy feat, but so far, she had kept her word.

Replacing the lid on the bottle of eyedrops, she turned to face the young woman. Celeste Jackson was petite. The woollen jumper she wore swamped her birdlike frame, making her look like a child playing dress up in her mother's wardrobe.

"Celeste, I presume?" Olivia held her hand out but let it drop back to her side when the gesture was ignored.

"You know right well who I am. You've been poking your nose into my business all week. Did you think I wouldn't find out? Well, I don't know how *your* team works but *ours* is a loyal bunch."

"That's important, especially considering the type of work you do." Olivia tried to imagine what Dr Quinn would do in this situation. The woman in front of her was obviously upset. If she was going to salvage anything useful from their conversation, she needed to get Celeste to calm down.

"Don't bother with your manipulative horseshit.

We all know what your little team is really like. You run around doing whatever you want, consequences be damned." Her look was pointed, and Olivia felt the urge to check the collar of her shirt was still buttoned. "You don't care who you hurt. You only care about clearing case files off your plate so you can have another commendation from on high."

"Celeste, I don't know what it is you think you know, but we're not trying to hurt anyone. We just want to find the people responsible for putting DI Appleton in the hospital."

Horror dawned on Celeste's face, letting Olivia know she'd screwed up.

"And you think I had something to do with it?"

"No, that's not what I'm saying."

"I would never hurt one of our own." Celeste covered her mouth with her hand and turned away. Her body was rigid, but Olivia had spent enough time with Dr Quinn to know there was something unspoken in the way she held herself. As Celeste moved her hand, the sleeve of her blouse rode up, exposing her wrist. The bruising was unmistakable. Olivia had seen enough women with marks like that to know a domestic abuse victim when she saw one.

Sensing Olivia's attention, Celeste jerked her sleeve down and turned away.

"Celeste, if there's anything you need—"

"Stay the fuck away from me!" She took a few steps forward and wrapped her arms around her chest. When she turned back, the myriad emotions

Olivia had seen just moments before were gone, replaced with a cold stare. "I won't let you throw me under the bus. I didn't do anything wrong, and digging around in my files and chatting to my colleagues is nothing more than a witch hunt. Everyone knows you've got nothing on me."

"Celeste, why did you delete the call log?" With nothing left to lose, Olivia decided to ask the question that had been burning on the tip of her tongue from the moment she'd realised who was standing in the bathroom with her.

"What call?"

"The call you took about DI Appleton's attack. You deleted it."

For a moment, confusion clouded Celeste's features but it was gone as quickly as it had appeared. "I never deleted any call, DC Crandell. The system glitched the following night. Ask any of the others who were on shift, and they'll all tell you the same thing. One minute, everything was fine and the next, the whole system went down. It was only for a couple of seconds, but it was enough to create panic." Her words sounded rehearsed to Olivia.

"Celeste, if someone is pressuring you. If somebody forced you to—"

"Just shut up." Celeste took a step towards Olivia as though she planned to physically enforce her words. Panic sparked in her eyes, an expression Olivia recognised only too well. "Just shut up," Celeste repeated. "You don't know what you're talking about. Nobody is forcing me to do anything. I come here, do my job, and that's it. Stop trying to twist everything I say."

Olivia held her hands up placatingly. "Celeste, *you* came to *me*, remember? I think you did that because you know this isn't right. Whoever attacked DI Appleton can't be allowed to get away with it."

"I don't know anything. I just need you to stop asking questions and poking your nose in where it doesn't belong. I can't help you."

Before Olivia could reply, Celeste pushed out through the bathroom door, leaving her to stare after the woman's retreating back.

CHAPTER SIXTEEN

SITTING in the beige tartan armchair next to the window, Harriet enjoyed the warmth of the sunshine that poured in through the glass. Splaying her fingers, she examined her short nails. The incessant ticking of the clock on the black, marble mantlepiece grew louder with every passing second.

The room was perfectly neutral. Nothing out of place. It had, to Harriet's mind at least, an almost unlived in feel. Not an easy feat, considering the room formed part of the Victorian terrace townhouse belonging to Dr Silva.

"Sorry for keeping you." Dr Silva swept into the room as though conjured by Harriet's thoughts. The silken, cream kimono style cover-up she wore trailed behind her like a delicate cape. Her mint green blouse was perfectly pressed, as were her stone-coloured linen trousers, making Harriet feel slovenly in her travel worn outfit.

"It's fine," Harriet said. "I was a little early."

Dr Silva paused and let her gaze slide over Harriet. "How are you, Harriet?"

"Fine." Harriet smiled and let her gaze fall to her hands again.

"You know that's not sufficient here." Dr Silva crossed to the matching, beige tartan chair opposite Harriet and settled into it. "We don't use words like, 'fine' here."

"Sometimes, fine is an apt description." Harriet could hear the challenge in her voice. She was behaving like a petulant child and that would help no one, least of all her. "I'm sorry." With a sigh, she met Dr Silva's gaze. "I'm just tired and I've had a lot on my mind."

"Would this have anything to do with the stories printed in the newspapers?"

Shame caused heat to spread from Harriet's chest, up her neck and into her face. "So, you've seen them then."

"I have." Dr Silva's tone was noncommittal.

"What did you think?" Harriet sat back in the chair and attempted to feign mild interest. Not that she really believed she would fool the woman sitting opposite. Dr Silva had known her far too long to be so easily led astray.

"I was concerned for you," Dr Silva said. "I know how deeply you care about the work you do. I know how much it means to you. And to have such an accusation levelled against you would be very difficult."

"To describe it as difficult is a kindness." Harriet smiled and allowed herself the luxury of examining the contents on the bookcase behind Dr Silva's chair.

Only the scratch of Dr Silva's pen on the paper of her leather-bound notebook was loud enough to be heard over the ticking of the clock.

"I sense there's something else on your mind, Harriet."

"I suppose there is." Harriet swallowed around the lump in the back of her throat. "You said I care deeply for the work I do."

Dr Silva settled her steely gaze on Harriet. The Roman blind prevented the sun's rays from reaching all the way across the room, leaving Dr Silva cloaked in shadow. This had the unusual effect of making her grey eyes appear darker than normal. The psychologist said nothing in response to Harriet, creating an uncomfortable void in the conversation.

Harriet understood the other woman's reasoning behind her behaviour. She wanted to create a place where Harriet could feel unhurried and unjudged. A place outside of the rest of the world, a place apart.

And for the most part it, worked. But Harriet didn't need a place set apart from everywhere else today. She needed somewhere that would help her solidify the thoughts in her mind. What she really needed was a friendly ear, someone who would listen and then help guide her chaotic thought-processes into something more rational. Who she needed was… Harriet banished the idea from her head.

"And I do care for my work," Harriet said, hunting around in the back of her mind for the right words. "But I'm not sure it's enough."

Dr Silva lifted her gaze from the pages of her notebook. "Oh?" There was genuine puzzlement in her face. "In what way is it not enough?"

"That's the part I'm struggling with," Harriet said. "Who am I really helping?"

"I'm sure your students would say you were helping them to fulfil their potential."

"But they don't need me for that," Harriet said. During her time in Ireland, she'd found herself with a lot of time to truly think about her work. Sure, writing up papers was important, and she wouldn't argue with the idea that teaching the next generation of psychologists to truly excel in their chosen field was vital to the future of the profession. But the more she dwelled on it, the less certain she was that it was the best use of her expertise.

She could do more. She needed to do more.

Dr Silva tilted her head to the side. "Are you thinking of leaving the university?"

Harriet's laugh was bitter. "Can you truly call it leaving if you're pushed?"

"I thought you said Dr Baig had reversed his decision on the suspension."

"He has."

Dr Silva scribbled a note in her pad. "I suppose I

can understand why you might still feel like you've been edged out."

Harriet nodded.

"However, do you think you might be using it as an excuse?"

"How so?" Harriet fought the urge to behave defensively, especially considering her sessions with Dr Silva inauspiciously resulted in her feeling stripped bare and utterly vulnerable. Was this how everyone else felt when they spoke with a psychologist?

"For quite some time now, you've spoken about being frustrated in your work at the university. From my perspective, it seems that type of work no longer fulfils you as you would like it to. In contrast, your work for the police has helped to make you feel more confident in what you have to offer. You speak of it bringing you a —" she flipped back through her notebook. "A kind of morbid happiness. You felt useful in a way you could never feel when working at the university."

"That is true," Harriet said. "But even my work with the police leaves me with a kind of longing. There's still something missing."

"And what do you think that might be?"

"I think I'm tired of always being too late." Harriet buried her face in her hands. "Everything I do with the police, while it helps to bring the victims the justice they need and provides closure to the families, it still feels like too little, too late."

Dr Silva, settled back into her chair. "And do you see a solution to this problem?"

Sighing, Harriet let her hands rest in her lap. "I don't want to give up my work with the police. Although, after everything that has happened, there's no guarantee they'll invite me back."

"But your name has been cleared of any wrongdoing."

Harriet gave the woman opposite a wry smile. "The media doesn't care about that. All they see is their next salacious headline. And people tend to believe that there's no smoke without fire. DCI Gregson and the others have to consider public perception. Without the goodwill of the people they are charged to protect, their job becomes infinitely more difficult. And I wouldn't want to make Drew's life any harder than it has to be."

The briefest flicker of a smile crossed Dr Silva's face. But if she had anything to say, she kept it to herself, and for that, Harriet was glad. "I'd like to work with the victims of violent crimes," Harriet said.

"You mentioned that you previously worked in a clinical setting, but you haven't said why you left."

"It was a long time ago." Pausing, Harriet twisted her fingers around the hem of her jumper.

"And you're not ready to talk about it yet?"

"Not yet," Harriet said. "The situation at the university brought a lot of things to light. Things I foolishly believed I'd dealt with."

"You know you're always welcome to discuss them here."

"I know." Harriet flashed the psychologist a smile. "I need to process things a little more in my own head, first. But as soon as I'm ready, I'll bring them up here, I promise."

"No need to make promises, Dr Quinn. These sessions are designed to help you do your job better. If you feel that not discussing something from your past benefits you here in the present, then I'm certainly not going to force you."

Suitably chastised, Harriet felt heat creep into her face.

Dr Silva glanced at her wristwatch. "Time's up." She glanced at Harriet. "Unless there's something more you need."

"No, it can wait." Harriet stood and picked her bag up from the floor. There was so much she hadn't found the courage to say. Clearly, she wasn't yet ready to deal with all of her demons head on. But that would come with time, she was certain of it. She knew enough about her own process to trust that it would tell her when the time had come to open up further.

Dr Silva stood and hesitated. "I'm sorry if I seemed a little abrupt."

Surprised by the other woman's admission, Harriet reached out and touched her hand to Dr Silva's arm. "You were fine."

Surprised, Dr Silva stared down at the place

where Harriet's fingers rested against her arm. "Good. I know I can be a little too clinical sometimes. Too many years spent working to a schedule, I suppose. Private practice is still relatively new to me."

She gestured for Harriet to move ahead of her. "Same time next week suit you?"

"That's fine," Harriet said. "I'll let you know if anything clashes."

A few moments later, Harriet was back in the safety of her own car. Dragging in a deep breath, she closed her eyes. She had put the inevitable off for long enough and there was nowhere else for her to go. The thought of going home filled her with dread but there was nothing else for it. She had run as far as she could, and now there was nowhere left to turn.

Sliding the key into the ignition, she started the engine. She would feel better once she was home. There really was nothing for her to fear. It was a lie she had told herself often to soothe the unease that turned over in her mind. But the lie was no longer soothing.

CHAPTER SEVENTEEN

MELISSA LEANED against the sink and struggled to fill a glass with water. She was taking her pain medication like clockwork. Popping each little white pill was all she had to look forward to.

A million times since Drew had dropped her at home, she had contemplated calling him and begging him to let her come back. She had mistakenly thought being at his house was hard. Being alone was so much worse.

If she wasn't crying because of the pain, then it was because of the frustration of her body not cooperating. And then there was her mind. What had once been her greatest asset had become a trap laced with misery. She couldn't sleep. There was no rest to be found. She'd tried binge watching some television shows, but her brain betrayed her at every turn with images of Chelsea and the darkness of that night.

Her grip slipped on the glass, and it tumbled into

the sink, shattering into a thousand jagged pieces. Seeing it glittering there sent her right back to the alley and the broken glass strewn across the ground. The sound of Chelsea's laboured breathing echoed in her ears.

"Please, make it stop." She squeezed her eyes shut, fighting to bury the memory before it could fully take hold.

The doorbell rang, jerking her away from the precipice in her mind. She glanced down at the glass in the sink, but it was just pieces of a broken tumbler. She wasn't back in that alley, she was home. She was safe.

That last piece of knowledge cut her to the bone. She was safe, but she'd failed to keep Chelsea safe.

The bell rang again, and Melissa hobbled towards the small hall. She was exhausted. Even crossing the short distance from the kitchen to the living room left her feeling wrung out. She used the furniture in her home like stepping stones, pausing at each piece long enough to take a breath. Finally, she reached the door and tugged it open.

DS Ben Mason stood sheepishly in the hall, his dark curly hair and navy coat still damp from the rain. Melissa gripped the frame, allowing it to hold her weight as she stared at him. Cold air drifted inside, curling around her ankles like an unwelcome ghost.

Ben opened his mouth, and Melissa took the opportunity to slam the door in his face. There was a perverse kind of satisfaction in witnessing the look of surprise that crossed his features as the door rushed towards him.

"Melissa, please. I came to see how you are."

"Fuck off." She hated that her voice was so hoarse. All the honey and lemon in the world couldn't soothe a throat made raw by screaming herself awake every time she drifted off.

"Come on. I know I messed up, but we're mates. When I heard what happened I—"

"You what? I bet you thought all your birthdays had come at once. That if I died, you'd be off the hook for double crossing me."

"Don't talk shit, Melissa. I was terrified. Nobody knew if you were going to pull through. I contacted Rich and everything."

"I bet he took your call" Melissa said, allowing her bitterness to coat her words.

"He said you were in a bad way, but your Mum was going to see about taking you back down South. I wanted to catch you before you left."

Melissa opened the door and then turned and hobbled back to the living room. "Lock the door when you come in. I'm not risking that bastard coming back to finish the job." She made it as far as her armchair and flopped down into its relative comfort. The pain was beginning to ramp up. It started like a dull ache, an itch she couldn't quite scratch. Then, as the seconds ticked by, it grew by degrees. Every breath, every small movement built on the pain until it was all she could think about. It screamed inside her head like a dentist's drill.

Melissa felt bad for not asking Drew how'd he'd coped after the Star Killer had tried to do him in. She'd seen the scars. The pain must have been excruciating.

Ben shuffled into the living room and paused. Melissa kept her eyes firmly shut as she struggled to return her breathing to a more normal pace.

"You look better than I expected," he said.

"You mean I only look half-dead?" Melissa cracked one eyelid.

"More like three-quarters. But hey, I love what you're doing with your face these days; the bruises really bring out the bloodshot colour of your eyes."

Despite herself, Melissa started to laugh. "You're a prick. You know that, right?"

Ben shrugged. "I'm flattered."

For a few brief moments, Melissa allowed herself the spark of joy that Ben's company brought. But like all joy in her life these days it faded faster than she would have liked. As the laughter faded, Melissa let the silence close around them.

Finally, Ben coughed awkwardly and made a move towards the couch. "Can I sit?"

"You really hurt me, you know."

The look of devastation that crossed his face surprised her. He hadn't seemed so beat up about it all when she'd confronted him that day. Amazing what a little guilt could do.

"I know I fucked up, Mel. If I could take it back, I would."

"Well, you can't. It's done. And anyway, it wouldn't make a difference now. I'm benched, whether I want to be or not. Gregson won't let me within fifty feet of this case because of what happened."

Ben stared down at his hands. "What if I told you there was a place for you on the task force they're setting up for this county lines drug ring?"

"I'd say nobody will let me play, Ben. We both know it."

"What if I could guarantee it. Would you come if I could get you in?"

"What, come to Scarborough? It wouldn't exactly be a stretch."

Ben shook his head. "Nah, not Scarborough. Leeds. That's where all the action is. If we want to get to the big boys, we need to go where they're doing all of their big business."

"I appreciate the offer, but that's never going to happen."

"Why not?"

"Well, ignoring the fact I'm not yet fit to get back to work, they tried to kill me, Ben. The powers that be won't want me investigating my own attempted murder."

"Ah, but that's where you're wrong," Ben said, a smug smile hovering on his lips. "You'll be investigating county lines drug gangs. Not murder, attempted or otherwise. It's a joint force effort. And they'll be only too happy to let you move over to Leeds after what happened. It's a fresh start, Mel."

He had a point. It was a chance at a new beginning. But that didn't change the fact that right now, it felt impossible.

Melissa stared down at her hands. There was a slight tremor, the first indication that she had missed the latest dose of her pain meds. She'd been so caught up in the conversation with Ben that the pain had taken a backseat for a change.

The moment she acknowledged that little fact, the pain came roaring back, and with it, the fear from that night. Sweat beaded on her brow and the tremors in her hands increased. She closed her eyes and tried to take a deep, steady breath, but she was instantly transported back to the alley.

The monster who had attacked her was there, pinning her to the ground, forcing her to listen to Chelsea's rattling breaths as they slowed and then stopped.

"Are you all right?" Ben's voice came from some distance away, but Melissa used it as an anchor to pull herself from the memory. How could she transfer to Leeds when her own mind was determined to destroy her? She wouldn't be an asset to the team, she would only hold them back.

"I don't think I can, Ben." There was a shake in her voice that left her feeling pathetic. "I've got a long road ahead."

"Nobody expects you to come over straight away." He sighed. "Just think about it, okay?"

Melissa shook her head. Her vision was beginning to narrow. "Just go. You've done your good Samaritan deed for the year. But you and I both know I'm fucked. I'll be lucky if they don't force me to take early retirement after this. And I don't need you here placating your guilty conscience by dangling my dream job in front of me when you know I don't stand a chance of getting there."

"Mel, that's not fair. I was just—"

"You felt bad, Ben. I get it. But you've done enough damage. You don't have to kick me when I'm down, too." Her voice was harsh and sounded nothing like her.

"When did you become such a hard-nosed bitch?"

"When I stopped taking crap from pissants like you." She needed him to go, and in that moment, she would have said anything to get him out the door. She knew she was being unnecessarily cruel. He didn't deserve this. She'd known him a long time and yes, he'd screwed up, but who hadn't?

"I'm not sticking around here just to be insulted." He hesitated. "I don't get you, Mel. Everything was fine." She could see the confusion on his face.

"Go on then, leave."

"Why are you doing this? The offer is real."

"Ben, go!"

"Mel, come on. Think about it."

"Fuck off, Wheelie Ben. And take your pity party of a job offer with you."

He stood in the middle of the living room and stared down at her. Emotions she couldn't read flitted across his face. Melissa wanted to feel remorse but at that moment, the pain in her body gave her no opportunity to feel anything but the burning in her nerve endings. What felt like an age later, Ben shook his head and crossed to the hall without a backwards glance.

When the front door slammed shut a moment later, Melissa managed to get to her feet. She hobbled down the hall and turned the key in the door before sliding the chain into place. Her knees buckled and she slid down the wall. The tears she had fought to hide from Ben coursed down her cheeks.

She'd been right; she'd be lucky if they didn't try to retire her. She was under no illusions regarding the severity of her injuries. Sure, she liked to put on a brave face, but she couldn't lie to herself.

She was afraid. Terrified, in fact. They had done their best to break her in the alley. And she couldn't shake the feeling that maybe they had succeeded. Not physically. Her body had taken a beating, but it would heal. It would take time, but it would happen. But the mental scarring from her attack was more difficult to quantify. Even now, as she sat slumped on the floor, safe in the hallway of her own apartment, she could feel that monster's hands on her, feel his breath across her face. What if he never left her mind?

That thought alone was enough to drive her to the brink of madness. For so long, she had trusted her mind to carry her through the horrors she had witnessed as part of her job. Not anymore. It had turned against her, and Melissa didn't know how to fix it.

CHAPTER EIGHTEEN

AMBROSE SAT down in his chair heavily and leaned back, causing it to creak loudly.

"Nothing new then?" Martina glanced at him over the top of the stack of files on her desk.

Ambrose gave a noncommittal groan and scrubbed his hand over his eyes. "The pathologist wants us to come down so he can run over the results."

Martina screwed her nose up in distaste. The last place she wanted to spend the remaining hours of her shift was trapped in the morgue. The smell would linger in her hair and clothes until she could get home for a shower. For some, the idea of going home was probably a comfort but not so for her. To her mind, going home was just another problem she wished she could postpone.

The situation with Mum had deteriorated

further. And while she had known it would happen, she was not prepared.

Her father's determination, while admirable, was making a difficult situation worse. When she'd suggested that they consider looking at some facilities for Mum to move into, he'd blown a gasket. Nobody was going to take his wife from him. She was ill, not a criminal to be locked away.

Martina sighed and closed her eyes. There had been a time when she'd admired her father's stubborn streak. Now though, she could understand why it had always bugged mum so much.

"I can see you're as thrilled about the idea as I am," Ambrose said wryly.

"Am I that transparent?" Martina reshuffled the files on her desk in search of a statement made by the neighbour.

"I can read you like a book," Ambrose said. "Go on then, tell me what's bothering you."

Martina sighed and sat back abruptly in her chair. "Have you seen the statement the neighbour made?"

Ambrose's brows snapped together. "The neighbour? The only statement we have from him is from the night the scene was discovered."

"And nobody followed up?" Martina couldn't keep the surprise from her voice. "Shouldn't we maybe have a word with him?"

"He hasn't got much to tell us, beyond the obvious."

"He was friends with the family. He might know something about the familial relationships."

Ambrose's expression brightened. "You want to know what he thinks of the son, don't you?"

Martina's face twisted into a grimace. "Is it wrong that I think the son knows more than he's telling us?"

Ambrose shrugged. "Nah, he was a bit too put together for someone who'd just received the news that his parents were dead."

Martina gathered her items together and slipped them into her rucksack. "So, you wouldn't mind if had a chat with the neighbour then, would you?"

Ambrose's mouth became a moue of displeasure. "You'd do anything not to come to the pathologist's office with me."

"I'll take that as a yes, then." She flashed him a broad smile before slipping into her jacket and hurrying from the office. She needed to get out before he changed his mind.

An hour later, she parked outside a large stone farmhouse set back from the road. As she switched off the ignition, two large black dogs came bounding across the yard in the direction of her car. Despite their size, their barks were high in pitch and Martina cringed, her hand frozen on the door handle.

It was still a decent walk to the front door. There was no way for her to avoid the canine confrontation. She contemplated beeping the horn in the hopes that it might bring someone from the household to her rescue, but that kind of behaviour would instantly make her look wea first impressions.

The dogs jumped and pranced alongside the driver's door as Martina started to push it open. Their yips grew louder; loud enough to drown out the hammering of her heartbeat.

Her sweaty palms slipped along the edge of the door as she placed one foot on the ground.

"Good dogs." Her voice sounded reedy and pathetic to her own ears. If Ambrose were here, he'd already have the dogs eating out of the palm of his hand.

But he's not here, Martina. So, get on with it.

Steeling herself, she pushed open the car door a little wider, giving herself barely enough room to slide out. "Good dogs," she said through gritted teeth. "Bugger off and let me get out of the car." The last was uttered beneath her breath.

Keeping her back pressed against the car's body, she put her rucksack between her and the excitable dogs. If they were going to lunge and take a chunk out of anything, better that it was the bag and not her arm.

"They know you're afraid." The voice came from somewhere behind her. If Martina had to guess, it came from the large sheds that occupied the space off to the left of the house.

"Twist, Dolly, heel."

The dog's tails dropped instantly. One started in

the direction of the disembodied voice. The other, however, stood its ground.

"Dolly, heel!" The sharp tone seemed to do the trick and Dolly scrambled in the direction of the stranger.

Relieved, Martina willed her heartbeat to slow its tempo. Turning, she gripped the side of the car and stared at the man across from her.

His tousled blond hair shone in the faint sunlight. His face and arms were tanned, suggesting to Martina that he was someone who spent a lot of time outdoors. The two black dogs sat next to his feet, their bodies pressed as close to his legs as possible.

He finished cleaning his hands on the piece of cloth he held and absentmindedly leaned down to stroke the head of one of the dogs.

"You all right?" His voice was low, casual even, but there was a hint of something else there. An uneasiness that surprised Martina.

"Yeah, I'm fine." She sucked a breath in and kept her gaze fixed firmly on the man instead of the dogs. "Are you Mr Phillips?"

He grinned at her before he shook his head. "That's funny, you're not the first person to come looking for Terry recently. Seems he's a popular guy. I'm Damien Parker." He jerked his thumb in the direction of the sheds. "I rent this from Mr Phillips."

Martina's eyebrows rose in surprise. "You rent the sheds?"

"The whole farm," he said. "Terry wanted to retire but he wasn't ready to sell up at the time. So, he rented it to me instead. I actually own the farm over the hill back that way." He jerked his chin in the direction of a distant hill, but Martina didn't bother to look.

"Is Mr Phillips around?"

Damien shook his head. "No, they went away. Terry's nerves were shot after that business up at the Hadfield's."

Martina's heart dropped. "Shit." Whoever had taken the initial statement from Terry Phillips had obviously not told him they would be following up. Then again, maybe they had, and Terry had just ignored it.

"Who should I tell him was looking for him?" Damian took a step in her direction. The dogs shifted with him as though they were glued to his legs.

"DC Martina Nicoll," she said, eyeing the dogs uneasily.

He rocked back on his heels, surprise widening his hazel eyes. "You're a police officer?"

Martina cocked her head to the side. "Yeah. What did you think I was?"

Damian shrugged but to Martina's mind at least the movement was a little too nonchalant. "Maybe a saleswoman. I don't know, I hadn't really thought about it too much. I didn't think you were a police officer though."

"Did you know the Hadfield family?"

Damian shook his head. "Not particularly well." He glanced down at the dogs and then seemed to change his mind. "Well, I suppose I knew them relatively well."

"Which one is it?"

Damian grinned. "Relatively well. I'd had a couple of chats with Mr Hadfield about renting out his land to me."

"And what did Mr Hadfield think about that idea?"

Damian's smile faded. "He was having none of it. Reckoned his son was going to take it over and he didn't want some stranger coming in and messing it all up." Damian sighed. "Not that I would have done anything like that. When you speak to Terry, he'll tell you that I run a tight ship here. I'm a hard worker and I don't believe in squandering opportunities."

"Were you upset that Mr Hadfield wasn't interested in your proposition?"

Damian's laughter took Martina and the two dogs at his feet by surprise. They scrambled up from their seated positions and started to yap excitedly.

"'Twist, Dolly, hush." Damian glanced at Martina. "You're scaring the nice detective lady."

Martina tried to loosen her grip on the strap of her rucksack, but her fingers refused to cooperate. Her muscles sang with tension as she watched the dogs for any sign that they were going to change their mind about obeying their owner.

"Not a fan of dogs I take it?" he said.

"What?" Martina's voice was a little higher than she would have liked.

"The dogs. You seem really nervous. I can put them in the shed if you like."

Martina hesitated.

"You're welcome to come over to the trailer and have a cup of tea. You've come all this way, after all. Seems a waste not to."

She nodded. "That would be great."

He pulled a face and Martina wondered if she'd made a mistake. "Full disclosure, I've mostly got camomile tea, but I might be able to scrounge you up a regular tea bag if you're lucky."

Martina felt a smile tug at the corners of her lips. "Camomile is fine."

With a satisfied jerk of his chin, Damian returned his attention to the dogs. "Come, Twist, come, Dolly." He turned and disappeared back through a side gate and the dogs trotted after him.

Martina took the opportunity to take in her surroundings. The farm was positioned low in a hollow, with the fields sloping upwards on all sides.

She took in a deep breath and wrinkled her nose as the scent of manure assaulted her senses. While it looked pretty enough, the idea of living out here in the country didn't appeal to her.

Damian appeared at the gate and pulled it open for her to follow him. "They're locked up tight, so you're safe."

She slipped through the gate and waited as he shut and locked it behind them. "This way."

He led the way across the yard. The muffled sound of the dogs barking reached her ears as they passed the first shed.

"It's not really fair," Martina mused.

"What's not fair?" Damian looked back at her over his shoulder.

"To lock them up just because of me."

He shrugged. "They're fine. They've got tons of space, and the back door of the shed is open if they want to run off some of their energy in the back field." His face broke into a wide grin. "They're not the smartest pair, so they probably won't figure that out until they tire themselves out from barking."

He paused next to a small caravan and pulled open the door.

"Do you live here?" Martina asked as she followed him inside.

"God, no. I just use this as a kitchen, so I'm not bothering the Phillips for hot water and the like." The caravan was equipped with banquette seating along the back wall, beneath a large window. "Grab a seat. Sorry it's so cramped. I did my best with it when I bought it."

"Where do you live?"

"Close to Goathland," he said, filling the kettle in the small sink. "I used to live around here when I was a boy, but my parents moved down south when I was ten."

Martina took a seat and smiled to herself as she noted the worn pattern on the oilcloth spread, and the wilting jam jar of wildflowers set out in the centre of the table.

"What brought you back to the area?"

Damian grimaced. "It's kind of a long story." He shot her a sideways look. "The short version is that I had a break down while I was working in London."

"I'm sorry," Martina said awkwardly.

He shrugged his broad shoulders. "Not your fault. And anyway, nothing to be sorry about. Best thing that ever happened, if you asked me." He turned towards her and carried two mugs of steaming tea back to the table. "Once I recovered, I packed the job in, cashed in on my flat and moved up here. Bought myself a small house and a plot of land and fell in love with farming."

The fragrant scent of the camomile tea tickled Martina's nose and she took a deep breath. When she looked up, it was to see Damian at the other side of the table grinning at her.

"Not many around these parts appreciate a good cup of herbal tea."

Wrapping her fingers around the chipped mug, Martina shrugged. "When you spend all day, every day, drinking tea and coffee, you learn to appreciate different things." She took a sip of the drink and glanced up at Damian in surprise. "This is amazing."

Colour spread up his cheeks and rushed towards his hairline. "I grow the camomile myself and then turn it into tea leaves. A bit of honey from some of the local hives, and it makes a lovely refreshing brew."

Martina took another sip and savoured the warmth as it spread down her throat and into her chest.

"I'm glad you like it," he said, pride edging his voice.

She set the cup back on the table. "I asked you earlier whether you were upset that Mr Hadfield hadn't liked your proposition."

"Oh, that." A wry smile tugged at the corners of Damian's mouth. But there was something in the way his shoulder's tensed that told Martina his nonchalant demeanour wasn't entirely honest. "It was fine. More than fine, really. Once I got stuck in here, really stuck in, I realised I'd bitten off more than I could chew."

"How so?"

His eyebrows rose, the only indication he'd heard her question as he kept his attention trained on the cup between his large, calloused hands.

"Terry is a good bloke but he's a bit of a pain in the arse too." Damian sighed. "It's not easy taking on a place like this. And it's made even more difficult with Terry constantly looking over my shoulder."

When he looked back up and met her eyes, Martina could see the naked honesty exposed in his expression.

"He's not happy with how you're running the farm?"

Damian shook his head. "Nothing I do is right, in his eyes."

"So why not leave?"

Damian shook his head. "I've sunk every penny into this place. If I pull out now, I'll lose it all. When I suggested to Terry that I was planning to approach Mr Hadfield, he wasn't happy about it. Between you, me, and the four walls, I think he's the reason Hadfield wasn't interested in my offer. When I got here, the farm was going to waste, too many fields left fallow. They should have brought in some sheep for the uneven terrain."

He cut himself off with a shake of his head that caused a curl to flop down onto his brow. "Listen to me going on. You're not interested in this shit."

Martina shook her head. "It sounds like the farm here was in trouble?"

Damien nodded. "This one and the Hadfield's. It was a money pit and how Hadfield has managed to keep his running for so long when it's obviously haemorrhaging money, I don't know." He took a mouthful of tea. "I honestly don't understand why they ran them into the ground the way they did."

Sitting back against the fabric cushion of the banquette seating, Martina tried to make sense of what she'd been told. "Why would they run them into the ground like that?"

Damian shrugged. "Like I said, I don't know.

Your guess is as good as mine. I haven't been able to work it out because it just makes no sense at all."

Martina took another thoughtful sip of her tea. "Were they close friends, Mr Hadfield and Mr Phillips?"

Damian screwed his face up into a grimace. "I wouldn't exactly call them close friends no. Maybe there was a time when they were, but recently, since I got here..." He gave a one shouldered shrug. "I don't think so."

Damian glanced out the window and swore. "I've got to go."

Martina glanced in the direction his attention was focused and spotted a couple of sheep making a great escape through a small gap in the fence.

With a smile, she thanked him for the tea as she followed him back to the car. "If you can think of anything else useful," she said as she exited through the gate. "'This is my number."

Damian took the card she offered and stared down at the name and constabulary symbol on the front. "You know, if you wanted to grab a drink sometime..."

Martina grimaced inwardly. He was a nice bloke and very easy to talk to, but considering the investigation they were running, it wouldn't be remotely professional to accept his offer.

As though he could sense her trepidation, he shook his head sheepishly. "Sorry, you've probably already got yourself a fella and here I am, putting my welly boots in it."

"It's not that," Martina said. "It's the investigation."

Understanding dawned quickly in Damian's hazel eyes. "Right, got you." He hesitated, scrubbing his hand across the back of his neck as he looked back down at the card. "Does that mean, if there was no investigation, you might say yes?"

Martina laughed. She had to admire his tenacity. Shrugging off the question, she returned to the car and, after unlocking it, tugged open the door.

"Maybe," was all she said. Colour mounted her cheeks as Damian's deep throated chuckle reached her. She slipped in behind the wheel and started the engine. *This is not me running away*, she thought as she carefully reversed out of the farmyard.

But as she made it to the road, she couldn't resist one last look back at Damian as he singlehandedly tried to wrangle his sheep back onto the correct side of the fence.

MARTINA'S PHONE BUZZED, alerting her to a phone call. Pulling over onto the side of the road, she stared at the number that pulsed on the screen. Her stomach knotted and without thinking about the consequences, she declined the call.

Dropping the phone back into the tray on the

console, she did her best to ignore the nervous butterflies that started up in her stomach.

Dad knew better than to call her when she was at work. She'd patiently explained to him more than once that she couldn't just drop everything and talk, no matter how much it pained her to ignore him

Edging back into traffic, she tried to put the guilt from her mind so she could concentrate on the road ahead.

CHAPTER NINETEEN

"I'M TELLING YOU, this is where they filmed *The Witcher*. I've seen pictures of Henry Cavill standing right here." Mariah indicated the large limestone cliffs surrounding them.

"You're such a bullshitter," Justin said with a shake of his head. "Why would Henry Cavill be filming *The Witcher* out here?"

"I'm not lying. Ask Tash."

"Ask Tash what?" The petite blonde caught up to them before whipping out her phone. It was the perfect place to take a selfie to share to her socials. Smoothing her hair back from her face, she carefully angled the phone.

"Tell him, this is where Henry Cavill was filming for *The Witcher*."

Tasha snapped the picture and pursed her lips as she looked over the results. The light wasn't great, but a filter would fix that.

"I'm not sure. I think so," she said, only half listening to the conversation going on around her. She angled the phone a second time, holding it in position while she watched Kyle scrambling over the rocks behind her. He chose that moment to look in her direction, a knowing grin spreading over his face as he caught her watching him.

"Shit!" Tasha swore beneath her breath as she hit a button and flipped the camera around before switching to video. She made a slow circle, taking in the tall limescale walls surrounding them.

"You know, if you wanted a picture, I'd be happy to pose for you." Kyle's voice in her ear sent a shiver down her spine.

"God, Kyle, don't be so conceited." She was aiming for nonchalant but missed it by a mile.

His smile broadened as he threw an arm around her shoulders, tucking her in against his body as though she was made to fit there. "Somebody learned a new word I see."

Shrugging him off, Tasha took a step away. Why had Mariah let Justin invite him? She knew how weird things were between them. If Tasha didn't know any better, she might think her friend was trying to sabotage her.

Not to be deterred, Kyle fell into step next to Tasha as she continued to film their surroundings.

"I've been thinking," Kyle said.

"That's a novelty," Tasha said drily.

Kyle hopped up onto a rock, moving easily across the uneven surface. He paused with his back to her he crouched down to retie the lace on his hiking boot.

Swallowing hard, Tasha swung away so she couldn't be caught staring a second time.

"We should grab a drink sometime." Kyle straightened up and hopped down from his perch. Ignoring him, Tasha dodged between two large boulders.

Was he really doing this now?

Kyle appeared in the gap, blocking her exit from between the rocks. "What do you say?"

"Kyle, stop messing around. I—"

A scream rent the air, the sound echoing off the limestone walls. In a flash, Kyle was off and running. He crossed the rocks and uneven terrain as though he were running on a flat track. Tasha's heart hammered against her ribs as she followed him.

Another scream and the sound of rocks skittering drew her attention upwards on the sheer rock face. Without much thought, she angled her phone camera up, along with her vision. The heavy, grey mist made it difficult to see much, but for a moment, Tasha was sure she saw a flash of canary yellow. It was there one second, and then gone before she could open her mouth to call out to Kyle.

Kyle came to a skidding halt as a shower of small rocks and debris fell around him. He yelled and doubled over giving Tasha the chance to catch up to him. A bloody gash where a jagged piece of rock had struck him had opened over his left eye.

"Kyle—"

The skittering of rocks was the only warning they had, and Kyle threw himself over Tasha pushing her back as another cascade of rocks tumbled over them.

A scream was cut off with a sickening thud. Silence followed, broken only by a few stray rocks rolling down the cliff face.

The seconds ticked by, and Tasha became aware of the frantic beat of Kyle's heart against her ear. Pushing against his chest, she stared up into his pale face. Ruby red blood contrasted starkly against the pallor of his skin.

"Are you all right?" His voice was a low rumble that faded into the background as Tasha peered past him.

The canary yellow looked odd against the grey limestone rocks. Like someone had taken a bucket of bright sunlight, given it form, and then poured it over the rocks. But it wasn't sunlight because sunlight didn't have red and black hair. Tasha's brain refused to put the pieces of the puzzle together as she stared past Kyle.

"Tash!" He shook her sharply, drawing her gaze away from the body.

It was a body. The splash of yellow was a coat. The hair was black, and the red slowly spreading across the rocks was blood. The pieces slowly fit together in her mind.

The yell they'd heard. A woman... a desperate woman who had fallen to the jagged rocks.

A scream spread up from the pit of Tasha's stomach, pouring out of her mouth until it reverberated and echoed around the rock face.

CHAPTER TWENTY

HARRIET SLID the key into the front door and opened the lock. The sound of paper *shushing* over the tile floor greeted her as she pushed the door inwards. Everything was exactly as she'd left it. It was a little dustier, but that was to be expected. Crouching down, she scooped up the post and set it aside on the table in the hall.

She closed the door and basked in the silence. The panic from before she'd gone to Ireland was long gone, along with the reporters who had camped outside on the street. But just because those things had returned to normal, did not mean everything was as it always had been. Wearily, she made her way down the hall and out into the kitchen. Some things were different now. She was different.

Setting down her bags, she filled the kettle and switched it on to boil. She grabbed a mug and dropped in a teabag. Pulling her phone from her pocket, she pulled up her contact list, her thumb hovering over Drew's name.

He'd asked her to let him know once she was back. A quick message was all it would take. Scrolling through her messenger app, she took note of the unanswered text messages she'd sent to David. He'd said she could call or text him anytime. That had clearly been a lie. As soon as everything had blown up in her life, he had ghosted her.

She had thought there could be something between them. The truth was a painful reminder of the damage Jonathan Connors had wrought in her life.

Closing the app, she tried to release the tension that tightened her shoulders. One more night to herself before she properly returned to the real world.

She put the phone down and grabbed her bags. When she was halfway up the stairs, the doorbell rang and she froze in her tracks. She contemplated ignoring it but quickly pushed the idea from her mind. She had nothing to be ashamed of. And hiding had not left her feeling any better.

Slowly returning down the stairs, she unlocked the door and let it swing open. The man on the step was well groomed. His shoulder length, light brown hair was swept back from his face and tucked fashionably behind his ears. His hazel eyes were warm and deep. Tiny gold flecks surrounding his irises caught the fading sunlight. The faint traces of lines on his face suggested somebody who spent a lot of time laughing or frowning. Harriet guessed it would be the former but at first glance she couldn't be entirely certain. An aquiline nose marred his otherwise symmetrical features, reducing his 'perfect Hollywood' good looks to something much more interesting.

His gaze found hers and his full, perfectly formed mouth quirked upwards at the corners into a broad smile. The expression flowed over his face, transforming and elevating his features, giving him a kind of boyish charm that hadn't been there a moment ago. His eyes crinkled at the corners, forming a familiar pattern, vindicating Harriet's initial assessment that here was a man who spent most of his time smiling.

"Can I help you?" she asked.

"Dr Quinn? Dr Harriet Quinn?"

"And you are?"

"I'm sorry, my name is Stephen. Stephen Jackson."

The name rang a bell in the back of her mind and Harriet decided to take a shot in the dark. "You're a journalist?"

He placed one broad hand over his chest, his smile turning contrite. "For my sins, yes. I'm an investigative journalist."

"What paper?"

"Freelance actually."

"A gun for hire." Harriet tried to mask the irritation in her voice. "I've got nothing to say."

"Look, I was sorry about what happened to you. The things they printed, well, there's no defending it."

"They wanted to sell papers, and they succeeded."

"But that doesn't make it right," Stephen said. He took a confident step forward.

"What do you want?"

"I wanted to talk to you about everything that happened. I wanted to hear your side of the story."

Harriet started to close the door. "I don't think so. As I said, I have nothing to say."

He moved faster than Harriet anticipated, jamming his foot in the door, preventing her from closing it completely. "Dr Quinn, you've spent your career trying to give a voice to those who don't have one. Let me do that for you. Let me give you a voice in all of this."

Harriet tightened her grip on the edge of the door. "I don't need a voice. It's over and done with."

"Are you really that naive?" One eyebrow raised towards his hairline. "From everything I've read about you, Dr Quinn, I wouldn't say naïveté is something that fits your character."

Harriet met his gaze steadily. "I have nothing to say."

He tilted his head to the side. "Oh, come on, Dr

Quinn. There must be something you want to get off your chest. We can help each other."

Harriet pushed against the door. "Remove your foot before I call the police."

"You and I both know they'll keep writing about you. Everyone knows there's no smoke without fire and with a history like yours, people will be only too happy to believe you capable of the terrible things they'll print."

She hesitated, and like a predator sensing weakness, Stephen smiled. "Your mother is a fascinating woman, Harriet. Did you forgive her because you feel a kinship with the darkness that drove her to murder your brother?"

Anger clogged the back of Harriet's throat making it difficult to think clearly. *Do not dignify him with an answer.* She did the only thing she could in the situation and pressed more firmly on the door, forcing him to remove his foot.

"Think about it, Dr Quinn."

She slammed the door in his face. The letter box flipped open, and Harriet realised he had crouched down. "You know they'll use your past against you. But I can help you. I can show everyone who you truly are."

Rather than stand there listening to him, she darted up the stairs. The more distance she put between them, the easier it was to block out his voice. But it wasn't until she closed the bedroom door that he was completely silenced.

Crossing to the window, Harriet opened the blinds and peered down at the street. Seconds ticked by, quickly turning into minutes as she waited at the window. When he stepped away from the door, he glanced upwards. Harriet's breath caught uncomfortably in the back of her throat as she shifted backwards, blending into the shadows of the room.

She watched as he studied the front facade of the house before finally turning and strolling off down the front path. Harriet continued to study him as he crossed the road and disappeared from sight. A moment later, the sound of an engine starting up interrupted the silence. Standing on tiptoe, Harriet tried to catch a glimpse of his car but there was nothing to see. The engine faded into the distance and Harriet slumped against the wall.

It wasn't exactly the welcome home she'd been hoping for. Then again, with everything that had happened, it could have been worse. Closing her eyes, she sighed. Was this her life now? Was she really measuring her interactions with people based on whether she believed a bad situation could have been worse?

She could not, would not live her life like this. Things needed to change. She sank onto the side of the bed and for the first time in a long while, she knew exactly what the change would be.

CHAPTER TWENTY-ONE

MARTINA FOUND Ambrose back at the station. The top button of his shirt was undone, and he looked a little worse for wear. His suit jacket was crumpled, discarded on the desk next to him.

She paused and watched him, his face buried in his hands as he stared blankly down at the surface of his desk.

Martina cleared her throat as she walked back to her seat. "I wasn't sure if you'd be here," she said, doing her best to ignore the sagging in his shoulders.

"I just got back." Ambrose's voice was muffled. When he finally raised his head to look at her, his features were strained.

Martina cocked a questioning eyebrow at him and settled into her chair.

Blowing out a breath, Ambrose tossed a folder across the desk to her. "Have you had lunch?"

His question took her by surprise as her fingers

brushed the edge of the brown paper folder. "No, why?"

"Good." That was all he said, but it was enough to cause the hairs on the back of her neck to stand to attention.

Martina set the folder in front of her and flipped it open. She scanned the pages, her mouth drying up as she discovered the gruesome details of the triple murder.

"This wasn't a run of the mill burglary," Ambrose said.

"Who would do something like this?" Martina's mouth was dry, her tongue thick, making it difficult to get the words out.

"I've never seen anything like it." Ambrose shrugged, a small gesture that belied the gravity of his words.

"Neither have I," Martina said. She could almost smell the coppery tang of blood as she read the catalogue of the wounds discovered by the forensic pathologist.

Closing the file, she sucked a breath through her mouth. It was an effort to prevent her mind from bringing the crime scene to life behind her eyelids. "Do we have anything back from forensics yet?"

Ambrose shook his head. "David has promised he should have something for us tomorrow."

Nodding, Martina pushed the file aside and turned her computer on.

"Any luck with Mr Phillips?" Ambrose asked.

Martina shook her head. "He wasn't there. But it wasn't altogether a wasted trip. I had a chat with the bloke renting the land from him."

"Mr Phillips rents out his farm? What, like one of those Airbnb things?"

Martina shook her head. "More like you'd rent a house. From what I could see, it was a much more permanent situation. Damian Parker. Nice, solid type."

"He have anything useful to add?"

Pursing her lips, Martina ran her thoughts back over the conversation they'd had. "A few things. He said Terry Phillips and Mr Hadfield were not as close as Phillips initially made out."

"Well, that's not a crime," Ambrose said. "Plus, that corroborates what the son said." He leaned back in his chair, ignoring the ominous creak emitted by the frame as he clasped his hands behind his head.

"He also said both farms were haemorrhaging money. He approached Mr Hadfield about renting out his land, but Hadfield wasn't having any of it."

Ambrose's expression turned thoughtful. "That can't have gone down too well with him."

Martina smiled. "I thought the same thing and I asked him as much. He said once he realised the state everything was in, he was glad Hadfield had turned him down. Said he'd bitten off more than he could chew with the farm he was renting from Phillips."

Martina leaned across the desk. "He also said,

Hadfield was adamant that his son was going to take over the farm."

Ambrose cocked an eyebrow at her. "That's not exactly new."

"Agreed," Martina said as she clicked through to the files on her computer. "But I made a few calls before I got back to the office."

Ambrose had straightened up in his chair. "And what did you find?"

"Well, Mr Phillips said in his original statement that Hadfield's son was away at Uni, studying Agriculture with Farm Business management. When I checked with the Newcastle University, they said he had enrolled but he dropped out two months ago."

"Why would he do that?"

"He dropped out voluntarily. It was either that or they were going to flunk him out."

Ambrose's expression had turned thoughtful. "That doesn't really prove anything."

"No," Martina ventured, "but that doesn't mean it's not interesting. If Mr Hadfield was expecting his son to take over the farm but the son had no interest in it..."

"Plenty of children have no interest in following in their parents' footsteps."

Martina conceded the point. "Mr Parker did say something interesting. He seemed surprised that Hadfield was able to keep the farm running. Looking into their finances might be worthwhile. Maybe he had creditors that we could talk to."

"It's better than what we've got so far, which is basically nothing."

"Do you think the DI will still refuse to entertain the idea of bringing in some outside help?"

Ambrose screwed his face into a grimace. "I really don't see him going for it. Maybe if we find something worthwhile in the financials, we'll be able to make a case for seeking outside assistance. But as it stands..." He shrugged. "It seems unlikely."

Martina nodded. "Then I'd better start looking into the financials."

Her phone rang, taking her by surprise. She picked it up and stared down at her father's number on the screen.

Unease wrapped its way around her spine, digging its tendrils into her like a creature latching onto its next meal.

"Everything all right?" Ambrose leaned a little closer as though he could sense the shift in her mood.

"I think so. I have to take this..." She got to her feet and made for the door.

She waited until she was in the hall before taking the call. "Dad, you know you're not supposed to--"

"Is this Martina Nicoll?" The unfamiliar voice took her completely by surprise.

"Yes, who is this? Where's my father?"

"My name is Claire Graham. I'm a paramedic. I've got your father here."

Before Martina could form words, Claire cut

across her. "He's fine. A little shook up. We've been trying to call you for a while."

White noise crowded Martina's brain, blotting out the voice of the paramedic on the other end of the line. "Is he hurt?" she finally managed to croak out.

"He's—"

"I want to speak to him," Martina said, finally finding her voice. "Let me speak to my father, please." The last word was gritted out between her teeth.

The sound of things being fumbled travelled down the line until finally, Dad's voice, a little wheezy, said, "Marty?"

Her heart broke to hear such vulnerability in her father's voice. "Yeah, dad, it's me. What happened? Is it mum?"

"She was upset, love. I tried…" His voice cracked and the sound sent guilt coursing in Martina's veins.

"Are you at home?"

"No. They're taking me to the hospital."

"All right, Dad, put Claire back on the phone."

Once she knew where they'd planned to take her father, Martina ended the call. She didn't care if it was rude or not. All she cared about was getting over to Scarborough hospital as quickly as she could. Her parents needed her.

You failed them. She tried to push the voice in her head aside but it refused to budge, a constant stream of guilt that soaked through her mind.

Returning to the office, she grabbed her coat and bag.

Ambrose looked her over. "What's wrong?"

"Family emergency. I've got to go."

He started to ask, but when he saw whatever emotion flooded her eyes, he stopped. He jerked his head in the direction of the door. "Go."

Martina did not need to be told twice.

CHAPTER TWENTY-TWO

DREW STARED down at the pages in front of him, his brain refusing to make sense of the words. Since he'd dropped Melissa back at her own apartment, he'd found himself unable to fully concentrate. Her words repeated on a loop through his head. It felt like something had been irrevocably changed between them.

Getting involved had been a mistake, they could both agree on that point. That type of co-dependency wasn't healthy for anyone. And Drew knew he carried his share of the blame. He'd known she was vulnerable after everything that had happened with Templeton. He knew her well enough to know that she was latching onto him because she felt adrift and she needed an anchor, and rather than let her find her feet with the team, he had tainted her entire experience.

Guilt weighed heavily on him. All he wanted to

do was pick up the phone and ask her how she was. Or better still, drive over there and make sure she was managing. But she had asked him not to. He could see that she wanted to do this alone. She needed to stand on her own two feet, and he could understand that. However, knowing that didn't make it any easier for him. He was so accustomed to shouldering responsibility and protecting those he cared about that having Melissa shut him out and block him from that role niggled at him like a toothache.

The phone on his desk rang, abruptly cutting off his circular thinking. Grabbing the handset, he answered without checking the caller ID.

"DI Haskell."

Wind whistled down the line and he could make out the faint trace of birds cawing in the background.

"Hello?" He pressed the phone a little more firmly against his ear and caught the sound of rustling plastic. Was this some kind of prank call?

"There it is. Hello, DI Haskell!" The voice jolted onto the line. "Sorry about that, I dropped the phone. It's a little scratched but nothing too egregious."

"Dr Sheridan?"

"Please, call me Tony." Tony huffed and puffed on the other end of the line like a man who had just run a marathon.

"Is everything all right, Tony? You sound a little..."

"Oh, it's nothing. I wanted to catch up with you about your little county lines issue."

Drew leaned back in his chair, a bemused smile playing over his face. Dr Sheridan's description was not quite how he would have described the situation. "Do you have anything I could use?"

"Maybe." Tony's voice faded, and the rustling of plastic returned.

"Dr Sheridan, if this isn't a convenient time."

"Good call," Tony said, his voice booming down the line again. "Give me five minutes and I'll call you back as soon as I get in home." The click of the call ending and the sound of the dial tone took Drew by surprise.

"You called me," Drew muttered. Replacing the receiver, he got up from his chair and grabbed the files from the pile on the floor. As he flipped them open, the sight of Melissa's handwriting tugged at his heart. If only she had shared with him.

Then again, how could she? He'd been so wrapped up with trying to clear Harriet's name that he hadn't given a moment's thought to Melissa or what she'd been dealing with.

Now was not the time to focus on the past. He couldn't change it, what was done was done. But he could help Mel now by finding the person responsible.

FORTY-FIVE MINUTES LATER, there was still no word from Dr Tony Sheridan. Drew skimmed the autopsy report on Angelica Dawson, flipping through the notes quickly. The bastard who had killed her had really done a number on her body. There was no doubt in Drew's mind that it was a message. Dr Sheridan had said as much the first time they'd spoken. Was it possible that there was more to the case than they'd initially thought? Had Melissa been lured into a trap?

Grabbing the phone, Drew quickly dialled Dr Sheridan's number from memory.

For a moment, he thought the phone would ring out. Finally, when he had all but given up hope of reaching Tony, the man in question answered. "Dr Sheridan's phone." Tony's voice crackled down the line. The sounds of the outside world were gone, replaced instead by the noise of a kettle boiling.

"Tony, it's DI Haskell. Is this a bad time?"

"DI Haskell...oh, yes. Was I supposed to call you back? I'm sorry, time got away from me. I had a quick look through my notes when I got in the door, and I'll admit I got a little carried away."

"I hope that means you have something good for me," Drew said. He flipped open the file on Chelsea Fraser and grimaced. She was just a child. How anyone could do such monstrous things made no sense to him.

"Well, I did a little bit of a deep dive on the whole psychology of county lines operations after we spoke. I was a little rusty on the details. And to be honest, we don't have much information in relation to the psychology behind it."

"That doesn't sound promising."

"Oh, don't let that put you off, DI Haskell. Many of the tactics used by these gangs are very similar to those used in cases of domestic violence. In fact, many gangs have connections to modern slavery, too, so it stands to reason we would see some overlap."

"You mentioned grooming the last time we spoke," Drew said.

"Yes, but it's not exactly the same kind of grooming used by sexual predators, although, there again we can see an overlap. Many of the children who are caught up in this kind of crime are sexually abused. Some are forced to prostitute themselves and are trafficked to other areas. However, true sexual predators tend to take their time with their intended target, often going to great lengths to ensure their hold on the victim is watertight. And they also go after much younger victims.

"In county lines, the victims are a little older, often on the cusp of adolescence. A kind of speed grooming is utilised and rather than it being older gang members doing the grooming, the victims are usually targeted by their peers and so-called friends. Other children who have already 'gone country'."

"You're telling me it's kids doing this to other kids? How can that be?" Drew stared down at the picture of Chelsea, unable to imagine how somebody so vulnerable could be a part of something so vicious.

"You only need look at the society we live in, DI Haskell, to find your answer. So much emphasis is placed on social standing. Teenagers are especially susceptible to this. Without the latest designer piece of clothing, or newest phone, they're vulnerable to ridicule by their peers. We live in a hyper-consumerist society where everyone is in search of fast money and easy success. Boys are socialised online to admire and seek out hyper masculinity. You only have to look to the success of some of the more controversial male influencers. Those who shy away from it are often ostracised from their social group which can be devastating. Nobody wants to be pushed out.

"And then the younger generations are constantly plugged in. This kind of 24/7 technological communication is the perfect breeding ground for individualised coercive and persuasive messaging. How would you cope if your friends were constantly extolling the benefits of their illegal activity?"

"I'd get new friends," Drew said smartly.

Tony laughed. The jovial sound travelled down the line, reminding Drew of similar conversations he'd shared with Harriet. He missed her. He missed sharing things with her and getting her unique view on the world.

"Said like an adult man confident in his own social standing. Children and teenagers, despite all indications to the contrary, are not yet fully formed.

They lack the confidence of their convictions because they have not yet had their mettle tested."

"But they're breaking the law. They have to know it's wrong."

"And by the time they might ever consider that possibility, it's too late. They're in too deep and to back out would mean dire consequences. A price little Chelsea paid in a truly horrific fashion."

"I've read the reports Melissa filed about Chelsea," Drew said. He wasn't entirely convinced by Dr Sheridan's assessment of the children's lack of responsibility for their actions. "She knew what she was doing. She was always quick to assert her rights. According to one of Melissa's reports, Chelsea even went so far as to describe it as a kind of lifestyle choice. That sounds like someone who knew exactly what they were doing."

"And I suppose when you were a teen, DI Haskell, you were always respectful of your elders. You didn't falsely believe you knew everything. You didn't wrongly assume were indestructible?"

"Well, I suppose..."

"What was that?"

"No, I was an idiot," Drew said finally. "If you asked my sister, she would tell you I was a know-it-all little shit."

"And so, you're beginning to understand a little of what these children are dealing with. Their dual status as both criminal and victim is a tricky line to walk."

"So how does any of this help me find the person responsible for Chelsea's murder and the attempted murder of DI Appleton?"

Tony fell silent. The seconds ticking by as Drew stared out into the room beyond. He watched as Gregson called Olivia and Maz into his office and felt his curiosity pique. A moment later, Jodie Meakin joined them.

"After reviewing the files you so kindly sent over, I'm inclined to modify my initial assessment of the situation, DI Haskell. This was a threat to your DI Appleton and the entire team. The fact that they used a child to send the threat tells me these people don't plan to just walk away. And when I look at the wider context of what was done to DI Appleton, the level of injury she sustained, the savagery involved in her attack, they want her to suffer. And as an extension of that, they want the unit to suffer."

Tony's words sent a shiver down Drew's spine.

"They're playing with you, DI Haskell. But make no mistake, this is a threat."

"What message are they trying to send us?"

Tony fell quiet, only the scratch of a pen on paper could be heard over the line. "I would hazard that they want you to know that they can come for you at any time and any place."

"Are you telling me DI Appleton is in danger?" Drew felt his hackles rise.

"Yes and no. I'm saying you're all under threat. There is something about this entire ordeal that feels personal. As though you and your team have personally offended somebody important. But the level of injuries suggests a sadistic streak. Whoever this person is, they enjoy inflicting pain, so I wouldn't imagine they will be in any rush to exact their revenge. They want to prolong it. I would expect them to find a way to get a message to your DI Appleton or your team. Something that will leave you in no doubt as to their intentions."

"Could you be wrong about this?" Drew knew as soon as the question left his mouth that Tony was not wrong. There were too many unanswered questions surrounding the case, and too many things that just didn't add up. After reading Chelsea's postmortem report, Drew had thought Melissa lucky to have survived. But if he were honest, he knew luck had nothing to do with it. They hadn't wanted to kill a police officer... yet.

Tony chuckled. "Of course I could be wrong, DI Haskell. While forensic psychology is a science, it's not an exact science. Nothing is when it comes to the human mind. There is still so much we don't fully understand. But if it's worth anything, I don't believe I am wrong. And I think if you spoke to Harriet about this, she would agree with my assessment of the case."

Drew sighed. "I think you're probably right. I just wish you weren't."

"Trust me, DI Haskell, I would love nothing more than to be wrong on this. I'll send over a written report for you to peruse. While it won't pinpoint an identity for you, it should help to fill in a few gaps you have in your case file. If I were to hazard a guess, I would suggest you look over your past cases. Something in there triggered this attack."

"You think it's somebody we locked up?"

"Or someone DI Appleton crossed paths with, as she seems to be at the centre of this. At any rate it gives you somewhere to start."

"Dr Sheridan, I don't know how to thank you. I really owe you for this."

"I said to call me Tony and it was my pleasure, DI Haskell. It was a nice diversion away from my own troubles."

"Anything you'd like assistance with?"

For a moment, Drew thought he might say yes.

Instead, he sighed. "No, DI Haskell. This is my own mess, and I need to stop avoiding it and face the truth head on. Look after yourself. And tell Harriet I said, 'hello,' will you?"

"Of course—"

The call ended abruptly, and Drew was left staring at the receiver.

The door to Gregson's office slammed open and Maz strode out. His face was ashen as he crossed the office with a determined stride. Jodie trailed him but said nothing. Drew watched as Max reached his desk, gathered up his belongings, and he exit through the front door.

Setting the phone down, Drew got to his feet in

time to see Olivia rush out of Gregson's room. She said something to Jodie, who indicated the main doors. Unease settled in Drew's gut.

For days now he had been so caught up in his thoughts, chasing his own tail that he'd been neglecting the team. He'd known Gregson was keeping something from him, but he hadn't pushed the matter, instead allowing the DCI to play his cards close to his chest. But something had changed. And considering the conversation he'd just had with Dr Sheridan, Drew knew he could not afford to be complacent any longer. The safety of the team depended on his ability to do his job to the highest standard.

Drawing in a breath, he squared his shoulders and made a beeline for Gregson's office. It was time to confront the situation head on.

CHAPTER TWENTY-THREE

"YOU TWO GET in here now and shut the door." There was a stoniness to Gregson's voice that took Olivia by surprise. The DCI was renowned for his mood swings, but this was a little much, even for him.

Olivia was the last into the office and she closed the door quietly behind her. When she turned to face Gregson, he was staring down at his hands, which were planted on the desk in front of him. Had he found out? Did he know she'd been spending time away from the desk?

From the corner of her eye, she glanced at Maz. He wouldn't have betrayed her. She was positive he had kept their secret. But if Maz hadn't mentioned anything, then who had?

Silence filled the room, eating into the oxygen, making it difficult to breathe.

A short rap on the door behind her made Olivia jump. Gregson beckoned the person to enter, and

Olivia's stomach sank as Jodie slipped into the room. Maz wouldn't have betrayed her to the boss, but he might have let it slip to Jodie. And as far as Olivia was concerned, she had no idea if the newest member of the group was trustworthy or not.

"Jodie..." Maz looked as confused as Olivia felt, which did nothing to make her feel better.

Jodie didn't acknowledge the DS. Instead, she shuffled quickly over to Gregson's desk, a sheaf of papers gripped tightly in her hands.

For a moment, everyone stood frozen. Olivia could Gregson was just waiting them out. Something was going on, and Olivia's stomach knotted uncomfortably.

"Sir, we think we might have something." Maz, who stood awkwardly to one side of Gregson's desk, broke first.

From her vantage point, Olivia noted just how uncertain her DS appeared in the presence of their superior. It was something she'd failed to notice before.

"Go on then, spit it out." Gregson looked tired. Exhausted in fact.

"We've been doing a little digging, sir..." Maz's hesitancy was beginning to grate even on Olivia. The urge to jump in and take over the conversation strong, but whenever they'd discussed talking to the DCI it had been agreed that it would sound better coming from Maz.

"Aye, well that's your job." Gregson made a point

of glaring at them both. "I don't suppose you came in here just to tell me that, so out with it. What have you got?"

Maz glanced in Olivia's direction. She didn't need to be a mind reader to know that his resolve was beginning to waver.

"Well, it's just..." Maz rubbed his hand across the back of his neck. "During this digging we came across some new information."

"And?"

"It's about the night DI Appleton was attacked."

"Christ, man, get on with it. I don't have all day."

"We've got a name, sir." Olivia couldn't contain her nervous energy any longer and blurted out the answer. They had more than a name, but baby steps were best.

The DCI's attention snapped towards her, and it took everything in her not to take a step back. DI Haskell made interacting with the DCI look like child's play. If she were honest, whenever she saw them together, they had an excellent rapport, something Olivia knew couldn't be true because as far as she'd heard, the Monk, was incapable of developing a rapport with anyone.

With nothing to lose, she chose to barrel ahead. "I've got some friends down in the Force Control room and while I was chatting with one in particular, he happened to mention something interesting." She took a breath, attempting to gauge Gregson's reaction to the information so far.

They'd agreed the story they would tell Gregson would be one made of half-truths. For instance, he did not need to know that she and Maz had taken it upon themselves to go and deliberately seek out the people who worked at Force Control based on a half-baked theory they'd pieced together from information Maz had gleaned while working with Jodie. Much better that the DCI think they had happened upon it.

Olivia chanced a look at Jodie. Did she know they had used her information as a jumping off point? It shouldn't have been possible.

Gregson frowned, and Olivia's heartbeat picked up.

"Well, this friend of mine mentioned that there was something strange with the way in which they received the call the night DI Appleton was attacked."

Maz found his voice again, his earlier anxiety replaced with eager excitement. "I've been through the call logs, sir, and from what we could find, there was no *official* call. Or if there ever was, it was deleted. An entire chunk of calls from that night were missing."

"Go on." There was something in Gregson's voice that made Olivia hesitate.

But if Maz noticed, he didn't pay it much heed. "According to those working in Force Control, there was a system wide glitch the following night that wiped a lot of their information. We haven't been able to recover it. And that makes it particularly difficult to trace who took the call. But that's where Olivia's mate comes in. He thinks there were two calls. One unofficial that didn't come through the normal channels and one that came in later from a bystander." Maz was beginning to babble, his excitement getting the better of him. "Olivia's friend thinks the person who took the first call was Celeste Jackson

"She wasn't officially on the roster for that night, she came in as a favour to cover for someone else. Sir, we think this Ms Jackson must know something about the assault, and we'd like your permission to bring her in so she can be questioned officially." Maz left out the part where Olivia had already spoken with Celeste. Olivia was grateful for small mercies.

The silence in the room once Maz had finished speaking was so absolute that Olivia could have dropped a pin on the floor and it would have echoed throughout the office.

Had they screwed up? Was there something they were missing?

Gregson dropped back in his chair and steepled his short fingers in front of him. "And I'm supposed to believe that you both just happened upon this information?" When neither replied, Gregson continued. "You must think I came down in the last shower. You..." He jabbed a finger in Olivia's direction. "...were placed on desk duty for a reason. If you're a member of this team, then you follow the rules same as everybody else."

"Sir, DC Crandell—"

Gregson cut Maz off before he could finish his sentence. "I don't want to hear it, Arya. We follow the rules or everything falls apart." Tutting, Gregson turned away in his chair. "Fuck!"

"Sir, we were just following the breadcrumbs." Olivia couldn't keep the misery from her voice. She'd screwed up. It didn't matter what she thought on the matter, the DCI was correct. The rules existed for a reason, and she'd gone against them.

"No, you went behind my back and used the information I was gathering to try and get ahead," Jodie's voice carried through the room like a crack of lightning.

"That's ridiculous. You're not the only one capable of police work."

"DS Arya was with me the day I found the missing piece in the call logs. He knew a part of what I'd discovered but not the whole. That was where you got your lead from."

"That's as maybe," Gregson said. He remained turned away. "But what's done is done." When he swung back around, his expression was a study in neutrality. "You say you want to speak with Celeste Jackson officially which tells me you've already spoken to her unofficially, is that right?"

"Well..." Maz ran his hand over the back of his neck.

"Yes or no."

"Yes." Olivia stared down at the ground, unable to meet the DCI's gaze.

"And who else knows you questioned her?"

"Sir, we didn't question her. It was just a conversation in the bathroom. She sought me out. And I didn't accuse her of anything."

Gregson pursed his lips and stared past them to the door. When he spoke again, his voice dropped several octaves. "What I'm about to tell you both in this room can go no further. Is that clear?"

Olivia nodded eagerly. From the corner of her eye, she spotted Maz stiffen.

"Ordinarily, I wouldn't have told any of you. But after you two went poking your noses in where they don't belong, my hands are tied." From a collection of files on his desk, Gregson pulled a blue one free and flipped it open.

Olivia tried to read the top page, but the type face was too small to make much sense from a distance.

"As you know, Ms Meakin came to speak with me a number of days ago. It seems she came to much the same conclusion as you two. The only difference being, Ms Meakin was far more discreet about her suspicions. I gave Ms Meakin the authority to dig a little deeper into Celeste Jackson. Discreetly, of course." He nodded in Jodie's direction.

Jodie straightened up. "I pulled phone records from the night of DI Appleton's attack and discovered two calls were made to Miss Jackson's phone around the time of the attack. Both calls were made from DI Appleton's phone. I traced the location of the phone. The first call was made in the general area of the attack. The second call, which happened a few minutes later, was made from a location some distance away from the attack site. This information, when shared with the DCI, gave him the evidence he needed to place Celeste Jackson under surveillance."

Olvia brightened. "Sir, this is amazing, we've got everything we need to bring her in."

Gregson shook his head. "We can't bring her in."

"Why not?" Olivia tried to keep the impatience from her voice. Yes, things were always more complicated when it came to investigating one of their own, but if what Jodie said was true, then they had more than enough to make a move.

"What I'm saying is that shortly after you two mavericks decided to conduct your own investigation independent of everybody else, it spooked Celeste Jackson. She decided to take an impromptu day off. She called in yesterday morning claiming to have the flu. And late yesterday evening an emergency call was made from Malham Cove." Gregson paused to take a breath, allowing the weight of his words to sink in. "It seemed a woman had taken a fall from the top of the limestone cliffs. I think you both know where this is going, don't you?" He sighed.

Olivia could see the colour drain from Maz's face, leaving him ashen, as understanding sank in with them both.

"She took her own life?" Olivia finally found her voice.

Gregson stared down at the report. "We can't be certain. The witnesses claim they saw a second car at the location, but we haven't been able to trace the owner."

Olivia's legs gave out beneath her. If she closed her eyes, she could see Celeste's face imprinted on the inside of her eyelids. The look on her face when Olivia had mentioned the call being deleted...

"Sir, there's something else I need to tell you." Olivia rubbed her sweaty palms over her thighs. He would be pissed but he needed to know. Without daring to look at him, Olivia swallowed and started to speak. "When I was speaking to Celeste, I noticed something."

"Go on." There was a stillness to Gregson's voice that made Olivia nervous.

"She had a lot of bruising on her arms."

"You never told me that," Maz interrupted.

"She tried to cover it up, but I saw it clearly. It was obviously caused by somebody grabbing her because I could see the individual finger marks. When I tried to ask her about it, she became defensive, but I could tell she was afraid. I think she was being coercively controlled."

"Is that all?" Gregson's gaze bore into her, making the room seem impossibly small and claustrophobic.

"No, sir," Olivia dug her nails into the palm of

her hand. "I asked her why she deleted the call, and she got really upset. She said it was the glitch that wiped everything. When I suggested that maybe someone was pressuring her, she became afraid. As though just by me suggesting it aloud whoever was pressuring her would find out."

"Anything else you want to tell me?" Gregson asked.

Hanging her head, Olivia tried to settle her nerves. "No, sir, that's all. We were going to come to you with the information—"

Gregson held his hand up, cutting her off before she could finish speaking. "I need time to think. For now, DS Arya, I'm suspending you effective immediately. Once all of this is straightened out, we'll reassess your future with the team."

Shock rendered Maz frozen where he stood.

"Sir, please, I—" Tears burned in the back of Olivia's throat. This was her fault. She had screwed up, not Maz. She was the one who should get suspended. He hadn't done anything wrong. If anything, he'd tried to tell her what a mistake it was not to go to the boss. He didn't deserve this.

"Get out." Gregson turned away, the dismissive note in his voice cut Olivia to the core. She knew she had screwed up, but this seemed excessive.

"Sir, I'm sorry I let you down. I'll gather my things and go." Maz left without looking at Olivia. She reached for him, but he shrugged away from her touch and left the door open as he stepped out into the main office. Jodie followed without a word.

"Sir, this isn't Maz's fault. If anyone deserves to be suspended, it's me. I'm the one who screwed up. I'm the one who—"

"He's your superior, DC Crandell, he should know better. Make no mistake, it was your reckless actions that put him in this position, but the buck stops with him." Gregson sighed. "You are to remain on desk duty for the foreseeable future. If I so much as see you standing at the coffee machine for a minute longer than necessary, I'll have your arse in a sling. Is that clear?"

"Yes sir..."

"Good, then go." He waved her away.

Olivia went in search of Maz the moment she left the office. But he was nowhere to be seen.

She spotted Jodie making her way back to her own office and hurried after her.

"Jodie, where did Maz go?"

Without looking up from the report in her hand, Jodie jerked her thumb in the direction of the front door. With a sinking heart, Olivia picked up her pace and made it to the door just in time to see Maz reversing from his car space.

Pushing out into the drizzly rain, Olivia tried to wave him down but if he saw her, he didn't acknowledge her. Instead, his eyes were fixed on the road ahead, his white knuckled grip on the steering wheel the only indication of his mood.

"Maz!" Olivia shouted to him and stepped out into the road, but he ignored her. He turned out onto the main road. Olivia watched his red taillights disappear into the distance.

"Shit!" She ran her hands back through her hair. It wasn't fair. Gregson should have suspended *her*. She was the one at fault. Guilt opened a pit in her stomach as realisation sank in. They were a team. If one of them messed up, it created a ripple effect throughout the group. And in this situation, her ripple had created a tidal wave that had left Celeste Jackson dead and seen Maz suspended.

"Shit, shit, shit!" Tears trailed down her cheeks, mingling with the rain that had started to come down hard and fast. The drops of water soaked through her shirt but that wasn't what chilled her to the bone. It was the knowledge that she was responsible for Celeste's death.

She'd thought life had taken enough from her when she'd fallen victim to Alfred Douglas. Just thinking about it was enough to cause the scar on her neck to prickle uncomfortably. But this was worse somehow. She'd never been afraid to suffer the consequences of her own actions, but being forced to sit back and watch on as others took the punishment for her mistakes cut deeper than Douglas' knife ever could.

She needed to fix this, but if she was honest with herself, she had no clue how.

CHAPTER TWENTY-FOUR

MARTINA SAT NEXT to her father's bed. watching him sleep. A rebreather oxygen mask had been fitted to his face. Martina had tried to make it more comfortable, but the blue strap continued to dig into his hollowed-out cheeks. He looked so small, fragile even. Outwardly, he'd got off relatively lightly. A few bumps and bruises from when Mum had attacked him during one of her episodes. The real problem, as the doctor had told her, was his heart.

Heart failure. A progressive and eventually fatal illness considering his already precarious health and near constant state of stress. If things did not change, then Mum, despite the grim nature of her illness, would outlive him.

Closing her eyes, Martina let her head rest on the back of the chair. Something had to change, and while she knew what that change needed to be, she was painfully aware that her father disagreed.

A quiet knock on the door drew her attention. Ambrose stood outside the window and when he smiled, Martina felt her strength begin to waver. Getting up from the chair quietly, she crept to the door and slipped out into the hall.

Ambrose said nothing as he noted the look on her face and pulled her into a bear hug. Normally, she would have pulled away, but it had been a long and gruelling twenty-four hours since her father had been admitted to the hospital, and Martina was grateful for the human contact.

Ambrose released her, and as she took a step back, Martina used the sleeve of her jumper to brush away the damp tears from her cheeks.

"You didn't have to come," she said quietly. The sound of the television, mingled with the laughter from visitors and patients in the ward across the hall, adding a surreal layer to the situation.

"I wanted to," Ambrose said. "Julie asked me to bring these." From beneath his anorak, he took a Tupperware box and handed it over. "They're Fat Rascals. But don't let the Tupperware fool you. You'll be relieved to know she didn't make them." He grinned at Martina. "She just wants everyone to think she bakes."

"Well, tell her I said thanks. It's really thoughtful. She honestly didn't have to."

Ambrose jerked his chin in the direction of the room. "How's the old man getting on?"

Martina tightened her grip on the box and tried

to force a level of brightness she didn't feel into her voice. "He's doing well. They said he'll be able to go home in a couple of days."

"What aren't you saying?"

Martina's head snapped up. "What do you mean?"

"Come on, I didn't become a detective for the health benefits. There's something you're not saying."

Leaning back against the wall, Martina blew out a breath. "Acute heart failure brought on by high blood pressure. Apparently, dad's been suffering from high blood pressure for a while now but never bothered to tell me. The GP prescribed medication but he's been so busy with Mum that he just stopped picking up his 'scripts." Martina swallowed around the lump in her throat. "The damage is..." Her voice failed her.

"Shit, I'm sorry." Ambrose patted her on the shoulder. "Has your mum been ill too?"

It dawned on Martina then that she had never actually told him, or anyone, about what was wrong with her mother. Shame and guilt had kept her silent about it. Not that she was ashamed of her mother's condition; it was more that she felt ashamed that she was so incapable of being the daughter her parents needed her to be.

Swallowing hard, she pushed away from the wall. "Fancy grabbing a coffee?"

"Will your dad be all right?"

Martina glanced back through the window. "He's sleeping. He won't miss me."

"Fine, but only if you let me have a Rascal. Julie only bought enough for you and her; said I was enough of a fat rascal already." Ambrose patted his belly, pride gleaming in his eyes.

"Somehow I doubt Julie said that to you."

"Are you accusing me of lying?" Ambrose clutched his chest in mock indignation.

"Here, have at it." Laughing, Martina handed the box over.

"WHY DIDN'T you say anything about what was going on at home?" Ambrose polished off the last of his Rascal before turning his attention to the sandwich he'd picked up in the hospital coffee shop.

"It wouldn't have changed anything," Martina said, staring down at her coffee. "People knowing about Mum won't bring her memory back. And it certainly won't make Dad any less stubborn about what needs to happen next." She sighed. "I just wish I knew what to say to him to make him understand that she needs more help than we can give her."

"If there's anything I can do..."

"Actually, there is," Martina said. Taking a deep mouthful of the black coffee, she grimaced as the molten liquid burned the tip of her tongue.

"Shoot."

"Take my mind off it. Has forensics come back with anything useful?"

Ambrose pursed his lips. "Someone did a crude clean up job in the bedroom. SOCOs think somebody was sick and then it was cleaned up with bleach."

"Do they think it was one of the victims?" Martina dumped the coffee in the bin before returning to her seat. "Considering the torture they endured, it would be understandable."

Munching on his sandwich, Ambrose shook his head. "They're not sure. They found prints but they match the family members."

"Why did nobody miss the family sooner?" Leaning back in her chair, Martina crossed her arms over her chest. "The daughter was still in school. Shouldn't they have noticed her absence?"

Finishing the last of his food, Ambrose dusted down the front of his shirt. "I'm going to follow up with the school but between that, the financials, going through the forensics, and the other interviews... Not to mention the other burglaries." The spark Martina had seen in his eye earlier was gone, and now he just looked exhausted.

"You need more help," she said.

Ambrose smiled. "I'll be fine. You just focus on your parents."

"No, Ambrose, I'll be back in tomorrow. I'd come in today, but I need to have a chat with Dad first." She swallowed around the lump in her throat.

"Something like this, we need more help. The guv can't expect us to—"

"You know as well as I do that he's not going to let us seek outside assistance."

Martina let her chin drop onto her chest. She did know. But that didn't mean she had to like or agree with it. "I should get back up there before Dad wakes up."

As they stood, Ambrose awkwardly patted her shoulder. "Don't feel like you need to rush back. I can manage my end of things. You just focus on your parents."

Martina tried to fix a smile on her face. Work didn't worry her but focusing on her parents did. Not that she could say that. Nobody would understand; they would assume she was being selfish, caring only about her own skin.

"Sure. But keep me in the loop and I'll see you tomorrow. And tell Julie I said thanks for the Rascals."

"I'll let her know." With a grin, Ambrose turned and ambled off down the hall, leaving Martina alone.

Her shoulders slumped as she thought about returning to her father's room. She contemplated buying another coffee, but knew she was only delaying the inevitable. They needed to make plans, and now was the best time to do it. Resigned to what lay ahead of her, she headed for the lifts.

CHAPTER TWENTY-FIVE

MISERY WEIGHED ON OLIVIA. She had screwed up, and now Maz was paying the price. It wasn't fair. She hadn't imagined the DCI would do something so drastic. Punishing her was one thing, but to scapegoat somebody else was too much.

That was her own guilt talking. She didn't honestly believe the DCI was scapegoating anyone. Maz was her superior; the buck did stop with him, but that didn't mean it still wasn't her fault. If she could just find some way to fix it, to redeem herself in the eyes of the DCI, then maybe, just maybe, he would lift Maz's suspension.

She stared at the stacks of files and reams of paper on her desk. She thought better on her feet and desk duty did nothing to get the sluggish gears in her brain moving. But what choice did she have? There had to be something here she could use. Something that would help them put the pieces of the puzzle together. They almost had it. There was just something they weren't seeing.

Grabbing the first sheaf of papers, Olivia started to comb through them. Surely something in here would give her the answers she needed.

And then it hit her. The night of the glitch. It had to have come from somewhere. Even now, when she closed her eyes, Olivia could see the look on Celeste's face when she'd suggested somebody was forcing her to cover up the crime. Everything she'd heard about Celeste suggested she wouldn't jeopardise her work. What had changed?

Olivia glanced towards Jodie's office. She would know how to find the answers. But would she help?

Olivia already knew the answer to that, so she stayed in her chair. Jodie had made her feelings crystal clear and there was no way she would help Olivia now. Sighing, she settled back and started to scan the paper in her hand.

Her stomach churned uncomfortably as she perused the pages of text messages Celeste and sent and received in the weeks leading up to her death. It was an invasion of her privacy. but what choice did she have?

A string of texts caught Olivia's eye. Celeste had saved the number in her phone under the name Foxy. Heat crawled up Olivia's cheeks as she read the pages of exchanges between both Celeste and Foxy. The relationship was an intense one and Olivia felt deeply uncomfortable reading about the intimate details of Celeste's sex life. And then the messages shifted. Foxy became more demanding, and the last text contained a hyperlink.

Turning to her computer, Olivia entered the link and waited for the page to load but the computer refused, stating the link had expired. Flopping back in her chair, she glared at the papers. There was just one person in the office who might be able to shed some light on the link.

Getting up from her desk, she crossed the room to Jodie's office. The constant hum of the computers unnerved her. There was something so terribly stifling and oppressive in the atmosphere. How could anyone work in here comfortably?

Making her way towards the corner of the room, Olivia spotted Jodie hunched over her keyboard. She was engrossed in the lines of code that flickered over her screen. If she had to spend all day staring at a screen like that, Olivia would lose her mind. Jodie, however, seemed at home here among the whirring of computer fans and the miles of wires.

"Jodie, can I get your input on something?"

"Can it wait?"

"Not really." Before Olivia could finish, Jodie had cleared the screen and spun around in her chair.

"What is it?" There was no denying the hostility in the other woman's voice.

"I was going through Celeste Jackson's texts recovered from her phone. Somebody sent her a link and I was hoping you could tell me what the link was for."

"Do you have a Facebook profile?" Olivia cocked her head to one side.

"Yeah. Why, what does that have to do with this?"

"If you can operate a Facebook page, then you know how to look up a link. You don't need me to do it for you." She turned back to her screen, the dismissal obvious.

"You really think I didn't already try—" Olivia cut herself off. "Look, I can tell you're pissed off at me but I need you to put that aside so we can work this case. Do you think you can do that?"

"I'm not going to take a fall for you the way Maz did. I won't shield your screw-ups."

"Fine," Olivia said. "And for the record, I didn't ask Maz to take the fall for me. The decision wasn't mine. I'd rather pay the price myself than have someone I care about pay it for me."

Jodie eyed her suspiciously. "Whatever." She thrust her hand out and waggled her fingers at Olivia. "Give me whatever you've got."

Handing over the pages, Olivia hovered at Jodie's shoulder as she scanned the texts.

"You don't have to watch me. Unlike you, I won't run off to the DCI with your lead."

Olivia swallowed a retort before it left her mouth and stepped back.

After a few minutes, Jodie sighed. "I can't help."

"But you haven't even tried the link."

"Let me guess; when you typed it in it said the link had expired."

Olivia nodded. "How did you know?"

"Because it's a dark web link. Probably a download of some dark web messenger service. Completely untraceable."

"Shit. So this is a dead end, too?"

Jodie shrugged and glanced down at the link again. "Whoever this Foxy is, they don't want a record of their conversations."

"Would Celeste have known this was dark web stuff?"

"Maybe, maybe not. It depends on how tech-savvy she was. But considering *you* didn't recognise it, probably not. Then again, she did wipe the system after DI Appleton's attack, so she was obviously pretty good around computers."

"Celeste said she had nothing to do with the glitch. She was adamant about it in fact."

"People lie."

Olivia sighed. Jodie was right; Celeste probably knew what she was doing. "And there's really nothing you can give me from this?"

Jodie chewed the tip of the pen in her hand. "As much as I hate to admit it, unless you can tell me the name of the…" She trailed off.

Olivia waited, impatience mounting as the woman next to her spun back to her screen and began to type furiously.

"What is it?" When Jodie didn't reply, Olivia moved closer and peered over the woman's shoulder. Not that it mattered. She couldn't make out what the code on the screen meant. It wasn't until a new window popped up with what looked to Olivia like CCTV footage. "Where is this?"

"Force Control," Jodie said. "I've been racking my brain trying to figure out how the glitch occurred, and this little link has given me an idea. Look at the date the message with the link was sent." Jodie jabbed her finger against the page.

"Three days before the attack on DI Appleton."

"Exactly. Her attacker was already planning to cover their tracks even before the attack happened."

"And what does that have to do with the CCTV outside Force Control?"

"Because I'm willing to bet Celeste didn't know the importance of that link. Something like this allows a third party to backdoor their way into a device. Now, if Celeste brought her phone to work with her, which we know she did, then Foxy could have used her phone to access the LAN and upload the virus that created the glitch."

"I still don't understand why—"

Jodie sighed. "Because in spite of Celeste's phone being the conduit, Foxy would still have needed to be nearby to breach the firewall and delete the files."

"You think Foxy went to Force Control?" Olivia's stomach twisted. If it were true, then this could be the missing link they'd been searching for."

"Bingo." Jodie spooled through the footage quickly. Seeing the images flash by so quickly hurt Olivia's eyes but she kept her attention riveted on the screen just the same.

"There!" Olivia pointed at the screen. Jodie paused and rewound a few frames before allowing it to play at normal speed. The seconds in the timer counted down and then Celeste appeared at the side of the building. Something moved in the lower right-hand corner of the image, but it was almost impossible to get a clear view.

"Is there not another angle we can view this from?"

"Hang on." Jodie hit the buttons on the keyboard and a second frame opened. This time, it was obvious that Celeste was talking to a person, but that person's face was obscured by a shadow cast by their black baseball cap.

"Shit." Olivia tried to contain her disappointment, but it was nearly impossible. It had been such a promising lead and now it was nothing more than another dead-end.

"Maybe, maybe not," Jodie whispered. She spooled the footage forwards, using the cameras in the car park to follow the stranger as they left Force Control. They turned out of the carpark and disappeared into a camera blind spot.

Olivia's frustration boiled over. "Who are these people? Why can't we catch a break?"

Jodie's gaze never left the screen. She clicked

through a few differed CCTV feeds before flopping back in her chair, a triumphant grin on her face. "Got you."

"What?" Olivia whirled back to the screen in time to see Jodie enlarge a screen capture of a number plate and a grainy image of a white car that looked suspiciously like a taxi. "I don't understand. How do you know this is the car we're after?"

"Because at the bottom of that road is a takeaway with a decent CCTV camera that takes in the street. During the timeframe we're searching for, nothing passes the takeaway. And yet a car passes through this junction a few minutes after our suspect disappears into the blackspot. It's not perfect but it's a start."

"It's more than a start, Jodie. It's bloody brilliant."

"We've got a name."

CHAPTER TWENTY-SIX

DENNIS SAT on the opposite side of the desk, his expression troubled. If Harriet didn't know any better, she might have said he looked concerned. But she knew better than to think something like this would cause him a moments concern. The moment Lila Uxley had backtracked on her story about Harriet's behaviour, Dr Baig had asked Harriet to return to work.

"I think you should think about this, Harriet." He spread his hands wide, a gesture meant to placate her.

"I have. My mind is made up." She leaned back in her chair. For the first time in her life, she genuinely felt at ease with her own decision.

Dennis shook his head. "No, I don't think so. I know that what happened before was unfortunate, but—"

"Unfortunate? Is that what we're calling it now?

The university allowed somebody to enrol under a false identity, for the sole purpose of damaging, no, *destroying* my reputation. And they very nearly succeeded."

"It was a mistake, Harriet. We all make them. You're not exactly above reproach yourself. If you had stayed on top of your student list as was agreed, this could have been prevented."

Harriet shook her head, letting her gaze fall to the empty spot on her wrist where her charm bracelet used to sit. Tilly had proudly informed her during their phone call a couple of days ago that she was taking very good care of it. And Harriet didn't doubt it. Still, it felt odd not to have something there to take its place.

"You know, I expected some push back from you, Dennis, but I didn't expect you to sink quite so low."

"You signed a contract with the university, Harriet, I'm within my right to enforce it."

"True, but once the term is over, I'm free to leave my contract."

He shook his head. "You're mistaken. That's not part of the—"

"Have you forgotten? My contract was adjusted when I started working with North Yorkshire Police. There is a clause which allows me to terminate my contract at the end of term so long as I give appropriate notice. I'm giving you plenty of notice. I'll see out the end of this term but then I'm done."

"And what do you plan to do then? I don't

imagine North Yorkshire Police have come back looking for your help. Even with the truth out in the open, bad press has a nasty habit of persisting."

"True, I don't see them offering me a position. But I have options." He did not need to know all her plans. It would just give him an excuse to try and talk her out of them.

"Well, I can't tell you how disappointed I am to hear this, Harriet. I was hoping we could put this all behind us."

"It was inevitable, Dennis. My attention has been splintered ever since I started working with the police. This will be better for all involved."

He sighed. "Are you sure there's nothing I can say to make you change your mind?"

"I'm very sure. It's time for a change."

Grumbling, Dennis leaned back in his chair and tented his fingers in front of him. "For what it's worth, I am sorry."

"That makes two of us, Dennis. But things change. People change. And this situation has taught me a valuable lesson."

"What might that be?"

"I shouldn't waste my life doing something I'm not entirely passionate about. I'm supposed to help people, I can see that now. But for so long, I've allowed fear to prevent me from doing the one thing I'm good at."

"What will you do if the police don't ask you to come back to work for them?"

Harriet shrugged. "I'm sure I'll think of something." She climbed to her feet.

"Have you spoken to her?"

Harriet knew who he was talking about without him ever having to say a name.

"No. I'm not sure I'd want to, either."

"That's understandable," Dennis said. "Still, it might help you to understand."

"What is there to understand? She tried to ruin my career."

"Yes, but wouldn't you like to know why? There must be a reason for it. Nobody wakes up one day and just decides to ruin a stranger's life. There's always a reason, a hidden meaning."

"I think I've got a pretty good idea what that hidden meaning might be," Harriet said. She didn't bother mentioning Jonathan's involvement with Lila Uxley. There was no proof that he was truly behind the young woman's behaviour, not that Harriet needed proof to guess the truth. On the other hand, it would be nice to know how Lila had wound up in Jonathan's web. All Harriet had to go on was the information Drew had given her.

No, this was something she was better off staying out of. Jonathan had already taken up far too much of her time. She wouldn't give him the satisfaction of taking anything more from her.

"I really should get going," she said. "I'll start back properly on Monday and finish out the term as promised."

Dennis stood and they shook hands over the top of the desk. "For what it's worth, Harriet, I am sorry."

"I know you are. But she fooled us all."

"No." He glanced down at his desk. "I should have listened to you. I should have trusted what you were telling me, but I didn't."

Harriet didn't say the words that hovered on the tip of her tongue. It felt too much like crowing over him and the situation. Instead, she gave his hand one last squeeze before releasing it. "It's all right, Dennis. This isn't the end of the world. It has given me the perspective I badly needed. In the end, it will all work out for the best. Just you wait and see."

"I want you to know that should you ever choose to come back to academia, there will always be a place for you here."

"I'll bear that in mind. Goodbye, Dennis."

She didn't wait for him to say anything else. Everything that needed to be said had been. Anything else was just prolonging an already difficult situation. She made it to the door before he spoke again.

"I really am sorry."

With one last look over her shoulder, Harriet smiled sadly at him. "I know."

CHAPTER TWENTY-SEVEN

"AND HOW SURE are you that this—"

"His name is Caz Popov, guv," Olivia said, reading from the sheet Jodie had printed out for them. "Got here four years ago and works as a taxi driver."

"Fine, this Caz Popov, how do we know this is the same person we're looking for in connection to DI Appleton's case?" Gregson leaned back in his chair.

Olivia had been nervous to approach him, especially after everything that had happened the last time she'd been in this office, but when she'd taken her news to DI Haskell, he had insisted she fill the DCI in.

"Ms Meakin did the hard work. She managed to trace him on CCTV on the night of the glitch at Force Control. She'd have to explain all the different ways she has connected him to the case, but it's all there in the file." Olivia fought the urge to chew her fingernails as Gregson flipped through the pages in front of him. If he decided they didn't have enough to bring Popov in, they would be back to square one again.

"What do you think, Haskell?" Gregson didn't bother to look up from the file.

DI Haskell stood to the side, propped against the wall. He'd already looked through the files but had yet to share his thoughts. Butterflies bumped and fluttered in Olivia's gut as she waited for him to speak.

"It's solid policing, sir," Drew said. "DC Crandell and Ms Meakin have knocked it out of the park."

"But is it enough? It's a lot of circumstantial evidence. We can't prove he was there at Force Control the night of the glitch. And we don't have any proof that he was involved with Celeste Jackson."

"But sir, the day Celeste fell, he was in the area," Olivia said.

"You said yourself he's a taxi driver. He could have been dropping a fare near Malham Cove."

"It's a bit of a stretch." Drew folded his arms over his chest. "But Ms Meakin seems pretty convinced that if we can bring her some of his electronics, she can work her magic and get us the hard proof we need."

The DCI tapped his fingers on the desk. Olivia

wasn't familiar enough with his body language to know if it was a favourable sign or not.

"Do we have an address?" Gregson finally broke the silence.

"He's got one in Pickering," Olivia piped up. She held her tongue on what she really wanted to say. She'd caused enough trouble. The last thing she wanted to do was push Gregson too far.

"I could do a drive by," Drew said. But Gregson was already shaking his head.

"Not a chance. If your mate Dr Sheridan is correct, he'll see you coming a mile off. No, we need someone they won't associate with this team. Give me a little time, I've got a plan."

"Care to share?" There was an edge to DI Haskell's voice that Olivia hadn't been expecting.

The look that Gregson gave DI Haskell was one of mild amusement. "I'll share in good time, DI Haskell. Dismissed."

CHAPTER TWENTY-EIGHT

JEREMY MOVED through the crowded pub, two full glasses clutched in his hands as he navigated the tiny gaps between the revellers.

From across the room, his gaze snagged on Kelly. He expected her to look happy. She'd been happy when he'd slipped away to get another round in. Instead, her expression was one of quiet discomfort.

Jeremy moved a little faster. Clearing the last group of people, he finally spotted the reason for her unhappiness.

Mark sat on the bench beside her. His body was pressed as close to hers as he could get without forcing her into his lap. The fingers of his right hand traced patterns over the bare skin of Kelly's arm. Her expression was pained, and she leaned back from him, struggling to put a little distance between them.

Mark's hand strayed to her stomach, where he

splayed his fingers against the small bump beneath her shirt.

Rage prickled beneath Jeremy's skin. Drink sloshed over the sides of the glasses as he picked up his pace. When he reached the table, he slammed the glasses down on the scarred wooden top.

Kelly jumped, raising her pale face to his. He could see the pleading in her gaze.

Mark kept his hand pressed to Kelly's stomach, almost possessively.

"I was just congratulating Kelly here on your forthcoming bundle of joy." He didn't bother to look in Jeremy's direction. "You know, if you and I had stayed together, Kels, this could have been my baby." He stroked her as though she belonged to him and Jeremy saw red.

"Get your fucking hands off her, Mark."

Mark finally glanced in his direction. "And there's the Jezza, I remember. Pity he was nowhere to be found the other night. We could have done with him that night."

Mark returned his attention to Kelly. "Did he tell you we went back into business together?"

Kelly's face went slack with fear. "No." She glanced at Jeremy, and he could see the question in her eyes.

Mark shot a curious look in Jeremy's direction. "You sure about that, Kels? You wouldn't be lying to me now, would you?"

Kelly glanced back at Mark, her gaze dropping to

the place where his hand was still stroking small circles over her belly.

"No, why would I?"

Mark released her and sat back suddenly. "No reason. He laughed mirthlessly. Kelly cringed against the fabric seat behind her.

Jeremy had promised he would never put her in such a position. When he'd left that life behind and he and Kelly had decided to really make a go of it, he'd sworn he was done with Mark's bullshit. He could see it all reflected in Kelly's face. The fear, the betrayal. The anger would come later.

"Our boy here was like a little lost lamb," Mark said. "Puked his guts up. I told him he was out of practice."

"That's enough, Mark." The words left Jeremy in a low growl.

"Now, now, Jezza. You shouldn't bite the hand that feeds you. The hand that clothes you and your pretty girlfriend."

"Jeremy..." Kelly looked at him, shock causing the remaining colour in her cheeks to leech away.

"Oh, he didn't tell you that he's back on the books?" The glee in Mark's voice almost saw Jeremy launch himself across the table. He imagined his fingers closing over Mark's shirt, dragging him out of his seat. He saw his fists smashing into the doughy flesh of Mark's face, crumpling it beneath his punches. He could hear the crunch of bone as he broke Mark's nose. He could also hear Kelly screaming, her voice high pitched and thin as blood coated his hands.

Jeremy blinked away the thoughts and discovered he was still standing on the opposite side of the table, his body unmoved. Mark studied him, the sly look in his eyes suggesting he knew exactly what Jeremy had been thinking.

"I'm not back on the books, Mark. We agreed, it was a one off. And I expect to be paid what I'm owed."

Mark laughed, the sound grating on Jeremy's nerves. "Oh, Jezza, I'd forgotten how much fun you could be. We both know you're not done. I've got another job coming up, and--"

"No." Jeremy pressed his hands to the table and leaned towards his former friend. "I'm done. It was a one-time only arrangement. We are done."

The joy faded from Mark's eyes, but his cold smile remained fixed in place. He shook his head and tutted. "You shouldn't be hasty about these things, Jezza."

"I told you then and I'm telling you now, we're done."

Mark stood abruptly, causing the drinks Jeremy had fetched from the bar to topple over, spilling their contents onto the ground.

"You'll be finished when I say you're finished." Mark pushed his face towards Jeremy. "I fucking own you."

From the corner of his eye, Jeremy spotted Kelly.

He saw fear in her face, the same fear he'd swore never to expose her to. He'd made a huge mistake. He knew that now. Getting involved with Mark again had been an error, but he could fix it. He couldn't take back what he'd done, but moving forward... he had a choice. And he knew what kind of future he wanted to have. Knew with a bone aching certainty that what he had with Kelly, the life they shared together, with the baby on the way, was it. There was absolutely nothing Mark could do to take that away from him.

If Kelly forgave him now for his mistake, he would spend the rest of his life making it up to her.

"Fuck off, Mark. You don't scare me. I was afraid, once. I'm not afraid of you anymore."

"One little phone call from me, Jezza and all of this--"

Before he could finish, Jeremy cut Mark off with a bark of laughter. "You can't touch me, Mark."

Jeremy straightened, using the not inconsiderable height difference between them to glare down at his former friend. "You see, I realised something, Mark. If you call the police and dob me in, I won't stay quiet."

Mark glared at him, rage and hatred mingling to form an emotion Jeremy had never seen before. Not that he cared; Mark needed to be brought down a peg or two and this was the way to do it.

The patrons gathered nearby had all gone silent and Jeremy knew they were listening to every word he said. He could tell from the way Mark's shoulders stiffened that he too knew the conversation was no longer private.

"One word from me, Mark, and everything you've built, everything you value, is gone."

"You wouldn't dare..."

"You come here, threatening me and mine, Mark." Jeremy drew in a breath. "I'll fucking do it. You turn me in, and I'll tell them everything I know. If I go down, you're coming with me. I mean it."

Mark stared at him for what felt like a lifetime but was probably more likely a heartbeat or two. Then he jerked back, and Jeremy tried not to show the surprise on his face.

The smile returned to Mark's mouth, and he grinned at both Jeremy and Kelly. "I had to be sure."

"What?" Jeremy stared at the other man, dumbfounded. "Sure of what?"

"That you meant it. It was so easy to pull you back in. One rough patch and a little bit of money trouble and you came running back to me like a lapdog." Mark shook his head and glanced at Kelly.

"I still care about you, Kels. I know you don't feel that way about me anymore." His eyes were filled with kindness. "But I needed to know that this ol' prick was worthy of you." He jerked a thumb in Jeremy's direction. "I didn't mean to freak you out." He sounded convincing enough. his words dripping with contrition.

He turned back to Jeremy and held his hand out. "No hard feelings, man, yeah?"

Shock rooted Jeremy to the spot. Was this real? Had it all been an act? It had felt real enough and yet... Jeremy glanced down at Kelly. Her expression had softened a little as she looked from Mark to Jeremy.

Seeing no other way, Jeremy took Mark's hand, and they shook over the table. Mark glanced down at the spilled drinks. "Shit, I spilled your pint. Let me make it up to you, Jezza. To show you there's no hard feelings."

Before Jeremy could say anything, Mark was rounding the table and heading for the bar.

Jeremy slid in next to Kelly and took her cold hand in his. "Are you all right?"

"Why didn't you tell me, Jeremy?"

"I didn't want you to worry." He sighed and let his hand fall from hers. "And we're desperate. With the baby coming, I needed to do something to give us some breathing space. And this was the only thing I could think of."

She lowered her voice. "But why would you go to him? We could have gone to my dad, or--"

Jeremy shook his head, cutting her off. "No. We could not go to your dad. He already thinks I'm a scumbag, Kelly. I don't need him knowing I'm struggling to look after you and our baby. He'll never forgive me."

"But Mark?"

Jeremy's mouth tightened into a grim line as he spotted Mark weaving his way back to the table. "There was no choice. I did what needed to be done. And when he pays up, we'll be sorted for the next few months. Maybe even more if I play my cards right and get that new job I want."

Mark slammed the glasses down on the table. "One drink with the lovebirds and then I'll leave you to your celebrations." He pushed the glasses across the table and grabbed his own glass, raising it in a toast. "To your future."

Jeremy shot Kelly a sideways look. She picked up her glass and with a steady hand, the person she had once been peeking out, and clinked her glass to Mark's. That just left Jeremy.

His hand closed around the frothy lager glass.

"To your future," Mark repeated as he thrust his glass roughly against Jeremy's. Jeremy mumbled a response, unease curling in the pit of his stomach as Mark kept his gaze pinned on him while he took a deep gulp from the pint.

"To the future," Jeremy said, half beneath his breath.

CHAPTER TWENTY-NINE

THE MONK BECKONED Drew into his office. "Shut the door after you."

Drew's skin practically hummed with energy. Ever since he'd heard the name Caz Popov all he'd wanted to do was get out there and track the bastard down. Not that the Monk was going to let him do it. Drew had a sneaking suspicion that he would be lucky if Gregson let him anywhere near the case because of his connection to DI Appleton. The fact that he had already kept him out of the loop on so much pertinent information already grated on Drew's nerves.

"I've sent a couple of uniforms around to check out Popov's house. But the word seems to be that he hasn't been seen at that address in quite some time."

Drew raised an eyebrow. "And where is that information coming from? Can we trust it?"

"Who knows what we can trust with this bloke?

Ms Meakin said he's a bit of a grey man. No record, and from what she can find, not much of a history either."

"Not exactly what I'd expect to see from somebody allegedly connected to the Marcovici family," Drew said.

"Then again, if they wanted someone to get close to a police officer, they needed someone who was basically a blank slate." Gregson sank back into his chair. "How is DI Appleton?"

"If I had to guess, not doing so great."

"Guess? I thought she was staying with you?"

Drew started to pace in the small space in front of Gregson's desk. "She wanted to go home. Said she needed some time to get things straight in her own head."

"But you've been checking in on her, right?" When Drew shook his head, one of Gregson's bushy eyebrows crawled up his forehead.

Good God, man, what is wrong with you? She was nearly killed. The last thing she needs is to be left alone."

"Melissa isn't like that, sir. If she says she needs space, then she does."

Gregson narrowed his gaze. "What happened between you two?"

The question took Drew by surprise. Despite his rough and gruff exterior, the DCI was far more perceptive than he liked to pretend.

"She broke it off," Drew said finally. It was

strange to say it out loud, but now that he had, it felt like a weight had been lifted from his shoulders.

"Took long enough," the monk said. "I figured she'd have kicked you to the kerb long ago considering all your hankering after Dr Quinn."

"I don't hanker—" Before Drew could finish speaking, the door to the office flew open and Olivia practically fell inside. She was breathing hard, as if she had run all the way there.

"Sir... Guv, you need to..." She gulped down a breath... "come downstairs. Popov--"

Drew didn't wait for her to finish the sentence before he rushed out. He was only vaguely aware that the detective constable and Gregson were following close behind.

"Haskell, wait!" The Monk's sharp tone brought Drew's headlong race downstairs to a halt. "Something's not right here."

"Popov is in custody, correct?"

"He's here," Olivia said. "He's not yet in custody."

"I don't understand." Drew looked from her to Gregson. "They picked him up and brought him in for questioning. What am I missing?"

"Popov wasn't picked up by the uniforms," Gregson said. "DC Crandell says Popov walked in of his own volition, with his solicitor, and turned himself in."

"That can't be right. Why would he do that? Somebody's got their wires crossed."

Olivia's hand automatically went to the collar of her shirt before dropping down to smooth down the front of the buttons. Drew had spotted her doing that action a number of times and it always happened when she appeared nervous.

"His solicitor is demanding they speak with the officer in charge of the case," Olivia said.

"Well, let's give them what they want," Drew said, taking another step downstairs.

"Drew, something about this is off," she said.

Drew paused before nodding. "No argument here. But what choice do we have? We were planning to bring him in anyway, and now that he's here, we might as well take full advantage."

"Fine, but I don't want you in there." Gregson's words sparked anger in the recesses of Drew's mind.

He'd known for a while that the Monk had some kind of problem with him. He hadn't broached the topic because he'd hoped it would blow over. But this was not something he could ignore any longer.

"What do you mean, I'm not going in there?" He tried to keep his tone measured.

"We can't give him what he wants. I want DC Green and DC Jacobson to do the interview."

Drew tried to swallow around the anger that blocked the back of his throat. "I need to be in there."

Gregson shook his head. "No, you don't. This is not about you trying to atone for your sins, Haskell. This is too important."

"Exactly! Which is why you need to—"

"You need to sit this one out, Drew. You're too close to the fire and you don't see it. Now I want you and DC Crandell to prep Tim and Karen before they go into the interview."

"Sir, think about this."

"I have. This is for the best." Gregson returned to the main office, leaving Drew and Olivia on the stairs.

Anger radiated throughout Drew's body. He contemplated ignoring the DCI's command. He'd get in trouble but he'd— he cut the thought off. Was the Monk right? Was he too close to the case to think clearly? He didn't have to search too far for the answer to that question.

"Fuck!" He gently banged his forehead against the wall.

"Sir, are you all right?" Olivia hovered on the top step, concern masking her face.

"As much as I'd like to say I am, I am not."

"If it's any consolation, sir, I don't think the DCI is making the right choice."

Sighing, Drew closed his eyes. "I wish I could agree."

"You think he's right?" she squeaked. A comical combination of shock and surprise widening her eyes.

"The bastard is right. All I want to do is barge into the interview room and throttle the little shit. And that's before I know for certain if he had anything to do with Melissa— DI Appleton's-- attack. That's no way to conduct an interview. We need someone who is removed from emotion, and Gregson knows it."

"I suppose so." Olivia didn't seem overly convinced.

"Come on let's prep the others. We need everyone firing on all cylinders if we're going to get somewhere on this."

With a jerk of her chin, Olivia let him pass before she followed him back to the office.

CHAPTER THIRTY

MELISSA WINCED and slipped in through the side door of the station. It had taken every ounce of her strength to get there and now that she had made it, her body felt entirely wiped. The moment her eyes fell on Drew, her resolve started to waver. He'd promised to contact her if something happened, yet it had been Jodie who had called to tell her they had someone in custody.

Drew's eyes widened in surprise as he watched her climb the stairs painstakingly slowly. "Mel, what are you doing here?"

"I'm here to see the piece of shit responsible for Chelsea's murder."

"We don't know that for sure."

"But you've got a good idea, yeah?" Melissa held her body ramrod straight, taking slow deep breaths in an attempt to slow her racing heart.

"He needs to be interviewed."

"Perfect, let me sit in."

Drew's eyebrows disappeared up his forehead. "You can't be serious."

"As a heart attack. Let me sit in. I'll know if it's him or not, and I can save us all a lot of wasted time."

"Even if I wanted to, I couldn't let you—"

"Couldn't, or wouldn't?" Melissa didn't bother to keep the challenge from her voice. The sting of his betrayal was fresh in her mind. When she'd asked him to keep her in the loop, after everything they'd gone through, she had mistakenly believed him when he'd said he would. But as usual, Drew wasn't thinking of her.

"Both actually."

"You're unbelievable, do you know that? I asked you to do one thing, Drew. One thing. And you couldn't even do that."

"What are you talking about?"

"I asked you to tell me if you had something. I asked to be brought in so I could see this through to the end. And you promised. You promised, Drew." Her voice cracked with emotion. She was exhausted, and the adrenaline she had relied on to get her this far was fading fast. Now that she was here, fear was beginning to worm its way under her skin. What if the man responsible for all of this really was here, just a few floors below her?

"Mel, you need to sit down. You don't look good." Drew tried to take her by the elbow, but she shrugged him off.

"I don't want your pity."

"DI Appleton, what are you doing here?" DCI Gregson's voice boomed through the hall.

Melissa shuffled around to face him. "I heard you had someone in custody…"

"And you thought what, that you'd come down here and make sure we're doing our jobs correctly?"

"I…" All the arguments she'd concocted on the drive over fled, leaving her mind blank.

"You need to go home, DI Appleton. You're still in recovery. You don't belong here."

His words hit her like a stinging slap to the face. "I need to know."

"And you will. As soon as we have something to share."

Melissa closed her eyes and let her body lean against the wall, grateful for its solid strength beneath her. "You don't understand. I need to know…"

Gregson said nothing, and for a moment, Melissa assumed he had walked away. When she chanced cracking an eyelid open, it was to find him studying her. "My office. Now."

"Let me help," Drew said, offering his arm.

"No. She made it here under her own power. She can walk the last few yards to my office without you propping her up." Gregson's tone brooked no argument, but Melissa could tell from the mutinous expression on Drew's face that he planned to do just that.

With a shake of her head, Melissa halted Drew

in his tracks. Gregson was right. She needed to prove she was capable. She might be down, but she was not out. And everyone needed to know that.

Gregson moved swiftly ahead of her, leading the way to the office. Every step she took sent fiery pain shooting through her body. By the time she made it, she was soaked in a film of cold sweat.

Gregson was already sitting in his chair behind the desk. "Sit."

Melissa tried to answer but her tongue refused to cooperate, so she complied silently. Easing her body into the chair caused stars to explode behind her eyelids. Finally, she was able to settle.

"I know you're going to tell me to go home," she croaked out.

"If you knew that, why come here at all?"

"Because I need to know if it's him. And if it is, I need to look him in the eye and tell him what a fucking coward he is for killing a child."

Gregson sighed and tented his fingers in front of him. "And this would do what exactly?"

"It'd make me feel better." A tremble had started in Melissa's hands. She locked her fingers together in her lap rather than betray her weakness. But that didn't stop the tremor from spreading up her hands and into her arms. The sensation moved quickly, spreading to her chest and stomach. The thought of looking that monster in the eye and saying anything at all to him terrified her. And Melissa hated herself for that. She was better than this, stronger than this.

"No, it won't."

"With all due respect, sir, you don't know anything about the situation."

"I know more than you think." When she didn't reply, he sighed. "Have you ever wondered why they call me the Monk?"

Melissa wasn't expecting the conversation to take such an odd turn, but she didn't have the energy to pretend she didn't know about his nickname. "No one was ever able to tell me."

Gregson's shark-like smile unnerved her.

"I worked a series of murders back in the late seventies when I was a young DC. It started with the body of a young man being found dumped outside Birmingham. He'd gone missing on a night out with a group of lads after work. A few months later a second body turned up. Six months after, there was a third. Nobody wanted to put the pieces together. Everybody said the cases were unconnected. Everybody except me."

Gregson got up from his seat and moved over to the shelves behind his desk. There, he opened a filing cabinet and withdrew a file.

"I pursued that case with a singular determination. I could see the patterns, I knew what was happening. At least two of the victims were confirmed homosexuals, and the injuries were consistent with crimes of a sexual nature. But the powers-that-be wanted nothing to do with it. The last thing they wanted was to admit to the public that we had somebody out there targeting young, gay men."

He dropped the file on the desk and slid it towards Melissa.

"Sir, I'm not sure what this has to do with me, or—"

"My pursuit of the one responsible isolated me from my colleagues. I refused to go out after work, preferring instead to stay late and work on my theory. I withdrew from my team, cutting myself off entirely. They started to call me the Monk behind my back, and then eventually to my face. Not that I cared. By hook or by crook I was going to catch the bastard."

As he was speaking, Melissa picked up the file and flipped through it. The crime scene photos made her cringe but something else caught her eye. A list of the names of the victims. The first name stood out.

"Gregson..."

DCI Gregson nodded. "Anthony Gregson was my younger brother. He was twenty-three when he was murdered. He was the first. And I was obsessed with finding the person responsible."

Gregson sat back down in his chair. "And then I got a lead."

"Let me guess, you went after this lead alone?" Melissa's gaze drifted over the notes.

"No. I asked for help," Gregson said surprising her. "But by then, my solitary and isolating behaviour had put me outside the team. They weren't interested. So, I went alone and got my head bashed in for my troubles. I'll never forget the look on my mother's face when I came round. She thought she would have to bury another son." Gregson fell silent.

"Sir, I'm sorry they let you down so badly. And I'm sorry about your brother but I really don't see—"

"I know you don't" Gregson said. "But the fact of the matter is this, DI Appleton: from the moment you arrived you have tried to keep yourself apart from this team. You have held the others at arm's length, including me. Every attempt to welcome you in has been rejected."

"So, you're telling me this team is isolating me like your team did to you?" Melissa set the file back down on the desk.

"Quite the opposite. From that experience I swore I would never again allow an officer to be isolated. I made a promise that when I was in a position of power, I would make damn sure my officers were a tight-knit-group. That they would always have each other's backs."

Melissa stared down at the bruises on the backs of her hands. "And then I turned up and ran around like a maverick, getting a child killed and myself injured."

"You made a mistake, it's true," Gregson said. "But I screwed up too."

Melissa's gaze whipped up to meet his. "How?"

"I should have done more to earn your trust. I should have tried harder, and if I had, then you would have understood why I made the decisions that I did."

"It's not your fault…"

"It's more my burden than it is yours, DI Appleton. I failed you. I failed you all. I know you think you need to go in there and face down the man responsible but I'm asking you to trust me to get this done. Let us support you now, the way we should have from the beginning…"

"Sir, I…"

"I'm asking you to trust me, Melissa. Let the team take some of the weight for a change."

"Did you catch the person responsible for the murder of your brother?"

For the first time, Melissa saw an emotion she couldn't read flit across Gregson's face. "No. It's still unsolved. I revisit the case every so often hoping against hope that something new will have shaken loose, but so far there's nothing."

"I'm sorry."

"It's not your fault."

She nodded. "Fine. I'll take a step back. But I want to know what he has to say, if that's all right with you."

Gregson thought about it for a moment and then nodded. "I can work with that."

CHAPTER THIRTY-ONE

DREW PACED BACK and forth in the small kitchen. Gregson had set Melissa up in her office along with PC Indira Shah and Olivia. Drew's mind kept replaying the way she had looked at him, as though he had betrayed her. He was just doing his job, something she should have understood.

DC Tim Green burst in through the office doors, his whoop of joy echoing through the space. DC Karen Jacobson followed at a much slower pace, her gaze still laser focused on the material in her arms.

"We got him," Tim said. "We nailed the prick!"

Drew emerged from the kitchen to see a small group of people gathering around the DCs. The door to Gregson's office opened at the same moment as Melissa's. Drew caught a glimpse of her chalk white face as she stood and hobbled to the door with help from PC Shah.

"What happened?" Gregson's voice which would

have normally silenced Tim could do nothing to quell the DC's excitement this time.

"He confessed. His solicitor had a whole statement prepared. We barely had to open our mouths in there."

Confusion wrapped itself around Drew. "What do you mean he confessed? Confessed to what?"

"Everything," Karen said, finally breaking her silence. She looked as confused as Drew felt. She self-consciously fidgeted with a thin necklace around her neck before she caught herself. Drew watched as she straightened her spine, and her expression becoming an unreadable mask. "He said he was the one responsible for the murders of Angelica Dawson, Chelsea Fraser, Celeste Jackson, and the attempted murder of DI Appleton. He knew the details of each case, things we never made public."

Drew shot a look at Gregson, but the other man was focused solely on Melissa.

"Did he give a motive?" There was something Drew was missing; he could feel it in the pit of his stomach.

"Said Angelica was making progress with Chelsea, and she needed to go. Then DI Appleton started poking her nose in, asking questions about his operations. Chelsea was already wobbling so he decided to send a message..." Karen trailed off and glanced down at her folders. "Celeste was an accident. They had been seeing each other for a few months,. He claims she knew everything, and when she found out about what he had done to DI Appleton, she panicked and wiped the system. When we started looking into it, he said she became erratic and threatened to go to the police. They agreed to meet at Malham Cove. Apparently, it's where they first met. They got into a fight , she was too close to the edge, and she went over."

"Are we buying this?" Drew asked, incredulity straining his voice.

"It's all a little convenient," Gregson said. "It's easy to pin it on Celeste because she's dead and can't defend herself."

Drew nodded. "Sir..."

"If you're about to ask if you can go in there and talk to him—" Gregson glanced over at Melissa who was clinging to the door frame of her office. Drew watched as she gave an almost imperceptible nod. With a sigh, Gregson looked at Drew. "Do it."

What had Gregson and Melissa discussed for him to have changed his mind so completely? Drew did not need to be asked twice.

Beckoning to Karen, he made for the stairs.

CHAPTER THIRTY-TWO

LATER THAT NIGHT, Jeremy stumbled back to the car with Kelly. His arm was tight around her shoulders. She was the only thing keeping him on his feet as they crossed the street.

"I love you. Do you know that?" His words were slurred but his mind had never felt so clear.

"Jeremy, I need you to concentrate." Kelly was pissed. Not drunk, just angry. He'd promised he wouldn't get rip-roaring drunk but after the situation with Mark, Jeremy had felt the tightness in his chest slowly unwind with each drink. And then there was the fact that the alcohol numbed the emotions he felt over everything he'd seen in that house.

They reached the car, and Kelly leaned him against the door as she fumbled to get the key.

When he closed his eyes now, he couldn't see any of the horrors he'd witnessed. But somewhere deep inside, he knew they were still there, waiting for him.

His eyelids slid open, and he stared down at the woman beside him. The mother of his unborn child. He loved her. God, he loved her. The emotion swelled inside him, growing larger until he was convinced it would burst out of his chest like the scene in Alien.

"What are you laughing about?" Kelly asked, finally looking up at him.

"I love you."

"You're drunk," she grumbled. returning her attention to the car.

"Doesn't mean what I'm saying isn't true."

"Jeremy, come on. We need to get home."

He pulled away from her and threw his arms wide. "I love you!" His voice bellowed, echoing up and down the dark street.

"Jeremy, you're going to wake everyone up," Kelly hissed. She grabbed his arm and tried to pull him back towards the car.

"I don't care who hears. I love you, Kelly. Always have, always will."

He saw the anger in her face soften at his words.

"There she is," he said, his voice turning hoarse. "There's the woman I love." He brushed his thumb against her cheek as he unsteadily closed the distance between them. Gently tilting her chin up, he lowered his lips to hers.

The kiss was tentative at first. Her mouth held the lingering taste of Coke, the only thing she could tolerate since she'd found out she was pregnant. He swept his tongue over her lower lip, deepening their embrace as he pushed her back against the car. His hands slid over her.

Kelly broke the kiss, her breathing erratic as she pressed her forehead against his chest. "We need to go home, Jeremy."

"I love you..." He tried to kiss her again, but she held him at bay with one hand planted firmly against his body.

"Home."

There would be no getting around her. She was sober and in full possession of her faculties, unlike him.

"Take me home, then," he said, a grin curving over his mouth. "And when we get in," he leaned down and whispered into her ear a promise of what was to come between them.

As he pulled back, he smiled at the rosy glow that flooded her cheeks.

"We'll see," was all she said as she pulled the car door open and ushered him inside.

CHAPTER THIRTY-THREE

CAZ POPOV WAS a tall thin man with fair hair and cold grey eyes. He lounged in the chair on the opposite side of the table, his body contorted in angles that Drew was certain could not be comfortable.

When they'd walked into the room, Caz had taken one look at Karen and rolled his eyes before tucking his chin against his chest and closing his eyes. Drew had hung back in the doorway, watching him feign sleep.

Closing the door gently, Drew took his seat, folding his large frame into the small chair. Why they couldn't have made the chairs in the interview rooms a little more comfortable had never made sense to him.

DC Jacobson shuffled her papers and cleared her throat before setting up the recording, giving her name and rank. Caz remained unmoved until she mentioned Drew's name. The moment she uttered the words DI Haskell, a frisson of excitement jolted through Caz's body.

He opened his eyes and stared across at Drew, a slow smile spreading across his wide mouth. Drew had watched a movie called *IT* a few months prior, and Popov reminded him of the clown, minus the make-up.

Straightening up, Caz placed his elbows on the table and propped his face up with his hands. "DI Haskell, I was hoping to see you."

"We've got a few questions to follow up from your earlier statement," Drew said. "Some things don't add up."

"My client has said all he is going to say." The solicitor, a small mouse-like man, fiddled nervously with his pen.

"I'd hoped Melissa might come with you." Popov flashed a chipped, toothy grin.

"You say Celeste Jackson's death was an accident, yet you admit to getting into an argument with her. Was this a physical altercation?"

Popov shook his head. "She was shouting and flapping her arms around like a demented harpy. I tried to warn her about the edge, but you know how women are, DI Haskell, they don't listen. And then she slipped and was gone before I could do anything."

"But why ask to meet up there at all? Why not

meet at your house, or her house? Why pick a place so remote?"

Popov's grin grew broader. "As I said in my earlier statement, it was where we met for the first time. I am a little bit of a romantic. I thought it might appeal to Celeste's softer side. It did not."

"We've got a witness who says Celeste had bruising on her arms."

"She was a clumsy woman."

"Fingertip bruising. The kind caused by someone grabbing Celeste hard enough to leave marks. And this witness says that Celeste was afraid."

"This witness wouldn't happen to be DC Crandell, would it?" Caz brushed invisible crumbs from the front of his cream jumper. "Celeste mentioned something about a busybody poking her nose in where it didn't belong."

Drew's discomfort grew. Popov knew so much about the team. Tony Sheridan's warning swirled in his mind, making it difficult to concentrate. There was something happening here that they just weren't seeing clearly.

"So, you didn't cause the bruising?" Karen asked.

Popov shrugged. "Who can say for sure. Celeste liked it rough in the bedroom. She was a kinky little thing, liked to feel me deep inside her. She liked it when I held her down and gave it to her hard. Maybe you like it that way too. You police officers are always wound so tightly. You need somebody willing to put you in your place. Someone to take control."

Drew watched Karen from the corner of his eye, but was pleased to see she was unmoved by Popov's deliberate attempt to make her uncomfortable.

"You liked to control Celeste?" Karen's voice was entirely neutral. "You liked hurting her?"

Popov pulled down the neck of his jumper, revealing bruising and scratch marks across the front of his chest. "Celeste gave as good as she got, and it was, as you ladies always insist, consensual."

"What about Chelsea? Did you control her too?"

Popov's grin returned. "Chelsea was a child. I am not a freak. She worked for me, nothing more."

"Doing what?" Drew leaned forward.

"I already said in my statement. Chelsea helped me deliver drugs. When she started to cause problems, I dealt with her and Melissa. Two birds with one stone."

"Why turn yourself in, Caz? Surely someone as smart as you wouldn't want to get caught."

Popov leaned back and crossed his ankle over his knee. "Maybe I felt bad about Celeste."

"But not Chelsea, or DI Appleton?" Drew kept his attention fixed on the man in front of him. All he wanted to do in that moment was reach across the table and throttle the life out of him.

"Chelsea was business, DI Haskell. It wasn't *personal*." There was something in the way he said the word personal that piqued Drew's interest.

"But DI Appleton *was* personal, is that what you're saying?"

"Dimitri and Oscar Kolokoff, DI Haskell. You remember them, correct?"

The sinking feeling in Drew's stomach grew. "They're dead."

Popov sprang forward in his chair, his upper body leaning over the table. "And all those responsible will pay, DI Haskell. Melissa was merely a taste of what is to come."

He dropped back into his seat and glanced at his nervous solicitor. "We are done. I have said all I would like to."

"Who is running the operation, Caz?" Drew had waited for the other shoe to drop and now that it had, he felt even more in the dark.

Caz grinned at him. "No comment."

THEY ASKED several more questions but Popov merely replied no comment to them all. In the end, Drew decided to end the interview. They had got as much from him as he'd been willing to share.

DC Karen Jacobson switched off the recording and gathered her items, but Drew remained seated.

From the other side of the table, Popov continued to grin at him like the cat who had got the cream.

"You know," Drew said, "you said it was just business where Chelsea Fraser was concerned. That you were not a...how did you phrase it?... a freak."

Popov's smile remained but had dimmed around the edges.

"During Chelsea's autopsy," Drew said, "they discovered she had been the victim of a very serious sexual assault prior to her murder. We recovered semen samples, and other bodily fluids. Not only that but they found evidence that she had been sexually assaulted several times in the past. Her little body carried the marks of countless injuries, some healed, some in the process of healing." Drew paused and blew out a breath. Popov's smile had disappeared entirely as he watched Drew through narrowed eyes.

"They found DNA under her fingernails too, proof that she fought back when she was held down."

"My client has already confessed to murdering Miss Fraser. This is uncalled for."

Ignoring the solicitor, Drew continued, "Do you know what they do in prison to men who rape little girls, Mr Popov?"

The colour drained from Popov's face until he was practically translucent.

Drew leaned closer and lowered his voice to a whisper. "The good news is it won't take long for you to find out." Without waiting for Popov to reply, Drew straightened up and strode out of the interview room.

CHAPTER THIRTY-FOUR

SOMETHING TUGGED at Jeremy's mind, pulling him from sleep. He opened his eyes and stared up at the white ceiling. An orange shaft of light cut across the expanse of space overhead. He followed the line, his head turning slowly over the pillow until he spotted the gap in the curtains that allowed the glow from the streetlamp to creep in.

"Jeremy..." He started, his body slowly catching up to his mind as he turned to face Kelly. She was sitting up in the bed, covers pulled up to her chest. Her hand lay on his arm, and she shook him. "Jeremy."

"What is it?" He was groggy. His throat was dry, his tongue rasping against the roof of his mouth like sandpaper. Even as he lay back against the pillows, the room started to spin slowly.

"I thought I heard something," she whispered.

She turned to glance down at him, her eyes still glazed with the remnants of sleep.

"It was nothing," he said, tugging her down towards him. "Probably just a dream." Alcohol numbed his senses. He was going to have one hell of a hangover in the morning.

She shook her head. "No, I really heard something."

He was more alert now, his body tensing in response to the fear he detected in her voice.

Jeremy stilled, straining to hear whatever had disturbed Kelly so much. Nothing stirred in their house, at least nothing he could detect.

"There's nothing, it was probably just something out on the street."

"Jeremy, I know what I heard. I'm not making it up."

Sighing, he brushed his hand down over his face and sat up in the bed, letting his feet swing down to the floor.

"What are you doing?" Kelly hissed in the darkness as he grabbed his jeans from where he'd discarded them earlier.

"Going to make sure everything is secure," he said, shooting her a smile in the dark. Her face was half illuminated in the light spearing through the curtains. She shook her head, her hair sliding over her shoulders.

"No, don't. Let's just call the police."

Jeremy scoffed and tried to smother the sound under his breath as Kelly gave him a dirty look.

"Jeremy, I know what I heard."

"We can't call the police just because you had a nightmare."

"It wasn't a nightmare. I think I heard..." she paused, her stillness unnerving him. She glanced at him. "Did you hear that?"

"Now you're just scaring yourself," Jeremy said, getting to his feet. "I'll go and check it out. You stay here." He stumbled, catching himself on the edge of the bed before he toppled to the floor.

"I'll come with you."

"No." Jeremy was firm. Even though he was sure it was nothing, he wasn't willing to risk her involvement. "You stay here. If you hear anything weird, call the police."

"You're scaring me."

He smiled at her, softening his words. "Babe, it's not going to come to that. Everything will be fine, just you wait and see." He crossed to the bottom of the bed and headed for the door. "Stay in here until I come back."

"Jeremy!" Her voice was little more than a whisper, but he heard her anyway and stopped.

"Yeah?"

"I think I heard glass breaking."

"It was probably somebody heading home after a few too many."

She started to shake her head, but he pulled open the door and slipped out into the hall. "Stay here."

Padding over the carpet, he made it to the top of the stairs without incident. The spinning had slowly eased but his brain was still fogged with drink. He held onto the banister because if he fell down the stairs now, Kelly would have his arse in a sling for being so careless. The house was wreathed in silence. He carried his phone in his hands, the flashlight app shining a small pool of light directly in front of him.

Pausing at the top of the steps, he listened, quieting his breathing so he could detect even the faintest sound. Nothing.

Sighing with relief, he started down the stairs. As he reached the third step from the bottom, it creaked beneath his weight. The bedroom door swung open, the sound of it swishing over the carpet a dead giveaway that Kelly hadn't stayed put.

He waited and a second later she appeared on the top landing. Her face, pale as moonlight, was filled with concern.

"Go back," he urged. "Everything is fine."

"I heard something else."

"It was me on the stairs," Jeremy said. He shifted in place allowing the creak of the floorboards beneath him to groan in response.

"Oh." Kelly's expression shifted, her fear fading a little.

"Go back to bed," he said again. "I'm going to get a

glass of water and do a quick sweep of the house before I come up."

Her hands flexed as she stood on the top step, uncertainty etched into the curve of her body. "You sure you don't want me to come with you?"

"Go back to bed and rest, Kels. I'll be right up." He smiled at her, hoping it would be enough to ease some of the tension she obviously still felt.

Finally, she listened to him. "Ok, but if you're not back in five minutes I'm calling the police."

Grinning, Jeremy shook his head. He waited until she had disappeared and the bedroom door had clicked shut before he carrying on down the stairs.

Padding to the front door, he was pleased to find it was still secure. He moved soundlessly through the living room, checking the windows to ensure they too remained locked.

When he was satisfied, he stopped at the bottom of the stairs and called up to reassure Kelly. Her response was muffled but he had a feeling she would be asleep before he made it back up to the bedroom.

With his throat still parched and burning, Jeremy headed for the kitchen. Flicking a switch, he watched as the small mood lights beneath the cupboards flickered into life. He could still remember the day Kelly had picked them out. She'd been so thrilled. Both of their families had struggled with poverty while they were growing up, his more than Kelly's. So, something as simple as mood lighting felt like an extravagance.

Fetching a glass from the cupboard, he crossed to the sink. Filling it, he returned to the table and sat. The cold crept in around his legs, like a cat curling around his ankles as it sought to steal his warmth.

A nearby car alarm blared, the sharp sound momentarily ripping through the silence so loudly it made Jeremy wince.

Too loud.

A cold breeze caused goosebumps to pebble his flesh. He glanced in the direction of the small utility room nestled off the kitchen.

Standing, he tried to calm the frantic beat of his heart as he crept to the half-closed door.

When he stepped into the utility room, something crunched underfoot. It took his brain a second to register the pain that bloomed in his toes.

Yelping, he took a step back as his eyes settled on the glass that littered the floor of the utility room. His gaze swept up to the door, glittering pieces of shattered glass still clung to the frame.

A hand clamped over Jeremy's mouth before the sound forming in the back of his throat could escape. Someone jerked him backwards, and a well-placed foot behind his legs sent him sprawling into the main area of the kitchen.

Jeremy hit the ground with a dull thud, the sound hardly registering in his mind as he struggled to get back up.

Before his thoughts could fully form, something fell on him. It was a person, their dark shape a blur, hands balled into fists that struck at him over and over.

He drew in a shuddering breath, trying to scream for Kelly to call the police. But something hard struck the side of his head, something harder than a fist.

Jeremy felt his brain rattle inside his skull, the force of the blow momentarily causing dark stars to explode behind his eyelids.

When he tried to open his eyes again, he found his eyelids were stuck together with something wet and warm that ran down from his hairline.

His mouth wasn't working properly. His jaw felt weird, stiff and out of place. There was the rag stuffed into his mouth, a strange taste covering his tongue.

"I wasn't sure you'd wake-up, Jezza." The voice came from somewhere to his left and Jeremy tried to move his head in that direction. But it was like his head was stuffed full of cotton wool, his brain struggling to put the pieces together.

As though sensing his inability to move properly, Mark's visage swam into view. His old friend winced as he took in Jeremy's face.

"Not looking too hot there, pal. I can't imagine you're feeling too good either." Mark clucked his tongue and shook his head sadly. "You know things didn't need to go like this."

Jeremy tried to speak around the rag. Claggy blood made it difficult to form words and anyway, his tongue was trapped beneath the foul-tasting gag.

Mark pulled it from his mouth and Jeremy thought, but couldn't be certain, that a couple of his teeth fell out after it. His jaw was still not functioning correctly, but he managed to form one garbled word.

"Why?"

Mark leaned over him, his smile tinged with sadness. "Because I know you, buddy. I offered you a chance to come back, but you used me. I thought you understood how things needed to be. I thought that after what you saw at that farmhouse that you got it."

Jeremy's mind wandered, his thoughts turning to Kelly upstairs. He needed to get up there, needed to protect her from the lunatic in the kitchen.

Jeremy groaned, struggling to sit up, but his body refused to do his bidding. There was a burning sensation in his ribs and every breath he sucked down failed to satisfy his starving lungs. Suffocating. He was suffocating.

Panic saw him thrash on the floor. He clutched out at Mark, grabbing him with bloodied hands.

"Sssh, mate, relax. Don't tax yourself." Mark pressed him back into the floor.

"Kelly..." Jeremy's tongue was too thick. The blood from his broken nose trickled into his mouth and down the back of his throat. It would drown him if he couldn't get up.

"Don't worry about her." Mark pulled back, crouching over Jeremy. "I didn't want this, Jezza. I thought you understood. I thought we could be a family again." Mark let his head hang down. "This is my failing."

When he looked at Jeremy again, there seemed to be genuine remorse lurking in his dark eyes. "It's not my call, mate. They make the rules, and we have to follow them. And when you break them..." Mark shrugged and reached into his pocket. When he raised his hand, Jeremy spotted a needle as it glinted in the half-light that filtered in through the kitchen window.

Mark moved fast, faster than Jeremy's eyes could follow. Despite the pain in his body, he felt the needle as it punched through his skin. Something burned as it spread through his neck. and he screwed up his eyes in response.

Mark patted him on the shoulder and pushed to his feet.

"I won't do any permanent damage to her, I promise. And when you're gone, I'll look after her. You've got my word on that."

It took a moment for his words to slide through the jumble of Jeremy's thoughts. When it did, Jeremy was filled with such intense fear that it muted his pain.

He tried to grab at Mark's leg, but his former friend stamped down on his fingers, crushing them beneath his boot tread.

"Don't prolong this, mate. Just go with it. I gave you the good stuff. It'll help. Just go with it."

Mark crammed the rag back in Jeremy's mouth

before he walked away, his boots crunching over the glass.

Jeremy lay there, the silence weighing on him as he fought to remain in control of his own thoughts. The seconds turned in minutes.

It was the screaming that pulled Jeremy from the twilight space his mind had slipped into.

Kelly…

He rolled onto his side. The drugs were beginning to take effect, and they curbed the edge of his pain. It had been years since he'd last indulged. Mark had done him a favour.

She was screaming his name, the terror in her voice drawing him to his feet. He barely registered the glass that spliced through the delicate flesh of his feet. Dragging his broken body into the kitchen, he clung to the counters as he propelled himself to the stairs.

He tried to call out to her, but his voice was too gravelly and low to be heard. Reaching the bottom of the stairs, Jeremy slumped onto the steps.

Kelly's screams were quieter now, as though something or someone was silencing her. Jeremy let the thought settle in his mind as he started the climb.

Digging his fingers into the carpet on each stair, he dragged himself slowly, inexorably, upwards. All the while, he chanted her name beneath his breath.

The bedroom door swung open, Kelly's quiet sobbing growing momentarily louder as a dark figure appeared. It took Jeremy a moment to realise the balaclava wearing shadow was Mark. Mark stood for a moment, struggling to close the belt on his jeans.

"Fucker..." The word slipped from Jeremy's mouth before he could stop himself.

Mark jerked his head up, his cold gaze settling on Jeremy slumped on the stairs.

Crossing the carpet, Mark crouched next to him. "I'd forgotten how tough you were." Shaking his head, Mark tutted softly to himself.

Jeremy made to grab him, but Mark shuffled back out of reach.

"Bastard..." Blood dripped on the floor beneath Jeremy's face, staining the carpet pink.

"When all of this is over, Jezza, I'll make it up to her. When you're gone, I'll treat her so well, she won't even remember your name."

Jeremy lunged forward, but Mark was already moving. He pushed up as Jeremy dragged his body upright. He couldn't see Mark's face beneath the mask, but Jeremy knew if he could, he'd see surprise etched into Mark's features.

The thought was gone before he could grab onto it. Mark took a step back and raised his leg.

When his boot connected with the centre of Jeremy's chest, the world slowed. He felt the pressure of Mark's kick as it propelled him backwards.

His hands scrabbled uselessly for the walls, the banister, anything to give him purchase. Anything that would save him.

His broken fingers found only air, and his body

tumbled backwards, the breath rushing from his chest as his spine cracked against the steps.

His legs went over his head and still he continued to fall. Time collapsed in on itself, prolonging the moment and speeding up all at once.

When he hit the bottom of the stairs, he felt his skull crack as it connected with the ground, like an egg carelessly dropped.

And then nothing at all.

CHAPTER THIRTY-FIVE

HARRIET CLIMBED from her car and pulled her coat tighter around her body before she hurried from the car park and into the imposing stone building. The feeling of being watched left her unnerved. She could feel the gazes, hear the whispers. Time had passed, and the tabloids had all moved on, but that had not stopped the rumours. People still looked at her like she was a criminal. She had tried to brush it off, pretend that everything was back to normal, but that just wasn't true.

She made it to the lobby of the building and was confronted by a large group of chattering students. Harriet kept her shoulders back and chin high as the conversations around her died away to silence.

"Good morning." Harriet tried to maintain a cheery facade as she edged through the crowd.

The students parted like a shoal of fish escaping a

much larger predator. The moment her back was turned, the chatter started up again. "That's her."

Picking up her pace, Harriet crossed the floor and made it to the stairs. Keeping her attention fixed on the ground in front of her, she tried to block out the gossip. On more than one occasion, she had wondered if returning had been a mistake.

Slipping in through the main door to her office, she was relieved to find the reception area empty. The idea of having to make small talk, no matter how well meaning it might be, left her cold. Most were not brave enough to ask her to her face about the situation, and those who were... well they usually believed in the old adage, that there was no smoke without fire.

Despite clearing her name, she was as much a pariah now as she had been when the articles first came out. And while she had agreed to see out the end of the term, judging by how few students turned up to her classes, Harriet wondered if continuing to beat a dead horse was worthwhile.

Her phone buzzed in her pocket, and she lifted it free and stared down at the screen. For a moment she thought it might be Drew, but was disappointed to learn it was just Dennis. She skimmed the message, pleased to see he had agreed to a meeting. Something needed to change. Continuing at the university was not really a viable option. The students who were skipping her lectures because they believed what they had read in the papers were only going to suffer.

If she could persuade Dr Baig that somebody else should take over, then perhaps something could be salvaged from the mess.

A knock on the door behind her caused Harriet's heartrate to skyrocket. The urge to hide washed over her but she dismissed it as ridiculous. *You've done nothing wrong. Get a grip.* While the voice in her head might be correct, it did nothing to diminish the very real feelings she was experiencing.

Pulling open the door, she was surprised to find Olivia on the other side.

"DC Crandell, what a lovely surprise." As soon as the words were out of Harriet's mouth, she knew just how true they were. She had refused to admit to herself just how much she had missed the team. It was like a piece of her life had been stolen from her and she had been cut adrift, unable to find a way back. And then there was Drew. The number of times she had picked up her phone to call him before losing her nerve. And the more time that passed, the harder it became.

"You're not busy, are you? I know I should have called first."

Harriet shook her head and stood aside to allow the other woman inside. "I'm never too busy for you. How have you been?"

"Oh, you know, muddling through." Olivia's smile was wan, and she touched her fingers to the collar of her shirt. As she watched her, Harriet wondered just how much of Olivia's behaviour was unconscious. A trauma response to everything she had been through.

"But how are *you*? How long have you been back? I can't imagine it was easy with all the gossip…" Olivia trailed off, colour spreading across her cheeks. "Sorry, I shouldn't have—"

Harriet smiled. "It's fine. You're right, it hasn't been easy. I was just thinking there needs to be a change. It's not fair on the students."

"What do you mean?" Olivia asked.

"Many of them stopped coming to class." Harriet swallowed hard. It wasn't easy to admit such vulnerability to another person. If it had been Drew, it wouldn't have been so difficult. But it wasn't Drew.

"Why would they stop…" Olivia trailed off. "They still believe you did something to Lila."

Harriet turned her gaze upwards to the ceiling, noting the water damage on the plaster work above her head. She'd never noticed it before, then again, she didn't have much occasion to stare at the ceiling.

"No smoke without fire, DC Crandell." With a sigh, she dropped her gaze. "I'm going to ask Dr Baig to have another lecturer take over my classes. I can't have the students suffering because—"

"You did nothing wrong."

"I know. But that doesn't change the fact that I need to do what is right for the students. If they continue to miss class, they will fail."

Olivia snorted. "You're a better woman than me,

Dr Quinn. If it were me, I'd let them fail. It'd serve them right."

The ghost of a smile crept onto Harriet's face. "I appreciate the sentiment, but it would be irresponsible of me to behave any other way. I have an obligation."

"You're still teaching the classes, right?" Olivia interrupted.

"Of course."

"Then you're already meeting your obligations. If they choose to ignore your attempts to educate them, that's not your problem."

"Well, I'm still going to try," Harriet said. "Dr Baig might refuse but I have to attempt to fix it."

Olivia shot her a sympathetic look before reaching into her bag and extracting a brown paper bag. "Well, I can't help you with that issue, but I can resolve another one. I thought you might like this back." She held the parcel out.

Gingerly, Harriet took the item. It was surprisingly heavy, and it took her a moment to guess at what it was. "My laptop?"

Olivia smiled. "Yeah. Jodie finished going through it and I figured you might need it. I would have returned it sooner, but I wasn't sure if you were back yet."

Harriet slipped it from the paper. When she had thought about the moment her laptop would be returned to her, she had always imagined it would be Drew handing it over.

"How did you know I was back?" Harriet asked, trying for nonchalance and falling short.

Olivia shifted awkwardly. "DI Haskell had some uniforms put on your place when everything blew up. It's just a drive-by to make sure everything is all right. They knew you'd returned."

Harriet set the laptop down on the reception desk, suddenly unsure of how to take the news. On one hand, it was typical of Drew to think of her and on the other, it was entirely reckless of him. If the tabloids got wind of what he was up to, it would only further tarnish the reputation of the force.

Olivia tapped her arm gently. "Don't worry about it, Dr Quinn. He has the blessing of the DCI. They didn't want to take the risk that something might happen to you. We've all been worried."

Harriet's smile was thin. "Hopefully it's behind me now and I can just move on with my life." Taking a deep breath, she decided to plunge ahead and ask the question that had been swirling around her brain. "How is DI Appleton?"

"I think we had a breakthrough with her case."

"You *think* you had a breakthrough?"

Olivia quickly filled her in on the details.

"And he just confessed to everything?" Harriet pursed her lips as Olivia nodded. "Why would he do that?"

With a shrug, Olivia picked up her bag. "I was hoping you could tell me."

"I wish I could. Nothing is ever so clean cut."

Musing, Harriet sat on the edge of the reception desk. "Perhaps Jodie should consider looking through his financial records to see if there's anything odd—"

"The DI already had her look through them. There was nothing. She's going through his electronics and tracking the contacts on his phones."

"Well, there must be something to be gained from it."

"Then again, maybe he really did all the things he said he did. If it walks like a duck…"

Harriet hid her smile. "I suppose. It certainly sounds like you all have it under control." She tried to hide the hurt from her voice, but Olivia picked up on it, nonetheless. She touched her hand to Harriet's arm.

"Things would be a lot easier if you were back with us. The team misses you, Dr Quinn."

"I appreciate that, but you've all obviously got everything under control. And that's how it should be. You're a strong team. You'll get through this, DS Arya included."

"He will. He just needs time."

Olivia looked as though she was going to say something else, but her phone buzzed. "Shit, I better get back or the DCI will have my hide."

Harriet contemplated asking Olivia to tell the team she was thinking of them, but at the last second, she changed her mind. She was trying to make a clean break. Sending a message back with Olivia would only confuse that.

"Look after yourself, Olivia. I'm here if you ever need me."

As Olivia headed for the door, she glanced back at Harriet. "I'll hold you to that." Pausing with her hand on the door handle, Olivia hesitated. "You know if you wanted to return, we would all have your back."

Harriet let her gaze drop to the floor. This was what she had been afraid of. All she had to do was look at the mess she had made of things at the university. Everything would only get worse if she tried to go back to the police. Even with her name cleared, there would be those out there who would take the opportunity to try and destroy Drew and the team. And as much as it hurt, Harriet could not allow that.

"I think it's better for everyone involved if we have a clean break. My staying away is the only thing that can protect all of you."

Olivia opened her mouth to argue, but Harriet shut her down with a head shake. "Deep down you know I'm right, Olivia. There are people who would be only too happy to see the team dismantled. We can't let that happen."

"It doesn't mean I have to like it," Olivia said grumpily. "But it was good to see you."

Harriet tapped her fingers on the laptop. "Thanks for returning this."

With a curt nod, Olivia slipped out into the hall. The door slammed shut behind her, leaving Harriet alone with her thoughts. She had spent so long pretending that she was fine without the camaraderie of the team. But seeing Olivia had shown her just how much she missed it. Working with Drew and the others had given her a sense of purpose that was now missing from her life. Thanks to Lila Uxley and Jonathan Connors, it had been ripped away from just when she was finally starting to feel like she belonged somewhere.

What made it worse was the knowledge that there was nowhere else on earth where she would feel that sense of belonging again. It was gone, broken beyond repair, and there was nothing she could do to fix it. It reminded her of the aftermath of her mother's attempt on her life and the moment she had realised Kyle would not be coming home. She was alone, then. And now, so many years later, she was alone, again.

Dropping down into the chair behind the desk, she allowed her tears to flow.

PART 2

TWO WEEKS LATER

CHAPTER THIRTY-SIX

OLIVIA SAT at the kitchen table, staring down into a bowl of soup cooling in front of her.

"Everything all right, love?" Her father's voice cut through her silent contemplation.

Painting a false smile on her face, Olivia met his grey-eyed gaze head on. "Fine, dad."

"Don't kid a kidder," he said, his canny eyes narrowing. "Something's eating at you. What is it?"

Olivia ducked her chin, hiding her smile. It still amused her that her father had the ability, even now, to make her feel like a little girl.

"Honestly, it's nothing. I was just thinking about work."

"They still got you chained to the desk?" He cocked a bushy eyebrow.

"Ken, don't brow beat the girl. If she wanted to tell you something, she'd have said so."

Olivia felt the gentle press of her mother's hand against her shoulder as she passed behind her.

"Nah, it's fine." She glanced at her father. "I'm still on the desk. But I'm hoping they'll clear me soon."

Her father glared at the slices of bread on the table as though each one had personally insulted him. "I don't know why you let them coddle you like that. I didn't raise my daughter to be sidelined."

"I'd hardly call being put on desk duty after I was injured in the line of duty sidelined, Dad." Olivia softened her words with a smile. "I'll be back out on the street in no time."

"They should have let me have five minutes with that cowardly bastard." Silence closed over the kitchen. From the corner of her eye, Olivia could see her mother frozen at the kitchen sink.

Olivia's gaze dipped, her attention snagging on the white knuckled grip her father had on his knife.

She reached out and placed a placating hand over his. "I'm fine now, Dad." Her voice was gentle.

He loosened his grip on the knife, allowing it to clatter to the tabletop as he took her hand in his.

"I'm fine," she repeated. Her words pulled him back from whatever place he'd retreated to in his mind.

He blinked back tears and swallowed hard. "I can see that. The fact that they can't is what baffles me." He coughed, brashly covering his emotions.

Olivia returned his forced smile with a warm one of her own. Even now, she could still remember the haunted look on her father's face when she'd woken up in the hospital and found him sitting next to her bed. He'd stayed with her until they'd kicked him out. But he had returned every day without fail, to read to her from the paper, as he had when she'd been small enough to sit on his knee. His presence had been all the encouragement Olivia had needed to get back on her feet as quickly as possible.

"What did I miss?" Robbie swept into the room. Before anyone could speak, he'd swiped a piece of buttered bread from the side of his father's plate.

"Your manners," Mum said. She tutted disapprovingly and started to return her attention to the sink. Before she could turn her back, Robbie moved to her side and planted a smacker on her cheek. He whirled out of reach before she could protest.

Not that she would. Robbie was the apple of their parents' eye, and as such could do no wrong.

Mum's cheeks turned rosy red, and she made a show of swiping at the spot where he'd kissed her cheek with a tea towel.

Robbie plopped down into his chair on the opposite side of the table, the slice of bread already half-eaten. His eating habits were legendary among the family. He had the appetite of a rugby team but never added an ounce of fat to his lanky frame.

He cocked an eyebrow in Olivia's direction as he caught her studying him.

"Still going around like a bride of Dracula, I see,"

he said. He popped the second half of the bread into his mouth and automatically reached for another.

"What?"

He gestured to his neck, indicating the polo neck Olivia had decided on for the day.

"Robbie!" Mum warned from behind him.

Olivia shrugged. "At least mine will improve with time. Pity the same can't be said for your face."

He chucked a chunk of bread at her head and Olivia ducked, allowing it to whizz harmlessly over her.

"You two are ridiculous!" Mum dropped the tea towel on the counter. "You're both adults, so behave like it, for once."

"Sorry, Mum," Olivia said sheepishly.

"Yeah, sorry..." Robbie mumbled.

He caught Olivia's eye and stuck his tongue out, drawing a grin from her. Within seconds, they had both dissolved into fits of giggles. The tension Olivia had been feeling before she'd arrived faded away as she relaxed into the camaraderie she felt with her family.

It had always been so easy with them.

"Did you see this?" Dad's voice cut through the laughter. He flicked the paper, straightening the pages as he placed them on the table in front of her. He jabbed a finger, scarred from years of working on fishing boats, at an article on the paper.

"Ken, is this really the best time? We're having our tea."

Olivia read quickly, her gaze scanning over the page. It was a small piece, covering a break-in involving a young couple on the outskirts of Brompton.

"Did you hear anything about it?" Dad leaned his elbows on the table.

Without paying much heed, Olivia shook her head. She devoured the words on the page, her mind running all the possible reasons for the crime. It was probably nothing. But there was something in the way the article was written which tugged at her. It lacked the usual salaciousness she'd come to expect with the papers. Then again, it also lacked details.

All she could glean from the piece was that a few weeks prior, the couple had been attacked in the early hours of a Saturday morning. Both had been taken to hospital with serious injuries, and one remained in critical condition. A quote from one of the family members caught Olivia's attention. "Home is supposed to be a haven, but nowhere is safe from these thugs. There's just no safe place anymore."

"I thought it would catch your eye," Dad said, his voice finally breaking through Olivia's thought process.

"Why this one?" She glanced up at him.

His response was a quick shrug. "No clue. Just thought it was a bit different to all the others."

Why her father had decided to become a fisherman was still a source of confusion to Olivia. The man had a mind like a steel trap, and as such would have made a fantastic detective. When she'd questioned him about it, he'd shrugged her questions off. His own father had been a fisherman, and his father before him. It was tradition.

The idea of being forced to do something was a foreign one to Olivia. And when she'd said as much to the man next to her, he'd just smiled at her. "The choices I've made gave you the privilege of choice," he'd informed her.

When she'd tried to press him further, he'd refused to answer any more of her questions. It still intrigued her.

Perhaps one day he would explain it to her.

"I should head out," Olivia said, getting to her feet.

"So soon?" Mum turned to her. "You've only been here a short while."

Olivia shook her head. "I really need to go. I've got a ton of stuff to do at home. Oscar will be pissed if I stay out any longer."

Mum snorted. "He'd survive another hour without you."

But Olivia already had her jacket on and was searching her pocket for her keys. "Sorry, Mum, duty calls."

Leaning down, she placed a quick kiss on her father's leathery cheek. Robbie gave her a quick salute, but his attention was riveted to the food that remained on the table. Mum followed her to the door, fretting and cajoling the entire time.

Olivia stepped out into the porch and turned back to her mother. "I promise I won't stay away this time."

"You'd better not. And your father is right," Her mum dropped her voice so she couldn't be heard over the raised voices coming from the kitchen. "Don't let them sideline you, Livvie." Livvie was the nickname her family had given her when she was young. But her mother rarely used it anymore. Hearing it coming from her now was jarring.

"Mum, I--"

"No, let me finish." The other woman held up her hand, effectively silencing Olivia without another word. "You made a mistake. But that doesn't give them the right to punish you forever. They need you as much as you need them. Don't you forget it." She leaned in, offering her cheek to Olivia.

Dutifully, Olivia pecked her mother on the cheek and allowed herself to be ushered out the door.

It wasn't until she was turning the key in the lock of her flat that she allowed the truth of her mother's words to sink in. They *did* need her. DI Haskell was not the type of man who suffered fools gladly, and he had requested that she stay on the team despite the mistakes she had made.

Stepping into the darkened hall, Olivia felt a fur covered body twine around her ankles. "Hello, Oscar," she said quietly. Flicking on the lights, she watched as the overweight ginger moggy threw himself down on the rug at her feet. He rolled onto his back, exposing the pale golden fur of his belly. A trap. One Olivia had fallen afoul of more times than she cared to count.

"Not today, Satan," she muttered, eyeing the cat as he reached one clawed foot in the direction of her black boots.

If he heard her, Oscar made no indication of it. Instead, his purrs only intensified as he rolled and stretched and made a giant fuss of himself against the rug.

Rolling her eyes, Olivia suppressed a smile as she stepped over his body and made her way to the kitchen. With a disgruntled *meep*, Oscar followed, beating her to the cupboard in spite of Olivia's head start.

As she dished out his food, her hands started to shake. And by the time she stood back to watch him eat, the tremors had spread up through her arms and into her spine. It was always the same. When she was alone, the fear and the panic returned. She could practically set her watch to it.

Turning her back on the cat, she gripped the edge of the counter top and closed her eyes. She drew in a deep, steadying breath, counting slowly backwards in an effort to bring her racing thoughts back under control.

Oscar's deep throated meow was the only warning she had before he leaped onto the counter and brushed his tail beneath her nose. She jerked back, surprised laughter bubbling out of her. Two luminous, green eyes stared back at her, as if to say, *what's your problem?*

Without a second thought, she swept him up into her arms and pressed her nose to his fur. Oscar meowed, before settling into her grip. Purring like a car without an exhaust, the cat pressed his nose against Olivia's throat.

The final dregs of tension ebbed slowly away from her body, leaving her feeling exhausted.

"Thanks, Oscar," she whispered against his warm body. He *meeped* in response and continued purring.

Rescuing Oscar had been Dr Quinn's idea after the incident at work. Initially, Olivia had fought the prospect of adopting an animal. She'd never been one of those children who'd dreamt of having a puppy. That had been Robbie's thing, not hers.

But Dr Quinn's quiet suggestion had stuck with her, burrowing its way into her brain until, one Saturday morning, Olivia found herself at a local cat rescue.

It had been love at first sight when she'd found Oscar, at least from her perspective. Oscar, on the other hand, couldn't have cared less about the prospect of finding his forever home with her. At least, he hadn't cared until she had whipped out a bag of treats.

Sensing the change in her mood, Oscar struggled

to escape her embrace. Setting him back down on the floor, she watched as he sashayed across the floor like he was taking part in his very own runway challenge from *RuPaul's Drag Race*.

Grinning, Olivia decided to settle down with a little television for the night with her feline companion.

CHAPTER THIRTY-SEVEN

HARRIET SETTLED back into her couch and curled her feet beneath her. Taking the afternoon to work from home was the best idea she'd had in a while. She picked up one of the papers she'd started working on before she'd left for Ireland, but the words bled into each other and refused to make any real sense.

Just as she was contemplating getting up to make a cup of tea, the doorbell rang. She froze. As time passed, it was getting easier to put her experience behind her, but hearing the doorbell still caused an almost Pavlovian response of fear.

Getting slowly to her feet, she tried to control her rapid heartbeat. Slipping out to the hall, she paused. The doorbell rang again. Through the coloured frosted glass of the door, she could make out the shadow of the person on the other side. She was certain of one thing; it wasn't Drew. She buried her disappointment.

Pausing with her hand on the wall, she contemplated returning to the living room and ignoring the uninvited caller entirely.

"Dr Quinn?" The female voice was familiar, but it still had the ability to take Harriet by surprise. Tugging open the door, she found herself face to face with DC Martina Nicoll.

"I was hoping I might find you at home." The detective constable smiled but Harriet could tell from the nervous way in which she held herself that she wasn't certain of her welcome.

"DC Nicoll, this is unexpected."

Martina's expression turned pensive, and she took a step back. "I shouldn't have come. This was a huge imposition. I'm sorry, I—"

"No, it's fine," Harriet said hurriedly. "You've taken me by surprise, that's all. I wasn't expecting company."

"I heard about the situation," Martina said. She coughed awkwardly and shoved her hands into the pockets of her jacket. "For what it's worth, Ambrose and I, we never thought you were capable of any wrongdoing."

"Everyone is capable of some kind of wrongdoing," Harriet said, before adding, "but I appreciate the sentiment nonetheless."

Martina nodded. "I suppose you might be right.

I've seen a lot of people do some terrible things. But..." she trailed off.

"Would you like to come in, DC Nicoll?"

"Please, call me Martina. I'm not here in an official capacity." She smiled apologetically. "I mean, I wish I was but..." she spread her hands in a gesture of helplessness.

"It's fine. Come on in." Harriet ushered her inside and closed the door. "I'm afraid I don't have anything to offer you beyond tea, and maybe coffee."

"I don't want to put you out," Martina said.

"You're not," Harriet said. "I was planning to put the kettle on before you arrived."

"Oh, well then, tea would be great. I've had more than enough coffee today."

Harriet directed her through to the kitchen and watched surreptitiously as Martina took a stool at the breakfast counter. The moments passed in comfortable silence as Harriet prepared the drinks. Martina didn't speak until Harriet had set a steaming cup of Yorkshire tea in front of her.

"What can I do for you?" Standing on the opposite side of the counter, Harriet leaned back against the cabinets, nursing her own mug of tea between her palms.

The mug had belonged to Drew. He'd jokingly told her that the cups she used were too small for him. He'd been right; she had watched him often enough struggling with the delicate handles on the bone

China cups she favoured. One night, he'd brought the mug in question. Harriet could remember the grin on his face when he'd told her he'd swiped it from the office kitchen. Of course, his mood had quickly faded when Harriet had suggested his act amounted to theft. Not that it had stopped him from using it.

When he'd moved into his new house, the mug had been overlooked, whether by design or just human error, Harriet couldn't be sure. And so, it had become a comfort blanket for her. She didn't want to admit it, but having the mug made it easier to pretend Drew's absence wasn't a gaping void in her life.

It really was much too big, more like a bowl than a mug. Only Drew would pick something like this.

"Well, it's interesting you should ask that." Martina kept her attention riveted to the cup in front of her. "I don't know if you've been watching the news lately."

Harriet shook her head. She had deliberately stayed away from the news ever since the situation with Misha—Lila, had erupted.

"Well, no matter," Martina said. "We picked up a case a few weeks ago. It's been all over the news. A family murdered in their home. Mum, Dad, and their teenage daughter." Martina swallowed hard. "Butchered, really. The crime scene was one of the worst I've seen. But forensics are all over the place with conflicting information and to be honest, it's virtually impossible to put the pieces together into something even remotely coherent."

Harriet cocked her head to the side. "I'm not sure what help I can be."

Martina took a mouthful of her tea and winced. "We don't have the resources to handle something like this."

From where Harriet stood, it sounded as though that admission had cost Martina dearly. She knew Martina was ambitious, and that admitting defeat would be no easy task for the young woman.

"And you were hoping I would have a word with DI Haskell?" Harriet guessed.

Martina pulled a face. "I hate to say it, but yeah. We could really do with a boost on this one. The media have turned it into a circus and social media is no better. Conspiracy theories have spiralled out of control. There's speculation that this is the work of some kind of serial killer--"

Something tugged at the back of Harriet's memory.

"—Which it isn't, but it's a believable theory, at least. Yesterday, I saw a post suggesting it was a mafia hit." Martina snorted. "A mafia hit. In Yorkshire. People have lost their minds."

"And what do you think?" Harriet asked.

Martina shook her head. "We've got no evidence to suggest anything of that nature. We know there was burglary, but the brutality of the murders just doesn't fit." Martina kept her gaze trained on the countertop. "I would ask you to look at the files, Dr Quinn, but after everything that happened and the media speculation surrounding this case—"

"You can't take the risk," Harriet said, her smile grim. "I understand, and I wouldn't ask you for the files. I haven't been cleared to work with the police. I might never get that clearance." Harriet sighed.

"But you didn't do anything," Martina said, incredulity staining her voice.

"No." Harriet sipped from her mug. "But mud sticks. If DCI Gregson were a smart man, he wouldn't let me near any of his cases ever again. The right kind of defence would have no problem poking holes in my credibility and the burden of proof falls on the Crown Prosecution." Harriet's stomach flip-flopped at the idea of never working alongside the team again. "I don't see it happening."

"Well, I'm sorry to hear that," Martina said, sounding shocked. "I really thought this would be a temporary thing."

Harriet cradled her mug, inhaling the steam as the taut silence stretched out between them. She could practically see the black cloud that hung over Martina, wrapping her in its dark cocoon.

"I'd be happy to speak with DI Haskell though, if that's really what you want," Harriet said.

Martina twisted her mouth into a half smile. "I wouldn't say it's what I want, but it's definitely what the case needs."

"Then consider it done. What does DS Scofield think of the plan?"

Martina twisted her fingers around her cup. "He doesn't know I came to you." Before Harriet could say anything, Martina added, "But he agrees in theory that we could do with DI Haskell's help."

"You mean he agreed you could use Drew's resources," Harriet said, a wry smile playing on her lips. She sighed. "Look, I'm happy to say it to Drew. I don't know what he'll do, but what I do know is that you don't want him calling up your sergeant with a proposal that he doesn't know is coming."

Martina nodded. "No, I don't want that." She remained thoughtful before she drank the last of her tea and grabbed her keys. "I really appreciate this, Dr Quinn. And for what it's worth, if it were up to me, I'd reinstate you immediately. I know I'm not the only one who sees your worth."

Harriet smiled. "Thank you."

Martina shrugged. "It's just what I think."

Harriet followed her to the door and unlocked it before letting the other woman step out onto the doorstep. "Good luck with your case. I have faith that you'll figure it out."

Martina's smile was worn around the edges. "I wish I had your faith, Dr Quinn. But maybe if DI Haskell can come up with something that allows everyone to work to their strengths, we'll find the person responsible."

"I trust Drew," Harriet said. "He'll want to help."

After they said their goodbyes, Harriet closed the door and leaned her forehead against the cool glass. So much for giving Drew space. Sighing, she heaved herself upright and made her way into the living room to get her phone.

HARRIET SAT in her car outside Drew's house. A mist had swept in off the sea as she'd crossed the moors and now it covered the windscreen, making it difficult to discern any details of the small cottage. There was a tremor in her hands as she gripped the steering wheel and listened to the gentle tick of the cooling engine.

It felt like a lifetime had passed since she'd last seen him. It had become painfully obvious on the journey over here that her staying away had less to do with needing space and more to do with the fact that she was nervous about seeing him.

She'd stood in the living room and stared at his number on her screen, unwilling or unable, she wasn't sure which, to make the call. In the end, she had decided that this was a conversation that needed to happen in person. And so, here she was.

Flexing her fingers over the steering wheel, she tried to steel her nerves. It was only Drew. She had come to his house a thousand times before. He was her friend.

Friend. The last time they had been together…

Harriet closed her eyes, remembering Drew's face when he'd barged his way into her hall, only to realise she wasn't alone. Something had changed between them that night, and Harriet couldn't shake the feeling that the damage was irreparable.

It was foolish and sentimental to think like that. They were work colleagues, friends and nothing more, thrown together by a shared desire to seek justice for those who couldn't seek it for themselves.

There could never be anything but that between them. But she had felt a shift, and now she couldn't shake that knowledge.

Get a grip, Harriet. She was grateful for the voice that piped up in the back of her mind.

She would just get out of the car, march up to the door and— Before she could finish the pep talk, the front door swung inwards, and Drew appeared.

He peered out into the gathering gloom, his corrugated brow smoothing as his face broke into a wide grin. He was out the door and across the gravel drive before Harriet could pull the keys from the ignition.

As Harriet stepped out of the car, Drew reached her and pulled her into a tight bear hug that squeezed the air from her lungs. It was easy to melt against him, to lean into the strength of his body as he held her close. She breathed in the scent of his aftershave, a combination of woodsmoke and leather, and felt the tension of the last few weeks finally seep out of her bones.

"You should have told me you were back," Drew said, his voice muffled against her. "I'd have come to see you."

"Well, I'm here now." She was unable to keep the smile from her voice.

"Drew?" The voice of DI Appleton drifted through the mist.

Harriet stiffened and slowly pulled away. Drew released her reluctantly and when he stepped back, Harriet could see DI Appleton in the door of the cottage.

Melissa's face was gaunt, faint shadows lurking beneath her eyes. Harriet knew she still had a long road of recovery ahead.

"Dr Quinn..." There was a resignation to Melissa's voice that took Harriet by surprise. "You're back then?"

"I've been back..." Harriet hesitated, her gaze sliding to Drew's face. "I've been back a while."

Something brightened in Melissa's eyes. Drew had gone rigid.

"When did you get back?" Drew asked, glancing down at her.

Harriet busied herself with her keys. "I'm not exactly sure. A few weeks at least."

"You stayed away." Drew's voice was flat. He took a step back from her.

"I thought it was for the best."

His jaw tightened and he gave a short nod of his

chin. "We just finished dinner but I'm sure I could find something..."

Harriet had already started to shake her head. "I'm fine, I already ate." It was a lie, but Drew didn't need to know that.

"Well, come in and tell us how things went in Ireland."

Harriet followed him back towards the house. As he reached the door, Melissa grabbed his arm, leaning her weight against him as he crossed the threshold. Drew seemed to be as surprised as Harriet was.

While she couldn't say she really knew DI Appleton, Harriet had always assumed her hard exterior would prevent her from asking for help. And as for appearing vulnerable? Well, it didn't fit with the personality traits she had always displayed in the past.

Then again, Harriet had been wrong about people before. She only needed to cast her mind back to Dr Jonathan Connors and Lila Uxley for proof of that.

She followed them as they made slow progress into the kitchen. As she entered the warm space, Harriet was surprised to discover that Drew had added a small couch. It sat next to the French doors overlooking the garden and it was piled with colourful cushions.

Harriet stood awkwardly to one side while Drew

helped Melissa to take a seat on the couch before turning back to Harriet.

"Something to drink?" There was an odd, strained expression that lurked around his eyes, and the tightness of his jaw left Harriet feeling that turning up unannounced had been a huge mistake.

"No, thanks, I'm fine…" She faltered before turning her attention to Melissa. "I was sorry to hear about the attack."

DI Appleton's demeanour shifted, her visage shuttering as her shoulders rounded and she hunched in on herself as though physically wounded by Harriet's words. "Thanks."

"Have they caught the people responsible?"

Melissa stared at her hands. "It's complicated. They picked someone up. but…" She shrugged.

"Well, if you ever need--"

"Thanks," Melissa said tightly. "I'll keep that in mind." A moment passed, and Harriet tightened her fingers around themselves as the tension ratcheted up in the room.

"Drew," Melissa said, her words cutting through the atmosphere. "I've got to make a call. I'll let you two catch up."

"Do you need me to get you anything?" Drew moved towards her like a moth to a flame.

Melissa shook her head and then glanced at Harriet. "Sorry, Dr Quinn. I'm not very good company these days."

"Don't worry about it," Harriet said. "I should

have called ahead. I'm sorry for barging in on you both and disturbing your evening."

Melissa looked from Harriet to Drew, her expression unreadable.

Drew held his hand out to help Melissa to her feet, but she brushed him away. She got to her feet carefully and padded to the door, Drew shadowing her movements like he expected her to drop at any time.

"I'm sorry about everything that happened with Lila Uxley," Melissa said. There was a hoarseness to her voice as though saying the words aloud caused her physical discomfort. "It was wrong. I wouldn't wish something like that on my worst enemy."

The phrasing was odd, Harriet thought, but before she could say anything else, Melissa spoke again.

"I can take it from here, Drew. You need to talk to Dr Quinn."

"Are you sure?" Drew raised an eyebrow at Melissa, but she simply nodded.

"I'm fine." She pushed away, and Harriet listened to the shuffling of her feet as she made her way slowly down the hall.

Lowering her voice, Harriet said, "How has she been?"

Shaking his head, Drew gestured for Harriet to follow him. "Let's take a walk."

A FEW MINUTES LATER, they were making their way down a steep flight of steps set into the side of the cliff. Drew moved confidently ahead, his long stride eating up the ground.

The sound of waves slapping against the sand intensified as they reached the promenade.

Harriet paused and stared at the sand and sea in front of her. The heavy, leaden sky kissed the landscape, making it virtually impossible to tell the difference between the horizon and the low-lying clouds.

"It's beautiful," Harriet said softly, drinking in the scenery. The salt air tickled her nose as she took a deep breath.

"We can take a walk on the beach if you'd like." Drew gestured to the beach below the promenade. "The tide won't be in for a while yet, and we can make it back up before it gets too dark."

Harriet cast him a sideways look. "You've really settled in here, haven't you?"

He nodded. "It's perfect."

Closing her eyes, Harriet let the sounds and the smells wash over her before she replied. "I can understand why you think that." Cracking an eyelid, she grinned at him. "I'm jealous that you have this on your doorstep."

"Come on." He started along the promenade and disappeared down a set of steps that led to the beach. Harriet followed. She glanced at the wet sand and then down at her low pumps.

"I'm not really wearing appropriate footwear," she called after him.

Drew's face broke into a wide grin as he started to roll up the bottom of his jeans before stripping off his boots and socks. "It's better without shoes. How else will you feel the sand between your toes?"

Seeing him like this took her by surprise. He was different, lighter. Had Melissa's accident brought them closer together? Harriet had noticed something different between them back at the house.

Drew took a couple of steps onto the beach and waited for her beyond a huddled groups of rocks that looked like sleeping giants gathered in front of the sea wall.

Harriet walked down the steps slowly. Sitting on the bottom step, she took off her shoes and socks. Cautiously, she touched the wet sand with her foot. The coldness of it caused goose bumps to rise on her arms.

It had been years since she'd walked on the sand. In fact, the last time, if she wasn't mistaken, had been when she was a child.

Crushing the memory down in the back of her mind, she tried to focus on the moment. She gasped as she took a step out onto the sand and her foot sank into a small puddle of freezing sea water.

"Oh my god," she whispered.

Drew chuckled. "I mean, you say you're jealous but I'm not sure you're cut out for this life if you can't handle a little puddle."

"It's bloody freezing, Drew."

He shrugged nonchalantly. "It's not cold, it's bracing."

Gritting her teeth, Harriet splashed through the puddle and stalked out past him. He fell easily into step next to her and they started down the beach, following the twinkling of the lights that were dotted along the length of the pier that lay in the distance.

From the corner of her eye, Harriet studied the man next to her. Despite the obvious difficulties he'd suffered during the last few weeks, Drew looked happier than she'd seen him in a long time. The tension that had sat on his shoulders back at the cottage was gone, no doubt blown away by the brisk breeze that cut across the open landscape.

"You seem different," Harriet mused.

"Do I?" The surprise that cut across Drew's features was genuine. "I think I'm just tired. But this is good." He spread his arms wide, gesturing to the wide-open expanse of space around them.

Shaking off his explanation, Harriet smiled at him. "No, I don't mean that. You're…" She struggled to pinpoint exactly what it was about him that had caught her attention. "I don't know if you're happier, or more relaxed. Maybe both?" She raised an eyebrow at him.

"I wouldn't say I'm more relaxed." Drew chuckled. "Work is busier than ever."

"Did you get the person responsible for Melissa's attack?"

His expression darkened, his brow drawing down as his mouth compressed into a thin line. "It's a long story." He quickly filled her in on everything that had happened. "They knew what they were doing. They're clearly organised." He sighed. "They could have killed her if they'd wanted to."

Harriet could detect the tumultuous emotions that dwelled beneath Drew's words. The urge to comfort him was strong. She could only imagine that the situation with Melissa had brought back to the surface all of his memories of Freya. "Melissa is strong. She wouldn't give up without a fight."

Drew nodded absently.

"You know I'm always here if you need someone to talk to. If you're finding it—"

Drew was already shaking his head. "I took your advice and contacted that psychologist you recommended."

It took Harriet a moment to put the pieces together in her brain.

"Tony Sheridan," Drew said. "Bit of an odd ball." The mischievous glint in Drew's eyes softened his words.

"Dr Sheridan can be a little unorthodox, but he knows what's he's about. You're in good hands." Even though she had been the one to give Drew the contact, there was still a small part of her that was hurt. Everyone had moved on so quickly without her. It seemed she was the only one who was still stuck.

"I had a visitor earlier," Harriet said, choosing to change the subject rather than dwell on the situation.

"Oh? Who was that?" The feigned nonchalance in his voice belied the look of consternation that flickered through his eyes.

"DC Martina Nicoll. She had a proposition for me." Harriet waited until Drew's expression cleared, and realisation dawned in his eyes.

"She's working on that triple murder, right?" he said.

Harriet nodded. "An entire family wiped out."

Drew glanced at her. "Well, not quite the entire family. There's a surviving son. He was at university at the time."

"You know all about it, then?"

Drew's expression was grim. "I know a little. Enough to know that it's an absolute shit show. DS Scofield is way out of his league on this one."

"Well, DC Nicoll would agree with you there. In fact--" Harriet hesitated, knowing that if she didn't present this exactly right, Drew would reject it outright simply on principal. "She thinks it would be helpful if the team would lend a hand."

"And what did you tell her?"

"I told her I would ask. Drew, you know better than most how difficult it can be to run an investigation without the proper resources."

"They have the same resources the rest of us get."

Harriet glared at him. "You and I know that's not true. Your budget is much larger—"

"Because the task force deals with much larger cases." Drew sighed. "I can't just go barging in there. It's not that simple. And even if I could—" He held a hand up to silence her, "Gregson would never go for it. He's getting enough flack as it is for the situation with Melissa. Top brass are demanding answers." He let his arms drop back to his side and turned so that his body faced hers. "You know I would help if I could."

"I know," Harriet said softly. She let her gaze drop to the sand beneath her feet. It had grown colder since they'd arrived, and her toes were starting to go numb.

"I'll see what I can do," Drew said suddenly.

Lifting her chin, she met his eyes. "Really?"

"Yeah, what's another impossible task? Isn't there a saying about doing as many as possible?"

Harriet laughed. "I think you've fumbled it a bit. It should be, *'Why, sometimes I've believed as many as six impossible things before breakfast.'* It's from Lewis Carroll's *Alice in Wonderland*."

Drew grinned. "I was close. Now, enough chat about that and tell me about Ireland. Is it as beautiful as Yorkshire?"

"Some might say so."

"Trick question," Drew said. "Nothing beats God's own county." He fell into step next to her. "Come on, I'll buy you a coffee from *Clara's* on the cliff and you can tell me everything."

She followed him back to the prom. Despite the

nip in the air, Harriet felt warm inside as she told Drew about the case she'd worked on and the budding relationship she was growing with her foster mother.

Drew listened attentively, only interrupting to ask her thoughtful questions. And by the time Harriet was ready to return home, she felt lighter than she had in a long time. Drew really was different. He was happy. And that, in turn, made Harriet happy. Even if they never worked together again, knowing that he was content took a weight off her shoulders.

CHAPTER THIRTY-EIGHT

OLIVIA SETTLED in behind her desk. Fatigue wracked her body, making her eyes blur as she piled the files up in front of her. It was a quiet morning, a small mercy she was more than grateful for. She'd been unable to rid her mind of the story her father had shown her in the paper.

After tossing and turning in bed, she'd given up and decided to gather as much information about the case as she could from online sources. Not that there was much to find.

However, being at work gave her options, so despite the fact that it was her day off, she had decided to come in under the pretence of getting some paperwork wrapped up.

Nobody needed to know what she was up to. She wasn't even sure what she was up to herself.

Clicking through to the report, she stared at the screen. The attack on the couple had been vicious.

Her gaze flew over the page. According to the attending officers, the place had been ransacked. A burglary gone wrong seemed to be the prevailing thought. But there was something about it that tugged at Olivia's brain. It felt wrong. She'd seen enough burglaries to know there was something off about this one.

It reminded her of something. She closed her eyes trying to recall the hazy memory that lurked in the recesses of her brain. Trying to force it only pushed the thought further out of reach. Frustrated, Olivia stood.

Maz was sat hunched over his desk, his attention riveted on his screen. Gregson had allowed him to return from his suspension a few days after they had charged Caz Popov. Despite her attempts to apologise, Maz evaded her at every turn. Not that she blamed him. Rather than approach DS Arya, she made a beeline for DI Haskell's office and rapped on the door.

"What?"

Unbothered by the harshness of his tone, Olivia pushed the door open. "Sir, there's something I want to discuss."

The DI waved his hand in the general vicinity of a chair buried beneath a mound of paperwork. Unlike the DCI's office, which was always immaculate, this space was crowded with papers, and files spilling their contents across every surface.

Olivia edged over to the chair and quickly set the

pile onto the floor. She took her seat and then waited as DI Haskell argued with himself over something on the computer.

Finally, he shoved the mouse away and sat back in his chair. "What can I do you for?"

"Guv, I noticed there was a break-in a couple of weeks back. A couple were attacked during the night, and I was wondering if I might take a look at it."

"Why?" The DI raised a brow at her as he grabbed his coffee cup and took a swig from the contents. "Christ, that's disgusting." Grimacing, he set the cup back on his desk and glared at it as though it had personally insulted him.

"Why what?"

"Why do you want to look at that case in particular? We've got more than enough work on our plate here. Why go looking for more?"

"It reminded me of something, sir. I thought maybe if I took a looked at the files and had a chat with the victims, I might be able—"

Drew shook his head, effectively cutting her off without ever having to say a word. "I get that you're feeling guilty over everything that happened, but this is not how you make amends."

Olivia dropped her gaze to her hands. "I know that. And with all due respect, guv, this is not about trying to make amends. The case is a nasty one and nobody is really looking at it but there's something off about the whole thing. It reminded me of the case a while back involving the woman we visited, Jessica

Tamblyn. We were looking for information on the Kolokoffs. Shortly after we had a chat with her, she was murdered in her flat."

DI Haskell remained silent, and Olivia took that as an invitation to carry on. "Nobody is looking at her death either. The moment they realised she was a prostitute, they decided she was probably killed over drugs, or her pimp went too far."

"And you don't believe either of those things." Drew kept his hands on the desk as he leaned back in his chair.

"Not at all. Neither does Dr Quinn…" Olivia swore inwardly as DI Haskell's expression became shuttered.

"You've been speaking to Dr Quinn?"

"Not about the case, sir. I just returned her laptop. Jodie was done with it, and I guessed Dr Quinn would need for her work."

"Good." DI Haskell's tone was dismissive. "Dr Quinn is not a member of this team anymore, so sharing information with her is strictly prohibited."

Olivia nodded. "Of course, sir."

Drew sighed. "If I let you go and speak with the victims --and that is a big 'if'-- I want you to take someone with you."

"Of course, guv."

"You've been cleared for duty but after your past behaviour, I don't want you out there alone."

Heat burned in Olivia's cheeks. On one hand, she was thrilled to be given her freedom from the desk, but on the other, the DI suggesting she needed a babysitter stung.

"Take Maz—"

"Sir, with all due respect, I don't think DS Arya wants anything to do with me."

"He's a member of this team. That means working together whether you want to or not. Plus, it'll give you a little bit of time to address the situation." As though he could read her panicked thoughts, he added, "It'll do you both good to clear the air."

Seeing no other choice, Olivia bit her tongue. She was finally being given a chance to get back out on the street; she wasn't going to look a gift horse in the mouth.

"Is that all?" DI Haskell cocked an eyebrow in her direction.

"That's everything, guv." Olivia escaped the office before he could change his mind. Pausing by her desk, she watched Maz. Judging by the way he was hunched over his desk, he was engrossed in the case file in front of him. How was she supposed to approach him when he'd made it perfectly clear that he wanted nothing to do with her?

She fingered the collar of her pale blue shirt, a shiver tracing lightly down her spine as she remembered the moment Alfred Douglas had jabbed the blade into her neck. Every night, she relived the moment at least once, sometimes more often. And every night, she woke in a cold sweat, her hand pressed to the scar on her throat.

But this was nothing like that. The fear she felt now was nothing like those cold sweat inducing nightmares. In some ways it was worse. She'd made a mistake where Alfred Douglas was concerned, and she had paid the price. But Maz was her friend, and her screw-up had nearly cost him his job. She needed to make it up to him somehow, but had no idea where to even begin.

"DS Arya, you're up." DI Haskell's voice rang out across the room before Olivia could summon the courage to do what needed to be done. Maz's head snapped up and he glanced in DI Haskell's direction in surprise.

"Of course, guv. Anything you need."

"I want you and DC Crandell to have a chat with the victims of a break-in over in Brompton. Nasty affair. Crandell will fill you in."

The surprise and joy Olivia had seen on Maz's face just mere seconds before disappeared, replaced with a dark scowl.

"Is there a problem, Arya?" There was no mistaking the challenge in DI Haskell's voice.

Maz merely gathered up his items and slipped on his coat. "No problem, guv."

Olivia did not need to be a detective to see that he was lying. Without looking at her, Maz made a beeline for the door, leaving Olivia with no choice but to trail after him.

"WHAT'S ALL THIS ABOUT THEN?" Maz finally broke his silence as Olivia slipped behind the steering wheel.

The fact that he hadn't tried to argue with her about which one of them would drive left her in no doubt as to his mood. The silence between them was not the usual kind; their easy camaraderie had been replaced by something harsh and cold.

"There was break-in over at Brompton. A couple were attacked in the middle of the night. Both sustained injuries. The man is currently in a coma over in James Cook in Middlesborough. I spoke to his partner a short while ago and she has agreed to meet us there."

"Fine." Maz settled back in his seat and glared out the passenger window. "Why has the DI sent us on a wild goose chase?"

Gripping the steering wheel, Olivia eased the car into traffic. "I asked him if I could look into the case. They have no leads and—"

"You what?" Maz turned to stare at her incredulously. "You're the reason we're doing this?"

"Yeah."

"Stop the car."

"Don't be ridiculous, Maz."

"I said stop the fucking car, DC Crandell." The way he used her title caused the breath to catch in the back of Olivia's throat. She had known he was angry, and she certainly couldn't blame him, but there was a part of her that had hoped they would patch things up. Hearing the tone in his voice quickly disabused her of that notion.

She pulled over and flicked off the engine before she turned to face him. "Go on, say it. I know you want to."

Maz shook his head. "You're unbelievable, you know that?"

"I said I was sorry. If I could have—"

"Cut the shit. I know you aren't sorry. You never are. You run into situations, never caring about the consequences or the potential damage to yourself or those around you."

"That's not fair, Maz. I never meant for—"

"And that's the problem, you never mean for anything… But everyone gets caught in the crosshairs of your recklessness."

"Nobody forced you to investigate alongside me, Arya. Don't pretend to be innocent in all of this. You were right there with me, in the thick of it."

He glanced down at his hands. "Don't you think I know that? I let you get away with constantly pushing the envelope. We were so stupid, and look what happened."

"If I could have taken your suspension, Maz, I would have. But I don't regret looking for the truth. DI Appleton was one of us…"

"And so was Celeste Jackson but that didn't stop us from getting her killed."

His declaration stunned Olivia into silence. Was that what he truly believed?

"We're not the reason she's dead."

"Aren't we? If we hadn't continued to dig, if we had just left it to Jodie to discreetly find the necessary proof, and then brought her in officially—"

"What? You think she'd still be alive? You think those bastards would have just rolled over and let her tell us everything she knew? Grow up, Maz. You know as well as I do that whether we'd have brought her in officially or not, she would have died. They set her up in the first place to take the fall, and the moment they were done with her, they killed her. I feel bad that she's dead, but I'm not responsible for it. I refuse to take ownership of that, and so should you."

He flexed his fingers, his gaze still trained on his hands. "I can't get her out of my head... I keep seeing the pictures from—"

Without thinking, Olivia reached across the space between them and gently touched her fingers to his shoulder. He flinched as though he'd been struck, but when he raised his gaze to her face, she could see unshed tears glittering in his eyes.

"This isn't on you, Maz. You can't carry everything."

He swallowed hard and nodded, his gaze returning to his hands. Tightening her grip on his shoulder, Olivia shook him gently. "I mean it, Maz. You did not kill Celeste. You're not responsible."

He flexed his fingers and flashed her a pained smile. "I'm fine. Let's go."

"Maz—"

"Don't."

That lone word was enough to silence Olivia entirely. She let her hand fall from his shoulder.

"Fill me in on what you know. I don't want to walk in there blind." He kept his attention fixed on the road ahead. Starting the engine, Olivia did as he asked, giving him as much information as she could remember.

And all the while, she couldn't escape the creeping fear that things would never be the same between them again.

CHAPTER THIRTY-NINE

OLIVIA KNOCKED SOFTLY on the door before letting herself in. She could feel Maz at her back as he quietly followed her. Just being back in the hospital was enough to spike Olivia's adrenaline. She could still remember the moment she had woken up in the sterile room and the fear she had felt. Everything had been such a jumble in her brain.

But this particular nightmare belonged to the young woman sitting next to the raised hospital bed, her shoulders hunched, head resting on the pristine white sheets, hand wrapped around the hand of the man in the bed.

The man in question, Jeremy Benson, was almost unrecognisable from the picture Olivia had seen in the file. His face looked puffy, skin doughy, and his eyes—which were shut—looked like two sunken pits. Beneath the harsh fluorescent lighting, Olivia could see the faint traces of bruising around his eyes. The tube in his mouth was hooked up to a large machine next to the bed. The rhythmic whoosh as it pushed oxygenated air in and out of his lungs caused Olivia's heart to subtly pick up its pace.

Ventilators unnerved her. She wasn't exactly sure why she had such a bizarre reaction to a machine she rationally knew was designed to support life. However, listening to the sound and watching the numbers change on the screen with each successful cycle of breathing left her uneasy. How precarious Jeremy's continued existence was. How easy it would be for it to come crashing down.

"Kelly Walker..." Olivia hated to break the young woman's rest. When she raised her head from the bed, Olivia felt even worse. Kelly was gaunt, with deep black circles beneath her eyes. And the look on her face was one Olivia had seen before, reflected back at her whenever she'd looked in the mirror in the early days after Alfred Douglas had attacked her.

"Yeah." Kelly's voice was flat.

"I'm DC Olivia Crandell. We spoke on the phone earlier. I asked if it was ok if we came by for a chat. This is my colleague DS Maz Arya."

Kelly nodded absentmindedly and returned her attention to the man in the bed. "Jeremy, these police officers are going to help us." Her voice was a whisper as she leaned over and spoke directly into his ear. As she straightened, she smoothed her hand back over his hair, a tender gesture that made Olivia feel as though she were intruding on an intimate moment.

Kelly stared down at him for a minute before returning her attention to Olivia and Maz. "Do you have news?"

Olivia couldn't be sure, but it sounded like there was a modicum of hope buried beneath the lifeless voice.

"We don't have any new information for you right now," Olivia said. "We're actually new to your case and I was hoping you could walk me through what happened that night."

Kelly closed her eyes, her knuckles whitening as she dug her fingertips into the sheets. "What's the point? You won't listen anyway."

"Why would you think that?" Olivia moved further into the room.

"Because the others didn't listen. Why would you be any different?" Kelly focused her attention on Olivia. "Even if he wakes up—and with every day that passes they say it's more and more unlikely—but even if he does come back, they said he'll be brain-damaged. He'll need around-the-clock care for the rest of his life. Jeremy wouldn't want that... he'd hate it."

"I'm very sorry—"

"I don't want your pity," Kelly spat the words out. "I want you to get the bastard who destroyed our lives."

"And we want that too," Maz said. "That's why we're here."

Olivia said, "Who do you think would do something like this?"

Kelly stiffened in her chair, her hand automatically moving to her stomach. "I…"

Sensing her faltering, Olivia decided to press a little harder. "Do you know who's responsible?"

"I'd like you to go," Kelly said abruptly. "You should be out there looking for the bloke who did this, not in here hassling me."

Olivia opened her mouth to argue but Maz touched her arm and shook his head. Swallowing the questions that crowded her, Olivia took a step back. "We really do want to help, Kelly."

Kelly squeezed her eyes shut, her body perfectly still. With a sigh, Olivia followed Maz to the door. As he opened it, Kelly shifted in her chair.

"Wait…"

Olivia's breath caught in the back of her throat, and she stilled.

Kelly faced them, her eyes full of unshed tears. "Jeremy would kill me if he knew I'd told you." She tossed a quick glance at the man in the bed. "I'd give anything to have him angry at me. But that won't ever happen again, will it?"

Olivia wanted to give the woman in front of her hope, but she also knew that doing so would sound trite, and that was the last thing Kelly needed.

"I don't like talking about it," Kelly said softly.

"Because it's my fault. He only got involved with him again because I got pregnant, and we needed money. Jeremy is a proud man. He wouldn't go to my dad for the cash. He wanted to provide for us, and when they let him go from his job, he was desperate, you know?" She glanced at Olivia before she shook her head. "Of course you don't. How could you?"

"I know what it's like to want something so bad you would do anything to get it. Desperation drives us to do things we wouldn't normally risk doing." Olivia deliberately kept her focus on Kelly and off Maz.

Swallowing hard, Kelly nodded jerkily. "Well, Jeremy was clearly feeling desperate. That's the only reason he went back to that monster." She took a deep steadying breath and fixed her attention on the man in the bed. "You should speak to Mark Robinson. I know it was him."

Olivia moved back into the room and took a seat next to Kelly. "How can you be so certain?"

Olivia didn't think it was possible for Kelly's face to grow any paler but the young woman visibly blanched. "I was involved with Mark before me and Jeremy… I didn't know it was him straight away. He was wearing a balaclava when he came into the bedroom."

"You never mentioned any of this in your previous statement," Maz interrupted, drawing a dark look from Olivia.

"I was ashamed. If I told you lot and Jeremy

woke up and he found out what happened... He wouldn't ever look at me the same."

The sinking feeling in the pit of Olivia's stomach grew. She hoped Kelly's story wasn't headed in the direction she feared.

"But he's not going to wake up now, is he? So, it doesn't matter that I'm damaged goods."

"Kelly—"

"Even though he was wearing a mask, and it was so dark..." She clenched her fists, her breath hitching as she spoke. "He pulled the mask off the lower half of his face when he got on the bed so he could kiss me." She sucked down a pained breath. "I begged him not to, said he might hurt the baby, and he laughed at that."

She fell silent for a moment. "I can still hear it, when I'm alone at night I can hear his laughter." She shuddered. "When he was on top of me, he did this thing he used to do all the time when we were together and we would, you know..."

Olivia touched her hand to Kelly's. The other woman jolted and glanced down at Olivia's fingers covering hers. She turned her hand, and for a moment Olivia thought she would withdraw from her touch. Instead, she wrapped her fingers tightly around Olivia's and squeezed hard.

"When he was holding me down and you know... he told me I was his 'good girl'. He said it over and over all while I was begging him to stop. And when he—" Kelly's voice broke, and she tightened her grip on Olivia's hand. "As he came, he bit me, just like he used to." Her other hand shook as she raised it to the neckline of her jumper and pulled it down to expose a bruised scar that looked suspiciously like teeth marks in her shoulder.

"Afterwards, he said things would go back to the way they used to be. He said he'd look after me, said Jeremy had helped him out with a big score when he'd cracked the safe. But he was having some issues shifting the larger items."

"Did he happen to mention what those larger items might be? Did he give you any other details about the job he did with Jeremy?"

Kelly swallowed hard and glanced down at the man in the bed. "I already know what the larger items are. Mark and Jeremy were involved together in a gang years ago. They would boost cars together. They moved on to bigger jobs, knocking over houses and businesses. When Jeremy was picked up after one burglary, they tried to pin it on him, but they couldn't link him to the scene. They got Mark instead and he did six months inside."

Kelly sighed and shifted in her chair. "Jeremy got out of the gang after that, cleaned his life up and got a job. We were happy…" Her voice broke then, and Olivia squeezed her hand.

"If Mark is talking about larger items, it means he's trying to shift some cars. He likes Land Rovers, but he'll take anything he can get his hands on."

"You've been very helpful, Kelly." Olivia kept

her hand in Kelly's, allowing the other woman to break down. "We'd like to get you in for a statement and we can get things rolling on your accusation of sexual assault."

Kelly shook her head and pulled her hand away from Olivia. "No, I can't. I've given you all I can. I took a risk telling you. If he finds out…" She sucked in a breath and her hand went back to her stomach. "The baby is all I have left of Jeremy. If Mark knew I told you, he would take that from me, too. He's not going to let me go. He's made that very clear."

"Kelly, you were subjected to a very serious sexual assault—"

Kelly snorted derisively. "Don't you think I know that? I was there. But this wasn't the first time Mark raped me. Why do you think I left him and chose Jeremy? I need you to get him for what he did to Jeremy. It's the only way…"

"Kelly, we'll do all we can, but your statement—"

Kelly leaned back in her chair, incredulity moulding her features. "You're not listening to me at all. I can't go against him like that. You need to find another way." She folded her arms over her chest. "I won't do it. I won't risk my baby's life." Her expression became mutinous.

Olivia raised her hand, a placating gesture. "I hear you. You've given us a lot to go on, and while I can't make any promises, we'll do our best."

Kelly's face crumpled. "You mean there's nothing you can do. Oh God, he's going to get away with it, isn't he?" Her voice became muffled as she buried her head in her hands.

Maz touched Olivia's shoulder, and she glanced up at him in surprise. He jerked his head towards the door, letting her know without having to open his mouth that they needed to leave.

"Kelly, is there someone we can contact to come and be with you?"

The young woman straightened her shoulders, brushing the tears from her face. "No. Mark will be here soon."

Olivia froze. "He's coming here?"

Kelly nodded and took Jeremy's hand in hers again. "I told you, he won't let me go. That's why I need you to get him."

Olivia sat for a moment, staring at the woman next to her. When Kelly looked at her, there was an emptiness in her eyes. "You need to go. Things are already—"

Olivia got to her feet before Kelly finished. "Of course, I'm sorry. We'll go." She made it as far as the door before she stopped and looked back at the couple. Kelly had placed her head back on the sheet next to Jeremy's hand. Her eyes were closed, but there was a stillness to her that frightened Olivia. She knew what desperation was. There had been plenty of nights after Alfred's attack where she had contemplated finishing the job he had started. Nights where she had felt she did not deserve to carry on. But she'd had people around her who had seen the darkness reflected in her. People who loved and cared for her. They had pulled her from the void she had slipped into.

After speaking to Kelly, Olivia knew the one who would have pulled her from the void was lying in the bed with a machine keeping his body functioning. But the machine could not restore the person he had been. It could not fix the damage sustained.

"I'm not supposed to say this," Olivia said. Maz froze next to her. "But I promise I will do everything in my power to bring him to justice."

Kelly turned her face so that she could focus on Olivia's face. "That's all I ask."

Olivia slipped out into the hall after Maz. His feelings on the matter were painted across his face but Olivia chose to keep quiet and keep walking.

CHAPTER FORTY

"SIR, there's something I wanted to speak to you about." Drew paused in the open doorway of the Monk's office.

The Monk—whose head was buried in a pile of paperwork—beckoned Drew inside. "Make it quick."

Drew dropped down into the chair across from the desk and leaned forward, propping his elbows on his knees. "I've got a favour to ask, sir."

The Monk paused and glanced up, his shrewd eyes raking over Drew's face. "What kind of favour?"

Screwing up his face, Drew shrugged. "The usual kind."

"So, nothing I'm going to like." Gregson sighed and leaned back in his chair. "All right, spit it out."

"Now that Popov is in custody and we're tying up loose ends—"

"If you think running down leads so we can make

this case as airtight as possible for CPS is just tying up loose ends, you need your head examined, man."

Drew grinned. "The case is already airtight, sir. Spending so much time on it is starting to feel like overkill, not to mention the fact that we're basically just raking over old ground. Ms Meakin is running down the last of his contacts. Unless something new comes out of that, we're spinning our wheels."

Gregson grunted but he didn't disagree, and Drew took that as a sign to continue.

"The team needs something new to sink its teeth into. Something that will help bring us all together after everything that has happened." He left out the part where Harriet was welcomed back to the team. As much as he wanted it to happen, he was only too aware just how risk averse The Monk truly was. With the precarious silence that had descended after Lila Uxley's arrest, Drew knew his boss would not fancy kicking the hornet's nest that was the British media back into high gear by bringing Harriet back on board.

No, if Drew wanted Harriet back, he would need to be strategic about it. He needed a case that only Harriet could help them with; one so important that Gregson would have no choice but to reinstate her. What he needed was a bloody miracle.

"And you happen to know what that something is, eh?" Before Drew could respond, the Monk continued. "Please tell me you're not going to ask for the 'murder farm'."

"Murder farm, sir?" Drew feigned ignorance. He'd heard the nickname assigned to the case in the press.

Gregson eyed Drew. "I may have been born at night, Haskell, but it wasn't last night. I know you're angling to get on that case. The answer is no."

"Sir, they're drowning over there. You and I both know they don't have the resources for something of this magnitude. I thought our task force was created for the express purpose of dealing with such complicated, and high-profile murders."

Gregson pinched the bridge of his nose and let his head rest on the back of his chair. "Ordinarily, I'd agree. And another time, I might be able to swing it. But everything that happened with Dr Quinn has left us in a bit of a bind. You and I both know we're not exactly popular around here. The other teams all believe we get too much. They feel if they were given the same kind of funding, then they would get the same results."

Drew snorted. He'd heard the gossip. It was nearly impossible to miss. If he were in their position, he'd probably feel the same way.

"Sir, with all due respect, the people who lost their lives in that house deserve our best. Now, I know DS Scofield will do his best with what he's been given, but it won't be enough. Don't let inter-office bollocks get in the way of bringing the bastard who murdered that family to justice."

Gregson looked bemused. "Tell me how you

really feel, DI Haskell." There was no denying the razor edge in the DCI's voice.

Drew knew he'd overstepped. "I'm sorry, sir, that was out of line."

Gregson waved the apology away. "Go. I won't make any promises, but I'll see if DI Brooks is in a sharing mood. If he's not, then I'm not going to press him."

Drew was already heading for the door, his step lighter than it had been.

"Do you hear me, Drew? If he's not interested in our help, I won't force him."

"Of course, sir. I understand." As far as Drew was concerned, the Monk had all but promised he would get them in on the case.

CHAPTER FORTY-ONE

MARTINA SCROLLED through the online brochure for the residential care home she'd been looking into after her father's accident. Things could not carry on with Mum as they were, no matter what her father said. As much as she hated the idea of handing her mother's care over to strangers, it was becoming painfully clear that she soon wouldn't have a choice.

She'd increased the nursing care for her mother, but the cost was beyond anything she could handle long term. She'd already burned through a large chunk of her own savings and when Dad had asked her to check his savings account, Martina had been dismayed to find it had dwindled to almost nothing. Not that he'd seemed surprised when she'd told him.

If anything, he'd seemed shocked to learn there was anything left at all. And when she'd asked him what had happened to the money, he'd looked at her as though she was ten years old again before patiently explaining that he'd hired some additional home help during the months prior. "Just some people to help keep the house looking nice. Your mother always did like a clean and tidy house. I don't want her thinking I'm letting her standards slip."

Martina flipped over to the calculations page for the level of care she'd been told her mother would need, and grimaced. How was she supposed to pay for it? She closed her eyes and sighed.

"It looks like we might have a lead after all," Ambrose said, next to her. Martina's eyes sprang open, and she watched him bounce excitedly on his feet, reminding her of a dog begging for table scraps.

Seeing Ambrose's behaviour brought a smile to Martina's lips. His movements seemed at odds with his hulking frame.

"The lab has come back with a DNA match in the system."

Martina immediately perked up. They'd all but given up hope of getting the person responsible. She'd hoped Dr Quinn could work some of her magic and help them out, but that seemed more impossible with each passing day.

"It can't be Andy Hadfield. I already checked his background, and there was nothing."

Ambrose grinned at her. "It's not Andy. They found trace amounts of vomit on the floor. Apparently, somebody tried to clean it up. They used bleach, but they missed a spot."

"Well, don't keep me in suspense," Martina said. "Tell me who our mystery person is."

"The DNA matched a Jeremy Benson. I've got his address here and—"

Something tugged at the back of Martina's mind. The name was familiar, but she couldn't quite remember why. "Wait, I know that name."

"I didn't see your name in his file, but you might have been part of the team that picked him up a few years back. He was picked up for burglary, but they had to drop the charges when they couldn't tie any of the stolen property to him." Ambrose flipped through the file in front of him. "Another bloke took the rap for it when he was caught trying to shift stolen items. A Mark Robinson."

Martina shook her head. "Nah, that doesn't ring any bells, but Jeremy does. It'll come to me, I'm sure. Shall we go and have a little chat with Jeremy? See if he has an answer for why his DNA is at the scene of a triple murder?"

With a smile, Ambrose snatched his coat from his chair. "I thought you'd never ask."

THE HOUSE WAS CLOAKED in darkness when Ambrose parked on the street outside. "Doesn't look like anyone is in," he said, leaning over the steering wheel so he could peer out through the windscreen.

"I'll knock." Martina was already pushing her

door open as she spoke. She slipped out into the drizzly rain and, with her head down, jogged up to the front door. She rapped sharply on the wood and waited. Turning to face the street, she scanned the houses nearby. With no answer, she knocked again, a little louder this time.

Moving from the front porch, Martina walked halfway down the path and then turned to stare back at the upper windows. Nothing.

Movement caught her eye, and she looked towards the next door neighbour's house. The curtains twitched and then dropped back into place. Without waiting, Martina made a beeline for the neighbour's front door. If she was lucky, she might get to find out when Jeremy was due home.

The front door of the house cracked open before Martina could reach for the knocker. The woman framed in the light that spilled from the hallway reminded Martina of her mother before she was ill. Despite being small, the woman's rounded frame was sturdy and she held the door open only wide enough to peer out into the rapidly darkening night.

"They're not in," she said, her accent betraying her Irish heritage.

"Can you tell me when I can expect them to return?" Martina moved closer and watched the woman flinch back into the hall. It wasn't until she was within touching distance of the door that Martina realised the safety chain was on.

The stranger gave a half shrug and started to close the door.

"Wait—" Martina fished in her pocket for her warrant card. "I'm DC Martina Nicoll. I'm looking for a Jeremy Benson."

The woman paused, her expression uncertain. "Let me take a closer look." She thrust a hand through the gap in the door. Martina handed the card over and waited.

Behind her she heard Ambrose huffing as he climbed from the car and slammed his door. The woman handed the card back and then glanced over Martina's shoulder to where Ambrose waited. "Is that fella with you?"

With the ghost of a smile, Martina nodded. "That's DS Ambrose Scofield. It's imperative we speak with Mr Benson, so if you could—"

The woman's expression grew sorrowful. "I don't think poor Jeremy will be speaking to anyone anytime soon."

"Why not? Has he left, or—"

"You lot really don't keep each other in the loop much, do ya? Jeremy's in the hospital." She slipped the chain from the door and let it swing wide. "Here, come in out of the rain. And tell that horse of a lad to get himself in here, too. I'll stick the kettle on. Will tea do?"

Before Martina could argue, the woman had shuffled quickly back into the house and disappeared from view. With no option but to follow, Martina glanced over at Ambrose.

"Come on then…" As soon as Ambrose reached her, Martina muttered beneath her breath, "Horse of a lad."

"What does that mean?"

Martina smiled. "I don't know, but it suits you, I think."

He pulled a face and followed her inside.

"Jeremy's been in hospital for a while now. The High Dependency Unit, I think Kelly said. She stays with him as much as she can. Poor thing is run ragged going back and forth, and her pregnant too."

"What happened exactly?" Ambrose asked.

Martina shot a sideways glance at Ambrose, who had managed to fold himself into the small Ikea rocking chair next to the couch. He was hunched forward, as though afraid that if he leaned too heavily on the frame, it would collapse beneath him. But it was the sight of his large hands holding the dainty bone China cup that brought Martina the most joy. It was like watching a grown man attend a doll's tea party.

The woman, who Martina had learned was Mrs Siobhan Hanrahan, set her own cup back on the side table next to her side of the couch. "They said it was a break-in. You know, like all those ones that have been going on around the place." She sighed. "I've been around the block a time or two and I've never seen a break-in like this."

The bells which had started to ring in Martina's brain earlier were now screaming. She'd heard something about a break-in and assault while she'd been in the hospital with her father, but she wasn't clear on the details.

"I was the one who called your lot that night. Fat lot of good that did. The fella responsible was long gone by the time the police arrived." She folded her hands in her lap, her fingers picking at a stray thread in her black trousers. "I was in bed watching an episode of *Killer in My Village*. I don't sleep very well since the doctor changed my heart medication. Anyway, it was the episode about that poor woman stabbed in Hertfordshire. Do you know the case?"

Martina shook her head and took a sip of tea.

"You should take a look at it. It might help, you know? So, there I am, sitting in bed watching telly when I hear all this noise from Kelly's house."

Colour suffused Siobhan's cheeks. "Now, I'm no prude but the walls are paper thin around here and I've mentioned this to Kelly before. But they're young and don't want some old biddy poking her nose in where it doesn't belong. So, I turned up the volume because it was getting into the meat of the episode." She trailed off and stared down into her cup. "Maybe if I hadn't... Well, there's nothing I can do now to change the past, is there?" Siobhan glanced at Martina and Ambrose before nodding to herself. "As I'm watching, I start hearing odd noises. And then the screaming started."

The colour slowly drained from Siobhan's face as she relived that night. "You hear stories, you know. And you see it on the telly but..." She swallowed. "I could hear the poor *creatúr* screaming for her life, and then it was muffled. There was this knocking, you know. Like a headboard on the wall. And I knew... I just knew. I used to be a nurse, but hearing that, I froze. I can remember my hands shook so much when I was trying to dial 999 that I wasn't sure I'd manage it." She took a breath and smoothed her hands down over her trousers as though that alone could help to clear the memories.

"I got out of bed and went round. The front door was wide open, and I found Kelly bleeding and crying on the floor next to Jeremy." The woman looked down at her hands. "I tried to help him, but there wasn't much I could do. Kelly was inconsolable... And it was hard to know what blood was hers and what came from Jeremy. I really thought she might lose the baby..."

Ambrose moved first. As she'd spoken, he had set his cup aside and now, he reached across the distance between his chair and hers and took her hand in his. "You did all you could, Siobhan. Not many people would help the way you did."

She gave a jerky nod. "No, I suppose many wouldn't. I'm not sure why not. The world feels darker than it used to be. People have seen too much, I suppose. Nothing surprises us anymore."

Martina said nothing but she agreed, nonetheless. Bad things had always happened, that never changed. What had changed was that people seemed to be getting more desensitised to the world around them. Whether that was caused by a constant bombardment of media, she didn't know. But something had shifted.

"You didn't say what you wanted to speak with Jeremy about," Siobhan said. "Nothing serious, I hope."

"It's nothing to worry about." Ambrose shared his most disarming smile with her. Martina had seen many people melt in the face of his charm, but Siobhan was not one of them.

"Don't give me that. You lot don't come knocking on doors at this time of the evening unless it's something important. Whatever it is, Jeremy won't be helping you anytime soon. The poor lad..."

"What hospital did you say he'd been taken to?" Martina edged forward in her chair.

"James Cook in Middlesborough. Such a long way for Kelly." She shook her head, tears shimmering in her eyes.

"We won't take any more of your time," Ambrose said, climbing carefully to his feet. "Thanks for the cuppa."

Siobhan struggled to her feet.

"No need," Ambrose said. "We can see ourselves out."

"I'm sure you can, but after everything I've just told you, I'd rather see you to the door so I can lock up again after. I always feel better with the chain on, and the deadbolt fastened."

Colour spread up Ambrose's neck. "Of course."

She shuffled after them down the hall, her slippers making a soft shushing noise as they passed over the worn carpet.

Once they'd said their goodbyes and were back on the street headed for the car, Martina finally broke her silence. "Well fuck. There goes our lead."

Ambrose shrugged. "I won't be happy until I see him in the bed. Maybe she's got it wrong. He might not be as bad as she said."

Martina chewed her lip but said nothing. There had been the ring of truth to Siobhan's words. Pulling her phone from her pocket, she did a quick Google search. Pausing at the side of the car, she held her phone up so Ambrose could see the news article.

"Well, fuck." His face twisted in anger as he unlocked the car and slipped in.

Returning her phone to its place, she followed his lead. The break in the case that had earlier seemed so promising was well and truly gone down the toilet. And there was not a damn thing anyone could do about it.

CHAPTER FORTY-TWO

OLIVIA CROSSED over to Maz's desk and waited for him to finish typing up his report. As though he could sense her eagerness, he slowed his pace to a crawl.

Finally, unable to wait a moment longer, she planted her hands on the desk, covering the pages of notes he was referring to. "We should tell Haskell everything we learned at the hospital."

Maz swung around in his chair. "We don't have a whole lot. We've got the word of someone who isn't willing to make a statement and a bloke in a coma."

"It's still something to go on," Olivia said.

"What's something to go on?" DI Haskell passed through the space, his coat over his arm and a coffee cup in his hand.

"We went to the hospital and—"

The DI shook his head, cutting Olivia off. "Save it for the meeting."

"Meeting?" Maz straightened in his chair.

"I'm calling a morning briefing. I want everyone in the conference room in five minutes. I just need to swing by the DCI's office first." He carried on without breaking his pace, reaching his office in just a few quick strides.

Olivia returned her attention to Maz, but he was too busy watching the DI to notice.

"You know, I get it," Olivia said softly.

"Get what?" Maz could not have sounded less interested in what she was saying. He would never forgive her for what had happened. And while she couldn't exactly blame him, she was also tired of apologising. There was nothing else she could do or say to change the past.

"Forget it," Olivia moved away, leaving Maz to his own thoughts.

TRUE TO HIS WORD, five minutes later, DI Haskell sat on the edge of the desk at the front of the largest room on their floor. They called it the Conference Room, but it was more like a dumping ground for broken chairs, extra desks, and a few unused whiteboards that had been procured when the task force had originally been set up.

Olivia sat near the back and watched as Maz and Jodie entered the room, their heads close together as they whispered conspiratorially to one another.

"This seat taken?" DC Green dropped into the chair next to Olivia, dragging her from her silent contemplation with a jolt.

"Does it look taken?" There was an edge to her words that she had not intended.

"Ouch, who pissed in your cornflakes?" Tim grinned at her, but upon seeing her expression, his smile wilted at the edges. "Look, I'll move if you want." He started to stand, a hurt look in his eyes.

"Don't be stupid. Sit." She grabbed his arm and forced him back into the chair. "It's not about you." Her gaze flickered back to Maz just as he threw his head back and laughed at something Jodie said.

"DS Arya still giving you the cold shoulder?"

"How did you know?"

"He's not exactly subtle about it," Tim said, leaning back into his chair and stretching his long, lean legs in front of him. "He's just pissed because the DCI held him responsible and put a black mark on his perfect little record."

Olivia eyed Tim. "That's a bit harsh."

"I don't think so." Tim glanced over at Maz. "Would the DI behave like that if Gregson pulled him up?" Without waiting for an answer, Tim continued, "No, he'd take it on the chin. The DI knows how to carry responsibility, the DS hasn't got a clue." Tim edged closer and lowered his voice to a whisper. "Haven't you ever wondered why he hasn't moved up in the ranks despite getting the rank of sergeant before the DI did?"

Olivia had never thought of it like that, but now that Tim had put the idea in her mind, she couldn't ignore it. He was right. A DS was supposed to show leadership skills, something Maz never did. If he wasn't told directly to do something by either the DCI or the DI, then he was happy to stay comfortable. How many times had Olivia been forced to coax him into following a lead with her? And while she was impulsive, a failing she was working on, he did not seem interested in smoothing out any of his issues.

DI Haskell cleared his throat, dragging everyone's attention to the front of the room. "Right, I want you all to hear it here first. As soon as I get the go ahead from the DCI, we'll be lending a hand on the triple murder that happened at the farmhouse in Saltergate Bank."

A frisson of excitement ran through the room and Olivia straightened up.

"We won't be taking the lead," the DI said. "This will still be—"

DCI Gregson chose that moment to enter the room. "Haskell, we need to talk."

"I was just getting the team up to speed on the case, sir."

Gregson's expression was thunderous. "You need to wrap this up."

As though he could read exactly what thoughts lay behind the DCI's expression, DI Haskell gave a curt nod. His face was unreadable as he turned back to the room. "What progress are you making on the Caz Popov follow-up?"

"I've been through his contacts, and while many of them have some form, I can't find any connection between them and anything we have," Jodie piped up.

Drew let his chin drop towards his chest as he leaned back against the desk. "So, we have nothing is what you're telling me. Are you sure there's nothing in his financials? Nothing we can use to show this is just a ruse to get us off the backs of the county lines gang Melissa was onto?"

Jodie shook her head. "There's nothing to see. I've searched everywhere. If he took money to make that confession, it never entered his accounts."

"Drew, we need to talk," Gregson said.

Scrubbing his hand over his mouth, DI Haskell nodded. "Fine, dismissed—"

"Sir, wait!" Olivia was already on her feet before he'd finished speaking.

The DI glanced in her direction before he shot a look at the DCI. "Fine, go on."

"As you know, I went to the hospital yesterday with DS Arya to speak with Kelly Walker about the break-in that happened."

"Make it fast, DC Crandell." There was a warning implicit in the DI's voice.

"It's not looking good for Jeremy Benson. According to his partner, the doctors are not confident that he will wake up. She alleges she was sexually assaulted during the attack--"

Confusion crossed DI Haskell's face. "I read through that file yesterday and her original statement does not mention a sexual assault."

Olivia swallowed hard. Maz caught her eye and shook his head.

"She claims she didn't bring up the assault earlier because she was afraid of what her partner would think if he found out. But now that she's convinced he won't wake-up..." Olivia trailed off.

"Fine. Take her statement and—"

"Sir, she doesn't want to make a statement."

DI Haskell had already started to move towards the back of the room, but he halted as her words sank in. "What?"

"She has reason to believe the man responsible for their attack will hurt her and her unborn child if she tries to accuse him."

"Did she give you a name?"

Olivia nodded and glanced down at her notes. "Mark Robinson. I've looked into—"

"Wait, did you say Mark Robinson?" Jodie cut her off.

"Yeah. Apparently, he and Jeremy were involved in some criminal activity when they were younger. Jeremy got out but Mark did a stint in prison, and when he came out, he climbed the rungs in the gang."

"What is it, Ms Meakin?" DI Haskell moved

back to the top of the room, ignoring the sharp look from the DCI.

"There's a Mark Robinson in Caz Popov's contacts. I don't know if they're one and the same—"

"But it needs checking out," DI Haskell said. "Let me know what you find."

"Good work, DC Crandell. Keep trying with the victim. Let's see if she can't give you something more to go on." DI Haskell hurried to the end of the room and disappeared out through the door before Olivia could utter another word.

"Good work!" Tim patted her on the shoulder, but Olivia ignored him.

Kelly had seemed adamant that she would not be willing to bring charges against Mark Robinson. And for Olivia, the idea of trying to force her into doing something she was so obviously terrified of doing did not sit well. Then again, she couldn't ignore DI Haskell's order.

"Shit."

CHAPTER FORTY-THREE

"DI BROOKS IS NOT interested in our help," Gregson said.

Drew stared at the DCI, waiting for him to continue, but when he said nothing else, Drew felt compelled to prompt him. "And..."

"And, what? That's it. DI Brooks does not want our assistance. He made it perfectly clear that he'd rather chew through his own leg than have us work on his case."

"Right, so who do we speak to now?"

DCI Gregson stared at him like he'd completely lost his mind. "Nobody. We don't speak to anyone else, DI Haskell. He doesn't want our help. That's it."

"Sir, I don't think I understand. You don't normally back down from a challenge."

"This isn't about backing down from a challenge, Haskell. This is playing nice with the other teams we work with. I can't just steamroll my way onto a case because you asked me to. We get invited, or it overlaps with something larger we're working on. You know how these things work."

Drew ran his hand down his face. "With all due respect, sir."

"Don't give me that shit. Whenever you start a sentence with that, you mean, 'with no respect'. Accept it, there's nothing I can do."

"This is too big for them, sir. Have you seen the papers recently? They're getting absolutely dragged through the mud because they have yet to come up with anything concrete. And it doesn't help that other farmers in the area are demanding answers. People are afraid."

Gregson dropped into his chair. "Don't you think I know that? But these things are delicate, Drew. After the shit show with Harriet, I have to tread carefully. There are already grumblings of wanting the team dismantled because it's such a huge drain on resources. We need the support of the other teams, not their ire."

Drew spun away. "That's crap. Everyone knows that what happened with Harriet, it wasn't her fault. This is just jealousy."

Gregson sighed. "You're probably right, but that doesn't change the fact that if we try and force our way in where we're not wanted, it'll come back to bite us on the arse."

Drew flexed his hands, curling and uncurling his fingers.

"Tell me you understand, Drew…"

Drew stared out into the office, ignoring the man behind him.

"Detective Inspector, tell me you understand what I'm saying to you."

"Aye, I hear you."

"I doubt that very much."

Drew turned back to face him. "What am I supposed to do, then?" He spread his hands wide. "It's not fair."

"The world isn't fair. But we do our best with what we're given."

"Still doesn't make it right." Seeing the look on Gregson's face, Drew nodded. "I understand, sir. I'll back off."

Without waiting, he pulled open the office door and left. DS Arya caught his eye as he crossed the floor, but Drew ignored him and made a beeline for the back stairs.

CHAPTER FORTY-FOUR

OLIVIA PAUSED in the hospital hallway. Kelly had been surprised when she had called but had agreed to meet. And now that she was here, Olivia could feel the knot which had formed in the pit of her stomach tightening. The idea of going in there to force Kelly to make a statement against the man she was so afraid of didn't sit right with her. But what choice did she have? Jodie had cross referenced the name Mark Robinson, and they were certain it was the same man. If he was capable of such a brutal attack, then it only stood to reason that he was worth looking into in connection with the attack on DI Appleton.

The more Olivia thought about it, the worse she felt. Her head was starting to throb and as she turned her head, a tell-tale sparkle at the edge of her vision told her that an aura migraine was on the way.

Swearing under her breath, she moved away from

the doors to the High Dependency Unit and hurried to a set of seats in the corridor. Quickly fishing through her bag, she grabbed a packet of Migraleve tablets and popped two of them into the palm of her hand. With her free hand, she grabbed her water bottle but was disappointed to discover it was already empty.

Scanning the corridor, she spotted a vending machine at the opposite end, next to a set of heavy double doors.

A couple of minutes later, can of Diet Coke in hand, she sat down on the chairs and blew out a breath. She didn't have a choice. No matter what her gut told her, Kelly needed to make a statement. The forensics report from Kelly and Jeremy's house gave them absolutely nothing to go on. If Mark had been in the house, they had not found any trace of him.

Not that it would stop them from trying to place him at the scene. Once he was in custody, Jodie would do a thorough dive on the location of his phone on the night in question. But Olivia had the sinking feeling that someone like Mark Robinson would not be caught so easily.

Leaning back in the plastic chairs, she let her head rest on the wall behind her. She closed her eyes, doing her best to ignore the waves of light that were slowly beginning to pulse on the inside of her eyelids.

Booming laughter echoed down the hall, bouncing off the walls and reverberating through the space. It made Olivia cringe. She'd heard that laugh before. Straightening up, she glanced down the hall and watched as DS Ambrose Scofield and DC Martina Nicoll came striding through the double doors.

DC Nicoll spotted her first, and paused. She nudged her colleague in the side and jerked her head in Olivia's direction. Olivia watched them approach, curiosity momentarily helping to chase the worst of her migraine away.

"She pulled it off, I see." DC Nicoll spoke first. A warm smile brightened her face, making her look young, almost vulnerable.

"Good to see you again," Olivia said, getting to her feet. "Who are we referring to?"

Confusion swept the smile from Martina's face. "Dr Quinn..." She shot a calculating glance at her colleague.

"Please tell me you didn't," DS Scofield grumbled.

"We need the help, Ambrose. Even you have to admit that."

Olivia watched the two of them bicker back and forth, reminding her of how it used to be between her and Maz.

"Dr Quinn hasn't spoken with me." Olivia saw a break in their conversation and took it. "However, our DCI made it very clear this morning that we were not to get involved in your case. Your DI was not best pleased to be asked."

"Brooks will have my arse in a sling for this," Ambrose muttered.

Martina's shrewd gaze flipped back to Olivia. "Then what are you doing here?"

"I'm following up with a victim regarding a serious assault. She agreed to speak with me. The DI wants me to persuade her to make a statement."

"You wouldn't by any chance be here to see Kelly Walker and Jeremy Benson?" DC Nicoll asked, raising a brow at Olivia.

"You know about the case?"

Martina glanced from Ambrose to Olivia, a wide smile curving her lips. "I think I might know a way we can persuade DI Brooks to agree to DI Haskell's team helping us out."

CHAPTER FORTY-FIVE

HARRIET SLIPPED the fluffy jumper on over her head just as the doorbell rang. Struggling to get it all the way on, she hurried out the hall to the door. She was beginning to release the fear she had felt around answering the door, but as she unlocked the bolt, a prickle of fear traced a finger up her spine.

The door swung open, revealing Drew standing on the doorstep. He held a bottle of wine in one hand and a plastic bag in the other.

"I thought I'd try and make up for the way I behaved the last time I was here…" He trailed off and smiled sheepishly at her. "If you've got plans, I can—"

"Don't be silly. Come in." She stood aside, holding the door wide.

"If David is here, I brought enough for everyone." Drew squeezed past her, bringing with him the scent of rain and leather.

"David isn't here," Harriet said, letting her gaze drop.

Drew paused, as though waiting for her to elaborate but she chose not to. When she said nothing, Drew shrugged and carried on into the kitchen.

"I can't say I'm sad about it," he said. "I'm bloody starving, and you know how I hate to share."

Harriet paused in the doorway and watched as Drew moved easily about in the space. He went to the cupboards and took out the plates before grabbing two glasses and setting them on the kitchen island.

"Drew, it's not that I'm not glad to see you, but…"

He stopped, leaning heavily on the kitchen counter. There was something in his eyes, something she wasn't used to seeing. Harriet tried to remember the last time she had seen such a haunted look in his gaze. The first time they had worked together, she had seen a glimmer of it, but she hadn't asked him about it. They hadn't known each other well enough for her to go poking her nose in. But now…

"You're wondering what I'm doing here."

Harriet nodded. "Yeah, I am."

"We're friends, aren't we?"

"Of course."

"So, can't friends do things like this?"

"Drew…"

"Melissa and I broke up."

For a moment, Harriet stared at him. The words refused to penetrate her brain.

"I don't understand. You were happy..."

Drew sighed. "That's not true. Melissa and I, we have a complicated history. But one thing I'm sure about, we're much better suited to being friends."

"I'm sorry."

Drew stared down at the countertop, the seconds slowly ticking by. "Honestly, I'm glad it's over. We weren't good for each other."

"I'm still sorry," Harriet said, slowly crossing into the space. "But if that's how you really feel about it, then I'm relieved for you."

"It is. I can't keep burying my head in the sand. Melissa was never the one for me..."

Drew raised his face and met her gaze head on. Harriet could feel his unspoken words. They pressed against her skin, and for a moment, she found herself wishing he would say what was on his mind. Instead, he grabbed the bottle opener and set about opening the wine with a sense of urgency.

"A toast," Drew said gruffly as he fought with the bottle. Finally, he pulled the cork free and poured two large measures of wine. He passed a glass to her and raised his. "To getting back on track."

Harriet let her glass touch his before taking a sip.

Drew didn't waste any time serving the food. He chatted amicably, but Harriet couldn't shake the feeling that there was something he wasn't telling her.

When they were settled in the living room, Harriet shifted on the cushion she'd placed on the floor and watched Drew on the other side of the coffee table. Unable to wait any longer, she decided to finally acknowledge the elephant in the room. "Why are you here?"

Drew shot a surprised look at her. "What do you mean? I told you, I'm here—"

Harriet shook her head and set her fork down on the side of her plate. "You forget, I know you, Drew Haskell. There's something you're not saying."

He jabbed his fork into a piece of chicken before cramming it into his mouth. Harriet waited impatiently as he chewed and swallowed. He shot a sideways look at her and grimaced before taking a big gulp of wine. "Fine. There is something."

"I knew it!"

"Look, I wanted to come because I really do miss…" He waved his hands in the air helplessly. "I miss what we have. I miss…" He cut himself off before he finished. "I wanted to come. But there's something I need your help with."

Harriet sat back against the couch. "Drew, I can't help. After everything that happened—"

He waved her concerns away. "As much as I want to, I can't ask you to come back officially… That's not my call to make. If it was, you would never have been shut out."

A small smile curled the corners of Harriet's mouth. "Then it's probably wise that you're not the one making those kinds of decisions." She sighed and smoothed down the front of her trousers. "Even if you were, I wouldn't come back." It pained her to say it.

"What? Why?"

"Because I've seen how vulnerable I make you and the team. I leave you open to the mercy of unscrupulous people who would seek to destroy everything good that you do."

"Don't be daft. We're not vulnerable because of you, Harriet. You make us stronger. You make us better."

"Thanks, but what I bring to the table is not enough. I've had a lot of time to think about this, Drew. You won't change my mind about it."

Drew shoved his hand back through his hair, causing it to stand on end. "You can't let those bastards win. You bailing is exactly what they want. They want you afraid... He wants you afraid and isolated and I'm sorry, but I won't let that happen."

She knew exactly who he was referring to. And while she hadn't heard from Dr Jonathan Connors since she'd returned from Ireland, she couldn't disagree with Drew's assessment of the situation.

"I..."

"Harriet," Drew leaned across the table and grabbed her hand in his. "Promise you won't cut yourself off from me..." He let his gaze drop to his hand on hers and slowly pulled away. "...From the team. You're one of us, whether you like it or not."

Her hand tingled where he had touched her and for a moment, Harriet's mouth refused to obey the commands from her brain. A beat later, she found her voice. "If it means that much to you, then I promise."

Drew nodded, a look of relief crossing his face. "Good. We can't let that prick win. I won't stop looking for a way to prove his connection to Lila Uxley and their plan to destroy your reputation."

"Jonathan is smart. He'll have some excuse ready so you can't pin anything on him. Not to mention, nobody will care. It's far more salacious to believe a psychologist working for the police is some kind of predator. Nobody wants to hear about a petty man hellbent on revenge because he was rejected."

Disgust washed over Drew's features as he took another mouthful of wine. "Blokes like that—"

Harriet cut him off. "Let's not ruin our evening by talking about someone like Connors. I'd much rather forget about him if I could."

"Sure, I understand." He sighed and picked up his fork, resuming his meal. She watched him for a few moments as he stabbed at the vegetables and chicken on his plate. Clearly, he was still thinking about Jonathan Connors, so Harriet did the only thing she could.

"What do you need my help with?"

Drew's head snapped up. "You said…"

"I know, but what kind of friend would I be if I turned you away when you needed me?"

Drew didn't waste a moment and climbed to his

feet. "Give me a second." He was gone before Harriet could utter a word.

She sat and waited as Drew disappeared into the kitchen and Harriet expected him to reappear any moment. Instead, her patience was rewarded with the sound of the front door slamming shut.

Confused, she stood and crossed to the bay window. Cracking the blinds, she peered out onto the street and caught sight of Drew crossing the road to his car. He remained a shadow as he clambered into the back seat. The seconds ticked by and Harriet watched in amazement as he got back out of the car, a large box in his arms. Setting her wine glass down on the coffee table, she hurried from the living room and into the hall.

Tugging the door open, she stood aside while Drew carried the box past her and into the living room.

"What's going on?" She closed and locked the door before following him inside.

"I went to Gregson and asked him permission to get in on the triple murder at Saltergate Bank."

"And he let you? Just like that?" Harriet didn't bother trying to hide her surprise. When she had spoken to Martina about the case, it had seemed like a long shot. And while she had faith in Drew, Harriet knew just how unbreakable the red tape of protocol could be.

"Not exactly. We managed to connect the case to

another we were looking into and through that we found a connection to Caz Popov."

"The man who admitted to trying to murder DI Appleton?"

Drew nodded. "You should have seen the look on the Monk's face when I told him we had a connection. But he was only too happy to take it to DI Brooks. What I wouldn't give to have been a fly on the wall when that conversation happened." Drew's grin pulled a smile from Harriet. It was good to see him so animated.

"So, what's all this?" She gestured to the box he held in his arms.

"I was hoping you would have a look through some of the reports I managed to get from Ambrose's team. I told him I was going to ask you, and he was fine about it."

Harriet folded her arms over her chest and approached the box slowly as though it contained a poisonous snake and not just a pile of paper. "I don't know, Drew. This could be a very bad idea."

He dumped the box onto the couch and pulled off the lid. "I've been through the information and to be honest we don't have much. Ambrose and Martina have suspicions but no evidence. We need somebody with an outside perspective to look it over and give us an idea of the direction we should be moving in."

Picking up the first file, Harriet sat down next to the box before she started to flip through the pages.

"You've clearly kept quite a bit from the media," she said, grimacing as she read through the report.

"We had to. It would comprise the case if they knew all the details."

Harriet made a non-committal noise, only half-listening to him as the details of the case began to pull her in.

HOURS LATER, Harriet sat back on the couch and sipped at her wine. "It's a mess."

Drew propped his body up on his elbow as he lounged on the floor. "There's just too many possibilities."

"There is, however, there's something off about the entire situation. The murders feel deeply personal but the burglary that has all the hallmarks of the other burglaries plaguing the area. They feel like two completely different scenarios."

"Exactly. But the forensics can't be ignored."

"No, it can't..." Harriet glanced down at the notes she had scribbled hastily. "And this Jeremy Benson, does he have a history of violence?"

"Petty thefts, back when he was a teen," Drew said. "A cash machine was ripped out of the wall at a Co-Op and there was a suspicion that Benson was involved. But he had an alibi, and they couldn't link him to the crime. Somebody else went down for it instead. By all accounts, Benson got out after that narrow escape and kept his nose clean. Until his DNA was found at the farmhouse."

"It makes no sense," Harriet said softly.

"I was going to head over to the farmhouse in the morning if you felt like joining?"

Feeling torn, Harriet hesitated. She wanted nothing more than to go with Drew. The desire to belong was overwhelming, but if the wrong people found out...

"Going through the information with you here, is one thing," she said.

"But you're worried what will happen if someone finds out." Drew sighed.

"I am, Drew. If this goes wrong, it could cost you everything."

"The place is closed off and nobody is going to be there, so if you're worried about being seen, you won't be. And honestly, it's a risk I'm willing to take. We need you on this." He sat up straight. "Come with me tomorrow, get a feel for the place. I know you like to walk through the crime scenes if you can."

Harriet glanced down at the crime scene photographs. "It would help. But, Drew, I told you, I can't come back."

"I know what you said, but you can't tell me that looking through this file hasn't felt right."

Harriet opened her mouth, a lie hovering on the tip of her tongue. It would be easier to tell him that doing this didn't give her a thrill. It would be easy to deny that for the first time in weeks she felt like she was right where she was supposed to be, doing exactly what she was meant to do. But Drew would see through it, and their relationship was not one built on lies.

"Drew, you know—"

"I'll make you a deal," Drew said. "Come with me tomorrow. And if walking through the scene helps you to come up with a theory, then I'll go to Gregson and talk to him about getting you officially reinstated. But if we get there and you still don't want to be involved, we can both walk away. No harm, no foul."

"Fine," she said.

Drew's grin was infectious as he reached across the table and held his hand out. "Shake on it."

Harriet took his hand in her own and felt his fingers tighten around hers. They shook on it. She would not lie to him. She couldn't. However, she knew she was not being honest with herself. She stared down at the place where his hand was wrapped around her own. Just how long could she keep lying to herself?

She slipped her hand from his.

"I should go." Drew stood and swayed unsteadily on his feet.

"Absolutely not," she said. "Your room is still available."

Drew shot her a sideways look. "My room, eh?"

Heat crept into her cheeks. "I don't have many

guests stay over. In fact, you are the only one... And, well, it still feels like your room."

An emotion she couldn't read passed over Drew's face. "What happened between you and David?"

The question took her by surprise. And for a moment, Harriet found herself unsure of what to say.

"Nothing," she said. "When the stories in the media continued to spiral, he cut contact. I suppose he thought I wasn't worth the risk."

Drew stared at her, shock written on his face. "You haven't spoken to him?"

"Not since that night you were here, no. I reached out a few times when I was in Ireland, but..." Harriet shrugged and then let her hands fall back to her sides. "I thought when you and he went completely radio silent on me, that..." She cut herself off, swallowing around the lump in her throat. David cutting her off had hurt, she couldn't deny it. But not hearing from Drew had been so much worse.

And when she'd received the call from Olivia to tell her about Lila Uxley and she'd realised Drew had been working to clear her name... She wasn't able to put into words how it had made her feel.

"I didn't cut you off," Drew said gruffly. "You really haven't heard from him?"

She shook her head. "Nothing."

"Bastard."

"It doesn't matter anymore. It's in the past."

"Harriet, I—" He took an unsteady step towards her.

"We should get some sleep." She cut him off. She couldn't be sure, but for a brief moment, she had been certain she had seen pity in his eyes, and that was not something she needed. It was over. Not that it had even really begun, and that was fine. But she did not need to hear Drew apologise and she did not want his pity. She had not pitied him when he'd told her it was over between him and Melissa.

Drew sobered instantly. "Of course, you're right. I'll see you in the morning." He made it to the door, then stopped. Tension sang in Harriet's muscles as he gripped the door frame, and she half expected him to say something else. He glanced back at her. "I'm really glad we did this, Harriet." He swallowed hard. "I missed this."

And then he was gone. She listened to his heavy tread on the stairs as he climbed them slowly. She held herself until the door to his room clicked shut. Dropping down onto the couch, she felt the tension slowly fade, leaving her feeling raw and exposed. Her mind ran over their conversation on a loop and so Harriet did the only thing that she knew would help. Grabbing the files, she settled back onto the couch and began to make notes.

CHAPTER FORTY-SIX

HARRIET REMAINED silent in the front passenger seat as Drew parked the car in front of the farmhouse. The property was remote, the frontage overlooking moorland that stretched for miles. Not that she could see much of the moorland. The space was wreathed in a thick mist that made visibility poor. The fog was so thick, it muffled the sounds of cars as they passed on the road behind them.

Harriet couldn't imagine feeling comfortable living in a place that was so isolated. Then again, perhaps that was just her brain making connections because it knew the intimate details of the crime that had been committed here.

Climbing from the car, she stood on the drive and stared up at the stone house. She already knew from the reports which room had belonged to Willow. Just thinking about the young teenage girl brought a lump to her throat.

It wasn't fair. Willow should still be alive and looking forward to school, and boys, and a life that was her own. Instead, she had been brutally slaughtered.

"Do you want to go in?" Drew said, breaking Harriet's train of thought.

"I thought I would have a walk around out here first, get a feel for the place. You go ahead."

Eyeing her speculatively, Drew rounded the car. "What are you thinking?"

Harriet ducked her head and concentrated on slipping her gloves on to keep out the worst of the biting cold. "We've only just got here."

"Yeah, but I know you spent all night going over the files."

She glanced up at him, schooling her features so as not to betray her surprise. "How could you...?"

"I got up early," Drew said. "When I came downstairs, I found you asleep on the couch with the files spread out around you."

"I wondered where the blanket had come from," she said, striking off in the direction of the side of the house. Drew followed and fell into step next to her. "The report said the patio doors were open when the first officer got here. But the report also mentions a window that was tampered with. The theory is that they got in through the window and left through the patio doors."

She nodded but kept her thoughts to herself.

Once they reached the back of the house, she studied the patio doors. "Which window was it?"

Drew pulled his notes out and flipped through the pages before he pointed to a section further along the back of the house. "It's over there." He moved away and Harriet followed, carefully keeping to the stone path that ran along the back of the house. Drew clambered through the flowerbed that sat below a small window.

"It's this one," he said, addressing his notes. "It opens into the utility room."

"I'd like to go inside now," Harriet said.

Without a word, Drew led her to the door and unlocked it. As Harriet followed him inside, she noted the way her breath formed little clouds in front of her face every time she exhaled. Black smudges covered the window and the window frames, and she did her best to ignore them.

She didn't wait for Drew, allowing her recollections from the reports to guide her way. She found herself in a large country kitchen. This room was somewhat untouched by the brutality that had taken place inside the house. In her mind, Harriet tried to imagine the family gathering together at the table for meals.

Everything she had read about the Hadfields suggested they were the type to come together for food. According to everyone who knew them, they were a close-knit unit. But the kitchen was cold and uninviting, the decor devoid of all personality. It was nothing like Harriet had imagined it to be.

A large black American fridge freezer sat against the back wall, its doors gleaming in the overhead lights. Harriet had expected to see some indications of family life but there was nothing, not even a magnet—a souvenir left over from a family holiday. It reminded her of the kitchen from her own childhood, before her mother's breakdown had driven them into the sea. There's had been a house, one with four walls, doors and windows, but it had never been a home. Was this the same?

She left the kitchen and entered the hall. The forensic team had left the metal stepping plates on the tile floor and Harriet moved onto the nearest one to avoid the rusty streak that snaked across the floor.

She turned slowly, scanning the walls for the spot where… Drew pointed it out before she could find it on her own.

"According to the forensic report, the blood spatter indicates Andrew Hadfield received the first blow to his head here."

Harriet's eyes tracked the marks on the wall to the place where a smeared handprint stained the beige paint.

"The first blow was enough to drive him to his knees. He tried to get up but blood cast-off suggests he received another blow to the back of his skull before he could rise. He crawled a few feet before collapsing at the bottom of the stairs."

Harriet noted the rusty smears on the bottom baluster along with what looked to her like another handprint.

"He was then dragged across the tiles and down the hall to the bathroom—"

As Drew spoke, Harriet moved down the hall, following the stepping plates until she reached the small toilet at the end of the hall.

"By all accounts, the first two blows to Andrew Hadfield's skull would have been enough to cause significant damage," she said quietly.

Drew stood behind her, his expression grim as he surveyed the scene over her shoulder. "The forensic pathologist believes it would have eventually proved fatal."

"So why the overkill?" Harriet indicated the room in front of her. The cistern lid was missing, no doubt removed by the SOCOs during their gathering of evidence. It had shattered during the continued attack on Andrew Hadfield. The individual had dragged his body to the toilet before they had removed the cistern lid and used it to obliterate his facial features.

"Andrew Hadfield was a big bloke. The blows sustained during the initial attack might have proved fatal but death wouldn't have been immediate. Maybe he started to come around and— Christ..." The rustle of papers told Harriet that Drew was reading the post-mortem report. "They found some cranial bone lodged in his nasal passageways and some broken pieces of his teeth in his stomach," Drew said. "The poor bastard swallowed and inhaled bits of his own face."

"It just doesn't make sense," Harriet said. "Why use such force if you just plan to steal farm machinery?" She had hoped that by coming to the house, she would get a better insight into the people who had lived here and, by extension, perhaps it would help to answer some of the questions raised by the reports. Rather than answer any of her questions, she was quickly discovering that being here only added to the mystery.

"We should go upstairs..." This was the part she was dreading the most. The reports, despite their detail, had not fully prepared her for seeing the place where Andrew Hadfield had died. And while his had been a terrible and violent death, the murders of Willow and her mother, Anna, were grislier than Harriet's worst nightmares.

They climbed the stairs together in silence. The hall was cold. Signs of the forensic team's work lay everywhere.

"It's down here," Drew said, pointing to a door at the end of the corridor.

Swallowing her discomfort, Harriet followed close behind him. Even Drew, as tough as he liked to pretend he was, paused outside the door and took a deep, steadying breath before crossing the threshold.

The bed was stripped down to the frame, but Harriet had seen the pictures of the scene and her mind instantly conjured images of the place at the time when Anna had died. There was a space on the floor where the forensic team had cut large sections of the carpet. The en-suite bathroom door caught her eye, and Harriet moved towards it, an invisible string pulling her forward.

She wasn't sure what she had expected to see, but she wasn't prepared for the stripped back room that awaited her. The bath, toilet, and sink remained in-situ, but all the trimmings had been stripped away. The bath panels had been removed, and pieces of the pipework were missing. Somehow, seeing the space so exposed made everything worse. This had been a place where a family had once shared a life and now the house had been reduced to its bare bones.

"'The SOCOs decided to take almost everything with them." Drew stood just inside the bedroom, his arms folded defensively across his chest.

Harriet stared at the empty bath. There was a faint line, no doubt a water line from when... She cut off her own train of thought.

"I brought the file with me," Drew said. "I thought it might help to see how everything was laid out."

Harriet shook her head and turned away. She did not need to see the photographs from the crime scene again. They were tattooed into her brain, a permanent fixture that she knew she would never be free of.

"He wanted Anna to watch," Harriet said quietly.

"Sorry, what?"

Harriet pointed to the place on the floor where sections of the carpet had been removed. "The attack on Willow started there. Maybe she heard a noise in her parents' room and…" Harriet trailed off and glanced back at the door. "No, she probably heard something elsewhere in the house and came to her parents for help."

"How can you be so sure?" There was no judgement in Drew's voice, only mild curiosity.

"If the attacker was in the room, there would be more of an indication of a struggle in the hall. The reports don't mention any evidence to support that theory. So, we can assume she made it into the room before she was caught."

"I thought the same," he said. "They found Willow's water bottle discarded on the stairs and one of her slippers in the hall. So, the working theory is that she was running from someone."

Harriet swallowed and wished she had something to rid her mouth of the bitter taste that coated her tongue. "The attack on Willow starts here and according to the SOCO's report, they found Willow's blood, saliva, and other bodily fluids on the bed covers." She closed her eyes and instantly regretted the action. Now that she was here, it was all too easy for her brain to replay the events as she believed they had unfolded on the fateful night.

Willow's terror would have been palpable. Despite working in this field for as long as she had, it still surprised Harriet to discover how cruel one human being could be to another.

"He wanted Anna to watch. Up close and personal. Everything that was being done to her daughter... That level of sadism is not common." Harriet did a slow turn in the room. "It feels personal."

"You think it was someone who knew the family?" Drew asked the question Harriet had been asking herself since she had started looking through the file the night before.

There was no way to be one hundred percent certain about anything. Forensic psychology was a science, but it wasn't always an exact one.

"It's one angle we shouldn't ignore. The way the murders were committed feels entirely different to the burglary. The torture, sexual assault, and murder of both Anna and Willow is very cohesive and heavily planned; one person who took their time to inflict as much suffering on each of them as they could. By comparison, we know there was more than one person here for the burglary because it would have taken more than one person to steal the farm machinery and the quad bikes."

"But what if you had the outside crew and then the people in here—"

"A thief wants to get in and out quickly, agreed?" Drew nodded, giving Harriet the opportunity to continue. "Spending too much time in the one place increases their chances of being caught."

She closed her eyes, and the crime scene photographs flashed through her mind unbidden. "The sheer level of torture and harm inflicted here would have taken time, Drew. Whoever did this knew they would not be disturbed. They knew the movements of the family. They knew they planned to go away and so they struck at a time when they were sure the family would not be missed for a significant period of time."

She balled her hands, digging her fingers into her palms. "They took their time. And then when they were done, they took the time to clean up."

"How can you be so sure?"

"Because despite the sexual assaults and the time spent with both Anna and Willow, no DNA was found on their bodies. He took the time to cut both Willow and Anna's fingernails and then used bleach to wash their bodies."

"What kind of lunatic does all that?" Drew jammed his hands into the pockets of his coat.

"Someone who is forensically aware enough to know that during an attack, DNA very often can be retrieved from beneath the fingernails."

"And the rest?" Drew raised a speculative eyebrow at her.

"He took as much pleasure in inflicting pain during the clean-up as he did while he tortured them." Harriet headed for the door. She needed to get out of the room and escape the images playing in her mind.

She made it down the hall and paused in front of another door. Pushing it open, she stepped inside and knew instantly it was Willow's room. The space was in a state of disarray, but Harriet could not tell if that had been caused by the SOCOs or if Willow kept her room messy.

Making her way through the space, Harriet sat on the edge of the mattress and tried to imagine the pretty teen in this room. A pair of headphones lay discarded on the rug next to the bed, and next to it, Harriet spotted the corner of a book poking out from beneath the bedframe.

Crouching down, she gripped the corner and pulled it free, only to discover it was not a book but a large sketch pad. Lifting it carefully onto the bed, she flipped it open. The first sketch was of a subsection of a thistle. A zoomed in photograph was pinned to the corner of the page and Harriet was impressed by the attention to detail the teen had shown in her work. She had clearly been very talented.

Harriet quickly scanned through the pages of sketches. She paused on a page in the middle, two hands entwined on what looked to her like the edge of a bed. Unlike the other pages, there was no photograph attached, but Harriet was keenly aware that at least one of the hands was wearing a band on their left ring finger. It was an odd picture, the level of detail in one of the hands suggested a drawing from life rather than something conjured from imagination.

"What have you found?" Drew's question caused Harriet to jump.

She moved aside, allowing him to peer over her shoulder to the sketch book.

"Whose is it?"

"I found it under Willow's bed."

"She was talented." Drew let his statement hang in the dead air between them.

"Whose hands do you think these are?" Harriet broke the silence as she got to her feet. The more she stared at the image, the more certain she was that it was a wedding band on the finger. There was an intimacy in the drawing that unnerved her, but she couldn't quite pinpoint why.

"No idea." Drew shrugged. "Have you seen enough here?"

Absentmindedly, Harriet nodded, her attention still fixed on the drawing pad.

"We can bring it with us," Drew said, finally breaking her concentration. "I've got some evidence bags in the boot of the car."

Reluctantly, Harriet agreed. She had seen enough. Her mind was swamped with imagery that she wished she did not need to see. But Drew had been right about one thing; it had been helpful to come here.

As she followed him back to the car, Harriet mulled over everything she had learned. It was impossible to have all the answers that Drew and the team needed but as she climbed back into the car next to Drew, she was certain of one thing.

Drew chucked his coat into the back seat of the car before he got in behind the steering wheel. "I thought coming here would have given me more—"

"Drew, you were right."

"I mean, I often am but you'll have to be a bit more specific." He twisted towards her in his seat and waited expectantly.

Drawing in a deep breath, she tried to settle her nerves. She had promised that she wouldn't do this, and yet… "I want back on the team."

"Are you sure?"

She stared down at her hands clasped in her lap. "It's the only thing I am sure of right now. I need this."

With a wide grin, Drew started the engine. "Then let's get you reinstated."

CHAPTER FORTY-SEVEN

OLIVIA SAT in the waiting area, watching people as they scurried by. After Martina and Ambrose had approached Kelly, she had stopped taking Olivia's calls. She had been understandably shocked by their line of questioning. Olivia had been surprised herself, but she had since read the forensic report. The DNA evidence was irrefutable. Jeremy had been inside that house. What role he had played there remained to be seen.

Her phone buzzed and she glanced down at the screen.

"*About to pick up Mark Robinson.*" The message from DC Green said. Olivia tried to stifle the kernel of jealousy that took root in her chest. DI Haskell had given Maz the choice of who to take with him. There had been a time when he would have picked her, no questions asked. That time was no more. And if Olivia was being honest, she was rapidly getting pissed off by his behaviour.

Sure, she had screwed up, but it wasn't as though he were blameless.

Scanning the hospital corridor, she spotted Kelly as she passed silently through the crowd. She looked like a sleepwalker, all shuffling feet and dazed expression.

Standing, Olivia continued to watch the other woman as she made for the doors. Following at a distance, Olivia observed her as she slipped out into the misty morning air.

She caught up to Kelly as the woman's body leaned back against the wall and her knees buckled and she dropped into a crouch. Kelly buried her face in her hands, shoulders shaking as she started to sob.

"Kelly…"

The other woman started, head snapping up as she wiped away her tears with the back of her hand. "No."

"Kelly, we need to talk."

"I don't want to speak to any of you lot. You're all a bunch of liars."

"I've never lied to you."

"Yeah, you did. You promised you'd get Mark, but it was all just a ruse to get close to me so you could try and pin something on Jeremy." She struggled to stand, and Olivia noted the bruising that ringed her wrists and disappeared beneath the sleeves of her jumper.

"What happened to your arms?"

Kelly pulled her sleeves down to cover the marks. "None of your fucking business."

"Kelly, did Mark do that?"

"What does it matter? I told you how dangerous he is. I told you what he did, but all you care about is pinning a murder on Jeremy when he's in that bed unable to defend himself." She started to cry in earnest, then; great big sobs that shook her small frame. "It's all my fault. If I had never crossed Mark, he wouldn't have come after Jeremy like that. He was trying to protect me and—"

Olivia went to Kelly and pulled her into a tight hug. For a moment, the other woman resisted before finally relenting. She allowed Olivia to hold her, her body shaking as the pain and anguish poured out of her.

Waiting until Kelly fell silent, Olivia released her and took a step back. "I'm not here to pin anything on Jeremy. I can promise you that."

Kelly's face was swollen and blotchy. She watched Olivia carefully with bloodshot eyes. "Why should I believe you?"

"Because I'm here to tell you that my colleagues are about to pick up Mark Robinson from his house."

Kelly stared blankly at her for a moment before succumbing to her tears again. Olivia gave her a moment before she decided to press on.

"But we need your help, Kelly." Olivia held her hand up, stopping the young woman before she could argue. "We don't have much evidence to hold him. The evidence recovered from your house wasn't enough."

"I told you, I can't."

"Without your help, Kelly, he's going to walk away from this." Olivia sucked in a breath, hating herself for what she was about to do. "And what will happen to you and the baby if he gets away with it scot-free?"

"He'll know I told you. He'll come after me."

"We can keep you safe, Kelly. Safer than you are now." Olivia looked pointedly at the marks on the other woman's wrists. "When did that happen?"

Kelly's gaze fell to the dark bruising, and she sighed, her shoulders dropping in defeat. "Last night. He was waiting for me outside the hospital when I nipped out for some air. He wanted me to come home with him, said being here with Jeremy was pointless, that we were just waiting for him to die..." She squeezed her eyes shut. "Says he wants to be a family, that he promised Jeremy he'd look after me and the baby."

"Kelly, is there anything you can give me that will help us put Mark behind bars?"

She shoved her hands into the pockets of her jeans. "You lot think Jeremy could hurt that family, but I know he wouldn't." She took a shaky breath. "Jeremy wasn't the violent type, not like Mark. If Jeremy was there, then it was because Mark needed him."

"Why would Mark need him?"

"Jeremy was always good with computers and codes and when he and Mark were younger, he got good at breaking into safes. It was a point of pride with him that he could do it." She hesitated, and Olivia watched as she twisted her fingers around the cuffs of her jumper.

Kelly took a breath and plunged ahead. "He was the only one who could do it, you know? Jeremy was happy to just have it as bragging rights. But Mark wanted to go for bigger scores. He was desperate to move up in the gang, and he saw Jeremy's abilities as his meal ticket.

"On the last job they did together, there was something Mark did that frightened Jeremy. He wouldn't tell me what it was, but I know it spooked him bad enough to want out. So, when the police came sniffing around, Jeremy snitched. Mark never knew, or if he did…"

Kelly let out a breath. "I need to know that you can get him."

Olivia felt torn. She wanted to promise Kelly that they would get Mark, but she knew that nothing was certain. If it were up to her, the likes of Mark Robinson would spend the rest of his life behind bars. But the world was not so cut and dry.

"We'll do our best. I can promise you that. But it wouldn't be fair of me to promise more than that."

Kelly stared down at the ground, and Olivia felt the possibility of getting something concrete from the young woman slipping away. Just when it seemed like Kelly would walk away, she thrust her hand into her pocket and withdrew it a moment later. "This might help." She held her hand out to Olivia and uncurled her fingers. In her palm sat a plain wedding band.

"I don't understand," Olivia said.

"Mark gave this to me when he came to see me after the attack. He said I could pawn it or sell it and get some cash for the baby." Kelly's voice was flat and devoid of all emotion. She stared down at the ring in the middle of her hand.

"Did he say where he got the ring?" Olivia's mouth was dry as she stared down at the plain gold band.

Kelly shook her head. "I asked, but he made a joke of it. Said if he told me he'd have to kill me. I tried to say no, but with Jeremy in a coma, Mark thinks we can go back to the way it used to be. I'm really afraid. I couldn't fight him off that night." She sighed. "It's the reason I've been spending my nights here. The waiting room is safer than home."

"And you think the ring was stolen?"

Kelly nodded and picked the ring up, holding it at an angle so that the engraving within was visible in the light.

A & A 17/08/03

"It's a wedding ring," Kelly said, stating the obvious. "After you came by here with the other officers, accusing Jeremy of those terrible things, I did a little digging." A shiver ran through Kelly, reminding Olivia just how long they had been standing outside for. "Anna and Andrew Hadfield. They were the couple in the farmhouse, right?"

"Where are you going with this?" Olivia had a pretty good idea where Kelly was steering the conversation, but she felt compelled to ask nonetheless.

"It didn't take much Googling to find out they got married the 17th of August 2003. It's the same date as the ring."

"Do you have any way of proving that it was Mark who gave you the ring?"

Kelly closed her fist, the ring disappearing from view. She wrapped her arms around her body as though that alone would protect her from the pain of Olivia's questions. "You don't give up do you? You think Jeremy gave me the ring."

"I'm just looking for a way to verify that Mark had the ring in his possession."

Kelly looked away, her gaze roaming over her surroundings. "He said if I needed it, he had more stuff."

"Excuse me?"

Kelly's face lit up. "I remember now; he said I could pawn it or sell it, and if it wasn't worth much, he had more."

"More jewellery?"

"Jewellery was always Mark's preferred form of currency. It was what he used to give me when we were together, and he would have me sell it on. I think it was just his way of trying to keep himself clean."

Olivia fished around in her pocket and pulled out a small evidence bag. She held it out to Kelly. "I'll get this checked out."

"Was that helpful?"

Olivia nodded, staring down at the ring. "It was. And if you would consider coming in and making a statement..."

Kelly nodded. "I know what you need, but I'm not sure." She stared down at her small bump. "If it were just me, I would."

"Kelly, I don't want this to sound insensitive, but what are you going to do if Jeremy doesn't wake up?"

"I can't think about that."

"I understand."

"But it's usually all I can think about," Kelly said. "If Jeremy dies, I'm going to leave. I can't stay here and risk Mark coming after us. And if Jeremy lives, then I'll stay as long as I can. But if you don't lock Mark up, I might have to cut and run anyway."

"Before you have to make any sort of long term decision, let me see what we can do about getting Mark off the board, eh?" Olivia tucked the evidence bag into her coat. "This really was helpful, Kelly. Look after yourself."

She left, giving the other woman the chance to

pull herself together before she returned to the lonely vigil next to her partner's bed. Olivia did not envy her for what difficulties lay ahead. Mark Robinson had a lot to answer for. And if the ring truly belonged to the Hadfields, then it was entirely possible that the team would crack the case before too long.

CHAPTER FORTY-EIGHT

DREW PARKED the car and tightened his grip on the steering wheel.

"Maybe I shouldn't be here," Harriet said.

"Look, the Monk is just going to have to get on board. We need you on this."

"You don't need me, Drew. The team is more than capable of working this out for yourselves." The self-deprecating note in Harriet's voice didn't go unnoticed by Drew. He wanted to reach across the distance between them and force her to understand just how much they needed her; how much *he* needed her. When she had been forced out, he had been cut adrift alongside her, and everything had gone to shit. No, he wouldn't make that mistake again. Gregson would reinstate her, or... Drew wasn't entirely sure what would happen if his boss didn't see the things his way.

"We might solve it," he said. "Then again, we might not. What I know for certain is that people would die, people we could save if you were working alongside us."

He cast a sideways glance at her and was pleased to see the ghost of a smile hovering on her lips.

"Right, let's get this over with. What's the worst that can happen?"

"ARE YOU OUT OF YOUR MIND?" Gregson's voice was loud enough to rattle the glass in his office door. "After everything I told you, you go and bring her to the crime scene and then back here? Have you lost your bloody mind, Haskell? What are you playing at?"

Drew fought the urge to tell the Monk to calm down. The man was apoplectic, his complexion more purple than normal, and Drew was genuinely concerned for his health.

"Sir, we need Dr Quinn. You and I both know how complicated a case like this can be."

"It's a burglary gone wrong, Drew. Stop trying to make a mountain out of a molehill."

"With all due respect, sir—"

"Don't bullshit me, Drew. With all due respect means no respect."

"I've been through the reports. DS Scofield and

his team weren't just drowning, they were nowhere near getting an arrest. And with every day that passes, we get further from finding the person responsible."

"I heard they got a DNA match at the scene."

"They did, and as I told you the man the DNA matched is currently in a coma in hospital and is unlikely to wake up. It's a lead to nowhere, sir."

Gregson huffed out a breath and stalked behind his desk before dropping into his chair. "Are you trying to destroy the team, DI Haskell?" As he spoke, he rummaged in the top drawer of his desk and pulled a bottle from within.

Taken aback, Drew shook his head. "Of course not, sir. I'm trying to make sure this team doesn't throw away one of the best assets we've ever had. I want our team to be the best there is."

Gregson popped a pill into his mouth, chewing it quickly. "And yet I distinctly remember explaining to you how some don't approve of our group. They think we're a drain on resources that could be better utilised if they were spread across the different forces. I did my best to hold them at bay because we got results and the only press we attracted was good. That reputation was damaged over everything that happened with Dr Quinn—"

"Sir, I really don't think it's fair to blame Harriet for something she had no control over."

"And normally, I would agree. But I have to look

out for our best interests. If we want to keep the team together, Dr Quinn cannot be a part of it. It gives the others ammunition to use against us."

"Sir, I really think—"

"It's done, Drew. You need to accept it. I won't authorise Dr Quinn's involvement in this or any other case. Now, you need to ask her to leave."

Disgust filled Drew's veins. He'd never known the Monk to shy away from a fight before. "I never thought I'd see the day when they turned you into a coward." He glared across the desk at his DCI.

The colour drained from Gregson's face, leaving him chalk white. A beat passed, and Drew watched as two spots of colour appeared high on the Monk's cheeks.

"Repeat that, DI Haskell." Gregson's voice had dropped, taking on an ominous tone that Drew had not heard before.

"You heard me. You're a coward if you let them—"

Gregson got to his feet so fast his chair thudded to the ground behind him. "You have no fucking idea the hoops I've jumped through just to keep this team together. I am many things, Drew, but a coward is not one of them. If you..." A look of confusion crossed the DCI's face, and he paused, flexing the fingers in his left hand like a man who had slept on it the wrong way.

Drew took a step forward, but the DCI shook his

head, the confusion dissipating as he returned his attention to the matter at hand. "You wouldn't last a minute if you were in my shoes, Haskell. You think you can do whatever you want now, because you're the golden boy. But I promise you, the minute you fuck up, they will eat you alive. I've been protecting you for years but no—"

This time Gregson cut off, a flash of pain crossing his face. He straightened and took a step back before folding at the waist and collapsing to the ground.

Shock propelled Drew into action. He flung open the office door and bellowed to those in the room beyond. "Ambulance, now!"

Without waiting for a response, he rounded the desk and reached for the man on the ground. Gregson's complexion was grey, his lips rapidly changing from blue to purple as his hands clutched at the place where his tie was nestled against the collar of his shirt.

"Sir..."

Gregson grimaced, his face screwing up as he wheezed and gasped.

Drew was only vaguely aware of the others who crowded into the office behind him. He continued to bark orders, informing them that he believed the DCI was suffering a heart attack and to inform the paramedics *en-route* of his condition.

Gregson opened his eyes, and Drew saw a combination of terror and panic flash across the DCI's face before the eyes rolled back in his head and he lost consciousness. The smell of fresh urine filled Drew's nose, and he was shocked to note the spreading wet patch on the front of Gregson's grey trousers.

Loosening the tie and shirt, Drew pressed his fingers to Gregson's throat and searched for a pulse.

CHAPTER FORTY-NINE

MARTINA STARED down into the cup of coffee clasped between her hands. The coffee shop buzzed with activity around her, but she was only vaguely aware of it. She could still see the look on Kelly's face when they had told her why they wanted to speak with Jeremy. A combination of devastation and something else. Something Martina had not been able to pinpoint.

Movement outside the window caught her eye and she watched as DC Crandell slipped inside. Martina didn't immediately signal her presence. Instead, she sank a little lower in her seat and studied the DC from afar.

She had been jealous of DI Haskell's task force team the moment she had heard of its creation. She had wondered what it was about DC Olivia Crandell that made her worthy of such a coveted space, while she continued to toil away in obscurity. In the end,

Martina had decided it mostly came down to luck. Olivia had been in the right place at the right time. That was all.

The same could probably be said for the rest of the task force. One could not discount the role luck played in such a situation. Of course, once you were a part of such a task force, it became a self-fulfilling prophecy that you would succeed at your job. When you had the resources and the backing of the top brass, it became easier to solve crimes. At least that was what Martina had told herself in the beginning.

But that had been before she had spent time with the team. Before she'd had the opportunity to see them up close, to work with them. She had seen just how hard they worked, how dedicated they were to finding answers. It didn't lessen the jealousy she felt; if anything, it made it worse. But now, rather than begrudge them the resources they had, she knew they had earned everything with blood, sweat, and tears.

Olivia caught her eye and raised her hand to wave. Martina returned the gesture, her smile warm as she beckoned the other woman over. The other DC made her way quickly through the crowd and paused at the table.

"Do you want another?" Olivia pointed to the cup Martina was nursing.

"No. If I drink anymore coffee today, I'll never sleep again."

Olivia grimaced. "I know the feeling, but after the afternoon I've had, I need it."

Olivia left and joined the queue at the counter. The line moved quickly, and within moments, she rejoined Martina with a large latte in a takeaway cup.

Dropping into the chair opposite Martina, Olivia blew the hair from her eyes and stretched her neck from side to side. "I think I made real progress with Kelly," she said, "She seemed a little more open to the idea of making a statement today. I really think she'll come in and give one. Especially if we can get this Mark Robinson off the streets. And she gave me something very interesting."

Martina leaned forward, propping her elbows on the tabletop. "Go on."

"She surrendered a ring. Said she got it from Mark Robinson. It looks like it came from the farm. The engraving on the inside seems to point in that direction. Obviously, we need to have it checked, but..." Olivia spread her hands wide. "It looks promising. Kelly said Robinson was having trouble shifting jewellery and mentioned there was more where that came from. Has there been any news from DS Scofield?"

Martina shook her head. "When they tried his last known address this morning, the guy there said he hadn't been around for a while. Your computer nerd is running down any connections in the hopes we get a hit."

She took a mouthful of the coffee and winced as it burned her tongue. "You said he had more jewellery that he hadn't yet shifted?"

Olivia flipped through her notepad. "Yup, Kelly said he would have her sell it on as a way to try and keep himself clean."

"We can always try local gold merchants and pawn shops," Martina said. Robinson had obviously gone to ground like a cockroach. Flushing him out would not be easy. "Kelly didn't give any indications that she might know where he was?"

Olivia started to shake her head and then paused. "Wait, he went to see her at the hospital last night. Told her he wanted her to come home with him, that there was no point waiting around for Jeremy to die."

"What are you thinking?" Martina couldn't hide her eagerness. She was tired of feeling like she was getting nowhere fast on this case. And aside from her own personal suspicions, which had amounted to nothing, Robinson was the first real lead they had.

"Well, what if he literally meant Kelly's home?"

Disappointment quenched Martina's hopes. "Don't you think Kelly would have mentioned that he was crashing at her place?"

"She might not know. She's been spending her nights in the hospital because she feels so unsafe after what happened. What if he has been squatting in her house and when he suggested going home, he meant it literally?"

"What a fucking creep. It would take some real brass balls to squat there like he didn't half kill some poor bloke and attack Kelly."

"True. But the more I hear about Mark Robinson, the more I'm inclined to believe it."

Abandoning the coffee, Martina stood and grabbed her coat. "I think we should go and check it out. Are you coming?"

Olivia's face broke into a wide smile as she got to her feet. "Definitely."

CHAPTER FIFTY

SITTING across the road from Kelly's house in an unmarked car, Olivia sank low in the passenger seat. They had been watching the house for less than ten minutes when they had seen signs of life within.

"I'm going to call it in," Olivia said, reaching for her phone.

"We need to be certain it's him," Martina said softly, her eyes never leaving the upstairs window where they had last seen movement.

"If it *is* him and he leaves—"

"Then we follow him," Martina said breezily, as though she had just mentioned the weather.

"It's not that simple, you know. We would—" Olivia cut off as the front door swung open and Mark Robinson strolled out. He pulled up his hood before he tucked his hands into the pockets of his tracksuit bottoms. They watched in silence as he glanced up and down the street before setting off in the direction of the end of the street.

"Shit, shit, shit..." Olivia muttered beneath her breath as she quickly fired off a text to Maz.

"Relax," Martina said. "I'll get out and follow him. It'll be easier on foot."

"This really doesn't seem like a good idea," Olivia said. "We should contact the others, regroup, and come up with a plan."

If Martina had heard her, she gave no indication of it as she climbed out of the car and closed the door gently behind her. From her vantage point, Olivia watched as the other DC pulled the hood up on her jacket to ward off the misty rain before setting off after their target.

A beep from her phone drew Olivia's attention to the screen.

Maz: Team *en-route*. Sit tight.

LESS THAN TWENTY minutes had passed when Olivia spotted Mark Robinson returning back up the street, a plastic bag swinging in his hand. DC Nicoll had already texted her, informing her of their suspect's movements. Apparently, he had taken a heated call in the corner shop, drawing the ire of the shopkeeper. However, it had not been enough to put Robinson off from buying lager, beans, and bread.

And now Olivia watched from a distance as he

happily made his way up the street, seemingly without a care in the world.

If Dr Quinn were here, she would have some kind of explanation for someone like Robinson. Olivia was not someone who could rationalise or understand how someone could commit such terrible and destructive acts and then behave as though they had done nothing wrong.

She sighed and searched for Robinson again. He sauntered along the pavement, his easy movements at odds with the way his eyes scanned back and forth. He was obviously searching for something. Maybe he had made Martina as she had followed him.

Olivia tried to slide even lower in the passenger seat. Despite parking the car a few doors down from the house, she still feared that she would be noticed.

A van pulled onto the street and Robinson hesitated. For the first time since Olivia had set eyes on him, he looked nervous. Olivia tried to get a good look at the van, but her line of sight was compromised by the way she was sitting.

The colour drained from Robinson's face as the van crawled along the side of the road towards him. There was obviously something at play here.

Robinson began to back pedal along the pavement as the van drew closer. Whatever was going on, he was afraid of whoever he thought was inside the vehicle. And if a scumbag like him was afraid, then it spelled bad news for Martina.

Scrambling from the car, Olivia jogged across the

street in the direction of Robinson and the van. Fear crawled into her throat as she watched the back doors of the van swing open. She got a brief glimpse of the interior and for a moment she was certain she saw two black clad figures.

"Mark Robinson," Olivia said, raising her voice to be heard above the rattle of the van's exhaust. "Police, don't move!"

Mark's eyes slid in her direction, and he dropped his plastic bag as he raised his hands over his head. "I give up. Arrest me. I give up!"

There was no denying the panic in his voice, and it would have been remiss of Olivia not to admit that she took some pleasure from hearing it.

The back doors of the van slammed shut and it swung out into the middle of the street. The squeal of tyres mingled with the smell of burning rubber as it took off down the residential street at speed and rounded the corner at the end without pausing at the junction.

Olivia fixed her gaze on the man in front of her as he started to lower his hands.

"Thanks for that, sugar tits—"

Before he could finish his sentence, Martina grabbed him from behind and drove him to the ground. "Mark Robinson, I'm arresting you on suspicion of murder."

Olivia was only half listening as Martina continued to speak. Pulling her phone from her pocket she made a note of the make and model of the van. Something that terrified Robinson enough to make him give himself up was something worth looking into.

CHAPTER FIFTY-ONE

"DREW, none of this is your fault." Harriet knew her words were falling on deaf ears as Drew continued to pace up and down the small space of his office.

She knew how much it had pained him not to get in the ambulance with DCI Gregson, but the team needed him, so he had sent DC Green instead.

"I drove him to this. If I hadn't pushed so hard—"

"Drew, listen to me. You did not cause this. No matter how hard you think you pushed him, you did not cause a heart attack. DCI Gregson has been under a lot of stress for a while now. We both know it's true." She paused as Drew dropped into a chair and buried his face in his hands.

A knock on the door pulled their attention. DS Arya poked his head inside, his expression grim. "Superintendent Burroughs is here, guv."

With a jerk of his head, Drew was on his feet and

halfway to the door before Harriet could stop him. As he passed her, she reached out and brushed her fingers against his shirt sleeve. Drew halted, his eyes haunted as he looked at her. She tightened her grip on him. She couldn't tell him that everything would be all right. He did not need to hear empty platitudes; he needed someone who could sit him down and reassure him that they would get through this. But Harriet knew Drew well enough that he would not listen to her or anyone right now.

Instead, she squeezed his arm, doing her best to comfort him. He closed his eyes and took a breath before letting some of the tension drop from his shoulders.

"It's fine. I'm fine." It was a lie. Harriet did not need to be a forensic psychologist to hear it in his voice. But she let him go all the same. If he needed to lie to himself right now, to get through this, then she would not stand in his way.

When he followed Maz out into the main office, Harriet let them go. Her presence would only complicate matters further. So, she did the only thing she could do in that moment, and started to work.

CHAPTER FIFTY-TWO

"SUPERINTENDENT BURROUGHS, good to see you again, sir. I just wish it was under better circumstances," Drew did his best to keep his voice light.

"It's a complete shit show, DI Haskell. The last thing we need is the DCI throwing in the towel when you're in the middle of such an important case. I told him not to take on so much, but would he listen?"

Burroughs paced along the corridor. "Well, none of that matters now. I'll keep the media off your back for as long as I can."

"What do you need from me, sir?"

Burroughs paused and eyed Drew seriously. "I know you like to do things a little differently. And your DCI gave you a lot of space. He did the heavy lifting with the top brass when they wanted to come down on you. I am not like that."

"Sir, the way we work, it requires—"

Burroughs cut him off with a wave of his hand. "You misunderstand me, DI Haskell. I don't need to know the intricacies of your team. What I'm telling you is that I am not your mother. I won't run around wiping your nose and kissing every scrape and scratch you get. That was Gregson's method. You get me the results and I will protect you. But if you get caught colouring outside the lines, I will leave you and your team out to dry. Am I clear?"

Inwardly bristling, Drew gave a curt nod.

"Good." Burroughs placed his hands behind his back. "I'm glad we could clear that up. Now what do you need from me?"

"Well, sir, we—"

"Remember, Haskell, I am not your mother."

"I understand, sir, but there is something I would like you to sign off on."

Burroughs shot him a speculative look. "Go on..."

"I would like Dr Quinn to be reinstated, effective immediately."

Pursing his lips, Burroughs resumed his pacing, the motion making Drew more nervous with every passing second. "And what happens if more allegations come out of the woodwork? Why should I risk that?"

Taking a deep breath, Drew decided to plunge ahead. "Dr Quinn is an asset to our team. She was unfairly targeted by a jealous colleague whose sole aim was to destroy her reputation. And he very nearly succeeded." Seeing that Burroughs was beginning to lose interest, Drew decided to go for broke. "And I am willing to vouch for her integrity, sir. If more allegations were to emerge—and I am sure they won't—I would be willing to fall on my sword."

"You would take responsibility for it if it went wrong?"

"I would, sir."

Burroughs smiled. It wasn't a pleasant sight. "That's quite the endorsement, DI Haskell. Dr Quinn must be an asset indeed." He headed for the door. "Consider her reinstated. But on your head be it if anything goes wrong."

Drew remained silent as the super left. He should have felt happier. Harriet was back on the team. Not only that, but they also had the support of the Superintendent. And at any other moment, Drew would have felt pleased. But with everything going on, he couldn't muster the necessary emotions. How could this feel like a win when they had already lost so much?

CHAPTER FIFTY-THREE

STARING out at the sea of expectant faces, Drew felt the weight of responsibility on his shoulders. If the shit hit the fan, he would take the fall, but it would be the team who paid the price. Was this how the DCI had felt all the time?

"As many of you already know, the DCI was taken to hospital earlier. We don't yet have an update on his condition. The last I heard was that they had rushed him into surgery. And while it's a very serious situation, we have to remember just how tough the DCI is." Drew took a shaky breath and caught Harriet's eye at the back of the room.

He had not had a chance to tell her about the news from the Superintendent before he'd called the briefing. But he knew her well enough to know she would understand.

"As soon as we have information on the DCI's condition, I will let you know. In the meantime, we need to keep things moving on our end. DCI Gregson would be the first one to have our arses in a sling if he thought we were sitting around twiddling our thumbs."

A low ripple of laughter passed through the room. It was a moment of light relief that was necessary. And Drew needed them to get their heads back in the game if they were to finish what the DCI had started.

"Now, where are we on Mark Robinson?"

"Sir, DC Crandell and DC Nicoll picked him up just a little over an hour ago. He's currently in processing."

Drew nodded. "Good. We need a strategy for questioning. Has the search of his address yielded anything useful?"

"Not yet, guv. He was squatting at another address. We've got people going through it now. They've recovered some items that may prove useful."

"Great. Where are we on the financial records for the Hadfields' farm?"

"Ms Meakin is getting the same run around from their financial advisor that we did, but I've got a feeling she won't be stopped for long," DS Scofield said, stretching his arms over his head so that his back arched, spine cracking loudly, drawing a look of surprise from PC Shah who sat next to him.

"Right, well tell Jodie I said she needs to stop toying with him and get the information we need. I also want a full work up on Robinson's financials and—"

"Guv, there's someone here to see you," DC Jacobson said from the door. "Says he needs to speak to the officer in charge."

"It can wait," Drew said. "DS Scofield, I want you to get everyone up to speed on what you know about the other burglaries prior to the Hadfield murders and—"

"Sir, he's really quite insistent." Jacobson looked uncomfortable and shifted from one foot to the other. "I don't think he's going to take no for an answer."

"Let me get finished up in here and I'll be out."

Her expression was pained but she withdrew and headed back to the corridor.

"On a final note, I want to let you all know Superintendent Burroughs has reinstated Dr Quinn effective immediately. So, any queries or questions you may have had, you can now feel confident in running them past her."

A murmur raced through the office and Drew was pleased to note nearly everyone looked pleased by the news.

"Right, that's all for now. You know what we need to do, let's get it done."

He moved away from the front of the room and made it as far as Harriet before anyone could catch up to him.

"He really reinstated me?" Harriet couldn't hide the surprise in her voice.

"He did."

"Wait, what did you promise him?" Alarm flashed in her eyes as she searched his face for any indication of the answer.

"Nothing. He realised your importance to the team and agreed."

"Drew, don't lie."

"Where is he!" The unfamiliar voice rang through the room like a bell, silencing every other conversation.

"Guv, I tried to keep him out," Jacobson's voice carried across the group.

Drew watched as she tried to corral a lanky young man back towards the doors. He looked familiar, and as Drew tried to remember where he'd seen him, it was Harriet who provided the answer.

"Andy Hadfield. I was hoping we would get the chance to speak with him…"

"Well, it looks like you'll get your wish," Drew inclined his head in the direction of his office before he gestured to DC Jacobson. "Let him through."

Hadfield shrugged arrogantly away from Karen and ploughed through the group of officers. "About fucking time," he muttered beneath his breath.

Drew fixed a smile on his face. He was aiming for polite but judging by the look of surprise Harriet gave him, he had probably missed it by a mile. "After you," he said, sweeping his hand towards his office door.

CHAPTER FIFTY-FOUR

"MR HADFIELD, it's good to finally meet you," Drew said as he closed the door behind Harriet. "I'm DI Drew Haskell. I'm heading up the team that has taken over your case."

Harriet moved quickly to the opposite side of the room, giving her a better vantage point from which to observe.

Andy Hadfield looked dishevelled. His blue T-shirt was stained and only half tucked into his jeans. He pushed a hand through his sandy brown hair, causing it to stick up. Glaring at Drew, his grey eyes were bright with barely contained rage.

"What the fuck were you playing at, keeping me out there? I'm not a trained dog; I'm a son grieving his parents."

"And sister," Harriet added.

"Excuse me, who the fuck are you?" The open hostility in Andy when he turned towards Harriet was surprising. "Of course I'm grieving my little sister. Do you think I'm a monster?"

"Of course not," Harriet said smoothly. As Drew opened his mouth, Harriet subtly caught his eye. "I'm a member of the team here. You can call me, Harriet."

Withholding information didn't sit well with her, but something about Andy's behaviour told her that if she informed him that she was a forensic psychologist, he would react badly. And right now, she was trying to understand the angry young man in front of her.

Andy let his gaze travel over her. His scrutiny would normally have made her uncomfortable, but she merely noted it as interesting.

"Whatever." Andy turned away, making his dismissal of her obvious. "When can I get back into my house? You've had it for long enough. I need to get in there."

"A very serious crime was committed there," Drew said, irritation colouring his words. "When I get the all-clear from the SOCOs, we will turn the house over to you."

"This is ridiculous. You can't hold my house prisoner. Can't you just tell them they're done?"

"It doesn't work like that, Andy," Harriet said placatingly. "It's important to process the scene correctly. We don't want to miss anything that might point us in the direction of the person responsible."

"I've watched enough *CSI* to know that if you

don't have something in the first twenty-four hours, you'll never have anything." He sounded so utterly sure of himself that it almost gave his statement a sense of credibility.

"Well, I don't mean to be combative," Drew said, "but the murder of your family wasn't produced by Jerry Bruckheimer, so it won't be so easily solved."

"You can't speak to me like that," Andy said, beginning to sound like a petulant child. "I'm a victim, too. My family was wiped out. I don't think I'm asking for too much when I ask when I can get back into my house."

With a sigh, Drew let go some of the tension he'd started to hold in his body. "You're right, I'm sorry. I should have been more understanding. I can't imagine how difficult this all must be for you."

Andy sniffed loudly and wiped at his dry eyes with the heel of his hand. "Thank you. I just can't believe they're gone."

"I'll see what I can do about turning your house over to you."

Drew appeared awkward, not that Harriet could blame him. There was something off about Andy's behaviour, and it wasn't just the pretence of crying. She half expected him to pull a tissue from his pocket so he could hide his inability to shed a tear.

"Andy, perhaps if you told us what it is you need from the house, we could help you to retrieve it."

Andy's attention snapped in Harriet's direction. "What I need is my house."

"It's just that returning there will be incredibly painful for you. It's bound to raise some ugly memories. Perhaps if DI Haskell and I were to escort you there ,we could—" Harriet caught sight of Drew shaking his head over the top of Andy's shoulder.

"That's why I need to get in there. I need to let the surveyor in so we can get a proper valuation on the property. I couldn't live there now, not after everything that's happened. Plus, I've got Uni and—"

"You're going to sell the farm?" Drew folded his arms over his broad chest.

"Obviously. I was going to take over from my father, it's why I'm studying agriculture and farm business management. But I couldn't possibly take it over now. Much better to sell up and get a fresh start."

"I'm sorry, I thought I read somewhere that you dropped out of your course." Harriet kept her tone conversational. Even if she was suspicious of his behaviour, she didn't want to spook him.

"Who told you that? Was it Cecelia? You can't believe everything she says."

"Cecelia is your girlfriend, is that correct?" Harriet said.

"Yeah, she's great. She might even be the one. But—" His voice dropped to a theatrical whisper, "she's prone to exaggeration. She means no harm—"

"Actually, it was the university who informed our colleagues." Harriet moved over to a chair and took a seat. Andy's behaviour was so far removed from anything she might have expected. Of course, you couldn't always predict the way grief would manifest. And in the scenario that Andy found himself, it was entirely possible the trauma of his family's murder could make his behaviour somewhat erratic.

Andy's demeanour shifted, growing more jovial with each passing moment. "And they said I dropped out?" His laughter was rich, and Harriet felt herself smile in response. "I suppose I can't blame them for their mistake. Their admin department is always so overwhelmed. But I didn't drop out. I decided to take a year off. I thought I would do a little travelling, you know, see the world before I get serious about things."

"What a wonderful idea," Harriet said. "Where are you hoping to go first?"

"I've always fancied doing a road trip across America. Or maybe an African safari." His smile was confident.

"Those are two very different experiences," Drew said casually. "Once in a lifetime trips by anyone's standards."

"Well, you only live once, right, DI Haskell? The death of my family has really put it into perspective how uncertain everything is. If I hadn't gone back to uni early, I might be dead too."

"And is that why you're in such a hurry to get the surveyor in to value the property?" Harriet asked. "Are you going to use some of the money to pay for your trip?"

Andy's expression turned thoughtful. "I just want to honour my family the best way I can. They would want me to be happy. My mother, especially, wanted only the best for me. She would appreciate what I'm doing."

"I'm sure she would," Harriet said thoughtfully. "Andy, can I ask, who do you think would do something like this to your family?"

Andy's face shuttered, his body tensing in response to her question. Much like his theatrical whispering of earlier, this too felt like a performance. As far as Harriet could tell, the only real reaction she had seen was the anger he'd shown at his perceived neglect, and even that had seemed like an extreme overreaction.

"I've been thinking about it since they died…" He paused and squeezed his eyes shut while pinching the bridge of his nose. "There's really only one person I can think of, but it's completely absurd."

"Anything you can tell us would be helpful," Harriet said gently.

"They were friends for years, I don't know why it all went wrong. But Terry Phillips is an angry man. He called by the house a few days before—" His voice choked up and he covered his eyes for a moment before taking a deep breath. "I'm sorry, it's just difficult to think about."

"Just take your time," Drew said.

"Thank you, I really appreciate it. Terry Phillips came to the house a few days before the murder. He was so angry. He barged into the house, demanding to see my father. There was a physical altercation and, well, he swore he would kill my father."

"He actually threatened to kill your father?" Drew straightened up and Harriet could tell this was new information to him.

"Yeah. I wouldn't mention it, but..." Andy spread his hands wide helplessly. "They're dead. I can't imagine anyone else would want to hurt them. They were such kind and generous people. And I miss them terribly..." He choked off and turned away.

Drew shot Harriet a look that suggested he wasn't sure what to do.

"Andy—"

"Where did you get that?" The sharpness of Andy's question surprised Harriet.

He was pointing at the notes spread on the small table in the corner of Drew's office. The drawing pad they had found in Willow's room was sitting on top, along with several of the images they had photographed.

"Oh," Harriet said, "we found that in Willow's room. I thought it was interesting—"

"Give it back!"

"Excuse me?"

"You shouldn't have that. You need to give it to me." Andy's body was stiff, and as Harriet glanced at him, she could see a vein throbbing in the side of his temple.

"It's evidence, Andy."

"It's not evidence. It's nothing. You need to give it back."

"Why does it upset you so much, Andy?" Harriet tried to gently steer the conversation in a constructive direction. She moved around him, trying to bring his attention back to her but Andy shoved her out of the way.

He grabbed for the pad, but Drew caught his arm, easily holding him back. "Nah mate, come on. You can't do that. The evidence stays here."

"It's fine, I'm fine!" Andy held his hands up, a gesture of surrender. When Drew released him, Andy shrugged away, shaking it off as he took a couple of steps back.

"Andy, I don't think Willow would mind me looking through the drawings," Harriet said. She studied his reactions carefully. There was something she wasn't quite seeing.

"I should go." The abruptness of his manner and the way he kept his attention fixed on the drawing pad as he had backpedalled to the door intrigued Harriet.

Andy pulled open the door before Harriet could say a thing.

"Wait—" Drew called after him, but Andy was already out the door.

"No, I need to go. There's so much I need to do." And then he was gone, his pace changing to a trot as he put distance between himself and the office.

"Well, that was weird," Drew said.

Harriet continued to watch the young man as he left the office.

"You want a coffee?" Drew said, pausing in the doorway.

"Sure..." Harriet was only half listening, her attention fixed on the drawing pad. Clearly something about it had spooked him, but what that was, she had no idea. The voice in the back of her mind told her it was not something she could ignore.

CHAPTER FIFTY-FIVE

RAISING A BROW AT HARRIET, Drew waited for her to share her thoughts. When she didn't, he knew he would have to prompt her. She was doing that thing again where she became so caught up in her own brain that she forgot not everyone around her was capable of mind reading.

"What is it? What have you figured out?"

"What?" She pulled her attention away from the photographs long enough to look at him.

"Something he did has set your spidey-sense tingling."

"My what sense?"

Drew chuckled and made a mental note to get Harriet to watch the Spiderman movies sometime, if only just so he could watch her grapple with the psychology of superheroes and their complexes.

"I just mean you've figured something out. You should share with the rest of the class."

She pulled a face and picked up the set of images before shuffling quickly through them. "Something about the pad really upset him. He has to know we'd remove items from the house."

"Maybe it was just a shock seeing it here. He probably wasn't expecting it."

"Maybe," Harriet said. Drew could tell she wasn't convinced. "I don't know, there was something about that meeting that felt off."

"He's young and his entire family was murdered," Drew said. "But I get what you're saying. There was something..."

DS Arya chose that moment to push open the door. "Sir, we're ready to get the interview with Mark Robinson underway."

"I'll be right there." Drew turned back to Harriet. "Rain check on the coffee."

"No problem," she said, her attention once again fixed on the drawing pad.

With a smile, Drew followed Maz out the door, but Harriet called after him.

"Drew, would it be all right if I went and had a chat with Willow's friend Sandra?"

"Sure thing. Just bring someone with you. I don't want a repeat of what happened with Robert Burton."

A pained look crossed Harriet's face and Drew instantly regretted his hasty words.

"Look, I didn't mean it like that—"

"No, it's fine. I get it. I do. Going to see Robert

was an error of judgement on my behalf. Things would have gone much more smoothly had I spoken to you and the team first."

"That's not what I meant," Drew sighed. He could just let it go and pretend the conversation had never happened, or he could do something that scared him witless. "I just want you to be safe, that's all."

Harriet froze, her attention fixed on him.

"I'm sorry, I—" He let his gaze drop. He wasn't sorry, not one bit. "Actually, I'm not sorry. I'm being honest, for once. And we're about to start the interview process with Robinson and I don't want to spend my time thinking more about you and wondering if you're safe or not. I need to concentrate on the situation at hand. So, no, I'm not sorry." The words rushed out of him a jumbled mess, but he didn't care. For once he had told her the truth.

The ghost of a smile hovered on her lips as she tucked a strand of dark curly hair behind her ear. It was a gesture he had come to associate with her feeling a little overwhelmed.

"I'm not sure you have to worry, Drew. I don't think I have anything to fear from a fourteen-year-old."

"Well, I'd still feel better if you brought somebody with you."

"I can do that."

"Good." Drew nodded decisively.

"Good," Harriet echoed the word.

He stood in the doorway for a moment longer before he cleared his throat and decided to move. "Right, I'll crack on here. Let me know how it goes."

"I will," Harriet said. "Good luck with Robinson."

"I hope he crumbles like a wet paper towel, but I doubt we'll be so lucky."

"You never know." She began to gather up her notes. "I'll keep you in the loop."

Without another word, Drew beat a hasty retreat. He had said enough. Anything more, and he was going to wind up saying something he couldn't take back. And there was too much going on to complicate matters further.

Joining the others, he watched as Harriet approached DC Nicoll. It only took a moment for Nicoll to agree to whatever Harriet had said and then they were both headed for the door. Discomfort twisted in the pit of Drew's stomach, and it took him several moments to realise he wished he was going with her.

CHAPTER FIFTY-SIX

DREW WATCHED through the cameras as every question Maz and Olivia put to Mark Robinson was met with a 'no comment' response. Just watching the smug look on his face was enough to enrage Drew. How could one man be so callous and calculated?

Maybe it would have been better if he'd asked Harriet to stay. She would probably have some sort of insight into Robinson's mindset, something they could use to their advantage. And right now, they needed every edge they could get.

When Maz and Olivia returned from the interview, they looked as defeated as Drew felt. Perching on the edge of a table, Drew watched on as Maz slammed his notes down onto his desk before slumping into his chair.

By comparison, Olivia controlled her feelings a little better. But Drew could still see through the thin veil of composure she hid behind.

"We need something that will make him want to talk," Maz said finally. "As it is, he knows we have nothing concrete to pin on him."

"We've got the ring, Kelly gave me," Olivia said.

"Yeah, but you know that won't hold up. He'll claim she must have got it from Jeremy and because we have Jeremy's DNA at the scene, the CPS won't push ahead on a 'he said, she said'." Seeing the look on Olivia's face, Maz hastily added. "It's not fair, but you know how it goes. They want a sure thing."

Olivia sighed and dropped back into her chair. "I know, I know. It doesn't mean I have to like it."

"Nobody likes it," Drew said. "Have they recovered anything useful from the house?"

"Ambrose and the others are currently going through it," Maz said.

"You and Olivia should help. We need an all-hands-on-deck approach—"

"Guv, I might have something useful." Jodie had paused inside the office door.

Drew waved her in. "What have you got?"

"I've been going through Mark Robinson's financial information. I was hoping we could maybe trace something back to the robbery."

She handed a printout over to him and then returned to the screen of her tablet.

"Go on," Drew said scanning the sheet in front of him. The rows of figures didn't mean much to him, but he trusted Jodie enough to know that if she were here, then those numbers would tell them something important.

"There were no direct deposits from anyone suspicious. However, when I cross referenced some messages in his WhatsApp along with the dates of deposits he made to his bank, I found an interesting connection."

"What messages?" Maz had joined them and was peering over Drew's shoulder at the statement.

"There are several contacts on his WhatsApp, but he regularly clears the threads. Luckily for us, he backs everything up to the cloud, so I was able to download past conversations. I found a conversation dating back to DI Appleton's attack. I matched the contact to Caz Popov and while he doesn't explicitly state what they're going to do, Mark is sent a time and address."

Jodie sucked in a breath and Drew could sense her excitement.

"What is it, Jodie?"

"The address was flagged two weeks ago for a welfare check. Residents in the area were concerned for a vulnerable young woman, Rosie Briggs, who has learning disabilities. Residents say she uses a mobility scooter which she keeps outside. They would regularly see her out and about. About four months ago, that changed. People started coming and going from the address at all hours of the day and night. And her neighbours noticed the mobility scooter had not moved in several weeks."

A sinking feeling opened in the pit of Drew's stomach as Jodie spoke.

"When they performed the welfare check, it was discovered that Rosie had been persuaded to share the house with a group of men. She was found in a back room of the property, in a bed. Based on the state she was found in, it's believed she had been confined there for some time. Rosie described the men as her friends—"

"They were cuckooing," Drew said.

Jodie glanced down at her tablet and nodded. "That's what it says in the report. They were using the house as a base for their activities. They persuaded Rosie to give them access to her bank account."

The colour in Jodie's cheeks faded as her gaze raked over the report. "During an interview, Rosie confided she was in a relationship with one of the men, a Simon Crane. She alleges that he would share her with his friends. She went on to say that it was fun, but some of the men were mean, and she showed the specialist officers some injuries she had sustained. They suspect she was prostituted, but it's still under investigation."

"And what does this address have to do with DI Appleton's attack?"

"Rosie described a night when another young girl was brought to the house. It upset her because she said the teen cried a lot and the men were mean to her. According to the evidence recovered from the house, some articles of clothing were recovered that match the items Chelsea Fraser was seen wearing on CCTV before she was abducted and murdered."

"Fuck…" Drew breathed the word out and began to pace. "Why weren't we informed of any of this before now?"

"It was all in the system, but nobody had put the pieces together."

"But how is Mark connected to DI Appleton's attack?"

"He allows the apps on his phone to track his location. I was able to place his phone in the same area as DI Appleton on the night she was attacked and Chelsea was murdered."

"This is fantastic work, Jodie."

"Guv, that's not all…"

Drew sat back on the edge of the desk. "Go on, what else have you got?"

CHAPTER FIFTY-SEVEN

"SO, tell me, why are we going to visit Sandra?" Martina steered the car carefully around the narrow country roads.

Harriet shuffled through her notes, pausing only long enough to take in the green scenery that flashed by on the other side of the glass. "Sandra was Willow's best friend. If anyone is going to be able to tell us about Willow, it's her."

"I'm not sure I understand," Martina said. Her gaze never left the road. A car appeared around a bend up ahead and she was forced to pull over into a passing place or risk losing a wing mirror. "Why is it so important that we get to know Willow? Wouldn't you be better positioned to work out who her killer is?"

Harriet suppressed a smile. People often thought her job entailed spending large amounts of time trying to get into the heads of killers. And while that was certainly an aspect of her work, it was only a small part of a much larger methodology.

"It's much easier to find out who the victim was," Harriet said, "Know the victim, and you'll be one step closer to knowing the perpetrator."

"Ok, now you've really lost me." Martina glanced over at her before returning her attention to the road.

"Every victim is chosen for a reason. Even when it appears random, there is something about the victim that the killer is attracted to."

"That sounds a little like victim blaming. What could Willow—a child—have done to attract a sadistic bastard like the one who murdered her?" The accusation hung between them.

"It's not something Willow did. Something about her attracted her killer. It could be as simple as the colour of her hair, or that she was the right age and in the right place, or she reminded him of someone he once knew. There was nothing Willow could have done to avoid it."

Harriet glanced down at the picture in the file of the young teen. So much potential snuffed out. Wasn't that always the way? "The moment he locked onto her, short of divine intervention, he was going to kill her. But to understand who he is, I need to know why her."

"And you think Sandra can tell you that?" DC Nicoll did nothing to hide the incredulity in her voice.

"If Willow is typical of teens her age, then there

will be very little that she won't have shared with her best friend. And even if there are things she hasn't shared, there are bound to be little cues that Sandra will have picked up on that I might be able to draw out of her."

They continued the drive in silence, but Harriet could tell that Martina was mulling over everything she had said. There was something DC Nicoll was holding back, but Harriet felt she did not know the detective well enough to question her on it. If it was something she wanted to share, then Harriet figured she would do so in her own time.

They parked in front of the house and Harriet sat for a moment, staring out at the misty rain as it blurred the windscreen. What lay ahead would not be easy. She was only too aware that questioning Sandra would cause pain and discomfort to the teen. If she could have avoided it, Harriet would have. The last thing she ever hoped to do was cause more pain and suffering; there was already more than enough of that in the world.

"Are you ready?" Martina tapped her arm and Harriet realised with a start that she had been silently contemplating for too long.

"Sorry, sometimes I get lost in my own thoughts."

Martina gave her an odd look before she shrugged it off and climbed out of the car. Harriet followed suit.

It would be easier if Drew were here. He was much easier to read. Or maybe that wasn't the case.

Perhaps he only appeared easier to read because of what they had been through together. They were comfortable with one another in ways Harriet had never been with anyone else.

She followed Martina to the door and waited in the rain as the DC rang the bell. The woman who opened the door appeared wary, and before Harriet or DC Nicoll could utter a word, she had stepped out onto the doorstep and pulled the door shut after her.

"I know you spoke to my husband, but I'm really not comfortable with this. Sandra has already been through so much. She doesn't need to be upset further. She's got exams to concentrate on and—"

Harriet stepped forward and reached her hand out to the woman in front of her. "Mrs Yates, my name is Dr Harriet Quinn, I was the one who spoke to your husband. And as I explained to him on the phone, I understand entirely where you're coming from. I don't want to upset Sandra further. That is absolutely the last thing I want to do. But your daughter knew Willow better than anyone, and we wouldn't be here if we didn't think it was important to the case."

As she spoke, Harriet observed the way the woman opposite picked obsessively at the skin along the edges of her nails.

"I can't have you upsetting her," Mrs Yates reiterated.

"And I promise, I will do my best not to," Harriet

said gently. "It's a painful subject but we really do need Sandra's help."

Mrs Yates' shoulders slumped, and she let her hands drop back to her side. "I suppose you'll keep hounding us until we cave. The journalists have been the same, vultures the lot of them." Anger coloured her words, and Harriet found she could completely understand the woman.

Mrs Yates stepped back and grudgingly ushered them inside.

MOMENTS LATER, Harriet and DC Nicoll were ensconced in a small living room. The grey wallpaper had hints of metallic tones that caught the light from the bare bulb overhead.

"I'm sorry everywhere is such a mess." Mrs Yates shrugged helplessly. "We're in the middle of decorating."

"No, this is perfect," Harriet said. "And thank you for the tea."

Mrs Yates nodded absently. "I'll call Sandra again. She probably has her headphones on." She disappeared into the hall and a moment later, the creak of floorboards echoed as she climbed the stairs.

The wallpapered walls were bare but, in the corner, Harriet could see a pile of framed photos stacked into a pile. She crossed the floor and picked up the first photo. A baby and toddler in a paddling pool grinned out of the image. Happiness radiated from the picture and Harriet felt her own mouth curve into a smile, as though the emotion from the photograph was contagious somehow.

Seeing the photograph highlighted the difference between this house and the Hadfield's. Despite the ongoing renovations and decorating, these photographs were obviously valued and were clearly intended to be hung on the wall. Harriet had not seen a single photograph in the Hadfield house. The walls had been almost completely bare throughout the property. Willow's room had been the only one that showed any kind of personality.

"Sorry to keep you waiting." Mrs Yates voice carried through the room. Harriet turned to find her standing with a young girl. Sandra's brown hair was perfectly straight and hung down around her heart shaped face. She kept her eyes trained on her Converse sneakers, not even raising her gaze when Harriet said hello.

"Sandra, did your mum explain why we're here today?"

Sandra shrugged and dropped into an armchair positioned in the bay window.

"We wanted to speak with you about Willow." Harriet perched on the edge of her seat opposite the teen. Sandra continued to keep her eyes averted but Harriet spotted a flicker of emotion as it crossed the teenager's face.

"You were best friends, is that correct?"

Sandra shrugged again.

"Being best friends, you must have told each other everything." Harriet paused, hoping it would give the young girl the chance to add something, anything. When she didn't, Harriet continued. "Was Willow ever worried or preoccupied by anything?"

Sandra shrugged and started to pluck invisible fibres from the sleeve of her black and red stripped cardigan.

"Did she ever confide in you that she was afraid?"

For a moment, Sandra hesitated as she reached for another invisible thread. Then the moment passed and the silent teen shrugged once again.

Reaching into her bag, Harriet pulled the photographed images from the drawing pad they had removed from the Hadfield house. She laid them carefully out on the coffee table, turning them so Sandra could see them clearly. "Willow was a talented artist—"

This drew an immediate response from Sandra. She snorted and tossed her hair back over her shoulder. "Why am I even here? You don't know anything about Willow. This is so stupid." She folded her arms over her chest and glared at the photos.

"You're right, we don't know anything about Willow. That's why we want to speak with you," Harriet said. "You knew her better than anyone." The teen had lapsed back into silence, but Harriet knew how to draw her out. "What is it about these pictures that made you react?"

Sandra glanced down at the photos of the drawings and rolled her eyes. "Willow wasn't into drawing. She liked music, like me. The only thing she could draw were stick figures. Those were done by Andy."

"We found the drawing pad under Willow's bed. Why would she hide it there if it belonged to her brother?" Harriet kept her voice neutral. If the drawings belonged to Andy, that might explain his reaction earlier. Then again, if the pad was his, why not just admit it?

"Andy's a real weirdo. He was always stealing things from Willow, creeping around in her bedroom when he thought no one would notice. Once when I..." Sandra cut off and folded her arms over her chest. "I don't want to talk about this anymore." The look on Sandra's face caused Harriet's stomach to flip uncomfortably.

"This must be incredibly difficult for you," Harriet said. "You must miss Willow terribly."

Sandra's bottom lip trembled, and she rubbed her sleeve against her eyes angrily, smearing black eyeliner onto her cheek.

"We did everything together. I can't believe she's gone. What kind of sick bastard would do that to her?" Sandra glanced up, making eye contact with Harriet for the first time since they had sat down to talk.

"That's why I'm here," Harriet said. "I'm trying to understand why anyone would want to hurt her."

"I heard it was some kind of robbery," Sandra said.

"We're looking into all possible avenues."

Sandra returned her attention to her jumper. "Whatever."

"Did Andy make Willow uncomfortable?"

"He was a weirdo. Of course he made her uncomfortably. He got off on it, too. If he could make her cry, it made him happy." Sandra's assault on her cardigan picked up in intensity. "I said I didn't want to talk about it. Willow wouldn't want me to grass."

"It's understandable that you would feel that way," Harriet said.

"So, I'm not talk about it anymore." Sandra followed her arms over her chest and slouched back into her chair.

Martina took the opportunity to sit forward in her seat. Her sudden movement surprised Harriet. She had been so silent during the conversation so far that Harriet had wondered if she would contribute at all.

"That's a nice sentiment." Martina propped her elbows on her thighs. "I'm sure Willow would really appreciate you having her back and keeping her secrets. The only problem, Sandra, is that Willow is dead, so she really can't appreciate anything you do for her anymore."

"DC Nicoll, that's a bit harsh," Mrs Yates interjected before Harriet could. "Sandra is more than aware that her friend is dead. So aware that she can't sleep at night because of nightmares."

Martina raised a placating hand. "I'm sorry about that, I really am. But that doesn't change the fact that we are looking for a killer and to do that we need to understand Willow better. Sandra is our only chance at doing just that." She turned her attention back to the teen, who was doing her best not to cry. "If you really care about your friend, you'll tell us what you know. Nothing you say can hurt Willow now. Somebody else already did that."

"That's enough!" Mrs Yates was on her feet in an instant. "I want you to leave."

"No, Mum, leave it."

"I won't have them come in here and traumatise you, love. I won't."

"Mum, I said leave it. They're right. Willow is dead. Telling her secrets now won't bring her back. But if it helps…" Sandra trailed off.

"What were you going to say earlier about Andy?" Harriet kept her tone gentle.

"One time I was there." She glanced at her mother. "It was right before I stopped going for sleepovers."

"I remember. You and Willow had a big fight." Puzzlement settled over Mrs Yates' face.

"Yeah. It was the middle of the night. Willow and I had gone to bed. We always shared because I was afraid to sleep on the floor in case of spiders.

Willow was already asleep, and I was trying to sleep but I was also looking at TikTok—"

"Sandra, how many times have I told you not to stay up all night looking at that phone?"

"Please, Mrs Yates, let her finish," Martina said.

"I heard footsteps in the hall, so I hid my phone under the pillow and pretended to be asleep. But I could see Andy as he came into the room. He came over and stood next to the bed. At first, I thought maybe he was going to wake Willow up, but he just kept standing there staring at us. And then—"

"Sandra Yates, did that boy touch you!" The shrill note in the mother's voice jolted Harriet.

"No, Mum. Yuck. Of course not!" Sandra's expression turned wary. "Forget it. I want to go back to my room now—"

"No way, you're going to finish what you were saying to these nice lady detectives, and when your father gets home, we're going to have a long chat."

"Mum." She drew out the word until it barely resembled a word and sounded more like a high-pitched whine.

"Sandra, we really do need you to tell us what happened," Martina said.

"He was just being weird, trying to upset us. He kept staring at us, and then he lifted the blankets off Willow." She swallowed hard. "When he touched her leg, she woke up and kicked him in the crotch. He was really pissed off, but he left after that. So there. Happy?" She aimed that last at her mother who was hovering over her like a clucking hen.

"What did Willow say?" The sinking feeling in the pit of Harriet's stomach continued to get worse. With every new thing she learned about the Hadfield siblings, her feelings of unease only increased.

"She was all freaked out—" Sandra hesitated.

"Go on, Sandra, it's really important you tell us."

The teen sighed as though the inconvenience of the conversation was too much for her. "She asked if Ricky ever did that to me."

"And Ricky is?" Martina asked.

"Ricky is my son," Mrs Yates said. "Sandra's older brother."

"And I told her no way. Ricky is a pain in the arse but he's not a creep. Willow said she caught Andy stealing a thong from her drawer once, and I made a joke about them being like the family from the *Chainsaw Massacre* movies, and she got so angry. We didn't talk for a while after that. I think I really hurt her feelings, but I didn't mean to. I was just so weirded out, you know?"

"Did Willow ever tell you anything else about Andy?"

Sandra was already shaking her head. "We never mentioned it again, and I was kind of relieved, because it was really weird."

"Sandra, one more question and we'll get out of your way. Did Willow ever keep a diary?"

"No. She wasn't really into that kind of thing. She kept everything on her phone or her laptop."

"We didn't recover her phone or her laptop at the house—"

"That doesn't matter," Sandra said, sliding her own phone out of her pocket. "She was obsessive about keeping everything backed up to the Cloud. And we swapped our logins, in case one of us got locked out. I can give you Willow's, if you like."

"That would be incredibly helpful," Harriet said.

As DC Nicoll took down the details, Harriet hoped it wouldn't be a waste of time. The killer had obviously taken Willow's electronics because he was afraid of what the police might find. But there was a chance that Willow's online backups had been overlooked.

CHAPTER FIFTY-EIGHT

DREW SETTLED into his chair and silently observed the man opposite. Maz joined him and quickly set the recording up.

Mark Robinson was a picture of calm. Evidently, he believed they couldn't connect him to any one crime. From the corner of his eye, he watched Maz lay the printouts Jodie had provided for them on the desk. Mark's eyes flickered to the rows of numbers, and Drew was pleased to see his shit-eating grin wilt at the edges.

"What is this?" The solicitor leaned forward, his eyes tracking over the pages.

"In the course of our investigation we were able to track some interesting financial movements on your account, Mark." Maz pulled out the sheets containing the WhatsApp messages between Mark and Caz Popov.

"Where did you get these?" Mark leaned

forward, his eyes practically bulging out of his head as he scanned the recovered messages.

"You recognise the conversation?" Maz slid another layer of sheets on top of the first.

"I've never seen this shit before in my life," Mark said, dropping back in his chair. "They can't do this." He turned to face his solicitor. "This is bullshit."

"Mark, we have more than enough evidence to connect you to several crimes," Drew said, finally breaking his silence. "We have location data that puts you at the scene of a serious assault of one DI Appleton. That same crime also resulted in the murder of a young girl, Chelsea Fraser. Does any of this sound familiar?"

Mark shook his head. "No fucking comment."

"We also have location data that puts you at a farmhouse at Saltergate Bank. We were able to recover this from your belongings." Drew gestured to a photograph that Maz produced from his case file. The receipt was from a pawn shop in York. "Is that your signature, Mark?"

"No comment," Mark's voice was growing more petulant.

"I think it is. It matches the signatures you made on your account when you were depositing cash into the bank."

"We had officers call into the pawn shop, and they recovered CCTV footage."

Maz withdrew several still images of Mark

Robinson from the file. In the pictures, it was plainly obvious that Mark was pawning jewellery.

"We've recovered the pieces, matching them to your receipt, and we have confirmation based on insurance information from the Hadfield's that the jewellery matches items stolen from the house."

"No comment," Robinson said again. But his voice wavered, and Drew knew it would only be a matter of time before he cracked.

"We also recovered some other very interesting information," Drew said. "Do you know a Terry Phillips?"

Mark glanced over at his solicitor. "I need to speak with you." He spoke quickly and in hushed tones, but Drew still heard him.

"I need some time to confer with my client," the solicitor said. "Is there somewhere private we can go?"

Drew nodded to Maz, who switched off the recording and gestured for Mark and the solicitor to follow him across the hall to another room.

Once alone, Drew sat back in his chair. They were beginning to finally get somewhere with the investigation. The only problem was, he couldn't shake the feeling that there was something he was missing. Mark Robinson was a nasty piece of work, there was no denying it, but Harriet had said the murders were personal, and so far they could find no personal connection between Robinson and the Hadfields.

Terry Phillips, on the other hand, was a different story. He had the motive and the personal connection to the family. There was just one problem: Terry Phillips had been out of the country during the window of time in which the Hadfields had been killed.

Leaving the interview room behind, Drew made his way down the corridor. Popping into a side room, he joined Ambrose and Olivia.

"What did they say?" Drew asked.

"They're willing to have one of us come over to interview Terry Phillips. We've tracked him down to an address in Mijas, Costa del Sol. If we can send someone, they'll meet us at the airport, and we can go from there."

"Fine. I'll have Superintendent Burroughs sign off on the paperwork."

Ambrose leaned back in his chair and stretched his arms over his head as he yawned. "Who are you going to send?"

"Why, are you angling for a free trip to Spain?"

Ambrose pulled a face. "As fun as that sounds, my Julie would have my head if I took off to Spain without her and the kids."

"Noted." Drew grinned at the other man. "I don't suppose you'd be much use to us without a head."

"I don't know," Ambrose said. "Julie might say it was an improvement."

Laughing, Drew headed for the door.

"Guv, what about charging Robinson with the

attack on Jeremy Benson and Kelly Walker?" The dark rings beneath Olivia's eyes told Drew just how little sleep she was running on. The last couple of months had taken their toll on them all. He would be glad when they could finally put everything behind them.

"Walker still hasn't come in to make a statement, so until we have something more concrete, there's no way we can move forward on it. As for the attack on Benson, I want to interview Robinson separately for that. Right now, we're going to keep the focus on his connection to Caz Popov and the Hadfields."

"Fine." She turned back to her work.

"Is there something you'd like to say, DC Crandell?"

"No, sir."

Frustration wormed its way through Drew's body. They were doing their best and moving as quickly as they could. Anything more, and they risked fucking up the entire investigation. Olivia should understand that. And yet...

"Any word on DCI Gregson?" Ambrose asked, breaking the tension.

Drew glanced at his phone and shook his head. "Nothing. Last I heard, he was still in surgery. Tim will let us know if anything changes."

Ambrose glanced over at Olivia and elbowed her gently in the ribs. "Fancy a cuppa?"

Olivia tried to say no, but Ambrose was not the kind of man that was easily denied. Drew watched on in admiration as he managed to convince the DC that she needed a break.

As Olivia left the room, Drew stopped Ambrose in the doorway. "Thanks, mate."

Dropping his focus to the floor, Ambrose shook his head. "Nothing to thank me for. She needs a break." He pulled a deep breath into his barrel chest. "She's right, though. Robinson needs to be held to account for his attack on that couple. Bastards like that cannot get away with whatever they want, otherwise what's even the point in being a copper?"

"I couldn't agree more," Drew said. "But when we go for him, I want it to stick. I don't want the CPS to wriggle out of it and claim insufficient evidence for prosecution."

"Aye, I hear you," Ambrose said. He clapped Drew on the shoulder.

Drew smiled and let Ambrose pass. Leaning back against the wall, he let his head drop onto his chest. He understood Olivia's frustration because it was his own. He wanted nothing more than to march into the interview room and throw the book at the smug prick. But the world didn't work like that. They needed to tread carefully, and that meant moving slowly. One mistake, and Robinson would walk. Drew could not have that on his conscience.

FORTY MINUTES LATER, Drew found himself back in the interview room. Gone was the carefree Mark Robinson from earlier. He stared down at his shoes, never once lifting his gaze as the solicitor cleared his throat.

"My client has prepared a statement, and he has instructed me to read it on his behalf. He will not be making any other comment other than the one I am about to read." The solicitor glanced in Robinson's direction. Getting no response, he went ahead.

"I, Mark Robinson, have no knowledge of any alleged attack on a DI Appleton. Nor do I have any knowledge of the murder of Chelsea Fraser.

"The next is a direct statement made by my client. Two months ago, I was approached by a man I knew. Terry Phillips. He owed me money. His farm was failing, and a planned sale of the land had fallen through. Terry Phillips blamed Andrew Hadfield for this. It was Terry Phillips' belief that if someone was to scare Andrew Hadfield and his family, he would then be persuaded to sell his farm to the developers.

"Terry Phillips provided me with dates when he knew the Hadfields would be at home. He also provided me with dates he believed they would be away on holiday. With this information, he engaged me as a means to intimidating the family into selling their farm by any means necessary.

"Terry Phillips said I should, 'do whatever it takes' to secure the sale. He indicated the Hadfield's daughter could be used to control the parents.

Phillips was very clear that I could use violence to ensure their compliance. He even seemed gleeful over the prospect of Andrew Hadfield needing hospital treatment.

"As I am not a violent person, I had no intention of doing as Terry Phillips suggested. However, due to Terry Phillips owing me a great deal of money, it was my decision to recoup my losses by robbing the farm when I knew the Hadfields would not be at home.

"I went to the farm with Jeremy Benson, with the sole intention of stealing enough items to cover Phillips' debts to me. Once there, we proceeded to remove all farm machinery, cars, and quad bikes from the property. Jeremy Benson then suggested we check the house. He was a very proficient thief, and he informed me that he had recently lost his job, and his girlfriend was now pregnant, meaning he was in need of money.

"Once inside the property we discovered the Hadfield family already dead. The smell was very strong and after the discovery, I was in a severe state of shock. I immediately left the property. However, Jeremy Benson insisted on continuing his search of the property. When he returned outside, he told me the smell had grown so strong that he had vomited on the floor. I did not interfere with the bodies, and I did not spend any length of time inside the house. This is all I am willing to say on the matter." The solicitor raised his face and glanced at Drew.

Drew leaned back in his chair. "That's quite the

statement, Mark. If you spent hardly any time in the property, how did you come to be in possession of the jewellery from the house?"

The solicitor glanced at Mark and subtly shook his head. "No comment," Mark said, his voice flat.

"You say Jeremy Benson wanted to remain in the house. Yet he was so disturbed by the scene that he was sick. I'm not sure I believe that. Maybe you were the one forcing him to stay in the house and he was sick as a result."

"No comment," Mark repeated.

"Mark, come on. You expect me to believe you had nothing to do with the murders of the Hadfields? You said yourself you knew when they would be at home. You admit you robbed them. Did it go too far? Did Andrew Hadfield fight back and you panicked?"

"I never touched them. They were already dead!" Mark straightened in his chair. "Terry Phillips is a lying bastard. He set me up. He probably killed them and then sent me there to take the blame. It's Terry Phillips you lot need to be talking to—"

"Mark, we agreed, no comment answers," the solicitor said.

"Fuck this shit. I didn't kill those people. I don't give a shit about them. And when you see Terry Phillips, you can tell that cowardly fuck that I'll make him sorry he ever crossed me!"

"Mr Robinson!" The solicitor was flustered as he tried to silence Robinson.

A knock at the door interrupted them.

"Interview suspended," Drew said, pushing to his feet. He nodded to Maz who ended the interview. Slipping out into the hall, Drew was surprised to find DC Karen Jacobson waiting for him.

"What is it? Is it Gregson? Is there news?"

She shook her head, her face pale. "It's not the DCI. Dr Quinn and DC Nicoll got back." She swallowed hard. "Guv, you really need to see this." Without waiting for a response, she hurried down the hall, leaving Drew with no choice but to follow.

CHAPTER FIFTY-NINE

HARRIET STARED AT THE SCREEN, unable to tear her gaze away. Deep down she had known it would be bad, but had she really expected this?

Jodie shoved her chair back violently and climbed unsteadily to her feet. "I need a moment. I —" And then she was gone, fleeing across the open office space as fast as her feet could carry her. Not that Harriet blamed her one bit. She wanted to flee, too. If she could have pried herself away from the computer, away from Willow's Cloud storage, she would have done it. But she couldn't. The suffering this child had gone through deserved to be witnessed.

Taking Jodie's seat, Harriet reached for the mouse with shaking hands. Clicking through the images, she felt bile climb the back of her throat.

"Oh my God..." Martina's voice barely penetrated the layer of shock that insulated Harriet from the rest of the world.

She clicked again and a video started to play. Willow's broken voice poured out of the speakers as she begged and pleaded with her abuser to stop.

Harriet hit pause on the video and the frozen image of Willow's tear-stained face was frozen in time on the screen.

"How could he?" Martina said. She stared at the screen for a moment more and then turned away.

Drew strode into the office, and from the corner of her eye, Harriet watched him move towards her. "Jacobson said you had something." He reached her side and Harriet turned towards him as his attention fixed on the screen.

"There are thousands of pictures and videos," she said, her voice barely rising above a whisper. "Most of them are of Willow. Some are videos downloaded from other places." She felt tears pricking at her eyes and she closed them. She wouldn't cry. Willow did not need her tears. She needed somebody to see what was happening to her. She needed someone who cared to notice the abuse she was suffering at the hands of her own brother.

"I don't understand," Drew said.

Without looking at the screen, Harriet hit play. She kept her gaze locked on Drew as he went slack jawed. The colour drained away from his face as the Andy in the video violated his sister. And then Harriet watched on as anger replaced the shock.

"Enough." Drew clenched his fists, turning away from the screen.

"We need to speak with him, this can't be ignored," Harriet said quietly. When Drew remained silent, Harriet started to fill in the blanks. "Willow kept the videos hidden in her Cloud storage. She downloaded them all. We think she took them from his computer. At least that's Jodie's working theory."

She sucked down a shaky breath. "And there's something else. We think we know when the murders were committed. Jodie has only done a cursory examination, but she says there is a pattern to Willow's behaviour. She backed up her files at roughly the same time every day. She backed them up on the Thursday as usual but there's nothing on the Friday, or any day after that. Jodie says she could be more certain if she had Willow's actual laptop to compare it to…"

"We'll go to his flat," Drew said. "If he's not there, somebody will know where he is."

"Drew, we need to approach this very carefully. If we go in too heavy, we'll spook him."

"I'm very fucking calm," Drew snapped. He caught himself, his shoulders dropping as he closed his eyes, and took a ragged breath. "Sorry."

"Don't apologise. I get it. I'm angry too."

He eyed her, his eyebrow rising, an unasked question.

"Say it," she challenged him.

"Do you think he killed his family?"

Harriet glanced back at the screen. They had seen the financial statements Willow had downloaded. Every penny Andy received from his parents for his tuition had been spent on extravagant items. Lavish dinners in expensive restaurants, all-expense paid holidays. His credit card debt was eyewatering. And when the cash had started to run dry, Andy had started to dip into his parents' savings. How he could have done any of it without his parents noticing, was something Harriet couldn't quite understand.

"Honestly, I think he's more than capable. If somebody challenged him, or threatened him, I could very well see him becoming violent. I can't diagnose him, but I would not be surprised to learn that he is a narcissist. The level of malignant narcissism displayed, his cruelty, the sense of grandiosity, and his lack of empathy all points towards it."

"Malignant narcissism that's a new one."

"It's more of a descriptor for the more severe cases. Malignant narcissism is generally categorised by its combination of narcissistic and psychopathic traits which I believe Andy displays."

"Well, whatever it is, if you think he's capable of murder, it's good enough for me. We should go, and you can fill me in on the way about what you learned from Sandra."

CHAPTER SIXTY

DREW TOOK THE LEAD, rapping harshly on the apartment door. Harriet hung back, shadowing his movements. He had seen a lot of things in his years with the force, but the video of Willow was a new low. How could somebody do that to another human? He often envied Harriet's ability to empathise with the worst of humanity, but this was a step too far even for him. There could be no empathy, no sympathy, for someone like Andy Hadfield.

The sound of a deadbolt being drawn back and the rattle of the door chain pulled Drew from his thoughts. The door cracked open, and a tear-soaked face peered out through the gap. The room behind her was in darkness, making it difficult to pick out any details.

"DI Haskell. This is my colleague Dr Harriet Quinn. We were wondering if we could speak with Andy Hadfield."

"He's not here." She sniffed and started to close the door, but Drew jammed his foot in the gap, halting her.

"We really need to speak with him."

The young woman's eyes widened, an automatic response to the edge in Drew's voice.

Harriet moved up next to him. "Cecelia, is it?"

"Yeah."

"Could we possibly come in?" Harriet spoke gently, as though the young woman on the other side of the door was a fragile thing that needed comfort.

"Ok..."

Drew withdrew his foot, and she closed the door, a moment later it swung open revealing that her white blouse was ripped. Blood, which had clearly come from her lip, had dried onto her collar. Her mascara was smeared onto her cheeks, but it did nothing to hide the red and purple bruise that was blooming around her right eye.

She hugged herself, her arm holding the ripped blouse in place. The movement revealed her ragged and torn nails.

Harriet was through the door before Drew could say a word. "You're safe now, Cecelia."

The young woman stared at Harriet for a moment, her wide eyes frightened, reminding Drew of a deer caught in the headlights. And then her knees buckled, and she collapsed into Harriet's arms as sobs shook her frame.

"I DON'T WANT to go to hospital," Cecelia said, the shrill note of panic unmistakable in her voice.

"But we should call someone to be with you," Harriet said. She sat next to Cecelia on the couch. Drew carried two mugs of steaming tea into the living room, feeling more like an oversized spare part than a DI in the North Yorkshire police force.

"I've already asked a friend to come over," Cecelia said quietly as she took the tea. "I'm sorry about trying to close the door in your face."

"Hazard of the job," Drew said easily. "Most people take one look at this ugly mug and try to slam the door. You're in good company."

She cracked a watery smile at that and turned her attention to the cup. "It's my fault. I shouldn't have pushed him."

"Can you tell us what happened?" Harriet angled her body towards the young woman giving her all her attention.

"I got a notice today," she said, her voice shaky.

"Take your time," Drew said.

She nodded. "I got a notice in the post. A speeding fine. But I never speed."

Drew tried to keep his sympathetic expression fixed in place. Nobody really believed that they drove too fast. What any of it had to do with Andy Hadfield though…

As though she could read Drew's mind Cecelia

added, "I don't. I swear. My dad was killed in a head on collision. The other driver was speeding, overtaking on the road. He wasn't paying attention and —" She swallowed around her pain. "Andy speeds, though. He thinks he's invincible. God's gift to driving. I told him about my dad, and he said if my dad was a better driver he wouldn't be dead."

Drew bit his tongue.

"I'm always telling him to slow down. He hates it." She hesitated. "I asked him about the fine, and he went ballistic. I've never seen him so angry."

"Why would he?" Harriet asked the question Drew was wondering.

"The fine was from some weeks back. A speed trap on the A169 near RAF Fylingdales. It's really close to Andy's parents' house. I assumed it was from when he was travelling back up here. He hates having to spend time with them. But after he lost his temper, I looked into it a little more..."

"What is it, Cecelia?" Drew leaned forward.

"Well, he came back from his parents' house on the Monday. But the camera caught the car speeding in the early hours of the Friday morning. I stayed over at a friend's house that night. We went out to celebrate our exam results and the party ended up continuing into the early hours back at her house, so I just stayed over. I definitely wasn't speeding on the A169."

"And where was Andy?" Harriet asked the question before Drew could.

"I thought he was at home in bed." Her voice trembled. "But now I'm not so sure."

THEY STAYED with Cecelia until her friend arrived. Drew had got on the phone the moment he had the details of the fine from Cecelia. Jodie had easily confirmed that the car was on the stretch of road the night they now believed the Hadfields had been murdered. But the real confirmation had come when Jodie had sent Drew the image the speed camera had captured.

"It's definitely him," Harriet said studying the picture as she sat next to Drew in the car.

"Means, motive, and opportunity," Drew said quietly. "He knows we're on his trail, doesn't he?"

"I think he knew from the moment he saw me with the sketch pad," Harriet said. "That's probably why he overreacted so badly to Cecelia questioning him. It made him paranoid, and he lashed out with violence."

"We need to put out a BOLO. Considering he has a head start on us, he could be anywhere."

But Harriet was already shaking her head. "He's not going to run, Drew. He's too arrogant for that."

"Then where is he?"

"He's gone back to the scene of the crime." She met his gaze head on. "Andy has gone home."

CHAPTER SIXTY-ONE

DREW WAS out of the car as soon as he parked it on the gravel driveway. Light spilled out from one of the upper windows, letting them know Harriet's hunch had been correct.

"You should wait in the car," Drew said.

"I can't let you go in there alone." Harriet moved past Drew and made her way to the front door, which was ajar. "It looks like he's expecting us."

Grumbling, Drew pushed Harriet behind him. "If you're coming in, then I at least need to go first. Hang back, please, Harriet."

Seeing the look on his face, Harriet nodded. "Fine."

"Good." Relief flooded Drew's features. "The others should be here soon and..." A crash from inside the property had them both moving into the hall.

The sound stopped as soon as they made it to the stairs and Harriet knew it was Andy's way of letting them know he was aware of their presence.

They climbed the stairs slowly, Drew moving stealthily ahead.

"Don't bother, DI Haskell, I'm not armed..." Andy's words carried out into the hall letting them know exactly where he was.

Shrugging, Drew climbed the last of the stairs quickly. He led the way down the hall and paused in the doorway to Willow's room.

"Come in, detective. Did you bring Dr Quinn with you too?" Andy's tone was syrupy sweet.

Harriet moved up next to Drew, meeting Andy's gaze head on. "Hello, Andy, good to see you again."

"I'm not sure I believe that." He grinned at her. "You know, I read all about you in the papers. Such terrible things they printed. Were any of them true?"

"You know as well as I do that you can't judge a book by its cover. They created a story to sell their papers, and it worked. You created a persona to fool those around you into believing you were the grieving son."

Andy shrugged. "It's not a persona, but I'm flattered you think I could do something so clever." He leaned back on the bed and patted the space next to him. "Come and sit with me, Dr Quinn. We can pretend we're having a civil conversation."

"You need to come with us, Andy," Drew interrupted.

Andy shot him a dirty look. "You don't get to decide, DI Haskell. Not if you want the truth."

"We already know the truth, Andy. We spoke to Cecelia." Harriet studied his expression, searching for any sign that her words had upset him. If she could get under his skin, he would begin to reveal things that he didn't necessarily want to.

"How is poor Cece? She's a bit of a drama queen, and just between us, she's a drinker. Ever since daddy darling popped off this mortal coil, she likes to drown her sorrows. She doesn't even remember when she gets behind the wheel of her car."

"You mean the speeding fine?" Drew quirked an eyebrow at Andy who nodded.

"She tried to blame me, imagine that."

"Why would she do that?" Harriet took a step forward, but Drew blocked her with his body.

"Beats me. She's cuckoo." He twirled his finger next to his temple signalling she was crazy.

"You left her pretty beat up—"

"That was self-defence," Andy said. "I regret hurting her, but she came at me all nails and teeth. What was I supposed to do, stand there and take it?"

"You're saying she attacked you?" Drew asked.

"She did."

"And did Willow attack you, too?" Harriet said. Her question had the desired effect. The smile on Andy's face faded instantly, replaced by a flicker of rage that he tried to hide.

"I don't know what you mean, Dr Quinn."

"Did she attack you all those times you pinned her down? What about when you raped her? Are you going to tell us that she started it?"

Andy feigned shock. "Why would you say that? I loved my sister. She was troubled, it's true. But I would never do the things you've suggested. And frankly I find it sick that you—"

Harriet's bitter laughter cut him off. "Andy, we both know the truth. You did such a good job hiding it. Nobody suspected the things you were doing. Nobody paid any attention, and all because you were so good at creating a false persona. But I've seen the photographs and the videos. It's over."

"How?"

"Willow downloaded the items from your computer. Even though you took her laptop and phone, she was obsessive about backing everything up to the Cloud. I'm guessing you tried to hack her account but couldn't."

For a moment, he stared at her ,and Harriet could see the cogs inside his mind turning over his options. "Willow was a clever girl. Much smarter than I gave her credit for. If I had known what she was up to, then maybe things could have been different." He sighed. "It doesn't mean I killed her, or my parents."

"We can place you here the night they were killed."

"How do you know when they were killed?"

"Again, because of Willow. She backed everything up on the Thursday night, but she didn't log into her accounts on Friday or any day after that."

"I see..." Andy stared at his surroundings. Sirens wailed in the distance growing ever closer with each passing second.

Drew stepped forward. "Andy Hadfield, I'm arresting you on suspicion—"

"You think you know so much. Willow was smart, I'll give her that. You said I created a persona, using it to hide what I was doing to my sister, but did you ask yourself where I learned to do that?"

Ice slithered down Harriet's spine. Where was he going with this?

"Where was the help for me when my own mother abused me? I've read all the articles about the horror killings at murder farm. And people keep asking how anyone could do something so terrible." He took a ragged breath. "My father knew what she was doing and said nothing. Willow suspected but did nothing. Our family was rotten to its core. I did the world a favour."

He reached over and flipped back the covers to reveal several empty pill bottles. "And I'll do you a favour now, too."

"Shit—" Drew sprang into action crossing the floor to Andy's side.

Harriet watched as he called for help and officers piled into the house. She watched Andy as paramedics arrived and they started to question him as they hooked him up to monitors and an IV drip.

And through it all, Harriet knew that he had not taken anything. She knew with a certainty all the way down to her bones that he would never endanger himself. After all, wasn't that the real reason he had murdered his family?

CHAPTER SIXTY-TWO

"HOW IS HE?" Harriet passed Drew a cup of machine coffee.

"You were right. They're keeping him for observation, but the doctors don't think he took anything at all. They found some tablets still floating in the toilet back at the house." He scrubbed his hand over his eyes.

"He regards himself too highly to harm himself. The moment he knew there was a chance of his parents finding out about him stealing their money, he killed the family. When Cecelia confronted him over the speeding fine, he attacked her. Being threatened triggers him to violence."

"Christ, I think I'll sleep for a week after this."

Harriet smiled at him. "I feel the same. How is Gregson?"

"He's out of surgery and in the ICU. The nurses

said as soon as he came around, he was demanding to see the reports and he wants a briefing in the morning. They've got their hands full with him."

Harriet snorted into her cup and burned her mouth. "Why can I visualise that so clearly?"

"Because you know the Monk." With a grin Drew looked at her. "We couldn't have done it without you."

"Of course you could. The team is solid."

He shook his head, his expression turning serious. "I couldn't have done it without you." He reached over and tucked a strand of hair behind her ear. "Please tell me you're going to keep working with us."

Harriet could hear the unspoken words beneath his question and for the first time she wasn't afraid.

"You're stuck with me, DI Haskell. For better or worse."

Grab the Next Book in the Series Now
Dark is the Mind

Thank you for reading this book. If you enjoyed it, please leave a review. I hate typos too but sometimes they slip through. Please send any errors you find to: bilindasheehan@gmail.com

They will be fixed ASAP! I'm grateful to eagle-eyed readers who contact me.

Sign up to my email list to receive a FREE DI Haskell & Quinn Novella.

https://dl.bookfunnel.com/q5vfej8w6w

GET THE NEXT BOOK!

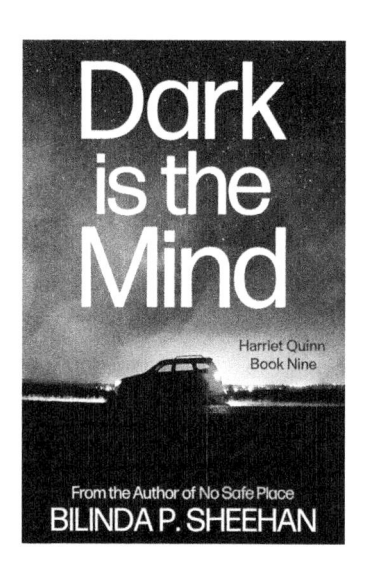

Harriet and DI Haskell return in the next book in the series.
Dark is the Mind

Join my mailing list

COME GET YOUR FREE BOOK!

Sign up to my mailing list to receive a FREE DI Haskell & Quinn Novella called, The Escape Room
https://dl.bookfunnel.com/q5vfej8w6w

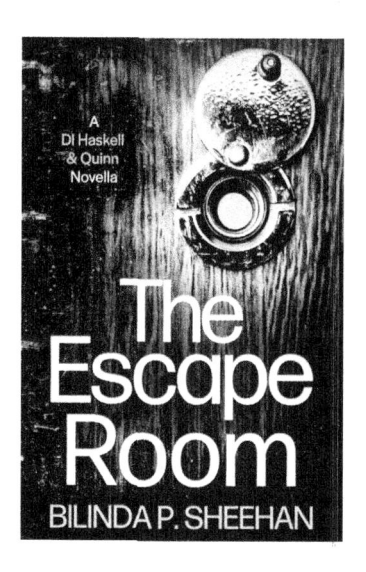

Come join me on Facebook
https://www.facebook.com/BilindaPSheehan/
Facebook: The Armchair Whodunnit's Book Club

Alternatively send me an email. I love to hear from readers and I reply to all my messages personally.

bilindasheehan@gmail.com

My website is bilindasheehan.com

ACKNOWLEDGMENTS

Thanks must go to Adam J. Wright for the use of his character Tony Sheridan. Without the use of aforementioned character, this book would not have been possible... Adam definitely did not make me say that. ;)

ALSO BY BILINDA P. SHEEHAN

Watch out for the next book coming soon from Bilinda P. Sheehan by joining her mailing list.

A Wicked Mercy - DI Haskell & Quinn Crime Thriller

Death in Pieces - DI Haskell & Quinn Crime Thriller Book 2

Splinter the Bone - DI Haskell & Quinn Crime Thriller Book 3

Hunting the Silence - DI Haskell & Quinn Crime Thriller Book 4

Hidden in Blood - DI Haskell & Quinn Crime Thriller Book 5

Place of Temptation - DI Haskell & Quinn Crime Thriller Book 6

Lake of Tears - DI Haskell & Quinn Crime Thriller Book 7

No Safe Place - DI Haskell & Quinn Crime Thriller Book 8

Dark is the Mind - DI Haskell & Quinn Crime Thriller Book 9

All the Lost Girls - A Gripping Psychological Thriller

Wednesday's Child - A Gripping Psychological Thriller

Printed in Great Britain
by Amazon

The Principles of Mechanics Presented in a New Form

The Principles of Mechanics Presented in a New Form

HEINRICH HERTZ
D.E. Jones and J.T. Walley, Translators

COSIMOCLASSICS

NEW YORK

The Principles of Mechanics Presented in a New Form
Cover © 2007 Cosimo, Inc.

For information, address:

Cosimo, P.O. Box 416
Old Chelsea Station
New York, NY 10113-0416

or visit our website at:
www.cosimobooks.com

The Principles of Mechanics Presented in a New Form was originally published in 1899.

Cover design by www.kerndesign.net

ISBN: 978-1-60206-294-8

All physicists agree that the problem of physics consists in tracing the phenomena of nature back to the simple laws of mechanics. But there is not the same agreement as to what these simple laws are. To most physicists they are simply Newton's laws of motion. But in reality these latter laws only obtain their inner significance and their physical meaning through the tacit assumption that the forces of which they speak are of a simple nature and possess simple properties.

——from the Author's Preface

EDITOR'S PREFACE

THE volume now published is Heinrich Hertz's last work. To it he devoted the last three years of his life. The general features were settled and the greater part of the book written within about a year; the remaining two years were spent in working up the details. At the end of this time the author regarded the first part of the book as quite finished, and the second half as practically finished. He had arranged to work once more through the second half. But soon his plans became only hopes, and his hopes were doomed to disappointment. Death was soon to claim him in the prime of his power. Shortly before he died he forwarded to the publishers the greater part of the manuscript. At the same time he sent for me and asked me to edit the book, in case he should not be able to see it through the press.

From first to last I have done this with the greatest care, seeking especially to give a faithful rendering of the sense of the original. I have also endeavoured, as far as possible, to retain the form; but to do this in all cases, without due reference to the contents and connection, would have been contrary to the author's wish. Hence I have slightly changed the form in places where, after careful study of the book, I felt convinced that the author would himself have made such changes. I have not thought it necessary to specify where these changes occur, inasmuch as none of them affect the sense. In order to guard against this I have carefully studied all the rough notes and earlier manuscripts of the work. Several of the first drafts had been carefully written out, and some of them are fuller than the manuscript as finally prepared for the press. With regard to two paragraphs of the work I have found it impossible to satisfy myself, the author's intention as to the final form having remained doubtful to me. I have marked these two paragraphs and have thought it best to leave them entirely unaltered.

After sending off the manuscript the author had noted certain corrections in a second copy; all these have been included before printing off. I have completed the references to earlier paragraphs of the book (of which few were given in the second part, and scarcely any in the last chapter), and have drawn up an index to the definitions and notation.

P. LENARD.

TRANSLATORS' NOTE

HERTZ'S *Principles of Mechanics* forms the third (and last) volume of his collected works, as edited by Dr. Philipp Lenard. English translations of the first and second volumes (*Miscellaneous Papers* and *Electric Waves*) have already been published.

The translation of the first two volumes was comparatively easy; the third has proved to be a more difficult undertaking. If it has been brought to a satisfactory conclusion this will be largely due to Professor Lenard, through whose hands the proof-sheets have passed. He has again, notwithstanding the pressure of other work, been good enough to advise and assist us from time to time, and we tender to him our warmest thanks.

We also desire to thank the publishers and printers for the extreme consideration shown by them while the book was being prepared for the press.

D. E. J.
J. T. W.

September 1899.

PREFACE BY H. VON HELMHOLTZ

ON the 1st of January 1894 Heinrich Hertz died. All who regard human progress as consisting in the broadest possible development of the intellectual faculties, and in the victory of the intellect over natural passions as well as over the forces of nature, must have heard with the deepest sorrow of the death of this highly favoured genius. Endowed with the rarest gifts of intellect and of character, he reaped during his lifetime (alas, so short!) a bounteous harvest which many of the most gifted investigators of the present century have tried in vain to gather. In old classical times it would have been said that he had fallen a victim to the envy of the gods. Here nature and fate appeared to have favoured in an exceptional manner the development of a human intellect embracing all that was requisite for the solution of the most difficult problems of science,—an intellect capable of the greatest acuteness and clearness in logical thought, as well as of the closest attention in observing apparently insignificant phenomena. The uninitiated readily pass these by without heeding them; but to the practised eye they point the way by which we can penetrate into the secrets of nature.

Heinrich Hertz seemed to be predestined to open up to mankind many of the secrets which nature has hitherto concealed from us; but all these hopes were frustrated by the malignant disease which, creeping slowly but surely on, robbed us of this precious life and of the achievements which it promised.

To me this has been a deep sorrow; for amongst all my

pupils I have ever regarded Hertz as the one who had penetrated furthest into my own circle of scientific thought, and it was to him that I looked with the greatest confidence for the further development and extension of my work.

Heinrich Rudolf Hertz was born on 22nd February 1857, in Hamburg, and was the eldest son of Dr. Hertz, who was then a barrister and subsequently became senator. Up to the time of his confirmation he was a pupil in one of the municipal primary schools (*Bürgerschulen*). After a year's preparation at home he entered the High School of his native town, the *Johanneum*; here he remained until 1875, when he received his certificate of matriculation. As a boy he won the appreciation of his parents and teachers by his high moral character. Already his pursuits showed his natural inclinations. While still attending school he worked of his own accord at the bench and lathe, on Sundays he attended the Trade School to practise geometrical drawing, and with the simplest appliances he constructed serviceable optical and mechanical instruments.

At the end of his school course he had to decide on his career, and chose that of an engineer. The modesty which in later years was such a characteristic feature of his nature, seems to have made him doubtful of his talent for theoretical science. He liked mechanical work, and felt surer of success in connection with it, because he already knew well enough what it meant and what it required. Perhaps, too, he was influenced by the tone prevailing in his native town and tending towards a practical life. It is in young men of unusual capacity that one most frequently observes this sort of timid modesty. They have a clear conception of the difficulties which have to be overcome before attaining the high ideal set before their minds; their strength must be tried by some practical test before they can secure the self-reliance requisite for their difficult task. And even in later years men of great ability are the less content with their own achievements the higher their capacity and ideals. The most gifted attain the highest and truest success because they are most keenly alive to the presence of imperfection and most unwearied in removing it.

For fully two years Heinrich Hertz remained in this state of doubt. Then, in the autumn of 1877, he decided upon an academic career; for as he grew in knowledge he grew in the conviction that only in scientific work could he find enduring satisfaction. In the autumn of 1878 he came to Berlin, and it was as an university student there, in the physical laboratory under my control, that I first made his acquaintance. Even while he was going through the elementary course of practical work, I saw that I had here to deal with a pupil of quite unusual talent; and when, towards the end of the summer semester, it fell to me to propound to the students a subject of physical research for a prize, I chose one in electromagnetics, in the belief that Hertz would feel an interest in it, and would attack it, as he did, with success.

In Germany at that time the laws of electromagnetics were deduced by most physicists from the hypothesis of W. Weber, who sought to trace back electric and magnetic phenomena to a modification of Newton's assumption of direct forces acting at a distance and in a straight line. With increasing distance these forces diminish in accordance with the same laws as those assigned by Newton to the force of gravitation, and held by Coulomb to apply to the action between pairs of electrified particles. The force was directly proportional to the product of the two quantities of electricity, and inversely proportional to the square of their distance apart; like quantities produced repulsion, unlike quantities attraction. Furthermore, in Weber's hypothesis it was assumed that this force was propagated through infinite space instantaneously, and with infinite velocity. The only difference between the views of W. Weber and of Coulomb consisted in this—that Weber assumed that the magnitude of the force between the two quantities of electricity might be affected by the velocity with which the two quantities approached towards or receded from one another, and also by the acceleration of such velocity.

Side by side with Weber's theory there existed a number of others, all of which had this in common—that they regarded the magnitude of the force expressed by Coulomb's law as being modified by the influence of some component of the velocity of the electrical quantities in motion. Such theories were advanced by F. E. Neumann, by his son C. Neumann, by Riemann, Grassmann, and subsequently by Clausius. Magnetised molecules were regarded as the axes of circular electric currents, in accordance with an analogy between their external effects previously discovered by Ampère.

This plentiful crop of hypotheses had become very unmanageable, and in dealing with them it was necessary to go through complicated calculations, resolutions of forces into their components in various directions, and so on. So at that time the domain of electromagnetics had become a pathless wilderness. Observed facts and deductions from exceedingly doubtful theories were inextricably mixed up together. With the object of clearing up this confusion I had set myself the task of surveying the region of electromagnetics, and of working out the distinctive consequences of the various theories, in order, wherever that was possible, to decide between them by suitable experiments.

I arrived at the following general result. The phenomena which completely closed currents produce by their circulation through continuous and closed metallic circuits, and which have this common property, that while they flow there is no considerable variation in the electric charges accumulated upon the various parts of the conductor,—all these phenomena can be equally well deduced from any of the above-mentioned hypotheses. The deductions which follow from them agree with Ampère's laws of electromagnetic action, with the laws discovered by Faraday and Lenz, and also with the laws of induced electric currents as generalised by F. E. Neumann. On the other hand, the deductions which follow from them in the case of conducting circuits which are not completely closed are essentially different. The accordance between the various theories and the facts which have been observed in the case of completely closed circuits is easily intelligible when we consider that closed currents of any desired strength can be maintained as long as we please—at any rate long enough to allow the forces exerted by them to exhibit plainly their effects; and that on this account the actual effects of such currents and their laws are well known and have been carefully investigated. Thus any divergence between any newly-advanced theory and any one of the known facts in this well-trodden region would soon attract attention and be used to disprove the theory.

But at the open ends of unclosed conductors between which insulating masses are interposed, every motion of electricity along the length of the conductor immediately causes an accumulation of electric charges; these are due to the surging of the electricity, which cannot force its way through the insulator, against the ends of the conductor. Between the electricity accumulated at the end and the electricity of the same kind which surges against it there is a force of repulsion; and an exceedingly short time suffices for this force to attain such magnitude that it completely checks the flow of the electricity. The surging then ceases; and after an instant of rest there follows a resurging of the accumulated electricity in the opposite direction.

To every one who was initiated into these matters it was then apparent that a complete understanding of the theory of electromagnetic phenomena could only be attained by a thorough investigation of the processes which occur during these very rapid surgings of unclosed currents. W. Weber had endeavoured to remove or lessen certain difficulties in his electromagnetic hypothesis by suggesting that electricity might possess a certain degree of inertia, such as ponderable matter exhibits. In the opening and closing of every electric current effects are produced which simulate the appearance of such electric inertia. These, however, arise from what is called electromagnetic induction, i.e. from a mutual action of neighbouring conductors upon each other, according to laws which have been well known since Faraday's time. True inertia should be proportional only to the mass of the electricity in motion, and independent of the position of the conductor. If anything of the kind existed we ought to be able to detect it by a retardation in electric oscillations, such as are produced by the sudden break of an electric current in metallic wires. In this manner it should be possible to find an upper limit to the magnitude of this electric inertia; and so I was led to propound the problem of carrying out experiments on the magnitude of extra-currents. Extra-currents in double-wound spirals, the currents traversing the branches in opposite directions, were suggested in the statement of the problem as being apparently best adapted for these experiments. Heinrich Hertz's first research of importance consisted in solving this problem. In it he gives a definite answer to the question propounded, and shows that of the extra-current in a double-wound spiral $\frac{1}{30}$ to $\frac{1}{20}$ at most could be ascribed to the effect of an inertia of electricity. The prize was awarded to him for this investigation.

But Hertz did not confine himself to the experiments which had been suggested. For he recognised that although the effects of induction are very much weaker in wires which are stretched out straight, they can be much more accurately calculated than in spirals of many turns; for in the latter he could not measure with accuracy the geometrical relations. Hence he used for further experiments a conductor consisting of two rectangles of straight wire; he now found that the extra-current due to inertia could at most not exceed $\frac{1}{250}$ of the magnitude of the induction current.

Investigations on the effect of centrifugal force in a rapidly rotating plate upon the motion of electricity passing through it, led him to find a still lower value to the upper limit of the inertia of electricity.

These experiments clearly impressed upon his mind the exceeding mobility of electricity, and pointed out to him the way towards his most important discoveries.

Meanwhile in England the ideas introduced by Faraday as

PREFACE BY H. VON HELMHOLTZ

to the nature of electricity were extending. These ideas, expressed as they were in abstract language difficult of comprehension, made but slow progress until they found in Clerk Maxwell a fitting interpreter. In explaining electrical phenomena Faraday was bent upon excluding all preconceived notions involving assumptions as to the existence of phenomena or substances which could not be directly perceived. Especially did he reject, as did Newton at the beginning of his career, the hypothesis of the existence of action-at-a-distance. What the older theories assumed seemed to him inconceivable—that direct actions could go on between bodies separated in space without any change taking place in the intervening medium. So he first sought for indications of changes in media lying between electrified bodies or between magnetic bodies. He succeeded in detecting magnetism or diamagnetism in nearly all the bodies which up to that time had been regarded as non-magnetic. He also showed that good insulators undergo a change when exposed to the action of electric force; this he denoted as the " dielectric polarisation of insulators."

It could not be denied that the attraction between two electrically charged bodies or between two magnet poles in the direction of their lines of force was considerably increased by introducing between them dielectrically or magnetically polarised media. On the other hand there was a repulsion across the lines of force. After these discoveries men were bound to recognise that a part of the magnetic and electric action was produced by the polarisation of the intervening medium; another part might still remain, and this might be due to action-at-a-distance.

Faraday and Maxwell inclined towards the simpler view that there was no action-at-a-distance; this hypothesis, which involved a complete upsetting of the conceptions hitherto current, was thrown into mathematical form and developed by Maxwell. According to it the seat of the changes which produce electrical phenomena must be sought only in the insulators; the polarisation and depolarisation of these are the real causes of the electrical disturbances which apparently take place in conductors. There were no longer any closed currents; for the accumulation of electric charges at the ends of a conductor, and the simultaneous dielectric polarisation of the medium between them, represented an equivalent electric motion in the intervening dielectric, thus completing the gap in the circuit.

Faraday had a very sure and profound insight into geometrical and mechanical questions; and he had already recognised that the distribution of electric action in space according to these new views must exactly agree with that found according to the older theory.

By the aid of mathematical analysis Maxwell confirmed this, and extended it into a complete theory of electromagnetics. For my own part, I fully recognised the force of the facts discovered by Faraday, and began to investigate the question whether actions-at-a-distance did really exist, and whether they must be taken into account. For I felt that scientific prudence required one to keep an open mind at first in such a complicated matter, and that the doubt might point the way to decisive experiments.

This was the state of the question at the time when Heinrich Hertz attacked it after completing the investigation which we have described.

It was an essential postulate of Maxwell's theory that the polarisation and depolarisation of an insulator should produce in its neighbourhood the same electromagnetic effects as a galvanic current in a conductor. It seemed to me that this should be capable of demonstration, and that it would constitute a problem of sufficient importance for one of the great prizes of the Berlin Academy.

In the Introduction to his interesting book, *Untersuchungen über die Austreitung der elektrischen Kraft*,[1] Hertz has described how his own discoveries grew out of the seeds thus

[1] [*Electric Waves.* London, Macmillan, 1893.]

sown by his contemporaries, and has done this in such an admirably clear manner that it is impossible for any one else to improve upon it or add anything of importance. His Introduction is of exceeding value as a perfectly frank and full account of one of the most important and suggestive discoveries. It is a pity that we do not possess more documents of this kind on the inner psychological history of science. We owe the author a debt of gratitude for allowing us to penetrate into the inmost working of his thoughts, and for recording even his temporary mistakes.

Something may, however, be added as to the consequences which follow from his discoveries.

The views which Hertz subsequently proved to be correct had been propounded, as we have already said, by Faraday and Maxwell before him as being possible, and even highly probable; but as yet they had not been actually verified. Hertz supplied the demonstration. The phenomena which guided him into the path of success were exceedingly insignificant, and could only have attracted the attention of an observer who was unusually acute, and able to see immediately the full importance of an unexpected phenomenon which others had passed by. It would have been a hopeless task to render visible by means of a galvanometer, or by any other experimental method in use at that time, the rapid oscillations of currents having a period as short as one ten-thousandth or even only a millionth of a second. For all finite forces require a certain time to produce finite velocities and to displace bodies of any weight, even when they are as light as the magnetic needles of our galvanometers usually are. But electric sparks can become visible between the ends of a conductor even when the potential at its ends only rises for a millionth of a second high enough to cause sparking across a minute air-gap. Through his earlier investigations Hertz was thoroughly familiar with the regularity and enormous velocity of these rapid electric oscillations; and when he essayed in this way to discover and render visible the most transient electric disturbances, success was not long in coming. He very soon discovered what were the conditions under which he could produce in unclosed conductors oscillations of sufficient regularity. He proceeded to examine their behaviour under the most varied circumstances, and thus determined the laws of their development. He next succeeded in measuring their wave-length in air and their velocity. In the whole investigation one scarcely knows which to admire most, his experimental skill or the acuteness of his reasoning, so happily are the two combined.

By these investigations Hertz has enriched physics with new and most interesting views respecting natural phenomena. There can no longer be any doubt that light-waves consist of electric vibrations in the all-pervading ether, and that the latter possesses the properties of an insulator and a magnetic medium. Electric oscillations in the ether occupy an intermediate position between the exceedingly rapid oscillations of light and the comparatively slow disturbances which are produced by a tuning-fork when thrown into vibration; but as regards their rate of propagation, the transverse nature of their vibrations, the consequent possibility of polarising them, their refraction and reflection, it can be shown that in all these respects they correspond completely to light and to heat-rays. The electric waves only lack the power of affecting the eye, as do also the dark heat-rays, whose frequency of oscillation is not high enough for this.

Here we have two great natural agencies—on the one hand light, which is so full of mystery and affects us in so many ways, and on the other hand electricity, which is equally mysterious, and perhaps even more varied in its manifestations: to have furnished a complete demonstration that these two are most closely connected together is to have achieved a great feat. From the standpoint of theoretical science it is perhaps even more important to be able to understand how apparent actions-at-a-distance really consist in a propagation of an action from one layer of an intervening medium to the next. Gravitation still remains an unsolved puzzle; as yet a satisfactory explanation of it has not been forthcoming, and we are still compelled to treat it as a pure action-at-a-distance.

Amongst scientific men Heinrich Hertz has secured enduring fame by his researches. But not through his work alone will his memory live; none of those who knew him can ever forget his uniform modesty, his warm recognition of the labours of others, or his genuine gratitude towards his teachers. To him it was enough to seek after truth; and this he did with all zeal and devotion, and without the slightest trace of self-seeking. Even when he had some right to claim discoveries as his own he preferred to remain quietly in the background. But although naturally quiet, he could be merry enough amongst his friends, and could enliven social intercourse by many an apt remark. He never made an enemy, although he knew how to judge slovenly work, and to appraise at its true value any pretentious claim to scientific recognition.

His career may be briefly sketched as follows. In the year 1880 he was appointed Demonstrator in the Physical Laboratory of the Berlin University. In 1883 he was induced by the Prussian Education Department (*Kultusministerium*) to go to Kiel with a view to his promotion to the office of Privat-docent there. In Easter of 1885 he was called to Karlsruhe as ordinary Professor of Physics at the Technical School. Here he made his most important discoveries, and it was during his stay at Karlsruhe that he married Miss Elizabeth Doll, the daughter of one of his colleagues. Two years later he received a call to the University of Bonn as ordinary Professor of Physics, and removed thither in Easter 1889.

Few as the remaining years of his life unfortunately were, they brought him ample proof that his work was recognised and honoured by his contemporaries. In the year 1888 he was awarded the Matteucci Medal of the Italian Scientific Society, in 1889 the La Caze Prize of the Paris Academy of Sciences and the Baumgartner Prize of the Imperial Academy of Vienna, in 1890 the Rumford Medal of the Royal Society, and in 1891 the Bressa Prize of the Turin Royal Academy. He was elected a corresponding member of the Academies of Berlin, Munich, Vienna, Göttingen, Rome, Turin, and Bologna, and of many other learned societies; and the Prussian Government awarded him the Order of the Crown.

He was not long spared to enjoy these honours. A painful abscess began to develop, and in November 1892 the disease became threatening. An operation performed at that time appeared to relieve the pain for a while. Hertz was able to carry on his lectures, but only with great effort, up to the 7th of December 1893. On New Year's day of 1894 death released him from his sufferings.

In the present treatise on the Principles of Mechanics, the last memorial of his labours here below, we again see how strong was his inclination to view scientific principles from the most general standpoint. In it he has endeavoured to give a consistent representation of a complete and connected system of mechanics, and to deduce all the separate special laws of this science from a single fundamental law which, logically considered, can, of course, only be regarded as a plausible hypothesis. In doing this he has reverted to the oldest theoretical conceptions, which may also be regarded as the simplest and most natural; and he propounds the question whether these do not suffice to enable us to deduce, by consistent and rigid methods of proof, all the recently discovered general principles of mechanics, even such as have only made their appearance as inductive generalisations.

The first scientific development of mechanics arose out of investigations on the equilibrium and motion of solid bodies which were directly connected with one another; we have examples of these in the simple mechanics, the lever, pulleys, inclined planes, etc. The law of virtual velocities is the earliest general solution of all the problems which thus arise. Later on Galileo developed the conception of inertia and of the accelerating action of force, although he represented this as consisting of a series of impulses. Newton first conceived the idea of action-at-a-distance, and showed how to determine it by the principle of equal action and reaction. It is well known that Newton, as well as his contemporaries, at first only accepted the idea of direct action-at-a-distance with the greatest reluctance.

From that time onwards Newton's idea and definition of force served as a basis for the further development of mechanics. Gradually men learned how to handle problems in which conservative forces were combined with fixed connections; of these the most general solution is given by d'Alembert's Principle. The chief general propositions in mechanics (such as the law of the motion of the centre of gravity, the law of areas for rotating systems, the principle of the conservation of *vis viva*, the principle of least action) have all been developed from the assumption of Newton's attributes of constant, and therefore conservative, forces of attraction between material points, and of the existence of fixed connections between them. They were originally discovered and proved only under these assumptions. Subsequently it was discovered by observation that the propositions thus deduced could claim a much more general validity in nature than that which followed from the mode in which they were demonstrated. Hence it was concluded that certain general characteristics of Newton's conservative forces of attraction were common to all the forces of nature; but no proof was forthcoming that this generalisation could be deduced from any common basis. Hertz has now endeavoured to furnish mechanics with such a fundamental conception from which all the laws of mechanics which have been recognised as of general validity can be deduced in a perfectly logical manner. He has done this with great acuteness, making use in an admirable manner of new and peculiar generalised kinematical ideas. He has chosen as his starting-point that of the oldest mechanical theories, namely, the conception that all mechanical processes go on as if the connections between the various parts which act upon each other were fixed. Of course he is obliged to make the further hypothesis that there are a large number of imperceptible masses with invisible motions, in order to explain the existence of forces between bodies which are not in direct contact with each other. Unfortunately he has not given examples illustrating the manner in which he supposed such hypothetical mechanism to act; to explain even the simplest cases of physical forces on these lines will clearly require much scientific insight and imaginative power. In this direction Hertz seems to have relied chiefly on the introduction of cyclical systems with invisible motions.

English physicists—*e.g.* Lord Kelvin, in his theory of vortex-atoms, and Maxwell, in his hypothesis of systems of cells with rotating contents, on which he bases his attempt at a mechanical explanation of electromagnetic processes—have evidently derived a fuller satisfaction from such explanations than from the simple representation of physical facts and laws in the most general form, as given in systems of differential equations. For my own part, I must admit that I have adhered to the latter mode of representation and have felt safer in so doing; yet I have no essential objections to raise against a method which has been adopted by three physicists of such eminence.

It is true that great difficulties have yet to be overcome before we can succeed in explaining the varied phenomena of physics in accordance with the system developed by Hertz. But in every respect his presentation of the *Principles of Mechanics* is a book which must be of the greatest interest to every reader who can appreciate a logical system of dynamics developed with the greatest ingenuity and in the most perfect mathematical form. In the future this book may prove of great heuristic value as a guide to the discovery of new and general characteristics of natural forces.

AUTHOR'S PREFACE

ALL physicists agree that the problem of physics consists in tracing the phenomena of nature back to the simple laws of mechanics. But there is not the same agreement as to what these simple laws are. To most physicists they are simply Newton's laws of motion. But in reality these latter laws only obtain their inner significance and their physical meaning through the tacit assumption that the forces of which they speak are of a simple nature and possess simple properties. But we have here no certainty as to what is simple and permissible, and what is not: it is just here that we no longer find any general agreement. Hence there arise actual differences of opinion as to whether this or that assumption is in accordance with the usual system of mechanics, or not. It is in the treatment of new problems that we recognise the existence of such open questions as a real bar to progress. So, for example, it is premature to attempt to base the equations of motion of the ether upon the laws of mechanics until we have obtained a perfect agreement as to what is understood by this name.

The problem which I have endeavoured to solve in the present investigation is the following:—To fill up the existing gaps and to give a complete and definite presentation of the laws of mechanics which shall be consistent with the state of our present knowledge, being neither too restricted nor too extensive in relation to the scope of this knowledge. The presentation must not be too restricted: there must be no natural motion which it does not embrace. On the other hand it must not be too extensive: it must admit of no motion whose occurrence in nature is excluded by the state of our present knowledge. Whether the presentation here given as the solution of this problem is the only possible one, or whether there are other and perhaps better possible ones, remains open. But that the presentation given is in every respect a possible one, I prove by developing its consequences, and showing that when fully unfolded it is capable of embracing the whole content of ordinary mechanics, so far as the latter relates only to the actual forces and connections of nature, and is not regarded as a field for mathematical exercises.

In the process of this development a theoretical discussion has grown into a treatise which contains a complete survey of all the more important general propositions in dynamics, and which may serve as a systematic text-book of this science. For several reasons it is not well suited for use as a first introduction; but for these very reasons it is the better suited to guide those who have already a fair mastery of mechanics as usually taught. It may lead them to a vantage-ground from which they can more clearly perceive the physical meaning of mechanical principles, how they are related to each other, and how far they hold good; from which the ideas of force and the other fundamental ideas of mechanics appear stripped of the last remnant of obscurity.

In his papers on the principle of least action and on cyclical systems,[1] von Helmholtz has already treated in an indirect manner the problem which is investigated in this book, and has given one possible solution of it. In the first set of papers he propounds and maintains the thesis that a system of mechanics which regards as of universal validity, not only Newton's laws, but also the special assumptions involved (in addition to these laws) in Hamilton's Principle,

[1] H. von Helmholtz, "Über die physikalische Bedeutung des Prinzips der kleinsten Wirkung," *Journal für die reine und angewandte Mathematik*, **100**, pp. 137-166, 213-222, 1887; "Prinzipien der Statik monocyklischer Systeme," *ibid.* **97**, pp. 111-140, 317-336, 1884.

AUTHOR'S PREFACE

would yet be able to embrace all the processes of nature. In the second set of papers the meaning and importance of concealed motions is for the first time treated in a general way. Both in its broad features and in its details my own investigation owes much to the above-mentioned papers: the chapter on cyclical systems is taken almost directly from them. Apart from matters of form, my own solution differs from that of von Helmholtz chiefly in two respects. Firstly, I endeavour from the start to keep the elements of mechanics free from that which von Helmholtz only removes by subsequent restriction from the mechanics previously developed. Secondly, in a certain sense I eliminate less from mechanics, inasmuch as I do not rely upon Hamilton's Principle or any other integral principle. The reasons for this and the consequences which arise from it are made clear in the book itself.

In his important paper on the physical applications of dynamics, J. J. Thomson [1] pursues a train of thought similar to that contained in von Helmholtz's papers. Here again the author develops the consequences of a system of dynamics based upon Newton's laws of motion and also upon other special assumptions which are not explicitly stated. I might have derived assistance from this paper as well; but as a matter of fact my own investigation had made considerable progress by the time I became familiar with it. I may say the same of the mathematical papers of Beltrami [2] and Lipschitz,[3] although these are of much older date. Still I found these very suggestive, as also the more recent presentation of their investigations which Darboux [4] has given with

[1] J. J. Thomson, "On some Applications of Dynamical Principles to Physical Phenomena," *Philosophical Transactions*, 176, II., pp. 307-342, 1885.

[2] Beltrami, "Sulla teoria generale dei parametri differenziali," *Memorie della Reale Accademia di Bologna*, 25 Febbrajo 1869.

[3] R. Lipschitz, "Untersuchungen eines Problems der Variationsrechnung, in welchem das Problem der Mechanik enthalten ist," *Journal für die reine und angewandte Mathematik*, 74, pp. 116-149, 1872. "Bemerkungen zu dem Princip des kleinsten Zwanges," *ibid.* 82, pp. 316-342, 1877.

[4] G. Darboux, *Leçons sur la théorie générale des surfaces*, livre v., chapitres vi. vii. viii., Paris, 1889.

additions of his own. I may have missed many mathematical papers which I could and should have consulted. In a general way I owe very much to Mach's splendid book on the *Development of Mechanics*.[1] I have naturally consulted the better-known text-books of general mechanics, and especially Thomson and Tait's comprehensive treatise.[2] The notes of a course of lectures on analytical dynamics by Borchardt, which I took down in the winter of 1878-79, have proved useful. These are the sources upon which I have drawn; in the text I shall only give such references as are requisite. As to the details I have nothing to bring forward which is new or which could not have been gleaned from many books. What I hope is new, and to this alone I attach value, is the arrangement and collocation of the whole—the logical or philosophical aspect of the matter. According as it marks an advance in this direction or not, my work will attain or fail of its object.

[1] E. Mach, *Die Mechanik in ihrer Entwickelung historisch-kritisch dargestellt*, Leipzig, 1883 (of this there is an English translation by T. J. M'Cormack, *The Science of Mechanics*, Chicago, 1893).

[2] Thomson and Tait, *Natural Philosophy*.

CONTENTS

	PAGE
INTRODUCTION	1

BOOK I

GEOMETRY AND KINEMATICS OF MATERIAL SYSTEMS

PREFATORY NOTE 45

CHAPTER I

TIME, SPACE, AND MASS 45

CHAPTER II

POSITIONS AND DISPLACEMENTS OF POINTS AND SYSTEMS . . 48

Position; Configuration and Absolute Position; Finite Displacements (*a*) of Points, (*b*) of Systems; Composition of Displacements.

CHAPTER III

INFINITELY SMALL DISPLACEMENTS AND PATHS OF A SYSTEM OF MATERIAL POINTS 61

Infinitely small Displacements; Displacements in the Direction of the Coordinates; Use of Partial Differential Coefficients; Paths of Systems.

CHAPTER IV

POSSIBLE AND IMPOSSIBLE DISPLACEMENTS. MATERIAL SYSTEMS   78

Connections ; Analytical Representation of Connections ; Freedom of Motion ; Displacements Perpendicular to Possible Displacements.

CHAPTER V

ON THE PATHS OF MATERIAL SYSTEMS 90

1. Straightest Paths ; 2. Shortest and Geodesic Paths ; 3. Relations between Straightest and Geodesic Paths.

CHAPTER VI

ON THE STRAIGHTEST DISTANCE IN HOLONOMOUS SYSTEMS . . 106

1. Surfaces of Positions ; 2. Straightest Distance.

CHAPTER VII

KINEMATICS 121

1. Vector Quantities with regard to a System ; 2. Motion of Systems, Velocity, Momentum, Acceleration, Energy, Use of Partial Differential Coefficients.

CONCLUDING NOTE ON BOOK I 135

BOOK II

MECHANICS OF MATERIAL SYSTEMS

PREFATORY NOTE 139

CHAPTER I

TIME, SPACE, AND MASS 139

CHAPTER II

THE FUNDAMENTAL LAW 144

The Law; its Justification, Limitation, and Analysis, Method of Applying it, Approximate Application.

CHAPTER III

MOTION OF FREE SYSTEMS 152

General Properties of the Motion: 1. Determinateness of the Motion; 2. Conservation of Energy; 3. Least Acceleration; 4. Shortest Path; 5. Shortest Time; 6. Least Time-Integral of the Energy. Analytical Representation: Differential Equations of the Motion. Internal Constraint of Systems. Holonomous Systems. Dynamical Models.

CHAPTER IV

MOTION OF UNFREE SYSTEMS 178

I. Guided Unfree System. II. Systems influenced by Forces: Introduction of Force, Action and Reaction, Composition of Forces, Motion under the Influence of Forces, Internal Constraint, Energy and Work, Equilibrium and Statics, Machines and Internal Forces, Measurement of Force.

CHAPTER V

SYSTEMS WITH CONCEALED MASSES 209

I. Cyclical Motion: Cyclical Systems, Forces and Force-Functions, Reciprocal Properties, Energy and Work, Time-Integral of the Energy. II. Concealed Cyclical Motion: Conservative Systems, Differential Equations of Motion, Integral Propositions for Holonomous Systems, Finite Equations of Motion for Holonomous Systems; Non-Conservative Systems.

CHAPTER VI

	PAGE
DISCONTINUITIES OF MOTION	253

Impulsive Force or Impulse; Composition of Impulses; Motion under the Influence of Impulses; Internal Constraint in Impact; Energy and Work; Impact of Two Systems.

CONCLUDING NOTE ON BOOK II 270

INDEX TO DEFINITIONS AND NOTATIONS 272

INTRODUCTION

THE most direct, and in a sense the most important, problem which our conscious knowledge of nature should enable us to solve is the anticipation of future events, so that we may arrange our present affairs in accordance with such anticipation. As a basis for the solution of this problem we always make use of our knowledge of events which have already occurred, obtained by chance observation or by prearranged experiment. In endeavouring thus to draw inferences as to the future from the past, we always adopt the following process. We form for ourselves images or symbols of external objects; and the form which we give them is such that the necessary consequents of the images in thought are always the images of the necessary consequents in nature of the things pictured. In order that this requirement may be satisfied, there must be a certain conformity between nature and our thought. Experience teaches us that the requirement can be satisfied, and hence that such a conformity does in fact exist. When from our accumulated previous experience we have once succeeded in deducing images of the desired nature, we can then in a short time develop by means of them, as by means of models, the consequences which in the external world only arise in a comparatively long time, or as the result of our own interposition. We are thus enabled to be in advance of the facts, and to decide as to present affairs in accordance with the insight so obtained. The images which we here speak of are our conceptions of things. With the things themselves they are in conformity in *one* important respect, namely, in satisfying the above-mentioned requirement. For our purpose it is not necessary that they should be in conformity with the things in any other respect whatever. As a matter of fact, we do not know, nor have we any means of knowing, whether our conceptions of things are in conformity with them in any other than this *one* fundamental respect.

The images which we may form of things are not determined without ambiguity by the requirement that the consequents of the images must be the images of the consequents. Various images of the same objects are possible, and these images may differ in various respects. We should at once denote as inadmissible all images which implicitly contradict the laws of our thought. Hence we postulate in the first place that all our images shall be logically permissible—or, briefly, that they shall be permissible. We shall denote as incorrect any permissible images, if their essential relations contradict the relations of external things, *i.e.* if they do not satisfy our first fundamental requirement. Hence we postulate in the second place that our images shall be correct. But two permissible and correct images of the same external objects may yet differ in respect of appropriateness. Of two images of the same object that is the more appropriate which pictures more of the essential relations of the object,—the one which we may call the more distinct. Of two images of equal distinctness the more appropriate is the one which contains, in addition to the essential characteristics, the smaller number of superfluous or empty relations,—the simpler of the two. Empty relations cannot be altogether avoided: they enter into the images because they are simply images,—images produced by our mind and necessarily affected by the characteristics of its mode of portrayal.

The postulates already mentioned are those which we assign to the images themselves: to a scientific representation of the images we assign different postulates. We require of this that it should lead us to a clear conception of what properties are to be ascribed to the images for the sake of permissibility, what for correctness, and what for appropriatenesss. Only thus can we attain the possibility of modifying and improving our images. What is ascriled to the images for the sake of appropriateness is contained in the notations, definitions, abbreviations, and, in short, all that we can arbitrarily add or take away. What enters into the images for the sake of correctness is contained in the results of experience, from which the images are built up. What enters into the images, in order that they may be permissible, is given by the nature of our mind. To the question whether an image is permissible or not, we can without ambiguity answer yes or no; and our decision will hold good for all time. And equally without ambiguity we can decide whether an image is correct or not; but only according to the state of our present experience, and permitting an appeal to later and riper experience. But we cannot decide without ambiguity whether an image is appropriate or not; as to this differences of opinion may arise. One image may be more suitable for one purpose, another for another; only by gradually testing many images can we finally succeed in obtaining the most appropriate.

Those are, in my opinion, the standpoints from which we must estimate the value of physical theories and the value of the representations of physical theories. They are the standpoints from which we shall here consider the representations which have been given of the Principles of Mechanics. We must first explain clearly what we denote by this name.

Strictly speaking, what was originally termed in mechanics a principle was such a statement as could not be traced back to other propositions in mechanics, but was regarded as a direct result obtained from other sources of knowledge. In the course of historical development it inevitably came to pass that propositions, which at one time and under special circumstances were rightly denoted as principles, wrongly retained these names. Since Lagrange's time it has frequently been remarked that the principles of the centre of gravity and of areas are in reality only propositions of a general nature. But we can with equal justice say that other so-called principles cannot bear this name, but must descend to the rank of propositions or corollaries, when the representation of mechanics becomes based upon one or more of the others. Thus the idea of a mechanical principle has not been kept sharply defined. W shall therefore retain for such propositions, when mentioning them separately, their customary names. But these separate concrete propositions are not what we shall have in mind when we speak simply and generally of the principles of mechanics: by this will be meant any selection from amongst such and similar propositions, which satisfies the requirement that the whole of mechanics can be developed from it by purely deductive reasoning without any further appeal to experience. In this sense the fundamental ideas of mechanics, together with the principles connecting them, represent the simplest image which physics can produce of things in the sensible world and the processes which occur in it. By varying the choice of the propositions which we take as fundamental, we can give various representations of the principles of mechanics. Hence we can thus obtain various images of things; and these images we can test and compare with each other in respect of permissibility, correctness, and appropriateness.

I

The customary representation of mechanics gives us a first image. By this we mean the representation, varying in detail but identical in essence, contained in almost all text-books which deal with the whole of mechanics, and in almost all courses of lectures which cover the whole of this science. This is the path by which the great army of students travel and are inducted into the mysteries of mechanics. It closely follows the course of historical development and the sequence of discoveries. Its principal stages are distinguished by the names of Archimedes, Galileo, Newton, Lagrange. The conceptions upon which this representation is based are the ideas of space, time, force, and mass. In it force is introduced as the cause of motion, existing before motion and independently of it. Space and force first appear by themselves, and their relations are treated of in statics. Kinematics, or the science of pure motion, confines itself to connecting the two ideas of space and time. Galileo's conception of inertia furnishes a connection between space, time, and mass alone. Not until Newton's Laws of Motion do the four fundamental ideas become connected with each other. These laws contain the seed of future developments; but they do not furnish any general expression for the influence of rigid spacial connections. Here d'Alembert's principle extends the general results of statics to the case of motion, and closes the series of independent fundamental statements which cannot be deduced from each other. From here on everything is deductive inference. In fact the above-mentioned ideas and laws are not only necessary but sufficient for the development of the whole of mechanics from them as a necessary consequence of thought; and all other so-called principles can be regarded as propositions and corollaries deduced by special assumptions. Hence the above ideas and laws give us, in the sense in which we have used the words, a first system of principles of mechanics, and at the same time the first general image of the natural motions of material bodies.

Now, at first sight, any doubt as to the logical permissibility of this image may seem very far-fetched. It seems almost inconceivable that we should find logical imperfections in a system which has been thoroughly and repeatedly considered by many of the ablest intellects. But before we abandon the investigation on this account, we should do well to inquire whether the system has always given satisfaction to these able intellects. It is really wonderful how easy it is to attach to the fundamental laws considerations which are quite in accordance with the usual modes of expression in mechanics, and which yet are an undoubted hindrance to clear thinking. Let us endeavour to give an example of this. We swing in a circle a stone tied to a string, and in so doing we are conscious of exerting a force upon the stone. This force constantly deflects the stone from its straight path. If we vary the force, the mass of the stone, and the length of the string, we find that the actual motion of the stone is always in accordance with Newton's second law. But now the third law requires an opposing force to the force exerted by the hand upon the stone. With regard to this opposing force the usual explanation is that the stone reacts upon the hand in consequence of centrifugal force, and that this centrifugal force is in fact exactly equal and opposite to that which we exert. Now is this mode of expression permissible? Is what we call centrifugal force anything else than the inertia of the stone? Can we, without destroying the clearness of our conceptions, take the effect of inertia twice into account,—firstly as mass, secondly as force? In our laws of motion, force was a cause of motion, and was present *before* the motion. Can we, without confusing our ideas, suddenly begin to speak of forces which arise through motion, which are a consequence of motion? Can we behave as if we had already asserted anything about forces of this new kind in our laws, as if by calling them forces we could invest them with the properties of forces? These questions must clearly be answered in the negative. The only possible explanation is that, properly speaking, centrifugal force is not a force at all. Its name, like the name *vis viva*, is accepted as a historic tradition; it is convenient to retain it, although we should rather apologise for its retention than endeavour to justify it. But, what now becomes of the demands of the third law, which requires a force exerted by the inert stone upon the hand, and which can only be satisfied by an actual force, not a mere name?

I do not regard these as artificial difficulties wantonly raised: they are objections which press for an answer. Is not their origin to be traced back to the fundamental laws? The force spoken of in the definition and in the first two laws acts upon a body in one definite direction. The sense of the third law is that forces always connect two bodies, and are directed from the first to the second as well as from the second to the first. It seems to me that the conception of force assumed and created in us by the third law on the one hand, and the first two laws on the other hand, are slightly different. This slight difference may be enough to produce the logical obscurity of which the consequences are manifest in the above example. It is not necessary to discuss further examples. We can appeal to general observations as evidence in support of the above-mentioned doubt.

As such, in the first place, I would mention the experience that it is exceedingly difficult to expound to thoughtful hearers the very introduction to mechanics without being occasionally embarrassed, without feeling tempted now and again to apologise, without wishing to get as quickly as possible over the rudiments, and on to examples which speak for themselves. I fancy that Newton himself must have felt this embarrassment when he gave the rather forced definition of mass as being the product of volume and density. I fancy that Thomson and Tait must also have felt it when they remarked that this is really more a definition of density than of mass, and nevertheless contented themselves with it as the only definition of mass. Lagrange, too, must have felt this embarrassment and the wish to get on at all costs; for he briefly introduces his Mechanics with the explanation that a force is a cause which imparts " or tends to impart" motion to a body; and he must certainly have felt the logical difficulty of such a definition. I find further evidence in the demonstrations of the elementary propositions of statics, such as the law of the parallelogram of forces, of virtual velocities, etc. Of such propositions we have numerous proofs given by eminent mathematicians. These claim to be rigid proofs; but, according to the opinion of other distinguished mathematicians, they in no way satisfy this claim. In a logically complete science, such as pure mathematics, such a difference of opinion is utterly inconceivable.

Weighty evidence seems to be furnished by the statements which one hears with wearisome frequency, that the nature of force is still a mystery, that one of the chief problems of physics is the investigation of the nature of force, and so on. In the same way electricians are continually attacked as to the nature of electricity. Now, why is it that people never in this way ask what is the nature of gold, or what is the nature of velocity ? Is the nature of gold better known to us than that of electricity, or the nature of velocity better than that of force ? Can we by our conceptions, by our words, completely represent the nature of any thing? Certainly not. I fancy the difference must lie in this. With the terms "velocity" and "gold" we connect a large number of relations to other terms; and between all these relations we find no contradictions which offend us. We are therefore satisfied and ask no further questions. But we have accumulated around the terms "force" and "electricity" more relations than can be completely reconciled amongst themselves. We have an obscure feeling of this and want to have things cleared up. Our confused wish finds expression in the confused question as to the nature of force and electricity. But the answer which we want is not really an answer to this question. It is not by finding out more and fresh relations and connections that it can be answered; but by removing the contradictions existing between those already known, and thus perhaps by reducing their number. When these painful contradictions are removed, the question as to the nature of force will not have been answered; but our minds, no longer vexed, will cease to ask illegitimate questions.

I have thrown such strong doubts upon the permissibility of this image that it might appear to be my intention to contest, and finally to deny, its permissibility. But my intention and conviction do not go so far as this. Even if the logical uncertainties, which have made us solicitous as to our fundamental ideas, do actually exist, they certainly have not prevented a single one of the numerous triumphs which mechanics has won in its applications. Hence, they cannot consist of contradictions between the essential characteristics of our image, nor, therefore, of contradictions between those relations of mechanics which correspond to the relations of things. They must rather lie in the unessential characteristics which we have ourselves arbitrarily worked into the essential content given by nature. If so, these dilemmas can be avoided. Perhaps our objections do not relate to the content of the image devised, but only to the form in which the content is represented. It is not going too far to say that this representation has never attained scientific completeness; it still fails to distinguish thoroughly and sharply between the elements in the image which arise from the necessities of thought, from experience, and from arbitrary choice. This is also the opinion of distinguished physicists who have thought over and discussed [1] these questions, although it cannot be said that all of them are in agreement.[2] This opinion also finds confirmation in the increasing care with which the logical analysis of the elements is carried out in the more recent text-books of mechanics.[3] We are con-

[1] See E. Mach, *The Science of Mechanics*, p. 244. See also in *Nature* (**48**, pp. 62, 101, 117, 126 and 166, 1893; and *Proc. Phys. Soc.* **12**, p. 289, 1893) a discussion on the foundations of dynamics introduced by Prof. Oliver Lodge and carried on in the Physical Society of London.
[2] See Thomson and Tait, *Natural Philosophy*, § 205 *et seq.*
[3] See E. Budde, *Allgemeine Mechanik der Punkte und starren Systeme*, p. 111-138

vinced, as are the authors of these text-books and the physicists referred to, that the existing defects are only defects in form; and that all indistinctness and uncertainty can be avoided by suitable arrangement of definitions and notations, and by due care in the mode of expression. In this sense we admit, as everyone does, the permissibility of the content of mechanics. But the dignity and importance of the subject demand, not simply that we should readily take for granted its logical clearness, but that we should endeavour to show it by a representation so perfect that there should no longer be any possibility of doubting it.

Upon the correctness of the image under consideration we can pronounce judgment more easily and with greater certainty of general assent. No one will deny that within the whole range of our experience up to the present the correctness is perfect; that all those characteristics of our image, which claim to represent observable relations of things, do really and correctly correspond to them. Our assurance, of course, is restricted to the range of previous experience: as far as future experience is concerned, there will yet be occasion to return to the question of correctness. To many this will seem to be excessive and absurd caution: to many physicists it appears simply inconceivable that any further experience whatever should find anything to alter in the firm foundations of mechanics. Nevertheless, that which is derived from experience can again be annulled by experience. This over-favourable opinion of the fundamental laws must obviously arise from the fact that the elements of experience are to a certain extent hidden in them and blended with the unalterable elements which are necessary consequences of our thought. Thus the logical indefiniteness of the representation, which we have just censured, has one advantage. It gives the foundations an appearance of immutability; and perhaps it was wise to introduce it in the beginnings of the science and to allow it to remain for a while. The correctness of the image in all cases was carefully provided for by making the reservation that, if need be, facts derived from experience should determine definitions or *vice versa*. In a perfect science such groping, such an appearance of certainty, is inadmissible.

(Berlin : 1890). The representation there given shows at the same time how great are the difficulties encountered in avoiding discrepancies in the use of the elements.

Mature knowledge regards logical clearness as of prime importance: only logically clear images does it test as to correctness; only correct images does it compare as to appropriateness. By pressure of circumstances the process is often reversed. Images are found to be suitable for a certain purpose; are next tested as to their correctness; and only in the last place purged of implied contradictions.

If there is any truth in what we have just stated, it seems only natural that the system of mechanics under consideration should prove most appropriate in its applications to those simple phenomena for which it was first devised, *i.e.* especially to the action of gravity and the problems of practical mechanics. But we should not be content with this. We should remember that we are not here representing the needs of daily life or the standpoint of past times; we are considering the whole range of present physical knowledge, and are, moreover, speaking of appropriateness in the special sense defined in the beginning of this introduction. Hence we are at once bound to ask,—Is this image perfectly distinct? Does it contain all the characteristics which our present knowledge enables us to distinguish in natural motions? Our answer is a decided—No. All the motions of which the fundamental laws admit, and which are treated of in mechanics as mathematical exercises, do not occur in nature. Of natural motions, forces, and fixed connections, we can predicate more than the accepted fundamental laws do. Since the middle of this century we have been firmly convinced that no forces actually exist in nature which would involve a violation of the principle of the conservation of energy. The conviction is much older that only such forces exist as can be represented as a sum of mutual actions between infinitely small elements of matter. Again, these elementary forces are not free. We can assert as a property which they are generally admitted to possess, that they are independent of absolute time and place. Other properties are disputed. Whether the elementary forces can only consist of attractions and repulsions along the line connecting the acting masses; whether their magnitude is determined only by the distance or whether it is also affected by the absolute or relative velocity;

whether the latter alone comes into consideration, or the acceleration or still higher differential coefficients as well—all these properties have been sometimes presumed, at other times questioned. Although there is such difference of opinion as to the precise properties which are to be attributed to the elementary forces, there is a general agreement that more of such general properties can be assigned, and can from existing observations be deduced, than are contained in the fundamental laws. We are convinced that the elementary forces must, so to speak, be of a simple nature. And what here holds for the forces, can be equally asserted of the fixed connections of bodies which are represented mathematically by equations of condition between the coordinates and whose effect is determined by d'Alembert's principle. It is mathematically possible to write down any finite or differential equation between coordinates and to require that it shall be satisfied; but it is not always possible to specify a natural, physical connection corresponding to such an equation: we often feel, indeed sometimes are convinced, that such a connection is by the nature of things excluded. And yet, how are we to restrict the permissible equations of condition? Where is the limiting line between them and the conceivable ones? To consider only finite equations of condition, as has often been done, is to go too far; for differential equations which are not integrable can actually occur as equations of condition in natural problems.

In short, then, so far as the forces, as well as the fixed relations, are concerned, our system of principles embraces all the natural motions; but it also includes very many motions which are not natural. A system which excludes the latter, or even a part of them, would picture more of the actual relations of things to each other, and would therefore in this sense be more appropriate. We are next bound to inquire as to the appropriateness of our image in a second direction. Is our image simple? Is it sparing in unessential characteristics —ones added by ourselves, permissibly and yet arbitrarily, to the essential and natural ones? In answering this question our thoughts again turn to the idea of force. It cannot be denied that in very many cases the forces which are used in mechanics for treating physical problems are simply sleeping partners, which keep out of the business altogether when actual facts have to be represented. In the simple relations with which mechanics originally dealt, this is not the case. The weight of a stone and the force exerted by the arm seem to be as real and as readily and directly perceptible as the motions which they produce. But it is otherwise when we turn to the motions of the stars. Here the forces have never been the objects of direct perception; all our previous experiences relate only to the apparent position of the stars. Nor do we expect in future to perceive the forces. The future experiences which we anticipate again relate only to the position of these luminous points in the heavens. It is only in the deduction of future experiences from the past that the forces of gravitation enter as transitory aids in the calculation, and then disappear from consideration. Precisely the same is true of the discussion of molecular forces, of chemical actions, and of many electric and magnetic actions. And if after more mature experience we return to the simple forces, whose existence we never doubted, we learn that these forces which we had perceived with convincing certainty, were after all not real. More mature mechanics tells us that what we believed to be simply the tendency of a body towards the earth, is not really such: it is the result, imagined only as a single force, of an inconceivable number of actual forces which attract the atoms of the body towards all the atoms of the universe. Here again the actual forces have never been the objects of previous experience; nor do we expect to come across them in future experiences. Only during the process of deducing future experiences from the past do they glide quietly in and out. But even if the forces have only been introduced by ourselves into nature, we should not on that account regard their introduction as inappropriate. We have felt sure from the beginning that unessential relations could not be altogether avoided in our images. All that we can ask is that these relations should, as far as possible, be restricted, and that a wise discretion should be observed in their use. But has physics always been sparing in the use of such relations? Has it not rather been compelled to fill the world to overflowing with forces of the most various kinds—with forces which never appeared in the phenomena, even with forces which only came into action in exceptional cases ? We see a piece of iron resting upon a table, and we accordingly imagine that no causes of motion —no forces—are there present. Physics, which is based upon the mechanics considered here and necessarily determined by this basis, teaches us otherwise. Through the force of gravitation every atom of the iron is attracted by every other atom in the universe. But every atom of the iron is magnetic, and is thus connected by fresh forces with every other magnetic atom in the universe. Again, bodies in the universe contain electricity in motion, and this latter exerts further complicated forces which attract every atom of the iron. In so far as' the parts of the iron themselves contain electricity, we have fresh forces to take into consideration; and in addition to these again various kinds of molecular forces. Some of these forces are not small: if only a part of these forces were effective, this part would suffice to tear the iron to pieces. But, in fact, all the forces are so adjusted amongst each other that the effect of the whole lot is zero; that in spite of a thousand existing causes of motion, no motion takes place; that the iron remains at rest. Now if we place these conceptions before unprejudiced persons, who will believe us ? Whom shall we convince that we are speaking of actual things, not images of a riotous imagination ? And it is for us to reflect whether we have really depicted the state of rest of the iron and its particles in a simple manner. Whether complications can be entirely avoided is questionable; but there can be no question that a system of mechanics which does avoid or exclude them is simpler, and in this sense more appropriate, than the one here considered; for this latter not only permits such conceptions, but directly obtrudes them upon us.

Let us now collect together as briefly as possible the doubts which have occurred to us in considering the customary mode of representing the principles of mechanics. As far as the form is concerned, we consider that the logical value of the separate statements is not defined with sufficient clearness. As far as the facts are concerned, it appears to us that the motions considered in mechanics do not exactly coincide with the natural motions under consideration. Many properties of the natural motions are not attended to in mechanics; many relations which are considered in mechanics are probably absent in nature. Even if these objections are acknowledged to be well founded, they should not lead us to imagine that the customary representation of mechanics is on that account either bound to or likely to lose its value and its privileged position; but they sufficiently justify us in looking out for other representations less liable to censure in these respects, and more closely conformable to the things which have to be represented.

II

There is a second image of mechanical processes which is of much more recent origin than the first. Its development from, and side by side with, the latter is closely connected with advances which physical science has made during the past few decades. Up to the middle of this century its ultimate aim was apparently to explain natural phenomena by tracing them back to innumerable actions-at-a-distance between the atoms of matter. This mode of conception corresponded completely to what we have spoken of as the first system of mechanical principles: each of the two was conditioned by the other. Now, towards the end of the century, physics has shown a preference for a different mode of thought. Influenced by the overpowering impression made by the discovery of the principle of the conservation of energy, it likes to treat the phenomena which occur in its domain as transformations of energy into new forms, and to regard as its ultimate aim the tracing back of the phenomena to the laws of the transformation of energy. This mode of treatment can also be applied from the beginning to the elementary phenomena of motion. There thus arises a new and different representation of mechanics, in which from the start the idea of force retires in favour of the idea of energy. It is this new image of the elementary processes of motion which we shall denote as the second; and to it we shall now devote our attention. In discussing the first image we had the advantage of being able to assume that it stood out plainly before the eyes of all physicists. With the second image this is not the case. It has never yet been portrayed in all its details. So far as I know, there is no text-book of mechanics which from the start teaches the subject from the standpoint of energy, and introduces the idea of energy before the idea of force. Perhaps there has never yet been a lecture on mechanics prepared according to this plan. But to the founders of the theory of energy it was evident that such a plan was possible; the remark has often been made that in this way the idea of force with its attendant difficulties could be avoided; and in special scientific applications chains of reasoning frequently occur which belong entirely to this mode of thought. Hence we can very well sketch the rough outlines of the image; we can give the general plan according to which such a representation of mechanics must be arranged. We here start, as in the case of the first image, from four independent fundamental ideas; and the relations of these to each other will form the contents of mechanics. Two of them—space and time—have a mathematical character; the other two—mass and energy—are introduced as physical entities which are present in given quantity, and cannot be destroyed or increased. In addition to explaining these matters, it will, of course, also be necessary to indicate clearly by what concrete experiences we ultimately establish the presence of mass and energy. We here assume this to be possible and to be done. It is obvious that the amount of energy connected with given masses depends upon the state of these masses. But it is as a general experience that we must first lay down that the energy present can always be split up into two parts, of which the one is determined solely by the relative positions of the masses, while the other depends upon their absolute velocities. The first part is defined as potential energy, the second as kinetic energy. The form of the dependence of kinetic energy upon the velocity of the moving bodies is in all cases the same, and is known. The form of the dependence of potential energy upon the position of the bodies cannot be generally stated; it rather constitutes the special nature and characteristic peculiarity of the masses under consideration. It is the problem of physics to ascertain from previous experience this form for the bodies which surround us in nature. Up to this point there come essentially into consideration only three elements—space, mass, energy, considered in relation to each other. In order to settle the relations of all the four fundamental ideas, and thereby the course in time of the phenomena, we make use of one of the integral principles of ordinary mechanics which involve in their statement the idea of energy. It is not of much importance which of these we select; we can and shall choose Hamilton's principle. We thus lay down as the sole fundamental law of mechanics, in accordance with experience, the proposition that every system of natural bodies moves just as if it were assigned the problem of attaining given positions in given times, and in such a manner that the average over the whole time of the difference between kinetic and potential energy shall be as small as possible. Although this law may not be simple in form, it nevertheless represents without ambiguity the transformations of energy, and enables us to predetermine completely the course of actual phenomena for the future. In stating this new law we lay down the last of the indispensable foundations of mechanics. All that we can further add are only mathematical deductions and certain simplifications of notation which, although expedient, are not necessary. Among these latter is the idea of force, which does not enter into the foundations. Its introduction is expedient when we are considering not only masses which are connected with constant quantities of energy, but also masses which give up energy to other masses or receive it from them. Still, it is not by any new experience that it is introduced, but by a definition which can be formed in more than one way. And accordingly the properties of the force so defined are not to be ascertained by experience, but are to be deduced from the definition and the fundamental laws. Even the confirmation of these properties by experience is superfluous, unless we doubt the correctness of the whole system. Hence the idea of force as such cannot in this system involve any logical difficulties : nor can it come in question in estimating the correctness of the system; it can only increase or diminish its appropriateness.

Somewhat after the manner indicated would the principles of mechanics have to be arranged in order to adapt them to the conception of energy. The question now is, whether this second image is preferable to the first. Let us therefore consider its advantages and disadvantages.

It will be best for us here to consider first the question of appropriateness, since it is in this respect that the improvement is most obvious. For, to begin with, our second image of natural motions is decidedly more distinct: it shows more of their peculiarities than the first does. When we wish to deduce Hamilton's principle from the general foundations of mechanics we have to add to the latter certain assumptions as to the acting forces and the character of contingent fixed connections. These assumptions are of the most general nature, but they indicate a corresponding number of important limitations of the motions represented by the principle. And, conversely, we can deduce from the principle a whole series of relations, especially of mutual relations between every kind of possible force, which are wanting in the principles of the first image; in the second image they are present, and likewise occur, which is the important point, in nature. To prove this is the object of the papers published by von Helmholtz under the title, *Ueber die physikalische Bedeutung des Prinzips der kleinsten Wirkung*. It would be more correct to say that the fact which has to be proved forms the discovery which is demonstrated and communicated in that paper. For it is truly a discovery to find that from such general assumptions, conclusions so distinct, so weighty, and so just can be drawn. We may then appeal to that paper for confirmation of our statement; and, inasmuch as it represents the furthest advance of physics at the present time, we may spare ourselves the question whether it be possible to conform yet more closely to nature, say by limiting the permissible forms of potential energy. We shall simply emphasise this, that in respect of simplicity as well, our present image avoids the stumbling-blocks which endangered the appropriateness of the first. For if we ask ourselves the real reasons why physics at the present time prefers to express itself in terms of energy, our answer will be, Because in this way it best avoids talking about things of which it knows very little, and which do not at all affect the essential statements under consideration. We have already had occasion to remark that in tracing back phenomena to force we are compelled to turn our attention continually to atoms and molecules. It is true that we are now convinced that ponderable matter consists of atoms; and we have definite notions of the magnitude of these atoms and of their motions in certain cases. But the form of the atoms, their connection, their motion in most cases—all these are entirely hidden from us; their number is in all cases immeasurably great. So that although our conception of atoms is in itself an important and interesting object for further investigation, it is in no wise specially fit to serve as a known and secure foundation for mathematical theories. To an investigator like Gustav Kirchhoff, who was accustomed to rigid reasoning, it almost gave pain to see atoms and their vibrations wilfully stuck in the middle of a theoretical deduction. The arbitrarily assumed properties of the atoms may not affect the final result. The result may be correct. Nevertheless the details of the deduction are in great part presumably false; the deduction is only in appearance a proof. The earlier mode of thought in physics scarcely allowed any choice or any way of escape. Herein lies the advantage of the conception of energy and of our second image of mechanics: that in the hypotheses of the problems there only enter characteristics which are directly accessible to experience, parameters, or arbitrary coordinates of the bodies under consideration; that the examination proceeds with the aid of these characteristics in a finite and complete form; and that the final result can again be directly translated into tangible experience. Beyond energy itself in its few forms, no auxiliary constructions enter into consideration. Our statements can be limited to the known peculiarities of the system of bodies under consideration, and we need not conceal our ignorance of the details by arbitrary and ineffectual hypotheses. All the steps in the deduction, as well as the final result, can be defended as correct and significant. These are the merits which have endeared this method to present-day physics. They are peculiar to our second image of mechanics: in the sense in which we have used the words they are to be regarded as advantages in respect of simplicity, and hence of appropriateness.

Unfortunately we begin to be uncertain as to the value of our system when we test its correctness and its logical permissibility. The question of correctness at once gives rise to legitimate doubts. Hamilton's principle can be deduced from the accepted foundations of Newtonian mechanics; but this does not by any means guarantee an accordance with nature. We have to remember that this deduction only follows if certain assumptions hold good; and also that our system claims not only to describe certain natural motions correctly, but to embrace all natural motions. We must therefore investigate whether these special assumptions which are made in addition to Newton's laws are universally true; and a single example from nature to the contrary would invalidate the correctness of our system as such, although it would not disturb in the least the validity of Hamilton's principle as a general proposition. The doubt is not so much whether our system includes the whole manifold [1] of forces, as whether it embraces the whole manifold of rigid connections which may arise between the bodies of nature. The application of Hamilton's principle to a material system does not exclude the existence of fixed connections between the chosen coordinates. But at any rate it requires that these connections be mathematically expressible by finite equations between the coordinates: it does not permit the occurrence of connections which can only be represented by differential equations. But nature itself does not appear to entirely exclude connections of this kind. They arise, for example, when bodies of three dimensions roll on one another without slipping. By such a connection, examples of which frequently occur, the position of the two bodies with respect to each other is only limited by the condition that they must always have one point of their surfaces common; but the freedom of motion of the bodies is further diminished by a degree. From the connection, then, there can be deduced more equations between the changes of the coordinates than between the coordinates themselves; hence there must amongst these equations be at least one non-integrable differential equation. Now Hamilton's principle cannot be applied to such a case; or, to speak more correctly, the application, which is mathematically possible, leads to results which are physically false. Let us restrict our consideration to the case of a sphere rolling without slipping upon a horizontal plane under the influence of its inertia alone. It is not difficult to see, without calculation, what motions the sphere can actually execute. We can also see what motions would correspond to Hamilton's principle; these would have to take place

[1] [*Mannigfaltigkeit* is thus rendered throughout.—*Tr.*]

in such a way that with constant *vis viva* the sphere would attain given positions in the shortest possible time. We can thus convince ourselves, without calculation, that the two kinds of motions exhibit very different characteristics. If we choose any initial and final positions of the sphere, it is clear that there is always one definite motion from the one to the other for which the time of motion, *i.e.* the Hamilton's integral, is a minimum. But, as a matter of fact, a natural motion from every position to every other is not possible without the co-operation of forces, even if the choice of the initial velocity is perfectly free. And even if we choose the initial and final positions so that a natural free motion between the two is possible, this will nevertheless not be the one which corresponds to a minimum of time. For certain initial and final positions the difference can be very striking. In this case a sphere moving in accordance with the principle would decidedly have the appearance of a living thing, steering its course consciously towards a given goal, while a sphere following the law of nature would give the impression of an inanimate mass spinning steadily towards it. It would be of no use to replace Hamilton's principle by the principle of least action or by any other integral principle, for there is but a slight difference of meaning between all these principles, and in the respect here considered they are quite equivalent. Only in one way can we defend the system and preserve it from the charge of incorrectness. We must decline to admit that rigid connections of the kind referred to do actually and strictly occur in nature. We must show that all so-called rolling without slipping is really rolling with a little slipping, and is therefore a case of friction. We have to rest our case upon this—that generally friction between surfaces is one of the processes which we have not yet been able to trace back to clearly understood causes; that the forces which come into play have only been ascertained quite empirically; and hence that the whole problem is one of those which we cannot at present handle without making use of force and the roundabout methods of ordinary mechanics. This defence is not quite convincing. For rolling without slipping does not contradict either the principle of energy or any other generally accepted law of physics. The process is one which is so nearly realised in the visible world that even integration machines are constructed on the assumption that it strictly takes place. We have scarcely any right, then, to exclude its occurrence as impossible, at any rate from the mechanics of unknown systems, such as the atoms or the parts of the ether. But even if we admit that the connections in question are only approximately realised in nature, the failure of Hamilton's principle still creates difficulties in these cases. We are bound to require of every fundamental law of our mechanical system, that when applied to approximately correct relations it should always lead to approximately correct results, not to results which are entirely false. For otherwise, since all the rigid connections which we draw from nature and introduce into the calculations correspond only approximately to the actual relations, we should get into a state of hopeless uncertainty as to which admitted of the application of the law and which not. And yet we do not wish to abandon entirely the defence which we have proposed. We should prefer to admit that the doubt is one which affects the appropriateness of the system, not its correctness, so that the disadvantages which arise from it may be outweighed by other advantages.

The real difficulties first meet us when we try to arrange the elements of the system in strict accordance with the requirements of logical permissibility. In introducing the idea of energy we cannot proceed in the usual way, starting with force, and proceeding from this to force-functions, to potential energy, and to energy in general. Such an arrangement would belong to the first representation of mechanics. Without assuming any previous consideration of mechanics, we have to specify by what simple, direct experiences we propose to define the presence of a store of energy, and the determination of its amount. In what precedes we have only assumed, not shown, that such a determination is possible. At the present time many distinguished physicists tend so much to attribute to energy the properties of a substance as to assume that every smallest portion of it is associated at every instant with a given place in space, and that through all the changes of place and all the transformations of the energy into new forms it retains its identity. These physicists must have the conviction that definitions of the required kind can be found; and it is therefore permissible to assume that such definitions can be given. But when we try to throw them into a concrete form, satisfactory to ourselves and likely to command general acceptance, we become perplexed. This mode of conception as a whole does not yet seem to have arrived at a satisfactory and conclusive result. At the very beginning there arises a special difficulty, from the circumstance that energy, which is alleged to resemble a substance, occurs in two such totally dissimilar forms as kinetic and potential energy. Kinetic energy itself does not really require any new fundamental determination, for it can be deduced from the ideas of velocity and mass; on the other hand potential energy, which does require to be settled independently, does not lend itself at all well to any definition which ascribes to it the properties of a substance. The amount of a substance is necessarily a positive quantity; but we never hesitate in assuming the potential energy contained in a system to be negative. When the amount of a substance is represented by an analytical expression, an additive constant in the expression has the same importance as the rest; but in the expression for the potential energy of a system an additive constant never has any meaning. Lastly, the amount of any substance contained in a physical system can only depend upon the state of the system itself; but the amount of potential energy contained in given matter depends upon the presence of distant masses which perhaps have never had any influence upon the system. If the universe, and therefore the number of such distant masses, is infinite, then the amount of many forms of potential energy contained in even finite quantities of matter is infinitely great. All these are difficulties which must be removed or avoided by the desired definition of energy. We do not assert that such a definition is impossible, but as yet we cannot say that it has been framed. The most prudent thing to do will be to regard it for the present as an open question, whether the system can be developed in logically unexceptionable form.

It may be worth while discussing here whether there is any justification for another objection which might be raised as to the permissibility of this second system. In order that an image of certain external things may in our sense be permissible, not only must its characteristics be consistent amongst themselves, but they must not contradict the characteristics of other images already established in our knowledge. On the strength of this it may be said to be inconceivable that Hamilton's principle, or any similar proposition, should really play the part of a fundamental law of mechanics, and be a fundamental law of nature. For the first thing that is to be expected of a fundamental law is simplicity and plainness, whereas Hamilton's principle, when we come to look into it, proves to be an exceedingly complicated statement. Not only does it make the present motion dependent upon consequences which can only exhibit themselves in the future, thereby attributing intentions to inanimate nature; but, what is much worse, it attributes to nature intentions which are void of meaning. For the integral, whose minimum is required by Hamilton's principle, has no simple physical meaning; and for nature it is an unintelligible aim to make a mathematical expression a minimum, or to bring its variation to zero. The usual answer, which physics nowadays keeps ready for such attacks, is that these considerations are based upon metaphysical assumptions; that physics has renounced these, and no longer recognises it as its duty to meet the demands of metaphysics. It no longer attaches weight to the reasons which used to be urged from the metaphysical side in favour of principles which indicate design in nature, and thus it cannot lend ear to objections of a metaphysical character against these same principles. If we had to decide upon such a matter we should not think it unfair to place ourselves rather on the side of the attack than of the defence. A doubt which makes an impression on our mind cannot be removed by calling it metaphysical; every thoughtful mind as such has needs which scientific men are accustomed to denote as metaphysical. Moreover, in the case in question, as indeed in all others, it is possible to show what are the sound and just sources of our needs. It is true we cannot *a priori* demand from nature simplicity, nor can we judge what in her opinion is simple. But with regard to images of our own creation we can lay down requirements. We are justified in deciding that if our images are well adapted to the things, the actual relations of the things must be represented by simple relations between the images.

And if the actual relations between the things can only be represented by complicated relations, which are not even intelligible to an unprepared mind, we decide that these images are not sufficiently well adapted to the things. Hence our requirement of simplicity does not apply to nature, but to the images thereof which we fashion; and our repugnance to a complicated statement as a fundamental law only expresses the conviction that, if the contents of the statement are correct and comprehensive, it can be stated in a simpler form by a more suitable choice of the fundamental conceptions. The same conviction finds expression in the desire we feel to penetrate from the external acquaintance with such a law to the deeper and real meaning which we are convinced it possesses. If this conception is correct, the objection brought forward does really justify a doubt as to the system; but it does not apply so much to its permissibility as to its appropriateness, and comes under consideration in deciding as to the latter. However, we need not return to the consideration of this.

If we once more glance over the merits which we were able to claim for this second image, we come to the conclusion that as a whole it is not quite satisfactory. Although the whole tendency of recent physics moves us to place the idea of energy in the foreground, and to use it as the corner-stone of our structure, it yet remains doubtful whether in so doing we can avoid the harshness and ruggedness which were so disagreeable in the first image. In fact I have discussed this second mode of representation at some length, not in order to urge its adoption, but rather to show why, after due trial, I have felt obliged to abandon it.

III

A third arrangement of the principles of mechanics is that which will be explained at length in this book. Its principal characteristics will be at once stated, so that it may be criticised in the same way as the other two. It differs from them in this important respect, that it only starts with three independent fundamental conceptions, namely, those of time, space, and mass. The problem which it has to solve is to represent the natural relations between these three, and between these three alone. The difficulties have hitherto been met with in connection with a fourth idea, such as the idea of force or of energy; this, as an independent fundamental conception, is here avoided. G. Kirchhoff has already made the remark in his *Text-book of Mechanics* that three independent conceptions are necessary and sufficient for the development of mechanics. Of course the deficiency in the manifold which thus results in the fundamental conceptions necessarily requires some complement. In our representation we endeavour to fill up the gap which occurs by the use of an hypothesis, which is not stated here for the first time; but it is not usual to introduce it in the very elements of mechanics. The nature of the hypothesis may be explained as follows.

If we try to understand the motions of bodies around us, and to refer them to simple and clear rules, paying attention only to what can be directly observed, our attempt will in general fail. We soon become aware that the totality of things visible and tangible do not form an universe conformable to law, in which the same results always follow from the same conditions. We become convinced that the manifold of the actual universe must be greater than the manifold of the universe which is directly revealed to us by our senses. If we wish to obtain an image of the universe which shall be well-rounded, complete, and conformable to law, we have to presuppose, behind the things which we see, other, invisible things—to imagine confederates concealed beyond the limits of our senses. These deep-lying influences we recognised in the first two representations; we imagined them to be entities of a special and peculiar kind, and so, in order to represent them in our image, we created the ideas of force and energy. But another way lies open to us. We may admit that there is a hidden something at work, and yet deny that this something belongs to a special category. We are free to assume that this hidden something is nought else than motion and mass again,—motion and mass which differ from the visible ones not in themselves but in relation to us and to our usual means of perception. Now this mode of conception is just our hypothesis. We assume that it is possible to conjoin with the visible masses of the universe other masses obeying the same laws, and of such a kind that the whole thereby becomes intelligible and conformable to law. We assume this to be possible everywhere and in all cases, and that there are no causes whatever of the phenomena other than those hereby admitted. What we are accustomed to denote as force and as energy now become nothing more than an action of mass and motion, but not necessarily of mass and motion recognisable by our coarse senses. Such explanations of force from processes of motion are usually called dynamical; and we have every reason for saying that physics at the present day regards such explanations with great favour. The forces connected with heat have been traced back with certainty to the concealed motions of tangible masses. Through Maxwell's labours the supposition that electro-magnetic forces are due to the motion of concealed masses has become almost a conviction. Lord Kelvin gives a prominent place to dynamical explanations of force; in his theory of vortex atoms he has endeavoured to present an image of the universe in accordance with this conception. In his investigation of cyclical systems von Helmholtz has treated the most important form of concealed motion fully, and in a manner that admits of general application; through him "concealed mass" and "concealed motion" have become current as technical expressions in German.[1] But if this hypothesis is capable of gradually eliminating the mysterious forces from mechanics, it can also entirely prevent their entering into mechanics. And if its use for the former purpose is in accordance with present tendencies of physics, the same must hold good of its use for the latter purpose. This is the leading thought from which we start. By following it out we arrive at the third image, the general outlines of which will now be sketched.

We first introduce the three independent fundamental ideas of time, space, and mass as objects of experience; and we specify the concrete sensible experiences by which time, mass, and space are to be determined. With regard to the masses we stipulate that, in addition to the masses recognisable by the senses, concealed masses can by hypothesis be

[1] [*Verborgene Masse; verborgene Bewegung.*]

introduced. We next bring together the relations which always obtain between these concrete experiences, and which we have to retain as the essential relations between the fundamental ideas. To begin with, we naturally connect the fundamental ideas in pairs. Relations between space and time alone form the subject of kinematics. There exists no connection between mass and time alone. Experience teaches us that between mass and space there exists a series of important relations. For we find certain purely spacial connections between the masses of nature: from the very beginning onwards through all time, and therefore independently of time, certain positions and certain changes of position are prescribed and associated as possible for these masses, and all others as impossible. Respecting these connections we can also assert generally that they only apply to the relative position of the masses amongst themselves; and further that they satisfy certain conditions of continuity, which find their mathematical expression in the fact that the connections themselves can always be represented by homogeneous linear equations between the first differentials of the magnitudes by which the positions of the masses are denoted. To investigate in detail the connections of definite material systems is not the business of mechanics, but of experimental physics: the distinguishing characteristics which differentiate the various material systems of nature from each other are, according to our conception, simply and solely the connections of their masses. Up to this point we have only considered the connections of the fundamental ideas in pairs: we now address ourselves to mechanics in the stricter sense, in which all three have to be considered together. We find that their general connection, in accordance with experience, can be epitomised in a single fundamental law, which exhibits a close analogy with the usual law of inertia. In accordance with the mode of expression which we shall use, it can be represented by the statement:—Every natural motion of an independent material system consists herein, that the system follows with uniform velocity one of its straightest paths. Of course this statement only becomes intelligible when we have given the necessary explanation of the mathematical mode of expression used; but the sense of the law can also be expressed in the usual language of mechanics. The law condenses into one single statement the usual law of inertia and Gauss's Principle of Least Constraint. It therefore asserts that if the connections of the system could be momentarily destroyed, its masses would become dispersed, moving in straight lines with uniform velocity; but that as this is impossible, they tend as nearly as possible to such a motion. In our image this fundamental law is the first proposition derived from experience in mechanics proper: it is also the last. From it, together with the admitted hypothesis of concealed masses and the normal connections, we can derive all the rest of mechanics by purely deductive reasoning. Around it we group the remaining general principles, according to their relations to it and to each other, as corollaries or as partial statements. We endeavour to show that the contents of mechanics, when arranged in this way, do not become less rich or manifold than its contents when it starts with four fundamental conceptions; at any rate not less rich or manifold than is required for the representation of nature. We soon find it convenient to introduce into our system the idea of force. However, it is not as something independent of us and apart from us that force now makes its appearance, but as a mathematical aid whose properties are entirely in our power. It cannot, therefore, in itself have anything mysterious to us. Thus according to our fundamental law, whenever two bodies belong to the same system, the motion of the one is determined by that of the other. The idea of force now comes in as follows. For assignable reasons we find it convenient to divide the determination of the one motion by the other into two steps. We thus say that the motion of the first body determines a force, and that this force then determines the motion of the second body. In this way force can with equal justice be regarded as being always a cause of motion, and at the same time a consequence of motion. Strictly speaking, it is a middle term conceived only between two motions. According to this conception the general properties of force must clearly follow as a necessary consequence of thought from the fundamental law; and if in possible experiences we see these properties confirmed, we can in no sense feel surprised, unless we are sceptical as to our fundamental law. Precisely the same is true of the idea of energy and of any other aids that may be introduced.

What has hitherto been stated relates to the physical content of the image, and nothing further need be said with regard to this; but it will be convenient to give here a brief explanation of the special mathematical form in which it will be represented. The physical content is quite independent of the mathematical form, and as the content differs from what is customary, it is perhaps not quite judicious to present it in a form which is itself unusual. But the form as well as the content only differ slightly from such as are familiar; and moreover they are so suited that they mutually assist one another. The essential characteristic of the terminology used consists in this, that instead of always starting from single points, it from the beginning conceives and considers whole systems of points. Every one is familiar with the expressions "position of a system of points," and "motion of a system of points." There is nothing unnatural in continuing this mode of expression, and denoting the aggregate of the positions traversed by a system in motion as its path. Every smallest part of this path is then a path-element. Of two path-elements one can be a part of the other: they then differ in magnitude and only in magnitude. But two path-elements which start from the same position may belong to different paths. In this case neither of the two forms part of the other: they differ in other respects than that of magnitude, and thus we say that they have different directions. It is true that these statements do not suffice to determine without ambiguity the characteristics of "magnitude" and "direction" for the motion of a system. But we can complete our definitions geometrically or analytically so that their consequences shall neither contradict themselves nor the statements we have made; and so that the magnitudes thus defined in the geometry of the system shall exactly correspond to the magnitudes which are denoted by the same names in the geometry of the point,—with which, indeed, they always coincide when the system is reduced to a point. Having determined the characteristics of magnitude and direction, we next call the path of a system straight if all its elements have the same direction, and curved if the direction of the elements changes from position to position. As in the geometry of the point, we measure curvature by the rate of variation of the direction with position. From these definitions we at once get a whole series of relations; and the number of these increases as soon as the freedom of motion of the system under consideration is limited by its connections. Certain classes of paths which are distinguished among the possible ones by peculiar simple properties then claim special attention. Of these the most important are those paths which at each of their positions have the least possible curvature: these we shall denote as the straightest paths of the system. These are the paths which are referred to in the fundamental law, and which have already been mentioned in stating it. Another important type consists of those paths which form the shortest connection between any two of their positions: these we shall denote as the shortest paths of the system. Under certain conditions the ideas of straightest and shortest paths coincide. The relation is perfectly familiar in connection with the theory of curved surfaces; nevertheless it does not hold good in general and under all circumstances. The compilation and arrangement of all the relations which arise here belong to the geometry of systems of points. The development of this geometry has a peculiar mathematical attraction; but we only pursue it as far as is required for the immediate purpose of applying it to physics. A system of n points presents a $3n$-manifold of motion,—although this may be reduced to any arbitrary number by the connections of the system. Hence there arise many analogies with the geometry of space of many dimensions; and these in part extend so far that the same propositions and notations can apply to both. But we must note that these analogies are only formal, and that, although they occasionally have an unusual appearance, our considerations refer without exception to concrete images of space as perceived by our senses. Hence all our statements represent possible experiences; if necessary, they could be confirmed by direct experiments, viz. by measurements made with models. Thus we need not fear the objection that in building up a science dependent upon experience, we have gone outside the world of experience. On the other hand, we are bound to answer the question how a new, unusual, and comprehensive mode of expression justifies itself; and what advantages we expect from using it. In answering this question we specify as the first advantage that it enables us to render the most general and comprehensive statements with great simplicity and brevity. In fact, propositions relating to whole systems do not require more words or more ideas than are usually employed in referring to a single point. Here the mechanics of a material system no longer appears as the expansion and complication of the mechanics of a single point; the latter, indeed, does not need independent investigation, or it only appears occasionally as a simplification and a special case. If it is urged that this simplicity is only artificial, we reply that in no other way can simple relations be secured than by artificial and well-considered adaptation of our ideas to the relations which have to be represented. But in this objection there may be involved the imputation that the mode of expression is not only artificial, but far-fetched and unnatural. To this we reply that there may be some justification for regarding the consideration of whole systems as being more natural and obvious than the consideration of single points. For, in reality, the material particle is simply an abstraction, whereas the material system is presented directly to us. All actual experience is obtained directly from systems; and it is only by processes of reasoning that we deduce conclusions as to possible experiences with single points. As a second merit, although not a very important one, we specify the advantage of the form in which our mathematical mode of expression enables us to state the fundamental law. Without this we should have to split it up into Newton's first law and Gauss's principle of least constraint. Both of these together would represent accurately the same facts; but in addition to these facts they would by implication contain something more, and this something more would be too much. In the first place they suggest the conception, which is foreign to our system of mechanics, that the connections of the material system might be destroyed; whereas we have denoted them as being permanent and indestructible throughout. In the second place we cannot, in using Gauss's principle, avoid suggesting the idea that we are not only stating a fact, but also the cause of this fact. We cannot assert that nature always keeps a certain quantity, which we call constraint, as small as possible, without suggesting that this quantity signifies something which is for nature itself a constraint,—an uncomfortable feeling. We cannot assert that nature acts like a judicious calculator reducing his observations, without suggesting that deliberate intention underlies the action. There is undoubtedly a special charm in such suggestions; and Gauss felt a natural delight in giving prominence to it in his beautiful discovery, which is of fundamental importance in our mechanics. Still, it must be confessed that the charm is that of mystery; we do not really believe that we can solve the enigma of the world by such half-suppressed allusions. Our own fundamental law entirely avoids any such suggestions. It exactly follows the form of the customary law of inertia, and like this it simply states a bare fact without any pretence of establishing it. And as it thereby becomes plain and unvarnished, in the same degree does it become more honest and truthful. Perhaps I am prejudiced in favour of the slight modification which I have made in Gauss's principle, and see in it advantages which will not be manifest to others. But I feel sure of general assent when I state as the third advantage of our method, that it throws a bright light upon Hamilton's method of treating mechanical problems by the aid of characteristic functions. During the sixty years since its discovery this mode of treatment has been well appreciated and much praised; but it has been regarded and treated more as a new branch of mechanics, and as if its growth and development had to proceed in its own way and independently of the usual mechanics. In our form of the mathematical representation, Hamilton's method, instead of having the character of a side branch, appears as the direct, natural, and, if one may so say, self-evident continuation of the elementary statements in all cases to which it is applicable. Further, our mode of representation gives prominence to this: that Hamilton's mode of treatment is not based, as is usually assumed, on the special physical foundations of mechanics; but that it is fundamentally a purely geometrical method, which can be established and developed quite independently of mechanics, and which has no closer connection with mechanics than any other of the geometrical methods employed in it. It has long since been remarked by mathematicians that Hamilton's method contains purely geometrical truths, and that a peculiar mode of expression, suitable to it, is required in order to express these clearly. But this fact has only come to light in a somewhat perplexing form, namely, in the analogies between ordinary mechanics and the geometry of space of many dimensions, which have been discovered by following out Hamilton's thoughts. Our mode of expression gives a simple and intelligible explanation of these analogies. It allows us to take advantage of them, and at the same time it avoids the unnatural admixture of supra-sensible abstractions with a branch of physics.

We have now sketched the content and form of our third image as far as can be done without trenching upon the contents of the book; far enough to enable us to submit it to criticism in respect of its permissibility, its correctness, and its appropriateness. I think that as far as logical permissibility is concerned it will be found to satisfy the most rigid requirements, and I trust that others will be of the same opinion. This merit of the representation I consider to be of the greatest importance, indeed of unique importance. Whether the image is more appropriate than another; whether it is capable of including all future experience; even whether it only embraces all present experience, all this I regard almost as nothing compared with the question whether it is in itself conclusive, pure and free from contradiction. For I have not attempted this task because mechanics has shown signs of inappropriateness in its applications, nor because it in any way conflicts with experience, but solely in order to rid myself of the oppressive feeling that to me its elements were not free from things obscure and unintelligible. What I have sought is not the only image of mechanics, nor yet the best image; I have only sought to find an intelligible image and to show by an example that this is possible and what it must look like. We cannot attain to perfection in any direction; and I must confess that, in spite of the pains I have taken with it, the image is not so convincingly clear but that in some points it may be exposed to doubt or may require defence. And yet it seems to me that of objections of a general nature there is only a single one which is so pertinent that it is worth while to anticipate and remove it. It relates to the nature of the rigid connections which we assume to exist between the masses, and which are absolutely indispensable in our system. Many physicists will at first be of opinion that by means of these connections forces are introduced into the elements of mechanics, and are introduced in a way which is secret, and therefore not permissible. For, they will assert, rigid connections are not conceivable without forces; they cannot come into existence except by the action of forces. To this we reply— Your assertion is correct for the mode of thought of ordinary mechanics, but it is not correct independently of this mode of thought; it does not carry conviction to a mind which considers the facts without prejudice and as if for the first time. Suppose we find in any way that the distance between two material particles remains constant at all times and under all circumstances. We can express this fact without making use of any other conceptions than those of space; and the value of the fact stated, as a fact, for the purpose of foreseeing future experience and for all other purposes, will be independent of any explanation of it which we may or may not possess. In no case will the value of the fact be increased, or our understanding of it improved, by putting it in the form—" Between these masses there acts a force which keeps them at a constant distance from one another," or " Between them there acts a force which makes it impossible for their distance to alter from its fixed value." But it will be urged that this latter explanation, although apparently only a ludicrous circumlocution, is nevertheless correct. For all the connections of the actual world are only approximately rigid; and the appearance of rigidity is only produced by the action of the elastic forces which continually annul the small deviations from the position of rest. To this we reply as follows:—With regard to rigid connections which are only approximately realised, our mechanics will naturally only state as a fact that they are approximately satisfied; and for the purpose of this statement the idea of force is not required. If we wish to proceed to a second approximation and to take into consideration the deviations, and with them the elastic forces, we shall make use of a dynamical explanation for these as for all forces. In seeking the actual rigid connections we shall perhaps have to descend to the world of atoms. But such considerations are out of place here; they do not affect the question whether it is logically permissible to treat of fixed connections as independent of forces and precedent to them. All that I wished to show was that this question must be answered in the affirmative, and this I believe I have done. This being so, we can deduce the properties and behaviour of the forces from the nature of the fixed connections without being guilty of a *petitio principii*. Other objections of a similar kind are possible, but I believe they can be removed in much the same way.

By way of giving expression to my desire to prove the logical purity of the system in all its details, I have thrown the representation into the older synthetic form. For this purpose the form used has the merit of compelling us to specify beforehand, definitely even if monotonously, the logical value which every important statement is intended to have. This makes it impossible to use the convenient reservations and ambiguities into which we are enticed by the wealth of combinations in ordinary speech. But the most important advantage of the form chosen is that it is always based upon what has already been proved, never upon what is to be proved later on : thus we are always sure of the whole chain if we sufficiently test each link as we proceed. In this respect I have endeavoured to carry out fully the obligations imposed by this mode of representation. At the same time it is obvious that the form by itself is no guarantee against error or oversight; and I hope that any chance defects will not be the more harshly criticised on account of the somewhat presumptuous mode of presentation. I trust that any such defects will be capable of improvement and will not affect any important point. Now and again, in order to avoid excessive prolixity, I have consciously abandoned to some extent the rigid strictness which this mode of representation properly requires. Before proceeding to mechanics proper, as dependent upon physical experience, I have naturally discussed those relations which follow simply and necessarily from the definitions adopted and from mathematics ; the connection of these latter with experience, if any, is of a different nature from that of the former. Moreover, there is no reason why the reader should not begin with the second book. The matter with which he is already familiar and the clear analogy with the dynamics of a particle will enable him easily to guess the purport of the propositions in the first book. If he admits the appropriateness of the mode of expression used, he can at any time return to the first book to convince himself of its permissibility.

We next turn to the second essential requirement which our image must satisfy. In the first place there is no doubt that the system correctly represents a very large number of natural motions. But this does not go far enough; the system must include all natural motions without exception. I think that this, too, can be asserted of it; at any rate in the sense that no definite phenomena can at present be mentioned which would be inconsistent with the system. We must of course admit that we cannot extend a rigid examination to all phenomena. Hence the system goes a little beyond the results of assured experience; it therefore has the character of a hypothesis which is accepted tentatively and awaits sudden refutation by a single example or gradual confirmation by a large number of examples. There are in especial two places in which we go beyond assured experience: firstly, in our limitation of the possible connections; secondly, in the dynamical explanation of force. What right have we to assert that all natural connections can be expressed by linear differential equations of the first order? With us this assumption is not a matter of secondary importance which we might do without. Our system stands or falls with it; for it raises the question whether our fundamental law is applicable to connections of the most general kind. And yet connections of a more general kind are not only conceivable, but they are permitted in ordinary mechanics without hesitation. There nothing prevents us from investigating the motion of a point where its path is only limited by the supposition that it makes a given angle with a given plane, or that its radius of curvature is always proportional to another given length. These are conditions which are not permissible in our system. But why are we certain that they are debarred by the nature of things? We might reply that these and similar connections cannot be realised by any practical mechanism; and in this respect we might appeal to the great authority of Helmholtz's name. But in every example possibilities might be overlooked; and ever so many examples would not suffice to substantiate the general assertion. It seems to me that the reason for our conviction should more properly be stated as follows. All connections of a system which are not embraced within the limits of our mechanics, indicate in one sense or another a discontinuous succession of its possible motions. But as a matter of fact it is an experience of the most general kind that nature exhibits continuity in infinitesimals everywhere and in every sense: an experience which has crystallised into firm conviction in the old proposition—*Natura non facit saltus*. In the text I have therefore laid stress upon this: that the permissible connections are defined solely by their continuity; and that their property of being represented by equations of a definite form is only deduced from this. We cannot attain to actual certainty in this way. For this old proposition is indefinite, and we cannot be sure how far it applies—how far it is the result of actual experience, and how far the result of arbitrary assumption. Thus the most conscientious plan is to admit that our assumption as to the permissible connections is of the nature of a tentatively accepted hypothesis. The same may be said with respect to the dynamical explanation of force. We may indeed prove that certain classes of concealed motions produce forces which, like actions-at-a-distance in nature, can be represented to any desired degree of approximation as differential coefficients of force-functions. It can be shown that the form of these force-functions may be of a very general nature; and in fact we do not deduce any restrictions for them. But on the other hand it remains for us to prove that any and every form of the force-functions can be realised; and hence it remains an open question whether such a mode of explanation may not fail to account for some one of the forms occurring in nature. Here again we can only bide our time so as to see whether our assumption is refuted, or whether it acquires greater and greater probability by the absence of any such refutation. We may regard it as a good omen that many distinguished physicists tend more and more to favour the hypothesis. I may mention Lord Kelvin's theory of vortex-atoms: this presents to us an image of the material universe which is in complete accord with the principles of our mechanics. And yet our mechanics in no wise demands such great simplicity and limitation of assumptions as Lord Kelvin has imposed upon himself. We need not abandon our fundamental propositions if we were to assume that the vortices revolved about rigid or flexible, but inextensible, nuclei; and instead of assuming simply incompressibility we might subject the all-pervading medium to much more complicated conditions, the most general form of which would be a matter for further investigation. Thus there appears to be no reason why the hypothesis admitted in our mechanics should not suffice to explain the phenomena.

We must, however, make one reservation. In the text we take the natural precaution of expressly limiting the range of our mechanics to inanimate nature; how far its laws extend beyond this we leave as quite an open question. As a matter of fact we cannot assert that the internal processes of life follow the same laws as the motions of inanimate bodies; nor can we assert that they follow different laws. According to appearance and general opinion there seems to be a fundamental difference. And the same feeling which impels us to exclude from the mechanics of the inanimate world as foreign every indication of an intention, of a sensation, of pleasure and pain,—this same feeling makes us unwilling to deprive our image of the animate world of these richer and more varied conceptions. Our fundamental law, although it may suffice for representing the motion of inanimate matter, appears (at any rate that is one's first and natural impression) too simple and narrow to account for even the lowest processes of life. It seems to me that this is not a disadvantage, but rather an advantage of our law. For while it allows us to survey the whole domain of mechanics, it shows us what are the limits of this domain. By giving us only bare facts, without attributing to them any appearance of necessity, it enables us to recognise that everything might be quite different. Perhaps such considerations will be regarded as out of place here. It is not usual to treat of them in the elements of the customary representation of mechanics. But there the complete vagueness of the forces introduced leaves room for free play. There is a tacit stipulation that, if need be, later on a contrast between the forces of animate and inanimate nature may be established. In our representation the outlines of the image are from the first so sharply delineated, that any subsequent perception of such an important division becomes almost impossible. We are therefore bound to refer to this matter at once, or to ignore it altogether.

As to the appropriateness of our third image we need not say much. In respect of distinctness and simplicity, as the contents of the book will show, we may assign to it about the same position as to the second image; and the merits to which we drew attention in the latter are also present here. But the permissible possibilities are somewhat more extensive than in the second image. For we pointed out that in the latter certain rigid connections were wanting; by our fundamental assumptions these are not excluded. And this extension is in accordance with nature, and is therefore a merit; nor does it prevent us from deducing the general properties of natural forces, in which lay the significance of the second image. The simplicity of this image, as of the second, is very apparent when we consider their physical applications. Here, too, we can confine our consideration to any characteristics of the material system which are accessible to observation. From their past changes we can deduce future ones by applying our fundamental law, without any necessity for knowing the positions of all the separate masses of the system, or for concealing our ignorance by arbitrary, ineffectual, and probably false hypotheses. But as compared with the second image, our third one exhibits simplicity also in adapting its conceptions so closely to nature that the essential relations of nature are represented by simple relations between the ideas. This is seen not only in the fundamental law, but also in its numerous general corollaries which correspond to the so-called principles of mechanics. Of course it must be admitted that this simplicity only obtains when we are dealing with systems which are completely known, and that it disappears as soon as concealed masses come in. But even in these cases the reason of the complication is perfectly obvious. The loss of simplicity is not due to nature, but to our imperfect knowledge of nature. The complications which arise are not simply a possible, but a necessary result of our special assumptions. It must also be admitted that the co-operation of concealed masses, which is the remote and special case from the standpoint of our mechanics, is the commonest case in the problems which occur in daily life and in the arts. Hence it will be well to point out again that we have only spoken of appropriateness in a special sense—in the sense of a mind which endeavours to embrace objectively the whole of our physical knowledge without considering the accidental position of man in nature, and to set forth this knowledge in a simple manner. The appropriateness of which we have spoken has no reference to practical applications or the needs of mankind. In respect of these latter it is scarcely possible that the usual representation of mechanics, which has been devised expressly for them, can ever be replaced by a more appropriate system. Our representation of mechanics bears towards the customary one somewhat the same relation that the systematic grammar of a language bears to a grammar devised for the purpose of enabling learners to become acquainted as quickly as possible with what they will require in daily life. The requirements of the two are very different, and they must differ widely in their arrangement if each is to be properly adapted to its purpose.

In conclusion, let us glance once more at the three images of mechanics which we have brought forward, and let us try to make a final and conclusive comparison between them. After what we have already said, we may leave the second image out of consideration. We shall put the first and third images on an equality with respect to permissibility, by assuming that the first image has been thrown into a form completely satisfactory from the logical point of view. This we have already assumed to be possible. We shall also put both images on an equality with respect to appropriateness, by assuming that the first image has been rendered complete by suitable additions, and that the advantages of both in different directions are of equal value. We shall then have as our sole criterion the correctness of the images: this is determined by the things themselves and does not depend on our arbitrary choice. And here it is important to observe that only one or the other of the two images can be correct: they cannot both at the same time be correct. For if we try to express as briefly as possible the essential relations of the two representations, we come to this. The first image assumes as the final constant elements in nature the relative accelerations of the masses with reference to each other: from these it incidentally deduces approximate, but only approximate, fixed relations between their positions. The third image assumes as the strictly invariable elements of nature fixed relations between the positions: from these it deduces when the phenomena require it approximately, but only approximately, invariable relative accelerations between the masses. Now, if we could perceive natural motions with sufficient accuracy, we should at once know whether in them the relative acceleration, or the relative relations of position, or both, are only approximately invariable. We should then know which of our two assumptions is false; or whether both are false; for they cannot both be simultaneously correct. The greater simplicity is on the side of the third image. What at first induces us to decide in favour of the first is the fact that in actions-at-a-distance we can actually exhibit relative accelerations which, up to the limits of our observation, appear to be invariable; whereas all fixed connections between the positions of tangible bodies are soon and easily perceived by our senses to be only approximately constant. But the situation changes in favour of the third image as soon as a more refined knowledge shows us that the assumption of invariable distance-forces only yields a first approximation to the truth; a case which has already arisen in the sphere of electric and magnetic forces. And the balance of evidence will be entirely in favour of the third image when a second approximation to the truth can be attained by tracing back the supposed actions-at-a-distance to motions in an all-pervading medium whose smallest parts are subjected to rigid connections; a case which also seems to be nearly realised in the same sphere. This is the field in which the decisive battle between these different fundamental assumptions of mechanics must be fought out. But in order to arrive at such a decision it is first necessary to consider thoroughly the existing possibilities in all directions. To develop them in one special direction is the object of this treatise,—an object which must necessarily be attained even if we are still far from a possible decision, and even if the decision should finally prove unfavourable to the image here developed.

BOOK I

GEOMETRY AND KINEMATICS OF
MATERIAL SYSTEMS

1. **Prefatory Note.** The subject-matter of the first book is completely independent of experience. All the assertions made are *a priori* judgments in Kant's sense. They are based upon the laws of the internal intuition of, and upon the logical forms followed by, the person who makes the assertions; with his external experience they have no other connection than these intuitions and forms may have.

CHAPTER I

TIME, SPACE, AND MASS

2. **Explanation.** The time of the first book is the time of our internal intuition. It is therefore a quantity such that the variations of the other quantities under consideration may be regarded as dependent upon its variation; whereas in itself it is always an independent variable.

The space of the first book is space as we conceive it. It is therefore the space of Euclid's geometry, with all the properties which this geometry ascribes to it. It is immaterial to us whether these properties are regarded as being given by the laws of our internal intuition, or as consequences of thought which necessarily follow from arbitrary definitions.

The mass of the first book will be introduced by a definition.

3. **Definition 1.** A material particle is a characteristic by which we associate without ambiguity a given point in

space at a given time with a given point in space at any other time.

Every material particle is invariable and indestructible. The points in space which are denoted at two different times by the same material particle, coincide when the times coincide. Rightly understood, the definition implies this.

4. **Definition 2.** The number of material particles in any space, compared with the number of material particles in some chosen space at a fixed time, is called the mass contained in the first space.

We may and shall consider the number of material particles in the space chosen for comparison to be infinitely great. The mass of the separate material particles will therefore, by the definition, be infinitely small. The mass in any given space may therefore have any rational or irrational value.

5. **Definition 3.** A finite or infinitely small mass, conceived as being contained in an infinitely small space, is called a material point.

A material point therefore consists of any number of material particles connected with each other. This number is always to be infinitely great: this we attain by supposing the material particles to be of a higher order of infinitesimals than those material points which are regarded as being of infinitely small mass. The masses of material points, and in especial the masses of infinitely small material points, may therefore bear to one another any rational or irrational ratio.

6. **Definition 4.** A number of material points considered simultaneously is called a system of material points, or briefly a system. The sum of the masses of the separate points is, by § 4, the mass of the system.

Hence a finite system consists of a finite number of finite material points, or of an infinite number of infinitely small material points, or of both. It is always permissible to regard a system of material points as being composed of an infinite number of material particles.

7. **Observation 1.** In what follows we shall always treat a finite system as consisting of a finite number of finite material points. But as we assign no upper limit to their number, and

no lower limit to their mass, our general statements will also include as a special case that in which the system contains an infinite number of infinitely small material points. We need not enter into the details required for the analytical treatment of this case.

8. **Observation 2.** A material point can be regarded as a special case and as the simplest example of a system of material points.

CHAPTER II

POSITIONS AND DISPLACEMENTS OF POINTS AND SYSTEMS

Position

9. Definition 1. The point of space which is indicated by a given particle at a given time is called the position of the particle at that time. The position of a material point is the common position of its particles.

10. Definition 2. The aggregate of the positions which all the points of a system simultaneously occupy is called the position of the system.

11. Definition 3. Any given position of a material point in infinite space is called a geometrically conceivable, or for shortness a conceivable, position of the point. The aggregate of any conceivable positions whatsoever of the points of a system is called a conceivable position of the system.

At any time two particles may differ as to their position, two material points as to their mass and their position, and two systems of material points as to the number, the mass, and the positions of their points. But, in accordance with the definitions which we have already given of them, particles, material points, and systems of material points cannot differ in any other respect.

12. Analytical Representation of the Position (a) of a Point.—The position of a material point can be represented analytically by means of its three rectangular coordinates referred to a set of fixed axes. These coordinates will always be denoted by x_1, x_2, x_3. Every conceivable position of the point implies a singly-determined value-system of these coordinates, and conversely every arbitrarily chosen value-system of the coordinates implies a singly-determined conceivable position of the point.

The position of a point can also be represented by any r quantities $p_1 \ldots p_\rho \ldots p_r$ whatsoever, provided we agree to associate continuously a given value-system of these quantities with a given position of the point, and conversely. The rectangular coordinates are then functions of these quantities, and conversely. The quantities p_ρ are called the general coordinates of the point. If $r > 3$, then for geometrical reasons $r - 3$ equations must exist between the quantities p_ρ which enable us to determine these quantities as functions of three independent quantities, for instance, x_1, x_2, x_3. However, we shall exclude dependence of the coordinates on one another on account of purely geometrical relations, and consequently it must always be understood that $r \gtreqless 3$. If $r < 3$, then all conceivable positions of the point cannot be represented by means of p_ρ, but only a portion of these positions. The positions not expressed in terms of p_ρ will be considered as being *eo ipso* excluded from discussion whilst we are using the coordinates p_ρ.

13. Analytical Representation (*b*) of a System.—The position of a system of n material points can be analytically represented by means of the $3n$ rectangular coordinates of the points of the system. These coordinates will be denoted by $x_1, x_2 \ldots x_\nu \ldots x_{3n}$, so that x_1, x_2, x_3 are the coordinates of the first point, $x_{3\mu-2}, x_{3\mu-1} x_{3\mu}$ the coordinates of the μth point. We shall call these $3n$ coordinates x_ν, the rectangular coordinates of the system. Every conceivable position of the system implies a singly-determined value-system of its rectangular coordinates, and conversely every arbitrarily chosen value-system of x_ν a singly-determined conceivable position of the system.

We may also consider the system as determined by means of any r quantities $p_1 \ldots p_\rho \ldots p_r$ whatever, as long as we agree to associate continuously a given value-system of these coordinates with a given position of the system, and conversely. The rectangular coordinates are therefore functions of these quantities, and conversely. The quantities p_ρ are called the general coordinates of the system. If $r > 3n$, then for geometrical reasons $r - 3n$ equations must exist between p_ρ. However, we shall assume that no geometrical relations exist between p_ρ, and consequently $r \gtreqless 3n$. If $r < 3n$, then all conceivable positions of the system cannot be expressed in terms of p_ρ, but only a portion of them. Those positions not expressed in terms of p_ρ will be considered as being *eo ipso* excluded from consideration when we are using the general coordinates p_ρ.

Configuration and Absolute Position

14. Definition 1. The aggregate of the relative positions of the points of a system is called the configuration of the system.

The configuration of the system and the absolute position of the configuration in space determine together the position of the system.

15. Definition 2. By a coordinate of configuration we mean any coordinate of the system whose value cannot change without the configuration of the system changing.

Whether a given coordinate is a coordinate of configuration or not does not depend on the choice of the remaining coordinates of the system.

16. Definition 3. By a coordinate of absolute position we mean any coordinate of the system through whose change the configuration of the system cannot be altered so long as the remaining coordinates of the system do not alter.

Whether a given coordinate is a coordinate of absolute position or not depends therefore on the choice of the remaining coordinates.

Corollaries

17. 1. A coordinate cannot be at one and the same time both a coordinate of configuration and a coordinate of absolute position. On the other hand, a given coordinate can and in general will be neither a coordinate of configuration nor a coordinate of absolute position.

18. 2. So long as $n > 3$, in every position $3n$ independent coordinates can be chosen in various ways, so that there are as many as $3n-6$ coordinates of configuration amongst them, but in no way so as to include more than $3n-6$ such coordinates.

For, let us choose from the coordinates the three distances of any three points of the system from each other, and the $3(n-3)$ distances of the remaining points from them; then we have $(3n-6)$ coordinates of configuration; and any $(3n-6)$ different functions of these distances give $(3n-6)$ coordinates of configuration of the system. Fewer coordinates of configuration can exist; for example, if we take the $3n$ rectangular coordinates, none exist. But there cannot be more than $(3n-6)$ coordinates of configuration amongst independent coordinates; for if, amongst the given coordinates of a system, there were more than $(3n-6)$ coordinates of configuration, then the latter could be expressed in terms of these $(3n-6)$ distances, and consequently would not be independent of one another.

19. 3. So long as $n > 3$, $3n$ independent coordinates for all conceivable positions of a system can be chosen in various ways so that there are amongst them as many as 6, but not more than 6 coordinates of absolute position.

For, let us choose the coordinates in such a manner that there are amongst them $(3n-6)$ coordinates of configuration, and take with them any 6 coordinates, say 6 of the rectangular coordinates of the system; then the last are *eo ipso* coordinates of absolute position, for no change in them changes the configuration so long as the rest are fixed. Fewer than 6 may exist; none exist, for instance, when we use the rectangular coordinates of the system. More than 6 cannot exist. For did more than 6 exist, then, for a particular choice of the coordinates, all conceivable configurations of the system would be determined by the remaining fewer than $3n-6$ coordinates; and consequently there would not be left $(3n-6)$ coordinates of configuration independent of one another for the system, which would be contrary to § 18.

20. 4. If $3n$ independent coordinates of a system of n points are so chosen that there are amongst them $(3n-6)$ coordinates of configuration, then the remaining 6 are necessarily coordinates of absolute position. And if these $3n$ coordinates are so chosen that 6 of them are coordinates of absolute

position, then the remaining $(3n - 6)$ are necessarily coordinates of configuration.

For, if there were amongst the latter even one which could be changed without altering the configuration of the system, then the absolute position of the configuration would be determined by more than 6 independent coordinates, which is impossible.

21. 5. Any quantity can be used as a coordinate of absolute position, provided its change alters the position of the system, and provided it is not itself a coordinate of configuration. Any 6 quantities which satisfy these conditions and are independent of one another, can be taken as coordinates of absolute position, and become coordinates of absolute position by the fact that no other quantities are associated with them as coordinates unless they have the properties of coordinates of configuration.

Finite Displacements

(a) Of Points

22. **Definition 1.** The passage of a material point from an initial to a final position, without regard to the time or manner of the passage, is called a displacement of the point from the initial position to the final one.

The displacement of a point is completely determined by its initial and final position. It is also completely known when we are given its initial position, its direction, and its magnitude.

23. **Observation 1.** The magnitude of the displacement of a point is equal to the distance of its final position from its initial one. Let the quantities x_ν be the rectangular coordinates of its initial position, and x_ν' the rectangular coordinates of its final position, then the magnitude s' of the displacement is the positive root of the equation

$$s'^2 = \sum_{1}^{3} {}_\nu (x_\nu' - x_\nu)^2.$$

24. **Observation 2.** The direction of a displacement is the direction of a straight line which is drawn from the initial

position of the point to the final one. Let s', x_ν, x_ν' have the same meaning as before, and let x_ν°, x_ν'', s'' be the coordinates of the initial and final positions, and the length of a second displacement, then the angle $\widehat{s's''}$ between the two displacements is given by the equation

$$s's'' \cos \widehat{s's''} = \sum_{1}^{3} {}_\nu (x_\nu' - x_\nu)(x_\nu'' - x_\nu^\circ) \qquad (i).$$

For, if we consider a triangle whose sides are equal in length to s' and s'', and the included angle equal to $\widehat{s's''}$, we obtain the equation

$$s'^2 + s''^2 - 2s's'' \cos \widehat{s's''} = \sum_{1}^{3} {}_\nu [(x_\nu' - x_\nu) - (x_\nu'' - x_\nu^\circ)]^2 \qquad (ii),$$

from which, together with § 23, equation (i) follows.

25. **Definition 2.** Two displacements of a point are said to be identical when they have the same initial and final positions; two displacements of a point are said to be equal when they have the same magnitude and direction; they are said to be parallel when they have the same direction.

26. **Note.** Let $x_1, x_2 \ldots x_k$ denote the k rectangular coordinates of a point in space of k dimensions, $x_1', x_2' \ldots x_k'$ the coordinates of a second point; then the additional statement that the distance between the two points is the positive root of the equation

$$s'^2 = \sum_{1}^{k} {}_\nu (x_\nu' - x_\nu)^2$$

extends the whole of the following investigation, as well as the whole of mechanics, to space of k dimensions, without necessitating anything but a change in the wording. No use will be made of this remark, but the investigation will refer, as stated at the beginning, simply to the space of Euclidian geometry.

(b) Of Systems

27. **Definition.** The passage of a system of material points from an initial position to a final one without regard to the time

or manner of the passage is called a displacement of the system from the initial to the final position.

The displacement of a system is completely known when we know its initial and final positions. It is also completely known when its initial position, and what are termed its direction and magnitude, are given.

28. **Notation.** It will be convenient to call the positive root of the arithmetic mean of the squares of a series of quantities their quadratic mean value.

29. **Definition a.** The magnitude of the displacement of a system is the quadratic mean value of the magnitudes of the displacements of all its particles.

The magnitude of the displacement which a system undergoes in moving from one position to another is called the distance between the two positions. The magnitude of a displacement is also called its length.

30. **Note.** The distance between two positions of a system is defined independently of the form of its analytical representation, and in particular is independent of the choice of the coordinates of the system.

31. **Problem.** To express the distance between two positions of a system in terms of its rectangular coordinates.

Let there be n material points in the system. Let x_ν be the value of one of the rectangular coordinates of the system before the displacement, and x_ν' the value of the same after the displacement. The coordinate x_ν is at the same time a coordinate of one of the points of the system: let the mass of this point be m_ν, ν ranges from 1 to $3n$, but all the $m_\nu's$ are not unequal, since for every μ from 1 to $3n$

$$m_{3\mu-2} = m_{3\mu-1} = m_{3\mu}.$$

If now η be the number of particles in the unit of mass, the mass m_ν contains $m_\nu\eta$ particles, and the whole mass m of the system $m.\eta$. Consequently, with this notation, the quadratic mean value s' of the displacements of all particles is the positive root of the equation

$$ms'^2 = \sum_{1}^{3n} m_\nu \, (x_\nu' - x_\nu)^2 \qquad \text{(i)},$$

and this root is therefore the required distance. Finally

$$m = \tfrac{1}{3}\sum_{1}^{3n} m_\nu \qquad \text{(ii)}.$$

32. Proposition. The distance between two positions of a system is always smaller than the sum of the distances of the two positions from a third.

Let the quantities x_ν', x_ν'', x_ν''' be the rectangular coordinates of the positions 1, 2, 3; let s_{12}, s_{13}, s_{23} be their distances from each other. For shortness write

$$\sqrt{\tfrac{m_\nu}{m}}(x_\nu''' - x_\nu') = a_\nu \qquad \sqrt{\tfrac{m_\nu}{m}}(x_\nu''' - x_\nu'') = b_\nu,$$

then $s_{13}^2 = \sum_{1}^{3n}\!a_\nu^2 \quad s_{23}^2 = \sum_{1}^{3n}\!b_\nu^2 \quad s_{12}^2 = \sum_{1}^{3n}(a_\nu - b_\nu)^2$. If then it were possible that $s_{12} > s_{13} + s_{23}$ we should get on squaring $s_{12}^2 - s_{13}^2 - s_{23}^2 > 2 s_{13} . s_{23}$, and on squaring again,

$$4\, s_{13}^2 s_{23}^2 - (s_{12}^2 - s_{13}^2 - s_{23}^2)^2 < 0.$$

This is, however, impossible, for, on substituting the values of s given as above, the left-hand side becomes

$$4 \sum_{1}^{3n}\!\sum_{1}^{3n}(a_\nu b_\mu - a_\mu b_\nu)^2,$$

which, being a sum of squares, is necessarily positive. Therefore our assumption was unwarranted, and consequently

$$s_{12} \leq s_{13} + s_{23}.$$

33. Corollary. It is therefore always possible to construct a plane triangle whose three sides are equal to the three distances of any three positions of a system from each other.

34. Definition b. The difference in direction between two displacements of a system from the same initial position is the included angle of a plane triangle which has the lengths of the two displacements as sides, and whose base is the distance between their final positions.

The difference in direction between two displacements is also called the angle between them, or their inclination towards one another.

35. **Note 1.** The inclination towards one another of two displacements with the same initial position is in all cases a singly-determined real angle, smaller than π.

For the triangle which determines that angle can always (§ 32) be drawn.

36. **Note 2.** The difference in direction between two displacements is defined independently of the form of the analytical representation, and in particular is independent of the choice of the coordinates used.

37. **Problem.** To express the angle between two displacements from the same initial position in terms of the rectangular coordinates of the initial and final positions.

Let the quantities x_ν be the coordinates of the common initial positions, x_ν' and x_ν'' the coordinates of the two final positions, s' and s'' the lengths of the two displacements, $\widehat{s's''}$ the included angle. By consideration of the plane triangle whose three sides are the three distances between the three positions, we obtain

$$2ms's'' \cos \widehat{s's''} = \sum_{1}^{3n} {}^\nu m_\nu (x_\nu' - x_\nu)^2 + \sum_{1}^{3n} {}^\nu m_\nu (x_\nu'' - x_\nu)^2 - \sum_{1}^{3n} {}^\nu m_\nu [(x_\nu'' - x_\nu) - (x_\nu - x_\nu)]^2,$$

and therefore

$$ms's'' \cos \widehat{s's''} = \sum_{1}^{3n} {}^\nu m_\nu (x_\nu'' - x_\nu)(x_\nu' - x_\nu) \qquad \text{(i)},$$

in which equation we consider s' and s'' expressed as in § 31 (i) in terms of the rectangular coordinates.

38. **Proposition.** Two displacements of a system from the same initial position have the angle between them equal to zero when the displacements of the individual points of both

the systems are parallel and correspondingly proportional, and conversely.

For, if the displacements of all points are parallel and proportional, then for all values of ν

$$x_\nu'' - x_\nu = \epsilon(x_\nu' - x_\nu),$$

where ϵ is the same constant factor for all values of ν. The right-hand side of equation § 37 (i) becomes therefore $m\epsilon s'^2$. Moreover $s'' = \epsilon s'$; thus by this equation $\cos \widehat{s's''} = 1$, and since $\widehat{s's''}$ is an interior angle of a triangle $s's'' = 0$ (§ 35).

Conversely when $\widehat{s's''} = 0$, $\cos \widehat{s's''} = 1$, and then the equation 37 (i) squared gives when the values of s' and s'' are substituted

$$0 = [\sum_1^{3n} \nu m_\nu(x_\nu'' - x_\nu)(x_\nu' - x_\nu)]^2 - \sum_1^{3n} \nu m_\nu(x_\nu'' - x_\nu)^2 \cdot \sum_1^{3n} \nu m_\nu(x_\nu' - x_\nu)^2$$

$$= \sum_1^{3n} \nu \sum_1^{3n} \mu m_\nu m_\mu [(x_\nu'' - x_\nu)(x_\mu' - x_\mu) - (x_\mu'' - x_\mu)(x_\nu' - x_\nu)]^2,$$

and this is only possible when for every value of μ and ν

$$\frac{x_\mu'' - x_\mu}{x_\nu'' - x_\nu} = \frac{x_\mu' - x_\mu}{x_\nu' - x_\nu};$$

wherefore the converse is proved.

39. Corollary 1. If two displacements from the same initial position have their inclinations to a third displacement from the same initial position zero, then their inclination to one another is zero.

All displacements whose inclinations to any given displacement are zero, have consequently their inclinations to each other zero. The common property of all such displacements is called their *direction*.

40. Corollary 2. When two displacements of a system have the same direction, they are equally inclined to a third displacement.

Thus all displacements from the same initial position, and having the same direction, make the same angle with all displacements which have another common direction. This angle is called the angle between the two directions or the inclination of the two directions.

41. Definition. Two displacements of a system are said to be identical when the displacements of the points of the two systems are identical. Two displacements are equal when the displacements of the individual points are equal and two displacements are parallel when the displacements of the individual points in both are parallel and correspondingly proportional.

42. Corollary. Two displacements of a system from different initial positions are parallel when each of them has the same direction as a displacement which passes through its initial position and is equal to the other displacement, and conversely.

43. Additional Note. By the difference in direction between two displacements of a system from different initial positions we mean the angle between either of them, and a parallel displacement to the other from its own initial position.

44. Problem. To express the angle between any two displacements of a system in terms of the rectangular coordinates of their four end positions.

Let s' and s'' be the magnitudes of the two displacements, and $\widehat{s's''}$ the angle between them. Let x_ν and x_ν' be the coordinates of the initial and final positions of the first, x_ν° and x_ν'', the coordinates of the initial and final positions of the second displacement. A displacement whose initial coordinates are x_ν, and whose final coordinates have the value $x_\nu + x_\nu'' - x_\nu^\circ$, has the same initial position as the first, and is equal to the second. Hence it makes with the first the required angle, for which we obtain the equation

$$m s' s'' \cos \widehat{s's''} = \sum_{1}^{3n} \nu\, m_\nu (x_\nu' - x_\nu)(x_\nu'' - x_\nu^\circ).$$

The same value is obtained if we choose a displacement through the initial position of the second, and equal to the first, and then find the angle between this and the second.

Our definition in § 43 was thus unique, and therefore permissible.

45. Definition. Two displacements of a system are said to be perpendicular to one another when the angle between them is a right angle.

46. Corollary 1. The necessary and sufficient analytical condition that two displacements should be perpendicular to one another is the equation

$$\sum_{1}^{3n} {}^{\nu} m_\nu (x_\nu' - x_\nu)(x_\nu'' - x_\nu^\circ) = 0,$$

in which use is made of the notation of § 44.

47. Corollary 2. In a system of n points there is from a given position a $(3n-1)$ manifold of displacements, and therefore a $(3n-2)$ manifold of directions conceivable which are perpendicular to a given direction.

48. Definition. The component of a displacement in a given direction is a displacement whose direction is the given direction, and whose magnitude is equal to the orthogonal projection of the magnitude of the given displacement upon the given direction.

Thus, if the magnitude of the given displacement is s, and it makes with the given direction the angle ω, then its component in this direction is equal to $s \cos \omega$.

The magnitude of the component in a given direction will be simply termed the component in that direction.

Composition of Displacements

49. Note. Let there be given to a system several displacements, which are equal to given displacements, and which are so related to one another that the final position of the preceding displacement is the initial position of the succeeding one, then the final position attained is independent of the succession of displacements.

Since this is true for the displacements which the individual points suffer, it must also be true for the system.

50. Definition 1. A displacement which carries the

system into the same final position as a succession of displacements, which are equal to given displacements, is called the sum of these given displacements.

51. **Definition 2.** The difference between a chosen displacement and another is a displacement whose sum, together with the latter one, gives the former.

52. **Corollary** (to § 49). The addition and subtraction of displacements is subject to the rules of algebraic addition and subtraction.

CHAPTER III

INFINITELY SMALL DISPLACEMENTS AND PATHS OF A SYSTEM OF MATERIAL POINTS

53. **Prefatory Note.** From here on we shall no longer deal with single material points by themselves, but shall regard their investigation as being included in that of systems. Hence what follows must be understood as referring always to displacements of systems, even when this is not expressly stated.

Infinitely Small Displacements

54. **Explanation.** A displacement is said to be infinitely small when its length is infinitely small.

The position of the infinitely small displacement is a position to which the bounding points of the displacement lie indefinitely near.

An infinitely small displacement is determined in magnitude and direction when we know its position, and the infinitely small changes which the coordinates of the system undergo owing to the displacement.

55. **Problem 1a.** To express the length ds of an infinitely small displacement in terms of the changes dx_ν of the $3n$ rectangular coordinates of the system.

If in equation § 31 (i) we substitute dx_ν for $x_\nu' - x_\nu$, we obtain

$$mds^2 = \sum_{1}^{3n} {}_\nu m_\nu dx_\nu^2.$$

56. Problem 1b. To express the angle $\overset{\wedge}{ss'}$ between two infinitely small displacements ds and ds' in terms of the changes dx_ν and dx_ν' in the $3n$ rectangular coordinates of the system.

If in the equation § 44 we substitute dx_ν for $x_\nu' - x_\nu$ and dx_ν' for $x_\nu'' - x_\nu^\circ$ we obtain

$$mdsds' \cos \overset{\wedge}{ss'} = \sum_{1}^{3n} {}_\nu m_\nu dx_\nu dx_\nu'.$$

This expression holds whether both displacements have the same position or not.

57. Problem 2a. To express the length ds of an infinitely small displacement in terms of the changes dp_ρ of the r general coordinates p_ρ of the system.

The rectangular coordinates x_ν are functions of the p_ρ's, and moreover of the p_ρ's alone, since they are completely determined by these, and since displacements of the system which are not expressible in terms of the changes of p_ρ are excluded from consideration (§ 13).

Putting now for shortness

$$\frac{\partial x_\nu}{\partial p_\rho} = a_{\nu\rho} \qquad \text{(i)},$$

we get $3n$ equations of the form

$$dx_\nu = \sum_{1}^{r} {}_\rho a_{\nu\rho} dp_\rho \qquad \text{(ii)},$$

where $a_{\nu\rho}$ are functions of the position, and can therefore be expressed as functions of p_ρ. Substituting these values in equation § 55, and putting for shortness

$$ma_{\rho\sigma} = \sum_{1}^{3n} {}_\nu m_\nu a_{\nu\rho} a_{\nu\sigma} \qquad \text{(iii)},$$

we get as the solution of the problem

$$ds^2 = \sum_{1}^{r} {}_\rho \sum_{1}^{r} {}_\sigma a_{\rho\sigma} dp_\rho dp_\sigma \qquad \text{(iv)}.$$

58. Problem 2b. To express the angle $\overset{\wedge}{ss'}$ between two infinitely small displacements of lengths ds and ds' and having the same position in terms of the changes dp_ρ and dp_ρ' in the r general coordinates p_ρ of the system.

We form the values of dx_ν' by means of § 57 (ii), and substitute these and the values of dx_ν in equation § 56. Remembering that for both displacements the values of the coordinates, and therefore of the quantities $a_{\rho\sigma}$, are equal, we obtain

$$dsds' \cos \widehat{ss'} = \sum_{1}^{r}{}_\rho \sum_{1}^{r}{}_\sigma a_{\rho\sigma} dp_\rho dp_\sigma'.$$

Properties of $a_{\rho\sigma}$ and $a_{\rho\sigma}$. Introduction of $b_{\rho\sigma}$.

59. 1. For all values of ρ, σ, τ (cf. § 57 (i)),

$$\frac{\partial a_{\rho\sigma}}{\partial p_\tau} = \frac{\partial a_{\rho\tau}}{\partial p_\sigma}.$$

60. 2. For all values of ρ and σ (cf. § 57 (iii)),

$$a_{\rho\sigma} = a_{\sigma\rho}.$$

61. 3. The number of the quantities $a_{\rho\sigma}$ is equal to $3nr$; the number of the quantities $a_{\rho\sigma}$ different from one another is $\frac{1}{2} r(r+1)$.

62. 4. For all values of ρ

$$a_{\rho\rho} > 0.$$

For all values of ρ and σ

$$a_{\rho\rho} a_{\sigma\sigma} - a^2_{\rho\sigma} > 0.$$

For the right-hand side of the equation § 57 (iv.), on account of its derivation from the equation § 55, is a necessarily positive quantity, whatever may be the values of dp_ρ. For this the foregoing inequalities are necessary conditions.

63. 5. For all values of ρ, σ, τ, the following equation holds,

$$\sum_{1}^{3n}{}_\nu m_\nu a_{\nu\sigma} \left(\frac{\partial a_{\nu\rho}}{\partial p_\tau} + \frac{\partial a_{\nu\tau}}{\partial p_\rho} \right) = m \left(\frac{\partial a_{\rho\sigma}}{\partial p_\tau} + \frac{\partial a_{\tau\sigma}}{\partial p_\rho} - \frac{\partial a_{\rho\tau}}{\partial p_\sigma} \right).$$

In order to prove this equation we must substitute on the right-hand side the values of $a_{\rho\sigma}$ given in § 57 (iii), and make use of the properties of $a_{\rho\sigma}$ given in § 59.

64. 6. Let the determinant formed by the r^2 quantities

$a_{\rho\sigma}$ be Δ. The factor of $a_{\rho\sigma}$ in Δ, divided by Δ will always be denoted by $b_{\rho\sigma}$. Thus we have as a definition

$$b_{\rho\sigma} = \frac{1}{\Delta}\frac{\partial \Delta}{\partial a_{\rho\sigma}}.$$

For all values of ρ and σ then

$$b_{\rho\sigma} = b_{\sigma\rho}.$$

The number of quantities $b_{\rho\sigma}$ different from one another is equal to $\frac{1}{2}r(r+1)$.

65. 7. The value of the expression

$$\sum_{1}^{r}{}_\rho a_{\rho\iota} b_{\rho\chi}$$

is equal to unity so long as $\iota = \chi$; its value is zero if ι and χ are different.

For if $\iota = \chi$, the expression $\sum_{1}^{r}{}_\rho a_{\rho\iota} b_{\rho\chi} \Delta$ represents the determinant Δ itself. If, however, ι and χ are different, it represents the determinant which results from Δ when the row $a_{\rho\chi}$ is replaced by the row $a_{\rho\iota}$. In this determinant two rows are equal, and consequently its value is zero.

66. 8. For all values of ι and χ we have the two equations

$$\sum_{1}^{r}{}_\rho \sum_{1}^{r}{}_\sigma b_{\rho\sigma} a_{\rho\iota} a_{\sigma\chi} = a_{\iota\chi},$$

$$\sum_{1}^{r}{}_\rho \sum_{1}^{r}{}_\sigma a_{\rho\sigma} b_{\rho\iota} b_{\sigma\chi} = b_{\iota\chi}.$$

For if we form by means of § 65 the value of the expression $\sum_{1}^{r}{}_\rho b_{\rho\sigma} a_{\rho\iota}$, or $\sum_{1}^{r}{}_\rho a_{\rho\sigma} b_{\rho\iota}$ for all values of σ from 1 to r, and then multiply the resulting equations one by one with $a_{\sigma\chi}$ or $b_{\sigma\chi}$ respectively, and add, the equations follow.

67. 9. Definite changes of the quantities $a_{\rho\sigma}$ involve definite changes of the quantities $b_{\rho\sigma}$. Let us denote by $\delta a_{\rho\sigma}$

and $\delta b_{\rho\sigma}$ any variation of $a_{\rho\sigma}$ and the resulting variation in $b_{\rho\sigma}$, then the following equations hold,

$$\sum_{\rho}^{r}\sum_{\sigma}^{r} a_{\rho\iota}a_{\sigma\chi}\delta b_{\rho\sigma} = -\delta a_{\iota\chi}$$

$$\sum_{\rho}^{r}\sum_{\sigma}^{r} b_{\rho\iota}b_{\sigma\chi}\delta a_{\rho\sigma} = -\delta b_{\iota\chi}.$$

If we vary the equations § 66 and make use of the results of § 65 the equations follow.

68. 10. If we vary in $a_{\rho\sigma}$ and $b_{\rho\sigma}$ only one definite coordinate, p_τ, on which they depend, then for every value of τ

$$\sum_{\rho}^{r}\sum_{\sigma}^{r} a_{\rho\iota}a_{\sigma\chi} \frac{\partial b_{\rho\sigma}}{\partial p_\tau} = -\frac{\partial a_{\iota\chi}}{\partial p_\tau},$$

$$\sum_{\rho}^{r}\sum_{\sigma}^{r} b_{\rho\iota}b_{\sigma\chi} \frac{\partial a_{\rho\sigma}}{\partial p_\tau} = -\frac{\partial b_{\iota\chi}}{\partial p_\tau}.$$

Displacements in the Direction of the Coordinates

69. **Definition 1.** A displacement in the direction of a definite coordinate is an infinitely small displacement in which only this one coordinate is changed without the remaining ones changing.

The direction of all the displacements in the direction of the same coordinate from the same position is the same; it is called the direction of the coordinate in that position.

70. **Note.** The direction of a coordinate depends on the choice of the remaining coordinates in use.

71. **Definition 2.** The reduced component of an infinitely small displacement in the direction of a given coordinate is the component of the displacement in the direction of the coordinate (§§ 48, 69) divided by the ratio of the change of the coordinate to a displacement in its own direction.

The reduced component in the direction of a coordinate is called for shortness the component along the coordinate.

Thus we speak of the component of a given displacement

in a given direction; we cannot speak of the reduced component in a given direction, but only of the reduced component of an infinitely small displacement in the direction of a coordinate.

72. Problem 1a. To express the inclination $\widehat{sx}_\nu$ of the displacement ds to the rectangular coordinate x_ν in terms of the $3n$ increments dx_ν.

In equation § 56, put the dx_ν's equal to zero for all values of ν, except the given one to which the problem refers. Then the direction of ds' is, by § 69, that of x_ν, and the angle $\widehat{ss}'$ becomes the required angle. Moreover, since by § 55 $mds'^2 = m_\nu dx_\nu'^2$, we get as solution

$$ds \cos \widehat{sx}_\nu = \sqrt{\frac{m_\nu}{m}} dx_\nu,$$

where for ds its value in terms of dx_ν is to be substituted.

73. Problem 1b. To express the components $\overline{dx}_\nu$ of the displacement ds along the rectangular coordinates x_ν in terms of the changes dx_ν of the coordinates.

Put $\widehat{sx}_\nu = 0$ in the foregoing proposition; then we get the displacement ds in the direction of the coordinate x_ν, and we observe that the ratio of the change of the coordinate to a displacement in its own direction is equal to dx_ν/ds, or to $\sqrt{m/m_\nu}$. The left-hand side of equation § 72 represents immediately the component of ds in the direction of x_ν; then if we divide the equation by $\sqrt{m/m_\nu}$ we obtain (§ 71) as the solution of the problem

$$\overline{dx}_\nu = \frac{m_\nu}{m} dx_\nu.$$

74. Problem 1c. To express the changes dx_ν of the rectangular coordinates in a displacement in terms of the reduced components of the displacement along these coordinates.

The solution of the foregoing problem gives immediately

$$dx_\nu = \frac{m}{m_\nu} \overline{dx}_\nu.$$

75. Problem 2a.

To express the inclination $\widehat{sp_\rho}$ of the displacement ds to the general coordinate p_ρ in terms of the r increments $dp_{\rho'}$.

Put in equation § 58 dp_ρ' zero for all values of ρ except the chosen one to which the problem refers. The direction of ds' is then by § 69 that of p_ρ, and the angle $\widehat{ss'}$ is the required angle. Since at the same time by § 57 $ds'^2 = a_{\rho\rho} dp'^2_\rho$, we obtain as solution of the problem

$$\sqrt{a_{\rho\rho}}\, ds \cos \widehat{sp_\rho} = \sum_{1}^{r}{}_\sigma a_{\rho\sigma} dp_\sigma,$$

where for ds its value in terms of dp_σ must be substituted.

76. Observation 1.

If in the foregoing expression we put all the dp_σ's equal to zero with the exception of a given one, say dp_σ, the direction of ds becomes the direction of this coordinate p_σ and the angle $\widehat{sp_\rho}$ becomes the angle $\widehat{p_\sigma p_\rho}$ which the coordinate p_σ makes with the coordinate p_ρ. Since at the same time $ds^2 = a_{\sigma\sigma} dp_\sigma^2$, we obtain for this angle

$$\cos \widehat{p_\sigma p_\rho} = \frac{a_{\rho\sigma}}{\sqrt{a_{\rho\rho} a_{\sigma\sigma}}},$$

and this angle is always, by § 62, a real angle.

77. Observation 2.

The coordinates p_ρ are called orthogonal when each of them is in every position perpendicular to the remaining ones. The necessary and sufficient condition is (§ 76) that $a_{\rho\sigma}$ should vanish whenever ρ and σ are different. For example, rectangular coordinates are orthogonal coordinates.

78. Problem 2b.

To express the components $\overline{dp_\rho}$ of the displacement ds along the coordinates p_ρ in terms of the increments dp_ρ of these coordinates in the displacement.

In equation § 75 put $\widehat{sp_\rho}$ equal to zero, and we get the displacement ds given by this equation in the direction of p_ρ; every dp_σ is zero except dp_ρ, and the equation thus becomes $\sqrt{a_{\rho\rho}}\, ds = a_{\rho\rho} dp_\rho$. The ratio of the change of p_ρ to a displacement in its own direction is thus $1/\sqrt{a_{\rho\rho}}$. If we remember that according to § 48 $ds \cos \widehat{sp_\rho}$ is the component of ds in the direction p_ρ and pay attention to definition § 71, we see that the left-hand side of the equation § 75 represents the reduced component along p_ρ and we obtain the expression,

$$\overline{dp}_\rho = \sqrt{a_{\rho\rho}}ds \cos \overset{\wedge}{sp}_\rho \qquad (i),$$

and thus

$$\overline{dp}_\rho = \sum_1^r {}_\sigma a_{\rho\sigma} dp_\sigma \qquad (ii).$$

79. Problem 2c. To express the increments dp_ρ of the coordinates, owing to a displacement ds, in terms of the components $\overline{dp}_\rho$ of the displacement along the coordinates p_ρ.

Using the equation § 78 (ii), along with the notation of § 64, we get immediately

$$dp_\rho = \sum_1^r {}_\sigma b_{\rho\sigma} \overline{dp}_\sigma.$$

80. Problem 3a. To express the components $\overline{dp}_\rho$ of a displacement along the general coordinates p_ρ in terms of the components $\overline{dx}_\nu$ of the displacement along the rectangular coordinates of the system.

We obtain successively by use of §§ 78, 57 (iii), 57 (ii), and 74,

$$\overline{dp}_\rho = \sum_1^r {}_\sigma a_{\rho\sigma} dp_\sigma = \sum_1^r {}_\sigma \sum_1^{3n} {}_\nu \frac{m_\nu}{m} a_{\nu\rho} a_{\nu\sigma} dp_\sigma$$

$$= \sum_1^{3n} {}_\nu \frac{m_\nu}{m} a_{\nu\rho} dx_\nu = \sum_1^{3n} {}_\nu a_{\nu\rho} \overline{dx}_\nu.$$

81. Problem 3b. To express the components $\overline{dx}_\nu$ of a displacement along the rectangular coordinates x_ν in terms of the components $\overline{dp}_\rho$ of the displacement along the general coordinates p_ρ of the system.

We obtain successively by means of §§ 73, 57 (ii), and 79,

$$\overline{dx}_\nu = \frac{m_\nu}{m} dx_\nu = \frac{m_\nu}{m} \sum_1^r {}_\sigma a_{\nu\sigma} dp_\sigma$$

$$= \frac{m_\nu}{m} \sum_1^r {}_\sigma a_{\nu\sigma} \sum_1^r {}_\rho b_{\rho\sigma} \overline{dp}_\rho,$$

thus, writing for shortness

III INFINITELY SMALL DISPLACEMENTS 69

$$\frac{m_\nu}{m}\sum_\sigma^r {}_1 a_{\nu\sigma}b_{\rho\sigma} = \beta_{\nu\rho} \qquad (i),$$

we obtain

$$\overline{dx}_\nu = \sum_\rho^r {}_1 \beta_{\nu\rho}\overline{dp}_\rho \qquad (ii).$$

82. Problem 4. To express the length of an infinitely small displacement in terms of its reduced components along the coordinates of the system.

If we employ the general coordinates p_ρ, we obtain by successive use of §§ 78 (ii) and 79 with the equation § 57 (iv)

$$ds^2 = \sum_\rho^r {}_1 \sum_\sigma^r {}_1 a_{\rho\sigma}dp_\rho dp_\sigma$$

$$= \sum_\rho^r {}_1 dp_\rho \overline{dp}_\rho = \sum_\rho^r {}_1 \sum_\sigma^r {}_1 b_{\rho\sigma}\overline{dp}_\rho \overline{dp}_\sigma.$$

83. If we employ rectangular coordinates these equations take the form

$$ds^2 = \sum_\nu^{3n} {}_1 \frac{m_\nu}{m} dx_\nu^2$$

$$= \sum_\nu^{3n} {}_1 dx_\nu \overline{dx}_\nu = \sum_\nu^{3n} {}_1 \frac{m}{m_\nu}\overline{dx}_\nu^2.$$

84. Problem 5a. To express the angle between two infinitely small displacements from any position in terms of the reduced components of both displacements along the rectangular coordinates.

By successive use of § 73 and § 74 in the equation § 56 we obtain the forms

$$dsds' \cos \widehat{ss'} = \sum_\nu^{3n} {}_1 \frac{m_\nu}{m} dx_\nu dx_\nu'$$

$$= \sum_\nu^{3n} {}_1 dx_\nu \overline{dx}_\nu' = \sum_\nu^{3n} {}_1 \overline{dx}_\nu dx_\nu' = \sum_\nu^{3n} {}_1 \frac{m}{m_\nu}\overline{dx}_\nu \overline{dx}_\nu'.$$

In these we must substitute for ds and ds' their values in terms of $\overline{dx}_\nu$ given in § 83.

85. Problem 5b. To express the angle between two

infinitely small displacements from the same position in terms of the components of the two displacements along the general coordinates p_ρ.

By successive use of §§ 78 and 79 in the equation § 58 we obtain the forms

$$dsds' \cos \widehat{ss'} = \sum_\rho^r \sum_\sigma^r a_{\rho\sigma} dp_\rho dp_\sigma'$$
$$= \sum_\rho^r dp_\rho d\bar{p}_\rho' = \sum_\rho^r d\bar{p}_\rho dp_\rho' = \sum_\rho^r \sum_\sigma^r b_{\rho\sigma} d\bar{p}_\rho d\bar{p}_\sigma'.$$

Here again we must substitute for ds and ds' their values in terms of $d\bar{p}_\rho$ given in § 82.

86. **Problem 6.** To express the angle between two infinitely small displacements in terms of the angles which both make with the coordinates of the system.

Divide the last of equations § 85 by $dsds'$ and remember that by § 78 (i)

$$\sqrt{a_{\rho\rho}} \cos \widehat{sp_\rho} = \frac{d\bar{p}_\rho}{ds}, \quad \sqrt{a_{\rho\rho}} \cos \widehat{s'p_\rho} = \frac{d\bar{p}_\rho'}{ds'},$$

we then obtain

$$\cos \widehat{ss'} = \sum_\rho^r \sum_\sigma^r b_{\rho\sigma} \sqrt{a_{\rho\rho} a_{\sigma\sigma}} \cos \widehat{sp_\rho} \cos \widehat{s'p_\sigma}.$$

87. When we employ rectangular coordinates the foregoing equation takes the form

$$\cos \widehat{ss'} = \sum_\nu^{3n} \cos \widehat{sx_\nu} \cos \widehat{s'x_\nu}.$$

It is to be noticed that the equation § 86 assumes the same position for the two displacements, whereas the equation of § 87 is free from this assumption.

88. **Proposition.** The r angles which any direction in a definite position makes with the r general coordinates are connected by the equation

$$\sum_\rho^r \sum_\sigma^r b_{\rho\sigma} \sqrt{a_{\rho\rho} a_{\sigma\sigma}} \cos \widehat{sp_\rho} \cos \widehat{sp_\sigma} = 1 ;$$

for this equation follows when in § 86 the directions of ds and ds' are made to coincide.

89. Corollary. In particular the $3n$ angles which any displacement of the system makes with the rectangular coordinates of the system satisfy the equation

$$\sum_{1}^{3n} \cos^2 \stackrel{\wedge}{sx_\nu} = 1.$$

Use of Partial Differential Coefficients

90. Notation. The length ds of an infinitely small displacement is determined by the values of the coordinates p_ρ of its position and their changes dp_ρ. If we change one of these constituent elements, whilst the rest remain constant, the resulting partial differential of ds will be denoted by $\partial_p ds$.

If we consider, as we may, the coordinates p_ρ and the components $\overline{dp}_\rho$ along them as the independent constituent elements of ds, then the resulting partial differential of ds will be denoted by $\partial_q ds$.

Other partial differentials of ds are of course possible, but it is not necessary for our purpose to specify them. The symbol ∂ds, which is usually used for them, will be retained, and will be more particularly defined on each occasion in words.

91. Note 1. The components of a displacement along the coordinates can be expressed as partial differential coefficients of the length of the displacement. Thus, by differentiating the equation § 57 (iv), and making use of § 78, we get

$$\overline{dp}_\rho = \tfrac{1}{2}\frac{\partial_p ds^2}{\partial dp_\rho} = ds\frac{\partial_p ds}{\partial dp_\rho}.$$

92. Note 2. The inclination of an infinitely small displacement to the coordinate p_ρ can be expressed by means of the partial differential coefficients of its length. Thus, using §§ 91 and 78,

$$\sqrt{a_{\rho\rho}} \cos \stackrel{\wedge}{sp}_\rho = \frac{\partial_p ds}{\partial dp_\rho}.$$

72   FIRST BOOK   CHAP.

93. **Observation.** In particular, if in §§ 91 and 92 we use rectangular coordinates we obtain

$$\overline{dx_\nu} = ds \frac{\partial ds}{\partial \overline{dx_\nu}} \qquad \text{(i)},$$

$$\sqrt{\frac{\overline{m_\nu}}{m}} \cos \overset{\wedge}{sx_\nu} = \frac{\partial ds}{\partial \overline{dx_\nu}} \qquad \text{(ii)},$$

where the meaning of the partial differentials is clear from what precedes.

94. **Note 3.** The changes which the coordinates p_ρ suffer in an infinitely small displacement can be expressed as partial differential coefficients of the length of the displacement. Thus, using the equations in §§ 82 and 79,

$$dp_\rho = \tfrac{1}{2} \frac{\partial_q ds^2}{\partial \overline{dp_\rho}} = ds \frac{\partial_q ds}{\partial \overline{dp_\rho}}.$$

95. **Note 4.** For all values of the index τ the following relation exists between the partial differential coefficients of ds—

$$\frac{\partial_p ds}{\partial p_\tau} = - \frac{\partial_q ds}{\partial p_\tau} \qquad \text{(i)}.$$

For

$$\frac{\partial_p ds}{\partial p_\tau} = \frac{1}{2ds} \sum_{1}^{\tau} {}_\rho \sum_{1}^{\tau} {}_\sigma \frac{\partial a_{\rho\sigma}}{\partial p_\tau} dp_\rho dp_\sigma,$$

and

$$\frac{\partial_q ds}{\partial p_\tau} = \frac{1}{2ds} \sum_{1}^{\tau} {}_\rho \sum_{1}^{\tau} {}_\sigma \frac{\partial b_{\rho\sigma}}{\partial p_\tau} \overline{dp_\rho} \overline{dp_\sigma}.$$

If we put in the first form for dp_ρ and dp_σ their values in terms of $\overline{dp_\rho}$ and $\overline{dp_\sigma}$ given in § 79, and make use of the relations in § 68 and the second form, the proof follows. In a similar manner we may proceed with the second form.

96. **Proposition.** If the position of an infinitely small displacement suffers two such changes, whereby the first time the components along the coordinates, and the second time the changes of the coordinates retain their original value, then the changes in the length of the displacement in both cases are equal, but of opposite signs.

PATHS OF SYSTEMS

For in the second case $\delta dp_\rho = 0$, whilst the coordinates p_ρ suffer the changes δp_ρ, and thus the change in the length of the displacement is given by

$$\delta_p ds = \sum_1^r \frac{\partial_p ds}{\partial p_\tau} \delta p_\tau \qquad \text{(i)}.$$

In the first case $\delta \overline{dp}_\rho = 0$, whilst the coordinates suffer the same changes δp_ρ so that

$$\delta_q ds = \sum_1^r \frac{\partial_q ds}{\partial p_\tau} \delta p_\tau \qquad \text{(ii)}.$$

From the equations (i) and (ii) and the equation § 95 (i) we get

$$\delta_p ds = - \delta_q ds.$$

Paths of Systems

Explanations

97. The aggregate of positions which a system occupies in its passage from one position to another is called a path of the system.

A path may also be considered as the aggregate of displacements which a system undergoes in its passage from one position to another.

98. A portion of the path which is limited by two infinitely near positions is called an element of the path. Such an element is an infinitely small displacement; it has both length and direction.

99. The direction of the path of a system in a given position is the direction of one of the elements of the path infinitely near that position.

The length of the path of a system between two of its positions is the sum of the lengths of the elements of the path between these positions.

100. **Analytical Representation.**—The path of a system is represented analytically when the coordinates of its positions

are given as functions of any one chosen variable. With every position of the path is a value of the variable associated. One of the coordinates themselves may serve as independent variable. It is frequently convenient to choose as independent variable the length of the path, measured from a given position of the path. The differential coefficients with regard to this chosen variable, and therefore with regard to the length of path, will be denoted in the manner of Lagrange by accents.

101. Definition 1. The path of a system is said to be straight when it has the same direction in all its positions.

102. Corollary. If a system describes a straight path, then its individual points describe straight lines, whose lengths measured from their starting-point are always proportional to one another (§ 38).

103. Definition 2. The path of a system is said to be curved when the direction of the path changes as we pass from one position to another. The rate of change of the direction with regard to the length of the path is called the curvature of the path.

The curvature of the path is therefore the limiting value of the ratio of the angle between two neighbouring elements to their distance.

104. Observation. The value of the curvature is therefore defined independently of the form of the analytical representation; hence, in particular, it is independent of the choice of the coordinates of the system.

105. Problem 1. To express the curvature c of the path in terms of the changes of the angles which the path makes with the rectangular coordinates of the system.

Let $d\epsilon$ be the angle between the direction of the path at the beginning and end of the path-element ds. Then by definition (§ 103)

$$c = \frac{d\epsilon}{ds}.$$

Let, further, $\cos \widehat{sx_\nu}$ be the cosine of the angle which the path makes with x_ν at the beginning of ds; and let

$\cos \widehat{sx}_\nu + d \cos \widehat{sx}_\nu$ be the value of the same quantity at the end of ds. Then, by equation § 87,

$$\cos(d\epsilon) = \sum_1^{3n} {}^\nu \cos \widehat{sx}_\nu (\cos \widehat{sx}_\nu + d \cos \widehat{sx}_\nu).$$

Further, by equation 89,

$$\sum_1^{3n} {}^\nu \cos^2 \widehat{sx}_\nu = 1,$$

and

$$\sum_1^{3n} {}^\nu (\cos \widehat{sx}_\nu + d \cos \widehat{sx}_\nu)^2 = 1.$$

If, then, we subtract twice the first equation from the sum of the last two we obtain

$$2 - 2\cos(d\epsilon) = d\epsilon^2 = \sum_1^{3n} {}^\nu (d \cos \widehat{sx}_\nu)^2,$$

and on dividing by ds^2

$$c^2 = \sum_1^{3n} {}^\nu \left(\frac{d \cos \widehat{sx}_\nu}{ds} \right)^2.$$

106. Problem 2. To express the curvature of the path in terms of the changes of the rectangular coordinates of the system with respect to the length of the path.

From § 72 we have (§ 100)

$$\cos \widehat{sx}_\nu = \sqrt{\frac{m_\nu}{m}} x_\nu',$$

and

$$(\cos \widehat{sx})' = \sqrt{\frac{m_\nu}{m}} x_\nu''.$$

Hence by § 105 the solution of the problem is

$$mc^2 = \sum_1^{3n} {}^\nu m_\nu x_\nu''^2.$$

107. Problem 3. To express the curvature of the path in terms of the changes in the rectangular coordinates, themselves considered as functions of any variable τ.

According to the rules of the differential calculus

$$x_\nu'' = \frac{d}{ds}\left(\frac{dx_\nu}{d\tau} \cdot \frac{d\tau}{ds}\right) = \left(\frac{d\tau}{ds}\right)^3 \left\{ \frac{ds}{d\tau} \cdot \frac{d^2x_\nu}{d\tau^2} - \frac{dx_\nu}{d\tau} \cdot \frac{d^2s}{d\tau^2} \right\}.$$

If we substitute this expression in c^2 and remember (§ 55) that

$$m\left(\frac{ds}{d\tau}\right)^2 = \sum_{1}^{3n}{}_\nu m_\nu \left(\frac{dx_\nu}{d\tau}\right)^2 \tag{i},$$

and

$$m\frac{ds}{d\tau} \cdot \frac{d^2s}{d\tau^2} = \sum_{1}^{3n}{}_\nu m_\nu \frac{dx_\nu}{d\tau} \cdot \frac{d^2x_\nu}{d\tau^2} \tag{ii},$$

we obtain

$$m\left(\frac{ds}{d\tau}\right)^4 c^2 = \sum_{1}^{3n}{}_\nu m_\nu \left(\frac{d^2x_\nu}{d\tau^2}\right)^2 - m\left(\frac{d^2s}{d\tau^2}\right)^2,$$

where for $ds/d\tau$ and $d^2s/d\tau^2$ their values determined by the foregoing equations are to be substituted.

108. **Problem 4.** To express the curvature of the path in terms of the changes in the general coordinates p_ρ of the system with regard to the length of the path.

Substitute in the expression § 106 instead of the rectangular coordinates, p_ρ, supposing x_ν'' expressed in terms of p_ρ' and p_ρ''.

Thus, by § 57 (ii),

$$x_\nu' = \sum_{1}^{r}{}_\rho a_{\nu\rho} p_\rho',$$

and hence

$$x_\nu'' = \sum_{1}^{r}{}_\rho (a_{\nu\rho} p_\rho'' + a_{\nu\rho}' p_\rho');$$

therefore

$$x_\nu''^2 = \sum_{1}^{r}{}_\rho \sum_{1}^{r}{}_\sigma (a_{\nu\rho} a_{\nu\sigma} p_\rho'' p_\sigma'' + 2 a_{\nu\rho}' a_{\nu\sigma} p_\rho' p_\sigma'' + a_{\nu\rho}' a_{\nu\sigma}' p_\nu' p_\sigma').$$

If we form these equations for all values of ν and multiply each of them by $\dfrac{m_\nu}{m}$ and then add, the left-hand side becomes c^2. The summation on the right with regard to ν can be obtained by aid of the quantities $a_{\rho\sigma}$ for the first two terms. For the first term we get immediately by § 57 (iii) $a_{\rho\sigma}$. For the coefficient of p_σ'' in the second term we have

$$2\sum_{1}^{r}{}_{\rho}p_{\rho}'\sum_{1}^{3n}{}_{\nu}\frac{m_{\nu}}{m}a_{\nu\sigma}a_{\nu\rho}' = 2\sum_{1}^{r}{}_{\rho}\sum_{1}^{r}{}_{\tau}p_{\rho}'p_{\tau}'\sum_{1}^{3n}{}_{\nu}\frac{m_{\nu}}{m}a_{\nu\sigma}\frac{da_{\nu\rho}}{dp_{\tau}}$$

$$= \sum_{1}^{r}{}_{\rho}\sum_{1}^{r}{}_{\tau}p_{\rho}'p_{\tau}'\sum_{1}^{3n}{}_{\nu}\frac{m_{\nu}}{m}a_{\nu\sigma}\left(\frac{\partial a_{\rho\nu}}{\partial p_{\tau}} + \frac{\partial a_{\nu\tau}}{\partial p_{\rho}}\right)$$

$$= \sum_{1}^{r}{}_{\rho}\sum_{1}^{r}{}_{\tau}p_{\rho}'p_{\tau}'\left(\frac{\partial a_{\rho\sigma}}{\partial p_{\tau}} + \frac{\partial a_{\tau\sigma}}{\partial p_{\rho}} - \frac{\partial a_{\rho\tau}}{\partial p_{\sigma}}\right) \quad \text{(by § 63)}$$

$$= \sum_{1}^{r}{}_{\rho}\sum_{1}^{r}{}_{\tau}p_{\rho}'p_{\tau}'\left(2\frac{\partial a_{\rho\sigma}}{\partial p_{\tau}} - \frac{\partial a_{\rho\tau}}{\partial p_{\sigma}}\right).$$

In the transition from the second to the third form, and from the fourth to the fifth, use is made of the fact that, when $F(\rho,\sigma)$ is any expression involving ρ and σ, then

$$\sum_{1}^{r}{}_{\rho}\sum_{1}^{r}{}_{\sigma}F(\rho,\sigma) \equiv \sum_{1}^{r}{}_{\rho}\sum_{1}^{r}{}_{\sigma}F(\sigma,\rho).$$

The coefficient of the third term cannot be expressed in terms of $a_{\rho\sigma}$. In order to make the connection with the rectangular coordinates disappear from the final result, let us put

$$a_{\rho\sigma\lambda\mu} = \sum_{1}^{3n}{}_{\nu}\frac{m_{\nu}}{m}\frac{\partial a_{\nu\sigma}}{\partial p_{\lambda}} \cdot \frac{\partial a_{\nu\rho}}{\partial p_{\mu}}.$$

Then we obtain

$$c^2 = \sum_{1}^{r}{}_{\rho}\sum_{1}^{r}{}_{\sigma}\left\{ a_{\rho\sigma}p_{\rho}''p_{\sigma}'' + \sum_{1}^{r}{}_{\tau}\left(2\frac{\partial a_{\rho\sigma}}{\partial p_{\tau}} - \frac{\partial a_{\rho\tau}}{\partial p_{\sigma}}\right)p_{\rho}'p_{\tau}'p_{\sigma}'' + \sum_{1}^{r}{}_{\lambda}\sum_{1}^{r}{}_{\mu}a_{\rho\sigma\lambda\mu}p_{\rho}'p_{\sigma}'p_{\lambda}'p_{\mu}' \right\}.$$

In these results the values of $a_{\rho\sigma}$ are given by means of § 57 as functions of p_{ρ}; the quantities $a_{\rho\sigma\lambda\mu}$ are to be regarded as newly introduced functions of the same quantities. The number of these newly introduced functions is equal to

$$\tfrac{1}{4}r^2(r+1)^2.$$

CHAPTER IV

POSSIBLE AND IMPOSSIBLE DISPLACEMENTS.
MATERIAL SYSTEMS

Explanations

109. There exists a connection between a series of material points when from a knowledge of some of the components of the displacements of those points we are able to state something as to the remaining components.

110. When connections exist between the points of a system, some of the conceivable displacements of the system are excluded from consideration, namely, those displacements of the system whose occurrence would contradict the statements above referred to. Conversely, every statement that some of the conceivable displacements of the system are excluded from consideration, implies a connection between the points of the system. The connections between the points of a system are completely given when for every conceivable displacement of the system it is known whether it is, or is not, excluded from our consideration.

111. Those displacements which are not excluded from our consideration are called possible ones, the others impossible ones. Possible displacements are also called virtual. They are always called possible displacements when as a narrower idea they are contrasted with conceivable displacements; they are only called virtual when as a broader idea they are contrasted with a narrower one, *e.g.* the case of actual displacements.

112. Possible paths are those paths which are composed of possible displacements. Possible positions are all those positions which can be reached *via* possible paths.

113. Thus all positions of possible paths are possible positions. But it is not to be understood that any conceivable path whatever through possible positions is also a possible path. On the contrary, a displacement between infinitely neighbouring possible positions may be an impossible displacement.

114. Between two possible positions there is always one possible path. For if from any one actual position even a single possible path can be drawn to each of the two positions, then these two paths must together form one possible path between the two positions; if no possible path could be drawn to one of the two, then would this position not be a possible position.

115. **Definition 1.** A connection of a system is said to be a continuous one when it is not inconsistent with the three following assumptions:—

1. That the knowledge of all possible finite displacements should be included in the knowledge of all possible infinitely small displacements.

2. That every possible infinitely small displacement can be traversed in a straight, continuous path.

3. That every infinitely small displacement, which is possible from a given position, is also possible from any infinitely neighbouring position, except for variations of the order of the distance between the positions or of a higher order.

116. **Corollary.** When only continuous connections exist in a system, the sum of any possible infinitely small displacements whatever from the same position is itself a possible displacement from the same position. (Superposition of infinitely small displacements.)

For, according to § 115 (3), the individual displacements may be performed successively, and consequently, by § 115 (2), the direct displacement from the initial position to the final one is itself a possible displacement.

117. **Definition 2.** A connection of a system is said to

be an internal one when it only affects the mutual position of the points of the system.

118. Corollary. When in a system only internal connections exist, every displacement of the system which does not alter the configuration is a possible displacement, and conversely.

119. Definition 3. A connection of a system is said to be normal (*gesetzmässiger*) when it exists independently of the time.

A normal connection is therefore implied in the statement that of the conceivable displacements of a system some are possible, others not, and this at all times or independently of the time.

120. Observation. So long as we treat solely of the geometry of systems, the difference between normal and abnormal connections does not appear, for in this case our investigations are not affected by the time. If the connections of a system are different at two different times, then for the present we must consider that we are dealing with two different systems. It will practically amount to the same thing if we assume that in this first book all the connections are normal.

121. Definition 1. A system of material points which is subject to no other than continuous connections is called a material system.

122. Definition 2. A material system which is subject to no other than internal and normal connections is called a free system.

123. Definition 3. A material system between whose possible positions all conceivable continuous motions are also possible motions is called a holonomous system.

The term means that such a system obeys integral (ὅλος) laws (νόμος), whereas material systems in general obey only differential conditions. (*Cf.* § 132 *infra.*)

Analytical Representation

124. Note. A system of material points satisfies the conditions of a material system when the differentials of its rectangular coordinates are subject to no other conditions than a series of homogeneous linear equations whose coefficients are continuous functions of possible values of the coordinates.

For the first kind of continuity which Definition 115 requires must be presupposed, when mention is made of the differentials of the coordinates of the system; the other two kinds of continuity are satisfied by the restriction of the differentials employed.

125. **Converse.** If a system of material points satisfies the conditions of a material system, then the differentials of its rectangular coordinates are subject to no other limitations than to a series of homogeneous linear equations, whose coefficients are continuous functions of possible values of the coordinates.

To prove this let us take a possible position of the system, and the possible displacements from it. For a given displacement the $3n$ increments dx_ν may be supposed to have to one another the ratios

$$\epsilon_{11} : \epsilon_{12} \ldots : \epsilon_{13n}.$$

If now we consider du_1 as any infinitely small quantity whatever, then by means of the set of equations

$$dx_\nu = \epsilon_{1\nu} du_1$$

a set of possible displacements is given. Now either all possible displacements are contained in these, or this is not the case. If not, then we must take a second displacement, which cannot be represented in this form, and for this the $3n$ increments dx_ν may bear to one another the ratios

$$\epsilon_{21} : \epsilon_{22} \ldots : \epsilon_{23n}.$$

Then taking any second infinitely small quantity du_2, by means of the set of equations

$$dx_\nu = \epsilon_{1\nu} du_1 + \epsilon_{2\nu} du_2,$$

by § 116 a more general set of possible displacements is given.

Now either all possible displacements are contained in this set, or not. If not, we must choose another such quantity du_3, and continue the process until, on account of the exhaustion of all possible displacements, it is not possible to continue it further. Its continuance becomes impossible when we have taken $3n$ such quantities du_λ; and then the expression

$$dx_\nu = \sum_1^{3n}{}_\lambda \epsilon_{\lambda\nu} du_\lambda \qquad (\text{i})$$

represents all possible displacements of the system, when all conceivable displacements are possible ones, and thus when no connections exist between the points of a system. In general the process must come to an end earlier, and all possible displacements may therefore be expressed by equations of condition of the form

$$dx_\nu = \sum_1^{l}{}_\lambda \epsilon_{\lambda\nu} du_\lambda,$$

where under all circumstances

$$l \lesseqgtr 3n.$$

In order that this form may be satisfied by arbitrarily chosen values of dx_ν, it is sufficient that the dx_ν's should satisfy the $3n-l$ linear homogeneous equations which result from the elimination of du_λ from the equations (i). The quantities $\epsilon_{\lambda\nu}$ must, according to § 115 (3), be continuous functions of the position. However (by § 124), the increments dx_ν are not to be subject to further limitations than these.

126. Observation. The number and the content of the equations which we obtain between dx_ν by the foregoing process, are independent of the particular choice of the displacements.

For if we take other displacements and express dx_ν in terms of other quantities dv_λ, then we can substitute the values of dx_ν in the equations which we have already obtained by elimination. If these are not identically satisfied then the quantities dv_λ would not be independent, which would be contrary to the assumption under which they are chosen. Thus these equations are identically satisfied, and cannot therefore be different from the equations or linear combinations of the equations which were obtained by elimination of the quantities dv_λ in terms of which the increments dx_ν are expressed. The number of equations obtained by means of du_λ can not be greater than the number obtained by means of dv_λ: neither can it be less; for then the converse process would show that the quantities du_λ would not be independent of one another.

127. Corollary 1. The connection of a material system can be completely expressed analytically by stating a single possible position of the system and a set of homogeneous linear equations between the differentials of its rectangular coordinates.

For relations between these differentials cannot by § 125 be given in any other manner than by such a set of equations. This does not exclude the existence of finite equations between the coordinates. However, all such finite equations can be completely replaced by means of a single possible position, and just as many homogeneous linear equations between the differentials. These last, however, must not be inconsistent with the given differential equations; they must either reduce to them, or must be associated with them in a complete representation.

128. Notation. The equations which represent the connection of a material system, in terms of its rectangular coordinates, will in future always be expressed in the following form

$$\sum_{1}^{3n} x_{\iota\nu} dx_\nu = 0.$$

It is to be understood that i such equations exist, and that the ι's have values from 1 to i. The quantities $x_{\iota\nu}$ are to be considered continuous functions of x_ν.

129. Corollary 2. The connection of a material system whose positions are expressed in terms of general coordinates can also be completely expressed analytically by stating a single possible position and a set of homogeneous linear equations between the differentials of the coordinates.

Using the general coordinates p_ρ whose number r is less than $3n$, a connection between the points of the system is *ipso facto* in existence. First suppose the connection to be completely expressed by the rectangular coordinates according to § 128. In the corresponding differential equations let the values of dx_ν be substituted in terms of dp_ρ by means of equation § 57 (ii). The resulting linear homogeneous equations can be so arranged that $3n - r$ of them are identically satisfied in consequence of the $3n-r$ equations which express the fact that the $3n$ quantities x_ν are functions of the r quantities p_ρ. The remaining $k = i - 3n + r$ equations between dp_ρ give completely all the equations between dx_ν, and therefore (§ 127), with a knowledge of one possible position, are sufficient to describe completely the connection of the system.

130. Notation. The equations which express the connection of a material system in the general coordinates p_ρ, will in future always be written in the form

$$\sum_{1}^{r}{}_\rho p_{\chi\rho} dp_\rho = 0.$$

They will be taken as k in number, and all values from 1 to k are to be given to χ. The quantities $p_{\chi\rho}$ are to be considered continuous functions of p_ρ.

131. Observation. The equations § 128 or § 130 are called the differential equations, or the equations of condition of the system.

132. Proposition. When from the differential equations of a material system an equal number of finite equations between the coordinates of the system can be deduced, the system is a holonomous system (§ 123).

For the coordinates of every possible position must satisfy the finite equations. The differences between the coordinates of two neighbouring positions satisfy consequently an equal number of homogeneous linear differential equations, and since these must not be inconsistent with the equal number of the differential equations of the system, they must satisfy these also. The displacement between any two possible positions is consequently a possible displacement, whence the assertion follows.

133. Converse. If a material system is holonomous, then its differential equations admit an equal number of finite or integral equations between the coordinates.

For let us take from the r coordinates of the system, between whose differentials the k equations exist, any, say the first $r - k$ as independent variables, and pass from any initial position of the system along different possible paths to a position for which the independent coordinates have given values. Now if with a continually changing path one arrived at continuously changing values of the remaining coordinates, consequently at different positions, these positions would be possible positions, and therefore the displacements between them would by hypothesis be possible displacements. There would then be a value-system of the differentials, different from zero, which would satisfy the differential equations, even when the first $r-k$ are put zero. This is not possible, for the equations are homogeneous and linear. Thus we must always arrive at the same values not only of the first $r-k$, but also of the remaining coordinates. The latter are consequently definite functions of the former. The k finite equations which express this are, since they cannot be inconsistent with the differential equations, integral equations of these latter.

Freedom of Motion

134. **Definition.** The number of infinitely small changes of the coordinates of a system that can be taken arbitrarily is called the number of free motions of the system, or the degree of freedom of its motion.

135. **Note 1.** The number of free motions of a system is equal to the number of its coordinates, diminished by the number of the differential equations of the system.

136. **Note 2.** The number of free motions of a material system is independent of the choice of the coordinates.

In the notation of §§ 128-130 the number of degrees of freedom is equal to $r-k$, or, by § 129, to $3n-i$, and is therefore always the same number, whatever numbers r and k may represent.

137. **Note 3.** The number of degrees of freedom of a system does not change with the position of the system.

For the connection being a continuous one, the number of degrees of freedom cannot differ by a finite quantity in neighbouring positions; thus, since a continuous change in this number is excluded, it does not change in finitely distant positions.

138. **Note 4.** The proof of the set of equations in § 125 furnishes a solution of the problem—To find, but not without trial, the number of degrees of freedom of a completely known material system. The number l of the auxiliary quantities du_λ found according to the method of that proof is the required number.

It is known that the possible positions of the system can be represented by means of r general coordinates p_ρ, and so in that proof these coordinates can be used instead of x_ν.

139. **Definition.** A coordinate of a material system whose changes can take place independently of the changes of the remainder of the coordinates is called a free coordinate of the system.

140. **Corollary.** A free coordinate does not appear in the differential equations of its system, and conversely every coordinate which does not appear in the differential equations of the system is a free coordinate.

141. **Observation 1.** Whether a given coordinate is a free coordinate or not depends on the choice of the remaining coordinates simultaneously employed.

For if a certain coordinate does not appear in the differential equations of the system, and we choose instead of one of those coordinates which do appear in the differential equations, a function of this and the first one as coordinate, then the first one loses its property of being a free coordinate, a property which it possessed until then.

142. **Observation 2.** In a free system every coordinate of absolute position is a free coordinate. See §§ 118 and 122.

143. **Proposition.** When the possible positions of a material system can be represented by means of coordinates which are all free, then the system is holonomous (§ 123).

For every displacement of the system between possible positions is expressed in terms of a value-system of the differentials of the free coordinates; every such value-system is possible since it is subject to no conditions, and therefore every displacement between possible positions is a possible **displacement.**

144. Converse. In a holonomous system all possible positions can be expressed in terms of free coordinates.

If a holonomous system has r coordinates, between which k differential equations exist, then k of the coordinates can be expressed as functions of the remaining $(r-k)$. (See § 133.) Hence these $r-k$ arbitrarily chosen coordinates determine completely the position of the system, and can by omission of the remaining coordinates be taken as free coordinates of the system. Also any $(r-k)$ functions of the original r coordinates may serve a similar purpose.

145. Observation 1. The number of free coordinates of a holonomous system is equal to the number of its degrees of freedom.

146. Observation 2. If the number of coordinates of a material system is equal to the number of its degrees of freedom, then all the coordinates are free coordinates, and the system is holonomous.

For should even a single differential equation between the coordinates exist, then the number of coordinates of the system would be greater than the number of degrees of freedom. The number of coordinates can not be less than the number of degrees of freedom.

147. Observation 3. The possible positions of a system, which is not holonomous, can not be fully represented by means of free coordinates alone.

For the opposite of this statement would be contrary to § 143.

Displacements Perpendicular to Possible Displacements

148. Proposition. If the r components $d\overline{p}_\rho$ of a displacement ds of a system along the coordinates p_ρ can be expressed by means of k quantities γ_χ in the form

$$d\overline{p}_\rho = \sum_1^k \varkappa \cdot p_{\chi\rho} \gamma_\chi,$$

where the $p_{\chi\rho}$'s are taken from the equations of condition of the system (§ 130), then the displacement is perpendicular to every possible displacement of the system from the same position.

Let ds' be the length of any possible displacement from the same position, and let dp_ρ' denote the changes of the coordinates owing to this displacement. If now we multiply the equations of the series, each with dp_ρ' and add them, then using equations § 85 and § 130

$$\sum_1^r {}_\rho d\bar{p}_\rho dp_\rho' = ds ds' \cos \widehat{ss'} = \sum_1^k {}_\chi \gamma_\chi \sum_1^r {}_\rho p_{\chi\rho} dp_\rho' = 0 ;$$

thus $\cos \widehat{ss'} = 0$; and $\widehat{ss'} = 90°$ as was to be proved.

149. Additional Note. The r components $d\bar{p}_\rho$ of a displacement ds along the coordinates p_ρ are singly determined when we know k of them, and know also that the displacement is perpendicular to every possible displacement of the system.

Let dp_ρ' be again the changes of p_ρ for any possible displacement. By means of the k equations of condition we can represent k of them as homogeneous linear functions of the remaining $(r-k)$, and then substitute these values in the equation

$$\sum_1^r {}_\rho d\bar{p}_\rho dp_\rho' = 0.$$

The dp_ρ''s appearing in this equation are now completely arbitrary, and thus the coefficient of each one of them must vanish. This gives $(r-k)$ homogeneous linear equations between $d\bar{p}_\rho$ which permit us to express $(r-k)$ of them as single-valued linear functions of the remaining k.

150. Converse. If a conceivable displacement is perpendicular to every possible displacement of a system, then its r components $d\bar{p}_\rho$ along p_ρ can always, by suitable choice of the k quantities γ_χ, be expressed in the form

$$d\bar{p}_\rho = \sum_1^k {}_\chi p_{\chi\rho} \gamma_\chi.$$

For if we determine the γ_χ's by means of k of these equations and calculate by means of these values all the components, we must obtain the given values of $\overline{dp_\rho}$. For the displacement so obtained is by § 148 perpendicular to all possible displacements, and has with the given displacement k components common. It has thus by § 149 all the r components along p_ρ common with the same.

CHAPTER V

SPECIAL PATHS OF MATERIAL SYSTEMS

1. Straightest Paths

151. Definition 1. An element of a path of a material system is said to be straighter than any other when it has a smaller curvature.

152. Definition 2. The straightest element is defined as a possible element, which is straighter than all other possible ones which have the same position and direction.

153. Definition 3. A path, all of whose elements are straightest elements, is called a straightest path.

154. Analytical Representation. All elements of a path of which one straightest element is the straightest, have the same position and direction; hence the values of their coordinates, and the first differentials of these coordinates with regard to the independent variables, are equal. The curvature, however, is determined not by means of these values alone, but also by means of the second differential coefficients of the coordinates. By the values of these the elements are distinguished, and for the straightest element the second differential coefficients must be such functions of the coordinates and of their first differential coefficients as make the curvature a minimum.

The equations which express this condition must be satisfied for all positions of a straightest path, and they are thus the differential equations of such a path.

155. Problem 1. To express the differential equations of the straightest paths of a material system in terms of the rectangular coordinates of the system.

Let us choose as independent variable the length of the path. Since only possible paths are to be considered, the $3n$ quantities x_ν' according to §§ 128 and 100 are subject to i equations of the form

$$\sum_{1}^{3n} x_{\iota\nu} x_\nu' = 0 \qquad \text{(i)}.$$

Thus the $3n$ quantities x_ν'' are subject to i equations of the form

$$\sum_{1}^{3n} x_{\iota\nu} x_\nu'' + \sum_{1}^{3n} \sum_{1}^{3n} \frac{\partial x_{\iota\nu}}{\partial x_\mu} x_\nu' x_\mu' = 0 \qquad \text{(ii)},$$

which follow from (i) by differentiation.

With the condition that these equations are not to be violated, the quantities x_ν'' will be determined so as to make the curvature c (§ 106), or what is the same thing, the value of $\tfrac{1}{2} c^2$, viz.,

$$\tfrac{1}{2} \sum_{1}^{3n} \frac{m_\nu}{m} x_\nu''^2 \qquad \text{(iii)},$$

a minimum.

According to the rules of the differential calculus, we proceed as follows:—

Multiply each of the equations (ii) by a factor to be determined later, which for the ιth equation we may denote by Ξ_ι; add the partial differential coefficients on the left-hand side of the resulting equations arranged according to each of the quantities x_ν'' to the partial differential coefficients of (iii) (the quantity which is to be made a minimum) arranged according to the same quantities; then finally put the result equal to zero, and we get $3n$ equations of the form

$$\frac{m_\nu}{m} x_\nu'' + \sum_{1}^{i} x_{\iota\nu} \Xi_\iota = 0 \qquad \text{(iv)};$$

which, together with the i equations (ii), give $3n + i$ linear but not homogeneous equations to determine the $3n + i$ quantities x_ν'' and Ξ_ι; and from these the values of these quantities can be found, and consequently the value of the least curvature. The satisfying of the equations (iv) at all positions of a possible path is thus a necessary condition that the path should be a straightest one, and the equations (iv) are therefore the required differential equations.

156. **Observation 1.** The equations (iv) are moreover the sufficient conditions for the occurrence of a minimum. For the second differential coefficients $\dfrac{\partial^2 c^2}{\partial x_\nu'' \partial x_\mu''}$ vanish whenever ν and μ are different, and are necessarily positive when ν and μ are equal. The value of the curvature thus admits no other special value.

The satisfying of equations (iv) for all positions of a possible path is thus the sufficient condition for a straightest path.

157. **Observation 2.** By use of § 72 the equations (iv) can be written in the form

$$\sqrt{\dfrac{m_\nu}{m}}\dfrac{d}{ds}\left(\cos \overset{\wedge}{sx_\nu}\right) = -\sum_1^i {}_\iota x_{\iota\nu} \Xi_\iota.$$

The equations (iv) therefore determine how the direction of a path must change from position to position in order that it may remain a straightest path; and moreover every single equation determines how the inclination of the path to a given rectangular coordinate changes.

158. **Problem 2.** To express the differential equations of the straightest paths of a material system in terms of the general coordinates of the system.

Choose again as independent variable the length of the path. The coordinates p_ρ and their differential coefficients p_ρ' satisfy (§ 130) the k equations

$$\sum_1^r {}_\rho p_{\chi\rho} p_\rho' = 0 \qquad \text{(i),}$$

thus the quantities p_ρ'' satisfy the equations

$$\sum_1^r {}_\rho p_{\chi\rho} p_\rho'' + \sum_1^r {}_\rho \sum_1^r {}_\sigma \dfrac{\partial p_{\chi\rho}}{\partial p_\sigma} p_\rho' p_\sigma' = 0 \qquad \text{(ii).}$$

From all values of p_ρ'' which satisfy these equations those are to be determined which make the value of c or $\tfrac{1}{2}c^2$, that is, the right-hand side of the equation § 108 (iii), a minimum. We proceed according to the rules of the differential calculus, as in § 155, and take Π_χ for the factor, with which we multiply the χth of equations (ii), and we obtain the necessary conditions for the minimum as r equations of the form

$$\sum_{1}^{r}{}_\sigma a_{\rho\sigma} p_\sigma'' + \sum_{1}^{r}{}_\sigma \sum_{1}^{r}{}_\tau \left(\frac{\partial a_{\rho\sigma}}{\partial p_\tau} - \tfrac{1}{2}\frac{\partial a_{\sigma\tau}}{\partial p_\rho}\right) p_\sigma' p_\tau' + \sum_{1}^{k}{}_\chi p_{\chi\rho} \Pi_\chi = 0 \quad \text{(iii)},$$

where to ρ in each equation a definite value from 1 to r has to be given. These make together with the equations (ii) $(r+k)$ linear but not homogeneous equations for the $(r+k)$ quantities p_ρ'' and Π_χ, by which these quantities, and thus the least curvature, can be found by § 108. The satisfying of equations (iii) for all positions of a possible path is the necessary condition that the path should be a straightest path.

159. **Observation 1.** The satisfying of equations (iii) is also the sufficient condition for a minimum, and thus for a straightest path. For the result of § 108 is only a transformation of § 106 for the curvature, and like § 156 this value in § 158 only admits one special value, which is a minimum.

160. **Observation 2.** By § 75 we have

$$\sqrt{a_{\rho\rho}} \cos \widehat{sp_\rho} = \sum_{1}^{r}{}_\sigma a_{\rho\sigma} p_\sigma';$$

and therefore

$$\frac{d}{ds}\left(\sqrt{a_{\rho\rho}} \cos \widehat{sp_\rho}\right) = \sum_{1}^{r}{}_\sigma a_{\rho\sigma} p_\sigma'' + \sum_{1}^{r}{}_\sigma \sum_{1}^{r}{}_\tau \frac{\partial a_{\rho\sigma}}{\partial p_\tau} p_\sigma' p_\tau'.$$

Thus the equations 158 (iii) can be written in the form

$$\frac{d}{ds}\left(\sqrt{a_{\rho\rho}} \cos \widehat{sp_\rho}\right) = \tfrac{1}{2}\sum_{1}^{r}{}_\sigma \sum_{1}^{r}{}_\tau \frac{\partial a_{\sigma\tau}}{\partial p_\rho} p_\sigma' p_\tau' - \sum_{1}^{k}{}_\chi p_{\chi\rho} \Pi_\chi.$$

The equations (158) (iii) determine thus how the direction of the path must change from position to position in order that it may remain a straightest path; and moreover every single equation determines how the inclination to a given coordinate p_ρ changes.

161. Proposition. From a given position in a given direction there is always one and only one straightest path possible.

For when a position and a direction in it are given, the equations 155 (iv) and 158 (iv) always give definite, and moreover unique, values for the change of direction; thus by means of the given quantities the initial position, the direction at the next element of the path, and therefore at the successive positions right to the final position, are singly determined.

162. Corollary. It is in general not possible to draw a straightest path from any position of a given system to any other position.

For since the manifold of possible displacements from a position is equal to the number of free motions of the system, the manifold of possible directions in any position and therefore the manifold of straightest paths from it is smaller by unity. The manifold of positions which are to be reached by straightest paths from a given position is thus again equal to the number of free motions. But the manifold of possible positions may be equal to the number of coordinates used, and is therefore in general greater than the former.

163. Note 1. In order to be able to express all straightest paths of a material system whose positions are denoted in terms of p_ρ, by equations between p_ρ it is not necessary to know any $3n$ functions whatever which fully determine the position of the separate points of the system as functions of p_ρ. It is sufficient that, together with the equations of condition of the system in terms of p_ρ, the $\frac{1}{2} r (r+1)$ functions $a_{\rho\sigma}$ of p_ρ should be known.

For the differential equations of the straightest paths can be explicitly written down when together with the $p_{\chi\rho}$'s the $a_{\rho\sigma}$'s are given as functions of p_ρ.

164. Note 2. In order to be able to express the straightest paths of a material system whose positions are denoted in terms of p_ρ by equations between p_ρ, it is sufficient to know, together with the equations of condition between p_ρ, the length of every possible infinitely small displacement as a function of these coordinates p_ρ and their changes.

For if ds is the expression for this length in the desired form, then

$$a_{\rho\sigma} = \frac{\partial^2 ds^2}{\partial dp_\rho \partial dp_\sigma}.$$

165. **Note 3.** In order to know the value of the curvature itself in any position of a straightest path, it is not sufficient to know the $\frac{1}{2}r(r+1)$ functions $a_{\rho\sigma}$. We require in addition the $\frac{1}{4}r^2(r+1)^2$ functions $a_{\rho\sigma\lambda\mu}$ (§ 108).

The knowledge of the position of all the separate points as functions of p_ρ is not necessary for the determination of the curvature itself.

2. Shortest and Geodesic Paths

166. **Definition 1.** The shortest path of a material system between two of its positions is a possible path between these positions, whose length is less than the length of any of the other infinitely neighbouring paths between the same positions.

167. **Note 1.** The definition does not exclude the possibility, which may actually arise, of there being more than one shortest path between the two positions. The shortest of these shortest paths is the absolutely shortest path. It is at the same time the shortest path which is at all possible between the two positions.

168. **Note 2.** Between any two possible positions of a material system there is always at least one shortest path possible.

For possible paths always exist between the two positions (§ 114), and consequently there is amongst them an absolutely shortest path which is shorter than the neighbouring ones,— such as, according to §§ 121, 115, it must possess,—and is consequently a shortest path.

169. **Note 3.** A shortest path between two positions is at the same time a shortest path between any two of its intermediate positions. Every portion of a shortest path is itself a shortest path.

170. **Note 4.** The length of a shortest path differs only by an infinitely small quantity of a higher order from the lengths of all neighbouring paths between the same end posi-

tions. By infinitely small quantities of the first order are meant the lengths of the displacements necessary to pass from a neighbouring path to the shortest path.

171. **Definition 2.** A geodesic path of a material system is any path whose length between any two of its positions differs only by an infinitely small quantity of a higher order from the lengths of any of the infinitely neighbouring paths whatever between the same positions.

172. **Note 1.** Every shortest path between any two positions is a geodesic path.

Thus the definition § 171 does not involve anything in the nature of an inconsistency, for there are paths which satisfy this definition.

173. **Note 2.** There is always at least one geodesic path possible between any two possible positions of a material system (§§ 168, 172).

174. **Note 3.** A geodesic path is not necessarily at the same time a shortest path between any two of its positions.

It cannot be concluded from the definition that every geodesic path is also a shortest path, and simple examples show that there are in fact geodesic paths which are not also shortest paths between their end positions. Such examples may be taken from the geometry of the single material point, that is, from ordinary geometry, and thus be assumed known.

175. **Note 4.** When between two positions there is only one geodesic path, then this is also a shortest path, and moreover the absolutely shortest path between the two positions.

For the opposite would by §§ 168 and 172 be contrary to the hypothesis.

176. **Note 5.** A geodesic path is always a shortest path between any two sufficiently neighbouring but still finitely distant positions on it.

There may be between any two positions of the geodesic path under consideration a number of other geodesic paths. The absolutely shortest path between the two positions must coincide with one of these paths (§ 172). If we now make the positions approach one another along the geodesic path considered, then the length of this path as well as the length of the absolutely shortest path tends to zero, whilst the remaining geodesic paths remain finite. At least, from a certain finite distance of the positions onwards the geodesic path, along which the two positions approach each other, must coincide with the absolutely shortest path.

177. Analytical Representation.—In order that a path may be a geodesic path, it is necessary and sufficient that the integral of the path-elements, (§ 99) viz.,

$$\int ds,$$

taken between any two positions of the path should not vary when any continuous variations are given to the coordinates of the positions of the path, it being only supposed (1) that these variations should vanish at the limits of the integral, and (2) that after the variation the coordinates and their differentials should satisfy the equations of condition of the system. The necessary and sufficient conditions for this are a set of differential equations, which the coordinates of the path, considered as functions of any single variable, must satisfy, and which are consequently the differential equations of the geodesic paths.

178. That these differential equations should be satisfied for all points of a possible path is also by § 172 the necessary condition that the path should be a shortest path, and hence these equations are also the differential equations of the shortest paths. The vanishing of the variation of the integral is, however, not also a sufficient condition that the path should be a shortest path between its bounding positions. It is further necessary that for every admissible variation of the coordinates the second variation of the integral should have an essentially positive value. For sufficiently near positions of a path, which satisfies the differential equations, this condition is always satisfied by § 176 of itself.

179. **Problem 1.** To express the differential equations of the geodesic paths of a material system in terms of its rectangular coordinates.

The $3n$ rectangular coordinates x_ν which are regarded as functions of any variable, must both before and after the variation satisfy (§ 128) the i equations

$$\sum_{1}^{3n}{}_\nu x_{\iota\nu} dx_\nu = 0 \qquad \text{(i)}.$$

The $3n$ variations δx_ν are therefore associated with the i equations which result from these after variation, viz.,

$$\sum_{1}^{3n}{}_\nu x_{\iota\nu} d\delta x_\nu + \sum_{1}^{3n}{}_\mu \sum_{1}^{3n}{}_\nu \frac{\partial x_{\iota\nu}}{\partial x_\mu} \delta x_\mu dx_\nu = 0 \qquad \text{(ii)}.$$

As the length ds of an element of the path does not depend on x_ν, but only on dx_ν, then its variation is

$$\delta ds = \sum_{1}^{3n}{}_\nu \frac{\partial ds}{\partial dx_\nu} \delta dx_\nu = \sum_{1}^{3n}{}_\nu \frac{\partial ds}{\partial dx_\nu} d\delta x_\nu \qquad \text{(iii)}.$$

This being understood,

$$\delta \int ds = \int \delta ds$$

must be made zero. According to the rules of the Calculus of Variations, we multiply each of the equations (ii) by a function of x_ν to be determined later, which for the ιth equation will be denoted by ξ_ι, and add the sum of the left-hand sides of the resulting equations, which sum is equal to zero, to the varied element of the integral. By partial integration we get rid of the differentials of the variations; finally we put the coefficients of each one of the arbitrary functions δx_ν equal to zero. We thus obtain $3n$ differential equations of the form

$$d\left(\frac{\partial ds}{\partial dx_\nu}\right) + \sum_{1}^{i}{}_\iota x_{\iota\nu} d\xi_\iota - \sum_{1}^{i}{}_\iota \sum_{1}^{3n}{}_\mu \left(\frac{\partial x_{\iota\mu}}{\partial x_\nu} - \frac{\partial x_{\iota\nu}}{\partial x_\mu}\right) \xi_\iota dx_\mu = 0 \qquad \text{(iv)},$$

which, together with the i equations (i), give $(3n+i)$ equations for the $(3n+i)$ functions x_ν and ξ_ι. These differential equations are necessary conditions for the vanishing of the variation of the integral; every geodesic path thus satisfies them, and consequently they represent the required solution.

180. **Observation 1.** The differential equations 179 (iv) are moreover the sufficient conditions that the path which satisfies them should be a geodesic path. For if these equations are satisfied, then the variation of the integral $\int ds$ becomes

equal to the series which results from partial integration under the integral sign; it thus becomes with the usual notation, the upper limit being denoted by 1 and the lower by 0,

$$\delta \int ds = \sum_{1}^{3n}{}_{\nu}\left[\left(\frac{\partial ds}{\partial dx_{\nu}} + \sum_{1}^{i}{}_{\iota} x_{1\nu}\xi_{\iota}\right)\delta x_{\nu}\right]_{0}^{1}.$$

If we make the variations δx_{ν} for any two positions of the path vanish, then the variation of the integral between these positions as limiting positions vanishes, and therefore the required sufficient analytical condition for a geodesic path is by § 177 satisfied.

181. Observation 2. Let us take the current length of the path as independent variable, then by use of §§ 55, 100, the equations 179 (iv), after division by ds, take the form

$$\frac{m_{\nu}}{m}x''_{\nu} + \sum_{1}^{i}{}_{\iota} x_{\iota\nu}\xi'_{\iota} - \sum_{1}^{i}{}_{\iota}\sum_{1}^{3n}{}_{\mu}\left(\frac{\partial x_{\iota\mu}}{\partial x_{\nu}} - \frac{\partial x_{\iota\nu}}{\partial x_{\mu}}\right)\xi_{\iota}x'_{\mu} = 0 \quad \text{(i)};$$

which, together with the i equations resulting from differentiating 179 (i), viz.,

$$\sum_{1}^{3n}{}_{\nu} x_{\iota\nu}x''_{\nu} + \sum_{1}^{3n}{}_{\nu}\sum_{1}^{3n}{}_{\mu}\frac{\partial x_{\iota\nu}}{\partial x_{\mu}}x'_{\nu}x'_{\mu} = 0 \quad \text{(ii)},$$

furnish $(3n + i)$ unhomogeneous, linear equations for the $(3n + i)$ quantities x''_{ν} and ξ'_{ι}, and thus permit these quantities to be expressed as single-valued functions of the quantities x_{ν}, x'_{ν}, ξ_{ι}.

182. Observation 3. By use of § 72 the equations 181 (i) can be put in the form

$$\sqrt{\frac{m_{\nu}}{m}}\frac{d}{ds}(\cos \widehat{sx_{\nu}}) = - \sum_{1}^{i}{}_{\iota} x_{\iota\nu}\xi'_{\iota} + \sum_{1}^{i}{}_{\iota}\sum_{1}^{3n}{}_{\mu}\left(\frac{\partial x_{\iota\mu}}{\partial x_{\nu}} - \frac{\partial x_{\iota\nu}}{\partial x_{\iota\mu}}\right)\xi_{\iota}x'_{\mu}.$$

The equations 181 (i) thus express how the direction of the path must continually change from a given initial value in order that it may remain a geodesic path; and moreover every single equation expresses how the inclination to a given rectangular coordinate changes.

183. Problem 2. To express the differential equations of the geodesic paths of a material system in terms of the general coordinates p_ρ.

The r coordinates p_ρ of the system are connected by the k equations

$$\sum_{1|}^{r} {}_\rho p_{\chi\rho} dp_\rho = 0 \qquad (i),$$

and thus the r variations by the equations

$$\sum_{1}^{r} {}_\rho p_{\chi\rho} d\delta p_\rho + \sum_{1}^{r} {}_\rho \sum_{1}^{r} {}_\sigma \frac{\partial p_{\chi\rho}}{\partial p_\sigma} \delta p_\sigma dp_\rho = 0 \qquad (ii).$$

Now the length ds of an infinitely small displacement depends not only on the differentials dp_ρ, but also on the values of p_ρ themselves, and thus

$$\delta ds = \sum_{1}^{r} {}_\rho \frac{\partial ds}{\partial dp_\rho} d\delta p_\rho + \sum_{1}^{r} {}_\rho \frac{\partial ds}{\partial p_\rho} \delta p_\rho.$$

This understood,

$$\delta \!\int\! ds = \int \delta ds \text{ must be made zero} \qquad (iii).$$

Then we proceed according to the rules of the Calculus of Variations as in § 179, and denoting the factor of the χth equation by π_χ we obtain the r differential equations

$$d\!\left(\frac{\partial ds}{\partial p_\rho}\right) - \frac{\partial ds}{\partial p_\rho} + \sum_{1}^{k} {}_\chi p_{\chi\rho} d\pi_\chi - \sum_{1}^{k} {}_\chi \sum_{1}^{r} {}_\sigma \!\left(\frac{\partial p_{\chi\sigma}}{\partial p_\rho} - \frac{\partial p_{\chi\rho}}{\partial p_\sigma}\right)\! \pi_\chi dp_\sigma = 0 \text{ (iv)},$$

which, together with the equations (i), give $(r+k)$ differential equations for the $(r+k)$ quantities p_ρ and π_χ as functions of the independent variables. These equations are the necessary conditions for the vanishing of the variation, and thus are satisfied in all positions of a geodesic path; they accordingly contain the solution of the problem.

184. Observation 1. The differential equations 183 (iv) are moreover the sufficient conditions that the path which satisfies them should be a geodesic path. For if these equations are satisfied, then the variation of the length of the path becomes (*cf.* § 180)

$$\delta\!\int\! ds = \sum_{1}^{r} {}_\rho \!\left[\left(\frac{\partial ds}{\partial dp_\rho} + \sum_{1}^{k} {}_\chi p_{\chi\rho}\pi_\chi\right)\! \delta p_\rho\right]_{0}^{1}.$$

If we make the variations δp_ρ of any two positions of the path vanish, then the variation of the integral between these positions as limits also vanishes, and therefore the required analytical condition for a geodesic path is satisfied (§ 177).

185. Observation 2. If we choose the length of the path as independent variable and divide the equations 183 (iv) by ds, and for ds substitute its value given by § 57 (iv) in terms of p_ρ and dp_ρ, we obtain the equations of the geodesic paths in the form of the r equations

$$\sum_1^r {}_\sigma a_{\rho\sigma} p_\sigma'' + \sum_1^r {}_\sigma \sum_1^r {}_\tau \left(\frac{\partial a_{\rho\sigma}}{\partial p_\tau} - \tfrac{1}{2}\frac{\partial a_{\sigma\tau}}{\partial p_\rho}\right) p_\sigma' p_\tau' + \sum_1^k {}_\chi p_{\chi\rho}\pi_\chi'$$
$$- \sum_1^k {}_\chi \sum_1^r {}_\sigma \left(\frac{\partial p_{\chi\sigma}}{\partial p_\rho} - \frac{\partial p_{\chi\rho}}{\partial p_\sigma}\right)\pi_\chi p_\sigma' = 0 \quad \text{(i)};$$

which, together with the k equations obtained from § 183 (i),

$$\sum_1^r {}_\rho p_{\rho\chi} p_\rho'' + \sum_1^r {}_\rho \sum_1^r {}_\sigma \frac{\partial p_{\chi\rho}}{\partial p_\sigma} p_\rho' p_\sigma' = 0 \quad \text{(ii)},$$

give $(r+k)$ unhomogeneous, linear equations for the $(r+k)$ quantities p_ρ'' and π_χ', and enable us to express these quantities as single-valued functions of p_ρ, p_ρ', and π_χ.

186. Observation 3. When by use of the length of the path as independent variable we consider the equation § 92, we obtain the equations 185 (i) in the form

$$\frac{d}{ds}\left(\sqrt{a_{\rho\rho}} \cos \widehat{sp_\rho}\right) = \tfrac{1}{2}\sum_1^r {}_\sigma \sum_1^r {}_\tau \frac{\partial a_{\sigma\tau}}{\partial p_\rho} p_\sigma' p_\tau' - \sum_1^k {}_\chi p_{\chi\rho}\pi_\chi'$$
$$+ \sum_1^r {}_\chi \sum_1^r {}_\sigma \left(\frac{\partial p_{\chi\sigma}}{\partial p_\rho} - \frac{\partial p_{\chi\rho}}{\partial p_\sigma}\right)\pi_\chi p_\sigma'.$$

Thus these equations again express how the direction of the path must change in order that the path may constantly remain geodesic; and moreover every single equation expresses how the inclination to a chosen coordinate p_ρ changes.

187. Note 1. A geodesic path is not completely known if we know the length and direction of one of its elements, but from a given position in a given direction there is in general an infinite series of geodesic paths possible.

When the quantities p_ρ, p_ρ' and the k quantities π_χ are given us for one position of the path, then they are (§ 185) also singly determined for the next element, and the continuation of the path is only possible in a single given manner. The knowledge of the direction of the path at that given position, however, only furnishes us with the quantities p_ρ and p_ρ', and this is not sufficient for the determination of the path, but admits, when particular conditions do not prevent, an infinity of the kth order of geodesic paths.

188. **Note 2.** When the differential equations of the system permit of no integral, consequently in the general case, $2r - k$ of the $2r$ quantities p_ρ and p_ρ' which determine a position and the direction at it, can be arbitrarily chosen, viz., the r quantities p_ρ and $r - k$ of the quantities p_ρ'. These $2r - k$ arbitrary values, together with the k arbitrary values of π_χ in that position, may be regarded as the $2r$ arbitrary constants which, together with the differential equations § 185 (i), determine a geodesic path, and must therefore exist in the integrals of these equations, for by § 173 it must be possible to connect every possible position of the system with every other by means of a geodesic path. For if the differential equations of the system furnish no finite relation between p_ρ, then every conceivable value-system of these quantities is a possible value-system; an arbitrary initial and final position are thus determined by means of these $2r$ arbitrary values of the coordinates.

189. **Note 3.** For every integral, which the differential equations of the material system admit, the number of the constants which determine uniquely a geodesic path diminishes by two.

For if from the equations of condition of the system l finite equations between p_ρ can be derived, then only $r - l$ of the r coordinates p_ρ can be arbitrarily chosen, and consequently of the $2r$ quantities p_ρ and p_ρ' which determine a position and a direction at it only $2r - l - k$. Further in this case the differential equations by multiplication by proper factors and by addition can be brought into such a form that l of them immediately give integrable equations, viz., those equations which are got by differentiation of the l finite relations. In each of these equations, one of which we may typify by the index λ, we get

$$\frac{\partial p_{\lambda\sigma}}{\partial p_\rho} - \frac{\partial p_{\lambda\rho}}{\partial p_\sigma} = 0.$$

Thus the corresponding quantities π_λ vanish from the equations 185 (i), and all the quantities p_ρ'' and π_χ' are singly determined in terms of the $k-l$ values of the remaining π_χ. On the whole, therefore, we have still $2r-2l$ arbitrary quantities; two have disappeared for every finite equation.

Finally, these $2r-2l$ arbitrary constants are always sufficient to connect every possible position of the system with every other by means of a geodesic path. If then l finite equations exist between p_ρ, it is sufficient to traverse the path in such a manner that two of its positions should each have $r-l$ coordinates common with the given positions; the coincidence of the remaining will then ensue of itself.

3. Relations between Straightest and Geodesic Paths

190. **Proposition.** In a holonomous system every geodesic path is a straightest path, and conversely.

To prove this let us use rectangular coordinates. Then if the system is holonomous, such a form may be given to the i equations of condition by multiplication by proper factors and addition in a proper order as to make every one of them directly integrable, namely, that form in which the left-hand side of each of them coincides with the exact differential of one of the i integrals of the equations. For every value-system of ι, μ, ν, then,

$$\frac{\partial x_{\iota\mu}}{\partial x_\nu} - \frac{\partial x_{\iota\nu}}{\partial x_\mu} = 0 \qquad (i),$$

and the differential equations of the geodesic paths by 181 (i) now become

$$\frac{m_\nu}{m} x_\nu'' + \sum_1^i {}_\iota x_{\iota\nu} \xi_\iota' = 0 \qquad (ii).$$

These equations differ only in notation from the equations of the straightest paths (§ 155 (iv)), viz.,

$$\frac{m_\nu}{m} x_\nu'' + \sum_1^i {}_\iota x_{1\nu} \Xi_\iota = 0 \qquad (iii),$$

as neither ξ_ι nor Ξ_ι appear in the remaining equations to be satisfied. Every possible path, which after a proper determination of ξ_ι satisfies the first of these equations, also satisfies the second when Ξ_ι is made equal to ξ_ι', and every solution of the second is also a solution of the first. The satisfying of the equations (ii) and (iii) is moreover a sufficient condition that the path should be a geodesic one or a straightest one.

191. Corollary 1. In a holonomous system only one geodesic path is possible from a possible position in a possible direction (§ 161).

192. Corollary 2. In a holonomous system there is always at the least one straightest path between any two possible positions (§ 173).

193. Proposition. If in a material system every geodesic path is also a straightest path, then the system is holonomous.

For from every possible position there is only one straightest path in a given direction by § 161, and consequently by hypothesis only one geodesic path. Moreover, it is possible by § 173 to reach every possible position by one of these paths. Thus the number of degrees of freedom of the system is equal to the number of its independent coordinates, and consequently by § 146 the system is holonomous.

194. Corollary. In a system which is not holonomous a geodesic path is not in general a straightest path.

This follows from the fact that in any direction there is only one straightest path, whereas many geodesic paths are possible (§ 161, 187).

195. Note. In a system which is not holonomous a straightest path is not in general a geodesic path.

The assertion is proved if examples of systems are given in which the straightest paths are not amongst the geodesic ones. Let us choose for simplicity a system in which there exists only a single unintegrable equation of condition between the r coordinates p_ρ of the system, and let this be

$$\sum_{1}^{r}{}_\rho p_{1\rho} p_\rho' = 0 \qquad \text{(i)}.$$

Let us now assume that every straightest path is also geodesic. Then for all possible systems of values of p_ρ and p_ρ' at least one system of values of p_ρ'' can be obtained so as to satisfy simultaneously the equations 158 (iv) and 185 (i). Then the equations obtained by subtraction of these equations in pairs, viz.,

$$p_{1\rho}\left(\Pi_1 - \pi_1'\right) + \pi_1 \sum_1^r {}_\sigma\left(\frac{\partial p_{1\sigma}}{\partial p_\rho} - \frac{\partial p_{1\rho}}{\partial p_\sigma}\right)p_\sigma' = 0,$$

are to be satisfied for all possible values of p_ρ and p_ρ'. But these are r equations for the single quantity $(\Pi_1 - \pi_1')/\pi_1$, and they are only consistent with one another when for all pairs of values of ρ and τ

$$\frac{1}{p_{1\rho}}\sum_1^r {}_\sigma\left(\frac{\partial p_{1\sigma}}{\partial p_\rho} - \frac{\partial p_{1\rho}}{\partial p_\sigma}\right)p_\sigma' = \frac{1}{p_{1\tau}}\sum_1^r {}_\sigma\left(\frac{\partial p_{1\sigma}}{\partial p_\tau} - \frac{\partial p_{1\tau}}{\partial p_\sigma}\right)p_\sigma'.$$

Let us now substitute in $(r - 1)$ of these equations independent of one another, by aid of equation (i), one of the quantities p_ρ' in terms of the remaining, then the ratios between the last are now entirely arbitrary quantities. The coefficient of each of these quantities must consequently vanish. We thus obtain as a necessary consequence of our assumption $(r - 1)^2$ equations between the r functions $p_{1\rho}$ and their r^2 first partial differential coefficients. In particular cases these equations can be satisfied, for they are satisfied when the equation (i) is integrable. But in general we have no right to make the functions $p_{1\rho}$ subject to even a single condition, and thus in general our assumption is unwarranted. Hence the statement is proved.

196. **Summary (190–195).** In holonomous systems the ideas of straightest and geodesic paths are completely identical as regards their content: in systems which are not holonomous neither of these ideas includes the other, but both have in general a completely different content.

CHAPTER VI

ON THE STRAIGHTEST DISTANCE IN HOLONOMOUS SYSTEMS

Prefatory Notes

197. This chapter is confined to holonomous systems alone, and by a system simply, is meant a holonomous one. It will therefore be assumed that the coordinates p_ρ of the system are all free coordinates. The number of these coordinates is equal to the number of degrees of freedom of the system, and is thus quite unarbitrary; we shall always denote them by r.

198. Straightest and geodesic paths in this chapter are the same (§ 196), and the common differential equations of these paths can be written in the form of the r equations

$$d\left(\sqrt{a_{\rho\rho}} \cos \widehat{sp_\rho}\right) = \frac{\partial ds}{\partial p_\rho},$$

which are obtained from § 186 or § 160, when we remember that for the chosen coordinates all the quantities $p_{\chi\rho}$ are zero.

199. As a consequence of this, we obtain from § 184 for the variation of the length of a path which satisfies the foregoing differential equations, that is for the length of a geodesic path,

$$\delta \!\int\! ds = \sum_{1}^{r}{}_\rho \left[\frac{\partial ds}{\partial dp_\rho} \delta p_\rho\right]_0^1,$$

or using § 92,

$$\delta \!\int\! ds = \sum_{1}^{r}{}_\rho \left[\sqrt{a_{\rho\rho}} \cos \widehat{sp_\rho} \,\delta p_\rho\right]_0^1,$$

where the quantities δp_ρ denote the variations of the coordinates of the final position, and $\cos \widehat{sp}_\rho$ the direction cosines of the final elements of the geodesic path under consideration.

1. Surfaces of Positions

200. **Definition.** By a surface of positions is meant, in general, a continuously connected aggregate of positions. In particular, however, here by surface will be understood an aggregate of possible positions of a holonomous system which is characterised by the fact that the coordinates of the positions which belong to it satisfy a single finite equation between them.

The aggregate of the positions which simultaneously belong to two or more surfaces we define as the intersection of these surfaces.

201. **Observation 1.** Through every position of a surface an infinite manifold of paths can be drawn, all of whose positions belong to the surface. We say of these paths that they belong to or lie on the surface; we employ the same expressions for the elements of the paths and for infinitely small displacements.

202. **Observation 2.** A path which does not lie on a surface has in general a finite number of positions common with it.

For the path is analytically expressed by means of $(r-1)$ equations between the coordinates of its positions, the surface by means of a single equation. By supposition the former equations are independent of the latter. Therefore in all they give r equations for the r coordinates of the common positions, which equations in general permit of none or a finite number of real solutions.

203. **Observation 3.** From any position of a surface a manifold of the $(r-1)$th order of infinitely small displacements is possible on the surface.

For of the r independent changes of the coordinates which characterise the displacement, $(r-1)$ can be arbitrarily chosen; the rth is then determined from the fact that the displacement lies along the given surface.

108   FIRST BOOK   CHAP.

204. **Proposition 1.** It is always possible to determine one, and in general only one, direction which is perpendicular to the $(r-1)$ different infinitely small displacements of a system from the same position (§ 197).

Let $d_\tau p_\rho$ be the change of the coordinate p_ρ for the τth of the $(r-1)$ displacements; let δp_ρ be the change of the coordinate p_ρ for a second displacement. The necessary and sufficient condition that the latter should be perpendicular to the former is that $(r-1)$ equations of the form (§ 58)

$$\sum_1^r{}_\rho \sum_1^r{}_\sigma a_{\rho\sigma} d_\tau p_\rho \delta p_\sigma = 0$$

should be satisfied. These, however, give $(r-1)$ unhomogeneous, linear equations for the $(r-1)$ ratios of δp_ρ to one another; they can thus always be satisfied, and in general only satisfied, by a single value-system of these ratios. In exceptional cases indeterminateness may arise; this may happen, for instance, when any three of the $(r-1)$ displacements are so chosen that every displacement which is perpendicular to two of them is also perpendicular to the third.

205. **Proposition 2.** If a direction is perpendicular to $(r-1)$ different displacements which lie on a surface in a given position, then it is perpendicular to every displacement which lies on the surface in that position.

The displacements, which lie on a surface in a given position, are characterised by the fact that the corresponding dp_ρ's satisfy a single homogeneous, linear relation between them, namely, the equation which is obtained by differentiation of the equation of the surface. If now the $(r-1)$ value-systems of $d_\tau p_\rho$ satisfy that equation, then so do also the quantities given by

$$dp_\rho = \sum_1^{r-1}{}_\tau \lambda_\tau d_\tau p_\rho,$$

where λ_τ denote arbitrary factors. Thus the dp_ρ's belong to any displacement on the surface, and moreover every displacement on the surface can be expressed in this form since it contains an arbitrary manifold of the $(r-1)$th order. By hypothesis now (§ 204)

$$\sum_{1}^{r}{}_{\rho}\sum_{1}^{r}{}_{\sigma} a_{\rho\sigma} d_\tau p_\rho \delta p_\sigma = 0 \;;$$

by multiplying these equations by λ_τ and adding we get

$$\sum_{1}^{r}{}_{\rho}\sum_{1}^{r}{}_{\sigma} a_{\rho\sigma} dp_\rho \delta p_\sigma = 0,$$

which is the required proof (§ 58).

206. **Definition.** A displacement from a position of a surface is said to be perpendicular to the surface when it is perpendicular to every displacement which lies on the surface in the same position.

207. **Corollary 1.** In every position of a surface there is always one, and in general only one, direction which is perpendicular to the surface.

208. **Corollary 2.** In every position of a surface it is always possible to draw one, and in general only one, straightest path perpendicular to the surface.

209. **Definition 1.** By a series of surfaces we mean an aggregate of surfaces whose equations (§ 200) differ y n the value of the contained constant.

210. **Notation.** Every series of surfaces can be analytically expressed by an equation of the form

R = constant,

which is obtained by the solution of the equation of one of the surfaces in terms of the variable constant; and in which the right-hand side denotes the possible values of this constant, whilst the left is a function of the coordinates p_ρ. To every surface of this series there corresponds a definite value of the constant, that is a definite value of the function R. Those surfaces, for which the value of the function R only differs by an infinitely small quantity, are called neighbouring surfaces.

211. **Definition 2.** An orthogonal trajectory of a series of surfaces is a path which cuts the series orthogonally, *i.e.* which is perpendicular to every surface of the series in the common positions (§ 202).

212. **Proposition.** In order that a path may be an orthogonal trajectory of the series

$$R = \text{constant} \qquad (i)$$

it is necessary and sufficient that it should satisfy in each of its positions r equations of the form

$$\sqrt{a_{\rho\rho}} \cos \widehat{sp}_\rho = f \frac{\partial R}{\partial p_\rho} \qquad (ii),$$

where the quantities $\widehat{sp}_\rho$ denote the inclinations of the path to the coordinates p_ρ, and f is a quantity identical for all the r equations, but which changes with a change of p_ρ.

Draw from the position under consideration an infinitely small displacement whose length is $\delta\sigma$, and denote the resulting changes of p_ρ and R by δp_ρ and δR, and let this displacement make an angle $\widehat{s\sigma}$ with the path considered; then multiply the equations (ii) each with the corresponding δp_ρ and add; we thus obtain (§§ 78 (i) and 85)

$$\delta\sigma \cos \widehat{s\sigma} = \sum_{1}^{r} {}_\rho f \frac{\partial R}{\partial p_\rho} \delta p_\rho = f\delta R \qquad (iii).$$

If now the displacement $\delta\sigma$ lies on a surface of the series (i), namely, that surface which has the position under consideration common with the path, then $\delta R = 0$, and thus $\widehat{s\sigma} = 90°$. The direction of the path is therefore perpendicular to the surface which it intersects (§ 206), and the equations (ii) are consequently the sufficient conditions that this should happen at every position. They are, moreover, the necessary conditions, since, apart from exceptional cases, at every position there is only one direction which satisfies the given requirement.

213. The orthogonal distance between two neighbouring surfaces of the series in any position is equal to

$$fdR.$$

For, let the displacement $\delta\sigma$ of the foregoing article coincide in direction and length with the portion of the orthogonal trajectory which lies between the two surfaces; then $\delta\sigma$ coincides with the distance under consideration, and the angle

$\overset{\wedge}{s\sigma}$ is equal to zero, and thus the proof follows from § 122 (iii).

214. The function f which enters into the equations of the orthogonal trajectory is a root of the equation

$$\frac{1}{f^2} = \sum_{1}^{r}{}_{\rho}\sum_{1}^{r}{}_{\sigma} b_{\rho\sigma}\frac{\partial R}{\partial p_\rho}\frac{\partial R}{\partial p_\sigma}.$$

For this equation follows when we substitute the value of the r direction cosines from § 212 (ii) in the equation § 88, which they must satisfy. The root to be chosen depends on whether we consider the direction of the trajectory positive along increasing or decreasing values of R.

2. Straightest Distance

215. **Definition.** By the straightest distance between two positions of a holonomous system is meant the length of one of the straightest paths connecting them.

216. **Observation.** Two positions may have more than one straightest distance. Amongst them are the lengths of the shortest paths between both positions, consequently, too, the length of the absolutely shortest path. When mention is made of the shortest distance between two positions as of a quantity determined without ambiguity, then the last is meant.

217. **Analytical Representation.** The straightest distance between two positions can be expressed as a function of the coordinates of these positions. That position which is regarded as the initial position will be denoted by 0, and its coordinates by $p_{\rho 0}$; whilst that position which is regarded as the final position will be denoted by 1, and its coordinates by $p_{\rho 1}$, so that the direction of the straightest path is positive from 0 to 1. The straightest distance for all value-systems of $p_{\rho 0}$ and $p_{\rho 1}$ is then a definite function of these $2r$ quantities. The analytical expression for the straightest distance, in terms of these variables, will be denoted by S, and for shortness this will be termed the straightest distance of the system.

218. **Observation 1.** The function S is in general a many-valued function of its independent variables. Of the branches of this function one and only one vanishes with the vanishing of the difference between $p_{\rho 0}$ and $p_{\rho 1}$. It is to this branch (§ 216) that we shall refer whenever we say that S is a given single-valued function.

219. **Observation 2.** The function S is symmetrical with regard to $p_{\rho 1}$ and $p_{\rho 0}$ in the sense that it does not change its value when for all values of ρ these quantities are interchanged.

For this interchange only implies an interchange of the final and initial position.

220. **Note.** When the straightest distance of a system is given in terms of any free coordinates, then all the straightest paths of the system are given in terms of these same coordinates, without its being necessary to know in what manner the position of the separate material points of the system depends on these coordinates.

For the straightest distance between any two infinitely near positions of the system is at the same time the length of the infinitely small displacement between them; but if this latter can be expressed in terms of the chosen coordinates, then the statement follows by § 163.

221. **Problem.** To obtain from the straightest distance of a system the expression for the length of its infinitely small displacements.

In S substitute for $p_{\rho 0}$, p_ρ, and for $p_{\rho 1}$, $p_\rho + \delta p_\rho$, and suppose δp_ρ to become very small. We already know (§ 57 (iv)) that the distance between the two positions is expressed as the quadratic root of a homogeneous quadratic function of δp_ρ. S itself cannot thus be expressed in a series of ascending powers of dp_ρ, but S^2 can, and in this expansion the quadratic terms must be the first which do not vanish. If, then, we denote by a bar that in the function under consideration $p_{\rho 0} = p_{\rho 1} = p_\rho$, we obtain for the distance between the two points, and therefore for the magnitude of the displacement, the expression

$$ds^2 = \tfrac{1}{2} \sum_\rho^r \sum_\sigma^r \overline{\left(\frac{\partial^2 S^2}{\partial p_{\rho 1} \partial p_{\sigma 1}}\right)} dp_\rho dp_\sigma,$$

and the function $a_{\rho\sigma}$ becomes
$$a_{\rho\sigma} = \tfrac{1}{2}\left(\overline{\frac{\partial^2 S^2}{\partial p_{\rho 1}\partial p_{\sigma 1}}}\right).$$
We might equally correctly have
$$a_{\rho\sigma} = \tfrac{1}{2}\left(\overline{\frac{\partial^2 S^2}{\partial p_{\rho 0}\partial p_{\sigma 0}}}\right).$$

These values of $a_{\rho\sigma}$ can be employed to obtain indirectly, from the function S, the straightest paths, but the following propositions enable us to determine them in a more direct way.

222. **Proposition.** A surface, all of whose positions have equal straightest distances from a fixed position, is cut orthogonally by all straightest paths through this fixed position.

Let $p_{\rho 0}$ be the coordinates of the fixed position and $p_{\rho 1}$ the coordinates of a position of the surface. Let us pass from the latter to another position of the surface for which $p_{\rho 1}$ has changed by $dp_{\rho 1}$. In this the straightest distance from the fixed position has, by hypothesis, not changed; but by § 199 it has changed by $\sum_{1}^{r}{}_{\rho}\sqrt{a_{\rho\rho 1}}\cos\widehat{sp}_{\rho 1}dp_{\rho 1}$, where $\widehat{sp}_{\rho 1}$ denotes the angle which the straightest path at 1 makes with the direction of p_ρ. Thus then
$$\sum_{1}^{r}{}_{\rho}\sqrt{a_{\rho\rho 1}}\cos\widehat{sp}_{\rho 1}dp_{\rho 1} = 0,$$

and this equation expresses that the shortest path is perpendicular to the displacement of $dp_{\rho 1}$ (§§ 85 and 78 (i)). Since this holds for any displacement which lies on the surface at 1, the proposition follows (§ 206).

223. **Corollary 1.** The straightest paths which pass through a fixed position are the orthogonal trajectories of a series of surfaces which satisfy the condition that all the positions of each one of them have the same distance from this fixed position.

224. **Corollary 2.** All the straightest paths which pass through the fixed position 0 satisfy the r equations
$$\sqrt{a_{\rho\rho 1}}\cos\widehat{sp}_{\rho 1} = \frac{\partial S}{\partial p_{\rho 1}} \qquad (i),$$

I

where $p_{\rho 1}$ are to be considered the coordinates of the variable position of the path, and $\cos \widehat{sp}_{\rho 1}$ the direction cosine of the path in this position.

For the equations (i) are the equations of the orthogonal trajectories of a series of surfaces which are represented by the equation

$$S = \text{constant} \qquad (\text{ii}).$$

For if S were any function of the variable coordinates $p_{\rho 1}$, then by § 212 the equations of the orthogonal trajectories would be

$$\sqrt{a_{\rho\rho 1}} \cos \widehat{sp}_{\rho 1} = f \frac{\partial S}{\partial p_{\rho 1}}, \qquad (\text{iii}),$$

and the perpendicular distance between two neighbouring surfaces would be equal to fdS. On account of the special nature (§§ 217, 222) of our function S, however, this distance is equal to dS itself, and consequently

$$f = 1 \qquad (\text{iv}),$$

and the general equations (iii) take the particular form (i).

225. Observation 1. The equations 224 (i), which are differential equations of the first order, can also be regarded as the equations of straightest paths in a finite form, if we regard $p_{\rho 0}$ as variable and the $2r$ quantities $p_{\rho 1}$ and $\widehat{sp}_{\rho 1}$ as constants.

For let us determine from these equations a series of positions 0 in such a manner that with fixed values of $p_{\rho 1}$, the values of $\widehat{sp}_{\rho 1}$ do not change, then we obtain positions 0 such that the straightest paths drawn from them towards the position 1 have in this position 1 a fixed direction. Since now only one straightest path having this property is possible, all the positions 0 so obtained must be on this one path; their aggregate forms this path and this last is expressed by the equations § 224 (i).

226. Observation 2. In the proof of § 222 we might equally well have made 1 the fixed and 0 the variable position. In place of the equations § 224 (i) we should then have obtained the equations

$$\sqrt{a_{\rho\rho 0}} \cos \widehat{sp}_{\rho 0} = -\frac{\partial S}{\partial p_{\rho 0}} \qquad (i).$$

The difference in the sign of the right-hand side results from the fact that the direction from the fixed position is now negative (§ 217). Like the equations § 224 (i), the equations § 226 (i) also represent straightest paths. They are the differential equations of the first order of all straightest paths which pass through the fixed position $p_{\rho 1}$, and at the same time the finite equations of a definite path which passes through the position $p_{\rho 0}$, and there makes with the coordinates the angles $\widehat{sp}_{\rho 0}$.

227. **Corollary 3.** The straightest distance S of a system satisfies, as a function of $p_{\rho 0}$, the partial differential equation of the first order

$$\sum_{\rho 1}^{r} \sum_{\sigma 1}^{r} b_{\rho\sigma 0} \frac{\partial S}{\partial p_{\rho 0}} \frac{\partial S}{\partial p_{\sigma 0}} = 1 \qquad (i),$$

and as a function of $p_{\rho 1}$ the partial differential equation of the first order

$$\sum_{\rho 1}^{r} \sum_{\sigma 1}^{r} b_{\rho\sigma 1} \frac{\partial S}{\partial p_{\rho 1}} \frac{\partial S}{\partial p_{\sigma 1}} = 1 \qquad (ii).$$

For both equations follow from § 214 and § 224 (iv); they are also immediately found when we substitute in § 88 the direction cosines of a straightest path expressed by means of S from § 224 (i) or 226 (i), which the angles of any inclination to the coordinates satisfy.

228. **Proposition.** If we erect at all positions of any surface straightest paths perpendicular to the surface, and cut off from each equal lengths, then the surface so obtained is cut orthogonally by each of these straightest paths.

Let the positions of the original surface be denoted by 0, and of the new surface by 1. Let $\widehat{sp}_{\rho 0}$ and $\widehat{sp}_{\rho 1}$ denote the angles which a chosen straightest path makes with the coordinates at the first and second surface respectively. If we proceed from this straightest path to any neighbouring one, then the length of the path changes (§ 199) by

$$\sum_{1}^{r}{}_\rho \sqrt{a_{\rho\rho 1}} \cos \widehat{sp}_{\rho 1} dp_{\rho 1} - \sum_{1}^{r}{}_\rho \sqrt{a_{\rho\rho 0}} \cos \widehat{sp}_{\rho 0} dp_{\rho 0},$$

where $dp_{\rho 1}$ and $dp_{\rho 0}$ denote the changes of p_ρ in the positions 1 and 0. But by construction this change is zero, and also by construction

$$\sum_{1}^{r}{}_\rho \sqrt{a_{\rho\rho 0}} \cos \widehat{sp}_{\rho 0} dp_\rho = 0,$$

for every path is perpendicular to the original surface.

Thus then also

$$\sum_{1}^{r}{}_\rho \sqrt{a_{\rho\rho 1}} \cos \widehat{sp}_{\rho 1} dp_{\rho 1} = 0\ ;$$

and since $dp_{\rho 1}$ denotes any displacement on the surface in the position 1, the conclusion follows.

229. **Corollary 1.** The orthogonal trajectories of any series of surfaces, each of which in all its positions has the same perpendicular straightest distance from its neighbouring ones, are straightest paths.

230. **Corollary 2.** If R is a function of the r coordinates p_ρ of such a nature that the equation

$$R = \text{constant} \qquad (i)$$

represents a series of surfaces each of which has in all its positions the same perpendicular straightest distance $d\text{R}$ from its neighbours, then the equations

$$\sqrt{a_{\rho\rho}} \cos \widehat{sp}_\rho = \frac{\partial \text{R}}{\partial p_\rho} \qquad (ii)$$

are the equations of the orthogonal trajectories, and consequently the equations of the straightest paths. And, moreover, these equations are differential equations of the first order for these paths.

For if R were any function whatever of p_ρ, then the equations 212 (ii) would represent the orthogonal trajectories of the series (i), and the perpendicular distance between two neighbouring surfaces would, by § 213, be equal to $fd\text{R}$. According to our particular hypothesis, however, this distance is constant and equal to $d\mathrm{R}$, consequently $f=1$, and thus the equations 212 (ii) reduce to the above-mentioned ones.

231. Corollary 3. If the equation
$$\mathrm{R} = \text{constant}$$
represents a series of surfaces of such a nature that each of them in all its positions has the same straightest orthogonal distance $d\mathrm{R}$ from its neighbours, then the function R satisfies the partial differential equation

$$\sum_{1}^{r}{}_{\rho}\sum_{1}^{r}{}_{\sigma} b_{\sigma\rho}\frac{\partial \mathrm{R}}{\partial p_\rho}\frac{\partial \mathrm{R}}{\partial p_\sigma'} = 1 \ ;$$

for this equation follows from § 214 and § 230. It is also immediately found when we substitute the direction cosines of a straightest path, given by § 230 (ii), in the equation § 88, which the angles of every inclination to the coordinates satisfy.

232. Proposition 1. (**Converse of § 231.**) If the function R satisfies the partial differential equation

$$\sum_{1}^{r}{}_{\rho}\sum_{1}^{r}{}_{\sigma} b_{\rho\sigma}\frac{\partial \mathrm{R}}{\partial p_\rho}\frac{\partial \mathrm{R}}{\partial p_\sigma} = 1,$$

then the equation
$$\mathrm{R} = \text{constant}$$
represents a series of surfaces of such a nature that each of them in all its positions has the same orthogonal straightest distance from its neighbours, and, moreover, this distance is measured by the change of R.

For if R were any function, then the orthogonal trajectories of the series would be given by equations of the form § 212 (ii), and the orthogonal distance between two neighbouring surfaces would in every position be $fd\mathrm{R}$. But by our special hypothesis as to the nature of R, $f=1$ (§ 214), and thus the proposition is true.

233. Proposition 2. If the function R of p_ρ is any solution of the partial differential equation

$$\sum_{1}^{r}{}_{\rho}\sum_{1}^{r}{}_{\sigma} b_{\rho\sigma}\frac{\partial \mathrm{R}}{\partial p_\rho}\frac{\partial \mathrm{R}}{\partial p_\sigma} = 1 \qquad\qquad \text{(i)},$$

then the equations

$$\sqrt{a_{\rho\rho}} \cos \widehat{sp_\rho} = \frac{\partial R}{\partial p_\rho} \qquad (ii)$$

are the equations of straightest paths. And, moreover, they are differential equations of the first order of the straightest paths represented by them.

This follows immediately from § 230 and § 232.

234. Observation. Although every path which is represented by the equations 233 (ii) is a straightest path, yet in general every straightest path cannot conversely be represented in this form. The manifold of straightest paths, which are contained in the given form, depends rather on the manifold which the function R as a solution of the differential equation possesses, that is on the number of its arbitrary constants.

In particular, however, if R is a complete solution, *i.e.* if R contains r arbitrary constants $a_0, a_1 \ldots a_{r-1}$, the first of which is the additive constant necessarily present, then all straightest paths of the system may be expressed in the form § 233 (ii). For the right-hand sides of these r equations (of which only $r-1$ are independent of one another) contain then $(r-1)$ constants which are sufficient to furnish an arbitrarily chosen direction of the path represented at an arbitrary position in terms of $(r-1)$ independent direction cosines. But if we can arbitrarily choose one position of the path represented, and its direction at this position, then we can represent all straightest paths.

235. Proposition 3. (Jacobi's Proposition.) Let R denote a complete solution of the differential equation

$$\sum_1^r {}_\rho \sum_1^{r_i} {}_\sigma b_{\rho\sigma} \frac{\partial R}{\partial p_\rho} \frac{\partial R}{\partial p_\sigma} = 1 \qquad (i),$$

and let its arbitrary constants, with the exception of the additive one, be $a_1, a_2 \ldots a_{r-1}$. Then the $(r-1)$ equations

$$\frac{\partial R}{\partial a_r} = \beta_r \qquad (ii),$$

where the β_r's are $(r-1)$ new arbitrary constants, give the equations of the straightest paths of the system in a finite form.

As proof we show that the paths which are represented by the equations (ii) are orthogonal trajectories of the series

$$R = \text{constant} \qquad (iii);$$

whence the proof follows by §§ 232 and 229.

In order now firstly to find the direction of the path represented, we differentiate the equations (ii) each in its own direction, *i.e.* we form these equations for two positions of the path at distance ds, in which p_ρ differs from its next value by dp_ρ, then we subtract and divide by ds. We thus obtain $(r-1)$ equations of the form

$$\sum_1^r {}_\sigma \frac{\partial^2 R}{\partial p_\sigma \partial a_\tau} \frac{\partial p_\sigma}{\partial s} = 0;$$

or, when we substitute in these by §§ 79 and 78 the direction cosines of the element of the path under consideration,

$$\sum_\rho^r \sqrt{a_{\rho\rho}} \cos \widehat{sp}_\rho \sum_1^r {}_\sigma b_{\rho\sigma} \frac{\partial^2 R}{\partial p_\sigma \partial a_\tau} = 0 \qquad (iv);$$

which equations give $(r-1)$ unhomogeneous, linear equations for the $(r-1)$ ratios of the direction cosines to one another.

Secondly, we notice that the equation (i) holds for all values of the constants a_τ; we can thus differentiate them with regard to these quantities, and we then obtain $(r-1)$ equations, which may be written in the form

$$\sum_1^r {}_\rho \frac{\partial R}{\partial p_\rho} \sum_1^r {}_\sigma b_{\rho\sigma} \frac{\partial^2 R}{\partial p_\sigma \partial a_\tau} = 0 \qquad (v),$$

and which express relations which the partial differential coefficients of R must satisfy as a consequence of our particular hypotheses with regard to this function.

If now the equations (ii) represent a definite path for the values of a_τ and β_τ under consideration, then from the equations (iv) must be obtained singly-determined values for the ratios of the direction cosines to one of them. But these same single values for the ratios of the quantities $\dfrac{\partial R}{\partial p_\rho}$ to one of them must be given by the equations (v). Thus if f is a factor which still remains to be determined, then

$$\sqrt{a_{\rho\rho}} \cos \overset{\wedge}{sp_\rho} = f\frac{\partial R}{\partial p_\rho}.$$

Thus by § 212 the path under consideration is the orthogonal trajectory of the series (iii), as was to be proved. The factor f is found equal to unity.

The hypothesis that the $(r-1)$ equations (ii) represent, for definite values of a_r and β_r, a definite path, would not be correct if these equations were not independent of one another. In that case the arbitrary constants would not be independent of one another, and the solution would not be, as was supposed, a complete one.

236. **Problem.** From any complete solution R of the differential equations 235 (i) to obtain the straightest distance S of the system.

By S is again to be understood the straightest distance between two positions 0 and 1 with the coordinates $p_{\rho 0}$ and $p_{\rho 1}$. In the $(r-1)$ equations, § 235 (ii), we substitute for p_ρ in the first place $p_{\rho 0}$, and in the second $p_{\rho 1}$. From the resulting $(2r-2)$ equations we eliminate β_r and express a_r as functions of $p_{\rho 0}$ and $p_{\rho 1}$. These functions are symmetrical with regard to $p_{\rho 0}$ and $p_{\rho 1}$, and give those values which a_r must have in order that the paths defined by them may pass through the definite positions 0 and 1.

We have then, in the first place, for any position 1, by §§ 224 (i) and 233 (ii),

$$\frac{\partial S}{\partial p_{\rho 1}} = \left(\frac{\partial R}{\partial p_\rho}\right)_1;$$

and secondly, for any position 0, by §§ 226 (i) and 233 (i),

$$\frac{\partial S}{\partial p_{\rho 0}} = -\left(\frac{\partial R}{\partial p_\rho}\right)_0.$$

We substitute in the right-hand side of these equations the values of a_r in terms of $p_{\rho 0}$ and $p_{\rho 1}$, and put p_ρ in the first equal to $p_{\rho 1}$, and in the second equal to $p_{\rho 0}$; we then obtain the first differential coefficients of S with regard to all the independent variables expressed as functions of these variables. S can then be found by a single integration.

CHAPTER VII

KINEMATICS

1. Vector Quantities with regard to a System

237. **Definition.** A vector quantity with regard to a system is any quantity which bears a relation to the system, and which has the same kind of mathematical manifold as a conceivable displacement of the system.

238. **Note 1.** A displacement of a system is itself a vector quantity with regard to the system. Every product of a displacement of the system with any scalar quantity whatever is a vector quantity with regard to the system.

239. **Note 2.** Every vector quantity with regard to a system can be represented geometrically by a conceivable displacement of the system. The direction of the displacement representing it is called the direction of the vector quantity. The measure of the representation can and will always be so chosen that the displacement representing it is indefinitely small. Every vector with regard to a system which changes with the position of the system can then be represented as an infinitely small displacement of the system from the position to which its instantaneous value belongs.

240. **Note 3.** A vector quantity with regard to a single material point is a vector in the ordinary sense of the word. Every vector with regard to a point can be represented by a geometrical displacement of the point; in particular, by an infinitely small displacement from its actual position.

241. **Note 4.** By components and reduced components

of a vector are meant those vectors of the same kind which are represented by the components and reduced components of that infinitely small displacement which represents the original vector (§§ 48, 71).

The reduced component of a definite vector in the direction of a coordinate p_ρ is called for short the component of the vector along p_ρ, or the vector along the coordinate p_ρ.

When no misunderstanding can arise, the magnitude of such a component is simply called a component or reduced component.

242. **Problem 1a.** To deduce the components k_ρ of a vector along the general coordinates p_ρ from the components h_ν along the $3n$ rectangular coordinates.

Let $d\bar{x}_\nu$ be the components along x_ν of that displacement which represents the vector quantity, and let $d\bar{p}_\rho$ be the components of the same displacement along p_ρ, then $d\bar{p}_\rho$ is given in terms of $d\bar{x}_\nu$ in § 80. But k_ρ and h_ν are respectively proportional to $d\bar{p}_\rho$ and $d\bar{x}_\rho$; consequently

$$k_\rho = \sum_{1}^{3n} {}_\nu a_{\nu\rho} h_\nu = \sum_{1}^{3n} {}_\nu \frac{\partial x_\nu}{\partial p_\rho} h_\nu.$$

243. **Problem 1b.** To deduce the components h_ν of a vector along rectangular coordinates, from the components k_ρ of the vector along p_ρ.

The equations § 242 give only r equations for the $3n$ quantities h_ν, from which the latter consequently cannot be found. In fact the problem is in general indeterminate. For all conceivable positions and displacements of a system cannot be expressed in terms of p_ρ but only a part of them, amongst which are the possible displacements.

The proposition can thus only be solved in the case when the given vector is parallel to a displacement which can be expressed in terms of p_ρ and its changes. In this case, by § 81,

$$h_\nu = \sum_{1}^{r} {}_\rho \beta_{\nu\rho} k_\rho.$$

244. **Problem 2a.** To determine the magnitude h of a vector, from its components h_ν along rectangular coordinates.

Using § 83 we obtain

$$h^2 = \sum_{1}^{3n} \nu \frac{m}{m_\nu} h_\nu^2.$$

245. Problem 2b. To determine the magnitude k of a vector in terms of its components k_ρ along the general co-ordinates p_ρ.

The problem is again, as in § 243, in general indeterminate.

A solution is only possible when the vector in question is parallel to a displacement which can be represented in terms of p_ρ, and then, by § 82,

$$k^2 = \sum_{1}^{r} \rho \sum_{1}^{r} \sigma\, b_{\rho\sigma} k_\rho k_\sigma.$$

246. Problem 3a. To find the components of a vector in the direction of any displacement ds from its components h_ν along x_ν.

If ds' denote the length and $\overline{dx_\nu}'$ the reduced components of the displacement by which we represent the vector, then the component of this displacement in the direction of ds is, by §§ 48 and 84,

$$ds' \cos \widehat{ss}' = \frac{1}{ds} \sum_{1}^{3n} \nu\, dx_\nu \overline{dx_\nu}'.$$

If we multiply this equation by the ratio of the magnitude of the vector to the length of the displacement by which it is represented, we obtain on the left-hand side the required component and on the right-hand side h_ν instead of $\overline{dx_\nu}'$; we thus get as a solution of the problem the required quantity equal to

$$\sum_{1}^{3n} \nu\, h_\nu \frac{dx_\nu}{ds},$$

or, by § 72, equal to

$$\sum_{1}^{3n} \nu \sqrt{\frac{m}{m_\nu}}\, h_\nu \cos \widehat{sx_\nu}.$$

247. Problem 3b. To find the components of a vector in the direction of any displacement ds, expressed in terms of p_ρ, from the components k_ρ along p_ρ.

If we employ the same method as in the previous problem we obtain by §§ 48 and 85 the required quantity equal to

$$\sum_{1}^{r}{}_\rho k_\rho \frac{dp_\rho}{ds},$$

or, by §§ 78 and 89, equal to

$$\sum_{1}^{r}{}_\rho \sum_{1}^{r}{}_\sigma b_{\rho\sigma} k_\rho \sqrt{a_{\sigma\sigma}} \cos \overset{\wedge}{sp_\sigma}.$$

248. Observation. Thus although in general all components of a vector are not determined by means of the quantities k_ρ, yet the components of the vector are determined by means of these quantities in all such directions as can be expressed in terms of p_ρ, and consequently in every possible direction.

249. Proposition 1. In order that the vector, whose components along p_ρ are the quantities k_ρ, may be perpendicular to a displacement for which p_ρ suffer the changes dp_ρ, it is necessary and sufficient that the equation

$$\sum_{1}^{r}{}_\rho k_\rho dp_\rho = 0$$

should be satisfied.

This follows from § 85 when we consider k_ρ proportional to $\overline{dp_\rho}'$.

250. Proposition 2. In order that the vector, whose components along p_ρ are k_ρ, should be perpendicular to every possible displacement of the system, it is necessary and sufficient that the r quantities k_ρ can be expressed in the form

$$k_\rho = \sum_{1}^{k}{}_\chi p_{\chi\rho} \cdot \gamma_\chi,$$

where $p_{\chi\rho}$ occur in the equations of condition of the system (§ 130) and γ_χ are quantities to be determined as we please.

This follows from §§ 148 and 150 when we consider k_ρ expressed by means of $\overline{dp_\rho}$.

251. Note 1. Vectors with regard to one and the same

system can be compounded and resolved like the conceivable displacements of the system.

Consequently, the compounding of the vectors of the same system follows the rules of algebraic addition.

252. **Note 2.** Vectors with regard to different systems are to be considered quantities of a different nature; they can neither be compounded nor added.

253. **Note 3.** A vector quantity with regard to a given system may be considered as a vector quantity of any more extended system of which the original forms a part.

254. **Problem 1.** The same vector quantities may, at one time, be considered as vector quantities with regard to a partial system, and, at another time, as vector quantities with regard to the complete system. From the components h_ν along the rectangular coordinates x_ν in the first case, the components h_ν' along the corresponding coordinates x_ν' in the second can be determined.

Let m be the mass of the partial system, m' the mass of the complete system. The coordinates x_ν of the partial system are at the same time coordinates of the complete system, only for clearness they are denoted as such by x_ν'. If now the partial system suffers any displacement, which is, of course, at the same time a displacement of the complete system, then $dx_\nu' = dx_\nu$ for the common coordinates, whereas $dx_\nu' = 0$ for the remaining ones. Now, by § 73 $m'\overline{dx_\nu'} = m_\nu\overline{dx_\nu'}$ and $m\overline{dx_\nu} = m_\nu\overline{dx_\nu}$, consequently $m'\overline{dx_\nu'} = m\overline{dx_\nu}$. In the case of a vector which is represented by means of this displacement, the component along x_ν is proportional to $\overline{dx_\nu}$, and that along x_ν' to $\overline{dx_\nu'}$. Thus we obtain

$$m'h_\nu' = mh_\nu$$

for every ν which the systems have in common, whereas for the remainder

$$h_\nu' = 0.$$

255. **Problem 2.** The same vector quantities may, at one time, be considered as vector quantities with regard to a partial system, and, at another time, as vector quantities with regard to the complete system. To determine, in the former

case, the components k_ρ' along the coordinates p_ρ' in terms of the components k_ρ along the coordinates p_ρ.

Let m be again the mass of the partial system, m' that of the complete. We assume that the coordinates p_ρ of the partial system are also coordinates of the complete system, only for clearness in the latter case they will be denoted by p_ρ'. Of the coordinates p_ρ' which are not common to the two systems we assume that they are not coordinates of the partial system. With these assumptions, an analogous consideration to the foregoing (§ 254) gives

$$m'k_\rho' = mk_\rho$$

for the common coordinates, whereas for the remainder

$$k_\rho' = 0.$$

But without the assumptions named the problem is indeterminate.

2. Motion of Systems

Explanations

256. (1) The passage of a system of material points from an initial position to a final one, considered with reference to the time and manner of the passage, is called a motion of the system from the initial to the final position (cf. § 27).

Consequently, in any definite motion the system describes a definite path, and moreover it describes definite lengths in definite times.

257. (2) Every motion of a system along a conceivable path is called a conceivable motion of the system (§ 11).

258. (3) Every motion of a system along a possible path is called a possible motion of the system (§ 112).

259. (4) Kinematics, or the theory of pure motion, treats of the conceivable and possible motions of systems.

So long as we deal only with normal systems (§§ 119, 120), kinematical investigations almost coincide with those of geometry. But when an abnormal system is investigated and the time appears in the equations of condition of the system, then kinematics possesses greater generality than geometry. However, it is not necessary to enter into purely kinematical investigations here; we may then be satisfied with the discussion of a series of fundamental ideas.

260. **Analytical Representation.** The motion of a system is analytically represented when in the representation of the path described, the time t is taken as independent variable, or, what is the same thing, when the coordinates of the position of the system are given as functions of the time.

Following Newton, the differential coefficients of all quantities with regard to the time will be denoted by dots.

Velocity

261. **Definition 1.** The instantaneous rate of motion of a system is called its velocity.

The velocity is determined by the change which the position of the system suffers in an infinitely small time, and by the time itself. It is measured by the ratio of these quantities which is independent of their absolute value.

By the condition of a system we shall mean its position and velocity.

262. **Corollary.** The velocity of a system may be regarded as a vector quantity with regard to the system. The direction of the velocity is then the direction of the instantaneous path-element; the magnitude of the velocity is equal to the differential coefficient of the length of path traversed with regard to the time.

The magnitude of the velocity is also called the velocity of the system along its path, or, when misunderstanding cannot arise, the velocity simply.

263. **Definition 2.** A motion of a system in which the velocity does not change its magnitude is called a uniform motion.

264. **Observation.** A straight motion of a system is motion in a straight path. In this motion the velocity does not change its direction.

265. **Problem 1.** To express the magnitude of the

velocity, its components and reduced components in the direction of the rectangular coordinates, in terms of the rates of change of these coordinates.

The magnitude v of the velocity is given by the positive root of the equation,

$$mv^2 = m\left(\frac{ds}{dt}\right)^2 = \sum_{1}^{3n}{}_\nu m_\nu \dot{x}_\nu^2.$$

Thus, then (§ 241), the components of the velocity in the direction of x_ν are equal to

$$\sqrt{\frac{m_\nu}{m}}\dot{x}_\nu,$$

and the reduced components in the same direction, or the components along x_ν, to

$$\frac{m_\nu}{m}\dot{x}_\nu.$$

266. **Observation.** The magnitude of the velocity of a system is the quadratic mean value of the magnitudes of the velocities of all its particles.

267. **Problem 2.** To express the magnitude of the velocity, its components and reduced components along the general coordinates p_ρ, in terms of the rates of change $\dot{p}_\rho$ of these coordinates.

By transformation of § 265 by means of § 57 we obtain the magnitude of the velocity as the positive root of the equation

$$v^2 = \sum_{1}^{r}{}_\rho \sum_{1}^{r}{}_\sigma a_{\sigma\rho}\dot{p}_\rho\dot{p}_\sigma.$$

Thence, by § 241, the components in direction of p_ρ are equal to

$$\frac{1}{\sqrt{a_{\rho\rho}}}\sum_{1}^{r}{}_\sigma a_{\rho\sigma}\dot{p}_\sigma,$$

and the reduced components in the same direction, or the components along p_ρ, to

$$\sum_{1}^{r}{}_\sigma a_{\rho\sigma}\dot{p}_\sigma.$$

Momentum

268. Definition. The product of the mass of a system into its velocity is called the quantity of motion, or momentum, of the system.

The momentum of the system is thus a vector quantity with regard to the system. The component of the momentum along any coordinate will usually be simply called the momentum of the system along this coordinate (§ 241).

269. Notation. The momenta of a system along the general coordinates p_ρ will always be denoted by q_ρ.

270. Problem 1. To express the momenta q_ρ of a system along p_ρ in terms of the rates of change of these coordinates.

From §§ 268 and 267 we obtain

$$q_\rho = m \sum_1^r {}_\sigma a_{\rho\sigma} \dot{p}_\sigma.$$

271. Problem 2. To express the rates of change of the general coordinates p_ρ in terms of the momenta of the system along these coordinates.

From the foregoing equation we obtain

$$\dot{p}_\rho = \frac{1}{m} \sum_1^r {}_\sigma b_{\rho\sigma} q_\sigma.$$

272. Observation. The velocity and the quantity of motion of a system are vectors with regard to the system of such a nature that they are always parallel to possible displacements of the system (§§ 243, 245).

Acceleration

273. Definition. The instantaneous rate of change of the velocity of a system is called its acceleration.

The acceleration is determined by the change which the velocity suffers in an infinitely small time and by the time itself; it is measured by the ratio of these two quantities which is independent of their absolute value.

274. Corollary. The acceleration of a system may be

regarded as a vector quantity with regard to the system. We take from the actual position of the system two displacements, of which the one represents the actual velocity, the other the velocity at the next instant; then the difference of these gives a new displacement, whose direction is the direction of the acceleration, whilst the magnitude of the acceleration is equal to the ratio of the length of this new displacement to the differential of the time.

275. **Problem 1.** To express the magnitude f of the acceleration and its components along the rectangular coordinates in terms of the differential coefficients of these coordinates with regard to the time.

The components of the velocity along x_ν, now, and after the time dt, are (§ 265)

$$\frac{m_\nu}{m}\dot{x}_\nu \quad \text{and} \quad \frac{m_\nu}{m}\dot{x}_\nu + \frac{m_\nu}{m}\ddot{x}_\nu dt,$$

the components of their difference are thus $\frac{m_\nu}{m}\ddot{x}_\nu dt$; the ratio of these to the time dt gives the components of the acceleration along x_ν equal to

$$\frac{m_\nu}{m}\ddot{x}_\nu,$$

whence by § 244 the magnitude of the acceleration is the positive root of the equation

$$mf^2 = \sum_1^{3n} m_\nu \ddot{x}_\nu^2$$

276. **Observation.** The magnitude of the acceleration of a material system is the quadratic mean value of the magnitudes of the accelerations of its particles.

277. **Problem 2.** To express the components f_ρ of the acceleration of a system along the general coordinates p_ρ, in terms of the differential coefficients of these with regard to the time.

By § 242,

$$f_\rho = \sum_1^{3n} \frac{m_\nu}{m} a_{\nu\rho} \ddot{x}_\nu,$$

and in this is to be substituted, as in § 108,

$$\ddot{x}_\nu = \sum_1^r {}_\sigma a_{\nu\sigma}\ddot{p}_\sigma + \sum_1^r {}_\sigma \sum_1^r {}_\tau \frac{\partial a_{\nu\sigma}}{\partial p_\tau}\dot{p}_\sigma\dot{p}_\tau.$$

Thus proceeding as in § 108 we obtain

$$f_\rho = \sum_1^r {}_\sigma a_{\rho\sigma}\ddot{p}_\sigma + \sum_1^r {}_\sigma \sum_1^r {}_\tau \left(\frac{\partial a_{\rho\sigma}}{\partial p_\tau} - \tfrac{1}{2}\frac{\partial a_{\sigma\tau}}{\partial p_\rho}\right)\dot{p}_\sigma\dot{p}_\tau.$$

278. Observation 1. The components of the acceleration are thus in general linear functions of the second differential coefficients of the coordinates, quadratic functions of the first differential coefficients, and implicit functions of the coordinates themselves.

279. Observation 2. The acceleration of a system is not necessarily parallel to a possible displacement of a system, nor even to a displacement which can be expressed by the coordinates p_ρ.

The components f_ρ do not therefore in general suffice to determine the magnitude of the acceleration nor even its components along all the rectangular coordinates (§§ 243, 245). On the other hand the quantities f_ρ are sufficient to determine the components of the acceleration in the direction of every one of the possible motions of the system (§ 248).

280. Problem 3. To find the component of the acceleration in the direction of the path.

The direction cosines of the path are by § 72 equal to $\sqrt{\dfrac{m_\nu}{m}}\dfrac{dx_\nu}{ds}$; and thus by § 265 to $\sqrt{\dfrac{m_\nu}{m}}\dfrac{\dot{x}_\nu}{v}$. Thence follows by § 246, with the help of § 275 for the tangential component f_t,

$$f_t = \sum_1^{3n} {}_\nu \frac{m_\nu}{m}\frac{\dot{x}_\nu \ddot{x}_\nu}{v} = \frac{dv}{dt} = \frac{d^2s}{dt^2} = \ddot{s},$$

where s is the current length of the path.

281. Note. If we resolve the acceleration of a system into two components, of which one is in the direction of the path and the other is perpendicular to the path, then the magnitude of the latter is equal to the product of the curvature of the path into the square of the velocity of the system in the path.

If, in equation § 107 (iii), we take the time t as independent variable, we obtain

$$mv^4c^2 = \sum_1^{3n} {}_\nu m_\nu \ddot{x}_\nu^2 - m\ddot{s}^2;$$

thus by use of §§ 275 and 280

$$v^4c^2 = f^2 - f_t^2.$$

If now we call the second, the radial or centrifugal component of the acceleration f_r, then $f^2 = f_t^2 + f_r^2$, for f_r and f_t are perpendicular to one another; consequently

$$f_r = cv^2,$$

as was to be proved.

Energy

282. Definition. The energy of a system is half the product of its mass into the square of the magnitude of its velocity.

283. Problem 1. To express the energy E of a system in terms of the rates of change of its rectangular coordinates.

By § 265

$$\mathrm{E} = \tfrac{1}{2}mv^2 = \tfrac{1}{2}\sum_1^{3n} {}_\nu m_\nu \dot{x}_\nu^2.$$

284. Corollary 1. The energy of a system is the sum of the energies of its particles.

285. Corollary 2. If several systems together form a greater system, then the energy of the latter is the sum of the energies of the former.

286. Problem 2. To express the energy of a system in terms of the rates of change of the general coordinates of the system and the momenta along these coordinates.

Using §§ 267, 270, 271, we obtain successively

$$\mathrm{E} = \tfrac{1}{2}m\sum_1^r {}_\rho \sum_1^r {}_\sigma a_{\rho\sigma}\dot{p}_\rho \dot{p}_\sigma \qquad \text{(i)}$$

$$= \tfrac{1}{2}\sum_1^r {}_\rho q_\rho \dot{p}_\rho \qquad \text{(ii)}$$

$$= \tfrac{1}{2}m \sum_{1}^{r} {}_{\rho} \sum_{1}^{r} {}_{\sigma} b_{\rho\sigma} \dot{q}_\rho \dot{q}_\sigma. \qquad \text{(iii)}.$$

287. **Observation** (on §§ 261-286). The velocity, momentum, acceleration, and energy of a system are defined independently of their analytical representation, and, in particular, independently of the choice of the coordinates of the system.

Use of Partial Differential Coefficients

288. **Notation** (*cf.* § 90). The partial differential of the energy E will be denoted by $\partial_p \mathrm{E}$ only when we consider the coordinates p_ρ and their rates of change $\dot{p}_\rho$ as the independent variable elements of the energy (§ 286 (i)).

The partial differential of the energy E will be denoted by $\partial_q \mathrm{E}$ only when we consider the coordinates p_ρ and the momenta q_ρ along these coordinates as the independent variable elements of the energy (§ 286 (iii)).

Either of these assumptions excludes the other. When misunderstanding cannot arise, any partial differential of E will be denoted as usual by $\partial \mathrm{E}$, *e.g.* the first or the second of those mentioned above, or any third kind.

289. **Note 1.** The momenta q_ρ of a system along the coordinates p_ρ may be expressed as partial differential coefficients of the energy of the system with regard to the rates of change of the coordinates.

For, by equation § 286 (i) and § 270 (cf. § 91),

$$q_\rho = \frac{\partial_p \mathrm{E}}{\partial \dot{p}_\rho}.$$

290. **Note 2.** The rates of change $\dot{p}_\rho$ of the coordinates p_ρ of a system may be expressed as partial differential coefficients of the energy of the system with regard to the momenta.

For, by equation § 286 (iii), and § 271 (cf. § 94),

$$\dot{p}_\rho = \frac{\partial_q \mathrm{E}}{\partial q_\rho}.$$

291. **Note 3.** The components f_ρ of the acceleration of a system along the coordinates p_ρ can be expressed as partial differential coefficients of the energy.

For, by equation 286 (i), firstly,

$$\frac{\partial_p E}{\partial \dot{p}_\rho} = m \sum_{1}^{r} {}_\sigma a_{\rho\sigma} \dot{p}_\sigma,$$

thus

$$\frac{d}{dt}\left(\frac{\partial_p E}{\partial \dot{p}_\rho}\right) = m \sum_{1}^{r} {}_\sigma a_{\rho\sigma} \ddot{p}_\sigma + m \sum_{1}^{r} {}_\sigma \sum_{1}^{r} {}_\tau \frac{\partial a_{\rho\sigma}}{\partial p_\tau} \dot{p}_\sigma \dot{p}_\tau;$$

and, secondly, by the same equation,

$$\frac{\partial_p E}{\partial p} = \tfrac{1}{2} m \sum_{1}^{r} {}_\sigma \sum_{1}^{r} {}_\tau \frac{\partial a_{\sigma\tau}}{\partial p_\rho} \dot{p}_\sigma \dot{p}_\tau.$$

By subtracting the second equation from the first and comparing with § 227,

$$mf_\rho = \frac{d}{dt}\left(\frac{\partial_p E}{\partial \dot{p}_\rho}\right) - \frac{\partial_p E}{\partial p_\rho} \qquad (i),$$

for which may be written (cf. § 289)

$$mf_\rho = \dot{q}_\rho - \frac{\partial_p E}{\partial p_\rho}.$$

292. **Note 4.** If we change one coordinate p_τ of a system twice by the same infinitely small amount, whereby the first time we let the rates of change of the coordinates, the second time the momenta along these coordinates, retain their original values, then the energy of the system in the two cases suffers an equal and opposite change.

For, if the equation § 95 (i) is multiplied by mds and divided by dt^2, we get

$$\frac{\partial_p E}{\partial p_\tau} = -\frac{\partial_q E}{\partial p_\tau},$$

which proves the statement.

293. **Proposition.** If the position of a system suffers twice the same infinitely small displacements whereby the first time the rates of change of the coordinates, and the second time the momenta along the coordinates, retain their original values, then the energy of the system in the two cases suffers an equal and opposite change.

For the change of the energy is in the first case

and in the second
$$\delta_p E = \sum_{1}^{r} {}_\tau \frac{\partial_p E}{\partial p_\tau} \delta p_\tau$$

$$\delta_q E = \sum_{1}^{r} {}_\tau \frac{\partial_q E}{\partial p_\tau} \delta p_\tau \, ;$$

thus then, by § 292,

$$\delta_p E = - \delta_q E.$$

294. **Corollary.** The components of the acceleration of a system along its coordinates p_ρ can also (by §§ 291 (ii) and 292) be expressed in the form

$$mf_\rho = \dot{q}_\rho + \frac{\partial_q E}{\partial p_\rho}.$$

Concluding Note on the First Book

295. As has already been stated in the prefatory note (§ 1), no appeal is made to experience in the investigations of this book. Consequently, if in the sequel we again meet with the results here obtained, we shall know that they are not obtained from experience but from the given laws of our intuition and thought, combined with a series of arbitrary statements.

It is true that the formation of the ideas and the development of their relations has only been performed with a view to possible experiences; it is thus none the less true that experience alone must decide on the value or worthlessness of our investigations. But the correctness or incorrectness of these investigations can be neither confirmed nor contradicted by any possible future experiences.

BOOK II

MECHANICS OF MATERIAL SYSTEMS

296. **Prefatory Note.** In this second book we shall understand times, spaces, and masses to be symbols for objects of external experience; symbols whose properties, however, are consistent with the properties that we have previously assigned to these quantities either by definition or as being forms of our internal intuition. Our statements concerning the relations between times, spaces, and masses must therefore satisfy henceforth not only the demands of thought, but must also be in accordance with possible, and, in particular, future experiences. These statements are based, therefore, not only on the laws of our intuition and thought, but in addition on experience. The part depending on the latter, in so far as it is not already contained in the fundamental ideas, will be comprised in a single general statement which we shall take for our Fundamental Law. No further appeal is made to experience. The question of the correctness of our statements is thus coincident with the question of the correctness or general validity of that single statement.

CHAPTER I

TIME, SPACE, AND MASS

297. Time, space, and mass in themselves are in no sense capable of being made the subjects of our experience, but only definite times, space-quantities, and masses. Any definite time, space-quantity, or mass may form the result of a definite experience. We make, that is to say, these conceptions symbols for objects of external experience in that we settle by what sensible perceptions we intend to determine definite

times, space-quantities, or masses. The relations which we state as existing between times, spaces, and masses, must then in future be looked upon as relations between these sensible perceptions.

298. **Rule 1.** We determine the duration of time by means of a chronometer, from the number of beats of its pendulum. The unit of duration is settled by arbitrary convention. To specify any given instant, we use the time that has elapsed between it and a certain instant determined by a further arbitrary convention.

This rule contains nothing empirical which can prevent us from considering time as an always independent and never dependent quantity which varies continuously from one value to another. The rule is also determinate and unique, except for the uncertainties which we always fail to eliminate from our experience, both past and future.

299. **Rule 2.** We determine space-relations according to the methods of practical geometry by means of a scale. The unit of length is settled by arbitrary convention. A given point in space is specified by its relative position with regard to a system of coordinates fixed with reference to the fixed stars and determined by convention.

We know by experience that we are never led into contradictions when we apply all the results of Euclidean geometry to space-relations determined in this manner. The rule is also determinate and unique, except for the uncertainties which we always fail to eliminate from our actual experience, both past and future.

300. **Rule 3.** The mass of bodies that we can handle is determined by weighing. The unit of mass is the mass of some body settled by arbitrary convention.

The mass of a tangible body as determined by this rule possesses the properties attributed to the ideally defined mass (§ 4). That is to say, it can be conceived as split up into any number of equal parts, each of which is indestructible and unchangeable and capable of being employed as a mark to refer, without ambiguity, a point of space at one time to a point of space at any other time (§ 3). The rule is also determinate and unique as regards bodies which we can handle, apart from the uncertainties which we cannot eliminate from our actual experience, either past or future.

301. **Addition to Rule 3.** We admit the presumption that in addition to the bodies which we can handle there are other bodies which we can neither handle, move, nor place in the balance, and to which Rule 3 has no application. The mass of such bodies can only be determined by hypothesis.

In such hypothesis we are at liberty to endow these masses only with those properties which are consistent with the properties of the ideally defined mass.

302. **Observation 1.** The three foregoing rules are not new definitions of the quantities time, space, and mass, which have been completely defined previously. They present rather the laws of transformation by means of which we translate external experience, *i.e.* concrete sensations and perceptions, into the symbolic language of the images of them which we form (*vide* Introduction), and by which conversely the necessary consequents of this image are again referred to the domain of possible sensible perceptions. Thus, only through these three rules can the symbols time, space, and mass become parts of our images of external objects. Again, only by these three rules are they subjected to further demands than are necessitated by our thought.

303. **Observation 2.** The indeterminateness which our rules involve and which we have acknowledged, does not arise from the indeterminateness of our images, nor of our laws of transformation, but from the indeterminateness of the external experience which has to be transformed. By this we mean that there is no actual method which, with the aid of our senses, determines time more accurately than can be done by the help of the best chronometer; nor position than when it is referred to a system of coordinates fixed with regard to the fixed stars; nor mass than when determined by the best balance.

304. **Observation 3.** There is, nevertheless, some apparent warrant for the question whether our three rules furnish true or absolute measures of time, space, and mass, and this

question must in all probability be answered in the negative, inasmuch as our rules are obviously in part fortuitous and arbitrary. In truth, however, this question needs no discussion here, not affecting the correctness of our statements, even if we attached to the question a definite meaning and answered it in the negative. It is sufficient that our rules determine such measures as enable us to express without ambiguity the results of past and future experiences. Should we agree to use other measures, then the form of our statements would suffer corresponding changes, but in such a manner that the experiences, both past and future, expressed thereby, would remain the same.

Material Systems

305. **Explanation.** By a material system is henceforth understood a system of concrete masses, whose properties are not inconsistent with the properties of the ideally defined material system (§ 121). Thus in a natural material system some positions and displacements are possible, others impossible; and the aggregate of possible positions and displacements satisfies the conditions of continuity (§ 121). In a natural free system the connections are independent of the position of the system relative to all masses not included in it, as well as of the time (§ 122).

306. **Note thereupon.** We know from experience that there is an actual content corresponding to the conceptions so defined.

For, firstly, experience teaches us that there are connections, and moreover continuous connections, between the masses of nature. There are thus material systems in the sense of § 305. We may even assert that other than continuous connections are not found in nature, and that, consequently, every natural system of material points is a material system.

Secondly, experience teaches us that the connections of a material system may be independent of its position relative to other systems, and of its absolute position. We may even assert that this independence always appears, so long as a material system is sufficiently distant in space from all other systems. Thus, there are systems which have only internal connections, and we possess also a general method for recognising and constructing such systems.

Thirdly and finally, experience teaches us that absolute time has no effect on the behaviour of natural systems which are only subject to internal connections. Every such natural system is thus subject only to normal (§ 119) connections and is therefore a free system. There are thus free systems in the sense of § 305, and we can construct free systems and recognise them as such independently of the statements which we shall have to make again concerning free systems.

307. **Observation.** The normal connections of free systems form those very properties which exist independently of the time. It is the problem of experimental physics to separate those finite groups of masses which can exist independently as free systems, from the infinite world of phenomena, and to deduce from those phenomena which occur in time and in connection with other systems those properties which are unaffected by time.

CHAPTER II

THE FUNDAMENTAL LAW

308. We consider the problem of mechanics to be to deduce from the properties of a material system which are independent of the time those phenomena which take place in time and the properties which depend on the time. For the solution of this problem we lay down the following, and only the following, fundamental law, inferred from experience.

309. **Fundamental Law.** Every free system persists in its state of rest or of uniform motion in a straightest path.

Systema omne liberum perseverare in statu suo quiescendi vel movendi uniformiter in directissimam.

310. **Note 1.** The fundamental law is so worded that its statement has reference only to free systems. But since a portion of a free system can be an unfree (*unfreies*) system, results may be deduced from the fundamental law which have reference to unfree systems.

311. **Note 2.** The aggregate of inferences with regard to a free system and its unfree portions which may be drawn from the fundamental law forms the content of mechanics. Our mechanics does not recognise other causes of motion than those which arise from the law. The knowledge of the fundamental law is, according to our view of it, not only necessary for the solution of the problem of mechanics, but also sufficient for this purpose, and this is an essential part of our assertion.

312. **Note 3. (Definition.)** Every motion of a free material system, or of its parts, which is consistent with the

fundamental law, we call a natural motion of the system in contradistinction to its conceivable and possible motions (§§ 257, 258).

Thus mechanics treats of the natural motions of free material systems and their parts.

313. **Note 4.** We consider a phenomenon of the material world to be mechanically and thereby physically explained when we have proved it a necessary consequence of the fundamental law and of those properties of material systems which are independent of the time.

314. **Note 5.** The complete explanation of the phenomena of the material world would therefore comprise: (1) their mechanical or physical explanation; (2) an explanation of the fundamental law; (3) the explanation of those properties of the material world which are independent of time. The second and third of these explanations we, however, regard as beyond the domain of physics.

Validity of the Fundamental Law

315. We consider the law to be the probable outcome of most general experience. More strictly, the law is stated as a hypothesis or assumption, which comprises many experiences, which is not contradicted by any experience, but which asserts more than can be proved by definite experience at the present time. For, as regards their relation to the fundamental law, the material systems of nature can be divided into three classes.

316. 1. The first class comprises those systems of bodies or parts of such systems which satisfy the conditions of a free system, as can be immediately seen from experience, and to which the fundamental law applies directly. Such are, for example, rigid bodies moving in free space or perfect fluids moving in closed vessels.

The fundamental law is deduced from experiences on such material systems. With regard to this first class it merely represents an experiential fact.

317. 2. The second class comprises those systems of bodies which do not immediately conform to the assumptions of

the fundamental law, or which do not at first sight obey the law, but which can be adapted to the assumptions or can be made to obey the law when, and in fact only when, to direct sensible experience certain definite hypotheses as to the nature of this experience are adjoined.

(*a*) Amongst these are included, firstly, those systems which do not seem to satisfy the condition of continuity in particular positions; *i.e.* those systems in which impulses, in the widest meaning of the term, occur. In this case it is sufficient to use the exceedingly probable hypothesis that all discontinuities are only apparent and vanish when we succeed in taking into consideration sufficiently small space- and time-quantities.

(*b*) Secondly, there are included amongst them those systems in which actions-at-a-distance, the forces due to heat and other causes of motion, not always fully understood, are in operation. When we bring to rest the tangible bodies of such systems, they do not remain in this state, but on being set free enter into a state of motion again. Thus, apparently, they do not obey the law. In this case it is highly probable that the tangible bodies are not the only masses, nor their visible motions the only motions of these systems, but that when we have reduced the visible motions of the tangible bodies to rest, other concealed motions still exist in the systems which are communicated to the tangible bodies again when we set them free. It appears that assumptions can always be made with regard to these concealed motions such that the complete systems obey the fundamental law.

As regards the second class of natural systems the law bears the character of a hypothesis which is in part highly probable, in part fairly probable, but which, as far as we can see, is always permissible.

318. 3. The third class of systems of bodies comprises those systems whose motions cannot be represented directly as necessary consequences of the law, and for which no definite hypotheses can be adduced to make them conformable to it. Amongst these are included, for instance, all systems which contain organic or living beings. We know, however, so little of all the systems included under this head, that it cannot be regarded as proved that such hypotheses are impossible,

and that the phenomena in these systems contradict the fundamental law.

Thus, then, with regard to the third class of systems of bodies the fundamental law has the character of a permissible hypothesis.

319. **Observation.** If we may assume that there is no free system in nature which is not conformable to the law, then we may consider any system whatever as such a free system, or as part of such a free system; so that, on this assumption, there is in nature no system whose motions cannot be determined by means of its connections and the fundamental law.

Limitation of the Fundamental Law

320. In a system of bodies which conforms to the fundamental law there is neither any new motion nor any cause of new motion, but only the continuance of the previous motion in a given simple manner. One can scarcely help denoting such a material system as an inanimate or lifeless one. If we were to extend the law to the whole of nature, as the most general free system, and to say—" The whole of nature pursues with uniform velocity a straightest path,"—we should offend against a feeling which is sound and natural. It is therefore prudent to limit the probable validity of the law to inanimate systems. This amounts to the statement that the law, applied to a system of the third class (§ 318), forms an improbable hypothesis.

321. No attention is, however, paid to this consideration, nor is it necessary, seeing that the law gives a permissible hypothesis if not a probable one. If it could be proved that living systems contradicted the hypothesis, then they would separate themselves from mechanics. In that case, but only in that case, our mechanics would require supplementing with reference to those unfree systems which, although themselves lifeless, are nevertheless parts of such free systems as contain living beings.

As far as we know, such a supplement could be formed,

namely, from the experience that animate systems never produce any different results on inanimate ones than those which can also be produced by an inanimate system. Thus it is possible to substitute for any animate system an inanimate one; this may replace the former in any particular problem under consideration, and its specification is requisite in order that we may reduce the given problem to a purely mechanical one.

322. **Observation.** In the usual presentation of mechanics such a reservation is omitted as superfluous and it is assumed that the fundamental laws include animate as well as inanimate nature. And, indeed, in that presentation it is permissible, because we give the freest play to the forms of the forces which there enter into the fundamental laws, and reserve to ourselves an opportunity of explaining, later and outside of mechanics, whether the forces of animate and inanimate nature are different, and what properties may distinguish the one from the other. In our presentation of the subject greater prudence is necessary, since a considerable number of experiences which primarily relate to inanimate nature only are already included in the principle itself, and the possibility of a later narrowing of the limits is much lessened.

Analysis of the Fundamental Law

323. The form in which we have stated the law purposely assimilates itself to the statement of Newton's First Law. However, this statement comprises three others independent of one another, namely, the following:—

1. Of the possible paths of a free system its straightest paths are the only one which it pursues.

2. Different free systems describe in identical times lengths of their paths proportional to each other.

3. Time, as measured by a chronometer (§ 298), increases proportionally to the length of the path of any one of the free moving systems.

The first two statements alone contain facts of a general nature derived from experience. The third only justifies our arbitrary rule for the measure of time, and only includes the particular experience that in certain respects a chronometer behaves as a free system, although, strictly speaking, it is not such.

Method of applying the Fundamental Law

324. When a given question with regard to the motion of a material system is asked, then one of the three following cases must necessarily arise :—

1. The question may be stated in such a manner that the fundamental law itself provides a definite answer. In this case, the problem is a definite mechanical one, and the application of the fundamental law gives its solution.

325. 2. The question may be stated in such a manner that the fundamental law itself does not directly furnish a definite reply, but one or more assumptions may be joined with the question by means of which the definite application of the law is rendered possible.

If only one such assumption is possible and we assume that the problem is a mechanical one, this assumption must also be an appropriate one; the problem can thus be considered as a definite mechanical one, and the application of the assumption and the fundamental law gives the solution.

If several assumptions are possible and we assume that the problem is a mechanical one, one of these assumptions must be appropriate; the problem may then be considered as an indeterminate mechanical one, and the application of the fundamental law to the different possible assumptions gives the possible solutions.

326. 3. The question may be stated in such wise that the fundamental law is insufficient for the solution and that no assumption may be joined to it such as to render the application of the law possible. In this case the question must contain assumptions contradicting the fundamental law or the properties of the system to which it relates; the proposition stated cannot then be considered a mechanical problem.

Approximate Application of the Fundamental Law

327. **Note.** When equations result from the given equations of condition of a system and the fundamental law, which have strictly the form of equations of condition, then for the determination of the motion of the system it is indifferent whether we consider the original equations alone, or instead of them the derived equations, as a representation of the connections of the system.

For if we omit from the series of original equations of condition all those which may be obtained analytically from the remainder and from the derived equations of condition, then only possible displacements, although in general not all the displacements which were possible according to the original equations, satisfy those of the original equations which are left and the derived equations. A path which was a straightest path under the original more general manifold will be one also *a fortiori* under the present more limited manifold. And since the natural paths must be included under this more limited manifold, the natural paths are the straightest amongst those which are possible by the present equations of condition. Thus the proof follows.

328. **Corollary 1.** If we know from experience that a system actually satisfies given equations of condition, then in applying the fundamental law it is quite indifferent whether these connections are original ones, *i.e.* whether they do not admit of a further physical explanation (§ 313), or whether they are connections which may be represented as necessary consequences of other connections and of the fundamental law, and which consequently admit of a mechanical explanation.

329. **Corollary 2.** If we know from experience that given equations of condition of a material system are only approximately but not completely satisfied, then it is still permissible to leave those equations of condition as an approximate representation of a true connection, and by applying the fundamental law to them to obtain approximate statements concerning the motion of the system, although it is quite certain that these approximate equations of condition do not

represent an original, continuous and normal connection, but can only be regarded as the approximate result of unknown connections and the fundamental law.

330. **Observation.** Every practical application of our mechanics is founded upon the foregoing corollary. For in all connections between sensible masses which physics discovers and mechanics uses, a sufficiently close investigation shows that they have only approximate validity, and therefore can only be derived connections. We are compelled to seek the ultimate connections in the world of atoms, and they are unknown to us. But even if they were known to us we could not apply them to practical purposes, but should have to proceed as we now do. For the complete control over any problem always requires that the number of variables should be extremely small, whereas a return to the connections amongst the atoms would require the introduction of an immense number of variables.

However, the fact that we may employ the fundamental law in the manner we do, is not to be regarded as a new experience in addition to the law, but is, as we have seen, a necessary consequence of the law itself.

CHAPTER III

MOTION OF FREE SYSTEMS

General Properties of the Motion

1. Determinateness of the Motion

331. **Proposition.** A natural motion of a free system is singly determined when the position and velocity of the system at any given time are known.

For the path of the system is singly determined (§ 161) by its position and the direction of its velocity; the constant velocity of the system in its path is given by the magnitude of the velocity at the initial time.

332. **Corollary 1.** The future and past conditions of a free system for all times are singly determined by its present condition (§ 261).

333. **Corollary 2.** If it were possible to reverse the velocity of a system in any position (a thing which would in no wise contravene the equations of condition of the system), then the system would pass through the positions of its former motion in reverse order.

334. **Note 1.** In a free holonomous system (§ 123) there is always a natural motion which carries the system in a given time from an arbitrarily given initial position to an arbitrarily given final one.

For a natural path is always possible between the two positions (§ 192). Any velocity is permissible in this path, and therefore such an one as makes the system traverse the given distance in the given time.

335. **Observation.** The foregoing note still holds when instead of the time of the transference the velocity of the system in its path or its energy is given.

336. **Note 2.** A free system which is not holonomous cannot be carried from every possible initial position to every possible final one by a natural motion (§ 162).

337. **Proposition.** A natural motion of a free holonomous system is determined by specifying two positions of the system at two given times.

For by these data the path of the system and its velocity in the path are determined.

338. **Observation 1.** The determination of a natural motion by means of two positions between which it takes place is in general not unique; it is unique so long as the distance between the two positions does not exceed a certain finite quantity and the length of the path described is of the order of this distance (cf. §§ 167, 172, 190, 176).

339. **Observation 2.** A natural motion of a free holonomous system, apart from the absolute value of the time, is also determined by two positions of the system and either the duration of the transference, or the velocity of the system in its path, or the energy of the system.

2. Conservation of Energy

340. **Proposition.** The energy of a free system in any motion does not change with the time.

For the energy (§ 282) is determined by the mass of the system, which is invariable, and the velocity in its path, which is also invariable.

341. **Observation 1.** Of the three partial statements into which the fundamental law can be subdivided (§ 323), only the second and third are needed for the proof of the proposition. We might also make the third unnecessary and render the proposition independent of any given method of measuring time by stating it in the form :—

The ratio of the energies of any two free systems in any motion does not change with the time.

342. **Observation 2.** The law of the conservation of energy is a necessary consequence of the fundamental law. Conversely, from the law of the conservation of energy the second partial statement (§ 323) of that law follows, but not the first, and consequently not the entire law. There might be free systems conceivable, for which the law of the conservation of energy held, and which nevertheless did not move in straightest paths. It is conceivable, for instance, that the law of the conservation of energy might also hold good for animated systems although these might not be embraced in our mechanics. Conversely, natural systems might be conceived which only moved in straightest paths, and for which nevertheless the law of the conservation of energy might not hold good.

343. **Observation 3.** Lately the opinion has been repeatedly expressed that the energy of a moving system is associated with a definite place and is propagated from place to place. On this account energy, in this respect as well as in respect to its indestructibility, has been compared with matter. This conception of energy is obviously very different from that implied in our method of treatment. We have no stronger reason for saying that the seat of the energy of a moving system is where the system is, than for saying that the seat of the velocity of a moving body is where the body is. But naturally this last mode of expression is never used.

3. Least Acceleration

344. **Proposition.** A free system moves in such a manner that the magnitude of its acceleration at any instant is the smallest which is consistent with the instantaneous position, the instantaneous velocity and the connections of the system.

For the square of the magnitude of the acceleration is by §§ 280, 281, equal to

$$v^4 c^2 + \dot{v}^2.$$

Now for the natural motion $\dot{v} = o$; v has a value given by the instantaneous velocity, and c has the least value which is consistent with the given direction of motion and the connections of the system. Hence the expression itself must take the smallest value consistent with the given circumstances.

345. **Observation 1.** The property of the natural motion stated in the above proposition determines this motion uniquely, and therefore the proposition can completely replace the fundamental law.

For if the expression $v^4 c^2 + \dot{v}^2$ is to become a minimum, firstly $\dot{v}$ must be zero, and consequently the system must traverse its path with constant velocity; secondly either v must be zero, in which case the system is at rest, or c must have the smallest value possible for the direction of the path, in which case the path is a straightest path.

346. **Observation 2.** Proposition 344 might be regarded as a preferable form of statement of the fundamental law, inasmuch as it condenses the law into a single indivisible statement, not only externally into one sentence. The chosen form, however, has the advantage of making its meaning clearer and more unmistakable.

4. Shortest Path

347. **Proposition.** The natural path of a free holonomous system between any two sufficiently near positions is shorter than any other possible path between the two positions.

For in a holonomous system a straightest path between any two sufficiently near positions is also a shortest one (§§ 190, 176).

348. **Observation 1.** If the restriction to sufficiently near positions is removed, then it can no longer be asserted that the natural path is shorter than all other paths, nor even that it is shorter than all neighbouring paths. However, the assertion contained in the foregoing proposition, that the variation of the length of the path vanishes in a transference to any neighbouring possible path, always holds (§§ 190, 171).

349. Observation 2. The foregoing proposition corresponds to the Principle of Least Action in the form given to it by Jacobi. If for the moment we take m_ν to be the mass, ds_ν the path-length described by the νth of the n points of the system in a given element of time, then the proposition asserts that the variation of the integral

$$\int ds = \frac{1}{\sqrt{m}} \int \sqrt{\sum_1^n {}_\nu m_\nu ds_\nu{}^2}$$

vanishes in the natural motion of the system, and this is Jacobi's form of that principle.

350. Observation 3. In order to establish more strictly the relation between the proposition of § 347 and Jacobi's Law, it is necessary to make the following statement:—According to the usual conception of mechanics the proposition contains a particular case of Jacobi's Law, viz., the case where no forces act.

Conversely, according to our conception, the assumptions of the complete Law of Jacobi are to be considered as less general. According to this conception Jacobi's Law is an adaptation of the proposition to particular relations and a modification of it to the assumptions in them.

351. Observation 4. The law of the conservation of energy is not postulated by the proposition of § 347, nor is the latter deduced from the law; they are quite independent of one another. In conjunction with the law of energy the proposition may completely replace the fundamental law, but only for holonomous systems. If the proposition were applied to other systems, it would certainly determine definite motions; but these motions would contradict the fundamental law (§ 194) and would consequently furnish false solutions of the stated mechanical problem.

5. Shortest Time

352. Proposition. The natural motion of a free holonomous system carries the system in a shorter time from a given initial position to a sufficiently near final one, than could be done with any other possible motion, with the same constant value of the energy.

For if the energy, and consequently the velocity in the path, are the same for all the motions compared, then the duration of the motion is proportional to the length of the path. Consequently it is the smallest for the shortest path, that is for the natural path.

353. **Observation.** If the restriction to sufficiently near positions is removed, then the time of the motion is no longer necessarily a minimum, but it still retains the property of always being equal for the natural path and for all its infinitely near possible paths (see § 348).

354. **Corollary 1.** For the natural motion of a free holonomous system between given sufficiently near final positions, the time-integral of the energy is always smaller than for any other possible motion performed with the same constant value of the energy.

For the time-integral is equal to the product of the given constant value of the energy and the duration of the transference.

355. **Observation 1.** The proposition of § 352, particularly in the form of § 354, contains Maupertuis' Principle of Least Action. If it is desired to establish more strictly its relation to this principle, we must express ourselves in the manner done in § 350.

356. **Observation 2.** The corollary § 354, and also the proposition § 352, assume for the motions compared with one another the constancy of the energy with the time. With the assumption that the natural motion is included in those compared, they are sufficient for its determination, and could replace the fundamental law, but only in the case of holonomous systems. Their assumptions applied to other systems would lead to false mechanical solutions.

357. **Corollary 2.** A free holonomous system is carried from its initial position in a given time through a greater straightest distance by its natural motion than by any other possible motion which takes place with the same constant value of the energy as the natural motion.

6. Least Time-Integral of the Energy

358. Proposition. The time-integral of the energy in the transference of a free holonomous system from a given initial position to a sufficiently near final one is smaller for the natural motion than for any other possible motion by which the system may pass from the given initial position to the final one in an equal time.

For firstly, if we compare only motions in one and the same path, of length S, then the time-integral attains its minimum value for that one in which the velocity v is constant. For since the sum of the quantities vdt has the given value S, then the sum of the quantities $v^2 dt$ will attain its smallest value only when all the v's are equal. But if the velocity is constant, then the time-integral of the energy is equal to $\frac{1}{2}mS^2/T$, where T is the duration of the transference. Since T is given, the time-integral of the energy for different paths of the system varies as the square of the length of the path; hence the first quantity, like the last, has its minimum value for the natural path.

359. Observation 1. If the limitation to sufficiently near positions is removed, then the time-integral of the energy will no longer necessarily be a minimum, but its variation, nevertheless, always vanishes in the transference to any other of the motions considered (*cf.* § 348).

360. Observation 2. The foregoing proposition corresponds to Hamilton's Principle. If it is desired to establish more closely its connection with this principle, we must use the mode of expression of § 300.

361. Observation 3. The proposition § 358 and the corollary § 354 agree in this, that amongst certain classes of possible motions they distinguish the natural motion by one and the same characteristic, viz., the minimum value of the time-integral of the energy. They differ essentially from one another in this, that they consider entirely different kinds of possible motions.

362. Observation 4. The law of the conservation of energy is a necessary consequence of the proposition in § 358;

and this proposition, employed as a principle, can therefore completely replace the fundamental law, but still only in its application to holonomous systems. If the restriction to holonomous systems is removed, then the proposition determines definite motions of the material systems; but these in general contradict the fundamental law, and are, therefore, mechanically considered, false solutions of the stated problem.

363. **Retrospect to §§ 347-362.** If we employ the properties of the natural motion stated in the propositions 347, 352, 354, and 358 as principles for the complete or partial determination of this motion, then we make the changes now entering into the condition of the system dependent on such peculiarities of the motion as can only appear in the future, and which often seem in human affairs as objects worth striving for. This circumstance has occasionally led physicists and philosophers to perceive in the laws of mechanics the expression of a conscious intention as to future aims, combined with a certain foresight as to the most suitable means for attaining them. Such a conception is, however, neither necessary nor permissible.

364. That such a conception of these principles is not necessary is shown by the fact that the properties of the natural motion which seem to indicate an intention can be recognised as the necessary consequences of a law in which one finds no expression of any intention as to the future.

365. That this conception of the principles is inadmissible is seen from the fact that the properties of the natural motion which appear to denote an outlook to future issues are not found in all natural motions. Had nature the design of aiming at a shortest path, a least expenditure of energy and a shortest time, it would be impossible to understand why there could be systems in which this design, although attainable, should still be regularly missed by nature.

366. If one wishes to recognise in the fact that a system always chooses a straightest path-element amongst all possible ones the expression of a definite intention, then this is allowable; the expression of a definite intention is then already seen in the fact that a natural system always chooses out

of all possible motions no arbitrary one, but always one which is determinable beforehand and is marked by particular characteristics.

Analytical Representations. Differential Equations of Motion

367. **Explanation.** By the differential equations of motion of a system we understand a set of differential equations in which the time is the independent variable, the coordinates of the system the dependent variables; and which, together with an initial position and initial velocity, uniquely determine the motion of the system (§ 331).

368. **Problem 1.** To express the differential equations of the motion of a free system in terms of its rectangular coordinates.

In § 155 (iv) we have found the differential equations of the straightest paths of the system in terms of the rectangular coordinates. In these equations we introduce the time t as independent variable instead of the length of the path. By the fundamental law, $ds/dt = v$ is independent of t, and consequently also of s. Thus we have

$$\dot{x}_\nu = x'_\nu \cdot v, \quad \ddot{x}_\nu = x''_\nu \cdot v^2.$$

We then multiply the equations 155 (iv) by mv^2 and put for shortness X_ι instead of $mv^2 \Xi_\iota$. We thus obtain as solution of the problem the $3n$ equations

$$m_\nu \ddot{x}_\nu + \sum_1^i {}_\iota x_{\iota\nu} X_\iota = 0 \qquad (i),$$

which with the i equations (*cf.* § 155 ii.)

$$\sum_1^{3n} {}_\nu x_{\iota\nu} \ddot{x}_\nu + \sum_1^{3n} {}_\nu \sum_1^{3n} {}_\mu \frac{\partial x_{\iota\nu}}{\partial x_\mu} \dot{x}_\nu \dot{x}_\mu = 0 \qquad (ii)$$

determine the $3n$ quantities $\ddot{x}_\nu$ and X_ι as single-valued functions of x_ν and $\dot{x}_\nu$.

369. **Observation 1.** The equations of motion of the free system in the form of § 368 are usually known as Lagrange's equations of the first form.

370. **Observation 2.** Every single equation of § 368 (i) gives us, after having first determined the quantities X_ι, the component of the acceleration of the system along one of the rectangular coordinates of the system.

371. **Problem 2.** To express the differential equations of motion of a free system in terms of its general coordinates p_ρ.

The differential equations of the straightest paths in terms of p_ρ are given in § 158 (iv). In these we introduce the time as independent variable instead of the length of the path; and we again note that according to the fundamental law

$$\dot{p}_\rho = p'_\rho v, \quad \ddot{p}_\rho = p''_\rho v^2.$$

We consequently multiply the equations § 158 (iv) by mv^2, and putting P_χ for $mv^2 \Pi_\chi$ we obtain as solution of the problem the r equations

$$m \left\{ \sum_1^r {}_\sigma a_{\rho\sigma} \ddot{p}_\sigma + \sum_1^r {}_\sigma \sum_1^r {}_\tau \left(\frac{\partial a_{\rho\sigma}}{\partial p_\tau} - \tfrac{1}{2} \frac{\partial a_{\sigma\tau}}{\partial p_\rho} \right) \dot{p}_\sigma \dot{p}_\tau \right\} + \sum_1^k {}_\chi p_{\chi\rho} P_\chi = 0 \quad \text{(i)},$$

which with the k equations (*cf.* § 158 (ii))

$$\sum_1^r {}_\rho p_{\chi\rho} \ddot{p}_\rho + \sum_1^r {}_\sigma \sum_1^r {}_\rho \frac{\partial p_{\chi\rho}}{\partial p_\sigma} \dot{p}_\rho \dot{p}_\sigma = 0 \quad \text{(ii)}$$

determine the $r + k$ quantities $\ddot{p}_\rho$ and P_χ as single-valued functions of p_ρ and $\dot{p}_\rho$.

372. **Observation.** If we make use of the notation of § 277 we can write the equations of motion of § 371 (i) in the form

$$mf_\rho + \sum_1^k {}_\chi p_{\chi\rho} P_\chi = 0.$$

If we assume that the quantities P_χ have been determined, each of these equations gives us the component of the acceleration along a given coordinate p_ρ expressed as a function of the instantaneous position and velocity of the system.

373. **Corollary 1.** If we express by using the notation of § 291 (i) the components of the acceleration in terms of the energy, then the equations of motion of a free system take the form

$$\frac{d}{dt}\left(\frac{\partial_p \mathrm{E}}{\partial \dot{p}_\rho}\right) - \frac{\partial_p \mathrm{E}}{\partial \dot{p}_\rho} + \sum_1^k {}_\chi p_{\chi\rho} \mathrm{P}_\chi = 0.$$

374. **Observation 1.** The differential equations of motion in this form are called also the generalised Lagrangian equations of motion or Lagrange's equations of the second form (*cf.* § 369).

375. **Observation 2.** If the coordinate p_ρ is a free coordinate, then it does not appear in the equations of condition of the system, and the quantities $p_{\chi\rho}$ are consequently all equal to zero. The equation of motion corresponding to p_ρ then becomes

$$\frac{d}{dt}\left(\frac{\partial_p \mathrm{E}}{\partial \dot{p}_\rho}\right) - \frac{\partial_p \mathrm{E}}{\partial p_\rho} = 0.$$

In a holonomous system all the equations of motion can be expressed in this simple form (§ 144).

376. **Corollary 2.** The equations of motion of a free holonomous system expressed in any r free coordinates p_ρ of the system can be written in the form of the $2r$ equations

$$q_\rho = \frac{\partial_p \mathrm{E}}{\partial \dot{p}_\rho} \qquad \text{(i)}$$

$$\dot{q}_\rho = \frac{\partial_p \mathrm{E}}{\partial p_\rho} \qquad \text{(ii).}$$

Of these the former contain only definitions; but the latter contain experiential facts. One can thus regard the equations of motion in this form as $2r$ differential equations of the first order for the $2r$ quantities p_ρ and q_ρ. These equations, together with the $2r$ initial values of the quantities, determine them for all times.

377. **Observation 1.** The equations 376 (i) and (ii) one might correctly term Poisson's form of the equations of motion.

378. **Observation 2.** From the equations § 376 there follow two reciprocal relations, analytically expressed by the equations

[from (ii)] $\qquad \dfrac{\partial_p \dot{q}_\rho}{\partial p_\sigma} = \dfrac{\partial_p \dot{q}_\sigma}{\partial p_\rho}$ \qquad (i) [from (i) and (ii)] $\quad \dfrac{\partial_p q_\rho}{\partial \dot{p}_\sigma} = \dfrac{\partial_p \dot{q}_\sigma}{\partial \dot{p}_\rho}$ \quad (ii),

and which possess a simple physical meaning. Both relations contain elements of experience and would not hold for every possible motion of the system. Hence they may, under certain conditions, be utilised for testing the fundamental law. A third analogous relation, deduced solely from § 376 (i), would only be a consequence of our definitions.

379. **Corollary 3.** The equations of motion of a free holonomous system in terms of any r free coordinates p_ρ of the system can be written in the form of the $2r$ equations (§§ 290, 289, 292, 375)

$$\dot{p}_\rho = \dfrac{\partial_q \mathrm{E}}{\partial q_\rho} \quad \text{(i)}$$

$$\dot{q}_\rho = -\dfrac{\partial_q \mathrm{E}}{\partial p_\rho} \quad \text{(ii).}$$

Of these the former contain only definitions; but the latter contain experiential facts. In this form also the equations of motion appear as $2r$ differential equations of the first order for the $2r$ quantities p_ρ and q_ρ. These equations, together with the $2r$ initial values of the quantities, determine them for all times.

380. **Observation 1.** The foregoing equations are usually known as the Hamiltonian form of the equations of motion for a free system.

381. **Observation 2.** Two reciprocal relations follow from the equations § 379, which are analytically expressed by the equations

$$\dfrac{\partial_q \dot{q}_\rho}{\partial p_\sigma} = \dfrac{\partial_q \dot{q}_\sigma}{\partial p_\rho} \quad \text{(i)}$$

$$\dfrac{\partial_q \dot{p}_\rho}{\partial q_\sigma} = -\dfrac{\partial_q \dot{q}_\sigma}{\partial q_\rho} \quad \text{(ii),}$$

and which possess a simple physical meaning. Both relations contain elements of experience and distinguish the natural motion from other possible motions. Hence they may conversely, under certain conditions, be utilised for testing the fundamental law. A third analogous relation, deduced solely from § 379 (i), would only be the consequence of our definitions, and would therefore have no mechanical significance.

It is necessary to insist on the fact that the equations 378 (i) and 381 (i) represent different statements, and not the same statements in a different form.

Internal Constraint of Systems

382. Proposition. A system of material points between which no connections exist, persists in its condition of rest or uniform motion in a straight path.

For in such a system the straight path is also the straightest.

383. Corollary 1. A free material point persists in its condition of rest or uniform motion in a straight path (Galileo's Law of Inertia or Newton's First Law).

384. Corollary 2. The acceleration of a system of material points between which no connections exist is zero. The connections between the points of a material system can thus be regarded as the cause owing to which the acceleration differs in general from zero.

385. Definition. The change in the acceleration caused by all the connections of a material system is called the constraint which the connections impose on the system; this change is also called for shortness the internal constraint, or, still shorter, the constraint of the system.

The constraint is measured by the difference between the actual acceleration of the system and the acceleration of that natural motion which would result on removal of all the equations of condition of the system; it is equal to the former diminished by the latter.

386. Corollary 1. The internal constraint of a system is, like the acceleration, a vector quantity with regard to the system.

387. Corollary 2. In a free system the internal constraint is equal to the acceleration of the system: it is here in fact only another mode of regarding the acceleration (§ 382).

388. Proposition 1. The magnitude of the constraint is at every instant smaller for the natural motion of a free system than for any other possible motion which coincides with it in position and velocity at the particular instant considered.

For· this statement is by § 387 only different in form from proposition § 344.

389. Corollary. Any connection which is added to the connections of the system already in existence increases the constraint of the system. The removal of any connection changes the natural motion in such a manner that the constraint is diminished.

390. Observation 1. The foregoing theorem corresponds to Gauss's Principle of Least Constraint. In order to present clearly its connection with this principle we should have to use the same mode of expression as in § 350.

391. Observation 2. Gauss's Principle and the Law of Inertia (§ 383) may together replace completely the fundamental principle, and that for all systems.

For they together are equivalent to the proposition § 344.

392. Proposition 2. The direction of the constraint in the natural motion of a free system is constantly perpendicular to every possible or virtual (§ 111) displacement of the system from its instantaneous position.

For the components of the constraint in a free system along the coordinates p_ρ are by § 387 equal to f_ρ, and may thus be written in the form

$$-\frac{1}{m}\sum_{1}^{k} {}_{\chi}p_{\chi\rho}\mathrm{P}_{\chi}.$$

Thus by § 250 they are perpendicular to every possible displacement of the system.

393. Symbolical Expression. If we denote by δp_ρ the changes of the coordinates p_ρ for any possible or virtual displacement of the system, then the equation

$$\sum_{1}^{r}{}_{\rho} f_\rho \delta p_\rho = 0 \qquad \text{(i)}$$

furnishes a symbolical expression of the foregoing proposition. For the equation replaces the proposition by § 249, and it is symbolical, since it stands as a symbol for an infinite number of equations.

If we use rectangular coordinates and denote by δx_ν the change of x_ν for any possible or virtual displacement, then the equation takes the form

$$\sum_{1}^{3n}{}_\nu m_\nu \ddot{x}_\nu \delta x_\nu = 0 \qquad \text{(ii)}.$$

394. **Observation 1.** The foregoing proposition, § 392, corresponds to d'Alembert's Principle; the equations 393 (i) and (ii) correspond to the usual expression of that principle. In order to establish clearly the relation between that principle and the proposition we should have to use the same mode of expression as in § 350.

395. **Observation 2.** From the condition that the constraint is perpendicular to every virtual displacement of the system we get by § 250 the equations of motion of the free system in the form § 372. Consequently d'Alembert's Principle can by itself replace the fundamental law, and that for all systems. Our fundamental law has over d'Alembert's Principle the advantage of a simpler and clearer meaning.

396. **Corollary 1.** In a free system the acceleration is always perpendicular to any possible displacement of the system from its instantaneous position.

397. **Corollary 2.** In the motion of a free system the acceleration is always perpendicular to the direction of the actual instantaneous motion.

398. **Corollary 3.** In the motion of a free system the component of the acceleration in any direction of a possible motion is always zero.

399. **Corollary 4.** The component of the acceleration of a free system in the direction of any free coordinate is always equal to zero.

400. **Proposition.** A free system moves in such a manner that the components of the acceleration in the direction of any coordinate of absolute position always remain zero, whatever is the internal connection between the points of the system.

For whatever is the connection of the system, every coordinate of its absolute position is a free coordinate (§ 142).

401. **Corollary.** If we choose the coordinates of a free system in all other respects arbitrarily, but so that there are amongst them six coordinates of absolute position (§ 19), we can without knowledge of the connection of the system, or without complete knowledge of it, write down immediately six differential equations of the motion of the system.

402. **Particular Selection of Coordinates.** The following choice of coordinates of absolute position is permissible for every system.

We denote by

$$a_1, a_2, a_3,$$

the arithmetic mean value of those rectangular coordinates of all particles which are respectively parallel to $x_1 x_2 x_3$. The quantities $a_1 a_2 a_3$ we consider as rectangular coordinates of a point of mean position, which we call the centre of gravity of the system. Through the centre of gravity we draw three straight lines parallel to the three coordinate axes. Through these three straight lines and all the particles we draw planes and denote by

$$\omega_1, \omega_2, \omega_3,$$

the arithmetic mean value of the inclinations of all the planes drawn through these straight lines to any one of them. The six quantities a and ω are variable quantities independent of each other, whose change necessarily causes a change in the position of the system, and which are not determined by the configuration alone. We can consequently make these six quantities coordinates of absolute position (§ 21), and we make them coordinates of absolute position so long as we introduce only coordinates of configuration for the remaining coordinates.

If we give a and ω any changes whilst we fix the remaining coordinates, the system moves as a rigid body.

We obtain then from purely geometrical considerations for the changes of the rectangular coordinates, when we allow the index ν to pass from 1 to n (§ 13),

$$\begin{cases} dx_{3\nu} = da_1 + (x_{3\nu-1} - a_2)d\omega_3 - (x_{3\nu-2} - a_3)d\omega_2 \\ dx_{3\nu-1} = da_2 + (x_{3\nu-2} - a_3)d\omega_1 - (x_{3\nu} - a_1)d\omega_3 \\ dx_{3\nu-2} = da_3 + (x_{3\nu} - a_1)d\omega_2 - (x_{3\nu-1} - a_2)d\omega_1 \end{cases} \quad \text{(i)}.$$

From this we can obtain, when we consider the x_ν's as functions of all the coordinates, the values of the partial differential coefficients of the x_ν's with respect to a and ω; thus, for instance,

$$\frac{\partial x_{3\nu}}{\partial a_1} = 1, \quad \frac{\partial x_{3\nu}}{\partial a_2} = 0, \quad \frac{\partial x_{3\nu}}{\partial a_3} = 0 \quad \text{(ii)},$$

$$\frac{\partial x_{3\nu}}{\partial \omega_1} = 0, \quad \frac{\partial x_{3\nu}}{\partial \omega_2} = -(x_{3\nu-2} - a_3), \quad \frac{\partial x_{3\nu}}{\partial \omega_3} = x_{3\nu-1} - a_2 \quad \text{(iii)}.$$

403. Corollary 1. As a consequence of the remark that the accelerations of the system along the coordinates a_1, a_2, a_3 must vanish (§ 400), we get the three equations

$$\sum_{1}^{n} {}_\nu m_\nu \ddot{x}_{3\nu} = 0, \quad \sum_{1}^{n} {}_\nu m_\nu \ddot{x}_{3\nu-1} = 0, \quad \sum_{1}^{n} {}_\nu m_\nu \ddot{x}_{3\nu-2} = 0.$$

For by § 242 and § 275 the acceleration along the coordinate a_1 of the centre of gravity is equal to

$$\sum_{1}^{3n} {}_\nu \frac{\partial x_\nu}{\partial a_1} \cdot \frac{m_\nu}{m} \ddot{x}_\nu,$$

therefore by § 402 (ii) equal to

$$\sum_{1}^{n} {}_\nu \frac{m_\nu}{m} \ddot{x}_{3\nu},$$

and similar expressions hold for the accelerations along a_2 and a_3.

404. Observation. The three equations § 403 can be immediately integrated twice and then express that the centre of gravity of a free system moves uniformly and in a straight line. This is known as the Principle of the Centre of Gravity.

405. Corollary 2. From the fact that the accelerations

of the system along the coordinates ω_1, ω_2, ω_3 must vanish (§ 400), we get the three equations

$$\sum_{1}^{n} \nu\, m_\nu(x_{3\nu-2}\ddot{x}_{3\nu-1} - x_{3\nu-1}\ddot{x}_{3\nu-2}) = 0$$

$$\sum_{1}^{n} \nu\, m_\nu(x_{3\nu}\ \ddot{x}_{3\nu-2} - x_{3\nu-2}\ddot{x}_{3\nu}\ ) = 0$$

$$\sum_{1}^{n} \nu\, m_\nu(x_{3\nu-1}\ddot{x}_{3\nu}\ \ - x_{3\nu}\ \ddot{x}_{3\nu-1}) = 0.$$

For by § 242 and § 275 the acceleration along ω_1 is equal to

$$\sum_{1}^{3n} \nu \frac{\partial x_\nu}{\partial \omega_1} \cdot \frac{m_\nu \ddot{x}_\nu}{m},$$

thus by § 402 (iii) equal to

$$\sum_{1}^{n} \nu \frac{m_\nu}{m} \Big\{ (x_{3\nu-2} - a_3)\ddot{x}_{3\nu-1} - (x_{3\nu-1} - a_2)\ddot{x}_{3\nu-2} \Big\},$$

then by using § 403 equal to

$$\sum_{1}^{n} \nu (x_{3\nu-2}\ddot{x}_{3\nu-1} - x_{3\nu-1}x_{3\nu-2}) ;$$

and corresponding values hold for the accelerations along ω_2 and ω_3.

406. **Observation.** These three equations contain the so-called Principle of Areas. These equations can be immediately integrated once, and then give the differential equations of the first order

$$\sum_{1}^{n} \nu\, m_\nu(x_{3\nu-2}\dot{x}_{3\nu-1} - x_{3\nu-1}\dot{x}_{3\nu-2}) = \text{const},$$

$$\sum_{1}^{n} \nu\, m_\nu(x_{3\nu}\ \dot{x}_{3\nu-2} - x_{3\nu-2}\dot{x}_{3\nu}\ ) = \text{const},$$

$$\sum_{1}^{n} \nu\, m_\nu(x_{3\nu-1}\dot{x}_{3\nu}\ \ - x_{3\nu}\ \dot{x}_{3\nu-1}) = \text{const}.$$

These admit of the following geometrical interpretation which suggests the name:—

Draw to each particle of the system from the origin a radius vector; then the sum of the projections of the areas described by these radii on each of the three coordinate planes increases uniformly with the time.

407. **Observation 1 (on §§ 402-406).** We have introduced the Principles of the Centre of Gravity and of Areas as particular cases of the general proposition § 400. We should not have been right in this, if we regarded, as is sometimes done, the essential features of these principles as lying in the fact that they furnish integrals of the equations of motion. One reason why this view seems to us inadmissible, is that the result derived from the Principle of Areas can only be called an integral in a figurative sense. We rather consider the essential features of the principles as lying in the fact that they furnish properties which are of general validity and can be stated quite independently of the particular connection of the system.

408. **Observation 2 (on §§ 402-406).** In deducing the Principles of the Centre of Gravity and of Areas as special cases of § 400 we have not made use of all the properties which the definitions assigned to a and ω. In fact, we might have been able to deduce these principles by using other coordinates, for instance, all coordinates which are in the same direction as a and ω without being identical with them. Of course, with any choice of coordinates, we should not obtain in every case six equations which would furnish a new physical meaning, or which would be quite independent of the equations § 403 and § 405; but they would always be those equations which result from the equations § 403 and § 405 by transformation to the chosen coordinates. But the proposition § 400 gives for all these different forms a common expression and physical meaning.

Holonomous Systems

409. **Note.** If the straightest distance (§ 217) is known for a holonomous system, then the equations of the straightest paths can be expressed in a finite form (§ 225). These paths, moreover, are the natural paths of the system, so long as it is

free; and all motions by which they could be traversed with a constant velocity, are natural motions of the system. The equations of motion of a free holonomous system can thus be expressed in a finite form.

410. **Problem.** To express the equations of motion of a free holonomous system by means of its straightest distance.

As before, let S be the straightest distance of the system, considered as a function of the free coordinates $p_{\rho 0}$ and $p_{\rho 1}$ of its initial and final positions. Let t_0 be the time at which the system passes through the initial position, and t_1 the time at which it passes through the final position. Then $t_1 - t_0$ is the duration of the motion, and thus

$$v = \frac{S}{t_1 - t_0} \qquad (i)$$

gives the constant velocity of the system in its path; its energy is given by

$$E = \tfrac{1}{2} m \frac{S^2}{(t_1 - t_0)^2} \qquad (ii),$$

and its momenta $q_{\rho 0}$ and $q_{\rho 1}$ at the times t_0 and t_1 by

$$\left. \begin{aligned} q_{\rho 0} &= m \frac{S}{t_1 - t_0} \sqrt{a_{\rho \rho 0}} \cos \widehat{sp_{\rho 0}} \\ q_{\rho 1} &= m \frac{S}{t_1 - t_0} \sqrt{a_{\rho \rho 1}} \cos \widehat{sp_{\rho 1}} \end{aligned} \right\} \qquad (iii).$$

For the equations of the straightest paths we find two forms in the equations § 224 (i) and § 226 (i). If we multiply these by $m/S(t_1 - t_0)$, or, what is the same thing (ii), by $\sqrt{2mE}$, we obtain the four following sets of r equations—

$$q_{\rho 1} = \tfrac{1}{2} \frac{m}{t_1 - t_0} \frac{\partial S^2}{\partial p_{\rho 1}} \qquad (iv)$$

$$q_{\rho 0} = - \tfrac{1}{2} \frac{m}{t_1 - t_0} \frac{\partial S^2}{\partial p_{\rho 0}} \qquad (v)$$

$$q_{\rho 1} = \sqrt{2mE} \frac{\partial S}{\partial p_{\rho 1}} \qquad (vi)$$

$$q_{\rho 0} = - \sqrt{2mE} \frac{\partial S}{\partial p_{\rho 0}} \qquad (vii).$$

Thus our problem is solved in a variety of ways.

For if we consider t_1 as the variable time, and consequently $p_{\rho 1}$ as the coordinates of the position changing with this time, the r equations (v) determine these r coordinates as finite functions of t_1, and the equations (vii) give us the same result if we associate with them the relation between E and t_1, i.e. the equation (ii). The $2r$ quantities $p_{\rho 0}$ and $q_{\rho 0}$ behave here as $2r$ arbitrary constants. From similar considerations the equations (iv), or (vi) and (ii), give us the equations of motion of the system; these are now in the form of differential equations of the first order, in which the r quantities $p_{\rho 0}$ behave as r arbitrary constants.

Or, if we consider, as is equally permissible, the time t_0 as the variable time, and thus the position 0 as the variable position, the equations (iv), or (vi) and (ii), give us the equations of motion in a finite form, with the time t_0 as independent, the quantities $p_{\rho 0}$ as dependent variables, and the quantities $p_{\rho 1}$ and $q_{\rho 1}$ as $2r$ arbitrary constants. Thus, again, the equations (v), or (vii) and (ii), give the equations of motion in the form of differential equations of the first order, in which $p_{\rho 1}$ behave as r arbitrary constants.

411. Corollary 1. If we put

$$\sqrt{2\mathrm{E}m} \cdot S = V \qquad (i),$$

and consider V as a function of $p_{\rho 0}$, $p_{\rho 1}$ and E, then the natural motions of the system can be expressed in the form

$$q_{\rho 1} = \frac{\partial V}{\partial p_{\rho 1}} \qquad (ii)$$

$$q_{\rho 0} = -\frac{\partial V}{\partial p_{\rho 0}} \qquad (iii)$$

$$t_1 - t_0 = \frac{\partial V}{\partial \mathrm{E}} \qquad (iv).$$

For the equations (ii) and (iii) coincide with the equations § 410 (vi) and (vii), and the equation (iv) follows from the equation (i) and § 410 (ii).

412. Observation. The function V here introduced is Hamilton's Characteristic Function of the System; Hamilton denotes it by the same symbol. Such a function, therefore, only exists for holonomous systems. Its mechanical meaning is this. Suppose that the system moves with given energy from a given initial to a given final position: then the characteristic function gives twice the value of that time-integral of the energy which results, considered as a function of that energy and of the coordinates of the initial and final positions.

For by equations 411 (i) and 410 (ii)

$$V = 2E(t_1 - t_0)$$

in value, but in form only when, on the right-hand side, we regard the duration of the motion $t_1 - t_0$ expressed as a function of E, $p_{\rho 1}$ and $p_{\rho 0}$.

413. **Proposition.** The characteristic function V of a free holonomous system satisfies the following two partial differential equations of the first order—

$$\frac{1}{2m}\sum_{1}^{r}{}_\rho \sum_{1}^{r}{}_\sigma b_{\rho\sigma 1}\frac{\partial V}{\partial p_{\rho 1}}\frac{\partial V}{\partial p_{\sigma 1}} = E$$

$$\frac{1}{2m}\sum_{1}^{r}{}_\rho \sum_{1}^{r}{}_\sigma b_{\rho\sigma 0}\frac{\partial V}{\partial p_{\rho 0}}\frac{\partial V}{\partial p_{\sigma 0}} = E.$$

For they are obtained by multiplying the equations § 227 for the straightest distance by $2mE$, and using equation § 411 (i).

414. **Corollary 2.** If we put

$$\frac{mS^2}{2(t_1 - t_0)} = P \qquad (i),$$

and regard P as a function of $p_{\rho 0}$, $p_{\rho 1}$, t_0 and t_1, the equations

$$q_{\rho 1} = \frac{\partial P}{\partial p_{\rho 1}} \qquad (ii)$$

$$q_{\rho 0} = -\frac{\partial P}{\partial P_{\rho 0}} \qquad (iii)$$

represent the natural motions of the system. The energy E of the system can be immediately obtained from P by means of the equations

$$\mathrm{E} = -\frac{\partial \mathrm{P}}{\partial t_1} = \frac{\partial \mathrm{P}}{\partial t_0} \qquad \text{(iv)}.$$

For the equations (ii) and (iii) coincide with the equations § 410 (iv) and (v), and the equations (iv) follow from (i) and § 410 (ii).

415. Observation. The function P, here introduced, is Hamilton's Principal Function of the System; it is called by Hamilton S. Such a function exists only for holonomous systems. Its mechanical meaning is this. Suppose that the system moves in a given time from a given initial to a given final position: then the Principal Function gives that value of the time-integral of the energy which results, considered as a function of that time and of the initial and final values of the coordinates.

For by equations § 414 (i) and 410 (ii)

$$\mathrm{P} = \mathrm{E}(t_1 - t_0)$$

as regards its value, but as regards it form only when we regard E, on the right-hand side, as a function of $p_{\rho 1}$, $p_{\rho 0}$, t_1 and t_0.

416. Proposition. The principal function of a holonomous system satisfies the two following partial differential equations of the first order—

$$\frac{1}{2m}\sum_{\rho}^{r}\sum_{\sigma}^{r} b_{\rho\sigma 1}\frac{\partial \mathrm{P}}{\partial p_{\rho 1}}\frac{\partial \mathrm{P}}{\partial p_{\sigma 1}} = -\frac{\partial \mathrm{P}}{\partial t_1}$$

$$\frac{1}{2m}\sum_{\rho}^{r}\sum_{\sigma}^{r} b_{\rho\sigma 0}\frac{\partial \mathrm{P}}{\partial p_{\rho 0}}\frac{\partial \mathrm{P}}{\partial p_{\sigma 0}} = \frac{\partial \mathrm{P}}{\partial t_0}.$$

For these are obtained when the equations § 227 are multiplied by (§ 410 (ii))

$$\frac{m\mathrm{S}^2}{2(t_1 - t_0)^2} = \mathrm{E}$$

and the relations § 414 (i) and (iv) made use of.

417. Observation on §§ 411-416. Starting from the differential equations § 227, we were able to consider in §§ 232-236 functions which were related to the straightest distance and capable of replacing it in all respects analytically, but without having the same simple geometrical meaning. In just the same way, starting from the differential equations §§ 413, 416, we can arrive at functions which are related to the characteristic and principal functions and analytically serve the same purpose, or even offer advantages over these; but their physical significance, on account of the mathematical complications, becomes more and more obscure. Such functions would be suitably denoted as Jacobi's Principal Functions and Characteristic Functions.

It appears, moreover, that even in the characteristic and principal functions it is only the simple idea of the straightest distance which appears, and this, too, somewhat indistinctly; so that the introduction of these two functions together and in addition to the straightest distance would have but little significance if all the systems to be considered were always, as here, completely known and free.

Dynamical Models

418. Definition. A material system is said to be a dynamical model of a second system when the connections of the first can be expressed by such coordinates as to satisfy the following conditions:—

(1) That the number of coordinates of the first system is equal to the number of the second.

(2) That with a suitable arrangement of the coordinates for both systems the same equations of condition exist.

(3) That by this arrangement of the coordinates the expression for the magnitude of a displacement agrees in both systems.

Any two of the coordinates so related to one another in the two systems are called corresponding coordinates. Corresponding positions, displacements, etc., are those positions, displacements, etc., in the two systems which involve similar values of the corresponding coordinates and their changes.

419. Corollary 1. If one system is a model of a second, then, conversely, the second is also a model of the first. If two systems are models of a third system, then each of these systems is also a model of the other. The model of the model of a system is also a model of the original system.

All systems which are models of one another are said to be dynamically similar.

420. **Corollary 2.** The property which one system possesses of being a model of another, is independent of the choice of the coordinates of one or the other system, although it is only clearly exhibited by a particular choice of coordinates.

421. **Corollary 3.** A system is not completely determined by the fact that it is a model of a given system. An infinite number of systems, quite different physically, can be models of one and the same system. Any given system is a model of an infinite number of totally different systems.

For the coordinates of the masses of the two systems which are models of one another can be quite different in number and can be totally different functions of the corresponding coordinates.

422. **Corollary 4.** The models of holonomous systems are themselves holonomous. The models of non-holonomous systems are themselves non-holonomous.

423. **Observation.** In order that a holonomous system may be a model of another, it is sufficient that both should have such free coordinates that the expression for the magnitude of the displacements of both systems should be the same.

424. **Proposition.** If two systems, each of which is a model of the other, have corresponding conditions at a definite time, then they have corresponding conditions at all times.

For by the equations of condition of a system, the expression for the magnitude of the displacement (§ 164) and the initial values of the coordinates and their change (§ 332), the course of these coordinates is determined for all times,— this being true whatever function of these coordinates the position of the masses of the system is.

425. **Corollary 1.** In order to determine beforehand the course of the natural motion of a material system, it is sufficient to have a model of that system. The model may be much simpler than the system whose motion it represents.

426. **Corollary 2.** If the same quantities are corresponding coordinates of a number of material systems which are models of one another, and if these corresponding coordinates alone are accessible to observation, then, so far as this limited observation is concerned, all these systems are not different from one another; they appear as like systems, however different in reality they may be in the number and the connection of their material points.

Thus it is impossible, from observation alone of the natural motions of a free system, *i.e.* without direct determination of its masses (§ 300), to obtain any wider knowledge of the connection of the system than that one could specify a model of the system.

427. **Observation 1.** If we admit generally and without limitation that hypothetical masses (§ 301) can exist in nature in addition to those which can be directly determined by the balance, then it is impossible to carry our knowledge of the connections of natural systems further than is involved in specifying models of the actual systems. We can then, in fact, have no knowledge as to whether the systems which we consider in mechanics agree in any other respect with the actual systems of nature which we intend to consider, than in this alone,—that the one set of systems are models of the other.

428. **Observation 2.** The relation of a dynamical model to the system of which it is regarded as the model, is precisely the same as the relation of the images which our mind forms of things to the things themselves. For if we regard the condition of the model as the representation of the condition of the system, then the consequents of this representation, which according to the laws of this representation must appear, are also the representation of the consequents which must proceed from the original object according to the laws of this original object. The agreement between mind and nature may therefore be likened to the agreement between two systems which are models of one another, and we can even account for this agreement by assuming that the mind is capable of making actual dynamical models of things, and of working with them.

CHAPTER IV

MOTION OF UNFREE SYSTEMS

429. Prefatory Note 1. Every unfree system we conceive to be à portion of a more extended free system; from our point of view there are no unfree systems for which this assumption does not obtain. If, however, we wish to emphasise this relation, we shall denote the unfree system as a partial system, and the free system of which it forms a part, as the complete system.

430. Prefatory Note 2. When a part of a free system is considered an unfree system it is assumed that the rest of the system is more or less unknown, so that an immediate application of the fundamental law is impossible. This deficiency of knowledge must in some way be met by special data. Such data can be given in various ways. As it is not our purpose to take every possible form for these data, we shall only consider two forms which, in previous developments of mechanics, have obtained special significance.

In the first form the motion of the unfree system is denoted as guided; whilst in the second we say that the motion is affected by forces.

I. Guided Unfree System

431. Definition. A guided motion of an unfree system is any motion which the system performs while the other masses of the complete system perform a determinate and prescribed motion. A system whose motion is guided is called a guided system.

432. Additional Note 1. A possible motion of a guided system is such a motion as is not inconsistent with the connection of the complete system and the prescribed motion of the other masses.

433. Additional Note 2. A natural motion of a guided system is such a motion as forms, with the prescribed motion of the remaining masses, a natural motion of the complete system.

434. Problem. To represent analytically the possible motions of a guided system.

Let the r quantities p_ρ be the general coordinates of the partial system considered, and the $\mathfrak{r}$ quantities $\mathfrak{p}_\rho$ be any coordinates whatever of the remaining masses of the complete system. The $r+\mathfrak{r}$ quantities p_ρ and $\mathfrak{p}_\rho$ are then general coordinates of the complete system, and its connections are expressible by a series of equations, say h in number, of the form

$$\sum_1^r {}_\rho p_{\chi\rho}\dot{p}_\rho + \sum_1^{\mathfrak{r}} {}_\rho \mathfrak{p}_{\chi\rho}\dot{\mathfrak{p}}_\rho = 0 \qquad \text{(i)},$$

where $p_{\chi\rho}$ and also $\mathfrak{p}_{\chi\rho}$ may be functions both of p_ρ and $\mathfrak{p}_\rho$. If now the motion of the masses whose coordinates are $\mathfrak{p}_\rho$ are determined, then the $\mathfrak{p}_\rho$'s are given functions of the time. The equations (i) are in part identically satisfied by these functions; in part they take, on substitution of these, the form of the r equations

$$\sum_1^r {}_\rho p_{\chi\rho}\dot{p}_\rho + p_{\chi t} = 0 \qquad \text{(ii)},$$

or

$$\sum_1^r {}_\rho p_{\chi\rho} dp_\rho + p_{\chi t} dt = 0 \qquad \text{(iii)},$$

which are called the equations of condition of the guided system, and in which $p_{\chi\rho}$ and $p_{\chi t}$ are now functions of p_ρ and the time t alone. All possible motions of the guided system satisfy these equations, and all motions which satisfy them are possible motions.

435. **Observation 1.** If the guided system is holonomous, then the differential equations (ii) and (iii) for it can be replaced by the same number of finite equations between the r coordinates of the system and the time t. The possible positions of a guided holonomous system can be expressed by coordinates which are subject to no other conditions than this, that a number of them are given functions of the time.

436. **Observation 2.** Thus the equations of condition of a guided system contain in general the time, and therefore the guided system, considered in itself, would be inconsistent with the requirements of normality (§ 119). Conversely, we now consider every system whose equations of condition in the ordinary language of mechanics contain the time explicitly, and which in our mode of expression is apparently abnormal, as a guided system, *i.e.* as a system which with other unknown masses satisfies the conditions of normality. If this assumption is permissible, then by it the problem is reduced to a determinate mechanical problem (§ 325). But if, owing to any particular form of the equations of condition, this assumption is not permissible, then these equations of condition already involve a contradiction to the fundamental law or its assumptions, and no questions asked concerning the system would be mechanical problems (§ 326).

437. **Observation 3.** The fundamental law is not directly applicable to a guided system. For the idea of straightest paths is only defined for normal connections (§ 120); and the internal connections of the guided system are abnormal. Some other characteristics must therefore be sought by which the natural motions of a guided system may be distinguished from the greater manifold of possible motions.

438. **Proposition 1.** A guided system, just like a free system, moves in such a manner that the magnitude of its acceleration is always smaller for the actual motion than for any other motion which satisfies the equations of condition and which, at the moment under consideration, coincides in position and velocity with the actual motion.

For the square of the magnitude of the acceleration of the complete system is equal to the sum of the corresponding quantities for the partial system and the remaining system, these quantities being multiplied by the masses of their systems and divided by the mass of the complete system. This sum, by § 344, is to be a minimum; the second member of the summation is supposed to be already determined and such a function of the time as allows the sum to be a minimum (§ 436); this minimum is then only obtained when the first member is made a minimum.

439. **Proposition 2.** A guided holonomous system, just like a free one, moves in such a manner that the time-integral of the energy in a motion between sufficiently near positions is smaller for the actual motion than for any other motion which satisfies the equations of condition, and which carries the system in the same time from the given initial to the final position.

For the time-integral of the energy for the complete system is equal to the sum of the corresponding quantities for the partial system and the remaining system. This sum is, by § 358, to be a minimum; the second member of the summation is supposed to be already determined and to be such as admits of a minimum sum; this minimum is then only obtained when the first member is made a minimum.

440. **Observation 1.** The two preceding propositions contain the adaptation of articles 344 and 358 to the special assumptions of this chapter. In the ordinary language of mechanics their contents could be put into the following form:—The Law of Least Acceleration and Hamilton's Principle still hold even where the equations of condition of a system contain the time explicitly.

441. **Observation 2.** The laws of energy, of the shortest path, and of the least time (§§ 340, 347, 352) can not be directly adapted in a similar manner to the assumptions of a guided system. In the ordinary language of mechanics this statement can be put in the following form:—The Principles of Energy and Least Action lose their validity when the equations of condition contain the time explicitly.

442. **Problem.** To obtain the differential equations of motion of a guided system.

Let, as before, m be the mass, p_ρ the coordinates, and f_ρ the accelerations along p_ρ for the guided system. Further, let $\mathfrak{m}$ be the mass and $\mathfrak{p}_\rho$ any coordinates of the remaining material points of the complete system. Thus p_ρ and $\mathfrak{p}_\rho$ may be taken as coordinates of the complete system. The components of the acceleration along these coordinates may be denoted for the complete system by f'_ρ and $\mathfrak{f}'_\rho$. Then the motion of the complete system is singly determined by its h equations of condition of the form § 434 (i), and by $r+\mathfrak{r}$ equation of motion of the form (§ 372)

$$(m+\mathfrak{m})f'_\rho + \sum_1^h \chi p_{\chi\rho} P_\chi = 0 \qquad (i)$$

$$(m+\mathfrak{m})\mathfrak{f}'_\rho + \sum_1^h \chi \mathfrak{p}_{\chi\rho} P_\chi = 0 \qquad (ii).$$

Now by hypothesis we have to regard the quantities $\mathfrak{p}_\rho$ as such determined functions of the time as identically satisfy the equations (ii), and through whose substitution the h equations of condition of the complete system are transformed into the k equations of condition (§ 434 (ii)) of the constrained system. Further, by § 255 we have

$$(m+\mathfrak{m})f'_\rho = mf_\rho \qquad (iii).$$

Thus we obtain as equations to be considered the r equations of motion

$$mf_\rho + \sum_1^k \chi p_{\chi\rho} P_\chi = 0 \qquad (iv),$$

and the k equations of condition

$$\sum_1^r \rho p_{\chi\rho} \dot{p}_\rho + p_{\chi t} = 0 \qquad (v).$$

These $(r+k)$ equations do not now contain any reference to the unknown masses of the complete system; and as they are sufficient for the unique determination of the $r+k$ quantities $\ddot{p}_\rho$ and P_χ, they contain the solution of the stated problem.

443. Corollary 1. The differential equations of motion of a guided system have the same form as those of a free system.

In the ordinary language of mechanics we may say that

the validity of this form does not depend on whether the equations of condition contain the time or not. The equations of motion of a guided system will therefore admit of exactly the same transformations as those of a free system (368 *et seq.*); but of course those forms which assume that all the coordinates are free will lose their applicability.

444. **Corollary 2.** A natural motion of a guided system is singly determined by a knowledge of the position and velocity of the system at any given time (*cf.* § 331).

445. **Note.** In a guided, as in a free system, the constraint is equal to the acceleration of the system.

For if all the equations of condition of a guided system are removed, then the material points of the system will be free points and the acceleration of the natural motion of the system will be zero (§ 385).

446. **Proposition 1.** The magnitude of the constraint at any instant in a guided system, as in a free one, is smaller for the natural motion than for any other possible motion which, at the moment considered, coincides with it in position and velocity.

The proof follows from §§ 445 and 448.

447. **Proposition 2.** In the natural motion of a guided system, as in that of a free system, the direction of the constraint is always perpendicular to every possible or virtual displacement of the system from its instantaneous position.

This follows from §§ 445 and 442 as in § 392.

448. **Observation.** The two foregoing propositions contain the adaptation of propositions 388 and 392 to the particular case of guided systems. In the usual language of mechanics they might be expressed in the following form:—Gauss's Principle of Least Constraint and d'Alembert's Principle retain their validity even when the equations of condition contain the time explicitly.

449. **Note.** When the coordinates $\mathfrak{p}_\rho$ of the complete system which appear together with p_ρ in the equations § 434 (i) are not functions of the time, but are constant, then the equations of condition of the guided system take the form

$$\sum_{1}^{r}{}_{\rho} p_{\chi\rho}\dot{p}_{\rho} = 0,$$

where the $p_{\chi\rho}$'s do not contain the time. The guided system appears in this case as a normal one, but it does not necessarily cease to be an unfree system. For $p_{\chi\rho}$ may be functions of the absolute position, whilst in the equations of condition of a free system they are independent of the absolute position.

In such guided, but nevertheless normal systems, the idea of the straightest path retains its applicability. It also follows that the fundamental law is immediately applicable to such systems; and all the propositions which have been proved for the motion of a free system also hold good for such systems, excepting only those which refer to absolute position, *i.e.* excepting only proposition 400 and its corollaries.

II. Systems acted on by-Forces

450. **Definition.** Two material systems are said to be directly coupled (*gekoppelt*) when one or more coordinates of the one are always equal to one or more coordinates of the other. Two systems will be simply said to be coupled when their coordinates can be so chosen that the systems become directly coupled. Coupled systems which are not directly coupled are said to be indirectly coupled.

451. **Corollary 1.** The coupling of two systems is a relation between them which is independent of our choice, and in particular independent of the choice of coordinates. But whether an existing coupling is direct or indirect does depend on the choice of coordinates, and is thus a question for our arbitrary determination.

452. **Corollary 2.** Every coupling which exists between two systems can be made direct by a proper choice of co-ordinates. When the contrary is not definitely expressed, we shall hereafter assume that this has been done. The coordinates of the coupled systems which are always equal we shall denote as their common coordinates.

453. **Corollary 3.** Each of two coupled systems is

necessarily an unfree system; but both together, or with other systems with which they are coupled, form a free system. When the contrary is not expressly stated it will be assumed in what follows that there is no coupling with more systems, so that the two coupled systems together form a free system.

454. Analytical Representation. Let p_ρ be the coordinates of the one, $\mathfrak{p}_\rho$ of the other system; then a coupling between the two systems is expressed by the fact that for one or more pairs of values of ρ and σ, p_ρ and $\mathfrak{p}_\sigma$ are always equal. We can, however, without restricting the generality, so arrange the indices that congruent coordinates in both systems have the same index. The systems are then coupled when for one or more values of ρ

$$\mathfrak{p}_\rho - p_\rho = 0 \qquad (\mathrm{i})$$

continually. From this equation the equations

$$\dot{\mathfrak{p}}_\rho - \dot{p}_\rho = 0 \qquad (\mathrm{ii})$$

or

$$d\mathfrak{p}_\rho - dp_\rho = 0 \qquad (\mathrm{iii})$$

immediately follow.

455. Definition. By a force we understand the independently conceived effect which one of two coupled systems, as a consequence of the fundamental law, exerts upon the motion of the other.

456. Corollary. To every force there is necessarily always a counterforce (*Gegenkraft*).

For the conception of the effect which the system, referred to in the definition as the second, produces upon the first, is by the definition itself also a force. Force and counterforce are reciprocal in the sense that we are free to consider either of them as the force or the counterforce.

457. Problem. To obtain an expression for the effect which one of two coupled systems produces upon the motion of the other.

Let m be the mass, and the r quantities p_ρ the coordinates of the first system; and let the k equations

$$\sum_1^r {}_\rho p_{\chi\rho} \dot{p}_\rho = 0 \qquad \text{(i)}$$

be its equations of condition. Let $\mathfrak{m}$ be the mass and the $\mathfrak{r}$ quantities $\mathfrak{p}_\rho$ the coordinates of the second system; and let the $\mathfrak{k}$ equations

$$\sum_1^r {}_\rho \mathfrak{p}_{\chi\rho} \dot{\mathfrak{p}}_\rho = 0 \qquad \text{(ii)}$$

be its equations of condition. Between the two there may further be for one or more, say h, values of ρ, equations of coupling of the form

$$\dot{\mathfrak{p}}_\rho - \dot{p}_\rho = 0 \qquad \text{(iii)}.$$

Let us now consider the motion of the first system under the action of the second, and regard it as a guided system. So long as the p_ρ's do not appear in the equations (iii) the accelerations along them are given by the equations (442)

$$m f_\rho + \sum_1^k {}_\chi p_{\chi\rho} P_\chi = 0 \qquad \text{(iv)};$$

but for those p_ρ's which appear in (iii) we must take into consideration these equations as well, and consequently multiply the coefficient of $\dot{p}_\rho$ in them, namely -1, by an undetermined factor which may be called P_ρ, and add the product to the left-hand side; thus, then, for these—

$$m f_\rho + \sum_1^k {}_\chi p_{\chi\rho} P_\chi - P_\rho = 0 \qquad \text{(v)}.$$

The appearance of the h quantities P_ρ in the equations of motion increases the number of unknowns in them by h, and for the determination of these h quantities the number of equations of condition is also increased by the h equations (iii), in which we must regard the $\dot{\mathfrak{p}}_\rho$'s as given explicit functions of the time. But if we assume that the quantities P_ρ are not unknown, but are given immediately as functions of the time, then the h equations (iii) and any knowledge of $\dot{\mathfrak{p}}_\rho$ and of the second system are unnecessary; the $k + r$ equations (i), (iv) and (v) are again sufficient for the unique determination of the $k + r$ unknowns P_χ and $\dot{p}_\rho$. The h factors P_ρ consequently represent completely the effect of the second system on the first, and their aggregate can be regarded as an analytical expression for this effect, as is required by the problem.

458. **Theorem 1.** If we wish to represent in a symmetrical manner the effect of the first system on the second, we must write the equations of coupling in the form

$$\dot{p}_\rho - \dot{\mathfrak{p}}_\rho = 0 \qquad \text{(i)},$$

and for the $\mathfrak{p}_\rho$'s which do not appear in (i) we have the following equations of motion

$$\mathfrak{m}\mathfrak{f}_\rho + \sum_1^k {}_\chi \mathfrak{p}_{\chi\rho} \mathfrak{P}_\chi = 0 \qquad \text{(ii)},$$

while for the remaining $\mathfrak{p}_\rho$'s they take the form

$$\mathfrak{m}\mathfrak{f}_\rho + \sum_1^k {}_\chi \mathfrak{p}_{\chi\rho} \mathfrak{P}_\chi - \mathfrak{P}_\rho = 0 \qquad \text{(iii)};$$

where by the $\mathfrak{P}_\rho$'s are understood the undetermined multipliers of equations (i). The aggregate of the $\mathfrak{P}_\rho$'s gives us an expression for the effect which the first at any instant has on the motion of the second.

459. **Theorem 2.** Thus we can write all equations of motion of the first system in the form

$$mf_\rho + \sum_1^k {}_\chi p_{\chi\rho} \mathrm{P}_\chi - \mathrm{P}_\rho = 0 \qquad \text{(i)},$$

and of the second in the form

$$\mathfrak{m}\mathfrak{f}_\rho + \sum_1^k {}_\chi \mathfrak{p}_{\chi\rho} \mathfrak{P}_\chi - \mathfrak{P}_\rho = 0 \qquad \text{(ii)},$$

when we decide (which is permissible, although arbitrary) that for all coordinates which are not coupled the quantities P_ρ and $\mathfrak{P}_\rho$ are to be zero. It is true that P_ρ and $\mathfrak{P}_\rho$ thereby lose their significance as a system of multipliers of the equations 457 (iii) and 458 (i); but they retain their significance as an expression for the effect which the one system has on the other.

460. **Analytical Representation of Force.** In accordance with the definition § 455 we may and shall decide that the aggregate of the quantities P_ρ, singly determined for all values of p_ρ by § 459, forms the analytical expression for the force

which the system $\mathfrak{p}_\rho$ exerts on the system p_ρ. In a similar manner the aggregate of the quantities $\mathfrak{P}_\rho$ forms the analytical expression for the force which the system p_ρ exerts on the system $\mathfrak{p}_\rho$. The individual quantities P_ρ or $\mathfrak{P}_\rho$ are called the components of the force along the corresponding coordinates p_ρ or $\mathfrak{p}_\rho$, or, for short, the forces along these coordinates.

By this determination we place ourselves in agreement with the existing notation of mechanics; and the necessity for securing such an agreement sufficiently justifies us in choosing this particular determination out of several permissible ones.

461. **Corollary 1.** The force which a system exerts on a second may be considered a vector quantity with regard to the second system: *i.e.* as a vector quantity whose components along the common coordinates are in general different from zero; whose components along the coordinates which are not common vanish; but whose components in such directions as cannot be expressed by changes of the coordinates used remain undetermined.

462. **Corollary 2.** The force which one system exerts on another may also be considered as a vector quantity with regard to the first system: *i.e.* as a vector quantity whose components along the common coordinates are in general different from zero; whose components along the coordinates which are not common vanish; but whose components in such directions as cannot be expressed by means of changes in the coordinates used remain undetermined.

463. **Observation.** Considered as vector quantities with regard to a system, every force contains components which depend on the choice of coordinates, *i.e.* on arbitrary convention. This arises from the fact that on the choice of coordinates depends the manifold of those motions of a system which we take into consideration; and in the direction of which we may therefore admit a possible effect.

464. **Note 1.** If a system is coupled successively with several other systems, and the same force is thereby exerted upon it by these systems, then its motion is the same, however much these ~~other~~ systems may differ amongst themselves.

We therefore speak (in accordance with definition § 455)

of the motion of a system under the influence or action of a force simply, without mentioning the other system to which it is due, and without which it could not be conceived.

465. **Note 2.** If a system is coupled successively with several other systems, and the same motion results, then it may exert upon each of these other systems the same force, even though these systems may be entirely different from each other.

We therefore speak (in accordance with definition § 455) of the force which a moving system exerts simply, without mentioning the other system upon which this force is exerted, and without which it could not be conceived.

466. **Note 3.** Since all forces which are simply spoken of as such can be no other than those which are exerted by material systems on material systems in accordance with the fundamental law, all forces must as a matter of course have certain properties common. The sources of all such common properties are the properties of material systems and the fundamental law.

Action and Reaction

467. **Notation.** (1) The components of the force which the $\mathfrak{p}_\rho$ system exerts on the p_ρ one, considered as vector quantities with regard to the p_ρ system, have already been denoted in § 460 by P_ρ. If we regard this same force as a vector quantity with regard to the system $\mathfrak{p}_\rho$, then its components along $\mathfrak{p}_\rho$ will be denoted by $\mathfrak{P}_\rho'$. Thus for all common coordinates

$$P_\rho = \mathfrak{P}_\rho'$$

identically.

(2) The components of the force which the p_ρ system exerts on the $\mathfrak{p}_\rho$ system, considered as vector quantities with regard to the $\mathfrak{p}_\rho$ system, have already been denoted in § 460 by $\mathfrak{P}_\rho$. If we regard this same force as a vector quantity with regard to the p_ρ system, then its components along p_ρ will be denoted by P_ρ'. Thus for all coordinates

$$\mathfrak{P}_\rho = P_\rho'$$

identically.

The forces exerted on a system are thus denoted by un-accented letters, whilst the forces exerted by a system are denoted by accented letters, as long as we regard them as vector quantities with regard to the system itself.

468. **Proposition.** Force and counterforce are always equal and opposite. By this is meant that their components, along each of the coordinates used, are equal and opposite; and this is equally true whether we regard force and counterforce as vector quantities with regard to the one or the other system.

For we may regard the two coupled systems (§ 457) as a single free system. Its mass is $m + \mathfrak{m}$, and its coordinates are p_ρ and $\mathfrak{p}_\rho$. Its equations of condition are the equations 457 (i) and (ii) and the equations of coupling as in 457 (iii). If in addition we denote the multipliers of the equations (i) by P_χ°, those of equation (ii) by $\mathfrak{P}_\chi^\circ$, and those of the equation (iii) by P_ρ°, then the equations of motion of the total system take the form

$$mf_\rho + \sum_1^k {}^\chi p_{\chi\rho} P_\chi^\circ - P_\rho^\circ = 0 \qquad (i)$$

$$\mathfrak{m}\mathfrak{f}_\rho + \sum_1^k {}^\chi \mathfrak{p}_{\chi\rho} \mathfrak{P}_\chi^\circ + P_\rho^\circ = 0 \qquad (ii),$$

where, for the coordinates that do not appear in the equations of coupling, the P_ρ°'s are to be put zero.

But the motion represented by these equations is that which before was considered as the motion of the separate systems. We consequently obtain a possible solution for the above equations when we substitute for f_ρ and $\mathfrak{f}_\rho$ their former values, and make

$$P_\chi^\circ = P_\chi, \quad \mathfrak{P}_\chi^\circ = \mathfrak{P}_\chi \qquad (iii),$$

and in (i)

$$P_\rho^\circ = P_r \qquad (iv),$$

and in (ii)

$$P_\rho^\circ = -\mathfrak{P}_\rho \qquad (v).$$

Moreover, since the undetermined multipliers are singly determined by the equations (i) and (ii), this possible solution is at the same time the only possible solution. Therefore the equations (iv) and (v) necessarily hold; thus from them

$$P_\rho = -\mathfrak{P}_\rho,$$

or, using the notation of § 467,

$$P_\rho = -P_\rho'$$
$$\mathfrak{P}_\rho = -\mathfrak{P}_\rho',$$

which proves the proposition.

469. **Observation 1.** The foregoing proposition corresponds to Newton's Third Law, and is also known as the Principle of Reaction. Nevertheless its content is not quite identical with that of Newton's Third Law. Their true relation is as follows:—

Newton's Law, as he intended it to be understood, contains our proposition completely; this is shown by the examples appended to his statement of the law.

But Newton's Law contains more. At least it is usually applied to actions-at-a-distance, *i.e.* to forces between bodies which have no common coordinates. But our mechanics does not recognise such actions. Thus in order to be able to adduce as a consequence of our proposition the fact that a planet attracts the sun with the same force that the sun attracts the planet, it is necessary that further data should be given as to the nature of the connection between the two bodies.

470. **Observation 2.** It is open to doubt, whether the extension of the application of the principle of reaction beyond what is contained in proposition 468 as to its form and content, can rightly be used as a fundamental principle of mechanics; or whether rather the actual and universally valid content of that principle has not been completely included in proposition 468.

As far as the form is concerned, it is manifest that the statement of the law is not quite clearly determined when applied to actions-at-a-distance. For when force and counter-force affect different bodies, it is not quite clear what is meant by opposite. For example, this is seen in the case of the mutual action between current-elements.

As far as the content is concerned, the application of the principle of reaction to actions-at-a-distance commonly found in mechanics manifestly represents an experiential fact, concerning the correctness of which in all cases people are beginning to be doubtful. For instance, in Electromagnetics we are almost convinced that the mutual action between moving magnets is not in all cases strictly subject to the principle.

Composition of Forces

471. Proposition. If a system is simultaneously coupled with several other systems, then the force which the aggregate of these systems exerts on the first is equal to the sum of the forces which the individual systems exert on it.

For let there be a system 1 of mass m and coordinates p_ρ, whose equations of condition are the k equations,

$$\sum_1^r {}_\rho p_{\chi\rho} \dot{p}_\rho = 0 \qquad \text{(i)},$$

and let this be simultaneously coupled with the systems 2, 3, etc., whose coordinates are $\mathfrak{p}_\rho''$, $\mathfrak{p}_\rho'''$, etc.

First consider the systems 2, 3, etc., as separate systems. Then the equations of coupling for every common coordinate p_ρ are to be written in the form

$$\dot{\mathfrak{p}}_\rho'' - \dot{p}_\rho = 0 \qquad \text{(ii)}$$
$$\dot{\mathfrak{p}}_\rho''' - \dot{p}_\rho = 0, \text{ etc.} \qquad \text{(iii)}.$$

If now we treat the system made up of 1, 2, 3, etc., as a free system, and denote the multipliers of the equations (i) by P_χ, those of (ii) by P_ρ'' and of (iii) by P_ρ''', etc., then we obtain the equations of motion of the system 1 in the form

$$mf_\rho + \sum_1^k {}_\chi p_{\chi\rho} P_\chi - P_\rho'' - P_\rho''' - \text{etc.} = 0 \qquad \text{(iv)},$$

where all the quantities P_ρ'', P_ρ''', etc., as well as P_χ are singly-determined quantities. P_ρ'', P_ρ''', etc., represent the components of the forces which the systems 2, 3, etc., respectively exert on the system 1.

Secondly, if we regard the systems 2, 3, etc., as forming one system, then for the quantities $\mathfrak{p}_\rho''$, $\mathfrak{p}_\rho'''$, etc., which by equations (ii), (iii), etc., are equal, one single coordinate $\mathfrak{p}_\rho$ can be used, and in place of those equations of coupling we have now for each common coordinate p_ρ the one equation

$$\dot{\mathfrak{p}}_\rho - \dot{p}_\rho = 0 \qquad (v).$$

If P_ρ is its multiplier, and we denote by P_χ° the multipliers of the equations (i) which correspond to the present system of equations of motion, then these take the form

$$mf_\rho + \sum_1^k \chi p_{\chi\rho} P_\chi^\circ - P_\rho = 0 \qquad (vi).$$

The P_ρ's represent the components of the total force exerted on the system 1.

Now this different mode of conception cannot alter the motion which ensues according to the fundamental law. Therefore a possible solution of the equations (vi) is obtained by using the former solution and putting

$$P_\chi^\circ = P_\chi \qquad (vii)$$
$$P_\rho = P_\rho'' + P_\rho''' + \ldots \qquad (viii).$$

Moreover, since there is only one possible solution, the foregoing is the one, and the equation (viii) which contains our proposition must necessarily hold.

472. **Corollary 1.** Any number of forces exerted on a system, or by a system, can be regarded as a single force, namely, that force which, considered as a vector quantity with regard to the system, is equal to the sum of these forces.

When we represent a number of forces in this way, we say that we compound them. The result of the composition is called the resultant of the individual forces.

473. **Corollary 2.** Any force exerted on a system, or by a system, can be conceived as a sum of any number of forces, namely, of any number of forces the sum of which, regarded as vector quantities with regard to the system, is equal to that original force.

When we represent a force in this way, we say that we resolve it; the forces which result from such a resolution we call the components of the original force.

474. **Observation.** The geometrical components of a force

along the coordinates can at the same time be considered components in the sense of § 473.

475. Definition. A force which is exerted by a single material point, or on a single material point, is called an elementary force.

476. Observation. As a rule, elementary mechanics means by forces only elementary forces. By way of distinction, the more general forms of forces hitherto considered by us are denoted as Lagrangian forces. Similarly we might denote the elementary forces as Galilean or Newtonian forces.

477. Corollary 1. Every elementary force can be represented by the geometrical displacement of a point, and therefore by a straight line given in magnitude and direction.

For each elementary force is a vector quantity with regard to a single point.

478. Corollary 2. The composition of the elementary forces, which act at the same point, is performed according to the method of geometrical composition and resolution of straight lines.

In particular, two forces acting at the same point can be combined into a single force, which is represented in magnitude and direction by the diagonal of a parallelogram whose sides represent these forces in magnitude and direction (Parallelogram of Forces).

479. Corollary 3. Every Lagrangian force can be represented as a sum of elementary forces, and is therefore capable of being resolved into elementary forces.

For every displacement of a system can be conceived as a sum of displacements of its individual points.

480. Corollary 4. The components of a force along the rectangular coordinates of the system on which the force acts, or which exerts the force, can be directly conceived as elementary forces, which act on the individual material points of the system.

Motion under the Action of Forces

481. Problem 1. To determine the motion of a material system under the action of a given force.

The solution follows directly from § 457. Let the P_ρ's be the given components of the force acting along p_ρ, then one uses the r equations

$$mf_\rho + \sum_1^k {}_\chi p_{\chi\rho} P_\chi = P_\rho$$

together with the k equations of condition of the system for the determination of the $r+k$ quantities $\ddot{p}_\rho$ and P_χ, and these equations are sufficient to determine them without ambiguity.

482. **Observation 1.** The equations of motion of a system acted on by forces have in rectangular coordinates the form of the $3n$ equations

$$m_\nu \ddot{x}_\nu + \sum_1^i {}_\iota x_{\iota\nu} X_\iota = X_\nu,$$

where the X_ν's are the components of the force along x_ν, and for the rest the notation of § 368 is used.

483. **Observation 2.** If the coordinate p_ρ is a free coordinate, then the equation of motion corresponding to it takes the simple form

$$mf_\rho = P_\rho,$$

If in a holonomous system all the coordinates p_ρ are free, then all the equations of motion of the system take this form, and these r equations are sufficient to determine the r quantities $\ddot{p}_\rho$.

484. **Corollary.** The natural motion of a material system from a given instant onwards is singly determined by position and velocity of the system at that instant and the knowledge of the forces acting on the system for all times from that instant onwards (*cf.* §§ 331, 444).

485. **Proposition.** The acceleration which a number of forces simultaneously acting produce in a system is equal to the sum of the accelerations which each force acting alone would produce.

For the equations of motion § 481 are linear in f_ρ and P_χ. Thus if the value-systems $f_{\rho 1}$ $P_{\chi 1}$, $f_{\rho 2}$ $P_{\chi 2}$, etc., are the solutions for these equations for the forces $P_{\rho 1}$, $P_{\rho 2}$, etc., then the value-system $f_{\rho1}+f_{\rho2}+\ldots$, $P_{\chi1}+P_{\chi2}\ldots$ is the solution for the force $P_{\rho1}+P_{\rho2}+\ldots$

486. **Observation.** The content of the above proposition can also be rendered by the statement that any number of simultaneously acting forces are independent of one another with regard to the acceleration which they produce. This principle has been known and used since Galileo's time.

487. **Corollary.** The acceleration which the resultant of any number of forces produces in a system is equal to the sum of the accelerations which the components acting alone would produce on the system (§§ 472, 473).

488. **Proposition.** If a force, as a vector quantity, is perpendicular to every possible displacement of a material system, then it has no effect on the motion of the system—and conversely.

For if π is such a force, then its components π_ρ along p_ρ have the form (§ 250)

$$\pi_\rho = \sum_{1}^{k} \chi p_{\chi\rho}\gamma_\chi.$$

If now this force be made to act on the system in addition to the force P, then the equations of motion can be written in the form

$$mf_\rho + \sum_{1}^{k} \chi p_{\chi\rho}\left(P_\chi - \gamma_\chi\right) = P_\rho.$$

In the solution of these equations with regard to $\ddot{p}_\rho$ and P_χ the P_χ's alone are increased by γ_χ; the $\ddot{p}_\rho$'s, which alone determine the motion, remain unaltered.

Conversely—if the addition of the components π_ρ to the right-hand side of the equations § 481 does not alter f_ρ, but only P_χ, then π_ρ can be written in the form

$$\pi_\rho = \sum_{1}^{k} \chi p_{\chi\rho}\gamma_\chi.$$

Thus the force π is perpendicular to every possible displacement of the system (§ 250).

489. **Observation.** The proposition states to what condition that part of a force, considered as a vector quantity, is subjected, which depends upon the choice of coordinates and therefore upon our will (§ 463). For this part must necessarily be such as to have no effect on the actual motion.

490. **Corollary.** Although the motion of a system can be obtained without ambiguity from a knowledge of the forces which act on the system, still the force which acts on a system can not be determined without ambiguity from the motion of the system.

491. **Problem 2.** To determine the force which a material system exerts in a given motion.

In accordance with § 467 we denote by P_ρ' the component of the force required along p_ρ; then by §§ 468 and 481 we get

$$P_\rho' = mf_\rho - \sum_1^k \chi p_{\chi\rho} P_\chi.$$

In these equations the f_ρ's are to be considered as given, and must, moreover, satisfy the equations of condition. The quantities P_χ are likewise determined, when that system is given with which the one considered is coupled. But when only the motion of the p_ρ system is given, the P_χ's remain unknown. The force which a moving system exerts is thus not completely determined by the knowledge of the motion of the system alone, but contains an undetermined summation whose components have the form

$$\pi_\rho = \sum_1^k \chi p_{\chi\rho} \gamma_\chi,$$

and which is therefore perpendicular to every possible displacement of the system.

492. **Observation.** Although all the components of the force exerted by a moving system are not singly determined by the motion of the system, yet the components in the direction of every possible displacement of the system are singly determined by its motion.

493. **Corollary.** The components of the force which a

moving system exerts in the direction of every free coordinate of the system are singly determined by the motion.

For if p_ρ is a free coordinate, then the $p_{\chi\rho}$'s vanish, and with them the undetermined series; thus the component of the force of the system along p_ρ can be written in the forms

$$P_\rho' = -mf_\rho \qquad (\S\ 491) \qquad \text{(i)}$$

$$= \frac{\partial_p E}{\partial p_\rho} - \frac{d}{dt}\left(\frac{\partial_p E}{\partial \dot{p}_\rho}\right) \qquad (\S\ 291)\ \text{(i)}\ \text{(ii)}$$

$$= \frac{\partial_p E}{\partial p_\rho} - \dot{q}_\rho \qquad (\S\ 291)\ \text{(ii)}\ \text{(iii)}$$

$$= -\frac{\partial_q E}{\partial p_\rho} - \dot{q}_\rho \qquad (\S\ 294) \qquad \text{(iv)}.$$

Internal Constraint

494. Proposition. The acceleration of a system of material points between which no connections exist, takes place in the direction of the force which acts on the system, and its magnitude is equal to the magnitude of the force, divided by the mass of the system.

For when no connections exist between the n points of a material system, then for every one of the $3n$ rectangular coordinates of the system (§ 482)

$$\frac{m_\nu}{m}\ddot{x}_\nu = \frac{X_\nu}{m};$$

but the left-hand side of the equation represents the components of the acceleration of the system along x_ν (§ 275).

495. Corollary. The acceleration of a single material point takes place in the direction of the force acting on it, and its magnitude is equal to the magnitude of the force, divided by the mass of the point (Newton's Second Law).

496. Observation. If connections exist between the points of a material system on which a force acts, then the acceleration of the system differs in general from that given by proposition

§ 494. We may thus regard the connections of the system as the cause of this difference, and by § 385 we have to denote this difference as the internal constraint of the system.

497. **Problem.** To determine the internal constraint of a system which moves under the action of forces.

The actual component of the acceleration of the system along the general coordinate p_ρ is f_ρ; the component which would arise if the equations of condition did not exist is (§ 494) P_ρ/m; the difference of the two quantities, or

$$z_\rho = f_\rho - \frac{P_\rho}{m} \qquad \text{(i)}$$

is thus the component of the constraint along p_ρ.

The knowledge of the components themselves along p_ρ is in general insufficient for the determination of the magnitude of the constraint. If, however, we use rectangular coordinates, we obtain for the component along x_ν

$$z_\nu = \frac{1}{m}(m_\nu \ddot{x}_\nu - X_\nu) \qquad \text{(ii)},$$

and consequently for the magnitude z of the constraint the positive root of the equation (§ 244)

$$mz^2 = \sum_1^{3n} {}_\nu \frac{1}{m_\nu}(m_\nu \ddot{x}_\nu - X_\nu)^2$$
$$= \sum_1^{3n} {}_\nu m_\nu \left(\ddot{x}_\nu - \frac{X_\nu}{m_\nu}\right)^2 \qquad \text{(iii)}.$$

498. **Proposition 1.** The magnitude of the constraint of a material system under the action of forces is at every instant, as in a free system, smaller for the natural motion than for any other possible motion which coincides with it, at the moment considered, in position and velocity.

For the necessary and sufficient condition that, with given values of X_ν, the quantity $\tfrac{1}{2}mz^2$ should be a minimum, is that the $3n$ equations, obtained as in § 155, viz.,

$$m_\nu \ddot{x}_\nu - X_\nu + \sum_1^i {}_\iota x_{\iota\nu} X_\iota = 0,$$

should be satisfied; where X_ι denote the i undetermined multipliers which with the $3n$ quantities $\ddot{x}_\nu$ are to be singly determined from these $3n$ equations and the i equations of condition of the system. But the foregoing equations give the same values for $\ddot{x}_\nu$ and X_ν as the corresponding equations for the natural motion (§ 482).

499. **Observation.** The foregoing proposition contains a complete statement of Gauss's Principle of Least Constraint. We might regard proposition 388 as a particular case of it. But according to our general conception we prefer to regard that proposition as the general one, and to consider the foregoing as the application of it to particular and more complex relations.

500. **Proposition 2.** In the natural motion of a system under the action of a force the direction of the constraint, as in the natural motion of a free system, is always perpendicular to every possible or virtual displacement of the system from its instantaneous position.

For by §§ 497 (i) and 481 the components of the constraint along p_ρ may be written in the form

$$z_\rho = -\frac{1}{m}\sum_1^k {}_\chi p_{\chi\rho} P_\chi.$$

The constraint as a vector quantity is thus (§ 250) perpendicular to every possible displacement of the system.

501. **Symbolical Expression.** If we denote by δp_ρ the changes of the coordinates p_ρ for any possible displacement of the system, then we can express the foregoing proposition by the following symbolical equation (*cf.* § 393)—

$$\sum_1^r {}_\rho\left(f_\rho - \frac{P_\rho}{m}\right)\delta p_\rho = 0 \qquad \text{(i)},$$

which in rectangular coordinates takes the form

$$\sum_1^{3n}{}_\nu(m_\nu\ddot{x}_\nu - X_\nu)\delta x_\nu = 0 \qquad \text{(ii)}.$$

502. **Observation.** Proposition § 500 contains the complete Principle of d'Alembert, and the equations § 501 (i) and (ii) the usual expression for it. With regard to the relation between

proposition § 500 and proposition § 392 the same remark is to be made as in § 499.

503. **Corollary 1.** The component of the acceleration of a material system in the direction of any possible motion is equal to the component of the force acting in this direction, divided by the mass of the system.

For the component of the constraint vanishes in the direction of every possible motion.

504. **Corollary 2.** The component of the acceleration of a material system in the direction of its actual motion is equal to the component of the force acting in that direction, divided by the mass of the system.

505. **Corollary 3.** The component of the acceleration of a material system along any free coordinate of the system is equal to the component of the force acting in that direction, divided by the mass of the system.

506. **Proposition.** In the natural motion of a material system under the action of forces the component of the acceleration along every coordinate of absolute position is always equal to the component of the force acting in that direction, divided by the mass of the system; and this holds good whatever the internal connection of the system is.

507. **Corollary 1.** If we choose the coordinates of a system in any manner so that there are six coordinates of absolute position amongst them, then we can with a knowledge of the forces acting on the system,—yet without a knowledge of the internal connection of the system,—always obtain six of the equations of motion of the system.

508. **Corollary 2.** In particular, if we arrange the coordinates of absolute position as in § 402, and apply the proposition to the direction of the three coordinates a_1, a_2, a_3, then we get the three equations

$$\sum_{1}^{n} {}_\nu m_\nu \ddot{x}_{3\nu} = \sum_{1}^{n} {}_\nu X_{3\nu}$$

$$\sum_{1}^{n} {}_\nu m_\nu \ddot{x}_{3\nu-1} = \sum_{1}^{n} {}_\nu X_{3\nu-1}$$

$$\sum_{1}^{n} \nu m_\nu \ddot{x}_{3\nu-2} = \sum_{1}^{n} \nu X_{3\nu-2}.$$

These three equations, which admit of the interpretation that the centre of gravity moves as if the whole mass were condensed at the centre of gravity and all the elementary forces applied there, form the so-called extended Principle of the Centre of Gravity (*cf.* § 404).

509. **Corollary 3.** Applied to the direction of the three coordinates of absolute position ω_1, ω_2, ω_3, the proposition gives the three equations

$$\sum_{1}^{n} \nu m_\nu(x_{3\nu-2}\ddot{x}_{3\nu-1} - x_{3\nu-1}\ddot{x}_{3\nu-2}) = \sum_{1}^{n} \nu (x_{3\nu-2}X_{3\nu-1} - x_{3\nu-1}X_{3\nu-2})$$

$$\sum_{1}^{n} \nu m_\nu(x_{3\nu}\ \ddot{x}_{3\nu-2} - x_{3\nu-2}\ddot{x}_{3\nu}\ ) = \sum_{1}^{n} \nu (x_{3\nu}\ X_{3\nu-2} - x_{3\nu-2}X_{3\nu}\ )$$

$$\sum_{1}^{n} \nu m_\nu(x_{3\nu-1}\ddot{x}_{3\nu}\ \ - x_{3\nu}\ \ddot{x}_{3\nu-1}) = \sum_{1}^{n} \nu (x_{3\nu-1}X_{3\nu}\ \ - x_{3\nu}\ X_{3\nu-1}).$$

These three equations form the so-called extended Principle of Areas (*cf.* § 406).

Energy, Work

510. **Definition.** The increase in the energy of a system, conceived as a consequence of force exerted on the system, is called the work of that force.

The work which a force performs in a given time is measured by the increase of the energy of the system on which it acts, in that time.

Any decrease in the energy owing to the action of force we consider a negative increase. The work of a force may thus be positive or negative.

511. **Corollary.** When a force acting on a system does a certain amount of work, the counterforce exerted by the system always does an equal and opposite amount of work.

For the latter work is equal to the increase of the energy of that system, with which the one under consideration is coupled; the sum of the energies of the two systems is, however, constant.

512. **Proposition.** The work which a force does on a system whilst it traverses an element of its path is equal to the product of the length of the element and the component of the force in its direction.

For the increase $d\mathrm{E}$ of the energy in the time-element dt, in which the element ds is traversed, is (§ 283)

$$d\mathrm{E} = m\,v\,\dot{v}\,dt = m\,\dot{v}\,ds.$$

By § 280 $\dot{v}$ is the component of the acceleration of the system in the direction of its path; thus by § 504 $m\dot{v}$ is the component of the force in that direction.

513. **Observation 1.** The work is also equal to the product of the magnitude of the force and the component of the element of the path in its direction.

514. **Observation 2.** If during the motion along the path-element ds the coordinates p_ρ suffer the changes dp_ρ, then the work done by the force is represented by the equation

$$d\mathrm{E} = \sum_{1}^{r} {}_\rho \mathrm{P}_\rho \delta p_\rho.$$

For the component of the force in the direction of the path-element is by § 247 equal to

$$\sum_{1}^{r} {}_\rho \mathrm{P}_\rho \frac{dp_\rho}{ds}.$$

515. **Corollary 1.** The force acting on a system does positive or negative work, according as the angle which it makes with the velocity of the system is smaller or greater than a right angle. If the force is perpendicular to the direction of motion, it does no work.

516. **Corollary 2.** A force which acts on a system at rest, does no work.

Equilibrium, Statics

517. **Definition.** We say that two or more forces which act on the same system are in equilibrium when any one of them counteracts the effect of the others, *i.e.* when the system moves

under the action of both, or of all of them, as though none of them existed.

518. **Proposition.** Two or more forces are in equilibrium when their sum is perpendicular to every possible (virtual) displacement of the system from its instantaneous position, and conversely.

The proposition follows immediately from §§ 471 and 488.

519. **Symbolical Expression.** If we denote by P_ρ', P_ρ'', etc., the components of the respective forces along p_ρ, and by δp_ρ the changes of p_ρ for any possible displacement of the system, then the foregoing proposition can be expressed in the form of the symbolical equations

$$\sum_{1}^{r}(P_\rho' + P_\rho'' + \ldots)\delta p_\rho = 0.$$

Cf. §§ 393, 501.

520. **Observation.** The foregoing proposition contains the Principle of Virtual Velocities (displacements, momenta), and the equation § 519 the usual analytical form of it.

521. **Corollary 1.** If several forces acting on a system are in equilibrium, then the sum of the work done by the forces in any possible (virtual) displacement of the system from its instantaneous position is zero, and conversely (Principle of Virtual Work).

For if we write the equation § 519 in the form

$$\sum_{1}^{r}P_\rho'\delta p_\rho + \sum_{1}^{r}P_\rho''\delta p_\rho + \ldots = 0,$$

then the proof follows by § 514.

522. **Corollary 2.** If two or more forces preserve equilibrium in a system, then the sum of their components in the direction of any possible motion of the system is zero.

523. **Corollary 3.** If two or more forces preserve equilibrium in a system, then the sum of their components along every free coordinate of the system vanishes.

524. **Proposition.** If two or more forces preserve equilibrium in a system, then the sum of their components along

any coordinate of absolute position is zero, no matter what may be the internal connection of the system.

525. **Observation.** Thus without a knowledge of the internal connection of a system, we can nevertheless always write down six necessary equations of condition for equilibrium. If we choose as coordinates of absolute position the six quantities $a_1 a_2 a_3$, $\omega_1 \omega_2 \omega_3$, which were introduced in § 402, then the foregoing proposition furnishes those six equations which correspond to the principles of the centre of gravity and of areas, and which Lagrange investigates in chapter iii. §§ 1 and 2 of the first part of the *Mécanique Analytique*.

526. **Note 1.** If two or more forces are in equilibrium when the system is in a given position and has a given velocity, then these forces are also in equilibrium in the same position, no matter what the velocity be.

For the condition of equilibrium does not contain the actual velocity of the system.

527. **Note 2.** If two or more forces are in equilibrium when the system is at rest, then the system continues in its state of rest. And conversely—if, notwithstanding the action of two or more forces, a system is at rest, then the forces on the system are in equilibrium.

528. **Corollary 1.** Two forces which, acting simultaneously on a system at rest, do not disturb the equilibrium of the system, have equal and opposite components in the direction of every possible motion of the system.

529. **Corollary 2.** Two forces which act successively on the same system at rest at the same time as other forces, and leave the system at rest, have the same components in the direction of every possible motion of the system.

530. **Observation.** From the last two corollaries the statical comparison of forces is deduced.

Machines and Internal Forces

531. **Definition.** A system whose masses are considered vanishingly small in comparison with the masses of the systems with which it is coupled, is called a machine.

A machine is thus completely represented, as to its effect on the motion of the other systems, by its equations of condition; the knowledge of the expression for the energy of the machine in terms of its coordinates is not necessary.

A machine is called simple when it has only one degree of freedom.

532. **Proposition.** So long as a machine moves with finite velocity the forces acting on the machine are continually in equilibrium.

For if these forces gave a component in the direction of any possible motion of the machine, then the component of the acceleration in this direction would be infinitely great on account of the vanishing mass (§ 504).

533. **Corollary.** There exists a series of homogeneous linear equations between the components of the forces acting on a machine along its coordinates, and their number is equal to the number of degrees of freedom of the machine. A simple machine is represented by a single homogeneous linear equation between the forces acting on its coordinates.

534. **Note 1.** If a machine is coupled as to all its coordinates with two or more material systems, then the mechanical connection produced between the latter can be analytically represented by a series of homogeneous linear differential equations between the coordinates of the connected systems. For in the equations of condition of the machine we can replace its coordinates by the equal coordinates of the connected systems.

Conversely, therefore, we can physically interpret any given analytical series of homogeneous linear differential equations between the coordinates of two or more systems as a mechanical connection of the kind which we denote as a coupling of these systems by means of the machine.

535. **Corollary.** If two or more systems are coupled by a machine, then the work done by each of the systems is equal and opposite to the work done by the other systems. Consequently no work is gained by coupling systems by a machine.

For the forces due to the systems preserve equilibrium in the machine, and thus the sum of the work done by them is zero.

536. **Note 2.** Any material system can in various ways be regarded as made up of two or more systems which

are coupled by machines. For if we divide up the masses of the system into several parts, and if p_ρ' are the coordinates of the first part, p_ρ'' of the second, etc., then we may consider those equations of condition of the complete system which only contain p_ρ', as equations of condition of the first partial system, those equations which only contain p_ρ'' as equations of condition of the second partial system, and so on; whilst those equations of condition of the complete system which contain p_ρ', p_ρ'' . . ., may be regarded as the equations of the machine coupling the partial systems.

The forces which in this permissible though arbitrary conception are exerted on the partial systems by the machine coupling them will be denoted as internal forces of the system.

537. **Corollary 1.** Every such series of internal forces may replace a portion of the connection of the system. For if we set aside those equations of condition of the whole system which represent the machines between the partial systems, but retain the forces exerted by the machines, then the system moves as before.

538. **Corollary 2.** The whole connection of a system can be set aside and replaced by a series of elementary forces which act on the individual material parts of the system.

For we may regard the individual points as partial systems, and the whole system as the aggregate of the partial systems coupled by machines.

539. **Corollary 3.** The internal forces which entirely or partially replace the connection of a system are always in equilibrium when acting on the original system.

For by § 532 they preserve equilibrium in the machines which form parts of the original system.

540. **Observation.** This last consideration is the one by which, in the usual development of mechanics, the transition is made from the laws of equilibrium (the Principle of Virtual Velocities) to the laws of motion (d'Alembert's Principle).

Measurement of Forces

541. Our considerations give three independent methods of measuring directly those components of the forces which

affect phenomena. By the application of any one of these three methods the forces can be made objects of direct experience, *i.e.* symbols for determinate connections of sensible perceptions.

542. The first method determines the force from the masses and motions of the system by which it is exerted. Physically this method is known as the measurement of force according to its origin. It is, for instance, applied on the assumption that equally stretched springs, equal quantities of explosive powder, etc., *ceteris paribus*, exert equal forces.

543. The second method determines the force by means of the masses and motions of the system on which it acts. In physics this method is known as the dynamical measurement of force. It was, for instance, applied by Newton when he deduced the force acting on the planets from their motion.

544. The third method determines the force by reducing it to equilibrium with known forces. This method is known as the statical method. For example, all measures of forces by the balance depend upon this.

545. When these three methods are used for the determination of one and the same force, paying attention to the relations deduced by us, they must lead in all cases to the same result, provided the fundamental law, on which our considerations are based, actually comprises correctly all possible mechanical experience.

CHAPTER V

SYSTEMS WITH CONCEALED MASSES

I. Cyclical Motion

546. **Definition 1.** A free coordinate of a system is said to be cyclical when the length of an infinitesimal displacement of the system does not depend on the value of the coordinate, but only on its change.

547. **Observation 1.** Cyclical coordinates exist; for instance, a rectangular coordinate of the system, when free, satisfies the definition. Cyclical coordinates can always be introduced, when infinitesimal displacements of the system are possible which do not involve a change in the mass-distribution in space, but only a cyclical interchange of the masses; hence the name. Cyclical coordinates may, however, appear under other circumstances, as the example of rectangular coordinates shows.

548. **Observation 2.** The energy of a system does not depend on the value of its cyclical coordinates, but only on their time-rates of change.

549. **Definition 2.** A cyclical system is a material system whose energy approximates sufficiently near to a homogeneous quadratic function of the rates of change of its cyclical coordinates.

A cyclical system is monocyclic, dicyclic, etc., according as it possesses one, two, etc., cyclical coordinates.

In a cyclical system the non-cyclical coordinates are also known as the parameters of the system; the rates of change of the cyclical coordinates are also called the cyclical intensities.

550. Observation 1. The condition that must be approximately satisfied for cyclical systems cannot be rigorously satisfied except in the case when the system possesses only cyclical coordinates.

For if a quantity is a coordinate of a system, then its change must involve a displacement of at least one material point of the system; the energy of this point is consequently a quadratic function of the rate of change of that coordinate, and the same holds for the energy of the system. Strictly speaking, then, the energy of any system contains necessarily the rates of change of all quantities which are coordinates of the system, and consequently the energy of a cyclical system contains the rates of change of its parameters.

551. Observation 2. But this condition for the appearance of a cyclical system can be satisfied to any degree of approximation so long as the system possesses cyclical coordinates.

It is, for instance, satisfied in the case when the parts of the energy which contain the rates of change of the parameters vanish in comparison with the parts which depend on the cyclical intensities. This is always possible by taking the rates of change of the parameters sufficiently small, or the cyclical intensities sufficiently great. As to how small the former must be taken or how great the latter, in order that a given degree of approximation may be attained, depends on the particular values of the coefficients in the expression for the energy.

In what follows it will always be assumed that the condition for a cyclical system is satisfied to such a degree of approximation that we may regard it as absolutely satisfied.

552. Notation. We shall denote the cyclical coordinates of the system by $\mathfrak{p}_\rho$, their number by $\mathfrak{r}$, and the momenta along $\mathfrak{p}_\rho$ by $\mathfrak{q}_\rho$. The r non-cyclical coordinates may be denoted by p_ρ, and their momenta along p_ρ by q_ρ. Let the mass of the cyclical system be $\mathfrak{m}$.

Let the external forces which act on the system have P_ρ as their components along p_ρ, and $\mathfrak{P}_\rho$ as their components along

$\mathfrak{p}_\rho$. The forces which the system itself exerts then have components along p_ρ, likewise along $\mathfrak{p}_\rho$, which by § 467 are to be denoted by P'_ρ and $\mathfrak{P}'_\rho$ respectively.

553. Corollary 1. The energy $\mathfrak{E}$ of a cyclical system can be written in the form

$$\mathfrak{E} = \tfrac{1}{2}m \sum_1^\tau{}^\rho \sum_1^\tau{}^\sigma \mathfrak{a}_{\rho\sigma} \dot{\mathfrak{p}}_\rho \dot{\mathfrak{p}}_\sigma$$

$$= \frac{1}{2m} \sum_1^\tau{}^\rho \sum_1^\tau{}^\sigma \mathfrak{b}_{\rho\sigma} \mathfrak{q}_\rho \mathfrak{q}_\sigma,$$

where $\mathfrak{a}_{\rho\sigma}$ and $\mathfrak{b}_{\rho\sigma}$ are functions of p_ρ alone, but not (§ 548) of $\mathfrak{p}_\rho$, while in other respects they have the same properties and connection as $a_{\rho\sigma}$ and $b_{\rho\sigma}$ (§ 59 et seq.).

If we consider $\mathfrak{E}$ a function of p_ρ and $\dot{\mathfrak{p}}_\rho$, as the first form represents it, then its partial differential may be denoted by $\partial_p \mathfrak{E}$; but if we regard it as a function of p_ρ and $\mathfrak{q}_\rho$, as the second form represents it, its partial differential may be denoted by $\partial_q \mathfrak{E}$ (cf. § 288).

554. Corollary 2. For all values of ρ the following equations hold—

$$\frac{\partial_p \mathfrak{E}}{\partial \dot{p}_\rho} = q_\rho = 0 \qquad (\text{§ 289}) \quad (\text{i})$$

$$\frac{\partial_q \mathfrak{E}}{\partial q_\rho} = \dot{p}_\rho = 0 \qquad (\text{§ 290}) \quad (\text{ii})$$

$$\frac{\partial_p \mathfrak{E}}{\partial \mathfrak{p}_\rho} = 0 \qquad (\text{iii})$$

$$\frac{\partial_q \mathfrak{E}}{\partial \mathfrak{p}_\rho} = 0 \qquad (\text{iv}).$$

These equations contain the peculiar characteristics of cyclical systems, and from them are deduced their special properties.

The equation (ii) repeats the observation (§ 550) that a contradiction exists between the assumption that the form of the energy is strictly the one assumed, and that nevertheless the p_ρ's are quantities which change with the time. We have then, conformably with § 551, to take the equation to mean that when $\mathfrak{E}$ has very approximately the chosen form, the p_ρ's must be considered as quantities which change very slowly.

Forces and Force-Functions

555. Problem 1. To determine the force P_ρ' which the cyclical system exerts along its parameter p_ρ.

By equations § 493 (iii) and (iv) and § 554 (i) we obtain

$$P_\rho' = \frac{\partial_p \mathfrak{E}}{\partial p_\rho} = -\frac{\partial_q \mathfrak{E}}{\partial p_\rho} \qquad (i),$$

or, in a more extended form,

$$P_\rho' = \tfrac{1}{2}\mathfrak{m} \sum_1^\mathfrak{r} {}_\sigma \sum_1^\mathfrak{r} {}_\tau \frac{\partial \mathfrak{a}_{\sigma\tau}}{\partial p_\rho} \dot{\mathfrak{p}}_\sigma \dot{\mathfrak{p}}_\tau$$

$$= -\frac{1}{2\mathfrak{m}} \sum_1^\mathfrak{r} {}_\sigma \sum_1^\mathfrak{r} {}_\tau \frac{\partial \mathfrak{b}_{\sigma\tau}}{\partial p_\rho} \mathfrak{q}_\sigma \mathfrak{q}_\tau \qquad (ii).$$

556. Corollary. The forces of a cyclical system along its parameters are independent of the rates of change of these parameters.

It is always assumed that these rates of change do not exceed the values which permit us to treat the system as a cyclical one. Thus in Electromagnetics the attractions between magnets are independent of the velocity of their motion, but only so long as this velocity is considerably less than the velocity of light.

557. Problem 2. To determine the force $\mathfrak{P}_\rho'$ which the cyclical system exerts along its cyclical coordinate $\mathfrak{p}_\rho$.

By equations § 493 (iii) and § 554 (iii) we obtain

$$\mathfrak{P}_\rho' = -\dot{\mathfrak{q}}_\rho \qquad (i).$$

When developed by § 270 we have

$$\mathfrak{q}_\rho = \mathfrak{m} \sum_1^\mathfrak{r} {}_\sigma \mathfrak{a}_{\rho\sigma} \dot{\mathfrak{p}}_\sigma \qquad (ii)$$

$$\mathfrak{P}_\rho' = -\mathfrak{m} \sum_1^\mathfrak{r} {}_\sigma \mathfrak{a}_{\rho\sigma} \ddot{\mathfrak{p}}_\sigma - \mathfrak{m} \sum_1^\mathfrak{r} {}_\sigma \sum_1^\mathfrak{r} {}_\tau \frac{\partial \mathfrak{a}_{\rho\sigma}}{\partial p_\tau} \dot{\mathfrak{p}}_\sigma \dot{p}_\tau \qquad (iii).$$

558. Corollary. If an external force acts on a cyclical system, and if its components along $\mathfrak{p}_\rho$ are $\mathfrak{P}_\rho$, then the changes of the cyclical momenta are given by the equation.

$$\dot{\mathfrak{q}}_\rho = \mathfrak{P}_\rho.$$

559. Proposition. When no forces act on the cyclical coordinates of a cyclical system, then all the cyclical momenta of the system are constant with regard to time.

For if the $\mathfrak{P}_\rho$'s are zero, then the foregoing equations give on integration

$$\mathfrak{q}_\rho = \text{constant}.$$

560. Definition. A motion of a cyclical system in which its cyclical momenta remain constant is called an adiabatic motion; and when its cyclical intensities remain constant it is called an isocyclic motion.

The cyclical system itself is called adiabatic or isocyclic when it is constrained to perform only adiabatic or isocyclic motions.

561. Observation 1. The analytical condition for adiabatic motion is that for all values of ρ

$$\dot{\mathfrak{q}}_\rho = 0, \quad \mathfrak{q}_\rho = \text{constant}.$$

The analytical condition for isocyclic motion is that for all values of ρ

$$\ddot{\mathfrak{p}}_\rho = 0, \quad \dot{\mathfrak{p}}_\rho = \text{constant}.$$

562. Observation 2. The motion of a cyclical system is adiabatic so long as no forces act along the cyclical coordinates; it is isocyclic when it is coupled as to its cyclical coordinates with other systems which possess constant rates of change for the coupled coordinates. Thus, in order that a motion may be isocyclic, appropriate forces must act on the cyclical coordinates.

563. Definition. If the forces of a cyclical system along its parameters can be expressed as the partial differential coefficients with regard to the parameters of a function of these parameters and some constant quantities, then this function is called the force-function of the cyclical system.

564. Proposition. There exists a force-function both for adiabatic and for isocyclic motion.

From § 555 (iii) for adiabatic motion we get

$$P_\rho' = -\frac{\partial}{\partial p_\rho} \sum_\sigma^r \sum_1^r \mathfrak{b}_{\sigma\tau} \frac{\mathfrak{q}_\sigma \mathfrak{q}_\tau}{2m} \qquad \text{(i)},$$

where the quantities $q_\sigma q_\tau/\mathfrak{m}$ are constants and the quantities $\mathfrak{b}_{\sigma\tau}$ functions of the parameters solely.

Similarly we get for isocyclic motion from § 555 (ii)

$$P_\rho' = \frac{\partial}{\partial p_\rho} \sum_\sigma^r \sum_\tau^r \mathfrak{a}_{\sigma\tau} \frac{\mathfrak{m}}{2} \dot{\mathfrak{p}}_\sigma \dot{\mathfrak{p}}_\tau \qquad \text{(ii)},$$

where the quantities $\mathfrak{m}\dot{\mathfrak{p}}_\sigma\dot{\mathfrak{p}}_\tau$ are constants and the quantities $\mathfrak{a}_{\sigma\tau}$ functions of the parameters solely.

565. Observation. We also distinguish the force-functions for adiabatic or isocyclic motions as adiabatic or isocyclic force-functions. There are other forms of motion of the system for which force-functions exist, but such a function does not exist for every given motion.

566. Additional Note 1. The force-function of an adiabatic system is equal to the decrease of the energy of the system, measured from some arbitrarily chosen initial condition. It is therefore equal to an arbitrary—*i.e.* not determined by definition—constant, diminished by the energy of the system.

567. Additional Note 2. The force-function of an isocyclic system is equal to the increase of the energy of the system measured from some arbitrarily chosen initial condition. It is therefore equal to the energy of the system diminished by an arbitrary constant.

Reciprocal Characteristics

568. Proposition 1a. If in an adiabatic system an increase of the parameter p_μ increases the component of the force along another parameter p_λ, then conversely an increase of p_λ increases the force along p_μ. Moreover, in an infinitesimally small increase, the quantitative relation between cause and effect is the same in both cases.

For in an adiabatic system we may regard the quantities p_ρ as sufficiently independent elements for determining P_ρ'; hence the equation § 564 (i), which holds for adiabatic systems, gives us

$$\frac{\partial P_\lambda'}{\partial p_\mu} = \frac{\partial P_\mu'}{\partial p_\lambda},$$

which proves the proposition.

569. **Proposition 1b.** If in an isocyclic system an increase of the parameter p_μ increases the component of the force along another parameter p_λ, then conversely an increase of p_λ increases the force along p_μ. Moreover, in an infinitesimal increase, the quantitative relation between cause and effect is the same in both cases.

For in an isocyclic system we may regard the quantities p_ρ as sufficiently independent elements for determining P_ρ': hence the equation § 564 (ii), which holds for isocyclic systems, gives us

$$\frac{\partial P_\lambda'}{\partial p_\mu} = \frac{\partial P_\mu'}{\partial p_\lambda},$$

which proves the proposition.

It is to be noted that this equation differs from the previous one in meaning although it is identical in form.

570. **Observation.** In order that the two foregoing propositions may admit of a physical application, it is sufficient that two parameters of the cyclical system and the forces along them should be accessible to direct observation.

571. **Proposition 2a.** If in a cyclical system an increase of the cyclical momentum $\mathfrak{q}_\mu$, with fixed values of the parameters, involves an increase of the force along the parameter p_λ, then the adiabatic increase of the parameter p_λ causes a decrease of the cyclical intensity $\dot{\mathfrak{p}}_\mu$, and conversely. Moreover, in an infinitesimal change the quantitative relation between cause and effect is the same in both cases.

For we have

$$P_\lambda' = -\frac{\partial_q \mathfrak{E}}{\partial p_\lambda}(555 \text{ (i)}), \quad \dot{\mathfrak{p}}_\mu = \frac{\partial_q \mathfrak{E}}{\partial \mathfrak{q}_\mu} \text{ (§ 290)};$$

thus

$$\frac{\partial P_\lambda'}{\partial \mathfrak{q}_\mu} = -\frac{\partial \dot{\mathfrak{p}}_\mu}{\partial p_\lambda} \qquad (i),$$

and the proposition furnishes the correct interpretation of this equation.

572. **Corollary.** If in a monocyclic system an increase of the cyclical intensity $\dot{\mathfrak{p}}$, with fixed values of the parameters, involves an increase of the force along the parameter p_λ, then

the adiabatic increase of the parameter p_λ causes a decrease of the cyclical intensity $\dot{\mathfrak{p}}$, and conversely.

For in a monocyclic system increase of the cyclical intensity always goes hand in hand with increase of the cyclical momentum, the parameters remaining fixed. In fact, for a monocyclic system

$$\mathfrak{q} = \mathfrak{m}\dot{\mathfrak{p}},$$

where $\mathfrak{a}$ is a necessarily positive (§ 62) function of the parameters of the system.

573. Proposition 2b. If in a cyclical system an increase of the cyclical intensity $\dot{\mathfrak{p}}_u$, the parameters remaining fixed, involves an increase of the force along the parameter p_λ, then the isocyclic increase of the parameter p_λ involves an increase of the cyclical momentum $\mathfrak{q}_\mu$, and conversely. Moreover, in an infinitesimal change the quantitative relation between cause and effect is the same in both cases.

For we have

$$P_\lambda' = \frac{\partial_p \mathfrak{E}}{\partial p_\lambda} \text{ (555(i))}, \quad \mathfrak{q}_\mu = \frac{\partial_p \mathfrak{E}}{\partial \dot{\mathfrak{p}}_\mu'} \text{ (289);}$$

thus

$$\frac{\partial P_\lambda'}{\partial \dot{\mathfrak{p}}_\mu} = \frac{\partial \mathfrak{q}_\mu}{\partial p_\lambda} \qquad (i),$$

and the proposition expresses this equation in words.

574. Corollary. If in a monocyclic system an increase of the cyclical momentum $\mathfrak{q}$ involves an increase of the force along the parameter p_λ, the parameters remaining fixed, then the isocyclic increase of the parameter p_λ involves an increase of the cyclical momentum $\mathfrak{q}$, and conversely.

The reason is the same as in § 572.

575. Observation. The foregoing propositions 2a and 2b admit of a physical application when it is possible to determine a cyclical intensity and also the corresponding cyclical momentum directly, *i.e.* to determine it without a knowledge of the coefficients $\mathfrak{a}_{\rho\sigma}$. This may happen. For instance, in Electrostatics the differences of potential of conductors correspond to cyclical intensities, the charges of the conductors to the cyclical momenta, and both quantities can be directly determined independently of one another.

The corollaries require only the direct determination either of the cyclical intensity or cyclical momentum.

576. **Proposition 3a.** If in a cyclical system a force exerted on the cyclical coordinate $\mathfrak{p}_\mu$ involves an increase with the time of the force along the parameter p_λ, then an adiabatic increase of the parameter p_λ causes a decrease of the cyclical intensity $\dot{\mathfrak{p}}_\mu$ and conversely. Moreover, in an infinitesimal change the quantitative relation between cause and effect is the same in both cases.

For if we regard on the left-hand side of equation § 571 (i) the changes $\partial P_\lambda'$ and $\partial \mathfrak{q}_\mu$ as happening in the time dt, and divide the differential coefficients in the numerator and denominator by this time dt and make use of equation § 558, where the change $\partial \mathfrak{q}_\mu$ is considered as the effect of the force $\mathfrak{P}_\mu$, then

$$\frac{\dot{P}_\lambda'}{\mathfrak{P}_\mu} = -\frac{\partial \dot{\mathfrak{p}}_\mu}{\partial p_\lambda},$$

and the proposition expresses fully this equation in words.

577. **Proposition 3b.**[1] If in a cyclical system an increase of the cyclical intensity $\dot{\mathfrak{p}}_\mu$, the parameters remaining fixed, involves an increase of the force along the parameter p_λ, then an isocyclic increase of the parameter p_λ involves a decrease of the force of the system along the cyclical coordinate $\mathfrak{p}_\mu$, and conversely. Moreover, in an infinitesimal change, the quantitative relation between cause and effect is the same in both cases.

For if we regard in the right-hand side of the equation § 573 (i) the changes $\partial \mathfrak{q}_\mu$ and ∂p_λ as occurring in the time dt, we can put

$$\partial \mathfrak{q}_\mu = \frac{d}{dt}\partial \mathfrak{q}_\mu \cdot dt = \partial \dot{\mathfrak{q}}_\mu dt = -\partial \mathfrak{P}_\mu' dt \quad (557 \text{ (i)})$$

$$\partial p_\lambda = \frac{d}{dt}\partial p_\lambda dt = \partial \dot{p}_\lambda dt;$$

thus that equation becomes

$$\frac{\partial P_\lambda'}{\partial \dot{\mathfrak{p}}_\mu} = -\frac{\partial \mathfrak{P}_\mu'}{\partial \dot{p}_\lambda},$$

and the proposition expresses this in words.

[1] Printed as in the original MSS.—ED.

218   SECOND BOOK   CHAP.

578. **Note.** The propositions **3a** and **3b** admit of a physical application when a cyclical intensity and also the corresponding cyclical force-component are accessible to direct observation. This happens, for instance, in Electromagnetics, and one can best illustrate the meanings of these theorems by translating them into the technical language of this branch of physics.

Energy and Work

579. **Proposition 1.** In the isocyclic motion of a cyclical system the work done on it through the coupling of its cyclical coordinates is always twice the work it does through the coupling of its parameters.

In the isocyclic motion $\ddot{\mathfrak{p}}_\rho$ is equal to zero for all values of ρ, and thus by § 514 and § 557 (iii) the work which the external forces acting on the cyclical coordinates perform in the unit of time is equal to

$$-\sum_1^{\mathfrak{r}}{}_\rho \mathfrak{P}_\rho' \dot{\mathfrak{p}}_\rho = \mathfrak{m} \sum_1^{\mathfrak{r}}{}_\rho \sum_1^{\mathfrak{r}}{}_\sigma \sum_1^r {}_\tau \frac{\partial \mathfrak{a}_{\rho\sigma}}{\partial p_\tau} \dot{\mathfrak{p}}_\sigma \dot{p}_\tau \dot{\mathfrak{p}}_\rho.$$

But the work which the system performs through the forces along the parameters, calculated for unit time, is found equal to

$$\sum_1^r {}_\rho \mathrm{P}_\rho' \dot{p}_\rho = \tfrac{1}{2} \mathfrak{m} \sum_1^r {}_\rho \sum_1^{\mathfrak{r}}{}_\sigma \sum_1^{\mathfrak{r}}{}_\tau \frac{\partial \mathfrak{a}_{\sigma\tau}}{\partial p_\rho} \dot{\mathfrak{p}}_\sigma \dot{\mathfrak{p}}_\tau \dot{p}_\rho$$

by the use of § 555 (ii).

The summations in both equations are identical except for the notation, and the value of the series in the first equation is therefore double that of the second.

580. **Corollary.** When an isocyclic system does work through the forces along its parameters, then the energy of the system increases at the same time, and by the same amount as the work done. When an isocyclic system has work done on it through the forces along its parameters, then the energy of the system decreases at the same time, and by the amount of the work done on it.

For the increase of the energy of the system is equal to the difference between the work done on it through its cyclic coordinates and the work it does through its parameters.

581. **Observation.** When an adiabatic system does work through the forces along its parameters, then the energy of the system decreases at the same time, and by the same amount as the work done. When an adiabatic system has work done on it by the forces along its parameters, then the energy of the system increases at the same time, and by the amount of work done.

For the work done on an adiabatic system through the cyclical coordinates is zero (§ 562).

582. **Proposition 2.** In an adiabatic displacement of a cyclical system the cyclical intensities always suffer changes in such a sense that the forces along the parameters caused by these changes do negative work.

Let the quantities p_ρ suffer the changes δp_ρ and the intensities $\dot{\mathfrak{p}}_\rho$ the changes $\delta\dot{\mathfrak{p}}_\rho$ from the displacement. If only the latter took place, then the forces P_ρ' would change by the amount (§ 555 (ii))

$$\delta P_\rho' = \mathfrak{m}\sum_1^{\mathfrak{r}}{}_\sigma \sum_1^{\mathfrak{r}}{}_\tau \frac{\partial \mathfrak{a}_{\sigma\tau}}{\partial p_\rho}\dot{\mathfrak{p}}_\sigma \delta\dot{\mathfrak{p}}_\tau,$$

and these $\delta P_\rho''$'s are what the proposition denotes as the forces caused by $\delta\dot{\mathfrak{p}}_\tau$. The work done by them is given by

$$\sum_1^{\mathfrak{r}}{}_\rho \delta P_\rho' \delta p_\rho = \mathfrak{m}\sum_1^{\mathfrak{r}}{}_\rho \sum_1^{\mathfrak{r}}{}_\sigma \sum_1^{\mathfrak{r}}{}_\tau \frac{\partial \mathfrak{a}_{\sigma\tau}}{\partial p_\rho}\dot{\mathfrak{p}}_\sigma \delta\dot{\mathfrak{p}}_\tau \delta p_\rho$$

$$= \mathfrak{m}\sum_1^{\mathfrak{r}}{}_\sigma \sum_1^{\mathfrak{r}}{}_\tau \delta\mathfrak{a}_{\sigma\tau}\dot{\mathfrak{p}}_\sigma \delta\dot{\mathfrak{p}}_\tau,$$

and the proof requires that this work should be necessarily negative. But for the adiabatic motion

$$\mathfrak{q}_\tau = \mathfrak{m}\sum_1^{\mathfrak{r}}{}_\sigma \mathfrak{a}_{\rho\sigma}\dot{\mathfrak{p}}_\sigma = \text{const},$$

thus

$$\sum_1^{\mathfrak{r}}{}_\sigma \delta\mathfrak{a}_{\sigma\tau}\dot{\mathfrak{p}}_\sigma = -\sum_1^{\mathfrak{r}}{}_\sigma \mathfrak{a}_{\sigma\tau}\delta\dot{\mathfrak{p}}_\sigma.$$

If we form these equations for all values of τ, multiply them in succession by the corresponding $\mathfrak{m}\delta\dot{\mathfrak{p}}_\tau$ and add them, we obtain on the left-hand side the foregoing expression for the work done, and on the right-hand side a necessarily positive quantity (§ 62), which completes the proof.

583. Corollary. In an adiabatic displacement of a cyclical system the cyclical intensities always suffer changes in such a sense that the forces caused by these changes tend to stop the motion which produces them.

This is in fact only another form of the foregoing proposition. It corresponds to Lenz's Law in Electromagnetics.

584. Note. In any infinitesimally small motion of a monocyclic system, the work received through the cyclical coordinates of the system bears the same ratio to the energy of the system as twice the increase of the cyclical momentum of the system does to this momentum.

For the work $d\mathfrak{Q}$ done through the cyclical coordinate $\mathfrak{p}$ in the time dt is given by

$$d\mathfrak{Q} = \mathfrak{P}d\mathfrak{p} = \dot{\mathfrak{q}}d\mathfrak{v} = \dot{\mathfrak{q}}\mathfrak{p}dt = \dot{\mathfrak{p}}d\mathfrak{q},$$

while the energy $\mathfrak{E}$ may be written

$$\mathfrak{E} = \tfrac{1}{2}\mathfrak{q}\dot{\mathfrak{p}},$$

thus

$$\frac{d\mathfrak{Q}}{\mathfrak{E}} = 2\frac{d\mathfrak{q}}{\mathfrak{q}},$$

which proves the proposition.

585. Corollary 1. In any motion of a monocyclic system the expression

$$\frac{d\mathfrak{Q}}{\mathfrak{E}}$$

is the complete differential of a function of the parameters and cyclical intensity of the system. This function is

$$2\log\frac{\mathfrak{q}}{\mathfrak{q}_0},$$

where $\mathfrak{q}_0$ denotes the cyclical momentum for an arbitrarily chosen initial position. This function is also called the entropy of the monocyclic system.

586. Corollary 2. The value of the integral

$$\int\frac{d\mathfrak{Q}}{\mathfrak{E}}$$

for any finite motion of a monocyclic system depends only on the condition of the system in its initial and final positions, and not on the condition at any intermediate position. The value of this integral is zero for every motion which carries the system back to its initial position.

For the value of this integral is equal to the difference between the entropy in the initial and final positions.

587. **Corollary 3.** In the adiabatic motion of a monocyclic system the entropy is constant. For in the adiabatic motion $\mathfrak{P}$, and consequently $d\mathfrak{Q}$, is equal to zero. Hence the adiabatic motion of a monocyclic system is called isentropic.

Time-Integral of the Energy

588. **Note 1.** If in the adiabatic motion of a cyclical system the cyclical coordinates $\mathfrak{p}_\rho$ change in a given finite time by $\bar{\mathfrak{p}}_\rho$, then the time-integral of the energy of the system for that time is equal to

$$\tfrac{1}{2}\sum_{1}^{r}{}_\rho \mathfrak{q}_\rho \bar{\mathfrak{p}}_\rho,$$

for the energy of the system can be written in the form (286 (ii))

$$\tfrac{1}{2}\sum_{1}^{r}{}_\rho \mathfrak{q}_\rho \dot{\mathfrak{p}}_\rho,$$

and for the adiabatic motion the $\mathfrak{q}_\rho$'s are constant.

589. **Note 2.** The variation of the time-integral of the energy of an adiabatic system when the motion of the system is varied depends—firstly, on the variation of the parameters during the whole time for which the integral is taken, and secondly, on the variations which the constant cyclical momenta of the system suffer.

590. **Notation.** We shall in what follows use the following notation :—δ will denote a variation by which the cyclical momenta suffer arbitrary variations,

δ_q a variation by which the cyclical momenta suffer no variations, and, finally, $\delta_\mathfrak{p}$ a variation by which the cyclical momenta suffer such variations that the initial and final values of the cyclical coordinates remain unaltered.

591. Corollary. From the notation we immediately get for all values of ρ

$$\delta_\mathfrak{q}\mathfrak{q}_\rho = 0, \quad \delta_\mathfrak{p}\bar{\mathfrak{p}}_\rho = 0,$$

and consequently by § 588 for any variations of the parameters

$$\delta_\mathfrak{q}\int \mathfrak{E}dt = \tfrac{1}{2}\sum_1^\mathfrak{r}{}_\rho\, \mathfrak{q}_\rho\delta_\mathfrak{q}\bar{\mathfrak{p}}_\rho \qquad (i)$$

$$\delta_\mathfrak{p}\int \mathfrak{E}dt = \tfrac{1}{2}\sum_1^\mathfrak{r}{}_\rho\, \bar{\mathfrak{p}}_\rho\delta_\mathfrak{p}\mathfrak{q}_\rho \qquad (ii).$$

592. Observation. In an adiabatic system it is always possible, and in general possible in only one way, to give the cyclical momenta such variations with any variation of the parameters that the initial and final values of the cyclical coordinates remain unaltered.

For from the general relation

$$\dot{\mathfrak{p}}_\rho = \frac{1}{\mathfrak{m}}\sum_1^\mathfrak{r}{}_\sigma\, \mathfrak{b}_{\rho\sigma}\mathfrak{q}_\sigma$$

it follows that in an adiabatic system, when the $\mathfrak{p}_\rho$'s change from the values $\mathfrak{p}_{\rho 0}$ to the values $\mathfrak{p}_{\rho 1}$,

$$\mathfrak{p}_{\rho 1} - \mathfrak{p}_{\rho 0} = \frac{1}{\mathfrak{m}}\sum_1^\mathfrak{r}{}_\sigma\, \mathfrak{q}_\sigma\int_0^1 \mathfrak{b}_{\rho\sigma}dt\,;$$

thus in any variation of the parameters and cyclical momenta

$$\delta\mathfrak{p}_{\rho 1} - \delta\mathfrak{p}_{\rho 0} = \frac{1}{\mathfrak{m}}\sum_1^\mathfrak{r}{}_\sigma\, \mathfrak{q}_\sigma\delta\int_0^1 \mathfrak{b}_{\rho\sigma}dt + \frac{1}{\mathfrak{m}}\sum_1^\mathfrak{r}{}_\sigma\, \delta\mathfrak{q}_\sigma\int_0^1 \mathfrak{b}_{\rho\sigma}dt.$$

These equations form $\mathfrak{r}$ unhomogeneous linear equations for the $\mathfrak{r}$ quantities $\delta\mathfrak{q}_\sigma$, and thus admit of one, and in general only one, solution—in particular in the case when the variations on the left-hand side vanish.

Variations of the kind denoted by $\delta_\mathfrak{p}$ are thus always possible with any variation of the parameters.

593. Proposition. In equal and arbitrary variations of the parameters in a given time the variations of the time-integral of the energy in an adiabatic system are equal and opposite when in the first instance the cyclical momenta of the system are not varied, and in the second are varied in such a manner that the initial and final values of the cyclical coordinates remain unaltered.

For in any variation

$$\delta \int \mathfrak{E} dt = \delta_q \int \mathfrak{E} dt + \sum_1^r \int \frac{\partial_q \mathfrak{E}}{\partial \mathfrak{q}_\rho} \delta \mathfrak{q}_\rho dt$$

$$= \delta_q \int \mathfrak{E} dt + \sum_1^r \bar{\mathfrak{p}}_\rho \delta \mathfrak{q}_\rho \,;$$

thus, in particular for a variation in which the initial and final values of $\mathfrak{p}_\rho$ remain unaltered,

$$\delta_\mathfrak{p} \int \mathfrak{E} dt = \delta_q \int \mathfrak{E} dt + \sum_1^r \bar{\mathfrak{p}}_\rho \delta_\mathfrak{p} \mathfrak{q}_\rho.$$

If twice the equation § 591 (ii) is subtracted from this, then

$$\delta_q \int \mathfrak{E} dt = - \delta_\mathfrak{p} \int \mathfrak{E} dt,$$

which proves the proposition.

With these we may compare the allied propositions § 96 and § 293.

II. Concealed Cyclical Motion

Explanations and Definitions

594. 1. We say that a system contains concealed masses when the position of all the masses of the system is not determined by means of those coordinates of the system which are accessible to observation, but only the position of a portion of them.

595. 2. Those masses whose position still remains unknown when the coordinates accessible to observation have been completely specified are called concealed masses, their

motions concealed motions, and their coordinates concealed coordinates. In contradistinction to these the remaining masses are called visible masses, their motions visible motions, and their coordinates visible coordinates.

596. 3. The problem which a system with concealed masses offers for the consideration of mechanics is the following:—To predetermine the motions of the visible masses of the system, or the changes of its visible coordinates, notwithstanding our ignorance of the position of the concealed masses.

597. 4. A system which contains concealed masses differs from a system without concealed masses only as regards our knowledge of the system. All the propositions hitherto made are therefore applicable to systems with concealed motions, if we understand by masses, coordinates, etc., all its masses, coordinates, etc. Thus alterations are only necessary when we restrict our propositions to the visible quantities. The problem can therefore be reduced to specifying what alterations our previous propositions must undergo, when by masses, coordinates, etc., we mean visible masses, coordinates, etc., only.

598. 5. It is evident that whether the problem is stated in the one form or the other, a solution cannot be obtained without some data as to the effect which the concealed masses produce on the motion of the visible masses. Such data are possible. A guided system, or a system under the action of forces, may be conceived as a system with concealed masses, if we consider either the unknown masses of the guiding system, or of the system producing the forces, as concealed. In general, however, in these cases it is possible also to ascertain physically the masses of the guiding system or of the system which exerts the forces, and it then rests with us to decide whether we regard them as concealed or not. But at present we are mainly interested in cases where a knowledge of the concealed masses cannot be obtained by physical observation.

599. 6. Continually recurrent motions, and therefore cyclical motions, are frequently concealed motions; for these, when existing alone, cause no change in the mass-distribution, nor therefore in the appearance of things. Thus to all appear-

ance the motion of a homogeneous fluid in a closed vessel is concealed; it is only rendered visible when its strictly cyclical character is destroyed by the introduction of dust or other such substances.

Conversely, concealed motions are almost always cyclical. For motions which do not recur continually must sooner or later produce a change in the mass-distribution, and therefore in the aspect of things, and thus become visible.

600. 7. Even cyclical motions cannot long retain their property of being concealed if we obtain means to affect the individual cyclical coordinates, and produce changes in the cyclical intensities. The manifold of our influence on the system is in this case as great as the actual manifold of the system, and we can argue from one to the other. The case is different, however, if any direct and arbitrary influence on the cyclical coordinates is permanently excluded. This may happen in adiabatic cyclical systems (§ 560), and in these we shall rather have to seek the motions which are concealed from our observation.

We therefore restrict our consideration of concealed motion in the first place to such cases. Our treatment, however, has the effect that even in these cases we treat the concealed motions as though they were visible, and only investigate subsequently which of our propositions are still applicable notwithstanding that they are now supposed to be concealed.

Conservative Systems

601. **Definition 1.** A material system which contains no other concealed masses than those which form adiabatic cyclical systems is called a conservative system.

The name is derived from a property of these systems which will appear later; at present it is sufficiently justified by its connection with the already established usage of mechanics.

602. **Observation.** Every conservative system may be regarded as consisting of two partial systems, of which one contains all the visible masses, the other all the concealed masses of the complete system. The coordinates of the

visible partial system, *i.e.* the visible coordinates of the complete system, are at the same time parameters of the concealed partial system.

We shall denote the mass of the visible partial system by m, its coordinates by p_ρ, and its momenta along p_ρ by q_ρ. The mass of the concealed partial system will be denoted by $\mathfrak{m}$, its coordinates by $\mathfrak{p}_\rho$, and its momenta along these coordinates by $\mathfrak{q}_\rho$.

603. **Definition 2.** By the force-function of a conservative system is meant the force-function of its concealed partial system (§ 563).

The force-function of a conservative system is thus in general given as a function of the visible coordinates and constant quantities, without any explicit statement of the connection between these constants and the momenta of the cyclical partial system. The form of this function is subject to no restriction by our considerations.

We shall denote the force-function of a conservative system by U.

604. **Note.** In order to fully determine the motion of the visible masses of a conservative system it is sufficient to know its force-function as a function of its visible coordinates, and this knowledge renders any further knowledge of the concealed masses of the system unnecessary.

For the forces which the concealed partial system exerts on the visible one can be completely obtained from the force-function in the given form, and these forces replace completely effect of the former on the latter (§ 457 *et seq.*).

605. **Definition 3.** That part of the energy of a conservative system which arises from the motion of its visible masses is called the kinetic energy of the whole system. In opposition thereto the energy of the concealed masses of the system is called the potential energy of the whole system.

Kinetic energy is also called *vis viva (lebendige Kraft)*. According to another and older mode of expression this term denotes twice the kinetic energy.

606. **Notation.** We shall denote the kinetic energy by T. T is thus a homogeneous quadratic function of $\dot{p}_\rho$ or of q_ρ; the coefficients of this function are functions of p_ρ. We shall

denote the partial differential of T by $\partial_p T$ when we regard p_ρ and $\dot p_\rho$ as variables independent of one another, but by $\partial_q T$ when we regard p_ρ and q_ρ as variables independent of one another.

The energy of the concealed cyclical partial system, *i.e.* the potential energy of the whole system, may be denoted as previously (§ 553) by $\mathfrak{E}$.

607. Observation. The kinetic and the potential energy of a conservative system do not differ in their nature, but only in the voluntary standpoint of our conception, or the involuntary limitation of our knowledge of the masses of the system. That energy, which from one particular standpoint of our conception or knowledge is to be denoted as potential, is from a different standpoint of our conception or knowledge denoted as kinetic.

608. Corollary 1. The energy of a conservative system is equal to the sum of its kinetic and potential energies.

We shall denote the total energy of the conservative system by E, and we thus have

$$E = T + \mathfrak{E}.$$

609. Corollary 2. In a free conservative system the sum of the potential and kinetic energies is constant in time. As the kinetic energy increases the potential energy decreases, and conversely (§ 340).

610. Corollary 3. In a free conservative system the difference between the kinetic energy and the force-function is constant in time; the kinetic energy and the force-function increase and decrease simultaneously and by the same amount (§ 566).

611. Definition 4. We shall call the difference between the kinetic energy and the force-function of a conservative system the mathematical or analytical energy of the system.

We shall denote the mathematical energy by h. It differs from the energy of the system only by a constant which is independent of the time and the position of the system, but is in general unknown. In mathematical applications it may completely take the place of the energy, but it lacks the physical meaning which the latter possesses.

612. Observation. The definition is represented by the equation

$$T - U = h \quad (i),$$

or

$$U + h = T \quad (ii).$$

If the conservative system is free, then the quantity h in this equation is a constant independent of the time, and the equation is then called the equation of energy for the conservative system.

From (ii) and § 608 we obtain the relation

$$U + h = E - \mathfrak{E} \quad (iii).$$

613. Definition 5. The time-integral of the kinetic energy of a system, taken between two definite times as limits, is called the action or " expenditure of power" (*Kraftaufwand*) between the two times.

The action in the motion of a conservative system during a given time is thus represented by the integral

$$\int T dt$$

taken between the initial and final values of that time.

614. Observation 1. If ds denotes a path-element of the visible partial system, and v its velocity in its path, then the action can be represented in the form of the integral

$$\frac{1}{2} m \int v ds$$

taken between the positions in which the system is found at the beginning and end of the time considered.

615. Observation 2. The name "action" (*Wirkung*) for the integral in the text has often been condemned as unsuitable. It is not easy to see, however, why the term "expenditure of power," invented by Jacobi, is better; nor why the term (*action*) originally chosen by Maupertuis should be preferred. All these names suggest conceptions which have nothing to do with the objects they denote. It is difficult to see how the summation of the energies existing at different times could yield anything else than a quantity for calculation, and it is not only difficult, but impossible, to find a suitable name, of simple meaning, for the integral in the text.

The other terms and notations introduced in this chapter are also justified less by their essential suitability than by the necessity of employing as much as possible the existing terms of mechanics.

Differential Equations of Motion

616. **Problem.** To form the differential equations of motion of a conservative system.

The solution of the problem consists only in specifying the equations of motion for the visible partial system. The mass of this portion is m, its coordinates p_ρ; let the k equations

$$\sum_1^r {}_\rho p_{\chi\rho} dp_\rho = 0 \tag{i}$$

be its equations of condition. Since the p_ρ's are at the same time the parameters of the concealed partial system, the components of the force which it exerts on the visible partial system are equal to $\partial U/\partial p_\rho$ (§ 563). Let an additional force act on the visible partial system on account of a coupling with other visible systems and let P_ρ be its components. Then the equations of motion of the system are by § 481

$$mf_\rho + \sum_k^1 {}_\chi p_{\chi\rho} P_\chi = \frac{\partial U}{\partial p_\rho} + P_\rho \tag{ii},$$

and these r equations, together with the k equations (i), are sufficient for the unique determination of the $r+k$ quantities $\ddot{p}_\rho$ and P_χ.

617. **Observation 1.** If the conservative system is free, then no external forces act on it, and the P_ρ's are zero; the equations of motion thus take the form

$$mf_\rho + \sum_1^k {}_\chi p_{\chi\rho} P_\chi = \frac{\partial U}{\partial p_\rho}.$$

618. **Observation 2.** In particular, if the coordinate p_ρ is a free coordinate of the visible partial system, then the equation of motion for the index $_\rho$ takes the form

$$mf_\rho = \frac{\partial U}{\partial p_\rho},$$

since then all the $p_{\chi\rho}$'s vanish.

619. **Observation 3.** If we substitute in the equations § 616-618 for the accelerations along p_ρ their different expressions from § 291, we obtain for these equations a series of different forms corresponding to the forms which we obtained for a completely known system in § 368 *et seq.*

620. **Corollary 1.** If in a holonomous conservative system all the p_ρ's are free coordinates, and we put for short

$$T + U = L,$$

then the equations of motion of the system may be expressed in the form of the $2r$ equations

$$q_\rho = \frac{\partial_p L}{\partial \dot{p}_\rho} \quad (i)$$

$$\dot{q}_\rho = \frac{\partial_p L}{\partial p_\rho} \quad (ii),$$

which may be regarded as so many differential equations of the first order for the $2r$ quantities p_ρ and q_ρ, and which, with given initial values, singly determine the course of these quantities.

For if we substitute the value of L, develop the partial differential coefficients and remember that U does not contain $\dot{p}_\rho$, and thus that

$$\frac{\partial_p U}{\partial \dot{p}_\rho} = 0, \qquad \frac{\partial_p U}{\partial p_\rho} = \frac{\partial U}{\partial p_\rho},$$

then we recognise that the equations (i) coincide with the relation between q_ρ and $\dot{p}_\rho$ which follows from the definitions, but that the equations (ii) coincide with the equations of motion in the form § 618 (§§ 289, 291).

621. **Observation.** The function L, by whose use the differential equations of motion take the simple form of the equations § 620 (i) and (ii), has been called Lagrange's function. This function consequently exists only for a holonomous system, and it is here equal to the difference between the kinetic and potential energies, except for an arbitrary constant.

622. **Corollary 2.** If in a holonomous conservative system all the p_ρ's are free coordinates, and we put for short

$$T - U = H,$$

then the equations of motion can be expressed in the form of the $2r$ equations

$$\dot{p}_\rho = \frac{\partial_q H}{\partial q_\rho} \qquad \text{(i)}$$

$$\dot{q}_\rho = -\frac{\partial_q H}{\partial p_\rho} \qquad \text{(ii)},$$

which may be regarded as so many partial differential equations of the first order for which the $2r$ quantities p_ρ and q_ρ, and which with given initial values, singly determine the course of these quantities.

For if we substitute the value of H, and remember that U does not contain q_ρ, and consequently that

$$\frac{\partial_q U}{\partial q_\rho} = 0, \qquad \frac{\partial_q U}{\partial p_\rho} = \frac{\partial U}{\partial p_\rho},$$

we see that the equations (i) represent the relation between q_ρ and $\dot{p}_\rho$ resulting from the definitions; while the equations (ii) coincide with the equations of motion (§ 618) deduced from experience (§§ 290, 294).

623. **Observation.** The function H, through whose use the equations of motion take the simple form given in § 622 (i) and (ii), is known as Hamilton's function. This function therefore exists only for a holonomous system, and for such a system is equal to the sum of the potential and kinetic energies, except for an arbitrary constant; it is also equal to the total energy of the system, except for an arbitrary constant.

In general it is permissible to define Hamilton's function for a system with any, not necessarily cyclic, concealed motions, by the equations § 622 (i) and (ii), *i.e.* as a function of the visible p_ρ's and q_ρ's through whose use (assuming there is such a function) the equations of motion take that simple form. With this more general definition, Hamilton's function is not always equal to the sum of the kinetic and potential energies.

624. **Note.** From the equations § 620 and § 622 the same reciprocal properties can be obtained for a system with concealed cycles as were deduced in § 378 and § 381 for a completely known system. This is unnecessary, but it is implied in these relations that each of them is valid quite independently of whether the coordinates, momenta, etc., appearing in them are visible or concealed coordinates, momenta, etc.

Integral Propositions for Holonomous Systems

625. Note 1. The integral

$$\int_{t_0}^{t_1} (T - U) dt$$

for the motion of a free holonomous system with concealed adiabatic cycles between sufficiently near positions 0 and 1 is smaller for the natural motion of the system than for any other possible motion by which both the visible and concealed coordinates pass in the same time from their initial to their final values.

For since $T - U$ is equal to the energy of the system, increased by a constant which is the same for all possible motions, the note is the same as proposition § 358 expressed by means of the notation just adopted.

626. Observation 1. If the restriction that the final positions should be sufficiently near is removed, then it can only be asserted that the variation of the integral vanishes in a transition to any one of the other motions considered. Using the notation of § 590 the statement takes the form that

$$\delta_p \int_{t_0}^{t_1} (T - U) dt = 0,$$

in a transition from the natural motion to any other possible motion, when the variations of the initial and final times as well as the initial and final values of the visible coordinates vanish (*cf.* § 359).

627. Observation 2. Note 1 distinguishes the natural motions from every other possible motion, and may therefore be used to determine the natural motion if it is actually possible to form the variation of Observation 1. But if, as is assumed, the cyclical coordinates are concealed, then the formation of variations of the form ∂_p is not possible, and the note, although still correct, becomes inapplicable.

628. Proposition 1. The integral

$$\int_{t_0}^{t_1} (T + U)dt$$

in the motion of a free holonomous system with concealed adiabatic cycles between sufficiently near positions of its visible masses is smaller for the natural motion than for any other possible motion which, in the same time and with the same momenta of the concealed cyclical motions, carries the visible coordinates from the given initial to the given final values.

The proof can be obtained by reference to Note 1, § 625. For this purpose we associate (as is possible by § 592) each one of the varied motions required by this proposition, with a second in which the visible coordinates undergo the same variation, but in which the cyclical momenta vary in such a manner that the initial and final values of the cyclical coordinates remain unaltered. We must denote, according to § 590, a variation by a transition to a motion of the first kind by δ_q, and a variation to the corresponding motion of the second kind by δ_p.

Now, firstly, since T depends on the visible coordinates alone,

$$\delta_q \int T dt = \delta_p \int T dt \qquad (i).$$

Secondly, since the duration of the motion is not varied, and $-U$ differs only by a constant from the energy of the cyclical motion (§ 566), we get by § 593

$$\delta_q \int U dt = - \delta_p \int U dt \qquad (ii).$$

Adding (i) and (ii) we get

$$\delta_q \int (T + U) dt = \delta_p \int (T - U) dt \qquad (iii).$$

Now by §§ 626, 625, the variation on the right-hand side has for the natural motion always a vanishing value, and for sufficiently near final positions a necessarily negative value, and therefore so has the variation on the left-hand side. Consequently the integral on the left has a minimum value for the natural motion between sufficiently near final positions; which proves the proposition.

629. **Observation 1.** If the restriction to sufficiently near positions is omitted, then it can only be asserted that the variation of the integral vanishes. The analytical expression for this statement is in our notation (in contradistinction to the statement of § 626)

$$\delta_q \int_{t_0}^{t_1} (T + U) dt = 0.$$

630. **Observation 2.** The property of the natural motion stated in the proposition distinguishes it without ambiguity from every other possible motion. The variation δ_q can be formed even though the cyclical motions are considered concealed; for its formation only requires that the constants appearing in the force-function should be left unvaried. The proposition can thus be used for the determination of the natural motion of conservative systems. Its validity is rigorously limited to holonomous systems.

631. **Observation 3.** The above proposition (§ 628) employed as in § 630 bears the name of Hamilton's Principle. Its physical meaning can in our opinion be no other than that of proposition § 358, from which we have deduced the principle. The principle represents the form which must be given to proposition § 358 in order that, notwithstanding our ignorance of the peculiarities of cyclical motion, it should remain applicable to the determination of the motion of the visible system.

632. **Note 2.** If we denote by ds a path-element of the visible masses of a free holonomous system which contains concealed adiabatic cycles, then the integral

$$\int_0^1 \frac{ds}{\sqrt{U + h}}$$

in a motion between sufficiently near positions 0 and 1 is smaller for the natural paths of the system than for any other possible paths by which the values both of the visible and cyclical coordinates pass from the given initial to the given final values. The quantity h is here to be considered a constant varying from one natural path to another, while for all the paths compared at any instant it is to be regarded as the same constant.

For if we introduce the time and make the arbitrary but permissible assumption that the system traverses the paths under consideration with a constant velocity, this being such that the constant h denotes the value of the analytical energy, then

$$T = U + h = \frac{1}{2}m\frac{ds^2}{dt^2} \qquad (i),$$

and thus the integral considered is equal to

$$\sqrt{\frac{2}{m}}\int_{t_0}^{t_1} dt.$$

The integral, except for the coefficient, is therefore equal to the duration of the motion. But this, by § 352 regarded as a consequence of § 347, is a minimum for a given value of the energy, *i.e.* of the constant h. Hence the content of this note is identical with that of proposition § 352, but is expressed by means of the notation since introduced.

633. Observation 1. If the restriction that the positions should be sufficiently near is omitted, then the vanishing of a variation only can be asserted: in our notation this statement is represented in the form

$$\delta_p \int_0^1 \frac{ds}{\sqrt{U+h}} = 0.$$

634. Observation 2. By means of the property stated in Note 2, the natural paths, which correspond to different values of the constant h, are uniquely distinguished from all other possible paths; and the proposition may be used for the determination of the natural paths of the system, if it is possible to form the variation δ_p. If, however, as is assumed, the peculiarities of the cyclical motion are concealed, then it is not possible to form this variation, and the note, although still correct, ceases to be applicable to the purpose in question.

635. **Proposition 2.**[1] In the motion of a free holonomous system which contains concealed adiabatic cycles, between two sufficiently near positions 0 and 1 of the visible masses, the integral

$$\int_0^1 \sqrt{U+h}\, ds$$

is smaller for the natural paths than for any other possible paths by which, with the same values of the concealed cyclical momenta and the constant h, the visible coordinates pass from the given initial values to the given final ones.

We again give the proof by a reference to the foregoing note (§ 632). For this purpose we introduce the time, and make the arbitrary but permissible assumption that the system traverses the paths considered with constant velocity, this being such that the constant h is equal to the mathematical energy. The integral can then be written in the form

$$\sqrt{\frac{2}{m}} \int_{t_0}^{t_1} (U+h)\, dt.$$

Further, we again associate, as is permissible by § 592, each one of the varied motions mentioned in the proposition with a second in which the visible coordinates undergo the same variation, and in which the constant h, and consequently the energy E, remains unaltered; the cyclical momenta must, however, vary in such a manner that the initial and final values of the cyclical coordinates retain their original values. A variation corresponding to the requirements of the proposition we shall again denote by δ_q, and a variation corresponding to the second motion by δ_p.

Now, firstly, for any variations δq_ρ of the cyclical momenta q_ρ (§ 566)

$$\delta \int (U+h)\, dt = \delta_q \int (U+h)\, dt + \sum_1^r \int \frac{\partial (U+h)}{\partial q_\rho} \delta q_\rho dt$$

$$= \delta_q \int (U+h) dt - \tfrac{1}{2} \sum_1^r \bar{p}_\rho \delta q_\rho,$$

thus in particular for a variation δ_p

[1] Printed as in the original MSS.—Ed.

$$\delta_p \int (U+h)dt = \delta_q \int (U+h)dt - \tfrac{1}{2} \sum_{1}^{r} {}_\rho \bar{\mathfrak{p}}_\rho \delta_p \mathfrak{q}_\rho \qquad \text{(i)}.$$

Secondly, we obtain from the equation § 612 (iii), remembering the relation § 588 and the constancy of E,

$$\int (U+h)dt = E(t_1 - t_0) - \tfrac{1}{2} \sum_{1}^{r} {}_\rho \bar{\mathfrak{p}}_\rho \mathfrak{q}_\rho,$$

thus by a variation of the kind δ_p

$$\delta_p \int (U+h)dt = E\delta_p(t_1 - t_0) - \tfrac{1}{2} \sum_{1}^{r} {}_\rho \bar{\mathfrak{p}}_\rho \delta_p \mathfrak{q}_\rho \qquad \text{(ii)}.$$

Subtraction of (i) and (ii) gives

$$\delta_q \int (U+h)dt = E\delta_p(t_1 - t_0) \qquad \text{(iii)};$$

or when, by aid of § 632 (i), we again eliminate the time,

$$\delta_q \int_0^1 \sqrt{U+h}\, ds = E\delta_p \int_0^1 \frac{ds}{\sqrt{U+h}} \qquad \text{(iv)}.$$

The variation on the right has always, by § 632, for the natural motion a vanishing, and for sufficiently near positions a negative value; and hence, since E is necessarily positive, the same holds for the variation on the left. The integral on the left has thus, for the natural motion and for sufficiently near final positions, a minimum value, which proves the proposition.

636. **Observation 1.** If the restriction that the positions should be sufficiently near is removed, then it can only be asserted that the variation of the integral vanishes. The analytical expression of this statement is in our notation (in contradistinction to § 633)

$$\delta_q \int_0^1 \sqrt{(U+h)}\, ds = 0.$$

637. **Observation 2.** For every value of the constant h the proposition distinguishes without ambiguity a natural path from all other possible paths. The property of natural paths which the proposition states, may therefore be used for

the determination of these paths; it can even be used if the cyclical motions are assumed to be concealed.

For the formation of the variation δ_q only requires that the constants appearing in the force-function should remain unaltered; the variation can thus be formed notwithstanding our ignorance of the peculiarities of cyclical motion.

638. Observation 3. Proposition 2, employed in the conception of the last observation, is Jacobi's form of the Principle of Least Action. For if, for the moment, we take m_ν to be the mass of the νth of the visible points of the system, ds_ν an element of the path of this point, then

$$mds^2 = \sum_1^n {}_\nu m_\nu ds_\nu{}^2,$$

and thus the integral for which we establish a minimum value is, except for coefficient,

$$\int \sqrt{U+h} \sqrt{\sum_1^n {}_\nu m_\nu ds_\nu{}^2},$$

which (again excepting a constant coefficient) is Jacobi's integral.

The physical meaning of Jacobi's Principle we conceive to be no other than that contained in propositions § 352 or § 347, from which it is deduced. It represents the form which we must give to that proposition in order that, notwithstanding our ignorance of the peculiarities of cyclical motions, it may be applicable to the determination of the motion of the visible system. The validity of Jacobi's Law is also confined to holonomous systems.

639. Proposition 3. In the motion of a free holonomous conservative system between sufficiently near positions, the time-integral of the kinetic energy is smaller for the natural motion than for any other possible motion which carries the system from the given initial to the given final values of the visible coordinates, and which is performed with the same given value of the mathematical energy which is constant with regard to the time.

For if we take h to be the given value of the mathematical energy, then for all the paths considered (§ 611)

$$T - U = h,$$

and thus the integral of which the proposition treats, viz.

$$\int_{t_0}^{t_1} T dt,$$

is (except for a constant coefficient) the integral of which Proposition 2 treats; the present proposition is thus only another mode of expressing the content of that proposition.

Observations similar to Nos. 1 and 2 after Proposition 2 are also applicable here.

640. **Observation.** Proposition § 639 expresses the Principle of Least Action as originally stated by Maupertuis. This form is preferable to Jacobi's in that it can be expressed more simply, and therefore appears to contain a simple physical meaning. But it has the disadvantage that it contains the time unnecessarily, inasmuch as the actual statement only determines the path of the system and not the motion in it; this motion being rather determined only by the note which is added, viz. that only motions with constant energy will be considered.

Retrospect to §§ 625-640

641. 1. From our investigations we see that, for the natural motion of a free conservative system, each one of the integrals

$$\int (T - U) dt, \qquad \int (T + U) dt,$$

$$\int \frac{ds}{\sqrt{U+h}}, \qquad \int \sqrt{U+h}\, ds,$$

$$\int T dt,$$

takes a special value under determined conditions. While the two upper integrals relate to the motion of the system, the others refer only to the path. The two integrals on the left relate to the case when all the coordinates of the system, even the cyclical ones, are considered, and when only those positions of the system are considered the same in which the latter coordinates as well as the former have the same values. The remaining integrals relate to the case when the cyclical coordinates are concealed, and when those positions of the system are considered the same in which the visible coordinates have the same values. The consideration of the last integral assumes the validity of the Principle of the Conservation of Energy; the consideration of the two upper ones allows the deduction of this principle; the two middle ones can be considered independently of this principle.

642. 2. The physical meaning of the two integrals on the left is extremely simple; the statements expressing them are immediate consequences of the fundamental law. The integrals on the right have lost their simple physical meaning; but the statement that they take special values for the natural motion always represents a form of the fundamental law, even though it be complicated and obscure. This has happened because the law has been adapted to complicated and obscure hypotheses. The statement which relates to the last integral has an illusory appearance of an independent and simple physical meaning.

Our method of proof was not chosen with a view to being as simple as possible, but to making the above relations stand out as clearly as possible.

643. 3. That Nature is not constituted so as to make any one of these integrals a minimum, is seen firstly from the fact that even in holonomous systems with a more extended motion a minimum does not always appear; and, secondly, from the fact that there are natural systems for which the minimum never appears, and for which the variation of these integrals never vanishes. An expression comprehending all the laws of natural motion cannot therefore be assigned to any of these integrals; and this justifies us in regarding the apparently simple meaning of the last integral as illusory.

Finite Equations of Motion for Holonomous Systems

644. **Note 1.** Let us denote by V' the value of the integral

$$\sqrt{\frac{m}{2}} \int_0^1 \frac{ds}{\sqrt{U+h}}$$

taken for the natural path between two value-systems of all the coordinates of a free holonomous system with adiabatic cycles, regarded as a function of the initial and final values of these coordinates, *i.e.* of $p_{\rho 0}$, $p_{\rho 1}$, and $\mathfrak{p}_{\rho 0}$, $\mathfrak{p}_{\rho 1}$, and the quantity h; then the expression

$$V'\sqrt{\frac{2E}{m+\mathfrak{m}}}$$

represents the straightest distance of the system. The notation is the same as we have used previously in this chapter.

By § 632 V′ is equal to the duration of the natural motion between the given positions, for the mathematical energy h. If then S is the straightest distance between the two positions, we get

$$E = \tfrac{1}{2}(m+\mathfrak{m})\frac{S^2}{V'^2},$$

from which the proof follows.

645. **Corollary.** By means of the function V′ the natural paths of the system considered may be represented in a concise form.

For if ds denotes an element of the path of the visible partial system, and $d\mathfrak{s}$ a similar quantity for the cyclical partial system, and $d\sigma$ for the complete system, then

$$(m+\mathfrak{m})d\sigma^2 = m\,ds^2 + \mathfrak{m}\,d\mathfrak{s}^2 \tag{i},$$

and therefore (§ 57) with the previous notation

$$d\sigma^2 = \sum_{1}^{r}{}_\rho \sum_{1}^{r}{}_\sigma \frac{m}{m+\mathfrak{m}} a_{\rho\sigma} dp_\rho dp_\sigma + \sum_{1}^{r}{}_\rho \sum_{1}^{r}{}_\sigma \frac{\mathfrak{m}}{m+\mathfrak{m}} \mathfrak{a}_{\rho\sigma} d\mathfrak{p}_\rho d\mathfrak{p}_\sigma. \tag{ii}$$

If $\widehat{\sigma p_\rho}$ and $\widehat{\sigma \mathfrak{p}_\rho}$ are the angles which the path of the complete system makes with the coordinates p_ρ and $\mathfrak{p}_\rho$ of that system, then the equations of the natural paths, after division of both sides by a constant factor, are obtained by §§ 224, 226 in the form

$$\sqrt{a_{\rho\rho 1}} \cos \sigma, p_{\rho 1} = \sqrt{\frac{2\mathrm{E}}{m}} \frac{\partial \mathrm{V}'}{\partial p_{\rho 1}} \qquad \text{(iii)}$$

$$\sqrt{a_{\rho\rho 0}} \cos \sigma, p_{\rho 0} = -\sqrt{\frac{2\mathrm{E}}{m}} \frac{\partial \mathrm{V}'}{\partial p_{\rho 0}} \qquad \text{(iv)}$$

$$\sqrt{\mathfrak{a}_{\rho\rho 1}} \cos \sigma, \mathfrak{p}_{\rho 1} = \sqrt{\frac{2\mathrm{E}}{\mathfrak{m}}} \frac{\partial \mathrm{V}'}{\partial \mathfrak{p}_{\rho 1}} \qquad \text{(v)}$$

$$\sqrt{\mathfrak{a}_{\rho\rho 0}} \cos \sigma, \mathfrak{p}_{\rho 0} = -\sqrt{\frac{2\mathrm{E}}{\mathfrak{m}}} \frac{\partial \mathrm{V}'}{\partial \mathfrak{p}_{\rho 0}} \qquad \text{(vi)},$$

and these equations admit of a dual interpretation, namely, either that they give the equations of the natural paths as differential equations of the first order or as equations of a finite form.

646. Observation. The foregoing equations (iii) to (vi) are correct in all cases, whether we regard the cyclical coordinates as visible or concealed. They cease, however, to be applicable if the latter be the case; for then the complete expression for V' is unknown and the equations cannot be developed.

647. Problem 1. To transform the foregoing equations of motion of a free holonomous system so that they remain applicable even when the cyclical motions of the system are concealed.

We denote by V the value of the integral

$$\sqrt{2m} \int_0^1 \sqrt{\mathrm{U}+h}\, ds,$$

taken for the natural path between two value-systems of the visible coordinates. In the determination of this natural path we shall regard the cyclical momenta in the force-function as invariable constants; V will therefore be considered a function of the initial and final values alone of the visible coordinates and the constant h. By § 635 (iv), for the transition from one natural path to another with visible coordinates varied in any manner,

$$\delta_q \sqrt{2m} \int_0^1 \sqrt{\mathrm{U}+h}\, ds = 2\mathrm{E}\delta_p \sqrt{\frac{m}{2}} \int_0^1 \frac{ds}{\sqrt{\mathrm{U}+h}} \qquad \text{(i)},$$

so that, in particular, in a transition from one natural path to any neighbouring natural path

$$\delta_q V = 2E\delta_p V' \qquad \text{(ii)},$$

therefore

$$\frac{\partial V}{\partial p_{\rho 1}} = 2E\frac{\partial V'}{\partial p_{\rho 1}}$$
$$\frac{\partial V}{\partial p_{\rho 0}} = 2E\frac{\partial V'}{\partial p_{\rho 0}} \qquad \text{(iii)}.$$

By the help of these equations we can eliminate the cyclical coordinates from the right-hand sides of the equations § 645 (iii) and (iv). Then for the left-hand sides we have to replace the angle $\widehat{\sigma p_\rho}$ by the angle $\widehat{sp_\rho}$. We then have, by § 645 (ii) (§ 75),

$$\sqrt{\frac{m}{m+\mathfrak{m}}}\sqrt{a_{\rho\rho}}d\sigma \cos \widehat{\sigma_,p_\rho} = \sum_1^r {}_\sigma \frac{m}{m+\mathfrak{m}} a_{\rho\sigma} dp_\sigma$$
$$= \frac{m}{m+\mathfrak{m}}\sqrt{a_{\rho\rho}}ds \cos \widehat{s_,p_\rho} \qquad \text{(iv)},$$

and further, from the equations

$$U + h = T = \tfrac{1}{2}m\frac{ds^2}{dt^2}$$

and

$$E = \tfrac{1}{2}(m+\mathfrak{m})\frac{d\sigma^2}{dt^2} \qquad \text{(v)},$$

by division

$$d\sigma = \sqrt{\frac{m}{m+\mathfrak{m}}}\sqrt{\frac{E}{U+h}}ds \qquad \text{(vi)};$$

thus from (iv) and (vi)

$$\cos \widehat{\sigma_,p_\rho} = \sqrt{\frac{U+h}{E}}\cos \widehat{s_,p_\rho} \qquad \text{(vii)}.$$

If now we substitute the result (iii) on the right, and the result (vii) on the left of the equations to be transformed, we obtain the equations

$$\sqrt{a_{\rho\rho 1}} \cos \widehat{s_,p_{\rho 1}} = \frac{1}{\sqrt{2m(U+h)_1}}\frac{\partial V}{\partial p_{\rho 1}},$$

$$\sqrt{a_{\rho\rho 0}} \cos s_{,}p_{\rho 0} = - \frac{1}{\sqrt{2m(\mathrm{U}+h)_0}} \frac{\partial \mathrm{V}}{\partial p_{\rho 0}} \qquad \text{(viii)},$$

which are the required transformations. For they no longer contain any quantities which refer to the concealed partial system, and they admit the dual interpretation that they present the natural paths of the visible partial system as differential equations of the first order, or in a finite form.

648. **Observation 1.** The function V does not contain the time and gives only the natural paths of the system, but not its motion in these paths. But since the natural paths are traversed with constant velocities, and we have already assigned the interpretation of analytical energy to the constant h appearing in V, it is easy to introduce the time as an independent variable in the equations. In the first place, the connection of the time with the length of the path, previously regarded as the independent variable, is given by the equation

$$\frac{\partial \mathrm{V}}{\partial h} = \sqrt{\frac{m}{2}} \int_0^1 \frac{ds}{\sqrt{\mathrm{U}+h}} = t_1 - t_0 \qquad \text{(i)}.$$

Thus we obtain after multiplication of the equations § 647 (viii) by

$$\sqrt{2m(\mathrm{U}+h)} = \sqrt{2m\mathrm{T}} = m\frac{ds}{dt},$$

and using § 75 and § 270,

$$q_{\rho 1} = \frac{\partial \mathrm{V}}{\partial p_{\rho 1}} \qquad \text{(ii)}$$

$$q_{\rho 0} = - \frac{\partial \mathrm{V}}{\partial p_{\rho 0}} \qquad \text{(iii)}.$$

Finally, we obtain for the value of the function itself,

$$\mathrm{V} = 2 \int_{t_0}^{t_1} \mathrm{T} dt \qquad \text{(iv)}.$$

In form these equations are much simpler than the equations of the foregoing problem, but the former have the advantage of containing one less independent variable.

649. **Observation 2.** The function V is the same function as Hamilton denoted by a similar symbol, and is known as the characteristic function of the conservative system. This statement agrees with that of § 412, for by the assumption made there that all coordinates were visible, the function here denoted by V is transformed into the function there denoted by the same symbol.

Finally, it appears that the characteristic function of a system, according to the now extended definition, is a quantity for calculation without any physical meaning. For, according as we treat greater or lesser parts of cyclical motions as concealed, we may write down different characteristic functions for the same system; and these serve the same purpose analytically although they possess different values for identical motions of the system.

650. **Proposition.** The characteristic function V of a conservative system satisfies the two partial differential equations of the first order

$$\frac{1}{2m}\sum_{1}^{r}{}_{\rho}\sum_{1}^{r}{}_{\sigma}b_{\rho\sigma 1}\frac{\partial V}{\partial p_{\rho 1}}\frac{\partial V}{\partial p_{\rho 1}} = (U+h)_1$$

$$\frac{1}{2m}\sum_{1}^{r}{}_{\rho}\sum_{1}^{r}{}_{\sigma}b_{\rho\sigma 0}\frac{\partial V}{\partial p_{\rho 0}}\frac{\partial V}{\partial p_{\sigma 0}} = (U+h)_0,$$

which correspond to the differential equations § 227 for the straightest distance.

For these equations are obtained by the substitution of the direction cosines from the equations § 647 (viii) in the equation § 88, which these direction cosines satisfy.

651. **Note 2.** If we denote by P' the value of the integral

$$\int_{t_0}^{t_1} (T-U)dt,$$

taken for the natural motion between two value-systems of all the coordinates of a free holonomous system with adiabatic cycles, and considered as a function of these values and the duration of the motion, then P' differs from the principal function of the system (§ 415) only by the product of the duration of the motion and an (unknown) constant.

For T − U differs from the energy of the system only by an (unknown) constant.

652. Corollary. With the aid of the function P′ the natural motions of the system can be expressed in a concise form.

In fact the difference between P′ and the principal function defined in § 415 does not prevent the immediate application of the equations § 414 (ii) and (iii), so that we obtain as equations of motion

$$q_{\rho_1} = \frac{\partial P'}{\partial p_{\rho_1}} \qquad (i)$$

$$q_{\rho_1} = -\frac{\partial P'}{\partial p_{\rho_0}} \qquad (ii)$$

$$q_{\rho_1} = \frac{\partial P'}{\partial \mathfrak{p}_{\rho_1}} \qquad (iii)$$

$$q_{\rho_0} = -\frac{\partial P'}{\partial \mathfrak{p}_{\rho_0}} \qquad (iv).$$

On the other hand the equation § 414 (iv) requires a slight modification; we obtain instead of it

$$h = -\frac{\partial P'}{\partial t_0} = \frac{\partial P'}{\partial t_1}.$$

653. Observation. The foregoing equations (i) to (iv) are correct in every case, whether all the coordinates are accessible to observation or not; but they cease to be applicable when the cyclical motions of the system are considered concealed.

654. Problem 2. To transform the foregoing equations of motion of a free holonomous system, so that they remain applicable even when the cyclical motions of the system are concealed.

We denote by P the value of the integral

$$\int_{t_0}^{t_1} (T + U)dt,$$

taken for the natural motion between the two value-systems of the visible coordinates existing at the times t_0 and t_1. In the determination of this natural motion the cyclical momenta contained in the constants of the force-function will be considered invariable, and P will thus be considered a function of the initial and final values alone of these coordinates and of the times t_0 and t_1.

Now, by § 628 (iii), for a transition from a natural motion to any neighbouring motion of equal duration, the equation

$$\delta_q \int (T + U) dt = \delta_p \int (T - U) dt$$

holds. If we apply this equation to the transition from a natural motion to a neighbouring natural motion of equal duration, we get

$$\delta_q P = \delta_p P',$$

thus

$$\frac{\partial P}{\partial p_{\rho_0}} = \frac{\partial P'}{\partial p_{\rho_0}}, \qquad \frac{\partial P}{\partial p_{\rho_1}} = \frac{\partial P'}{\partial p_{\rho_1}}.$$

By means of these equations we eliminate the concealed coordinates from the right of equations § 652. For the left, it is sufficient to remark that the momentum q_ρ of the whole system along p_ρ is also the momentum of the visible partial system along p_ρ, regarded as a coordinate of this partial system. We then obtain as equations of motion of the visible partial system

$$q_{\rho_1} = \frac{\partial P}{\partial p_{\rho_1}} \qquad \text{(i)},$$

$$q_{\rho_0} = -\frac{\partial P}{\partial p_{\rho_0}} \qquad \text{(ii)},$$

which are the required transformations.

655. **Observation 1.** The function P here introduced is the function which Hamilton denoted by S, and is known as the principal function of the conservative system. This statement agrees with § 415, for by the assumption there made, that all the coordinates are visible, the present function P transforms into the function there denoted by the same symbol.

656. **Observation 2.** The value of the principal function for a definite transference is related to the characteristic function in a simple manner. For by a simple transformation we obtain

$$\int_{t_0}^{t_1}(T+U)dt = \int_{t_0}^{t_1}(2U+h)dt$$

$$= \sqrt{2m}\int_0^1 \sqrt{U+h}\,ds - \sqrt{\frac{m}{2}}\int_0^1 \frac{h\,ds}{\sqrt{U+h}}.$$

Thus (§§ 647, 644)

$$P = V - h(t_1 - t_0) \qquad (i),$$

where we have to regard the quantity h introduced on the right-hand side, in V and in the second summation, as a function of $(t_1 - t_0)$, p_{ρ_0} and p_{ρ_1}.

Conversely,

$$V = P + h(t_1 - t_0) \qquad (ii),$$

where, on the right-hand side in P and in the second summation, the quantity $(t_1 - t_0)$ is regarded as a function of h, p_{ρ_0} and p_{ρ_1}.

657. **Observation 3.** The analytical energy h does not appear in the principal function. Still it can be indirectly deduced from it by means of the equations § 654 (i), (ii), § 286 (iii) and § 612 (i). It can also be directly expressed by means of P. For if we change on the right-hand side of § 656 (i) t_1 and t_0, but not p_{ρ_1} and p_{ρ_0}, and denote by dh the change of h which necessarily results therefrom, we get

$$dP = \frac{\partial V}{\partial h}dh - h\,d(t_1 - t_0) - (t_1 - t_0)dh,$$

and thus, by § 648 (i),

$$dP = -h\,d(t_1 - t_0),$$

from which follows

$$h = -\frac{\partial P}{\partial t_1} = \frac{\partial P}{\partial t_0}.$$

658. **Proposition.** The principal function P of a conservative system satisfies the two differential equations of the first order

$$\frac{1}{2m}\sum_{1}^{r}{}_{\rho}\sum_{1}^{r}{}_{\sigma} b_{\rho\sigma}\frac{\partial P}{\partial p_{\rho_1}}\frac{\partial P}{\partial p_{\sigma_1}} + \frac{\partial P}{\partial t_1} = U_1$$

$$\frac{1}{2m}\sum_{1}^{r}{}_\rho\sum_{1}^{r}{}_\sigma b_{\rho\sigma}\frac{\partial P}{\partial p_{\rho_0}}\frac{\partial P}{\partial p_{\sigma_0}} - \frac{\partial P}{\partial t_o^1} = U_0,$$

which correspond to the differential equations § 227 for the straightest distance.

For these equations are obtained when the analytical energy h is expressed in terms of the differential coefficients of P, the first time directly by means of § 657, and the second time indirectly by means of § 612 (i) and § 654 (i), (ii).

Retrospect to §§ 644-658

659. 1. In §§ 644-658 there are given four finite representations of the motion of a holonomous system with adiabatic cycles. In the first and third all the coordinates of the system were considered capable of being observed, and in the second and fourth the cyclical coordinates were treated as concealed. The first and third representation, which led to the characteristic function, essentially gave only the path of the system and corresponded to the Principle of Least Action. The second and fourth, which led to the principal function, gave the motion completely, and corresponded to Hamilton's Principle.

660. 2. All the four representations have the same simple physical sense, and in all of them the cause of the mathematical complexity is the same. The simple physical sense consists in the fact that the natural paths are always straightest paths, and in the purely geometrical connections of these paths with the straightest distance in holonomous systems. The cause of the mathematical complexity consists in this, that we did not always treat in the same manner all the essential elements for determining the motion, but eliminated some of them as concealed. We may also say that difference in the treatment consists in the fact that for some coordinates the initial and final values were the elements introduced, and for others the initial velocities. Our course of investigation was not adopted as being the simplest possible, but rather as putting this relation as clearly as possible.

661. 3. Further representations of the motion of a

holonomous system could be given by eliminating other coordinates, or by introducing for the visible coordinates as well, not their initial and final values, but other quantities as elements; or by proceeding from the partial differential equations, § 650 or § 658, in the same manner as is done for the straightest distance in §§ 232 *et seq.* Such representations may in particular cases have certain mathematical advantages, as Jacobi has shown in a comprehensive manner. But the further one proceeds in this direction the more is the physical meaning obscured under its mathematical form, and the more the functions used take the character of auxiliary constructions with which it is no longer possible to associate a physical meaning.

Non-Conservative Systems

Explanations and Notes

662. 1. If a material system contains only such concealed masses as are in adiabatic cyclical motion, then if the visible coordinates are under our free control it is possible at every instant to transform back the energy which has become the energy of the concealed masses, into the energy of the visible masses. The visible energy once residing in the system may therefore be permanently retained as visible energy.

It is on account of this property that we have called these systems conservative. For the same reason we denote the forces exerted by the concealed masses of such systems as conservative forces.

663. 2. On the other hand, those systems in which we cannot sufficiently control the visible coordinates so as to retransform the concealed energy at every instant into visible energy are called non-conservative, and the forces of their concealed masses non-conservative forces. Non-conservative systems in which the energy tends to change from the energy of the visible masses into that of the concealed masses, but not conversely, are called dissipative systems, and the forces due to their concealed masses dissipative forces.

664. 3. In general the systems and forces of nature are non-conservative if concealed masses come into consideration. This circumstance is a necessary consequence of the fact that conservative systems are exceptions, and even exceptions attained only more or less approximately (§ 550); so that for any natural system taken at random the probability of its being conservative is infinitely small. Again we know by experience that the systems and forces of nature are dissipative if concealed masses come into consideration. This circumstance is sufficiently explained by the hypothesis that in nature the number of concealed masses and of their degrees of freedom is infinitely great compared with the number of visible masses and their visible coordinates; so that for any motion taken at random the probability of the energy concentrating itself in a special direction from that large number of masses into this definite and small number is infinitely small.

665. 4. The difference between conservative and dissipative systems of forces does not lie in nature, but results simply from the voluntary restriction of our conception, or the involuntary limitation of our knowledge of natural systems. If all the masses of nature were considered visible, then the difference would cease to exist, and all the forces of nature could be regarded as conservative forces.

666. 5. Conservative forces appear in general as differential coefficients of force-functions, *i.e.* as such functions of the visible coordinates of the system as are independent of the time. The non-conservative forces depend in general on the first and higher differential coefficients of the visible coordinates with regard to the time. With any given analytical form of a force of either kind, the question may be raised whether this form is consistent with the assumptions of our mechanics, or the reverse.

667. To this question an answer cannot in general be given; in particular cases it is to be judged from the following considerations :—

(1) If it can be shown that there exists a normal continuous system which exerts forces of the given form, then it is proved that the given form satisfies the postulates of our mechanics.

(2) If it can be proved that the existence of such a system is impossible, then it is shown that the given form contradicts our mechanics.

(3) If it can be shown that there exists in nature any system which we know by experience to exert forces of the given form, then we consider it thereby proved that the given form is consistent with our mechanics.

If no one of the three cases happens, then the question must remain an open one. Should such a form of force be found as would be rejected by the second consideration, but permitted by the third, then the insufficiency of the hypothesis on which our mechanics reposes, and in consequence the insufficiency of our mechanics itself, would be proved.

CHAPTER VI

DISCONTINUITIES OF MOTION

Explanations and Notes

668. 1. All systems of material points to which the fundamental law in accordance with its assumptions is applicable must possess continuous connections. Hence the coefficients of all the equations of condition of such systems are throughout continuous functions of the position (§ 124). This, however, does not prevent these functions from changing very quickly near given positions, so that the equations have, in positions very near to one another, coefficients which differ by finite quantities.

669. 2. When the system considered passes through such a position of very rapid change, then a complete knowledge of its motion requires a complete knowledge of the equations of condition during the rapid change itself. Certain statements may, however, be made concerning the motion even when the form of the equations of condition of the system is given only before and after the place of its sudden change. If we limit ourselves to this class of statements, then it is analytically simpler to pay no attention to the special manner of the change, and to use the equations of condition as though their coefficients were discontinuous. In this case the system is regarded as discontinuous, owing to the voluntary limitation imposed by our mode of treatment.

670. 3. But it may happen that while our physical means permit us to completely investigate the connection of a system

in other respects, they are yet insufficient to investigate it at the places of very sudden change, although we are convinced, and indeed may physically prove, that even here this connection is continuous. If this happens we are compelled to represent the connection analytically as discontinuous, unless we renounce the possibility of a single representation of it. In this case the system must be regarded as discontinuous on account of the involuntary limitation of our knowledge of the system.

671. 4. Conversely, if the coefficients of the equations of condition of a system are directly given as discontinuous functions of the position, without a knowledge of how these functions are obtained, then we assume that one of the two cases previously mentioned happens. We regard the given equations only as an incomplete and approximate presentation of the true and continuous form. We therefore assume, from this very fact, that a complete determination of the motion of such a system is not required of us, but only the specification of those statements which can be made notwithstanding the incomplete knowledge of the system, with the supposition that even in the positions of discontinuity the unknown connection is in reality continuous.

672. 5. If a system passes through a point of very rapid change with a finite velocity, then its equations of condition undergo finite changes in a vanishing time. If during the whole change the system is in reality normal, as the fundamental law assumes, then, to all appearances, it ceases to be normal at the instant of its passing through that position, although this has not actually occurred. Hence if a system is given us analytically, and if its equations of condition are independent of the time but at a certain moment instantaneously take a new form, then we consider the equations of condition at this moment as only an approximate representation of another connection, unknown and perhaps more intricate, but at the same time not only continuous but also normal. Hence we assume again that a complete determination of the motion of the system is not required of us, but only a specification of those statements which, notwithstanding our ignorance, can be made by means of the fundamental law, with the supposi-

tion that even at the time of the discontinuity the true connection of the system is continuous and normal.

673. 6. When we regard all positions and times of discontinuity in the foregoing manner we have renounced the investigation of actually discontinuous systems. The fundamental law, too, would not be applicable to these. This restriction, however, does not imply a refusal to investigate any natural system whatever, for everything points to the conclusion, that there are in nature only apparent, and not actual, discontinuities. That the motion of systems through apparent positions of discontinuity is not completely determined by the fundamental law alone, corresponds entirely with the physical experience that the knowledge of a system before and after a position of discontinuity is not sufficient to determine completely the change of the motion during the passage through that position.

Impulsive Forces or Impulses

674. **Note.** If a system passes through a position of discontinuity, then its velocity undergoes a change of finite magnitude. The differential coefficients of the coordinates with regard to the time suddenly jump to new values.

For immediately before and after such a position these differential coefficients, and consequently the components of that velocity, must satisfy linear equations with finitely different coefficients.

675. **Corollary 1.** In a motion through a position of discontinuity the acceleration becomes infinitely great, but in such a manner that the time-integral of the acceleration taken for the time of the motion retains in general a finite value.

For this time-integral is the change of the velocity which in general is finite.

676. **Corollary 2.** If the equations of condition of one of two or more coupled systems are subject to discontinuity, then in the motion through this discontinuity the force acting between the systems becomes in general infinitely great, but in such a manner that the time-integral of the force, taken for the time of the motion, remains finite.

For in general the components of the acceleration of the discontinuous system along the common coordinates become infinite in the sense of Corollary 1. But since the coefficients of the equations of condition remain finite during the discontinuity, the force is of the order of the acceleration.

677. **Definition.** An impulsive force or impulse is the time-integral of the force exerted by one system on another during the motion through a position of discontinuity, taken for the duration of the motion through this position.

678. **Observation.** When all the systems considered have finite velocities, finite and infinitesimal, but not infinite impulses, may appear. In what follows we shall assume the impulses to be finite.

679. **Corollary 1.** To every impulse there is always a counter-impulse. It is the time-integral of the force which the system regarded as the second exerts on the first.

680. **Corollary 2.** An impulse is always exerted by, as well as exerted on, a system which suffers a discontinuity of motion; it is not conceivable without two such systems mutually acting on one another.

We may speak of impulses simply without expressly mentioning the systems which cause or suffer them, for exactly the same reasons as we thus speak of forces.

681. **Corollary 3.** An impulse may always be considered as a vector quantity with regard to that system which causes it, as well as with regard to that system on which it acts. Its components along the common coordinates are in general different from zero; its components along the coordinates which are not common are zero; its components in directions which cannot be expressed in terms of the coordinates used remain undetermined.

For this statement holds for the force of which the impulse is the time-integral.

682. **Notation.** If a system with the coordinates p_ρ suffers a discontinuity of motion, then we shall denote the components along p_ρ of the impulse which acts on the system, by J_ρ. But the components of the impulse which the system causes along p_ρ will be denoted by J_ρ'. For the second system whose co-

ordinates are denoted by $\mathfrak{p}_\rho$, the corresponding quantities will be denoted by $\mathfrak{J}_\rho$ and $\mathfrak{J}_\rho'$ respectively (*cf.* § 467). Thus, then,

$$J_\rho = \mathfrak{J}_\rho',$$
$$\mathfrak{J}_\rho = J_\rho',$$

identically.

683. Proposition. An impulse and its counter-impulse are always equal and opposite, *i.e.* their components along every coordinate are equal and opposite whether we consider these quantities as vector quantities with regard to the one system, or with regard to the other system.

For an impulse and its counter-impulse can also be regarded as is the time-integrals of force and counter-force (*cf.* § 468).

With the notation employed the proposition is given by the equation

$$J_\rho = -J_\rho'$$
$$\mathfrak{J}_\rho = -\mathfrak{J}_\rho'.$$

Composition of Impulses

684. Proposition. If a system is simultaneously coupled with other systems, then any impulse which the aggregate of these systems exerts is equal to the sum of the impulses exerted by the several systems.

For the proposition holds at every instant during the impulses for the acting forces (§ 471), and therefore also for their integrals, *i.e.* for the impulses.

685. Corollary. If impulses simultaneously act on the same system or are exerted by the same system, they can be compounded and resolved by the rules for the composition and resolution of vector quantities. We speak of the components of an impulse and of resultant impulses in the same sense as we speak of the components of forces and resultant forces (*cf.* §§ 472-474).

686. Definition. An impulse which is exerted by or on a single material point is called an elementary impulse.

687. Corollary 1. Every impulse which is exerted by or on a material system can be resolved into a series of elementary impulses (*cf.* § 479).

688. **Corollary 2.** The composition and resolution of elementary impulses are performed by means of the rules for the composition and resolution of geometrical quantities. (Parallelogram of impulses.) (*Cf.* § 478.)

Motion under the Action of Impulses

689. **Problem 1.** To determine the motion of a material system under the action of a given impulse.

The solution of the problem consists simply in stating the change which the velocity of the system suffers through the impulse. Let the system considered be the same as in § 481; let us denote by P_ρ the components of the infinite force which acts on the system during the impulse, then, by § 481, during this time,

$$mf_\rho + \sum_1^k {}_\chi p_{\chi\rho} P_\chi = P_\rho \qquad (i).$$

Multiply this equation by dt and integrate for the duration of the impulse. Since the values of the coordinates during this time are constant,

$$m\int f_\rho dt = q_{\rho 1} - q_{\rho 0} \qquad (ii),$$

where we denote quantities before the impulse by the index 0 and after by the index 1. We have further, by § 682,

$$\int P_\rho dt = J_\rho \qquad (iii),$$

and putting for short

$$\int P_\chi dt = J_\chi \qquad (iv),$$

we obtain r equations of the form

$$q_{\rho 1} - q_{\rho 0} + \sum_1^k {}_\chi p_{\chi\rho} J_\chi = J_\rho \qquad (v).$$

Since the velocity of the system before and after the impulse must satisfy the connections of the system, we obtain from

VI DISCONTINUITIES OF MOTION 259

the k equations of condition of the system, k equations of the form

$$\sum_{1}^{r}{}_{\rho}p_{\chi\rho}(\dot{p}_{\rho 1}-\dot{p}_{\rho 0})=0 \qquad \text{(vi)},$$

which, with the equations (v), may be regarded as $k+r$ unhomogeneous linear equations for the $k+r$ quantities $\dot{p}_{\rho 1}-\dot{p}_{\rho 0}$ and J_{χ}, or for the $k+r$ quantities $q_{\rho 1}-q_{\rho 0}$ and J_{χ}; and they singly determine these quantities, and therefore the change in the velocity of the system.

690. Observation 1. If the velocity of the system before the impulse is given, and thus the quantities $q_{\rho 0}$ and $\dot{p}_{\rho 0}$ known, then we may regard the r equations § 689 (v), together with the k equations § 689 (vi), or, what is the same thing, the k equations

$$\sum_{1}^{r}{}_{\rho}p_{\chi\rho}\dot{p}_{\rho 1}=0,$$

as $r+k$ unhomogeneous linear equations for the $r+k$ quantities $\dot{p}_{\rho 1}$ and J_{χ}, which singly determine these quantities, and therefore the velocity of the system after the impulse.

691. Observation 2. If we use rectangular coordinates and denote the component of the impulse along x_ν by I_ν, then the equations of the impulse take the form of the $3n$ equations

$$m_\nu(\dot{x}_{\nu 1}-\dot{x}_{\nu 0})+\sum_{1}^{i}{}_\iota x_{\iota\nu}\mathrm{I}_\iota=\mathrm{I}_\nu \qquad \text{(i)},$$

which, with the i equations deduced from the equations of condition, namely,

$$\sum_{1}^{3n}{}_\nu x_{\iota\nu}(\dot{x}_{\nu 1}-\dot{x}_{\nu 0})=0 \qquad \text{(ii)},$$

singly determine the $3n$ components $\dot{x}_{\nu 1}-\dot{x}_{\nu 0}$ of the change of the velocity and the i quantities I_ι.

692. Observation 3. If the coordinate p_ρ is a free coordinate, then the corresponding quantities $p_{\chi\rho}$ are zero, and the equation of impulse relative to p_ρ takes the simple form

$$q_{\rho 1}-q_{\rho 0}=\mathrm{J}_\rho.$$

If in a holonomous system all the coordinates are free, then all the equations take this form, and the resulting r equations are sufficient to determine the r quantities $\dot{p}_{\rho 1} - \dot{p}_{\rho 0}$, which are known linear functions of the quantities $q_{\rho 1} - q_{\rho 0}$, immediately given by these equations.

693. **Corollary 1 (to § 689).** In order to impress suddenly on a system at rest a given possible velocity, it is sufficient to apply to the system an impulse in the given direction and equal in magnitude to the product of the given velocity and the mass of the system.

For if $q_{\rho 0} = 0$, and the given values of $\dot{p}_{\rho 1}$ satisfy the equations of condition, then the assumption

$$J_\chi = 0$$
$$J_\rho = q_{\rho 1}$$

satisfies the equations § 689 (v) and (vi).

694. **Corollary 2.** In order to bring a moving system suddenly to rest in its instantaneous position, it is sufficient to apply to the system an impulse opposite in direction and equal in magnitude to the product of the velocity of the system and its mass.

For if $q_{\rho 1} = 0$, and if the quantities $\dot{p}_{\rho 0}$ satisfy the equations of condition of the system, then the assumption

$$J_\chi = 0$$
$$J_\rho = -q_{\rho 0}$$

satisfies the equations § 689 (v) and (vi).

695. **Proposition.** The change of velocity which several impulses, acting simultaneously, produce in a system is the sum of the changes of velocity which the impulses, acting singly, would produce.

All impulses are considered as acting simultaneously which take place within a vanishing time, without regard to their succession in this time.

The theorem follows (*cf.* § 485) from the linear form of the equations § 689 (v) and (vi), and it can also be regarded as an immediate consequence of § 485.

696. **Observation.** The content of the foregoing pro-

position may also be expressed by the usual statement that several simultaneous impulses are quite independent as regards the velocity which they produce.

697. **Proposition.** If the direction of an impulse is perpendicular to every possible displacement of the system on which it acts, then the impulse produces no effect on the motion of the system. And conversely: If an impulse produces no effect on the motion of the system on which it acts, then it is perpendicular to every possible displacement of the system.

The proposition may be regarded as an immediate consequence of § 488, or it can be deduced from the equations § 689 (v) and (vi).

698. **Note.** Although the change of motion which an impulse produces can be singly determined when we know the impulse, yet the impulse cannot conversely be singly determined when we know the sudden change of motion which it has produced.

699. **Problem 2.** To determine the impulse which a material system exerts in a given sudden change of motion.

As in § 682 we denote the components of the impulse by J'_ρ, and by §§ 683 and 689 (v) these are

$$J'_\rho = -q_{\rho 1} + q_{\rho 0} - \sum_1^k {}_x p_{\chi\rho} J_\chi.$$

In this equation $q_{\rho 1}$ and $q_{\rho 0}$ are determined by the data of the problem, but the J_χ's are not so given unless the motion of the second system on which the impulse acts is also given. The solution of the problem is thus not determinate, but contains an undetermined summation which represents an impulse perpendicular to every possible displacement of the system.

700. **Observation 1.** Although all the components of the impulse which a system exerts in a sudden change of motion are not determined by the change of motion of the system, still all the components in the direction of a possible motion are determined by this change.

701. **Observation 2.** Although all the components of the

impulse which a system exerts in a sudden change of motion are not determined by the change of motion of the system, yet every component in the direction of a free coordinate is singly determined by this change.

702. **Observation 3.** If p_ρ is a free coordinate, then the impulse exerted in the direction of this coordinate can be written in the form

$$J'_\rho = -q_{\rho 1} + q_{\rho 0}$$
$$= -\left(\frac{\partial_p E}{\partial \dot{p}_\rho}\right)_1 + \left(\frac{\partial_p E}{\partial \dot{p}_\rho}\right)_0.$$

Internal Constraint in an Impulse

703. **Note 1.** If an impulse acts on a system of material points between which no connections exist, it produces a change of velocity whose direction is that of the impulse, and whose magnitude is equal to the magnitude of the impulse divided by the mass of the system.

704. **Note 2.** If connections exist between the points of the system, then the change of velocity differs in general from that given in the foregoing remark. The connections of the system may thus be considered the causes of this difference.

705. **Definition.** By internal constraint, or constraint simply, in an impulse, we mean the alteration which all the connections of a system produce in the change of velocity of the system due to the impulse.

The constraint in an impulse is measured by the difference between the actual change of velocity and that change of velocity which would take place if all the equations of condition of the system were removed; it is equal to the former diminished by the latter.

706. **Corollary.** The constraint in an impulse is the time-integral of the internal constraint of the system taken for its whole duration.

707. **Problem.** To determine the constraint of a system in an impulse.

We shall denote the components of the constraint along p_ρ

by Z_ρ. If then we multiply the equation § 497 (i) by mdt and integrate for the duration of the impulse, we obtain

$$mZ_\rho = q_{\rho 1} - q_{\rho 0} - J_\rho \qquad \text{(i)}.$$

The components along any coordinates are not in general sufficient for the determination of the magnitude of the constraint. If, therefore, we use rectangular coordinates and denote the component of the constraint along x_ν by Z_ν, we obtain

$$mZ_\nu = m_\nu(\dot{x}_{\nu 1} - \dot{x}_{\nu 0}) - I_\nu \qquad \text{(ii)};$$

then the magnitude Z of the constraint is the positive root of the equation

$$mZ^2 = \sum_1^{3n} {}_\nu m_\nu \left(\dot{x}_{\nu 1} - \dot{x}_{\nu 0} - \frac{I_\nu}{m_\nu} \right)^2.$$

708. Proposition 1. The magnitude of the constraint in an impulse is smaller for the natural change of motion than it would be for any other possible change of motion.

For the necessary and sufficient condition (*cf.* §§ 155, 498) that with given values of I_ν the quantity $\tfrac{1}{2}mZ^2$ should be a minimum, is given by the $3n$ equations

$$m_\nu(\dot{x}_{\nu 1} - \dot{x}_{\nu 0}) - I_\nu + \sum_1^i {}_\iota x_{\iota \nu} I_\iota = 0,$$

where the quantities I_ι denote any undetermined multipliers, and these with the i equations

$$\sum_1^{3n} {}_\nu x_{\iota \nu}(\dot{x}_{\nu 1} - \dot{x}_{\nu 0}) = 0$$

singly determine the $3n + i$ quantities $\dot{x}_{\nu 1} - \dot{x}_{\nu 0}$ and I_ι. But since the equations coincide with the equations of motion (§ 691) of the system, they are satisfied by the natural changes of velocity, and only by these.

709. Observation. The foregoing theorem contains the adaptation of Gauss's Principle of Least Constraint to the particular case of impulses.

710. Corollary. If, owing to the connections of the system, the angle between an impulse and the change of velocity caused by it is not zero (§ 703), then this angle is as small as possible, consistently with the connections of the system.

For, if we draw a plane triangle whose sides represent the magnitude of the impulse divided by the mass of the system, the magnitude of any possible change of velocity and the magnitude of the difference of these two quantities, that is to say, the constraint which corresponds to this change of velocity, then the angle ϵ included between the first two sides represents the angle between the impulse and the change of velocity (§ 34). Now a possible change of velocity in a given direction may take all values; but amongst all the changes of velocity in given directions, the natural one can only be that in which the constraint is perpendicular to the change of velocity (§ 708). If, then, we restrict ourselves to those changes of velocity which are subject to this consideration, all the triangles to be drawn are right-angled, and the hypothenuse is equal in all and is given. But the side opposite to the angle ϵ is smaller for the natural change of velocity than for any other (§ 708); therefore, for this change of velocity the angle ϵ itself is a minimum, which proves the proposition.

711. **Proposition 2.** The direction of the constraint in an impulse is perpendicular to every possible (virtual) displacement of the system from its instantaneous position.

For by §§ 707, 689, the components of the constraint can be represented in the form

$$-\frac{1}{m}\sum_{1}^{k}{}_\chi p_{\chi\rho} \mathrm{J}_\chi.$$

Thus (§ 250) the constraint as a vector quantity is perpendicular to every possible displacement of the system. The proposition may also be immediately deduced from § 500.

712. **Symbolical Expression.** If we denote by δp_ρ the changes of the coordinates p_ρ for every possible displacement of the system, then the foregoing proposition can be expressed in the form of the symbolical equation

$$\sum_{1}^{r}{}_\rho (q_{\rho 1} - q_{\rho 0} - \mathrm{J}_\rho)\delta p_\rho = 0 \qquad (\mathrm{i}),$$

which, for rectangular coordinates, takes the form

$$\sum_{1}^{3n} {}_\nu [m_\nu(\dot{x}_{\nu 1} - \dot{x}_{\nu 0}) - \mathrm{I}_\nu]\delta x_\nu = 0 \qquad \text{(ii)}$$

(*cf.* §§ 393, 501).

713. Observation. The foregoing proposition (§ 711) contains the adaptation of d'Alembert's Principle to the particular case of impulses, and the symbolical form § 712 is the usual expression for this adaptation.

714. Corollary 1. The component of the change of motion in the direction of every possible motion produced by an impulse is equal to the component of the impulse in that direction divided by the mass of the system.

715. Corollary 2. The component of the change of motion produced by an impulse in the direction of every free coordinate is equal to the component of the impulse along this coordinate divided by the mass of the system.

716. Corollary 3. The component of the velocity along every coordinate of absolute position changes by an amount which is equal to the component of the impulse acting in that direction divided by the mass of the system—whatever be the connections of the system.

717. Observation. Without any knowledge, or without a complete knowledge of the connection between the masses of a system, we can always find six equations for the motion of a system under the action of an impulse. If we choose as coordinates of absolute position the six quantities a_1, a_2, a_3, ω_1, ω_2, ω_3, introduced in § 402, then the six equations which we obtain represent the adaptation of the Principle of the Centre of Gravity and of Areas to the particular case of impulses.

Energy, Work

718. Definition. The increase of the energy of a system produced by an impulse acting on the system is called the work of the impulse.

Any decrease of the energy owing to an impulse is regarded as a negative increase. Thus the work of an impulse may be positive or negative.

719. Corollary. The work of an impulse is the time-integral of the work performed by that force whose time-integral is the impulse.

720. Proposition. The work of an impulse is equal to the product of the magnitude of the impulse and the component in its direction of the mean value of the initial and final velocities of the system.

For whatever may be the actual values of the force acting during the time of the impulse and the motion of the system during this time, the final motion, and consequently the work of the impulse, will be the same as though the force acted with a constant mean value in the direction of the impulse. Now, if we make this simple assumption, then, firstly, the magnitude of the force acting is equal to the magnitude of the impulse divided by its duration. Secondly, the velocity changes uniformly from its initial to its final value, and its mean value is the arithmetic mean of the initial and final values. The component of the portion of the path described during the impulse is, however, equal to the component of that mean value, multiplied by the time. Then, if we calculate by § 513 the work performed by the force during its time of application, *i.e.* the work of the impulse, the time drops out and the proposition follows.

721. Observation. With the notation hitherto used, the analytical expression for the proposition is the statement that the work of the impulse is equal to

$$\tfrac{1}{2}\sum_{1}^{r}{}_\rho J_\rho(\dot{p}_{\rho 1} + \dot{p}_{\rho 0}).$$

722. Corollary 1. The work of an impulse is equal to the product of the impulse and the component of the original velocity taken in its direction, increased by half the product of the magnitude of the impulse and the component in its direction of the change of velocity produced by it.

The analytical expression for this is that the work of the impulse is equal to

$$\sum_{1}^{r}{}_\rho J_\rho \dot{p}_{\rho 0} + \tfrac{1}{2}\sum_{1}^{r}{}_\rho J_\rho(\dot{p}_{\rho 1} - \dot{p}_{\rho 0}),$$

which coincides with § 721.

723. Corollary 2. The work of an impulse which sets in motion a system at rest is equal to half the product of the impulse, and the component in its direction of the velocity produced by it.

For if the quantities $\dot{p}_{\rho 0}$ are zero, then the work of the impulse is

$$\tfrac{1}{2}\sum_{1}^{r}{}_{\rho}J_{\rho}\dot{p}_{\rho 1}.$$

724. Proposition. If a system at rest is set in motion by an impulse, then it moves in that direction in which the impulse performs the most work, *i.e.* in which it performs more work than it would if it were compelled to move in any other direction by additional connections. (The so-called Bertrand's Law.)

For if J is the magnitude of the impulse, v that of the velocity produced, and ϵ the angle between them, then for every original or additional connection we have by § 714

$$v = \frac{J}{m}\cos \epsilon.$$

Thus the work of the impulse is by § 723 equal to

$$\tfrac{1}{2}Jv\cos \epsilon = \frac{J^2}{2m}\cos^2 \epsilon.$$

But the angle ϵ for the natural action of the impulse takes (§ 710) the smallest value consistent with the original connection, and consequently ϵ can only be increased by any additional connection, *i.e.* $\cos^2 \epsilon$ decreased, which proves the proposition.

725. Corollary. The energy which an impulse on a system at rest produces in that system is greater the fewer the connections of the system. The greatest possible value of that energy, which, however, can only be attained by dropping all the connections, is equal to the square of the magnitude of the impulse divided by twice the mass of the system.

Impact of Two Systems

Explanations

726. 1. We say that two systems impinge when they behave as though they had been coupled for a very short time.

We assume this coupling to be direct by assuming (§ 452) a special choice of the coordinates of the two systems.

727. 2. We have to conceive such a temporary coupling as a permanent coupling of the two systems with a third unknown system which possesses the property that it in general has no effect on their motion, but that in the immediate neighbourhood of those positions in which certain coordinates of the one system are equal to certain coordinates of the other it constrains these coordinates to remain temporarily equal. We call such coordinates the common coordinates of the two systems.

728. 3. Before and after the impact the rates of change of the coordinates of each of the two systems are subject simply to the equations of condition of its own system. But during the impulse the rates of change of the common coordinates are also related by the equations of coupling. These rates of change, then, just like the coordinates themselves, must during the impulse have become respectively equal and must have remained so for a time. But the time in which this takes place we regard as vanishingly small, and what takes place during this time as quite unknown. We consider the systems only before and after the impulse, and expect that only such information with regard to the impact will be required as can be given without a knowledge of what takes place during the impact.

729. **Problem.** To determine the subsequent motion of two impinging systems from their motion before the impact, as far as is possible without a knowledge of what takes place during the impulse.

Let the quantities p_ρ be the r coordinates of the one system and $\mathfrak{p}_\rho$ the r coordinates of the other. Let the number of common coordinates be s. In the impact each of the systems suffers an impulse; let the components of the impulse on the first system be J_ρ and on the second $\mathfrak{J}_\rho$. Quantities before and after the impulse will be distinguished by the indices 0 and 1.

Now, in the first place, for all coordinates of the first system equations of the form § 689 (v) hold good, and for all coordinates of the second system corresponding equations. In the second place, the impulses which the two systems suffer stand in the relation of impulse and counter-impulse, and consequently for all common coordinates we have by §§ 682, 683,

$$J_\rho = -\mathfrak{J}_\rho,$$

and for all the coordinates of the two systems which are not common,

$$J_\rho = 0, \quad \mathfrak{J}_\rho = 0.$$

If now we combine the two relations we obtain for the s common coordinates, s equations of the form

$$q_{\rho 1} - q_{\rho 0} + \sum_1^k {}_\times p_{\chi\rho} J_\chi = -\mathfrak{q}_{\rho 1} + \mathfrak{q}_{\rho 0} - \sum_1^{\mathfrak{k}} {}_\times \mathfrak{p}_{\chi\rho} \mathfrak{J}_\chi \quad \text{(i)};$$

while for the $(r-s)+(\mathfrak{r}-s)$ coordinates which are not common, $r-s$ equations of the form

$$q_{\rho 1} - q_{\rho 0} + \sum_1^k {}_\times p_{\chi\rho} J_\chi = 0 \qquad \text{(ii)}$$

and $(\mathfrak{r}-s)$ of the form

$$\mathfrak{q}_{\rho 1} - \mathfrak{q}_{\rho 0} + \sum_1^{\mathfrak{t}} {}_\times \mathfrak{p}_{\chi\rho} \mathfrak{J}_\chi = 0 \qquad \text{(iii)}$$

are obtained. The equations (i), (ii), (iii), together with the $k+\mathfrak{k}$ equations of condition of the two systems, we may regard as equations for the quantities $\dot{p}_{\rho 1}$ and $\dot{\mathfrak{p}}_{\rho 1}$, which determine the motion of the system after the impulse, and for the quantities J_χ and $\mathfrak{J}_\chi$. We have thus altogether $r+\mathfrak{r}-s+k+\mathfrak{k}$ unhomogeneous linear equations which the $r+\mathfrak{r}+k+\mathfrak{k}$ unknowns must satisfy and which contain the requirements of the problem.

730. **Observation.** If the coordinates p_ρ and $\mathfrak{p}_\rho$ are free coordinates of their systems, then the equations of impact can be written in a simpler form. By paying attention to the common coordinates of the system, s equations of the form

$$q_{\rho 1} + \mathfrak{q}_{\rho 1} = q_{\rho 0} + \mathfrak{q}_{\rho 0} \qquad \text{(i)}$$

will be obtained; for the coordinates of the first system which are not common, $r-s$ equations of the form

$$q_{\rho 1} = q_{\rho 0} \qquad \text{(ii)};$$

and for the coordinates of the second system which are not common, $\mathfrak{r} - s$ equations of the form

$$\mathfrak{q}_{\rho 1} = \mathfrak{q}_{\rho 0} \qquad \text{(iii)};$$

these give $r + \mathfrak{r} - s$ equations to determine the $r + \mathfrak{r}$ unknowns $\dot{p}_{\rho 1}$ and $\dot{\mathfrak{p}}_{\rho 1}$.

731. Corollary 1. The motion of two systems after impact is not completely determined by their motion before impact and the general laws of mechanics, but its determination requires also a knowledge of further relations obtained from other sources. The number of these additional necessary relations is equal to the number of common coordinates during the impact.

732. Corollary 2. If in an impact it is possible to obtain, in addition to the relations deduced from the general laws of mechanics, as many linear equations for the components of the velocity after the impact as there are common coordinates, then the motion after the impact is singly determined by means of the previous motion.

733. Observation. The special relations which are necessary for the determination of the motion in an impact, and which do not spring from the general laws of mechanics, depend on the special nature of that system which causes the coupling and whose peculiarities are not known to us in detail. It is this concealed system which takes up the energy lost by the impinging systems, or which supplies the energy gained by the impinging systems. The first case occurs, for instance, in an inelastic impact where the immediate neighbourhood of the point of impact is to be regarded as the coupling system. The second case occurs in explosions. The detailed consideration of these special relations is, however, not a part of general mechanics.

Concluding Note on the Second Book

734. In this second book our object has not been to determine the necessary relations between the creations of our own mind, but rather to consider the experiential connections between

the objects of our external observation. It was therefore inevitable that our investigations should be founded not only on the laws of thought, but also on the results of previous experience. As the necessary contribution of experience, we thus took from our observation of nature the fundamental law.

735. At first it might have appeared that the fundamental law was far from sufficient to embrace the whole extent of facts which nature offers us and the representation of which is already contained in the ordinary system of mechanics. For while the fundamental law assumes continuous and normal connections, the common applications of mechanics bring us face to face with discontinuous and abnormal connections as well. And while the fundamental law expressly refers to free systems only, we are also compelled to investigate unfree systems. Even all the normal, continuous, and free systems of nature do not conform immediately to the law, but seem to be partly in contradiction to it. We saw, however, that we could also investigate abnormal and discontinuous systems if we regarded their abnormalities and discontinuities as only apparent; that we could also follow the motion of unfree systems if we conceived them as portions of free systems; that, finally, even systems apparently contradicting the fundamental law could be rendered conformable to it by admitting the possibility of concealed masses in them. Although we have associated with the fundamental law neither additional experiential facts nor arbitrary assumptions, yet we have been able to range over the whole domain covered by mechanics in general. Nor does our special hypothesis prevent us from understanding that mechanics could and must have been developed in the manner in which it actually has developed.

In conclusion, then, we may assert that the fundamental law is not only necessary but also sufficient to represent completely the part which experience plays in the general laws of mechanics.

INDEX TO DEFINITIONS AND NOTATIONS

(Numbers refer to paragraphs.)

ACCELERATION, 273
Action, 613
Adiabatic motion, 560
Analytical energy, 611
Angle between two displacements, 34, 43

COMMON coordinates, 452
Component of a displacement, 48
Components along the coordinates, 71, 241; of a force, 473; of an impulse, 685; of a vector, 241
Concealed masses, motions, coordinates, 595
Conceivable motion, 257; position, 11
Condition of a system, 261
Configuration, 14
Connection, 109
Conservative systems, forces, 601, 662
Constraint, 385; in impact, 705
Continuous connection, 115
Coordinates of absolute position, 16; of configuration, 15
Counter-force, 456
Counter-impulse, 679
Coupled systems, 450
Coupling, 450
Curvature of a path, 103
Cyclical coordinates, 546; intensity, 549; system, 549

DEGREES of freedom, 134
Difference between two displacements, 51; in direction between two displacements, 34, 43
Differential equations of motion, 367; of a system, 131
Direction of a coordinate, 69; displacement, 24, 39; path, 99; vector quantity, 239
Displacement, 22, 27; in direction of a coordinate, 69; perpendicular to a surface, 206
Displacements perpendicular to one another, 45

Dissipative forces, systems, 663
Distance between two positions, 29

ELEMENTARY force, 475; impulse, 686
Equations of condition, 131; motion, 367
Energy, 282
Entropy, 585
Equal displacements, 25, 41
Equilibrium, 517

FORCE, 455; along the coordinates, 460
Force-function, 563; of a conservative system, 603
Free coordinate, 139; system, 122
Freedom of motion, 134

GEODESIC path, 171
Guided motion, system, 431

HOLONOMOUS system, 123

IDENTICAL displacements, 25, 41
Impossible displacements, 111
Impulse, impulsive force, 677
Inclination of two displacements, 34, 43
Internal connection, 117; constraint, 385; do. in impact, 705
Infinitely small displacement, 54
Isocyclic motion, 560

KINETIC energy, 605

LENGTH of a path, 99; of a displacement, 23, 29

MAGNITUDE of a displacement, 23, 29
Machines, 531
Mass, 4, 300
Material particle, 3; point, 5; system, 121
Mathematical energy, 611
Model of a system, 418
Momentum, 268; along a coordinate, 268
Monocyclic system, 549
Motion, 256

PRINCIPLES OF MECHANICS

NATURAL motion, 312
Non-conservative systems, forces, 663
Normal connection, 119

ORTHOGONAL trajectory, 211

PARALLEL displacements, 25, 41
Parameter, 549
Path-element, 98
Path of a system, 97
Perpendicular displacements to one another, 45; to a surface, 206
Position, 9, 10, 54
Possible displacements, 111; motion, 258; paths, positions, 112
Potential energy, 605

QUADRATIC mean value, 28
Quantity of motion, 268

REACTION, 679
Reduced components, 71, 241
Resultant of forces, 472
Resulting impulse, 685

SERIES of surfaces, 209
Shortest path, 166
Space, 2, 299
Straight path, 101
Straighter element of path, 157
Straightest element of path, 152; distance, 215; path, 153
Sum of two displacements, 50
Surfaces of positions, 200
System of material points, 6; with concealed masses, 594

TIME, 2, 298
Trajectory (orthogonal), 211

UNIFORM motion, 263

VECTOR quantity, 237
Velocity, 261
Virtual displacements, 111
Visible masses, motions, coordinates, 595
Vis viva, 605

WORK of a force, of an impulse, 510, 718

INDEX

(Numbers refer to paragraphs.)

x_ν The $3n$ rectangular coordinates of a system, 13.

p_ρ, $\mathfrak{p}_\rho$ The r or $\mathfrak{r}$ general coordinates of a system, 13.

m_ν Mass of a material point, 31.

m, $\mathfrak{m}$ Whole mass of a system, 31.

ds Length of an infinitely small displacement, of a path-element, 55, 57.

$s \overset{\wedge}{p_\rho}$ Inclination of a path-element to the coordinate p_ρ, 75.

$a_{\nu\rho}$, $a_{\rho\sigma}$, $b_{\rho\sigma}$; $\mathfrak{a}_{\rho\sigma}$, $\mathfrak{b}_{\rho\sigma}$, 57, 64; 553.

c Curvature of a path, 105.

$x_{\iota\nu}$, $p_{\chi\rho}$, $\mathfrak{p}_{\chi\rho}$ Coefficients of the equations of condition, 128, 130.

X_ν, P_χ, $\mathfrak{P}_\chi$ Multipliers, 368, 371.

s Straightest distance of a system, 217.

t Time, 260.

v Magnitude of the velocity of a system, 265.

q_ρ $\mathfrak{q}_\rho$ Reduced components of the momenta of a system, 269.

f; f_ρ Magnitude; reduced components of the acceleration, 275, 277.

E $\begin{cases} \text{Energy of a system, 283.} \\ \text{Total energy of a conservative system, 608.} \end{cases}$

$\mathfrak{E}$ $\begin{cases} \text{Energy of a cyclical system, 553.} \\ \text{Potential energy of a conservative system, 606.} \end{cases}$

T Kinetic energy of a conservative system, 606.

P_ρ, $P_\rho{'}$, $\mathfrak{P}_\rho$, $\mathfrak{P}_\rho{'}$, X_ν Reduced components of a force, 460, 467, 482, 552.

J_ρ, $J_\rho{'}$, $\mathfrak{J}_\rho$, $\mathfrak{J}_\rho{'}$, I_ν Reduced components of an impulse, 682, 691.

∂_p, ∂_q; $\partial_\mathfrak{p}$, $\partial_\mathfrak{q}$ 90, 288, 606; 553.

$\delta_\mathfrak{p}$, $\delta_\mathfrak{q}$ 590.

Accents ($x_\nu{'}$, $x_\nu{''}$, $p_\rho{'}$, etc.) denote, when nothing else is stated, differential coefficients with regard to the length of the path, 100.

Dots ($\dot{p}_\rho$, $\dot{q}_\rho$, $\ddot{p}_\rho$, etc.) denote differential coefficients with regard to the time, 260.

Indices 0 and 1 ($p_{\rho 0}$, $p_{\rho 1}$, $a_{\rho\sigma 0}$, etc.), 217.

$\bar{\mathfrak{p}}_\rho$ 588.

d'Alembert's principle, 394, 448, 502, 713.

Hamilton's principle, 360, 440, 631; form of the equations of motion, 380; function, 623; characteristic function, 412, 655; principal function, 415, 655.

Jacobi's principal functions and characteristic functions, 417.

Lagrange's equations of motion, 369, 374; conditions of equilibrium, 525; forces, 476; function, 621.

Newton's first law, 383; second law, 495; third law, 469.

Principle of the conservation of energy, 340, 441; of least action, Maupertuis' form, 355, 441, 640; do., Jacobi's form, 349, 441, 638; of least constraint, 390, 448, 709; of the centre of gravity and of areas, 404, 406, 508, 509, 717; of virtual velocities, 520; of virtual work, 521.

Poisson's form of the equations of motion, 377.

COSIMO

COSIMO is a specialty publisher of books and publications that inspire, inform and engage readers. Our mission is to offer unique books to niche audiences around the world.

COSIMO BOOKS publishes books and publications for innovative authors, non-profit organizations and businesses. **COSIMO BOOKS** specializes in bringing books back into print, publishing new books quickly and effectively, and making these publications available to readers around the world.

COSIMO CLASSICS offers a collection of distinctive titles by the great authors and thinkers throughout the ages. At **COSIMO CLASSICS** timeless classics find a new life as affordable books, covering a variety of subjects including: *Business, Economics, History, Personal Development, Philosophy, Religion and Spirituality,* and much more!

COSIMO REPORTS publishes public reports that affect your world: from global trends to the economy, and from health to geo-politics.

FOR MORE INFORMATION CONTACT US AT
INFO@COSIMOBOOKS.COM

- ❋ If you are a book-lover interested in our current catalog of books.

- ❋ If you are a bookstore, book club or anyone else interested in special discounts for bulk purchases

- ❋ If you are an author who wants to get published

- ❋ if you are an organization or business seeking to publish books and other publications for your members, donors or customers

**COSIMO BOOKS ARE ALWAYS
AVAILABLE AT ONLINE BOOKSTORES**

VISIT COSIMOBOOKS.COM
BE INSPIRED, BE INFORMED

Printed by BoD™in Norderstedt, Germany